ANDRE DUBUS'S
Selected Stories

"There isn't a better short story writer in America."
—*Minneapolis Tribune*

"Not since Flannery O'Connor has there been a writer who explores so compellingly the polarities of violence and redemption, anger and tenderness, sexuality and asceticism."
—*Boston Herald*

"Dubus writes like a pilot pushing the envelope—continually testing fiction's limits, pressing up against that line that separates drama from melodrama, sentiment from sentimentality, pathos from bathos, and redefining it....Few characters in contemporary fiction talk as freely, seriously or straight from the heart as Dubus's. They tell us stories, but more than that they give us their lives....If there is salvation in fiction, it must come from a place where there are this many true voices."
—*Village Voice*

"Mr. Dubus is a shrewd student of people who come to accept pain as a fair price for pleasure, and to view right and wrong as a matter of degree; without moralizing, he suggests that their self-inflicted punishments are often worse than what a just court, or a just God, would decree."
—*The New Yorker*

"His power is ominous and genuine."
—*Vanity Fair*

"Dubus the stylist gets better and better, like the sort of wine his characters would never drink....Joan [the mother of the boy who's at the center of *Voices From the Moon*] knows what all the characters in [it] will eventually learn. 'When I'm alone at night,' she tells her [older] son Larry, 'I look out my window, and it comes to me, we don't have to live great lives, we just have to understand and survive the ones we've got.' It's that simple and that complicated."
—James Kaufman, *St. Louis Dispatch*

SELECTED STORIES OF
ANDRE DUBUS

MR. CHARLES GILLIGAN,
THANKS FOR GIVING
OF YOURSELF, TO YOUR CLASSES,
TO MY EMILY.
I THINK THIS IS A GRITTY,
DELICIOUS, PROFOUND BOOK.
THAT'S WHY I WANT YOU TO
HAVE IT ALSO.
PEACE!
RON SWEET

G93

VINTAGE CONTEMPORARIES

Vintage Books
A Division of Random House, Inc.
New York

ANDRE
DUBUS

*Selected
Stories*

First Vintage Contemporaries Edition, December 1989

Copyright © 1975, 1977, 1980, 1983, 1984, 1986, 1988 by Andre Dubus

"The Curse" first appeared in *Playboy* (January 1988); "They Now Live in Texas" in *Indiana Review*, Vol. 10, Numbers 1 and 2 (Spring 1987).

Library of Congress Cataloging-in-Publication Data
Dubus, Andre, 1936-
    [Short stories. Selections]
    Selected stories / Andre Dubus.—1st Vintage Books ed.
       p.   cm.—(Vintage contemporaries)
    ISBN 0-679-72533-4 : $9.95
    I. Title.
  PS3554.U265A6   1989
813'.54—dc20   89-40273
                                           CIP

Manufactured in the United States of America
10 9 8 7 6 5 4 3 2 1

TO MY CHILDREN

Suzanne, b. 16 August 1958
Andre, 11 September 1959
Jeb, 29 November 1960
Nicole, 3 February 1963
Cadence, 11 June 1982
Madeleine, 10 January 1987

I prayed for the tree to have a long and healthy life till it dies, and a strong trunk.

Cadence Dubus, August 1987

You have to be lying flat on your back to look straight up.

Judith Tranberg,
Registered Physical Therapist, July 1987

If your eyes are sound, your whole body will be full of light.

St. Luke, Chapter 11

CONTENTS

SELECTED STORIES OF
ANDRE DUBUS

MIRANDA OVER THE VALLEY

ALL THAT DAY she thought of Michaelis: as she packed for school in Boston and confirmed her reservation and, in Woodland Hills, did shopping which she knew was foolish: as though she were going to some primitive land, she bought deodorant and bath powder and shampoo, and nylons and leotards for the cold. At one o'clock she was driving the Corvette past cracked tan earth and dry brush, it was a no smoking zone and she put out her cigarette and thought: Now he has finished his lunch and they have gone back to the roof, he's not wearing his shirt, he has a handkerchief tied around his head so sweat won't burn his eyes; he's kneeling down nailing shingles. She saw them eating dinner, her last good Mexican food until she flew west again at Thanksgiving, but she could not see the evening beyond dinner. She saw enchiladas and Margaritas, she saw them talking, she talked with him now driving to the shopping center, but after that she saw nothing. And she was afraid. In the evening she brushed her long dark hair and waited for him and she opened the front door when he rang; he was tall, he was tanned from his summer work, and he shook her father's hand and kissed her mother's cheek. Miranda liked the approval in her parents' eyes, and she took his arm as they walked out to the driveway, to his old and dented Plymouth parked behind the Corvette. They went to dinner and then drove and then stopped on Mulholland Drive, high above the fog lying over the San Fernando Valley, and out her window she saw stars and a lone cloud slowly passing the moon. She took his thick curly hair in one hand and kissed him and with her tongue she told him yes, told him again and again while she waited for him to know she was saying yes.

The next day her parents and Michaelis took her to the airport. She met Holly at the terminal and they flew to Boston. She was eighteen years old.

She lived with Holly in a second-floor apartment Holly found on Beacon Street. It was large, and its wide, tall windows overlooked the old, shaded street. They put a red carpet in the living room and red curtains at the windows. Holly's boyfriend, who went to school in Rhode Island, built them a bar in one corner, at the carpet's edge. Holly was a year older than Miranda, this was her second year at Boston University, and the boys who came to the apartment were boys she had known last year. There were also some new ones, and soon Holly was making love with one of them. His name was Brian. When he came to the apartment Miranda watched him and listened to him, but she could neither like him nor dislike him, because she could not understand who he was. He was a student and for him the university was a stalled escalator: he leaned against its handrails, he looked about him and talked and gestured with his hands, his pale face laughed and he stroked his beard, and his hair tossed at his neck. But there was no motion about him.

When he spent the night, Holly unfolded the day bed in the living room and Miranda had the bedroom to herself. She lay on her twin bed at the window and listened to rock music from an all-night FM station; still there were times when, over the music, she could hear Holly moaning in the next room. The sounds and her images always excited her, but sometimes they made her sad too; for on most weekends Tom drove up from Providence and on Friday and Saturday nights Miranda fell asleep after the same sounds had hushed. Brian knew about Tom and seemed as indifferent to his weekend horns as he was to an incomplete in a course or the theft of his bicycle, which he left on the sidewalk outside a Cambridge bar one Sunday afternoon.

Tom knew nothing about Holly's week nights. The lottery had spared him, so he was a graduate student in history and, though he tried not to, at least once each visit he spoke of the diminishing number of teaching jobs. He was robust and shyly candid and

Miranda liked him very much. She liked Holly very much too and she did not want to feel disapproval, but there it was in her heart when she heard the week night sounds and then the weekend sounds, and when she looked at Tom's red face and thick brown moustache and thinning hair. One night in late September Miranda and Holly went to a movie and when they came home they sat at the bar in the living room and drank a glass of wine. After a second glass Miranda said Tom had built a nice bar. Then she asked if he was coming this weekend. Holly said he was.

'I'd feel divided,' Miranda said, and she looked at Holly's long blonde hair and at the brown, yellow-tinted eyes that watched her like a wise and preying cat.

Then it was early October and she was afraid. At first it was only for moments which struck her at whim: sometimes in class or as she walked home on cool afternoons she remembered and was afraid. But she did not really believe, so she was only afraid when memory caught her off guard, before she could reassure herself that no one was that unlucky. Another week went by and she told Holly she was late.

'You can't be,' Holly said.

'No. No, it must be something else.'

'What would you do?'

She didn't know. She didn't know anything except that now she was afraid most of the time. Always she was waiting. Whether she was in class or talking to Holly or some other friend, even while she slept and dreamed, she was waiting for that flow of blood that would empty her womb whether it held a child or not. Although she did not think of womb, of child, of miscarriage. She hoped only for blood.

Then October was running out and she knew her luck was too. Late Halloween afternoon she went to the office of a young gyne-cologist who had the hands of a woman, a plump face and thin, pouting lips. He kept looking at his wrist watch. He asked if she planned to keep the child and when she told him yes he said that if she were still in Boston a month from now to come see him. As she was leaving, the receptionist asked her for twenty dollars. Mi-randa wrote a check, then went out to the street where dusk had descended and where groups of small witches, skeletons, devils, and ghosts in sheets moved past her as she stopped to light a cigarette; she followed in the wake of their voices. Holly was home. When Miranda told her she said: 'Oh Jesus. Oh Jesus Jesus Jesus.'

'I'm all right,' Miranda said. She noticed that she sounded as if she were reciting something. 'I'm all right. I'm not in trouble, I'm only having a baby. It's too early to call Michaelis. It's only three o'clock in California. He'll still be at school. I'd like to rest a while then eat a nice meal.'

'We only have hamburger. I'll go out and get us some steaks.'

'Here.'

'No. It's my treat.'

While Holly was gone, Miranda put on Simon and Garfunkel and the Beatles and lay on the couch. The doorbell rang and she went downstairs and gave candy to the children. She and Holly had bought the candy yesterday: candy corn, jelly beans, bags of small Tootsie Rolls, orange slices, and chocolate kisses; and now, pouring candy into the children's paper bags, smiling and praising costumes, she remembered how frightened she was yesterday in the store: looking at the cellophane bags of candy, she had felt she did not have the courage to grow a minute older and therefore would not. Now as she passed out the candy she felt numb, stationary, as though she were suspended out of time and could see each second as it passed, and each of them went on without her.

She went upstairs and lay on the couch and the doorbell rang again. The children in this group were costumed too, but older, twelve or thirteen, and one of the girls asked for a cigarette. Miranda told her to take candy or nothing. When she went upstairs she was very tired. She had been to three classes, and she had walked in the cold to the doctor's and back. While the Beatles were singing she went to sleep. The doorbell rang but she didn't answer; she went back into her deep sleep. When Holly came in talking, Miranda woke up, her heart fast with fright. Holly put on the Rolling Stones and broiled the steaks and they drank Burgundy. During dinner Brian called, saying he wanted to come over, but Holly told him to make it tomorrow.

At eight o'clock, when it was five in California, Miranda went to the bedroom and closed the door and sat on her bed. The phone was on the bedside table. She lowered her hand to the receiver but did not lift it. She gazed at her face in the reflecting window. She was still frozen out of time, and she was afraid that if Michaelis wasn't home, if the phone rang and rang against the walls of his empty apartment, something would happen to her, something she could not control, she would go mad in Holly's arms. Then she turned away from her face in the window and looked at the numbers as she dialed; his phone rang only twice and then he answered and time had started again.

'Happy Halloween,' she said.

'Trick or treat.'

'Trick,' she said. 'I'm pregnant.' He was silent. She closed her eyes and squeezed the phone, as though her touch could travel too, as her voice did, and she saw the vast night between their two coasts, saw the telephone lines crossing the dark mountains and plains and mountains between them.

'It's about two months, is that right?'

'It was September second.'

'I know. Do you want to get married?'

'Do you?'

'Of course I do. If that's what you're thinking about.'

'I'm not thinking about anything. I saw the doctor this afternoon and I haven't thought about anything.'

'Look: do you want to do it at Thanksgiving? That'll give me time to arrange things, I have to find out about blood tests and stuff, and your folks'll need some time—you want me to talk to them?'

'No, I will.'

'Okay, and then after Thanksgiving you can go back and finish the semester. At least you'll have that done. I can be looking for another apartment. This is all right for me, *may*be all right for two, but with a—' He stopped.

'Are you sure you want to?'

'Of course I am. It just sounded strange, saying it.'

'You didn't say it.'

'Oh. Anyway, we'll need more room.'

'I didn't think he'd do that,' Holly said. She was sitting on the living room carpet, drinking tea. Miranda could not sit down; she stood at the window over Beacon Street, she went to the bar for a cigarette, she moved back to the window. 'I just didn't think he would,' Holly said.

'You didn't want him to.'

'Are you really going to get *mar*ried?'

'I love him.'

'He's your first one.'

'My first one. You mean the first one I've made love with.'

'Yes.'

'And that's how you mean it.'

'That's how. And you've only done *that* once.'

'That's not what it means to me.'

'How would you know? You've never had anybody else.'

'But you have.'

'What's that mean.'

'I guess it means look at yourself.'

'All right. I'll look at myself. I've never had to get married, and I've never had to get an abortion, and nobody owns me.'

'I want to be owned.'

'You do?'

'Yes. The way you are now, you have to lie.'

'I don't lie to Tom. He doesn't ask.'

'I don't mean just that. I don't know what I mean; it's just all of it. I have to go outside for a minute. I have to walk outside.'

She put on her coat as she went down the gray-carpeted stairs. She walked to the corner and then up the dead-end street and climbed the steps of the walk that crossed Storrow Drive. As she climbed she held the iron railing, but it was cold and she had forgotten her gloves. She put her hands in her pockets. She stood on the walk and watched the cars coming and passing beneath her and listened to their tires on the wet street. To her right was the Charles River, wide and black and cold. On sunny days it was blue and in the fall she had watched sailboats on it. Beyond the river were the lights of Cambridge; she thought of the bars there and the warm students drinking beer and she wanted Michaelis with her now. She knew that: she wanted him. She had wanted him for a long time but she had told him no, had even gone many times to his apartment and still told him no, because all the time she was thinking. On that last night she wasn't thinking, and she had not done any thinking since then: she had moved through September and October in the fearful certainty of love, and she still had that as she stood shivering above the street, looking out at the black river and the lights on the other side.

She phoned her parents at nine-fifteen, during their cocktail hour. Her mother talked on the phone in the breakfast room, and her father went to his den and used the phone there. He would be wearing a cardigan and drinking a martini. Her mother would be wearing a dress; nearly always she put on a dress at the end of the day. She would be sitting on the stool by the phone, facing the blackboard where Miranda and her two older brothers had read messages when they came home from school, and written their own. Once, when she was a little girl, she had come home and read: *Pussycat, I'm playing golf. I'll be home at four, in time to pay Maria.* And she had written: *Maria was not here. I feel sick and I am going to bed.* Beyond her mother's head, the sun would be setting over the bluff behind the house; part of the pool would be in the bluff's shadow, the water close to the house still and sunlit blue. The sun would be coming through the sliding glass doors that opened to the pool and the lawn, those glass doors that one morning when she was twelve she opened and, looking down, saw a small rattlesnake coiled sleeping in the shade on the flagstone inches from her bare feet. As she shut the doors and cried out for her father it raised its head and started to rattle. Her father came running bare-chested in pajama pants; then he went to his room and got a small automatic he kept in his drawer and shot the snake as it slithered across the stones. Sunlight would be coming through those doors now and into the breakfast room and shining on her mother in a bright dress.

'Fly home tomorrow,' her mother said.

'Well, I'll be home at Thanksgiving. Michaelis said he'd arrange it for then.'

'We'd like to see you before *that*,' her mother said.

'And don't worry,' her father said. 'You're not the first good kids to get into a little trouble.'

That night she fell asleep listening to her father's deep and soothing voice as it drew her back through October and September, by her long hair (but gently) dragging her into August and the house in Woodland Hills, the pepper trees hanging long over the sidewalks, on summer mornings coffee at the glass table beside the pool and at sixteen (with her father) a cigarette too, though not with her mother until she was seventeen; in the morning she woke to his voice and she heard it on the plane and could not read *Time* or *Holiday* or *Antigone*, and it was his voice she descended through in the night above Los Angeles, although it was Michaelis who waited for her, who embraced her. When they got home and she hugged her father she held him tightly and for a moment she had no volition and wanted none. Just before kissing her mother, Miranda looked at her eyes: they were green and they told her she had been foolish; then Miranda kissed her, held her, and in her own tightening arms she felt again her resolve.

They went to the breakfast room. Before they started talking, Miranda went outside and looked at the pool and lawn in the dark. Fog was settling; tops of trees touched the sky above the bluff. She went in and sat at one end of the table, facing her father and the glass doors behind him. They reflected the room. Her father's neck and bald head were brown from playing golf, his thin moustache clipped, more gray than she had remembered, and there was more gray too (or more than she had seen, thinking of him in Boston) in the short brown hair at the sides of his head. He was drinking brandy. Or he had a snifter of brandy in front of him, but he mostly handled it; he picked it up and put it down; he ran his finger around the rim; he warmed it in his cupped hands but didn't drink; with thumb and fingers he turned it on the table. He was smoking a very thin cigar, and now and then he cheated and inhaled. Her mother sat to his left, at the side of the table; she had pulled her chair close to his end of the table and turned it so she faced Miranda and Michaelis. Her hair had been growing darker for years and she had kept it blonde and long. Her skin was tough and tan, her face lined, weathered, and she wore bracelets that jangled. She was drinking brandy and listening, though she appeared not listening so much as hearing again lines she had played to for a hundred nights, and waiting for her cue. Miranda mostly watched her father, because he was talking, though sometimes she glanced at Michaelis; he was the one she wanted to watch, but she didn't; for she didn't want anyone, not even him, to see how much she was appealing to him. He sat to her left, his chair was pulled toward her so that he faced her parents, and when she looked at him she saw his quiet profile, his dark curly hair, his large hand holding the can of Coors, and his right shoulder, which was turned slightly away from her. She wanted to see his eyes but she did not really need to; for in the way he occupied space, quiet, attentive, nodding, his arms that were so often spread and in motion now close to his chest, she saw and felt what she had seen at the airport: above his jocular mouth the eyes had told her he had not been living well with his fear.

'—so it's not Mother and me that counts. It's *you* two. We've got to think about what's best for you two.'

'And the baby,' Miranda said.

'Come on, sweetheart. That's not a baby. It's just something you're piping blood into.'

'It's alive; that's why you want me to kill it.'

'Sweetheart—'

'Do you *really* want it?' her mother said.

'Yes.'

'I don't believe you. You mean you're happy about it? You're *glad* you're pregnant?'

'I can do it.'

'You can have a baby, sure,' her father said. 'But what about Michaelis? Do you know how much studying there is in law school?'

'I can work,' she said.

'I thought you were having a baby,' her mother said.

'I can work.'

'And hire a Mexican woman to take care of your child.'

'I can work!'

'You're being foolish.'

Her father touched her mother's arm.

'Wait, honey. Listen, sweetheart, I know you can work. That's not the point. The point is, why suffer? Jesus, sweetheart, you're eighteen years old. You've never had to live out there. The hospital and those Goddamn doctors will own you. And you've got to eat once in a while. Michaelis, have another beer.'

Michaelis got up and as he moved behind Miranda's chair she held up her wine glass and he took it. When he came back with his beer and her glass of wine he said: 'I can do it.'

'Maybe you shouldn't,' her mother said. 'Whether you can or not. Maybe it won't be good for Miranda. What are you going to be, pussycat—a dumb little housewife? Your husband will be out in the world, he'll be growing, and all you'll know is diapers and Gerbers. You've got to finish college—' It was so far away now: blackboards, large uncurtained windows looking out at nothing, at other walls, other windows; talking, note-taking; talking, talking, talking . . . She looked at Michaelis; he was watching her mother, listening. '—You can't make marriage the be-all and end-all. Because if you do it won't work. Listen: from the looks of things we've got one of the few solid marriages around. But it took work, pussycat. Work.' Her eyes gleamed with the victory of that work, the necessity for it. 'And we were older. I was twenty-six, I'd been to school, I'd worked; you see the difference it makes? After all these years with this guy—and believe me some of them have been like standing in the rain—now that I'm getting old and going blind from charcoal smoke at least I know I didn't give anything up to get married. Except my independence. But I was fed up with that. And all right: I'll tell you something else too. I'd had other relationships. With men. That helped too. There—' she lightly smacked the table '— that's my confession for the night.'

But her face was not the face of someone confessing. In her smile, which appeared intentionally hesitant, intentionally vulnerable, and in the crinkling tan flesh at the corners of her eyes, in the wide green eyes themselves, and in the tone of finality in her throaty voice—there: now it's out, I've told you everything, that's how much I care, the voice said; her smacking of the table with a palm said— Miranda sensed a coaxing trick that she did not want to understand. But she did understand and she sat hating her mother, whose eyes and smile were telling her that making love with Michaelis was a natural but subsidiary part of growing up; that finally what she felt that night and since (and before: the long, muddled days and nights when she was not so much trying to decide but to free herself so she could make love without deciding) amounted now to nothing more than anxiety over baby fat and pimples. It meant nothing. Miranda this fall meant nothing. She would outgrow the way she felt. She would look back on those feelings with amused nostalgia as she could now look back on grapefruit and cottage cheese, and the creams she had applied on her face at night, the camouflaging powder during the day.

'You see,' her father said, 'we don't object to you having a lover. Hell, we can't. What scares us, though, is you being unhappy: and the odds are that you *will* be. Now think of it the other way. Try to, sweetheart. I've never forced you to do anything—I've never been *a*ble to—and I'm not forcing you now. I only want you to look at it from a different side for a while. You and Mother fly to New York—' She felt sentenced to death. Her legs were cool and weak, her heart beat faster within images of her cool, tense body under lights, violated. '—the pill, then you're safe. Both of you. You have three years to grow. You can go back to school—'

'To be *what*?' she said. 'To be *what*,' and she wiped her eyes.

'That's exactly it,' her mother said. 'You don't know yet what you want to be but you say you're ready to get married.'

She had not said that. She had said something altogether different, though she couldn't explain it, could not even explain it to herself. When they said married they were not talking about her. That was not what she wanted. Perhaps she wanted nothing. Except to be left alone as she was in Boston to listen to the fearful pulsations of her body; to listen to them; to sleep with them; wake with them. It was not groceries. She saw brown bags, cans. That was not it. She watched Michaelis. He was listening to them, and in his eyes she saw relieved and grateful capitulation. In his eyes that night his passion was like fear. He was listening to them, he was nodding, and now they were offering the gift, wrapped in her father's voice: '—So much better that way, so much more sensible. And this Christmas, say right after Christmas, you could go to Acapulco. Just the two of you. It's nice at that time of year, you know? It could be your Christmas present. The trip could.'

She smiled before she knew she was smiling; slightly she shook her head, feeling the smile like a bandage: they were giving her a honeymoon, her honeymoon lover in the Acapulco hotel after he had been sucked from her womb. She would have cried, but she felt dry inside, she was tired, and she knew the night was ended.

'I was afraid on Mulholland Drive. I was afraid in Boston. It was the most important thing there was. How I was afraid all the time.' Her parents' faces were troubled with compassion; they loved her; in her father's eyes she saw her own pain. 'I kept wanting not to be afraid, and it was all I thought about. Then I stopped wanting that. I was afraid, and it was me, and it was all right. Now we can go to Acapulco.' She looked at Michaelis. He looked at her, guilty, ashamed; then he looked at her parents as though to draw from them some rational poise; but it didn't work, and he lowered his eyes to his beer can. 'Michaelis? Do you want to go to Acapulco?'

Still he looked down. He had won and lost, and his unhappy face struggled to endure both. He shrugged his shoulders, but only slightly, little more than a twitch, as if in mid-shrug he had realized what a cowardly gesture the night had brought him to. That was how she would most often remember him: even later when she would see him, when she would make love with him (but only one more time), she would not see the nearly healed face he turned to her, but his face as it was now, the eyes downcast; and his broad shoulders in their halted shrug.

It was not remorse she felt. It was dying. In the mornings she woke with it, and as she brushed her hair and ate yogurt or toast and honey and coffee and walked with Holly to school as the November days grew colder, she felt that ropes of her own blood trailed from her back and were knotted in New York, on that morning, and that she could not move forward because she could not go back to free herself. And she could not write to Michaelis. She tried, and she wrote letters like this:—*the lit exam wasn't as hard as I expected. I love reading the Greeks. The first snow has fallen, and it's lovely and I like looking out the window at it and walking in it. I've learned to make a snow angel. You lie on your back in the snow and you spread your arms and legs, like doing jumping jacks, and then you stand up carefully and you've left an angel in the snow, with big, spreading wings. Love, Miranda.* When she wrote *love* she wanted to draw lines through it, to cover it with ink, for she felt she was lying. Or not that. It was the word that lied, and when she shaped it with her pen she felt the false letters, and heard the hollow sound of the word.

She did not like being alone anymore. Before, she had liked coming home in the late afternoon and putting on records and studying or writing to Michaelis or just lying on the couch near the sunset window until Holly came home. But now that time of day (and it was a dark time, winter coming, the days growing short) was like the other time: morning, waking, when there was death in her soul, in her blood, and she thought of the dead thing she wouldn't call by name, and she wished for courage in the past, wished she had gone somewhere alone, New Hampshire or Maine, a small house in the woods, and lived alone with the snow and the fireplace and a general store down the road and read books and walked in the woods while her body grew, and it grew. She would not call it anything even when she imagined February's swollen belly; that would be in June; the second of June. Already she would not think June when she knew she would say: Today is probably the day my baby would have been born. So she could not be alone anymore, not even in this apartment she loved, this city she loved.

She thought of it as a gentle city. And she felt gentle too, and tender. One morning she saw a small yellow dog struck by a car; the dog was not killed; it ran yelping on three legs, holding up the fourth, quivering, and Miranda could feel the pain in that hind leg moving through the cold air. She could not see blood in movies anymore. She read the reviews, took their warnings, stayed away. Sometimes when she saw children on the street she was sad; and there were times when she longed for her own childhood. She remembered what it was like not knowing anything, and she felt sorry for herself because what she knew now was killing her, she felt creeping death in her breast, and bitterly she regretted the bad luck that had brought her this far, this alone; and so she wanted it all to be gone, November and October and September, she wanted to be a virgin again, to go back even past that, to be so young she didn't know virgin from not-virgin. She knew this was dangerous. She knew that nearly everything she was feeling now was dangerous, and so was her not-feeling: her emptiness when she wrote to her parents and Michaelis; in classrooms she felt abstract; when people came to the apartment she talked with them, she got high with them, but she was only a voice. She neither greeted them nor told them goodbye with her body; she touched no one; or, if she did, she wasn't aware of it; if anyone touched her they touched nothing. One night as she was going to bed stoned she said to Holly: 'I'm a piece of chalk.' She thought of seeing a psychiatrist but believed (had to believe) that all this would leave her.

On days when she got home before Holly, she put on music and spent every moment waiting for Holly. Sometimes, waiting, she drank wine or smoked a pipe, and the waiting was not so bad; although sometimes with wine it was worse, the wine seemed to relax her in the wrong way, so that her memory and dread and predictions were even sharper, more cruel. With dope the waiting was always easier. She was worried about drinking alone, smoking alone; but she was finally only vaguely worried. The trouble she was in was too deep for her to worry about its surfaces. When Holly came home, short of breath from climbing the stairs, her fair cheeks reddened from the cold and her blonde hair damp with snow like drops of dew, Miranda talked and talked while they cooked, and she ate heartily, and felt that eating was helping her, as though she were recovering from an illness of the flesh.

Her parents and Michaelis wanted her to fly home at Thanksgiving but she went to Maine with Diane, a friend from school. Holly told her parents she was going too, and she went to Rhode Island with Tom. Diane's parents lived in a large brick house overlooking the sea. They were cheerful and affluent, and they were tall and slender like Diane, who had freckles that were fading as winter came. There was a younger brother who was tall and quiet and did not shave yet, and his cheeks were smooth as a girl's. Around him Miranda felt old.

She had never seen the Atlantic in winter. On Thanksgiving morning she woke before Diane and sat at the window. The sky was gray, a wind was blowing, the lawn sloping down to the sea was snow, and the wind blew gusts of it like powder toward the house. The lawn ended at the beach, at dark rocks; the rocks went out into the sea, into the gray, cold waves. Beyond the rocks she saw a seal swimming. She watched it, sleek and brown and purposeful, going under, coming up. She quickly dressed in corduroy pants and sweater and boots and coat and went downstairs; she heard Diane's parents having coffee in the kitchen, and quietly went outside and down the slippery lawn to the narrow strip of sand and the rocks. But the seal was gone. She stood looking out at the sea. Once she realized she had been daydreaming, though she could not recall what it was she dreamed; but for a minute or longer she had not known where she was, and when she turned from her dreaming to look at the house, to locate herself, there was a moment when she did not know the names of the people inside. Then she began walking back and forth in front of the house, looking into the wind at the sea. Before long a light snow came blowing in on the salt wind. She turned her face to it. I suppose I don't love Diane, she told herself. For a moment I forgot her name.

Then it was December, a long Saturday afternoon that was gray without snow, and Holly was gone for the weekend. In late afternoon Miranda left the lighted apartment and a paper she was writing and walked up Beacon Street. The street and sidewalks were wet and the gutters held gray, dirty snow. She walked to the Public Garden where there were trees and clean snow, and on a bridge

over a frozen pond she stopped and watched children skating. Then
she walked through the Garden and across the street to the Common;
the sidewalks around it were crowded, the Hare Krishna people
were out too, with their shaved heads and pigtails and their robes
in the cold, chanting their prayer. She did not see any winos. In
warm weather they slept on the grass or sat staring from benches,
wearing old, dark suits and sometimes a soiled hat. But now they
were gone, and where, she wondered, did they go when the sky
turns cold? She walked across the Common to the State House;
against the gray sky its gold dome looked odd, like something im-
ported from another country. Then she walked home. Already dusk
was coming, and she didn't want to be alone. When she got home
Brian was ringing the doorbell.

'Holly's not here,' she said.

'I know. Are you here?'

'Sometimes. Come on up.'

He was tall and he wore a fatigue jacket. She looked away from
his face, reached in her pocket for the key; she felt him wanting
her, it was like a current from his body, and she felt it as she opened
the door and as they climbed the stairs. In the apartment she gave
him a beer.

'Are you hungry?' she said.

'No.'

'I am. If I cook something, will you eat it?'

'Sure.'

'There's chicken. Is chicken all right? Broiled?'

'Chicken? Why not?'

He followed her to the kitchen. While she cooked they talked
and he had another beer and she drank wine. She wasn't hungry
anymore. She knew something would happen and she was waiting
for it, waiting to see what she would do. She cooked and they ate
and then went to the living room and smoked a pipe on the couch.
When he took off her sweater she nearly said let's go to bed, but
she didn't. She closed her eyes and waited and when he was undressed she kissed his bearded face. Her eyes were closed. She felt
wicked and that excited her; he was very thin; her body was quick
and wanton; but her heart was a stone; her heart was a clock; her
heart was a watching eye. Then he shuddered and his weight rested
on her and she said: 'You bastard.'

He left her. He sat at the end of the couch, at her feet; he took a swallow of beer and leaned back and looked at the ceiling.

'I saw it downstairs,' he said. 'You wanted to ball.'

'Don't call it that.'

He looked at her; then he leaned over and picked up his socks.

'No,' she said. 'Call it that.' He put on his socks. 'Say it again.'

'What are you playing?'

'I'm not. I don't play anymore. It's all—What are you doing?'

'I'm putting on my pants.' He was standing, buckling his belt. He picked up his sweater from the floor.

'No,' she said. 'I'm cold.'

'Get dressed.'

'I don't want you to go. Let's get in bed.'

'That'll be the second time tonight I do something you want me to. Will I be a bastard again?'

'No. I'm just screwed up, Brian, that's all.'

'Who isn't?'

In bed he was ribs and hip bone against her side and she liked resting her head on his long hard arm.

'What's the matter?' he said. 'You worried about that guy in California?'

'He's not there anymore.'

'Where'd he go?'

'He's still there. Things happened.'

'Have you had many guys?'

'Just him and you. You won't tell Holly, will you?'

'Why should I?'

'How long have you been in school?'

'Six years, on and off.'

'What will you do?'

'They haven't told me yet.'

'Michaelis is going to be a lawyer.'

'Good for him.'

'I used to love him.'

'Figures.'

'He's going to work with Chicanos. I won't be with him now. For a whole year I thought about that. I was going to marry him and have a baby and carry it like a papoose on the picket lines. We wouldn't have much money. That was it for a whole year and I was feeling all that when I made love with him, it was my first time and I hurt and I bled and I probably wasn't any good, but my God I felt wonderful. I felt like I was going to heaven.'

'You better cheer up, man. There's other guys.'

'Oh yes, I know: there are other guys. Miranda will have other guys.'

Her heart did not change: not that night when they made love again, nor Sunday morning waking to his hands. Late Sunday night Holly came home and Miranda woke up but until Holly was undressed and in bed she pretended she was asleep so Holly wouldn't turn on the lights. Then she pretended to wake up because she wanted to talk to Holly before, in the morning, she saw her face.

'How was your weekend?'

'Fine. What did you do?'

'Stayed in the apartment and studied.'

She lit a cigarette. Holly came over and took one from the pack. Miranda did not look at her: she closed her eyes and smoked and felt the sour cold of the lie. Holly was back in bed, talking into the distance of the lie, and Miranda listened and answered and lay tense in bed, for she was so many different Mirandas: the one with Holly now and the one who made love with Brian (balled; balled; she was sure) and the one who didn't want to make love with Brian (b——); and beneath or among those there were perhaps two other Mirandas, and suddenly she almost cried, remembering September and October when she was afraid, but she was one Miranda Jones. She sat up quickly, too quickly, so that Holly stopped talking and then said: 'What's wrong?'

'Nothing. I just want another cigarette.'

'You should get out next weekend.'

'Probably.'

'Come to Providence with me.'

'What would I do?'

'I don't know. Whatever you do here. And we can get you a date.'

'Maybe I will. Probably I won't, though.'

Tuesday after dinner Brian came over. He sat on the couch with Holly, and Miranda faced them from a chair. She tried not to look directly at him but she could not help herself: she drank too much beer and she watched him. He kept talking. Her nakedness was not in his face. She felt it was in hers, though, when Holly's hand dropped to his thigh and rested there. She was not jealous; she did not love Brian; she felt as though something were spilled in the room, something foul and shameful, and no one dared look at it, and no one would clean it up. I'm supposed to be cool, she told herself as she went to the refrigerator and opened three cans of beer. She opened Brian's last. It was his because it was on the left and she would carry it in her left hand and she remembered his hands. I am not for this world, she thought. Or it isn't for me. It's not because I'm eighteen either. Michaelis is twenty-two; he will get brown in the sun talking to Chicanos, he will smell of beer and onions, but his spirit won't rise; Michaelis is of the world, he will be a lawyer.

She brought Holly and Brian their beer. I'm supposed to be cool, she told herself as she watched Holly's hand on his leg, watched his talking face where she didn't live. And where did she live? Whose eyes will hold me, whose eyes will know me when my own eyes look back at me in the morning and I am not in them? I'm supposed to be cool, she told herself as she went to her room and felt the room move as she settled heavily under the blankets; she was bloated with beer, she knew in the morning her mouth would be dry, her stomach heavy and liquid. From the living room the sounds came. It's not me. She was drunk and for a moment she thought she had said it aloud. It's not me they're doing it to. I don't love him. She remembered his hard, thin legs between hers and she saw him with Holly and wary as a thief her hand slid down and she moved against it. It's not me they're doing it to. She listened to the sounds from the other room and moved within them against her hand.

In his bed in his apartment Michaelis held her and his large, dark eyes were wet, and she spoke to him and kissed and dried his tears, though she felt nothing for them; she gave them her lips as she might have given coins to a beggar. She could feel nothing except that it was strange for him to cry; she did not believe she would ever cry again; not for love. It was her first night home, they had left her house three hours earlier, left her mother's voice whose gaiety could not veil her fear and its warning: 'Don't be late,' she said, meaning don't spend the night, don't drive our own nails through our hands; already her mother's eyes (and, yes, her father's too) were hesitant, vulpine. How can we get our daughter back? the eyes said. We have saved her. But now how do we get her back? Her parents' hands and arms were loving; they held her tightly; they drew her to their hearts. The arms and eyes told her not to go to Acapulco after Christmas; not to want to go. No matter. She did not want to go. Michaelis's arms were tight and loving too, he lay on his side, his body spent from loving her, and now she was spending his soul too, watching it drip on his cheeks: '—It didn't mean anything. Don't cry. We won't go to Acapulco. I don't think I'll sleep with Brian again, but we won't go to Acapulco. I want to do other things. I don't know what they'll be yet. You'll have a good life, Michaelis. Don't worry: you will. It'll be a fine life. Don't be sad. Things end, that's all. But you'll be fine. Do you want to take me home now? Or do you want me to stay a while. I'll stay the night if you want—'

She propped on an elbow and looked at him. He had stopped crying, his cheeks glistened still, and he lay on his back now, staring at the ceiling. She could see in his face that he would not make love with her again or, for some time, with anyone else. She watched him until she didn't need to anymore. Then she called a taxi and put on her clothes. When she heard the taxi's horn she left Michaelis lying naked in the dark.

THE WINTER FATHER

for Pat

THE JACKMAN'S MARRIAGE had been adulterous and violent, but in its last days, they became a couple again, as they might have if one of them were slowly dying. They wept together, looked into each other's eyes without guile, distrust, or hatred, and they planned Peter's time with the children. On his last night at home, he and Norma, tenderly, without a word, made love. Next evening, when he got home from Boston, they called David and Kathi in from the snow and brought them to the kitchen.

David was eight, slender, with light brown hair nearly to his shoulders, a face that was still pretty; he seemed always hungry, and Peter liked watching him eat. Kathi was six, had long red hair and a face that Peter had fallen in love with, a face that had once been pierced by glass the shape of a long dagger blade. In early spring a year ago: he still had not taken the storm windows off the screen doors; he was bringing his lunch to the patio, he did not know Kathi was following him, and holding his plate and mug he had pushed the door open with his shoulder, stepped outside, heard the crash and her scream, and turned to see her gripping then pulling the long shard from her cheek. She got it out before he reached her. He picked her up and pressed his handkerchief to the wound, midway between her eye and throat, and held her as he phoned his doctor who said he would meet them at the hospital and do the stitching himself because it was cosmetic and that beautiful face should not be touched by residents. Norma was not at home. Kathi lay on the car seat beside him and he held his handkerchief on her cheek, and in the hospital he held her hands while she lay on the table. The doctor said it would only take about four stitches and it would be better without anesthetic, because sometimes that puffed the skin, and he wanted to fit the cut together perfectly, for the scar; he told this very gently to Kathi, and he said as she grew, the scar would move down her face and finally would be under her jaw. Then she and Peter squeezed each other's hands as the doctor stitched and she gritted her teeth and stared at pain.

She was like that when he and Norma told them. It was David who suddenly cried, begged them not to get a divorce, and then fled to his room and would not come out, would not help Peter load his car, and only emerged from the house as Peter was driving away: a small running shape in the dark, charging the car, picking up something and throwing it, missing, crying *You bum You bum You bum* . . .

Drunk that night in his apartment whose rent he had paid and keys received yesterday morning before last night's grave lovemaking with Norma, he gained through the blur of bourbon an intense focus on his children's faces as he and Norma spoke: We fight too much, we've tried to live together but can't; you'll see, you'll be better off too, you'll be with Daddy for dinner on Wednesday nights, and on Saturdays and Sundays you'll do things with him. In his kitchen he watched their faces.

Next day he went to the radio station. After the news at noon he was on; often, as the records played, he imagined his children last night, while he and Norma were talking, and after he was gone. Perhaps she took them out to dinner, let them stay up late, flanking her on the couch in front of the television. When he talked he listened to his voice: it sounded as it did every weekday afternoon. At four he was finished. In the parking lot he felt as though, with stooped shoulders, he were limping. He started the forty-minute drive northward, for the first time in twelve years going home to empty rooms. When he reached the town where he lived he stopped at a small store and bought two lamb chops and a package of frozen peas. *I will take one thing at a time*, he told himself. Crossing the sidewalk to his car, in that short space, he felt the limp again, the stooped shoulders. He wondered if he looked like a man who had survived an accident which had killed others.

That was on a Thursday. When he woke Saturday morning, his first thought was a wish: that Norma would phone and tell him they were sick, and he should wait to see them Wednesday. He amended his wish, lay waiting for his own body to let him know it was sick, out for the weekend. In late morning he drove to their coastal town; he had moved fifteen miles inland. Already the snow-ploughed streets and country roads leading to their house felt like parts of his body: intestines, lung, heart-fiber lying from his door to theirs. When they were born he had smoked in the waiting room with the others. Now he was giving birth: stirruped, on his back, waves of pain. There would be no release, no cutting of the cord. Nor did he want it. He wanted to grow a cord.

Walking up their shovelled walk and ringing the doorbell, he felt at the same time like an inept salesman and a con man. He heard their voices, watched the door as though watching the sounds he heard, looking at the point where their faces would appear, but when the door opened he was looking at Norma's waist; then up to her face, lipsticked, her short brown hair soft from that morning's washing. For years she had not looked this way on a Saturday morning. Her eyes held him: the nest of pain was there, the shyness, the coiled anger; but there was another shimmer: she was taking a new marriage vow: This is the way we shall love our children now; watch how well I can do it. She smiled and said: 'Come in out of the cold and have a cup of coffee.'

In the living room he crouched to embrace the hesitant children. Only their faces were hesitant. In his arms they squeezed, pressed, kissed. David's hard arms absolved them both of Wednesday night. Through their hair Peter said pleasantly to Norma that he'd skip the coffee this time. Grabbing caps and unfurling coats, they left the house, holding hands to the car.

He showed them his apartment: they had never showered behind glass; they slid the doors back and forth. Sand washing down the drain, their flesh sunburned, a watermelon waiting in the refrigerator . . .

'This summer—'

They turned from the glass, looked up at him.

'When we go to the beach. We can come back here and shower.'

Their faces reflected his bright promise, and they followed him to the kitchen; on the counter were two cans of kidney beans, Jalapeño peppers, seasonings. Norma kept her seasonings in small jars, and two years ago when David was six and came home bullied and afraid of next day at school, Peter asked him if the boy was bigger than he was, and when David said 'A lot,' and showed him the boy's height with one hand, his breadth with two, Peter took the glass stopper from the cinnamon jar, tied it in a handkerchief corner, and struck his palm with it, so David would know how hard it was, would believe in it. Next morning David took it with him. On the schoolground, when the bully shoved him, he swung it up from his back pocket and down on the boy's forehead. The boy cried and went away. After school David found him on the sidewalk and hit his jaw with the weapon he had sat on all day, chased him two blocks swinging at his head, and came home with delighted eyes, no damp traces of yesterday's shame and fright, and Peter's own pain and rage turned to pride, then caution, and he spoke gently, told David to carry it for a week or so more, but not to use it unless the bully attacked; told him we must control our pleasure in giving pain.

Now reaching into the refrigerator he felt the children behind him; then he knew it was not them he felt, for in the bathroom when he spoke to their faces he had also felt a presence to his rear, watching, listening. It was the walls, it was fatherhood, it was himself. He was not an early drinker but he wanted an ale now; looked at the brown bottles long enough to fear and dislike his reason for wanting one, then he poured two glasses of apple cider and, for himself, cider and club soda. He sat at the table and watched David slice a Jalapeño over the beans, and said: 'Don't ever touch one of those and take a leak without washing your hands first.'

'Why?'

'I did it once. Think about it.'

'Wow.'

They talked of flavors as Kathi, with her eyes just above rim-level of the pot, her wrists in the steam, poured honey, and shook paprika, basil, parsley, Worcestershire, wine vinegar. In a bowl they mixed ground meat with a raw egg: jammed their hands into it, fingers touching; scooped and squeezed meat and onion and celery between their fingers; the kitchen smelled of bay leaf in the simmering beans, and then of broiling meat. They talked about the food as they ate, pressing thick hamburgers to fit their mouths, and only then Peter heard the white silence coming at them like afternoon snow. They cleaned the counter and table and what they had used; and they spoke briefly, quietly, they smoothly passed things; and when Peter turned off the faucet, all sound stopped, the kitchen was multiplied by silence, the apartment's walls grew longer, the floors wider, the ceilings higher. Peter walked the distance to his bedroom, looked at his watch, then quickly turned to the morning paper's television listing, and called: 'Hey! *The Magnificent Seven*'s coming on.'

'All *right*,' David said, and they hurried down the short hall, light footsteps whose sounds he could name: Kathi's, David's, Kathi's. He lay between them, bellies down, on the bed.

'Is this our third time or fourth?' Kathi said.

'I think our fourth. We saw it in a theater once.'

'I could see it every week,' David said.

'Except when Charles Bronson dies,' Kathi said. 'But I like when the little kids put flowers on his grave. And when he spanks them.'

The winter sunlight beamed through the bedroom window, the afternoon moving past him and his children. Driving them home he imitated Yul Brynner, Eli Wallach, Charles Bronson; the children praised his voices, laughed, and in front of their house they kissed him and asked what they were going to do tomorrow. He said he didn't know yet; he would call in the morning, and he watched them go up the walk between snow as high as Kathi's waist. At the door they turned and waved; he tapped the horn twice, and drove away.

That night he could not sleep. He read *Macbeth*, woke propped against the pillows, the bedside lamp on, the small book at his side. He put it on the table, turned out the light, moved the pillows down, and slept. Next afternoon he took David and Kathi to a movie.

He did not bring them to his apartment again, unless they were on the way to another place, and their time in the apartment was purposeful and short: Saturday morning cartoons, then lunch before going to a movie or museum. Early in the week he began reading the movie section of the paper, looking for matinees. Every weekend they went to a movie, and sometimes two, in their towns and other small towns and in Boston. On the third Saturday he took them to a PG movie which was bloody and erotic enough to make him feel ashamed and irresponsible as he sat between his children in the theater. Driving home, he asked them about the movie until he believed it had not frightened them, or made them curious about bodies and urges they did not yet have. After that, he saw all PG movies before taking them, and he was angry at mothers who left their children at the theater and picked them up when the movie was over; and left him to listen to their children exclaiming at death, laughing at love; and often they roamed the aisles going to the concession stand, and distracted him from this weekly entertainment which he suspected he waited for and enjoyed more than David and Kathi. He had not been an indiscriminate moviegoer since he was a child. Now what had started as a duty was pleasurable, relaxing. He knew that beneath this lay a base of cowardice. But he told himself it would pass. A time would come when he and Kathi and David could sit in his living room, talking like three friends who had known each other for eight and six years.

Most of his listeners on weekday afternoons were women. Between love songs he began talking to them about movie ratings. He said not to trust them. He asked what they felt about violence and sex in movies, whether or not they were bad for children. He told them he didn't know; that many of the fairy tales and all the comic books of his boyhood were violent; and so were the westerns and serials on Saturday afternoons. But there was no blood. And he chided the women about letting their children go to the movies alone.

He got letters and read them in his apartment at night. Some thanked him for his advice about ratings. Many told him it was all right for him to talk, he wasn't with the kids every afternoon after school and all weekends and holidays and summer; the management of the theater was responsible for quiet and order during the movies; they were showing the movies to attract children and they were glad to take the money. The children came home happy and did not complain about other children being noisy. Maybe he should stop going to matinees, should leave his kids there and pick them up when it was over. *It's almost what I'm doing*, he thought; and he stopped talking about movies to the afternoon women.

He found a sledding hill: steep and long, and at its base a large frozen pond. David and Kathi went with him to buy his sled, and with a thermos of hot chocolate they drove to the hill near his apartment. Parked cars lined the road, and children and some parents were on the hill's broad top. Red-faced children climbed back, pulling their sleds with ropes. Peter sledded first; he knew the ice on the pond was safe, but he was beginning to handle fatherhood as he did guns: always as if they were loaded, when he knew they were not. There was a satisfaction in preventing even dangers which did not exist.

The snow was hard and slick, rushed beneath him; he went over a bump, rose from the sled, nearly lost it, slammed down on it, legs outstretched, gloved hands steering around the next bump but not the next one suddenly rising toward his face, and he pressed against the sled, hugged the wood-shock to his chest, yelled with delight at children moving slowly upward, hit the edge of the pond and sledded straight out, looking at the evergreens on its far bank. The sled stopped near the middle of the pond; he stood and waved to the top of the hill, squinting at sun and bright snow, then two silhouettes waved back and he saw Kathi's long red hair. Holding the sled's rope he walked on ice, moving to his left as David started down and Kathi stood waiting, leaning on her sled. He told himself he was a fool: had lived winters with his children, yet this was the first sled he had bought for himself; sometimes he had gone with them because they asked him to, and he had used their sleds. But he had never found a sledding hill. He had driven past them, seen the small figures on their crests and slopes, but no more. Watching David swerve around a bump and Kathi, at the top, pushing her sled, then dropping onto it, he forgave himself; there was still time; already it had begun.

But on that first afternoon of sledding he made a mistake: within an hour his feet were painfully cold, his trousers wet and his legs cold; David and Kathi wore snow pants. Beneath his parka he was sweating. Then he knew they felt the same, yet they would sled as long as he did, because of the point and edges of divorce that pierced and cut all their time together.

'I'm freezing,' he said. 'I can't move my toes.'

'Me too,' David said.

'Let's go down one more time,' Kathi said.

Then he took them home. It was only three o'clock.

After that he took them sledding on weekend mornings. They brought clothes with them, and after sledding they went to his apartment and showered. They loved the glass doors. On the first day they argued about who would shower first, until Peter flipped a coin and David won and Peter said Kathi would have the first shower next time and they would take turns that way. They showered long and when Peter's turn came the water was barely warm and he was quickly in and out. Then in dry clothes they ate lunch and went to a movie.

Or to another place, and one night drinking bourbon in his living room, lights off so he could watch the snow falling, the yellowed, gentle swirl at the corner streetlight, the quick flakes at his window, banking on the sill, and across the street the grey-white motion lowering the sky and making the evergreens look distant, he thought of owning a huge building to save divorced fathers. Free admission. A place of swimming pool, badminton and tennis courts, movie theaters, restaurants, soda fountains, batting cages, a zoo, an art gallery, a circus, aquarium, science museum, hundreds of restrooms, two always in sight, everything in the tender charge of women trained in first aid and Montessori, no uniforms, their only style warmth and cheer. A father could spend entire days there, weekend after weekend, so in winter there would not be all this planning and driving. He had made his cowardice urbane, mobile, and sophisticated; but perhaps at its essence cowardice knows it is apparent: he believed David and Kathi knew that their afternoons at the aquarium, the Museum of Fine Arts, the Science Museum, were houses Peter had built, where they could be together as they were before, with one difference: there was always entertainment. Frenetic as they were, he preferred weekends to the Wednesday nights when they ate together. At first he thought it was shyness. Yet they talked easily, often about their work, theirs at school, his as a disc jockey. When he was not with the children he spent much time thinking about what they said to each other. And he saw that, in his eight years as a father, he had been attentive, respectful, amusing; he had taught and disciplined. But no: not now: when they were too loud in the car or they fought, he held onto his anger, his heart buffetted with it, and spoke calmly, as though to another man's children, for he was afraid that if he scolded as he had before, the day would be spoiled, they would not have the evening at home, the sleeping in the same house, to heal them; and they might not want to go with him next day or two nights from now or two days. During their eight and six years with him, he had shown them love, and made them laugh. But now he knew that he had remained a secret from them. What did they know about him? What did he know about them?

He would tell them about his loneliness, and what he had learned about himself. When he wasn't with them, he was lonely all the time, except while he was running or working, and sometimes at the station he felt it waiting for him in the parking lot, on the highway, in his apartment. He thought much about it, like an athletic man considering a sprained ligament, changing his exercises to include it. He separated his days into parts, thought about each one, and learned that all of them were not bad. When the alarm woke him in the winter dark, the new day and waiting night were the grey of the room, and they pressed down on him, fetid repetitions bent on smothering his spirit before he rose from the bed. But he got up quickly, made the bed while the sheets still held his warmth, and once in the kitchen with coffee and newspaper he moved into the first part of the day: bacon smell and solemn disc jockeys with classical music, an hour or more at the kitchen table, as near-peaceful as he dared hope for; and was grateful for too, as it went with him to the living room, to the chair at the southeast window where, pausing to watch traffic and look at the snow and winter branches of elms and maples in the park across the street, he sat in sun-warmth and entered the cadence of Shakespeare. In mid-morning, he Vaselined his face and genitals and, wearing layers of nylon, he ran two and a half miles down the road which, at his corner, was a town road of close houses but soon was climbing and dropping past farms and meadows; at the crest of a hill, where he could see the curves of trees on the banks of the Merrimack, he turned and ran back.

The second part began with ignition and seat belt, driving forty minutes on the highway, no buildings or billboards, low icicled cliffs and long white hills, and fields and woods in the angled winter sun, and in the silent car he received his afternoon self: heard the music he had chosen, popular music he would not listen to at home but had come to accept and barely listen to at work, heard his voice in mime and jest and remark, often merry, sometimes showing off and knowing it, but not much, no more than he had earned. That part of his day behind glass and microphone, with its comfort drawn from combining the familiar with the spontaneous, took him to four o'clock.

The next four hours, he learned, were not only the time he had to prepare for, but also the lair of his loneliness, the source of every quick chill of loss, each sudden whisper of dread and futility: for if he could spend them with a woman he loved, drink and cook and eat with her while day changed to night (though now, in winter, night came as he drove home), he and this woman huddled in the light and warmth of living room and kitchen, gin and meat, then his days until four and nights after eight would demand less from him of will, give more to him of hopeful direction. After dinner he listened to jazz and read fiction or watched an old movie on television until, without lust or even the need of a sleeping woman beside him, he went to bed: a blessing, but a disturbing one. He had assumed, as a husband and then an adulterous one, that his need for a woman was as carnal as it was spiritual. But now celibacy was easy; when he imagined a woman, she was drinking with him, eating dinner. So his most intense and perhaps his only need for a woman was then; and all the reasons for the end of his marriage became distant, blurred, and he wondered if the only reason he was alone now was a misogyny he had never recognized: that he did not even want a woman except at the day's end, and had borne all the other hours of woman-presence only to have her comfort as the clock's hands moved through their worst angles of the day.

Planning to tell all this to David and Kathi, knowing he would need gin to do it, he was frightened, already shy as if they sat with him now in the living room. A good sign: if he were afraid, then it took courage; if it took courage, then it must be right. He drank more bourbon than he thought he did, and went to bed excited by intimacy and love.

He slept off everything. In the morning he woke so amused at himself that, if he had not been alone, he would have laughed aloud. He imagined telling his children, over egg rolls and martinis and Shirley Temples, about his loneliness and his rituals to combat it. And *that* would be his new fatherhood, smelling of duck sauce and hot mustard and gin. Swallowing aspirins and orange juice, he saw clearly why he and the children were uncomfortable together, especially at Wednesday night dinners: when he lived with them, their talk had usually dealt with the immediate (I don't like playing with Cindy anymore; she's too bossy. I wish it would snow; it's no use being cold if it doesn't snow); they spoke at dinner and breakfast and, during holidays and summer, at lunch; in the car and stores while running errands; on the summer lawn while he prepared charcoal; and in their beds when he went to tell them goodnight; most of the time their talk was deep only because it was affectionate and tribal, sounds made between creatures sharing the same blood. Now their talk was the same, but it did not feel the same. They talked in his car and in places he took them, and the car and each place would not let them forget they were there because of divorce.

So their talk had felt evasive, fragile, contrived, and his drunken answer last night had been more talk: courageous, painful, honest. *My God*, he thought, as in a light snow that morning he ran out of his hangover, into lucidity. *I was going to have a Goddamn therapy session with my own children.* Breathing the smell of new snow and winter air he thought of this fool Peter Jackman, swallowing his bite of pork fried rice, and saying: And what do you feel at school? About the divorce, I mean. Are you ashamed around the other kids? He thought of the useless reopening and sometimes celebrating of wounds he and Norma had done with the marriage counselor, a pleasant and smart woman, but what could she do when all she had to work with was wounds? After each session he and Norma had driven home, usually mute, always in despair. Then, running faster, he imagined a house where he lived and the children came on Friday nights and stayed all weekend, played with their friends during the day, came and left the house as they needed, for food, drink, bathroom, diversion, and at night they relaxed together as a family; saw himself reading as they painted and drew at the kitchen table . . .

That night they ate dinner at a seafood restaurant thirty minutes from their town. When he drove them home he stayed outside their house for a while, the three of them sitting in front for warmth; they talked about summer and no school and no heavy clothes and no getting up early when it was still dark outside. He told them it was his favorite season too because of baseball and the sea. Next morning when he got into his car, the inside of his windshield was iced. He used the small plastic scraper from his glove compartment. As he scraped the middle and right side, he realized the grey ice curling and falling from the glass was the frozen breath of his children.

At a bar in the town where his children lived, he met a woman. This was on a Saturday night, after he had taken them home from the Museum of Fine Arts. They had liked Monet and Cézanne, had shown him light and color they thought were pretty. He told them Cézanne's *The Turn in the Road* was his favorite, that every time he came here he stood looking at it and he wanted to be walking up that road, toward the houses. But all afternoon he had known they were restless. They had not sledded that morning. Peter had gone out drinking the night before, with his only married friend who could leave his wife at home without paying even a subtle price, and he had slept through the time for sledding, had apologized when they phoned and woke him, and on the drive to the museum had told them he and Sibley (whom they knew as a friend of their mother too) had been having fun and had lost track of time until the bar closed. So perhaps they wanted to be outdoors. Or perhaps it was the old resonance of place again, the walls and ceiling of the museum, even the paintings telling them: You are here because your father left home.

He went to the bar for a sandwich, and stayed. Years ago he had come here often, on the way home from work, or at night with Norma. It was a neighborhood bar then, where professional fishermen and lobstermen and other men who worked with their hands drank, and sometimes brought their wives. Then someone from Boston bought it, put photographs and drawings of fishing and pleasure boats on the walls, built a kitchen which turned out quiche and crêpes, hired young women to tend the bar, and musicians to play folk and bluegrass. The old customers left. The new ones were couples and people trying to be a couple for at least the night, and that is why Peter stayed after eating his sandwich.

Within an hour she came in and sat at the bar, one empty chair away from him: a woman in her late twenties, dark eyes and light brown hair. Soon they were talking. He liked her because she smiled a lot. He also liked her drink: Jack Daniel's on the rocks. Her name was Mary Ann; her last name kept eluding him. She was a market researcher, and like many people Peter knew, she seemed to dismiss her work, though she was apparently good at it; her vocation was recreation: she skied down and across; backpacked; skated; camped; ran and swam. He began to imagine doing things with her, and he felt more insidious than if he were imagining passion: he saw her leading him and Kathi and David up a mountain trail. He told her he spent much of his life prone or sitting, except for a daily five-mile run, a habit from the Marine Corps (she gave him the sneer and he said: Come on, that was a long time ago, it was peacetime, it was fun), and he ran now for the same reasons everyone else did, or at least everyone he knew who ran: the catharsis, which kept his body feeling good, and his mind more or less sane. He said he had not slept in a tent since the Marines; probably because of the Marines. He said he wished he did as many things as she did, and he told her why. Some time in his bed during the night, she said: 'They probably did like the paintings. At least you're not taking them to all those movies now.'

'We still go about once a week.'

'Did you know Lennie's has free matinees for children? On Sunday afternoons?'

'No.'

'I have a divorced friend; she takes her kids almost every Sunday.'

'Why don't we go tomorrow?'

'With your kids?'

'If you don't mind.'

'Sure. I like kids. I'd like to have one of my own, without a husband.'

As he kissed her belly he imagined her helping him pitch the large tent he would buy, the four of them on a weekend of cold brook and trees on a mountainside, a fire, bacon in the skillet . . .

In the morning he scrambled their eggs, then phoned Norma. He had a general dislike of telephones: talking to his own hand gripping plastic, pacing, looking about the room; the timing of hanging up was tricky. Nearly all these conversations left him feeling as disconnected as the phone itself. But talking with Norma was different: he marvelled at how easy it was. The distance and disembodiment he felt on the phone with others were good here. He and Norma had hurt each other deeply, and their bodies had absorbed the pain: it was the stomach that tightened, the hands that shook, the breast that swelled then shrivelled. Now fleshless they could talk by phone, even with warmth, perhaps alive from the time when their bodies were at ease together. He thought of having a huge house where he could live with his family, seeing Norma only at meals, shared for the children, he and Norma talking to David and Kathi; their own talk would be on extension phones in their separate wings: they would discuss the children, and details of running the house. This was of course the way they had finally lived, without the separate wings, the phones. And one of their justifications as they talked of divorce was that the children would be harmed, growing up in a house with parents who did not love each other, who rarely touched, and then by accident. There had been moments near the end when, brushing against each other in the kitchen, one of them would say: Sorry. Now as Mary Ann Brighi (he had waked knowing her last name) spread jam on toast, he phoned.

'I met this woman last night.'

Mary Ann smiled; Norma's voice did.

'It's about time. I was worried about your arm going.'

'What about you?'

'I'm doing all right.'

'Do you bring them home?'

'It's not them, and I get a sitter.'

'But he comes to the house? To take you out?'

'Peter?'

'What.'

'What are we talking about?'

'I was wondering what the kids would think if Mary Ann came along this afternoon.'

'What they'll think is Mary Ann's coming along this afternoon.'

'You're sure that's all?'

'Unless you fuck in front of them.'

He turned his face from Mary Ann, but she had already seen his blush; he looked at her smiling with toast crumbs on her teeth. He wished he were married and lovemaking were simple. But after cleaning the kitchen he felt passion again, though not much; in his mind he was introducing the children to Mary Ann. He would make sure he talked to them, did not leave them out while he talked to her. He was making love while he thought this; he hoped they would like her; again he saw them hiking up a trail through pines, stopping for Kathi and David to rest; a sudden bounding deer; the camp beside the stream; he thanked his member for doing its work down there while the rest of him was in the mountains in New Hampshire.

As he walked with David and Kathi he held their hands; they were looking at her face watching them from the car window.

'She's a new friend of mine,' he said. 'Just a friend. She wants to show us this night club where children can go on Sunday afternoons.'

From the back seat they shook hands, peered at her, glanced at Peter, their eyes making him feel that like adults they could sense when people were lovers; he adjusted the rearview mirror, watched their faces, decided he was seeing jumbled and vulnerable curiosity: Who was she? Would she marry their father? Would they like her? Would their mother be sad? And the night club confused them.

'Isn't that where people go drink?' Kathi said.

'It's afternoon too,' David said.

Not for Peter; the sky was grey, the time was grey, dark was coming, and all at once he felt utterly without will; all the strength he had drawn on to be with his children left him like one long spurt of arterial blood: all his time with his children was grey, with night coming; it would always be; nothing would change: like three people cursed in an old myth they would forever be thirty-three and eight and six, in this car on slick or salted roads, going from one place to another. He disapproved of but understood those divorced fathers who fled to live in a different pain far away. Beneath his despair, he saw himself and his children sledding under a lovely blue sky, heard them laughing in movies, watching in awe like love a circling blue shark in the aquarium's tank; but these seemed beyond recapture.

He entered the highway going south, and that quick transition of hands and head and eyes as he moved into fast traffic snapped him out of himself, into the sound of Mary Ann's voice: with none of the rising and falling rhythm of nursery talk, she was telling them, as if speaking to a young man and woman she had just met, about Lennie's. How Lennie believed children should hear good music, not just the stuff on the radio. She talked about jazz. She hummed some phrases of 'Somewhere Over the Rainbow,' then improvised. They would hear Gerry Mulligan today, she said, and as she talked about the different saxophones, Peter looked in the mirror at their listening faces.

'And Lennie has a cook from Tijuana in Mexico,' Mary Ann said. 'She makes the best chili around.'

Walking into Lennie's with a pretty woman and his two healthy and pretty children, he did not feel like a divorced father looking for something to do; always in other places he was certain he looked that way, and often he felt guilty when talking with waitresses. He paid the cover charge for himself and Mary Ann and she said: All right, but I buy the first two rounds, and he led her and the children to a table near the bandstand. He placed the children between him and Mary Ann. Bourbon, Cokes, bowls of chili. The room was filling and Peter saw that at most tables there were children with parents, usually one parent, usually a father. He watched his children listening to Mulligan. His fingers tapped the table with the drummer. He looked warmly at Mary Ann's profile until she turned and smiled at him.

Often Mulligan talked to the children, explained how his saxophone worked; his voice was cheerful, joking, never serious, as he talked about the guitar and bass and piano and drums. He clowned laughter from the children in the dark. Kathi and David turned to each other and Peter to share their laughter. During the music they listened intently. Their hands tapped the table. They grinned at Peter and Mary Ann. At intermission Mulligan said he wanted to meet the children. While his group went to the dressing room he sat on the edge of the bandstand and waved the children forward. Kathi and David talked about going. Each would go if the other would. They took napkins for autographs and, holding hands, walked between tables and joined the children standing around Mulligan. When it was their turn he talked to them, signed their napkins, kissed their foreheads. They hurried back to Peter.

'He's *neat*,' Kathi said.

'What did you talk about?'

'He asked our names,' David said.

'And if we liked winter out here.'

'And if we played an instrument.'

'What kind of music we liked.'

'What did you tell him?'

'Jazz like his.'

The second set ended at nearly seven; bourbon-high, Peter drove carefully, listening to Mary Ann and the children talking about Mulligan and his music and warmth. Then David and Kathi were gone, running up the sidewalk to tell Norma, and show their autographed napkins, and Peter followed Mary Ann's directions to her apartment.

'I've been in the same clothes since last night,' she said.

In her apartment, as unkempt as his, they showered together, hurried damp-haired and chilled to her bed.

'This is the happiest day I've had since the marriage ended,' he said.

But when he went home and was alone in his bed, he saw his cowardice again. All the warmth of his day left him, and he lay in the dark, knowing that he should have been wily enough to understand that the afternoon's sweetness and ease meant he had escaped: had put together a family for the day. That afternoon Kathi had spilled a Coke; before Peter noticed, Mary Ann was cleaning the table with cocktail napkins, smiling at Kathi, talking to her under the music, lifting a hand to the waitress.

Next night he took Mary Ann to dinner and driving to her apartment, it seemed to him that since the end of his marriage, dinner had become disproportionate: alone at home it was a task he forced himself to do, with his children it was a fragile rite, and with old friends who alternately fed him and Norma he felt vaguely criminal. Now he must once again face his failures over a plate of food. He and Mary Ann had slept little the past two nights, and at the restaurant she told him she had worked hard all day, yet she looked fresh and strong, while he was too tired to imagine making love after dinner. With his second martini, he said: 'I used you yesterday. With my kids.'

'There's a better word.'

'All right: needed.'

'I knew that.'

'You did?'

'We had fun.'

'I can't do it anymore.'

'Don't be so hard on yourself. You probably spend more time with them now than when you lived together.'

'I do. So does Norma. But that's not it. It's how much I wanted your help, and started hoping for it. Next Sunday. And in summer: the sort of stuff you do, camping and hiking; when we talked about it Saturday night—'

'I knew that too. I thought it was sweet.'

He leaned back in his chair, sipped his drink. Tonight he would break his martini rule, have a third before dinner. He loved women who knew and forgave his motives before he knew and confessed them.

But he would not take her with the children again. He was with her often; she wanted a lover, she said, not love, not what it still did to men and women. He did not tell her he thought they were using each other in a way that might have been cynical, if it were not so frightening. He simply followed her, became one of those who make love with their friends. But she was his only woman friend, and he did not know how many men shared her. When she told him she would not be home this night or that weekend, he held his questions. He held onto his heart too, and forced himself to make her a part of the times when he was alone. He had married young, and life to him was surrounded by the sounds and touches of a family. Now in this foreign land he felt so vulnerably strange that at times it seemed near madness as he gave Mary Ann a function in his time, ranking somewhere among his running and his work.

When the children asked about her, he said they were still friends. Once Kathi asked why she never came to Lennie's anymore, and he said her work kept her pretty busy and she had other friends she did things with, and he liked being alone with them anyway. But then he was afraid the children thought she had not liked them; so, twice a month, he brought Mary Ann to Lennie's.

He and the children went every Sunday. And that was how the cold months passed, beginning with the New Year, because Peter and Norma had waited until after Christmas to end the marriage: the movies and sledding, museums and aquarium, the restaurants; always they were on the road, and whenever he looked at his car he thought of the children. How many conversations while looking through the windshield? How many times had the doors slammed shut and they re-entered or left his life? Winter ended slowly. April was cold and in May Peter and the children still wore sweaters or windbreakers, and on two weekends there was rain, and everything they did together was indoors. But when the month ended, Peter thought it was not the weather but the patterns of winter that had kept them driving from place to place.

Then it was June and they were out of school and Peter took his vacation. Norma worked, and by nine in the morning he and Kathi and David were driving to the sea. They took a large blanket and tucked its corners into the sand so it wouldn't flap in the wind, and they lay oiled in the sun. On the first day they talked of winter, how they could feel the sun warming their ribs, as they had watched it warming the earth during the long thaw. It was a beach with gentle currents and a gradual slope out to sea but Peter told them, as he had every summer, about undertow: that if ever they were caught in one, they must not swim against it; they must let it take them out and then they must swim parallel to the beach until the current shifted and they could swim back in with it. He could not imagine his children being calm enough to do that, for he was afraid of water and only enjoyed body-surfing near the beach, but he told them anyway. Then he said it would not happen because he would always test the current first.

In those first two weeks the three of them ran into the water and body-surfed only a few minutes, for it was too cold still, and they had to leave it until their flesh was warm again. They would not be able to stay in long until July. Peter showed them the different colors of summer, told them why on humid days the sky and ocean were paler blue, and on dry days they were darker, more beautiful, and the trees they passed on the roads to the beach were brighter green. He bought a whiffle ball and bat and kept them in the trunk of his car and they played at the beach. The children dug holes, made castles, Peter watched, slept, and in late morning he ran. From a large thermos they drank lemonade or juice; and they ate lunch all day, the children grazing on fruit and the sandwiches he had made before his breakfast. Then he took them to his apartment for showers, and they helped carry in the ice chest and thermos and blanket and their knapsack of clothes. Kathi and David still took turns showering first, and they stayed in longer, but now in summer the water was still hot when his turn came. Then he drove them home to Norma, his skin red and pleasantly burning; then tan.

When his vacation ended they spent all sunny weekends at the sea, and even grey days that were warm. The children became braver about the cold, and forced him to go in with them and body-surf. But they could stay longer than he could, and he left to lie on the blanket and watch them, to make sure they stayed in shallow water. He made them promise to wait on the beach while he ran. He went in the water to cool his body from the sun, but mostly he lay on the blanket, reading, and watching the children wading out to the breakers and riding them in. Kathi and David did not always stay together. One left to walk the beach alone. Another played with strangers, or children who were there most days too. One built a castle. Another body-surfed. And, often, one would come to the blanket and drink and take a sandwich from the ice chest, would sit eating and drinking beside Peter, offer him a bite, a swallow. And on all those beach days Peter's shyness and apprehension were gone. It's the sea, he said to Mary Ann one night.

And it was: for on that day, a long Saturday at the beach, when he had all day felt peace and father-love and sun and salt water, he had understood why now in summer he and his children were as he had yearned for them to be in winter: they were no longer confined to car or buildings to remind them why they were there. The long beach and the sea were their lawn; the blanket their home; the ice chest and thermos their kitchen. They lived as a family again. While he ran and David dug in the sand until he reached water and Kathi looked for pretty shells for her room, the blanket waited for them. It was the place they wandered back to: for food, for drink, for rest, their talk as casual as between children and father arriving, through separate doors, at the kitchen sink for water, the refrigerator for an orange. Then one left for the surf; another slept in the sun, lips stained with grape juice. He had wanted to tell the children about it, but it was too much to tell, and the beach was no place for such talk anyway, and he also guessed they knew. So that afternoon when they were all lying on the blanket, on their backs, the children flanking him, he simply said: 'Divorced kids go to the beach more than married ones.'

'Why?' Kathi said.

'Because married people do chores and errands on weekends. No kid-days.'

'I love the beach,' David said.

'So do I,' Peter said.

He looked at Kathi.

'You don't like it, huh?'

She took her arm from her eyes and looked at him. His urge was to turn away. She looked at him for a long time; her eyes were too tender, too wise, and he wished she could have learned both later, and differently; in her eyes he saw the car in winter, heard its doors closing and closing, their talk and the sounds of heater and engine and tires on the road, and the places the car took them. Then she held his hand, and closed her eyes.

'I wish it was summer all year round,' she said.

He watched her face, rosy tan now, lightly freckled; her small scar was already lower. Holding her hand, he reached over for David's, and closed his eyes against the sun. His legs touched theirs. After a while he heard them sleeping. Then he slept.

WAITING

JUANITA CREEHAN WAS a waitress in a piano bar near Camp Pendleton, California. She had been a widow for twelve years, and her most intense memory of her marriage was an imagined one: Patrick's death in the Chosin Reservoir. After Starkey got back from Korea, he and Mary came to her apartment, and he told Juanita how it happened: they were attacking a hill, and when they cleared it they went down to the road and heard that Patrick had caught it. Starkey went over to the second platoon to look at him.

'What did they do to him?' Juanita said.

'They wrapped him in a shelter half and put him in a truck.'

She thought of the road of frozen mud and snow; she had never seen snow but now when it fell or lay white in her mind it was always death. Many nights she drank and talked with Starkey and Mary, and she asked Starkey for more details of the Reservoir, and sometimes she disliked him for being alive, or disliked Mary for having him alive. She had been tolerant of Mary's infidelity while Starkey was gone, for she understood her loneliness and dread; but now she could not forgive her, and often she looked quickly into Mary's eyes, and knew that her look was unforgiving. Years later, when she heard they were divorced, she was both pleased and angry. At the end of those nights of listening to Starkey, she went to bed and saw the hills and sky, and howitzers and trucks and troops on the road. She saw Patrick lying in the snow while the platoon moved up the hill; she saw them wrap him in the shelter half and lift him to the bed of the truck.

Some nights she descended further into the images. First she saw Patrick walking. He was the platoon sergeant, twenty-six years old. He walked on the side of the road, watching his troops and the hills. He had lost weight, was thinner than ever (my little bantam rooster, she had called him), his cheeks were sunken, and on them was a thin red beard. She no longer felt her own body. She was inside his: she felt the weight of helmet and rifle and parka; the cold feet; and the will to keep the body going, to believe that each step took him and his men closer to the sea. Through his green eyes and fever-warmth she looked up the road: a howitzer bounced behind a truck; Lieutenant Dobson, walking ahead on the road, wore a parka hood under his helmet; she could see none of his flesh as he looked once up at the sky. She heard boots on the hard earth, the breathing and coughing of troops, saw their breath-plumes in the air. She scanned the hills on both sides of the road, looked down at her boots moving toward the sea; glanced to her left at the files of young troops, then looked to the right again, at a snow-covered hill without trees, and then her chest and belly were struck and she was suddenly ill: she felt not pain but nausea, and a sense of futility at living this long and walking this far as her body seemed to melt into the snow . . .

On a summer night in 1962, for the first time in her life, she woke with a man and had to remember his name. She lay beside the strange weight of his body and listened to his breath, then remembered who he was: Roy Hodges, a sergeant major, who last night had talked with her when she brought his drinks, and the rest of the time he watched her, and when she went to the restroom she looked at her tan face and blonde hair; near the end of the evening he asked if he could take her home; she said she had a car but he could follow her, she'd like to have a drink, and they drank vodka at her kitchen table. Now she did not want to touch him, or wake him and tell him to go. She got up, found her clothes on the floor and dressed; quietly she opened a drawer and took a sweater and put it on her shoulders like a cape. Her purse was in the kitchen. She found it in the dark, on the floor beside her chair, and went out of the apartment and crossed the cool damp grass to her car.

With the windshield wipers sweeping dew, she drove down a hill and through town to the beach. She locked her purse in the car and sat on loose sand and watched the sea. Black waves broke with a white slap, then a roar. She sat huddled in the cool air.

Then she walked. To her left the sea was loud and dark, and she thought of Vicente Torrez with the pistol in his lap: a slender Mexican boy who in high school had teased her about being named Juanita, when she had no Mexican blood. Blonde gringita, he called her, and his eyes looked curiously at her, as if her name were an invitation to him, but he didn't know how to answer it. Five years after high school, while she was married to Patrick, she read in the paper that he had shot himself. There was no photograph, so she read the story to know if this were the same Vicente, and she wanted it to be him. He had been a cab driver in San Diego, and had lived alone. The second and final paragraph told of the year he was graduated from the high school in San Diego, and listed his survivors: his parents, brothers, sisters. So it was Vicente, with the tight pants and teasing face and that question in his eyes: Could you be my girl? Love me? Someone she once knew had sat alone in his apartment and shot himself; yet her feeling was so close to erotic that she was frightened. Patrick came home in late afternoon and she watched through the window as he walked uniformed across the lawn (it was winter: he was wearing green) and when he came inside she held him and told him and then she was crying, seeing Vicente sitting in a dirty and disorderly room, sitting on the edge of his bed and reaching that moment when he wanted more than anything else not to be Vicente, and crying into Patrick's chest she said: 'I wonder if he knew somebody would cry; I wonder if he wouldn't have done it; if that would have seen him through till tomorrow—' The word tomorrow stayed in her heart. She saw it in her mind, its letters printed across the black and white image of Vicente sitting on the bed with the pistol, and she loosened Patrick's tie and began to unbutton his green blouse.

She was looking out at the sea as she walked, and she stepped into a shallow pool left by the tide; the water covered her sandalled feet and was cool and she stood in it. Then she stepped out and walked on. For a year after Patrick was killed she took sleeping pills. She remembered lying in bed and waiting for the pill to work, and the first signals in her fingers, her hands: the slow-coming dullness, and she would touch her face, its skin faintly tingling, going numb, then she was aware only of the shallow sound and peaceful act of her slow breathing.

Juanita Jody Noury Creehan. Her mother had named her, given her a choice that would not change her initials if later she called herself Jody. Her mother's maiden name had been Miller. She looked up at the sky: it was clear, stars and a quarter-moon. Noury Creehan: both names from men. She stepped out of her sandals, toe against heel, toe against heel, heart beating as though unclothing for yet another man, remembering the confessions when she was in high school, remembering tenderly as if she were mother to herself as a young girl. Petting: always she called it that, whispering through lattice and veil, because that was the word the priests used in the confessional and when they came to the Saturday morning catechism classes for talks with the junior and senior girls; and the word the nuns used too on Saturday mornings, black-robed and looking never-petted themselves, so the word seemed strange on their tongues. The priests looked as if they had petted, or some of them did, probably only because they were men, they had hands and faces she liked to watch, voices she liked to hear.

Petting, for the bared and handled and suckled breasts, her blouse unbuttoned, and her pants off and skirt pulled up for the finger; the boys' pants on and unzipped as they gasped, thick warmth on her hand, white faint thumping on the dashboard. She confessed her own finger too, and while petting was a vague word and kept her secrets, masturbation was stark and hid nothing, exposed her in the confessional like the woman in the photograph that Ruth had shown her: a Mexican woman of about thirty, sitting naked in an armchair, legs spread, hand on her mound, and her face caught forever in passion real or posed.

Then finally in high school it was Billy Campbell in the spring of her junior year, quick-coming Billy dropping the Trojan out of the car window, the last of her guilt dropping with it, so that after one more confession she knew she had kneeled and whispered to a priest for the last time. Young and hot and pretty, she could not imagine committing any sin that was not sexual. When she was thirty there was no one to tell that sometimes she could not bear knowing what she knew: that no one would help her, not ever again. That was the year she gained weight and changed sizes and did not replace her black dress, though she liked herself in black, liked her blonde hair touching it. She began selecting colors which in the store were merely colors; but when she thought of them on her body and bed, they seemed to hold possibilities: sheets and pillow-cases of yellow and pink and pale blue, and all her underwear was pastel, so she could start each day by stepping into color. Many of those days she spent at the beach, body-surfing and swimming beyond the breakers and sleeping in the sun, or walking there in cool months. Once a bartender told her that waitresses and barten-ders should have a month off every year and go to a cabin in the mountains and not smile once. Just to relax the facial muscles, he said; maybe they go, like pitchers' arms. Her days were short, for she slept late, and her evenings long; and most days she was relieved when it was time to go to work, to the costume-smile and chatter that some nights she brought home with a gentle man, and next day she had that warmth to remember as she lay on the beach.

She unbuttoned and unzipped her skirt, let it fall to the sand; pulled down her pants and stepped out of them. She took off the sweater and blouse and shivering dropped them, then reached around for the clasp of her brassiere. She walked across wet sand, into the rushing touch of sea. She walked through a breaking wave, sand moving under her feet, current pulling and pushing her farther out, and she walked with it and stood breast-deep, watching the surface coming from the lighter dome of the sky. A black swell rose toward her and curled, foam skimming its crest like quick smoke; she turned to the beach, watched the wave over her shoulder: breaking it took her with head down and outstretched arms pointing, eyes open to dark and fast white foam, then she scraped sand with breasts and feet, belly and thighs, and lay breathing salt-taste as water hissed away from her legs. She stood and crossed the beach, toward her clothes.

He was sleeping. In the dark she undressed and left her clothes on the floor and took a nightgown to the bathroom. She showered and washed her hair and when she went to the bedroom he said: 'Do you always get up when it's still night?'

'I couldn't sleep.'

She got into bed; he placed a hand on her leg and she shifted away and he did not touch her again.

'In three months I'll be thirty-nine.'

'Thirty-nine's not bad.'

'I was born in the afternoon. They didn't have any others.'

'What time is it?'

'Almost five.'

'It's going to be a long day.'

'Not for me. I'll sleep.'

'Night worker.'

'They were Catholics, but they probably used something anyway. Maybe I was a diaphragm baby. I feel like one a lot of the time.'

'What's that supposed to mean?'

'Like I sneaked into the movie and I'm waiting for the usher to come get me.'

'Tell him to shove off.'

'Not this usher.'

'You talking about dying?'

'No.'

'What then?'

'I don't know. But he's one shit of an usher.'

She believed she could not sleep until he left. But when she closed her eyes she felt it coming in her legs and arms and breath, and gratefully she yielded to it: near-dreaming, she saw herself standing naked in the dark waves. One struck her breast and she wheeled slow and graceful, salt water black in her eyes and lovely in her mouth, hair touching sand as she turned then rose and floated in swift tenderness out to sea.

KILLINGS

O N THE AUGUST morning when Matt Fowler buried his youngest son, Frank, who had lived for twenty-one years, eight months, and four days, Matt's older son, Steve, turned to him as the family left the grave and walked between their friends, and said: 'I should kill him.' He was twenty-eight, his brown hair starting to thin in front where he used to have a cowlick. He bit his lower lip, wiped his eyes, then said it again. Ruth's arm, linked with Matt's, tightened; he looked at her. Beneath her eyes there was swelling from the three days she had suffered. At the limousine Matt stopped and looked back at the grave, the casket, and the Congregationalist minister who he thought had probably had a difficult job with the eulogy though he hadn't seemed to, and the old funeral director who was saying something to the six young pallbearers. The grave was on a hill and overlooked the Merrimack, which he could not see from where he stood; he looked at the opposite bank, at the apple orchard with its symmetrically planted trees going up a hill.

Next day Steve drove with his wife back to Baltimore where he managed the branch office of a bank, and Cathleen, the middle child, drove with her husband back to Syracuse. They had left the grandchildren with friends. A month after the funeral Matt played poker at Willis Trottier's because Ruth, who knew this was the second time he had been invited, told him to go, he couldn't sit home with her for the rest of her life, she was all right. After the game Willis went outside to tell everyone goodnight and, when the others had driven away, he walked with Matt to his car. Willis was a short, silver-haired man who had opened a diner after World War II, his trade then mostly very early breakfast, which he cooked, and then lunch for the men who worked at the leather and shoe factories. He now owned a large restaurant.

'He walks the Goddamn streets,' Matt said.

'I know. He was in my place last night, at the bar. With a girl.'

'I don't see him. I'm in the store all the time. Ruth sees him. She sees him too much. She was at Sunnyhurst today getting cigarettes and aspirin, and there he was. She can't even go out for cigarettes and aspirin. It's killing her.'

'Come back in for a drink.'

Matt looked at his watch. Ruth would be asleep. He walked with Willis back into the house, pausing at the steps to look at the starlit sky. It was a cool summer night; he thought vaguely of the Red Sox, did not even know if they were at home tonight; since it happened he had not been able to think about any of the small pleasures he believed he had earned, as he had earned also what was shattered now forever: the quietly harried and quietly pleasurable days of fatherhood. They went inside. Willis's wife, Martha, had gone to bed hours ago, in the rear of the large house which was rigged with burglar and fire alarms. They went downstairs to the game room: the television set suspended from the ceiling, the pool table, the poker table with beer cans, cards, chips, filled ashtrays, and the six chairs where Matt and his friends had sat, the friends picking up the old banter as though he had only been away on vacation; but he could see the affection and courtesy in their eyes. Willis went behind the bar and mixed them each a Scotch and soda; he stayed behind the bar and looked at Matt sitting on the stool.

'How often have you thought about it?' Willis said.

'Every day since he got out. I didn't think about bail. I thought I wouldn't have to worry about him for years. She sees him all the time. It makes her cry.'

'He was in my place a long time last night. He'll be back.'

'Maybe he won't.'

'The band. He likes the band.'

'What's he doing now?'

'He's tending bar up to Hampton Beach. For a friend. Ever notice even the worst bastard always has friends? He couldn't get work in town. It's just tourists and kids up to Hampton. Nobody knows him. If they do, they don't care. They drink what he mixes.'

'Nobody tells me about him.'

'I hate him, Matt. My boys went to school with him. He was the same then. Know what he'll do? Five at the most. Remember that woman about seven years ago? Shot her husband and dropped him off the bridge in the Merrimack with a hundred pound sack of cement and said all the way through it that nobody helped her. Know where she is now? She's in Lawrence now, a secretary. And whoever helped her, where the hell is he?'

'I've got a .38 I've had for years. I take it to the store now. I tell Ruth it's for the night deposits. I tell her things have changed: we got junkies here now too. Lots of people without jobs. She knows though.'

'What does she know?'

'She knows I started carrying it after the first time she saw him in town. She knows it's in case I see him, and there's some kind of a situation—'

He stopped, looked at Willis, and finished his drink. Willis mixed him another.

'What kind of a situation?'

'Where he did something to me. Where I could get away with it.'

'How does Ruth feel about that?'

'She doesn't know.'

'You said she does, she's got it figured out.'

He thought of her that afternoon: when she went into Sunny-hurst, Strout was waiting at the counter while the clerk bagged the things he had bought; she turned down an aisle and looked at soup cans until he left.

'Ruth would shoot him herself, if she thought she could hit him.'

'You got a permit?'

'No.'

'I do. You could get a year for that.'

'Maybe I'll get one. Or maybe I won't. Maybe I'll just stop bring-ing it to the store.'

Richard Strout was twenty-six years old, a high school athlete, football scholarship to the University of Massachusetts where he lasted for almost two semesters before quitting in advance of the final grades that would have forced him not to return. People then said: Dickie can do the work; he just doesn't want to. He came home and did construction work for his father but refused his father's offer to learn the business; his two older brothers had learned it, so that Strout and Sons trucks going about town, and signs on construction sites, now slashed wounds into Matt Fowler's life. Then Richard married a young girl and became a bartender, his salary and tips augmented and perhaps sometimes matched by his father, who also posted his bond. So his friends, his enemies (he had those: fist fights or, more often, boys and then young men who had not fought him when they thought they should have), and those who simply knew him by face and name, had a series of images of him which they recalled when they heard of the killing: the high school running back, the young drunk in bars, the oblivious hard-hatted young man eating lunch at a counter, the bartender who could perhaps be called courteous but not more than that: as he tended bar, his dark eyes and dark, wide-jawed face appeared less sullen, near blank.

One night he beat Frank. Frank was living at home and waiting for September, for graduate school in economics, and working as a lifeguard at Salisbury Beach, where he met Mary Ann Strout, in her first month of separation. She spent most days at the beach with her two sons. Before ten o'clock one night Frank came home; he had driven to the hospital first, and he walked into the living room with stitches over his right eye and both lips bright and swollen.

'I'm all right,' he said, when Matt and Ruth stood up, and Matt turned off the television, letting Ruth get to him first: the tall, muscled but slender suntanned boy. Frank tried to smile at them but couldn't because of his lips.

'It was her husband, wasn't it?' Ruth said.

'Ex,' Frank said. 'He dropped in.'

Matt gently held Frank's jaw and turned his face to the light, looked at the stitches, the blood under the white of the eye, the bruised flesh.

'Press charges,' Matt said.

'No.'

'What's to stop him from doing it again? Did you hit him at all? Enough so he won't want to next time?

'I don't think I touched him.'

'So what are you going to do?'

'Take karate,' Frank said, and tried again to smile.

'That's not the problem,' Ruth said.

'You know you like her,' Frank said.

'I like a lot of people. What about the boys? Did they see it?'

'They were asleep.'

'Did you leave her alone with him?'

'He left first. She was yelling at him. I believe she had a skillet in her hand.'

'Oh for God's sake,' Ruth said.

Matt had been dealing with that too: at the dinner table on evenings when Frank wasn't home, was eating with Mary Ann; or, on the other nights—and Frank was with her every night—he talked with Ruth while they watched television, or lay in bed with the windows open and he smelled the night air and imagined, with both pride and muted sorrow, Frank in Mary Ann's arms. Ruth didn't like it because Mary Ann was in the process of divorce, because she had two children, because she was four years older than Frank, and finally—she told this in bed, where she had during all of their marriage told him of her deepest feelings: of love, of passion, of fears about one of the children, of pain Matt had caused her or she had caused him—she was against it because of what she had heard: that the marriage had gone bad early, and for most of it Richard and Mary Ann had both played around.

'That can't be true,' Matt said. 'Strout wouldn't have stood for it.'

'Maybe he loves her.'

'He's too hot-tempered. He couldn't have taken that.'

But Matt knew Strout had taken it, for he had heard the stories too. He wondered who had told them to Ruth; and he felt vaguely annoyed and isolated: living with her for thirty-one years and still not knowing what she talked about with her friends. On these summer nights he did not so much argue with her as try to comfort her, but finally there was no difference between the two: she had concrete objections, which he tried to overcome. And in his attempt to do this, he neglected his own objections, which were the same as hers, so that as he spoke to her he felt as disembodied as he sometimes did in the store when he helped a man choose a blouse or dress or piece of costume jewelry for his wife.

'The divorce doesn't mean anything,' he said. 'She was young and maybe she liked his looks and then after a while she realized she was living with a bastard. I see it as a positive thing.'

'She's not divorced yet.'

'It's the same thing. Massachusetts has crazy laws, that's all. Her age is no problem. What's it matter when she was born? And that other business: even if it's true, which it probably isn't, it's got nothing to do with Frank, it's in the past. And the kids are no problem. She's been married six years; she ought to have kids. Frank likes them. He plays with them. And he's not going to marry her anyway, so it's not a problem of money.'

'Then what's he doing with her?'

'She probably loves him, Ruth. Girls always have. Why can't we just leave it at that?'

'He got home at six o'clock Tuesday morning.'

'I didn't know you knew. I've already talked to him about it.'

Which he had: since he believed almost nothing he told Ruth, he went to Frank with what he believed. The night before, he had followed Frank to the car after dinner.

'You wouldn't make much of a burglar,' he said.

'How's that?'

Matt was looking up at him; Frank was six feet tall, an inch and a half taller than Matt, who had been proud when Frank at seventeen outgrew him; he had only felt uncomfortable when he had to reprimand or caution him. He touched Frank's bicep, thought of the young taut passionate body, believed he could sense the desire, and again he felt the pride and sorrow and envy too, not knowing whether he was envious of Frank or Mary Ann.

'When you came in yesterday morning, I woke up. One of these mornings your mother will. And I'm the one who'll have to talk to her. She won't interfere with you. Okay? I know it means—' But he stopped, thinking: I know it means getting up and leaving that suntanned girl and going sleepy to the car, I know—

'Okay,' Frank said, and touched Matt's shoulder and got into the car.

There had been other talks, but the only long one was their first one: a night driving to Fenway Park, Matt having ordered the tickets so they could talk, and knowing when Frank said yes, he would go, that he knew the talk was coming too. It took them forty minutes to get to Boston, and they talked about Mary Ann until they joined the city traffic along the Charles River, blue in the late sun. Frank told him all the things that Matt would later pretend to believe when he told them to Ruth.

'It seems like a lot for a young guy to take on,' Matt finally said.

'Sometimes it is. But she's worth it.'

'Are you thinking about getting married?'

'We haven't talked about it. She can't for over a year. I've got school.'

'I *do* like her,' Matt said.

He did. Some evenings, when the long summer sun was still low in the sky, Frank brought her home; they came into the house smelling of suntan lotion and the sea, and Matt gave them gin and tonics and started the charcoal in the backyard, and looked at Mary Ann in the lawn chair: long and very light brown hair (Matt thinking that twenty years ago she would have dyed it blonde), and the long brown legs he loved to look at; her face was pretty; she had probably never in her adult life gone unnoticed into a public place. It was in her wide brown eyes that she looked older than Frank; after a few drinks Matt thought what he saw in her eyes was something erotic, testament to the rumors about her; but he knew it wasn't that, or all that: she had, very young, been through a sort of pain that his children, and he and Ruth, had been spared. In the moments of his recognizing that pain, he wanted to tenderly touch her hair, wanted with some gesture to give her solace and hope. And he would glance at Frank, and hope they would love each other, hope Frank would soothe that pain in her heart, take it from her eyes; and her divorce, her age, and her children did not matter at all. On the first two evenings she did not bring her boys, and then Ruth asked her to bring them next time. In bed that night Ruth said, 'She hasn't brought them because she's embarrassed. She shouldn't feel embarrassed.'

Richard Strout shot Frank in front of the boys. They were sitting on the living room floor watching television, Frank sitting on the couch, and Mary Ann just returning from the kitchen with a tray of sandwiches. Strout came in the front door and shot Frank twice in the chest and once in the face with a 9 mm. automatic. Then he looked at the boys and Mary Ann, and went home to wait for the police.

It seemed to Matt that from the time Mary Ann called weeping to tell him until now, a Saturday night in September, sitting in the car with Willis, parked beside Strout's car, waiting for the bar to close, that he had not so much moved through his life as wandered through it, his spirit like a dazed body bumping into furniture and corners. He had always been a fearful father: when his children were young, at the start of each summer he thought of them drowning in a pond or the sea, and he was relieved when he came home in the evenings and they were there; usually that relief was his only acknowledgment of his fear, which he never spoke of, and which he controlled within his heart. As he had when they were very young and all of them in turn, Cathleen too, were drawn to the high oak in the backyard, and had to climb it. Smiling, he watched them, imagining the fall: and he was poised to catch the small body before it hit the earth. Or his legs were poised; his hands were in his pockets or his arms were folded and, for the child looking down, he appeared relaxed and confident while his heart beat with the two words he wanted to call out but did not: *Don't fall*. In winter he was less afraid: he made sure the ice would hold him before they skated, and he brought or sent them to places where they could sled without ending in the street. So he and his children had survived their childhood, and he only worried about them when he knew they were driving a long distance, and then he lost Frank in a way no father expected to lose his son, and he felt that all the fears he had borne while they were growing up, and all the grief he had been afraid of, had backed up like a huge wave and struck him on the beach and swept him out to sea. Each day he felt the same and when he was able to forget how he felt, when he was able to force himself not to feel that way, the eyes of his clerks and customers defeated him. He wished those eyes were oblivious, even cold; he felt he was withering in their tenderness. And beneath his listless wandering, every day in his soul he shot Richard Strout in the face; while Ruth, going about town on errands, kept seeing him. And at nights in bed she would hold Matt and cry, or sometimes she was silent and Matt would touch her tightening arm, her clenched fist.

As his own right fist was now, squeezing the butt of the revolver, the last of the drinkers having left the bar, talking to each other, going to their separate cars which were in the lot in front of the bar, out of Matt's vision. He heard their voices, their cars, and then the ocean again, across the street. The tide was in and sometimes it smacked the sea wall. Through the windshield he looked at the dark red side wall of the bar, and then to his left, past Willis, at Strout's car, and through its windows he could see the now-emptied parking lot, the road, the sea wall. He could smell the sea.

The front door of the bar opened and closed again and Willis looked at Matt then at the corner of the building; when Strout came around it alone Matt got out of the car, giving up the hope he had kept all night (and for the past week) that Strout would come out with friends, and Willis would simply drive away; thinking: *All right then. All right*; and he went around the front of Willis's car, and at Strout's he stopped and aimed over the hood at Strout's blue shirt ten feet away. Willis was aiming too, crouched on Matt's left, his elbow resting on the hood.

'Mr. Fowler,' Strout said. He looked at each of them, and at the guns. 'Mr. Trottier.'

Then Matt, watching the parking lot and the road, walked quickly between the car and the building and stood behind Strout. He took one leather glove from his pocket and put it on his left hand.

'Don't talk. Unlock the front and back and get in.'

Strout unlocked the front door, reached in and unlocked the back, then got in, and Matt slid into the back seat, closed the door with his gloved hand, and touched Strout's head once with the muzzle.

'It's cocked. Drive to your house.'

When Strout looked over his shoulder to back the car, Matt aimed at his temple and did not look at his eyes.

'Drive slowly," he said. "Don't try to get stopped.'

They drove across the empty front lot and onto the road, Willis's headlights shining into the car; then back through town, the sea wall on the left hiding the beach, though far out Matt could see the ocean; he uncocked the revolver; on the right were the places, most with their neon signs off, that did so much business in summer: the lounges and cafés and pizza houses, the street itself empty of traffic, the way he and Willis had known it would be when they decided to take Strout at the bar rather than knock on his door at two o'clock one morning and risk that one insomniac neighbor. Matt had not told Willis he was afraid he could not be alone with Strout for very long, smell his smells, feel the presence of his flesh, hear his voice, and then shoot him. They left the beach town and then were on the high bridge over the channel: to the left the smacking curling white at the breakwater and beyond that the dark sea and the full moon, and down to his right the small fishing boats bobbing at anchor in the cove. When they left the bridge, the sea was blocked by abandoned beach cottages, and Matt's left hand was sweating in the glove. Out here in the dark in the car he believed Ruth knew. Willis had come to his house at eleven and asked if he wanted a nightcap; Matt went to the bedroom for his wallet, put the gloves in one trouser pocket and the .38 in the other and went back to the living room, his hand in his pocket covering the bulge of the cool cylinder pressed against his fingers, the butt against his palm. When Ruth said goodnight she looked at his face, and he felt she could see in his eyes the gun, and the night he was going to. But he knew he couldn't trust what he saw. Willis's wife had taken her sleeping pill, which gave her eight hours—the reason, Willis had told Matt, he had the alarms installed, for nights when he was late at the restaurant—and when it was all done and Willis got home he would leave ice and a trace of Scotch and soda in two glasses in the game room and tell Martha in the morning that he had left the restaurant early and brought Matt home for a drink.

'He was making it with my wife.' Strout's voice was careful, not pleading.

Matt pressed the muzzle against Strout's head, pressed it harder than he wanted to, feeling through the gun Strout's head flinching and moving forward; then he lowered the gun to his lap.

'Don't talk,' he said.

Strout did not speak again. They turned west, drove past the Dairy Queen closed until spring, and the two lobster restaurants that faced each other and were crowded all summer and were now also closed, onto the short bridge crossing the tidal stream, and over the engine Matt could hear through his open window the water rushing inland under the bridge; looking to his left he saw its swift moonlit current going back into the marsh which, leaving the bridge, they entered: the salt marsh stretching out on both sides, the grass tall in patches but mostly low and leaning earthward as though windblown, a large dark rock sitting as though it rested on nothing but itself, and shallow pools reflecting the bright moon.

Beyond the marsh they drove through woods, Matt thinking now of the hole he and Willis had dug last Sunday afternoon after telling their wives they were going to Fenway Park. They listened to the game on a transistor radio, but heard none of it as they dug into the soft earth on the knoll they had chosen because elms and maples sheltered it. Already some leaves had fallen. When the hole was deep enough they covered it and the piled earth with dead branches, then cleaned their shoes and pants and went to a restaurant farther up in New Hampshire where they ate sandwiches and drank beer and watched the rest of the game on television. Looking at the back of Strout's head he thought of Frank's grave; he had not been back to it; but he would go before winter, and its second burial of snow.

He thought of Frank sitting on the couch and perhaps talking to the children as they watched television, imagined him feeling young and strong, still warmed from the sun at the beach, and feeling loved, hearing Mary Ann moving about in the kitchen, hearing her walking into the living room; maybe he looked up at her and maybe she said something, looking at him over the tray of sandwiches, smiling at him, saying something the way women do when they offer food as a gift, then the front door opening and this son of a bitch coming in and Frank seeing that he meant the gun in his hand, this son of a bitch and his gun the last person and thing Frank saw on earth.

When they drove into town the streets were nearly empty: a few slow cars, a policeman walking his beat past the darkened fronts of stores. Strout and Matt both glanced at him as they drove by. They were on the main street, and all the stoplights were blinking yellow. Willis and Matt had talked about that too: the lights changed at midnight, so there would be no place Strout had to stop and where he might try to run. Strout turned down the block where he lived and Willis's headlights were no longer with Matt in the back seat. They had planned that too, had decided it was best for just the one car to go to the house, and again Matt had said nothing about his fear of being alone with Strout, especially in his house: a duplex, dark as all the houses on the street were, the street itself lit at the corner of each block. As Strout turned into the driveway Matt thought of the one insomniac neighbor, thought of some man or woman sitting alone in the dark living room, watching the all-night channel from Boston. When Strout stopped the car near the front of the house, Matt said: 'Drive it to the back.'

He touched Strout's head with the muzzle.

'You wouldn't have it cocked, would you? For when I put on the brakes.'

Matt cocked it, and said: 'It is now.'

Strout waited a moment; then he eased the car forward, the engine doing little more than idling, and as they approached the garage he gently braked. Matt opened the door, then took off the glove and put it in his pocket. He stepped out and shut the door with his hip and said: 'All right.'

Strout looked at the gun, then got out, and Matt followed him across the grass, and as Strout unlocked the door Matt looked quickly at the row of small backyards on either side, and scattered tall trees, some evergreens, others not, and he thought of the red and yellow leaves on the trees over the hole, saw them falling soon, probably in two weeks, dropping slowly, covering. Strout stepped into the kitchen.

'Turn on the light.'

Strout reached to the wall switch, and in the light Matt looked at his wide back, the dark blue shirt, the white belt, the red plaid pants.

'Where's your suitcase?'

'My suitcase?'

'Where is it.'

'In the bedroom closet.'

'That's where we're going then. When we get to a door you stop and turn on the light.'

They crossed the kitchen, Matt glancing at the sink and stove and refrigerator: no dishes in the sink or even the dish rack beside it, no grease splashings on the stove, the refrigrator door clean and white. He did not want to look at any more but he looked quickly at all he could see: in the living room magazines and newspapers in a wicker basket, clean ashtrays, a record player, the records shelved next to it, then down the hall where, near the bedroom door, hung a color photograph of Mary Ann and the two boys sitting on a lawn—there was no house in the picture—Mary Ann smiling at the camera or Strout or whoever held the camera, smiling as she had on Matt's lawn this summer while he waited for the charcoal and they all talked and he looked at her brown legs and at Frank touching her arm, her shoulder, her hair; he moved down the hall with her smile in his mind, wondering: was that when they were both playing around and she was smiling like that at him and they were happy, even sometimes, making it worth it? He recalled her eyes, the pain in them, and he was conscious of the circles of love he was touching with the hand that held the revolver so tightly now as Strout stopped at the door at the end of the hall.

'There's no wall switch.'

'Where's the light?'

'By the bed.'

'Let's go.'

Matt stayed a pace behind, then Strout leaned over and the room was lighted: the bed, a double one, was neatly made; the ashtray on the bedside table clean, the bureau top dustless, and no photographs; probably so the girl—who *was* she?—would not have to see Mary Ann in the bedroom she believed was theirs. But because Matt was a father and a husband, though never an ex-husband, he knew (and did not want to know) that this bedroom had never been theirs alone. Strout turned around; Matt looked at his lips, his wide jaw, and thought of Frank's doomed and fearful eyes looking up from the couch.

'Where's Mr. Trottier?"

'He's waiting. Pack clothes for warm weather.'

'What's going on?'

'You're jumping bail.'

'Mr. Fowler—'

He pointed the cocked revolver at Strout's face. The barrel trembled but not much, not as much as he had expected. Strout went to the closet and got the suitcase from the floor and opened it on the bed. As he went to the bureau, he said: 'He was making it with my wife. I'd go pick up my kids and he'd be there. Sometimes he spent the night. My boys told me.'

He did not look at Matt as he spoke. He opened the top drawer and Matt stepped closer so he could see Strout's hands: underwear and socks, the socks rolled, the underwear folded and stacked. He took them back to the bed, arranged them neatly in the suitcase, then from the closet he was taking shirts and trousers and a jacket; he laid them on the bed and Matt followed him to the bathroom and watched from the door while he packed his shaving kit; watched in the bedroom as he folded and packed those things a person accumulated and that became part of him so that at times in the store Matt felt he was selling more than clothes.

'I wanted to try to get together with her again.' He was bent over the suitcase. 'I couldn't even talk to her. He was always with her. I'm going to jail for it; if I ever get out I'll be an old man. Isn't that enough?'

'You're not going to jail.'

Strout closed the suitcase and faced Matt, looking at the gun. Matt went to his rear, so Strout was between him and the lighted hall; then using his handkerchief he turned off the lamp and said: 'Let's go.'

They went down the hall, Matt looking again at the photograph, and through the living room and kitchen, Matt turning off the lights and talking, frightened that he was talking, that he was telling this lie he had not planned: 'It's the trial. We can't go through that, my wife and me. So you're leaving. We've got you a ticket, and a job. A friend of Mr. Trottier's. Out west. My wife keeps seeing you. We can't have that anymore.'

Matt turned out the kitchen light and put the handkerchief in his pocket, and they went down the two brick steps and across the lawn. Strout put the suitcase on the floor of the back seat, then got into the front seat and Matt got in the back and put on his glove and shut the door.

'They'll catch me. They'll check passenger lists.'

'We didn't use your name.'

'They'll figure that out too. You think I wouldn't have done it myself if it was that easy?'

He backed into the street, Matt looking down the gun barrel but not at the profiled face beyond it.

'You were alone,' Matt said. 'We've got it worked out.'

'There's no planes this time of night, Mr. Fowler.'

'Go back through town. Then north on 125.'

They came to the corner and turned, and now Willis's headlights were in the car with Matt.

'Why north, Mr. Fowler?"

'Somebody's going to keep you for a while. They'll take you to the airport.' He uncocked the hammer and lowered the revolver to his lap and said wearily: 'No more talking.'

As they drove back through town, Matt's body sagged, going limp with his spirit and its new and false bond with Strout, the hope his lie had given Strout. He had grown up in this town whose streets had become places of apprehension and pain for Ruth as she drove and walked, doing what she had to do; and for him too, if only in his mind as he worked and chatted six days a week in his store; he wondered now if his lie would have worked, if sending Strout away would have been enough; but then he knew that just thinking of Strout in Montana or whatever place lay at the end of the lie he had told, thinking of him walking the streets there, loving a girl there (who *was* she?) would be enough to slowly rot the rest of his days. And Ruth's. Again he was certain that she knew, that she was waiting for him.

They were in New Hampshire now, on the narrow highway, passing the shopping center at the state line, and then houses and small stores and sandwich shops. There were few cars on the road. After ten minutes he raised his trembling hand, touched Strout's neck with the gun, and said: 'Turn in up here. At the dirt road.'

Strout flicked on the indicator and slowed.

'Mr Fowler?'

'They're waiting here.'

Strout turned very slowly, easing his neck away from the gun. In the moonlight the road was light brown, lighter and yellowed where the headlights shone; weeds and a few trees grew on either side of it, and ahead of them were the woods.

'There's nothing back here, Mr. Fowler.'

'It's for your car. You don't think we'd leave it at the airport, do you?'

He watched Strout's large, big-knuckled hands tighten on the wheel, saw Frank's face that night: not the stitches and bruised eye and swollen lips, but his own hand gently touching Frank's jaw, turning his wounds to the light. They rounded a bend in the road and were out of sight of the highway: tall trees all around them now, hiding the moon. When they reached the abandoned gravel pit on the left, the bare flat earth and steep pale embankment behind it, and the black crowns of trees at its top, Matt said: 'Stop here.'

Strout stopped but did not turn off the engine. Matt pressed the gun hard against his neck, and he straightened in the seat and looked in the rearview mirror, Matt's eyes meeting his in the glass for an instant before looking at the hair at the end of the gun barrel.

'Turn it off.'

Strout did, then held the wheel with two hands, and looked in the mirror.

'I'll do twenty years, Mr. Fowler; at least. I'll be forty-six years old.'

'That's nine years younger than I am,' Matt said, and got out and took off the glove and kicked the door shut. He aimed at Strout's ear and pulled back the hammer. Willis's headlights were off and Matt heard him walking on the soft thin layer of dust, the hard earth beneath it. Strout opened the door, sat for a moment in the interior light, then stepped out onto the road. Now his face was pleading. Matt did not look at his eyes, but he could see it in the lips.

'Just get the suitcase. They're right up the road.'

Willis was beside him now, to his left. Strout looked at both guns. Then he opened the back door, leaned in, and with a jerk brought the suitcase out. He was turning to face them when Matt said: 'Just walk up the road. Just ahead.'

Strout turned to walk, the suitcase in his right hand, and Matt and Willis followed; as Strout cleared the front of his car he dropped the suitcase and, ducking, took one step that was the beginning of a sprint to his right. The gun kicked in Matt's hand, and the explosion of the shot surrounded him, isolated him in a nimbus of sound that cut him off from all his time, all his history, isolated him standing absolutely still on the dirt road with the gun in his hand, looking down at Richard Strout squirming on his belly, kicking one leg behind him, pushing himself forward, toward the woods. Then Matt went to him and shot him once in the back of the head.

Driving south to Boston, wearing both gloves now, staying in the middle lane and looking often in the rearview mirror at Willis's headlights, he relived the suitcase dropping, the quick dip and turn of Strout's back, and the kick of the gun, the sound of the shot. When he walked to Strout, he still existed within the first shot, still trembled and breathed with it. The second shot and the burial seemed to be happening to someone else, someone he was watching. He and Willis each held an arm and pulled Strout face-down off the road and into the woods, his bouncing sliding belt white under the trees where it was so dark that when they stopped at the top of the knoll, panting and sweating, Matt could not see where Strout's blue shirt ended and the earth began. They pulled off the branches then dragged Strout to the edge of the hole and went behind him and lifted his legs and pushed him in. They stood still for a moment. The woods were quiet save for their breathing, and Matt remembered hearing the movements of birds and small animals after the first shot. Or maybe he had not heard them. Willis went down to the road. Matt could see him clearly out on the tan dirt, could see the glint of Strout's car and, beyond the road, the gravel pit. Willis came back up the knoll with the suitcase. He dropped it in the hole and took off his gloves and they went down to his car for the spades. They worked quietly. Sometimes they paused to listen to the woods. When they were finished Willis turned on his flashlight and they covered the earth with leaves and branches and then went down to the spot in front of the car, and while Matt held the light Willis crouched and sprinkled dust on the blood, backing up till he reached the grass and leaves, then he used leaves until they had worked up to the grave again. They did not stop. They walked around the grave and through the woods, using the light on the ground, looking up through the trees to where they ended at the lake. Neither of them spoke above the sounds of their heavy and clumsy strides through low brush and over fallen branches. Then they reached it: wide and dark, lapping softly at the bank, pine needles smooth under Matt's feet, moonlight on the lake, a small island near its middle, with black, tall evergreens. He took out the gun and threw for the island: taking two steps back on the pine needles, striding with the throw and going to one knee as he followed through, looking up to see the dark shapeless object arcing downward, splashing.

They left Strout's car in Boston, in front of an apartment building on Commonwealth Avenue. When they got back to town Willis drove slowly over the bridge and Matt threw the keys into the Merrimack. The sky was turning light. Willis let him out a block from his house, and walking home he listened for sounds from the houses he passed. They were quiet. A light was on in his living room. He turned it off and undressed in there, and went softly toward the bedroom; in the hall he smelled the smoke, and he stood in the bedroom doorway and looked at the orange of her cigarette in the dark. The curtains were closed. He went to the closet and put his shoes on the floor and felt for a hanger.

'Did you do it?' she said.

He went down the hall to the bathroom and in the dark he washed his hands and face. Then he went to her, lay on his back, and pulled the sheet up to his throat.

'Are you all right?' she said.

'I think so.'

Now she touched him, lying on her side, her hand on his belly, his thigh.

'Tell me,' she said.

He started from the beginning, in the parking lot at the bar; but soon with his eyes closed and Ruth petting him, he spoke of Strout's house: the order, the woman presence, the picture on the wall.

'The way she was smiling,' he said.

'What about it?'

'I don't know. Did you ever see Strout's girl? When you saw him in town?'

'No.'

'I wonder who she was.'

Then he thought: *not was: is. Sleeping now she is his girl.* He opened his eyes, then closed them again. There was more light beyond the curtains. With Ruth now he left Strout's house and told again his lie to Strout, gave him again that hope that Strout must have for a while believed, else he would have to believe only the gun pointed at him for the last two hours of his life. And with Ruth he saw again the dropping suitcase, the darting move to the right: and he told of the first shot, feeling her hand on him but his heart isolated still, beating on the road still in that explosion like thunder. He told her the rest, but the words had no images for him, he did not see himself doing what the words said he had done; he only saw himself on that road.

'We can't tell the other kids,' she said. 'It'll hurt them, thinking he got away. But we mustn't.'

'No.'

She was holding him, wanting him, and he wished he could make love with her but he could not. He saw Frank and Mary Ann making love in her bed, their eyes closed, their bodies brown and smelling of the sea; the other girl was faceless, bodiless, but he felt her sleeping now; and he saw Frank and Strout, their faces alive; he saw red and yellow leaves falling to the earth, then snow: falling and freezing and falling; and holding Ruth, his cheek touching her breast, he shuddered with a sob that he kept silent in his heart.

THE PRETTY GIRL

But because thou art lukewarm, and neither cold nor hot,
I am about to vomit thee out of my mouth. . . .
                                        Saint John, *The Apocalypse*

For Roger Rath, out among the stars

I DON'T KNOW HOW I feel till I hold that steel. That was always true: I might have a cold, or one of those days when everything is hard to do because you're tired for no reason at all except that you're alive, and I'd work out, and by the time I got in the shower I couldn't remember how I felt before I lifted; it was like that part of the day was yesterday, and now I was starting a new one. Or a hangover: some of my friends and my brother too are hair-of-the-dog people, but I've never done that and I never will, because a drink in the morning shuts down the whole day, and anyway I can't stand the smell of it in the morning and my stomach tells me it would like a Coke or a milkshake, but it is not about to stand for a prank like a shot of vodka or even a beer.

It was drunk out last night, Alex says. And I always say: *A severe drunk front moved in around midnight.* We've been saying that since I was seventeen and he was twenty-one. On a morning after one of those, when I can read the words in the *Boston Globe* but I can't remember them long enough to understand the story, I work out. If it's my off day from weights, I run or go to the Y and swim. Then the hangover is gone. Even the sick ones: some days I've thought I'd either blow my lunch on the bench or get myself squared away and, for the first few sets, as I pushed the bar up from my chest, the booze tried to come up too, with whatever I'd eaten during the night, and I'd swallow and push the iron all the way up and bring it down again, and some of my sweat was cool. Then I'd do it again and again, and add some weights, and do it again till I got a pump, and the blood rushed through my muscles and flushed out the lactic acid, and sweat soaked my shorts and tank shirt, the bench under my back was slick, and all the poison was gone from my body. From my head too, and for the rest of the day, unless something really bothered me, like having to file my tax return, or car trouble, I was as peaceful as I can ever be. Because I get along with people, and they don't treat me the way they treat some; in this world it helps to be big. That's not why I work out, but it's not a bad reason, and one that little guys should think about. The weather doesn't harass me either. New Englanders are always bitching about one thing or another. Once Alex said: *I think they just like to bitch, because when you get down to it, the truth is the Celtics and Patriots and Red Sox and Bruins are all good to watch, and we're lucky they're here, and we've got the ocean and pretty country to hunt and fish and ski in, and you don't have to be rich to get there.* He's right. But I don't bitch about the weather: I like rain and snow and heat and cold, and the only effect they have on me is what I wear to go out in them. The weather up here is female, and goes from one mood to another, and I love her for that.

So as long as I'm working out, I have good days, except for those things that happen to you like dead batteries and forms to fill out. If I skip my workouts I start feeling confused and distracted, then I get tense, and drinking and talking aren't good, they just make it worse, then I don't want to get out of bed in the morning. I've had days like that, when I might not have got up at all if finally I didn't have to piss. An hour with the iron and everything is back in place again, and I don't know what was troubling me or why in the first place I went those eight or twelve or however many days without lifting. But it doesn't matter. Because it's over, and I can write my name on a check or say it out loud again without feeling like a liar. This is Raymond Yarborough, I say into the phone, and I feel my words, my name, go out over the wire, and he says the car is ready and it'll be seventy-eight dollars and sixty-five cents. I tell him I'll come get it now, and I walk out into the world I'd left for a while and it feels like mine again. I like stepping on it and breathing it. I walk to the bank first and cash a check because the garage won't take one unless you have a major credit card, which I don't because

I don't believe in buying something, even gas, that I don't have the money for. I always have enough money because I don't buy anything I can't eat or drink. Or almost anything. At the bank window I write a check to Cash and sign both sides and talk to the girl. I tell her she's looking good and I like her sweater and the new way she's got her hair done. I'm not making a move; I feel good and I want to see her smiling.

But for a week or two now, up here at Alex's place in New Hampshire, the iron hasn't worked for me. While I'm pumping I forget Polly, or at least I feel like I have, but in the shower she's back again. I got to her once, back in June: she was scared like a wild animal, a small one without any natural weapons, like a wounded rabbit, the way they quiver in your hand and look at you when you pick them up to knock their heads against trees or rocks. But I think she started to like it anyways, and if I had wanted to, I could have made her come. But that's Polly. I've known her about twelve years, since I was fourteen, and I think I knew her better when we were kids than I ever did after high school when we started going together and then got married. In school I knew she was smart and pretty and tried to look sexy before she was. I still don't know much more. That's not true: I can write down a lot that I know about her, and I did that one cold night early last spring, about fifty pages on a legal pad, but all of it was what she said to me and what she thought I said to her and what she did. I still didn't understand why she was that way, why we couldn't just be at peace with one another, in the evenings drink some beer or booze, talking about this and that, then eat some dinner, and be easy about things, which is what I thought we got married for.

We were camping at a lake and not catching any trout when we decided to get married. We talked about it on the second night, lying in our sleeping bags in the tent. In the morning I woke up feeling like the ground was blessed, a sacred place of Indians. I was twenty-two years old, and I thought about dying; it still seemed many years away, but I felt closer to it, like I could see the rest of my life in that tent while Polly slept, and it didn't matter that at the end of it I'd die. I was very happy, and I thought of my oldest brother, Kingsley, dead in the war we lost, and I talked to him for a while, told him I wished he was here so he could see how good I felt, and could be the best man. Then I talked to Alex and told him he'd be the best man. Then I was asleep again, and when I woke up Polly was handing me a cup of coffee and I could hear the campfire crackling. Late that afternoon we left the ground but I kept the tent; I didn't bring it back to the rental place. I had a tent of my own, a two-man, but I rented a big one so Polly could walk around in it, and arrange the food and cooler and gear, the way women turn places into houses, even motel rooms. There are some that don't, but they're not the kind you want to be with for the whole nine yards; when a woman is a slob, she's even worse than a man. They had my deposit, but they phoned me. I told them we had an accident and the tent was at the bottom of Lake Willoughby up in Vermont, up in what they call the Northern Kingdom. He asked me what it was doing in the lake. I said I had no way of knowing because that lake was formed by a glacier and is so deep in places that nobody could know even how far down it was, much less what it was doing. He said *on* the lake, what was it doing *on* the lake? Did my boat capsize? I said, What boat? He had been growling, but this time he barked: then how did the tent get in the fucking lake? I pitched it there, I said. That's the accident I'm talking about. Then he howled: the deposit didn't cover the cost of the tent. I told him to start getting more deposit, and hung up. That tent is out here at Alex's, folded up and resting on the rafters in the garage. This place was Kingsley's, and when his wife married again she wanted to give it to me and Alex, but Alex said that wasn't right, he knew Kingsley would want her to do that, and at the same time he knew Kingsley would expect us to turn it down and give her some money; their marriage was good, and she has his kid, my niece Olivia who's nearly ten now. I was still in school, so Alex bought it.

What I thought we had—I know we had it—in the tent that morning didn't last, and even though I don't understand why everything changed as fast as our weather does, I blame her because I tried so hard and was the way I always was before, when she loved me; I changed toward her and cursed her and slapped her around when every day was bad and the nights worse. There are things you can do in the daytime that make you feel like your marriage isn't a cage with rattlesnakes on the floor, that you can handle it: not just working out, but driving around for a whole afternoon just getting eggs and light bulbs and dry cleaning and a watchband and some socks. You listen to music in the car and look at people in their cars (I've noticed often you'll see a young girl driving alone, smiling to herself; maybe it's the disc jockey, maybe it's what she's thinking), and you talk to people in their stores (I always try to go to small stores, even for food), and your life seems better than it was when you walked out of the house with the car key. But at night there's nothing to distract you; and besides at night is when you really feel married, and need to; and there you are in the living room with all those snakes on the floor. I was tending bar five nights a week then, so two nights were terrible and sad, and on the others I came home tired and crept into the house and bed, feeling like I was doing something wrong, something I didn't want her to wake up and see. Then near the end Vinnie DeLuca was in that bed on the nights I worked, and I found out and that was the end.

I treated her well. I shared the housework, like my brothers and I did growing up. I've never known a woman who couldn't cook better than I do, but still I can put a meal on the table, and I did that, either fried or barbecued; I cooked on the grill outside all year round; I like cooking out while snow is falling. I washed the dishes when she cooked, and sometimes remembered to vacuum, and I did a lot of the errands, because she hated that, probably because she went to supermarkets and never talked to anybody, while I just didn't quite enjoy it.

Never marry a woman who doesn't know what she wants, and knows she doesn't. Mom never knew what she wanted either, but I don't think she knew she didn't, and that's why she's stayed steady through the years. She still brings her Luckies to the table. When I was little I believed Mom was what a wife should look like. I never thought much about what a wife should be like. She was very pretty then and she still is, though you have to look at her for a while to see it. Or I guess other people do, who are looking for pretty women to be young, or the other way around, and when they see a woman in her fifties they don't really look at her until they have to, until they're sitting down talking to her, and seeing her eyes and the way she smiles. But I don't need that closer look. She's outdoors a lot and has good lines in her face, the kind of lines that make me trust someone.

Mom wants Lucky Strikes and coffee, iced in summer after the hot cups in the morning, and bourbon when the sun is low. When she has those she's all right, let it rain where we're camping or the black flies find us fishing. During the blizzard of 1978 Mom ran out of Luckies and Jim Beam, and the coffee beans were low; the old man laughs about it, he says she was showing a lot of courage, but he thought he better do something fast or be snowed in with a crazy woman, so he went on cross-country skis into town and came back with a carton and a bottle and a can of coffee in his parka pockets. I tried to stop you, she says when they joke about it. Not as hard as you've tried to stop me going other places, the old man says. The truth is, it was not dangerous, only three miles into town from their house, and I know the old man was happy for an excuse to get out into the storm and work up a sweat. Younger, he wouldn't have needed an excuse, but I think his age makes him believe when there's a blizzard he should stay indoors. He's buried a few friends. At the store he got to in the snow they only had regular coffee, not the beans that Mom buys at two or three stores you have to drive to. He says when he came home she grabbed the carton first and had one lit before he was out of his ski mask, and she had two drinks poured while he was taking off his boots; then she held up the can of coffee and said: Who drinks this? You have a girl friend you were thinking about? He took the drink from her and said I don't have time for a girl friend. And she said I know you don't. They didn't tell us any more of that story; I know there'd be a fire going, and I like to think he was down to his long underwear by then, and he took that off and they lay in front of the fireplace. But probably they just had bourbon and teased one another and the old man took a shower and they went upstairs to sleep.

I hope the doctors never tell Mom she has to give up her Luckies and coffee and bourbon. You may call that an addiction. So what is my pumping iron? What is Polly?

She would say I raped her in June and so would her cop father and the rest of her family, if she told them, which she probably did because she moved back in with them. But maybe she didn't tell them. She didn't press charges; Alex keeps in touch with what's going on down there, and he lets me know. But I've stayed up here anyway. It's hard to explain: the night I did it I naturally crossed the state line and came up here to the boondocks; I knew when they didn't find me at home or at work, Polly would tell them to try here, but it was a good place to wait for a night and a day, a good place to make plans. In the morning I called Alex and he spoke to a friend on the force and called me back and said, Nothing yet. Late that afternoon he called again, said, Nothing yet. So I stayed here the second night, and next morning and afternoon he called me again, so I stayed a third night and a fourth and fifth, because every day he called and said there was nothing yet. By then I had missed two nights of a job I liked, tending bar at Newburyport, where I got good tips and could have girls if I wanted them. I knew that a girl would help, maybe do more than that, maybe fix everything for me. But having a girl was just an idea, like thinking about a part of the country where you might want to live if you ever stopped loving the place where you were.

So I wanted to want a girl, but I didn't, not even when these two pretty ones came in almost every night I worked and sat at the bar and talked to me when I had the time, and gave me signs with their eyes and the way they joked with me and laughed at each other. I could have had either one, and I don't know how the other one would have taken it. Sometimes I thought about taking both of them back to my place, which is maybe what they had in mind anyway, but that wouldn't be the same as having a girl I wanted to want, and I couldn't get interested enough to go through the trouble. Once, before Polly, I went to a wedding where everyone got drunk on champagne. I noticed then something I hadn't noticed before: girls get horny at weddings. I ended up with two friends of the bride; I had known them before, but not much. They were dressed up and looking very good, and when the party broke up we went to a bar, a crowded bar with a lot of light, one of those places where the management figures it draws a crowd with all kinds in it, so one way to keep down fights and especially guys pulling knives is have the place lit up like a library. I sat between them at the bar and rubbed their thighs, and after we drank some more I had a hand up each of them; it was late spring and their legs were moist, squeezing my hands; then they opened a little, enough; I don't remember if they did this at the same time or one was first. Then I got my hands in their pants. The bar was crowded and people were standing behind us, drinking in groups and pairs, buying drinks over the girls' shoulders, and I was stroking clitoris. When I told Alex this he said, How did you drink and smoke? I said I don't know. But I do know that I kept talking and pretending to each girl that I was only touching her. I got the drinking done too. Maybe they came at the bar, but pretty soon I couldn't take it anymore, and I got them out of there. But in the car I suddenly knew how drunk and tired I was; I was afraid I couldn't make it with both of them, so I took the plump one to her apartment and we told her good night like a couple of innocent people going home drunk from a wedding. Then I brought the other one to my place, and we had a good night, but every time I thought of the bar I was sorry I took the plump one home. Probably the girl with me was sorry too, because in the morning I took a shower and when I got out, the bed was made and she was gone. She left a nice note, but it was strange anyway, and made the whole night feel like a bad mistake, and I thought since it didn't really matter who I got in bed with, it should have been the one that was plump. She was good-looking and I'm sure was not lonesome or hard up for a man, but still for the rest of the day and that night I felt sorry when I remembered her leaving the car and walking up the walk to her apartment building, because you know how women are, and she was bound to feel then that her friend was slender and she wasn't and that was the only reason she was going home alone drunk, with juicy underpants. She was right, and that's why I felt so bad. Next day I decided to stop thinking about her. I do that a lot: you do some things you wish you hadn't, and thinking about them afterward doesn't do any good for anybody, and finally you just feel like your heart has the flu. None of this is why I didn't take the two girls this summer back to my place.

What is hard to explain is why, when I knew Polly wasn't going to press charges, I stayed here instead of giving my boss some almost true story. I thought of some he would believe, or at least accept because he likes me and I do good work, something just a few feet short of saying Hey, lookit, I was running from a rape charge. But I didn't go back, except one night to my apartment for my fishing gear and guns and clothes and groceries. Nothing else in there belonged to me.

When I came up here that night I did it, I went to my place first and loaded the jeep with my weights and bench and power stands. So when I knew nobody was after me, all I did was work out, lifting on three days and running and swimming in the lake on the others. That was first thing in the morning, which was noon for everybody else. Every day was sunny, and in the afternoons I sat on a deck chair on the wharf, with a cooler of beer. Near sundown I rowed out in the boat and fished for bass and pickerel. If I caught one big enough for dinner, I stopped fishing and let the boat drift till dark, then rowed back and ate my fish. So all day and most of the night I was thinking, and most of that was about why I wasn't going back. All I finally knew was something had changed. I had liked my life till that night in June, except for what Polly was doing to it, but you've got to be able to separate those things, and I still believe I did, or at least tried to hard enough so that sometimes I did, often enough to know my life wasn't a bad one and I was luckier than most. Then I went to her house that night and I felt her throat under the Kabar, then her belly under it. I don't just mean I could feel the blade touching her, the way you can cut cheese with your eyes closed; it wasn't like that, the blade moving through air, then stopping because something—her throat, her belly—was in the way. No: I felt her skin touching the steel, like the blade was a finger of mine.

They would call it rape and assault with a deadly weapon, but those words don't apply to me and Polly. I was taking back my wife for a while; and taking back, for a while anyway, some of what she took from me. That is what it felt like: I went to her place torn and came out mended. Then she was torn, so I was back in her life for a while. All night I was happy and I kept getting hard, driving north and up here at Alex's, just remembering. All I could come up with in the days and nights after that, thinking about why I didn't go back to my apartment and working the bar, was that time in my life seemed flat and stale now, like an old glass of beer.

But I have to leave again, go back there for a while. Everything this summer is breaking down to for a while, which it seems is as long as I can keep peaceful. Now after my workout I get in the hot shower feeling strong and fresh, and rub the bar of soap over my biceps and pecs, they're hard and still pumped up: then I start to lose what the workout was really for, because nobody works out for just the body, I don't care what they may say, and it could be that those who don't lift or run or swim or something don't need to because they've got most of the time what the rest of us go for on the bench or road or in the pool, though I'm not talking about the ones who just drink and do drugs. Then again, I've known a lot of women who didn't need booze or drugs or a workout, while

I've never known a man who didn't need one or the other, if not both. It would be interesting to meet one someday. So I flex into the spray, make the muscles feel closer to the hot water, but I've lost it: that feeling you get after a workout, that yesterday is gone and last night too, that today is right here in the shower, inside your body; there is nothing out there past the curtain that can bring you down, and you can take all the time you want to turn the water hotter and circle and flex and stretch under it, because the time is yours like the water is; when you're pumped like that you can't even think about death, at least not your own; or about any of the other petty crap you have to deal with just to have a good day; you end up with two or three minutes of cold water, and by the time you're drying off, the pump is easing down into a relaxed state that almost feels like muscle fatigue but it isn't: it's what you lifted all that iron for, and it'll take you like a stream does a trout, cool and easy the rest of the day.

I've lost that now: in the shower I see Polly walking around town smiling at people, talking to them on this warm dry August day. I don't let myself think anymore about her under or on top of or whatever and however with Vinnie DeLuca. I went through that place already, and I'm not going back there again. I can forget the past. Mom still grieves for Kingsley, but I don't. Instead of remembering him the way he was all those years, I think of him now, like he's forever twenty years old out there in the pines around the lake, out there on the water, and in it; Alex and I took all his stuff out of here and gave it to his wife and Mom. What I can't forget is right now. I can't forget that Polly's walking around happy, breathing today into her body. And not thinking about me. Or, if she does, she's still happy, she's still got her day, and she's draining mine like the water running out of the tub. So lately after my workout I stand in the shower and change the pictures; then I take a sandwich and the beer cooler out to the wharf and look at the pictures some more; I do this into the night, and I've stopped fishing or whatever I was doing in the boat. Instead of looking at pictures of Polly happy, I've been looking at Polly scared shitless, Polly fucked up, Polly paying. It's time to do some more terrorizing.

So today when the sun is going down I phone Alex. The lake is in a good-sized woods, and the trees are old and tall; the sun is behind them long before the sky loses its light and color, and turns the lake black. The house faces west and, from that shore, shadows are coming out onto the water. But the rest of it is blue, and so is the sky above the trees. I drink a beer at the phone and look out the screen window at the lake.

'Is she still living with Steve?' I say to Alex. A month ago he came out here for a few beers and told me he heard she'd moved out of her folks' house, into Steve Buckland's place.

'Far as I know,' Alex says.

'So when's he heading north?'

Steve is the biggest man I know, and he has never worked out; he's also the strongest man I know, and it's lucky for a lot of people he is also the most laid back and cheerful man I know, even when he's managed to put away enough booze to get drunk, which is a lot for a man his size. I've never seen him in a fight, and if he ever was in one, I know I would've heard about it, because guys would talk about that for a long time; but I've seen him break up a few when he's tending bar down to Timmy's, and I've seen him come out from the bar at closing time when a lot of the guys are cocked and don't want to leave, and he herds them right out the door like sheep. He has a huge belly that doesn't fool anybody into throwing a punch at him, and he moves fast. Also, we're not good friends, I only know him from the bar, but I like him, he's a good man, and I do not want to fuck over his life with my problem; besides, the word is that Polly is just staying with him till he goes north, but they're not fucking, then she'll sublet his place (he lives on a lake too; Alex is right about New England) while he stays in a cabin he and some guys have in New Hampshire, and after hunting season he'll ski, and he won't come back till late spring. Alex says he's leaving after Labor Day weekend. I have nothing against Steve, but Vinnie DeLuca is another matter. So I ask Alex about that gentleman's schedule.

'He's a bouncer at Old Colony. I think they call him a doorman.'

'I'll bounce his ass.'

'He might be carrying something, you know. With that job.'

'Shit. You think anybody'd let that asshole carry a gun?'

'Sure they would, but I was thinking blackjack. Want me to come along?'

'No, I'm all set.'

'If you change your mind, I'll be here.'

I know he will. He always has been, and I'm lucky to have a brother who's a friend too; I'm so lucky, I even had two of them; or unlucky because now I only have the one, depending on how I feel about things at the time I'm thinking of my brothers. I bring a beer out and sit on the wharf and watch the trees on the east side of the lake go from green to black as the sun sets beyond the tall woods. Then the sky is dark and I get another beer and listen to the lake sloshing against the bank, like someone is walking on it out there in the middle, his steps pushing the water around, and I think about Kingsley in the war. At first I don't want to, then I give in to it, and I picture him crawling in the jungle. He bought it from a mine; they didn't tell us if he was in a rice paddy or open field or jungle, but I always think of him in jungle because he loved to hunt in the woods and was so quiet in there. After a while I swallow and tighten my chest and let out some air. Polly said I was afraid to cry because it wasn't macho. That's not true. I sure the fuck cried when Mom and the old man told me and Alex about Kingsley, there in the kitchen, and I would've cried no matter who was there to watch. I fight crying because it empties you so you can't do anything about what's making you cry. So I stop thinking about Kingsley, that big good-looking wonderful son of a bitch with that look he had on his face when he was hunting, like he could see through the trees, as he stepped on a mine or tripped a wire. By the time I stop thinking about him, I know what else I'll do tonight, after I deal with Mr. DeLuca a.k.a. the doorman of Old Colony.

It is a rowdy bar at the north end of town, with a band and a lot of girls, and it draws people from out of town instead of just regulars, so it gets rough in there. I sit in my jeep in the parking lot fifteen minutes before closing. The band is gone, but the parking lot is still full. At one o'clock they start coming out, loud in bunches and couples. Some leave right away, but a lot of them stand around, some drinking what they sneaked out of the bar. The place takes about twenty minutes to empty; I know that's done when I see Vinnie come into the doorway, following the last people to leave. He stands there smoking a cigarette. He's short and wide like I am, and he is wearing a leisure suit with his shirt collar out over the lapels. He's got a chain around his neck. The cruiser turns into the parking lot, as I figured it would; the cops drive very slowly through the crowd, stopping here and there for a word; they pass in front of me and go to the end of the lot and hang a slow U and come back; people are in their cars now and driving off. I feel like slouching down but will not do this for a cop, even to get DeLuca. The truth is I'm probably the only one in the parking lot planning a felony. They pass me, looking at the cars leaving and the people still getting into cars, then they follow everybody out of the lot and up the road. Vinnie will either come right out or stay inside and drink while the waitresses and one bartender clean the place and the other bartender counts the money and puts it in the safe. It's amazing how many places there are to rob at night, when you think about it; if that's what you like. I hate a fucking thief. Polly used to shoplift in high school, and when she told me about it, years later, telling it like it was something cute she and her pals did, I didn't think it was funny, though I was supposed to. There are five cars spread around the lot. I don't know what he's driving, so I just sit watching the door, but he stays inside, the fucker getting his free drinks and sitting on a barstool watching the sweeping and table-wiping and the dirty ashtrays stacking up on the bar and the bartender washing them. Maybe he's making it with one of the waitresses, which I hope he isn't. I do not want to kick his ass with a woman there. If he comes out with a bartender or even both of them, it's a problem I can handle: either they'll jump me or try to get between us, or run for the phone, but I'll get him. With a woman, you never know. Some of them like to watch. But she might start screaming or crying or get a tire iron and knock the back of my head out my nose.

He comes out with three women. The women are smoking, so I figure they just finished their work and haven't been sitting around with a drink, they're tired and want to go home. A lot of people don't know what a long, hard job that is. I'm right: they all stand on the little porch, but he's not touching any of them, or even standing close; then they come down the steps and one woman heads for a car down on the left near the road, and the other two go to my right, toward the car at the high end of the lot, and he comes for the one straight ahead of him, off to my left maybe a couple of hundred feet. The TransAm: I should have known. I'm out the door and we're both walking at right angles to his car. He looks at me once, then looks straight ahead. Headlights are on his blue suit, and the two women drive down and pass behind him;

the other one is just getting to her car, and she waves and they toot the horn, and turn onto the road. I get to the car first and plant myself in front of it and watch his chain. It's gold and something hangs from it, a disc of some kind.

'Ray,' he says, and stops. 'How's it going, Ray?' His voice is smooth and deep in his throat, but I can see his eyes now. They look sad, the way scared eyes do. His skin is dark and he is hairy and his shirt is unbuttoned enough to show this, and the swell of his pecs. I think of Alex, and look at Vinnie's hands down by his jacket pockets; I'm looking at his face too, and I keep seeing the gold chain, a short one around his neck so the disc shows high on his chest. My legs are shaky and cool and I need a deep breath, but I don't take it; I swing a left above the chain, see it hit his jaw, then my right is there in his face, and I'm in the eye of the storm, I don't hear us, I don't feel my fists hitting him, but I see them; when my head rocks he's hit me; I hit him fast and his face has a trapped look, then he's inside my arms, grabbing them, his head down, and I turn with him and push him onto the car, his back on the hood. There is a light on his face, and blood; I hold him down with my left hand on his throat and pound him with the right. There is a lot of blood on his mouth and nose and some on his forehead and under an eye. He is limp under my hand, and when I let him go he slides down the hood and his back swings forward like he's sitting up, and he drops between me and the grill. He lies on his side. My foot cocks to kick him but I stop it, looking at his face. The face is enough. The sky feels small, like I could breathe it all in. Then I look into the light. It's the headlights of the waitress's car, the one alone; it's stopped about twenty feet away with the engine running and the lights aimed at me. She's standing beside the car, yelling. I look around. Nobody else is in the lot; it feels small too. I look down at DeLuca, then at her. She's cursing me. I wave at her and walk to my jeep. She is calling me a motherfucking, cocksucking string of other things. I like this girl. With the lights off, I back the jeep up away from the club and make a wide half-circle around her to the road, so she can't read my plates. I pull out and turn on the lights.

I take a beer from the cooler on the floor and light a cigarette. My hands are shaky, but it's the good kind. Kingsley taught me about adrenaline, long before he used it over there, when I started first grade, which for boys means start learning to fight too. He said when you start to tremble, that's not fear, it just feels like it; it's to help you, so put it to use. That is why I didn't say to DeLuca the things I thought of saying. When I know I have to fight I never talk. Adrenaline makes guys start talking at each other, and you can use it up; I hold it in till I've got to either yell or have action.

The street is wide and quiet, most of the houses dark. I pass a cemetery and a school. I don't know why it is, but I know of four schools in this town either next to or across the street from a cemetery. I'm talking elementary schools too. Maybe it's an old custom, but it's weird looking at little girls and boys on a playground, and next door or across the street are all those tombstones over the dead. King is buried in one with trees and no school or anything else around but woods and the Merrimack River. The sky is lit up with stars and moon, the kind of night you could drive in with your lights off if you were the only one on the road, just follow the grey pavement and look at the dark trees and the sky and listen to the air rushing at the window. I turn on the radio and get onto 495 north. My knuckles are sore but the fingers work fine. I suck down the beer and get another from under the ice, and it feels good on my hand. I'm getting WOKQ from Dover, New Hampshire. Every redneck from southern Maine to Boston listens to that station. New Hampshire is also a redneck state, though the natives don't know it because they get snow every winter. When King was at Camp LeJeune he wrote to the family and said they could move New Hampshire down there and everybody would be happy except for the heat, which he wasn't happy with either. The heat got to him in Nam too; he wrote and said the insects and heat and being wet so much of the time were the worst part. I think about that a lot; was he just saying that so we wouldn't worry, or did he mean it? Most of the time I think he meant it, which taught me something I already knew but didn't always know that I knew: it gets down to what's happening to you right now, and if you're hot and wet and itching, that's what you deal with. You'll end up tripping a mine anyways, so you might as well fight the bugs and stay cool and dry till then.

Mostly there's woods on the sides of the highway. People are driving it fast tonight. I pull into the right lane, Crystal Gayle is singing sad, and take the exit. I hope Waylon comes on; I'm in a

Waylon mood. I cross the highway on the overpass, cars going under
me without a sound I can hear over Crystal, and go on a two-lane
into the town square of Merrimac, where they leave off the *k*. I
don't know why. The square has a rotary and some lights and is
empty. I turn right onto 110, two-lane and hilly with curves, and
I have to piss. It's not just beer, it's nerve-piss, and I shiver holding
it in. Nobody's on the road, and when I turn left toward the lake
I cut the lights and can see clearly: the road is narrow with trees
on its sides, and up ahead where the road turns left, there are trees
too, a thin line of them at the side of the lake. I shift down and
turn and back up and turn, and park it facing 110. I take the gasoline
can from behind my seat, then piss on the grass, looking up at the
stars and smelling the pines among the trees. I carry the gasoline
can in my left hand, the side away from the road, and walk on
grass, close to the trees. I have on my newest jeans, the darkest I've
got, and a dark blue shirt with long sleeves. My fingers try to stiffen,
holding the can. That's from DeLuca, maybe the first one, that
came up from behind my ass and got his jaw; he saw it but only in
time to turn his face from it a little, so all he did was stretch his
jaw out for me to hit. He should have dropped his chin, caught it
on the head. I hear the lake, then see it through the trees. It's bigger
than ours but there are more houses too, all around it, and in summer
they're filled. We only have a few houses, on the east and north
sides, because it's way out in the boondocks and the west and south
sides belong to some nature outfit that a rich guy gave his land to,
and all you can do there is hike and look at trees and birds. The
road turns left, between the woods and the backs of houses, and I
follow it near the trees. A dog barks and some others pick it up.
But it's just the bitchy barking of pets, there's not a serious one in
there, and I keep walking, and nobody talks to the dogs or comes
out for a look, and they stop.

All the houses are so close together I won't see Steve's until I'm
at it. I know it's on this road and it's brown. King wrote to me and
Alex once from there; he didn't want the folks to read it; he wrote
about patrols and ambushes. He said *Don't get me wrong, I wish right
now I was back there with you guys and a case of Bud in the cooler out on
a boat pulling in mackerel. They must be in, about now. But I'll say this:
I'll never feel the adrenaline like this again, not even with blue fish or deer
or kicking ass. I understand now what makes bankers and such go skydiving*

on Saturdays. Then I see Polly's red Subaru and Steve's van, and I freeze, then lower the can to the ground and kneel beside it. I wonder if this is close to what King felt. When I think of the arsenal Steve's got inside, I believe maybe it is. I kneel listening. There's a breeze and the water lapping in front of the house. I listen some more, then unscrew the cap and get up to a crouch and cross the road. I stand behind his van and look up and down the road and in the yards next door. Every yard is small, every house is small, no rich man's lake here, but people that work. Her car and the van are side by side in a short dirt driveway; on the right, by the corner of the house, there's a woodpile. I look at the dark windows, then go for the wood. I'm right under a window, and all I can hear is the breeze and the water. I move up the side of the house, under windows, toward the lake. At the front yard I stop, breathing through my mouth but slow and quiet as I can. There's a tree that looks like an oak in the yard, then the wharf. He's got a cement patio with some chairs and a hammock and a barbecue grill and table with empty beer bottles on it. I run to the lake side of the tree and press my back against it; he has a short wharf with an outboard and a canoe. I look around the tree at the front of the house. Then I step toward the lake, move out far enough so I'm past the branches—it's an oak—and I start pouring: walking backward parallel to the house that I'm watching all the time, and when I clear it, I turn and back toward the road, watching Steve's and the house on my left too. The gasoline is loud, back and forth in the can, and pouring onto the grass.

I back up past their cars and my back is stiff, I'm breathing short and quiet and need more of it but won't; I make a wide circle around their cars, and take the can cap from my pocket and drop it there, and go around the house again, the corner with the woodpile, and I back toward the lake, checking the other house on my left now, my head going back and forth but mostly forth, waiting for Steve to stick a Goddamn .30-06 or 12-guage out one of the windows, then I'm past the house and feeling the lake behind me and I keep going to the tree and around it, and all I can smell is gasoline. I empty the can near where I started so the lines will meet. Then I straighten up and step down off a low concrete wall to the beach. I go up the beach past three houses, then out between them to the road, and I cross it and lay the can in the woods. Then I cross again and stand at the road with her car and his van between me and the house. I look down till I see the gas cap. Then I take one match from a book and strike it and hold it to the others; they catch with a hiss, and I toss them at the cap: the gasoline flares with a whoosh and runs left and right and dances around the corners into the breeze, curving every which way, and I run back into the road where I can look past the house in time to see the flames coming at each other around the house, doing some front-yard patterns like ice skaters where I emptied the can. Then they meet and I am running on the grass beside the road, down the road and around the corner, on the grass in the dark by the woods, to my jeep up there. The key is in my hand.

In the upstairs bedroom she wakes to firelight and flickering shadows on the walls that do not yet feel like her own, and she is so startled out of sleep that she is for a moment displaced, long enough for this summer's fear—that no walls and roof will ever feel like her own —to rise in her heart before it is dissipated by this new fear she has waked to; then she is throwing back the sheet and crossing the floor. Out the front window she looks at sinuous flames surrounding the yard between her and the lake; calling Steve, she goes to the side window and looks down at fire, then into the back room where Steve's mattress on the floor is empty, still made since morning. She steps on and over it, to the rear window overlooking the yard and car and van and the ring of fire. She switches on the stair light and descends, calling; by the bottom step she knows she is not trapped and her voice softens, becomes quizzical. Downstairs is a kitchen, darkened save for the wavering light on the walls, and a living room where he sleeps sitting on the couch, his feet on the coffee table, the room smelling of beer and cigarette smoke.

'Steve?' He stirs, shakes his head, drops his feet to the floor. She points out the wide front window. 'Look.'

He is up, out the front door, turning on the faucet and pulling the coiled hose across the patio. In places the fire has spread toward the house, but it is waning and burns close to the ground.

'It's all around,' she says, as, facing the lake, he moves the hose in an arc; neighbor men shout and she trots to either side of the house and sees them: the men next door with their hoses and wives and children. Steve belches loudly; she turns and sees him pissing on the fire, using his left hand, while his right moves the hose. He yells thanks over each shoulder; the men call back. The fire is out, and Steve soaks the front lawn, then both sides, joining his stream with the others. He asks her to turn it off, and he coils the hose and she follows him to the backyard. The two men come, and their wives take the children inside.

'Jeesum Crow,' one says. 'What do you figure that was about?'

'Tooth fairy,' Steve says, and offers them a beer. They accept, their voices mischievous as they excuse themselves for drinking at this hour after being wakened. They blame the fire. Polly has come to understand this about men: they need mischief and will even pretend a twelve-ounce can of beer is wicked if that will make them feel collusive while drinking it. Steve brings out four bottles, surprises her by handing her one he had not offered; she is pleased and touches his hand and thanks him as she takes it. She sits on the back stoop and watches the men standing, listens to their strange talk: about who would want to do such a thing, and what did a guy want to get out of doing it, and if they could figure out what he was trying to get done, then maybe they could get an idea of who it might be. But their tone will not stay serious, moves from inquisitive to jestful, without pattern or even harmony: while one supposes aloud that teenaged vandals chose the house at random and another agrees and says it's time for the selectmen to talk strict curfew and for the Goddamn cops to do some enforcing, the first one cackles and wheezes about a teenaged girl he watched water skiing this afternoon, how she could come to his house any night and light some fire. They clap hands on shoulders, grab an arm and pull and push. Steve takes in the empties and brings out four more.

Polly goes upstairs for cigarettes and stands at the back window, looking down at them. Steve has slept in here since she moved in; some nights, some days, one of them has stood in the short hall between their rooms and tapped on the door, with a frequency and need like that of a couple who have lived long together: not often, and not from passion, but often enough for release from carnal solitude. She does not want to join the men in the yard and does not want to be alone in the house; she goes downstairs and sits on the stoop, smoking, and staring at the woods beyond them. She imagines Ray lying under the trees, watching, his knife in his hand. One of the men stoops and rises with something he shows the others.

A cap from a gasoline can, they say. Sitting between the house and the men, she still feels exposed, has the urge to look behind her, and she smokes deeply and presses her fingers against her temples, rubs her eyes to push away her images of him softly paddling a canoe on the lake, standing on the front lawn, creeping into hiding in the living room, up the stairs to her bedroom; in the closet there. The men are leaving. They tell her good night, and she stands and thanks them. Steve comes to her, three bottles in his large hand. He places the other on her shoulder.

'Looks like your ex is back,' he says.

'Yes.'

'Dumb asshole.'

'Yes.'

Vinnie is a bruise on the pillow, and from a suspended bottle of something clear, a tube goes to his left arm and ends under tape. He is asleep. She stands in the doorway, wanting to leave; then quietly she goes in, to the right side of the bed. His flesh is black and purple under both eyes, on the bridge of his nose, and his right jaw; cotton is stuffed in his nostrils; his breath hisses between swollen lips, the upper one stitched. Polly has not written a card for the zinnias she cut from her mother's garden but, even so, she can let him wake to them and phone later, come back later, do whatever later. When she puts them on the bedside table, his eyes open.

'I brought you some flowers,' she says. She looks over her shoulder at the door, then takes from her purse a brown-bagged pint of vodka. Smiling, she pulls out the bottle so he can see the label, then drops it into the bag. He only watches her. She cannot tell whether his eyes show more than pain. She pushes the vodka under his pillows.

'Do you hurt?'

'Drugs,' he says, through his teeth, only his lips moving, spreading in a grimace.

'Oh Jesus. Your jaw's broken?'

He nods.

'Will you hurt if I sit here?'

'No.'

She sits on the side of the bed and takes his right hand lying on the sheet, softly rubs his bare forearm, watching the rise and fall of his dark hair, its ends sun-bleached gold. His arm is wide and hard with muscle, her own looks delicate, and as she imagines Ray's chest and neck swelling with rage, a cool shiver rises from her legs to her chest. She reaches for her purse on the bedside table.

'Can I smoke in here?'

'I guess.'

He sounds angry; she knows it is because his jaw is wired, but still she feels he is angry at her and ought to be. She finds an ashtray in the drawer of the bedside table, cocks her head at the hanging bottle of fluid, and says: 'Is that your food?'

'Saline. Eat with a straw.'

'Can you smoke?'

'Don't know.'

She holds her cigarette between his lips, on the right side, away from the stitches. She cannot feel him drawing on it; he nods, she removes it, and he exhales a thin stream.

'Are you hurt anywhere else? Your body?'

'No. How did you know?'

'My father called me.' She offers the cigarette, he nods, and as he draws on it, she says: 'He said you're not pressing charges.'

His face rolls away from the cigarette, he blows smoke toward the tube rising from his arm, then looks at her, and she knows what she first saw in his eyes and mistook for pain.

'I don't blame you,' she says. 'I wouldn't either. In June he came into my apartment with a fucking knife and raped me. I was afraid to do anything, and I kept thinking he was gone. *Really* gone, like California or someplace. Because Dad checked at where he worked and his apartment, and he never went back after that night. Even if I knew he hadn't gone, I wouldn't have. Because he's fucking *crazy*.'

She stands and takes her cigarettes and disposable lighter from her purse and puts them on the table.

'I'll leave you these. I have to go. I'll be back.'

Her eyes are filling. Besides Steve, Vinnie is the only person outside her family she has told about the rape, but his eyes did not change when she said it; could not change, she knows, for the sorrow in them is so deep. She has known him in passion and mirth, and kissing his forehead, his unbruised left cheek, his chin, she feels as dangerous as Ray, more dangerous with her slender body and pretty face.

'I guess it wasn't worth it,' she says.
'Nothing is. I'm all broken.'

Sometimes, on her days off that summer, she put on a dress and went to Timmy's in early afternoon to drink. It was never crowded then, and always the table by the window was empty, and she sat there and watched the Main Street traffic and the people walking outside in the heat; or, in the rain, cars with lights and windshield wipers on, the faces of drivers and passengers blurred by rain and dripping windows.

She slept late. She was twenty-six and, for as long as she could remember, she had hated waking early; now that she worked at night, she not only was able to sleep late, but had to; she lived at home and no longer felt, as she had when she was younger and woke to the family voices, that she had wasted daylight sleeping while everyone else had lived half a day. There had been many voices then, but now two brothers and a sister had grown and moved away, and only Margaret was at home. She was seventeen and drank a glass of wine at some family dinners, had never, she said, had a cigarette in her mouth, had not said but was certainly a virgin, and early in the morning jogged for miles on the country roads near their home; during blizzards, hard rain, and days when ice on the roads slowed her pace, she ran around the indoor basketball court at the YMCA. She received Communion every Sunday and, in the Lenten season, every day. She was dark and pretty, but Polly thought all that virtue had left its mark on her face, and it would never be the sort that makes men change their lives.

Polly liked her sister, and was more amused than annoyed by the way she lived. She could not understand what pleasures Margaret drew from running and not drinking or smoking dope or even cigarettes, and from virginity. She did understand Margaret's religion, and sometimes she wished that being a Catholic were as easy for her as it was for Margaret. Then she envied Margaret, but when envy became scorn she fought it by imagining Margaret on a date; certainly she felt passion, so maybe her sacramental life was not at all easy. Maybe waking up and jogging weren't either; and she would remember her own high school years when, if you wanted friends and did not want to do what the friends did, you had to be very strong. So those times when she envied, then scorned Margaret ended with her wondering if perhaps all of Margaret's life was good because she willed it.

Polly went to Mass every Sunday, but did not receive communion because she had not been in the state of grace for a long time, and she did not confess because she knew that she could not be absolved of fornication and adultery while wearing an intrauterine device whose presence belied her firm intention of not sinning again. She was not certain that her lovemaking since the end of her marriage was a sin, or one serious enough to forbid her receiving, for she did not feel bad about it, except when she wished during and afterward that she had not gone to bed with someone, and that had to do with making a bad choice. She had never confessed her adultery while she was married to Raymond Yarborough, though she knew she had been wrong, had felt wicked as well as frightened; but, remembering now (she had filed for divorce and changed her name back to Comeau), her short affair with Vinnie when the marriage was in its final months was diminished by her sharper memory of Raymond yelling at her that she was a spoiled, fucked-up cunt not worth a shit to anybody, Raymond slapping her, and, on the last night, hitting her with his fist and leaving her unconscious on the bedroom floor, where she woke hearing Jerry Jeff Walker on the record player in the living room and a beer bottle landing on others in the wastebasket. Her car key was in there with him, so she climbed out the window and ran until she was nauseated and her legs were weak and trembling; then she walked, and in two hours she was home. She had to wake them to get in, and her mother put ice on her jaw, Margaret held her hand and stroked her hair, and her father took his gun and nightstick and drove to the apartment, but Raymond was gone in his jeep, taking with him his weights and bench and power stands, fishing rods and tackle box, two shotguns and a .22 rifle, the hunting knife he bought in memory of his brother, his knapsack and toilet articles and some clothes. When she moved from that apartment two weeks later, she filled a garbage bag with his clothes and Vietnam books, most of them hardcover, and left it on the curb; as she drove away, she looked in the rear view mirror at the green bulk and said aloud: 'Adiós, motherfucker.'

She also did not go to confession because, as well as not feeling bad about her sexual adventures, and knowing that she would not give them up anyway, she did believe that in some way her life was not a good one, but in a way the Church had not defined. Neither could she: even on those rare and mysterious nights when drinking saddened her and she went to bed drunk and disliking herself and woke hung over and regretful, she did not and could not know what about herself she disliked and regretted. So she could not confess, but she went to Mass with her family every Sunday and had gone when she lived alone, because it was one religious act she could perform, and she was afraid that neglecting it would finally lead her to a fearful loneliness she could not bear.

Dressing for Mass was different from dressing for any other place, and she liked having her morning coffee and cigarette while, without anticipating drinks or dinner or a man or work or anything at all, she put on makeup and a dress and heels; and she liked entering the church where the large doors closed behind her and she walked down the aisle under the high, curved white ceiling, and between stained-glass windows in the white walls whose lower halves were dark brown wood, as the altar was and the large cross with a bronze Christ hanging from the wall behind it. When she was with her family, her father chose a pew and stood at it while Margaret went in, then Polly, then her parents; alone, she looked for a pew near the middle with an aisle seat. She kneeled on the padded kneeler, her arms on the smooth old wood of the pew in front of her, and looked at the altar and crucifix and the stained-glass window behind them; then sat and looked at people sitting in front of her on both sides of the aisle. There was a scent of perfume and sometimes leather from purses and coats, tingeing that smell she only breathed here: a blending of cool, dry basement air with sunlight and melting candle wax. As the priest entered wearing green vestments, she rose and sang with the others, listened to her voice among theirs, read the Confiteor aloud with them, felt forgiven as she read *in what I have done and in what I have failed to do*, those simple and general words as precise as she could be about the life, a week older each Sunday, that followed her like a bridal train into church where, for forty minutes or so, her mind was suspended, much as it was when she lay near sleep at the beach. She did not pray with concentration, but she did not think either, and her mind wandered from the Mass to the faces of people around her. At the offertory she sang with them and, later, stood and read the Lord's Prayer aloud; then the priest said *Let us now offer each other a sign of peace* and, smiling, she shook the hands of people in front of her and behind her, saying *Peace be with you.*

She liked to watch them receive communion: children and teen-agers and women and men going slowly in two lines up the center aisle and in single lines up both side aisles, to the four waiting priests. Coming back, they chewed or dissolved the host in their mouths. Sometimes a small boy looked about and smiled. But she only saw children when they crossed her vision; she watched the others: the old, whose faces had lost any sign of beauty or even pleasure, and were gentle now, peacefully dazed, with God on their tongues; the pretty and handsome young, and the young who were plain or homely; and, in their thirties and forties and fifties, women and men who had lost the singularity of youth, their bodies unattractive, most of them too heavy, and no face was pretty or plain, handsome or homely, and all of these returned to their pews with clasped hands and bowed heads, their faces both serious and calm. She tenderly watched them. Now that she was going to Mass with her family, she watched them too, the three dark faces with downcast eyes: slender Margaret with her finely concave cheeks, and no makeup, her lips and brow bearing no trace of the sullen prudery she some-times turned on Polly, sometimes on everyone; her plump mother, the shortest in the family now, grey lacing her black hair, and her frownlike face one of weariness in repose, looking as it would later in the day when, reading the paper, she would fall asleep on the couch; her father, tall and broad, his shirt and coat tight across his chest, his hair thick and black, and on his face the look of peaceful concentration she saw when he was fishing; and she felt merciful toward them, and toward herself, not only for her guilt or shame because she could not receive (they did not speak to her about it, or about anything else she did, not even—except Margaret—with their eyes), but for her sense and, often at Mass, her conviction that she was a bad woman. She rose and sang as the priest and altar boys walked up the aisle and out the front of the church; then people filled the aisle and she moved with them into the day.

She had always liked boys and was very pretty, so she had never had a close girl friend. In high school she had the friends you need, to keep from being alone, and to go with to places where boys were. Those friendships felt deep because at their heart were shared guilt and the fond trust that comes from it. They existed in, and because of, those years of sexual abeyance when boys shunned their company and went together to playing fields and woods and lakes and the sea. The girls went to houses. Waiting to be old enough to drive, waiting for those two or three years in their lives when a car's function would not be conveyance but privacy, they gathered at the homes of girls whose mothers had jobs. They sat on the bed and floor and smoked cigarettes.

Sometimes they smoked marijuana too, and at slumber parties, when the parents had gone to bed, they drank beer or wine bought for them by an older friend or brother or sister. But cigarettes were their first and favorite wickedness, and they delightfully entered their addiction, not because they wanted to draw tobacco smoke into their lungs, but because they wanted to be girls who smoked. Within two or three years, cigarette packs in their purses would be as ordinary as wallets and combs; but at fourteen and fifteen, simply looking at the alluring colored pack among their cosmetics excited them with the knowledge that a time of their lives had ended, and a new and promising time was coming. The smooth cellophane covering the pack, the cigarette between their fingers and lips, the taste and feel of smoke, and blowing it into the air, struck in them a sensual chord they had not known they had. They watched one another. They always did that: looked at breasts, knew who had gained or lost weight, had a pimple, had washed her hair or had it done in a beauty parlor, and, if shown the contents of a friend's closet, would know her name. They watched as a girl nodded toward a colored disposable lighter, smiled if smoke watered her eyes, watched the fingers holding the cigarette, the shape of her lips around the tip, the angle of her wrist.

So they were friends in that secret life they had to have; then they were older and in cars, and what they had been waiting for happened. They shared that too, and knew who was late, who was taking the pill, who was trusting luck. Their language was normally profane, but when talking about what they did with boys, they said *had sex, slept with, oral sex, penis.* Then they graduated and spread outward from the high school and the houses where they had gathered, to nearby colleges and jobs within the county. Only one, who married a soldier, moved out of the state. The others lived close enough to keep seeing each other, and in the first year out of high school some of them did; but they all had different lives, and loved men who did not know each other, and soon they only met by chance, and talked on sidewalks or at coffee counters.

Since then Polly had met women she liked, but she felt they did not like her. When she thought about them, she knew she could be wrong, could be feeling only her own discomfort. With her girlhood friends she had developed a style that pleased men. But talking with a woman was scrutiny, and always she was conscious of her makeup, her pretty face, her long black hair, and the way her hands moved with a cigarette, a glass, patting her hair in place at the brow, pushing it back from a cheek. She studied the other woman too, seeing her as a man would; comparing her, as a man would, with herself; and this mutual disassembly made them wary and finally mistrustful. At times Polly envied the friendships of men, who seemed to compete with each other in everything from wit to strength, but never in attractiveness or over women; or girls like Margaret, who did nothing at all with her beauty, so that, seeing her in a group of girls, you would have to look closely to know she was the prettiest. But she knew there was more, knew that when she was in love she did not have the energy and time to become a woman's friend, to go beyond the critical eye, the cautious heart. Even men she did not love, but liked and wanted, distracted her too much for that. She went to Timmy's alone.

But not lonely: she went on days when, waking late, and eating a sandwich or eggs alone in the kitchen, she waited, her mind like a blank movie screen, to know what she wanted to do with her day. She saw herself lying on a towel at the beach; shopping at the mall or in Boston; going to Steve's house to swim in the lake or, if he wanted to run the boat, water-ski; wearing one of her new dresses and drinking at Timmy's. That was it, on this hot day in July: she wanted to be the woman in a summer dress, sitting at the table by the window. She chose the salmon one with shoulder straps, cut to the top of her breasts and nearly to the small of her back. Then she took the pistol from the drawer of her bedside table and put it in her purse. By one o'clock she was at the table, sipping her first vodka and tonic, opening a pack of cigarettes, amused at herself as she tasted lime and smelled tobacco, because she still loved smoking and drinking as she had ten years ago when they were secret pleasures, still at times (and today was one) felt in the lifted glass and fondled pack a glimmer of promise from out there beyond the window and the town, as if the pack and glass were conduits between the mysterious sensuous rhythms of the world and her own.

She looked out the window at people in cars and walking in the hot sunlight. Al was the afternoon bartender, a man in his fifties, who let her sit quietly, only talking to her when she went to the bar for another drink. Men came in out of the heat, alone or in pairs, and drank a beer and left. She drank slowly, glanced at the men as they came and went, kept her back to the bar, listened to them talking with Al. For the first two hours, while she had three drinks, her mood was the one that had come to her at the kitchen table. Had someone approached and spoken, she would have blinked at the face while she waited for the person's name to emerge from wherever her mind had been. She sat peacefully looking out the window, and at times, when she realized that she was having precisely the afternoon she had wanted, and how rare it was now and had been for years to have the feeling you had wanted and planned for, her heart beat faster with a sense of freedom, of generosity; and in those moments she nearly bought the bar a round, but did not, knowing then someone would talk to her, and what she had now would be lost, dissipated into an afternoon of babble and laughter. But the fourth drink shifted something under her mood, as though it rested on a foundation that vodka had begun to dissolve.

Now when she noticed her purse beside her hand, she did not think of money but of the pistol. Looking out at people passing on foot or in cars, she no longer saw each of them as someone who loved and hoped under that brilliant, hot sky; they became parts again, as the cars did, and the Chevrolet building across the street where behind the glass front girls spoke into telephones and salesmen talked to couples, and as the sky itself did: parts of his town, the boundaries of her life.

She saw her life as, at best, a small circle: one year as a commuting student, driving her mother's car twenty minutes to Merrimack College, a Catholic school with secular faculty, leaving home in the morning and returning after classes as she had since kindergarten, discovering in that year—or forcing her parents to discover what she had known since ninth grade—that she was not a student, simply because she was not interested. She could learn anything they taught, and do the work, and get the grades, but in college she was free to do none of this, and she chose to do only enough to accumulate eight Cs and convince her parents that she was, not unlike themselves, a person whose strengths were not meant to be educated in schools.

She did not know why she was not interested. In June, when her first and last year of college was a month behind her, she remembered it with neither fondness nor regret, as she might have recalled movies she had seen with boys she did not love. She had written grammatical compositions she did not feel or believe, choosing topics that seemed both approachable and pleasing to the teacher. She discovered a pattern: all topics were approachable if she simply rendered them, with an opening statement, proper paragraphs, and a conclusion; and every topic was difficult if she began to immerse in it; but always she withdrew. In one course she saw herself: in sociology, with amusement, anger, resignation, and a suspended curiosity that lasted for weeks, she learned of the hunters, the gatherers, the farmers, saw herself and her parents defined by survival; and industrialization bringing about the clock that, on her bedside table, she regarded as a thing which was not inanimate but a conscience run on electricity, and she was delighted, knowing that people had once lived in accord with the sun and weather, and that punctuality and times for work and food and not-work and sleep were later imposed upon them, as she felt now they were imposed upon her.

In her other classes she listened, often with excitement, to a million dead at Borodino, Bismarck's uniting Germany, Chamberlain at Munich, Hitler invading Russia on the twenty-second of June because Napoleon did, all of these people and their actions equally in her past, kaleidoscopic, having no causal sequence whose end was her own birth and first eighteen years. She could say 'On honeydew he hath fed / And drunk the milk of paradise' and '. . . the women come and go / Talking of Michelangelo,' but they, and Captain Vere hanging Billy Budd, and Huck choosing Nigger Jim and hell, joined Socrates and his hemlock and Bonhoeffer's making an evil act good by performing it for a friend, and conifers and deciduous trees, pistils and stamens, and the generals and presidents and emperors and kings, all like dust motes in the sunlight of that early summer, when she went to work so she could move to an apartment an hour's walk from the house she had lived in for nineteen years, and which she forced herself to call *my parents' house* instead of home until that became habitual.

She was a clerk in a department store in town. The store was old and had not changed its customs: it had no cash registers. She worked in the linen department, and placed bills and coins into a cylinder and put that in a tube which, by vacuum, took the money to a small room upstairs where women she never met sent change down. She worked six days a week and spent the money on rent and heat and a used Ford she bought for nine hundred and eighty-five dollars; she kept food for breakfasts and lunches in her refrigerator, and ate dinners with her parents or dates or bought pieces of fish, chicken, or meat on the way home from work. On Sundays she went to the beach.

A maternal uncle was a jeweler and owned a store, and in fall she went to work for him, learned enough about cameras and watches to help customers narrow their choices to two or three; then her uncle came from his desk, and compared watches or cameras with a fervor that made their purchase seem as fraught with possibilities of happiness and sorrow as choosing a lover. She liked the absolute cleanliness of the store, with its vacuumed carpets and polished glass, its lack of any distinctive odors, and liked to believe what she did smell was sparkle from the showcases. Her grey-haired uncle always wore a white shirt and bow tie; he told her neckties got in the way of his work, the parts of watches he bent over with loupe and tweezers and screwdriver and hand remover. She said nothing about a tie clasp, but thought of them, even glanced at their shelf. She liked them, and all the other small things in their boxes on the shelves: cuff links and rings and pins and earrings. She liked touching them with customers.

She worked on Saturdays, but on Wednesday afternoons her uncle closed the store. It was an old custom in the town, and most doctors and lawyers and dentists and many owners of small stores kept it still. She had grown up with those Wednesday afternoons when she could not get money at the bank or see a doctor or buy a blouse, but now they were holidays for her. She had been in school so much of her life that she did not think of a year as January to January, but September to June and, outside of measured time, the respite of summer. Now her roads to and from work wound between trees that were orange and scarlet and yellow, then standing naked among pines whose branches a month later held snow, and for the first time in her memory autumn's colors did not mean a school desk and homework, and snow the beginning of the end of half a year and Christmas holidays. One evening in December, as she crossed her lawn, she stopped and looked down at the snow nearly as high as her boots; in one arm she cradled a bag of groceries; and looking at the snow, she knew, as if for the first time, though she had believed she had known and wanted it for years, that spring's trickle of this very snow would not mean now or ever again the beginning of the end of the final half-year, the harbinger of those three months when she lived the way they did before factory whistles and clocks.

The bag seemed heavier, and she shifted its weight and held it more tightly. Then she went inside and up two flights of stairs and into her apartment. She put the groceries on the kitchen table and sat looking from the bag to her wet boots with snow rimming the soles and melting on the instep. She took off her gloves and un-buttoned her coat and put her damp beret on the table. For a long time she had not been afraid of people or the chances of a day, for she believed she could bear the normal pain of being alive: her heart had been broken by girls and boys, and she had borne that, and she had broken hearts and borne that too, and embarrassment and shame and humiliation and failure, and she was not one of those who, once or more wounded, waited fearfully for the next mistake or cruelty or portion of bad luck. But she was afraid of what she was going through now: having more than one feeling at once, so that feeling proud and strong and despairing and resigned, she sat suspended in fear. *So this is the real world they always talked about.* She said it aloud: 'the real world,' testing its sound in the silence; for always, when they said it, their tone was one of warning, and worse, something not only bitter and defeated but vindictive as well, the same tone they had when they said *I told you so.* She groped into the bag, slowly tore open a beer carton as she looked at the kitchen walls and potted plants in the window, drew out a bottle, twisted off the cap, but did not drink. Her hand went into her purse, came out with cigarettes and lighter, placed them beside the beer. She hooked a toe under the other chair, pulled it closer, and rested both feet on it. *I don't believe it. And if you don't believe it, it's not true, except dying.*

What she did believe through that winter and spring was that she had entered the real world of her town, its time and work and leisure, and she looked back on her years of growing up as something that had happened to her outside of the life she now lived, as though childhood and her teens (she would soon be twenty) were, like those thirteen summers from kindergarten until the year of college, a time so free of what time meant to her now that it was not time but a sanctuary from it. Now, having had those years to become herself so she could enter the very heart of the town, the business street built along the Merrimack, where she joined the rhythmic exchange of things and energy and time for money, she knew she had to move through the town, and out of it. But, wanting that motion, she could not define it, for it had nothing to do with place or even people, but something within herself: a catapult, waiting for both release and direction, that would send her away from these old streets, some still of brick, and old brick leather factories, most of them closed but all of them so bleak, so dimly lit beyond their dirty windows that, driving or even walking past one, you could not tell whether anyone worked inside.

On a Wednesday afternoon in May, at a bar in Newburyport, where the Merrimack flowed through marshes to the sea, she sat alone on the second-floor sun deck, among couples in their twenties drinking at picnic tables. She sat on a bench along the railing, her back to the late-afternoon sun, and watched the drinkers, and anchored sailboats and fishing boats, and boats coming in. A small fishing boat followed by screaming gulls tied up at the wharf beside the bar, and she stood so she could look down at it. She had not fished with her father since she started working; she would call him tonight—no, she would finish this drink and go there for dinner and ask him if he'd like to go Sunday after Mass. Then Raymond Yarborough came around the cabin, at the bow, swinging a plastic bag of fish over his left shoulder. One of the men—there were six—gave him a beer. Her hand was up in a wave, her mouth open to call, but she stopped and watched. He had a beard now, brown and thick; he was shirtless and sunburned. She wore a white Mexican dress and knew how pretty she looked standing up there with the sun on her face and the sky behind her, and she waited. He lifted the bag of fish to the wharf and joined the others scrubbing the cleaning boards and deck. Then he went into the cabin and came out wearing a denim work shirt and looked up and laughed.

'Polly Comeau, what are you doing up there?'

She wondered about that, six years later, on the July afternoon at Timmy's; and wondered why, from that evening on, she not only believed her life had changed but knew that indeed it had (though she was never comfortable with, never sure of, the distinction between believing something about your life and that something also being true). But something did happen: when Ray became not the boy she had known in high school but her lover, then husband, she felt both released and received, no longer in the town, a piece of its streets and time, but of the town, having broken free of its gravity, so that standing behind the jewelry counter she did not feel rooted or even stationary; and driving to and from work, or pushing a cart between grocery shelves, were a new sort of motion whose end was not the jewelry store, the apartment, the supermarket cash register, but herself, the woman she saw in Raymond's face.

In her sleep she knew she was dreaming: she was waitressing at the Harbor Schooner, but inside it looked like the gymnasium in high school with tables for prom night, and the party of four she was serving changed to a crowd, some were familiar, and she strained to know them; then her father was frying squid in the kitchen and she was there with a tray, and he said *Give them all the squid they want*; then a hand was on her mouth and she woke with her right hand pushing his wrist and her left prying his fingers, and in that instant before opening her eyes, when her dream dissolved into darkness, she knew it was Ray. She was on her back and he was straddling her legs. She kneed him but he moved forward and she struck bone. He sat on her thighs and his right hand went to his back and she heard the snap, and the blade leaving its sheath; then he was holding it close to her face, his dark-bladed knife; in the moonlight she saw the silver line of its edge. Then its point touched her throat, and his hand left her mouth.

'Turn over,' he said.

He rose to his knees, and she turned on her stomach, her back and throat waiting for the knife, but then his knees were between her legs, his hand under her stomach, lifting: she kneeled with her face in the pillow, heard his buckle and snap and zipper and pants slipping down his legs; he pushed her nightgown up her back, the knife's edge touched her stomach, and he was in, rocking her back and forth. She gripped the pillow and tensed her legs, trying to remain motionless, but his thrusts drove her forward, and her legs like springs forced her to recoil, so she was moving with him, and always on her tightened stomach the knife flickered, his breathing faster and louder then Ah Ah Ah, a tremor of his flesh against hers, the knife scraping toward her ribs and breasts, then gone, and he was too; above his breathing and her own she heard the ascent of pants, the zipper and snap and buckle, but no sheating of the blade, so the knife itself had, in the air above her as she collapsed forward, its own sound of blood and night: but please God oh Jesus please not her gripping the pillow, her chin pressed down covering her throat, not her in the white Mexican dress with her new sunburn standing at the rail, seeing now Christ looking down through her on the sun deck that May afternoon to her crouched beneath the knife—

'Good, Polly. You got a little juiced after a while. Good.'

His weight shifted, then he was on the floor. She heard him cut the telephone cord.

'See you later, Polly.'

His steps on the floor were soft: he shut the door and in the corridor he was quiet as night. Her grip on the pillow loosened; her hands opened; still she waited. Then slowly and quietly she rolled over and got out of bed and tiptoed to the door and locked it again. She lit a cigarette, sat on the toilet in the dark, wiped and flushed and went to the window beside the bed, where she stood behind the open curtain and looked down at the empty street. She listened for his jeep starting, heard only slow and occasional cars moving blocks away, in town, and the distant voices and laughter of an outdoor party, and country music from a nearby window. She dressed and went down the hall and three flights of stairs and outside, pausing on the front steps to look at the street and parked cars and, on the apartment's lawn and lawns on both sides of it and across the street, the shadowed trunks of trees. She could not hear the sounds of the party or the music from the record player. Then he was dripping out of her and she went up the stairs and sat on the toilet while he pattered into the water, then scrubbed her hands, went out again, down the walk, and turned left, walking quickly in the middle of the sidewalk between tree trunks and parked cars, and looked at each of them and over her shoulders and between the cars for two and a half blocks to the closed drugstore, lighted in the rear where the counter was. In the phone booth she stood facing the street; the light came on when she closed the door, so she opened it and called her father.

She knew his steps in the hall and opened the door before he knocked. He was not in uniform, but he wore his cartridge belt and holstered .38. She hugged his deep, hard chest, and his arms were around her, one hand patting her back, and when he asked what Ray had done to her, she looked up at his wide sunburned face, his black hair and green eyes like her own, then rested her face on his chest and soft old chamois shirt, and said: 'He had his knife. He touched me with it. My throat. My stomach. He cut the phone wire—' His patting hand stopped. 'The door was locked and I was asleep, he doesn't even *have* a credit card, I don't know what he used, I woke up with his hand on my mouth then he had that big knife, that Marine knife.'

His mouth touched her hair, her scalp, and he said: 'He raped you?'

She nodded against his chest; he squeezed her, then his hands were holding her waist and he lifted her and his shoulders swung to the left and he put her down, as though moving her out of his path so he could walk to the bed, the wall, through it into the third-story night. But he did not move. He inhaled with a hiss and held it, then blew it out and did it again, and struck his left palm with his right fist, the open hand gripping the fist, and he stood breathing fast, the hand and fist pushing against each other. He was looking at the bed, and she wished she had made it.

'You better come home.'

'I want to.'

'Then I'm going look for him.'

'Yes.'

'You have anything to drink?'

'Wine and beer.'

When he turned the corner into the kitchen, she straightened the sheets; he came back while she was pulling the spread over the pillows.

'I'll call Mom,' he said. He stood by the bed, his hands on the phone. 'Then we'll go to the hospital.'

'I'm all right.'

He held the cord, looking at its severed end.

'They take care of you, in case you're pregnant.'

'I'm all right.'

He swallowed from the bottle, his eyes still on the cord. Then he looked at her.

'Just take something for tonight. We can come back tomorrow.'

She packed an overnight bag and he took it from her; in the corridor he put his arm around her shoulders, held her going slowly down the stairs and outside to his pickup; with a hand on her elbow he helped her up to the seat. While he drove he opened a beer she had not seen him take from the apartment. She smoked and watched the town through the windshield and open window: Main Street descending past the city hall and courthouse, between the library and a park, to the river; she looked across the river at the street climbing again and, above the streetlights, trees and two church steeples. On the bridge she saw herself on her knees, her face on the pillow, Ray plunging, Ray lying naked and dead on her apartment floor, her father standing above him. She looked at the broad river, then they were off the bridge and climbing again, past Wendy's and McDonald's and Timmy's, all closed. She wanted to speak, or be able to; she wanted to turn and look at her father, but she had to be cleansed first, a shower, six showers, twelve; and time; but it was not only that.

It was her life itself; that was the sin she wanted hidden from her father and the houses and sleeping people they passed; and she wanted to forgive herself but could not because there was no single act or even pattern she could isolate and redeem. There was something about her heart, so that now glimpsing herself waiting on tables, sleeping, eating, walking in town on a spring afternoon, buying a summer blouse, she felt that her every action and simplest moments were soiled by an evil she could not name.

Next day after lunch he brought her to a small studio; displayed behind its front window and on its walls were photographs, most in color, of families, brides and grooms, and what she assumed were pictures to commemorate graduation from high school: girls in dresses, boys in jackets and ties. The studio smelled of accumulated cigarette smoke and filled ashtrays, and the woman coughed while she seated Polly on a stool in the dim room at the rear. The woman seemed to be in her fifties; her skin had a yellow hue, and Polly did not want to touch anything, as if the walls and stool, like the handkerchief of a person with a cold, bore traces of the woman's tenuous mortality. She looked at the camera and prepared her face by thinking about its beauty until she felt it. They were Polaroid pictures; as she stood beside her father at the front desk, glancing at portraits to find someone she knew, so she could defy with knowledge what she defied now with instinct, could say to herself: *I know him, her, them; they're not like that at all; are fucked up too*, and, her breath recoiling from the odor of the woman's lungs that permeated the walls and pictures, she looked down at the desk, at her face as it had been only minutes ago in the back room. With scissors, the woman trimmed it. She watched the blade cutting through her breasts. The black-and-white face was not angry or hating or fearful or guilty; she did not know what it was but very serious and not pretty.

At City Hall they went to the detectives' office at the rear of the police station. Two detectives sat at desks, one writing, one drinking coffee. They greeted her father, and she stood in the doorway while he went to the desk of the coffee-drinker, a short man wearing a silver revolver behind his hip. Then her father leaned over him, hiding all but his hand on the coffee cup, and she watched her father's uniformed back, listened to his low voice without words. The other detective frowned as he wrote. Her father turned and beckoned: 'Okay, Polly.'

The detective rose to meet her, and she shook his hand and did not hear his name. His voice was gentle, as if soothing her while dressing a wound; he led her across the room and explained what he was doing as he rolled her right forefinger on ink, then on the license. There was a sink and he told her to use the soap and water, the paper towels, then brought her to his desk where her father waited, and held a chair for her. It had a cushioned seat, but a straight wooden back and no arms, so she sat erect, feeling like a supplicant, as she checked answers on a form he gave her (she was not a convicted felon, a drunk, an addict) and answered questions he asked her as he typed on her license: *one twenty-six, black* (he looked at her eyes and said: 'Pretty eyes, Polly'), *green*. He gave her the card and signed the front and looked at the back where he had typed *Dark* under Complexion, *Waitress* under Occupation, and, under Reason for Issuing License: *Protection*. He said the chief would sign the license, then it would go to Boston and return laminated in two weeks; he offered them coffee, they said no, and he walked them to the office door, his hand reaching up to rest on her father's shoulder. The other detective was still writing. In the truck, she said: 'He was nice.'

The gun, her father said, looked like a scaled-down Colt .45: a .380 automatic which they bought because it was used and cost a hundred and fifteen dollars (though he would have paid three hundred, in cash and gladly, for the .38 snubnose she looked at and held first; they were in the store within twenty hours of his bringing her home, then driving to Newburyport, to Ray's empty apartment, where he had kicked open the locked door and looked around enough to see in the floor dust the two bars of clean wood where the weight-lifting bench had been, and the clean circles of varying sizes left by the steel plates and power stands); and because of the way it felt in her hand, light enough so it seemed an extension of her wrist, a part of her palm, its steel and its wooden grips like her skinned bone, and heavy enough so she felt both safe and powerful, and the power seemed not the gun's but her own; and because of its size, which she measured as one and a half Marlboro boxes long, and its shape, flat, so she could carry it concealed in the front pocket of her jeans, when she left home without a purse.

They bought it in Kittery, Maine, less than an hour's drive up New Hampshire's short coast, at the Kittery Trading Post, where as a virgin, then not one but still young enough to keep that as secret as the cigarettes in her purse, she had gone with her father to buy surf rods and spinning rods, parkas, chamois and flannel shirts. It was also the store where Ray, while shopping for a pocketknife, had seen and bought (*I had to*, he told her) a replica of the World War II Marine knife, with the globe and anchor emblem on its sheath. It came in a box, on whose top was a reproduction of the knife's original blueprint from 1942. When he came home, he held the box toward her, said *Look what I found*, his voice alerting her; in his face she saw the same nuance of shy tenderness, so until she looked down at the box she believed he had brought her a gift. *I don't need it*, he said, as she drew it from the sheath, felt its edge, stroked its blood gutter. *But, see, we gave all his stuff away.* That was when she understood he had been talking about Kingsley, and she had again that experience peculiar to marriage, of entering a conversation that had been active for hours in her husband's mind. Now she brought her father to the showcase of knives and showed him, and he said: 'Unless he's good with it at thirty feet, he might as well not have it at all. Not now, anyways.'

Next day, in the sunlit evening of daylight savings time, at an old gravel pit grown with weeds and enclosed by woods on three sides, with a dirt road at one end and a bluff at the other, her father propped a silhouette of a man's torso and head against the bluff, walked twenty paces from it, and gave her the pistol. He had bought it in his name, because she was waiting for the license, and he could not receive the gun in Maine, so a clerk from the Trading Post, who lived in Massachusetts where he was also a gun dealer, brought it home to Amesbury, and her father got it during his lunch hour.

'It loads just like the .22,' he said.

A squirrel chattered in the trees on the bluff. She pushed seven bullets into the magazine, slid it into the handle, and, pointing the gun at the bluff, pulled the slide to the rear and let it snap forward; the hammer was cocked, and she pushed up the safety. Then he told her to take out the magazine and eject the chambered shell: it flipped to the ground, and he wiped it on his pants and gave it to her and told her to load it again; he kept her loading and unloading for ten minutes or so, saying he was damned if he'd get her shot making a mistake with a gun that was supposed to protect her.

'Shoot it like you did the .22 and aim for his middle.'

He had taught her to shoot his Colt .22, and she had shot with him on weekends in spring and summer and fall until her midteens, when her pleasures changed and she went with him just often enough to keep him from being hurt because she had outgrown shooting cans and being with him for two hours of a good afternoon; or often enough to keep her from believing he was hurt. She stood profiled to the target, aimed with one extended hand, thumbed the safety off, and, looking over the cocked hammer and barrel at the shape of a man, could not fire.

'The Miller can,' she said, and, shifting her feet, aimed at the can at the base of the bluff, held her breath, and squeezed to an explosion that shocked her ears and pushed her arm up and back as dust flew a yard short of the can.

'Jesus *Christ*.'

'Reminds me of what I forgot,' he said and, standing behind her, he pulled back her hair and gently pushed cotton into her ears. 'Better go for the target. They didn't make that gun to hit something little.'

'It's the head. If we could fold it back.'

He patted her shoulder.

'Just aim for the middle, and shoot that piece of cardboard.'

Cardboard, she told herself as she lined up the sights on the torso's black middle and fired six times, but *shoulder* she thought when she saw the first hole, *missed, stomach, chest, shoulder, stomach*, and she felt clandestine and solemn, as though performing a strange ritual that would forever change her. She was suddenly tired. As she loaded the magazine, images of the past two nights and two days assaulted her, filled her memory so she could not recall doing anything during that time except kneeling between a knife and Ray's cock, riding in her father's truck—home, to the studio, to City Hall, to Kittery, home, to this woods—and being photographed and fingerprinted and questioned and pointing guns at the walls and ceiling of the store, and tomorrow night she had to wait tables, always wiping them, emptying ashtrays, bantering, smiling, soberly watching them get drunk, their voices louder than the jukebox playing music she would like in any other place. She fired, not trying to think *cardboard*, yielding to the target's shape and going further, seeing it not as any man but Ray, so that now as holes appeared and her arm recoiled from the shots muted by cotton and she breathed the smell of gunpowder, and reloaded and fired seven more times and seven more, she saw him attacking her and falling, attacking her and falling, and she faced the target and aimed with both hands at head and throat and chest, and once heard herself exhale: '*Yes.*'

Two weeks later her father brought her license home, but he had told her not to wait for it, no judge would send her to jail, knowing she had applied, and knowing why. So from that afternoon's shooting on, she carried it everywhere: in her purse, jeans, shorts, beach bag, in her skirt pocket at work and on the car seat beside her as, at two in the morning, she drove home, where she put it in the drawer of her bedside table and left her windows open to the summer air. At Timmy's on that sunlit afternoon in July she rested her hand on it, rubbed its handle under the soft leather of her purse. She knew she was probably drunk by police or medical standards, but not by her own. Her skin seemed thickened, so she could feel more sharply the leather and the pistol handle beneath it than her fingers themselves when she rubbed them together. For a good while she had been unaware of having legs and feet; her cheeks and lips were numb; sometimes she felt an elbow on the table, or the base of her spine, or her thighs when they pressed on the chair's edge, then she shifted her weight. But she was not drunk because she knew she was: she knew her reflexes were too slow for driving, and she would have to concentrate to walk without weaving to the ladies' room. She also knew that the monologue coming to her was true; they always were. She listened to what her mind told her when it was free of the flesh: sometimes after making love, or waking in the morning, or lying on the beach for those minutes before the sun warmed her to sleep, or when she had drunk enough, either alone or with someone who would listen with her; but for a long time there had been no one like that.

Only three men were at the bar now. She brought her glass and ashtray to it, told Al to fill one and empty the other, and took two cocktail napkins. She paid and tipped, then sat at the table and wiped it dry with the napkins, and waited for Steve. At ten to five he came in, wearing a short-sleeved plaid shirt, his stomach not hanging but protruding over his jeans. Halfway to the bar he saw her watching him and smiled, his hand lifting. She waved him to her and looked at his narrow hips as he came.

'Steve? Can I talk to you a minute?'

He glanced over her at the bar, said he was early, and sat. Even now in July, his arms and face looked newly sunburned, his hair and beard, which grew below his open collar, more golden.

'You're one of those guys who look good everywhere,' she said. 'Doing sports outside, drinking in a bar—you know what I mean? Like some guys look right for a bar, but you see them on a boat or something, and they look like somebody on vacation.'

'Some girls too.'

She focused on his lips and teeth.

'You're always smiling, Steve. Don't you ever get down? I've never seen you down.'

'No time for it.'

'No time for it. What did you do today, with all your time?'

'Went out for cod this morning—'

'Did you catch any?'

'Six. Came back to the lake, charcoaled a couple of fillets, and crapped out in the hammock. What's wrong—you down?'

'Me? No, I'm buzzed. But let me tell you: I've been thinking. I'm going to ask you a favor, and if it's *any* kind of *hassle*, you say no, all right? But I think it might be good for both of us. Okay? But if it's not—'

'What is it?'

'No, but wait. I'm sitting here, right? and looking out the window and thinking, and I've got to leave home. See'—she leaned forward, placed her hands on his wrists, and lowered her voice—'I'm living with my folks because I had a nice apartment and I liked being there, but last month, last month Ray broke in one night while I was sleeping and he held a knife on me and raped me.' She did not know what she had expected from his face, but it surprised her: he looked hurt and sad, and he nodded, then slowly shook his head. 'So I moved in with my folks. I was scared. I mean, it's not as bad as some girls get it, from some stranger, like that poor fifteen-year-old last year hitchhiking and he had a knife and made her *blow* him; it was just Ray, you know, but still—I've got a gun too, a permit, the whole thing.' He nodded. 'It's right here, in my purse.'

'That's the way it is now.'

'What is?'

'Whatever. Women need things; you're built too small to be safe anymore.'

'Steve, I got to move. But I'm still scared of having my own place. I was thinking, see, if I could move in with you, then I could do it gradually, you know? And when you leave in the fall I could sublet, I'd pay the whole rent for you till you get back, and by then—when do you come back?'

'Around April.'

'I'd be ready. Maybe I'd move to Amesbury or Newburyport. Maybe even Boston. I don't know why I said Boston. Isn't it funny it's right there and nobody ever goes to live there?'

'Not me. Spend your life walking on concrete? Sure: move in whenever you want.'

'Really? I won't be a problem. I can cook too—'

'So can I. Here.' He reached into his pocket, brought out a key ring and gave her a key. 'Anytime. Call me before, and I'll help you move.'

'No. No, I won't bring much: just, you know, clothes and cassette player and stuff. My folks won't like this.'

'Why not?'

'They'll think we're shacking up.'

'What are you, twenty-five?'

'Six.'

'So?'

'I know. It'll be all right. It's just I keep giving them such a bad time.'

'Hey: *you*'re the one having the bad time.'

'Okay. Can I move in tonight? No, I'm too buzzed. Tomorrow?'

'Tonight, tomorrow. Better bring sheets and a pillow.'

'I can't believe it.' He looked at the bar, then smiled at her and stood. 'All worked out, just like that. Jesus, you're saving my life, Steve. I'll start paying half the rent right away, and look: I'll stay out of the way, right? If you bring a girl home, I won't *be* there. I'll be shut up in my room, quiet as a mouse. I'll go to my folks' for the night, if you want.'

'No problem. Don't you even want to know how much the rent is?'

'I don't even *care*,' and she stood and put her arm around his back, her fingers just reaching his other side, and walked with him to the bar.

Polly's father comes down the slope of the lawn toward the wharf and I'm scared even while I look past him at the pickup I heard on the road, then down the driveway, and I look at his jeans and shirt, then I'm not scared anymore. For a second there, I thought Polly or maybe Vinnie had pressed some charges, but it all comes together at once: he's not in a cruiser and he's got no New Hampshire cops with him and he's wearing civvies, if you can call it that when he's wearing his gun and his nightstick too. I decide to stay in the deck chair. He steps onto the wharf and keeps coming and I decide to take a swallow of beer too. The can's almost empty and I tilt my head back; the sun is behind me, getting near the treetops across the lake. I'm wearing gym shorts and nothing else. I open the cooler and drop in the empty and take another; I know what my body looks like, with a sweat glisten and muscles moving while I shift in the chair to pull a beer out of the ice, while I open it, while I hold it up to him as he stops spread-legged in front of me.

'Want a beer, John?'

I don't know what pisses him off most, the beer or *John*; his chest starts working with his breath, then he slaps the can and it rolls foaming on the wharf, stops at the space between two boards.

'You don't like Miller,' I say. 'I think I got a Bud in there.'

He unsnaps his nightstick, moves it from his left hand to his right, then lowers it, holding it down at arm's length, gripping it hard and resting its end in his left hand. This time I don't shift: I watch his eyes and pull the cooler to me and reach down through the ice and water. I open the beer and take a long swallow.

'*Ass*hole,' he says. 'You want to *rape* somebody, *ass*hole? You want to set fucking *fires*?'

I watch his eyes. At the bottom of my vision I see the stick moving up and down, tapping his left hand. I lower the beer to the wharf and his eyes go with it, just a glance, his head twitching left and down; I grab the stick with my left hand and let the beer drop and get my right on it too. He holds on and I pull myself out of the chair, looking up at his eyes and pushing the stick down. My chest is close to his; we stand there holding the stick.

'What's the gun for, John?' I've got an overhand grip; I work my wrists up and down, turning the stick, and his face gets red as he holds on. I don't stop. 'You want to waste me, John? Huh? Go for it.'

I'm pumping: I can raise and lower the stick and his arms and shoulders till the sun goes down, and now he knows it and he knows I know it; he is sweating and his teeth are clenched and his face is very red with the sun on it. All at once I know I will not hurt him; this comes as fast as laughing, is like laughing.

'Go for the gun, John. And they'll cut it out of your ass.' I walk him backward a few steps, just to watch him keep his balance. 'They can take Polly's nose out too.'

'Fucker,' he says through his teeth.

'Yes I did, John. Lots of times. On the first date too. Did she tell you that?' He tries to shove me back and lift the stick; all he does is strain. 'It wasn't a date, even. I came in from fishing, and there she was, drinking at Michael's. We went to her place and fucked, and know what she said? After? She said, Once you get the clothes off, the rest is easy. Now what the fuck does *that* mean, John? What does that *mean*?'

I'm ahead of him again. Before he gets to the gun my left hand is on it; I swing the stick up above my head, his left hand still on it; I unsnap the holster and start lifting the gun up against his hand pressing down; it comes slowly but it never stops, and his elbow bends as his hand goes up his ribs. When the gun clears the holster he shifts his grip, grabs it at the cylinder, but his fingers slip off and claw air as I throw it backward over my shoulder and grab his wrist before the gun splashes. I lift the stick as high as I can. He still has some reach, so I jerk it down and free, and throw it with a backhand sidearm into the lake. He is panting. I am too, but I shut my mouth on it.

'Go home, John.'

'You leave her alone.'

He is breathing so hard and is so red that I get a picture of him on his back on the wharf and I'm breathing into his mouth.

'Go get some dinner, John.'

'You—' Then he has to cough; it nearly doubles him over, and he turns to the railing and holds it, leans over it, and hacks up a lunger. I turn away and pick up the beer I dropped. There's still some in it; I drink that and take one from the ice, then look at him again. He's standing straight, away from the rail.

'You leave her alone,' he says. 'Fire last night. What are you, crazy? DeLuca.'

'DeLuca who?'

He lifts a hand, waves it from side to side, shakes his head.

'I don't care shit about DeLuca,' he says. 'Let it go, Ray. You do anything to her, I'll bring help.'

'Good. Bring your buddies. What are friends for, that's what I say.'

'I mean it.'

'I know you do. Now go on home before that club floats in and we have to start all over.'

He looks at me. That's all he does for a while, then he turns and goes up the wharf, wiping his face on his bare arm. He walks like he's limping, but he's not. I get another beer and follow him up the lawn to his pickup. By the time he climbs in and starts it, I'm at his window. I toss the beer past him, onto the seat. He doesn't look at me. He backs and turns and I wait for gravel to fly, but he goes slowly up the driveway like the truck is tired too. At the road he stops and looks both ways. Then the beer comes out the window onto the lawn, and he's out on the blacktop, turning right, then he's gone beyond a corner of woods.

Last night waiting tables she was tired, and the muscles in her back and legs hurt. She blamed that afternoon's water skiing, and worked the dining room until the kitchen closed, then went upstairs to the bar and worked there, watching the clock, wiping her brow, sometimes shuddering as a chill spread up her back. She took orders at tables, repeated them to the bartender, garnished the drinks, subtracted in her mind, made change, and thanked for tips, but all that was ever in her mind was the bed at Steve's and herself in it. At one o'clock the Harbor Schooner closed, and when the last drinkers had gone down the stairs, the bartender said: 'What'll it be tonight?' and she went to the bar with the other two waitresses, scanned the bottles, shaking her head, wanting to want a drink because always she had one after work, but the bottles, even vodka, even tequila, could have been cruets of vinegar. She lit a cigarette and asked for a Coke.

'You feeling all right?' he said.

'I think I'm sick,' and she left the cigarette and carried the Coke, finishing it with long swallows and getting another, as she helped clean the tables, empty the ashtrays, and stack them on the bar.

She wakes at two o'clock in the heat of Labor Day weekend's Sunday afternoon, remembers waking several times, once or more when the room was not so brightly lit, so hot; and remembers she could not keep her eyes open long enough to escape the depth of her sleep. Her eyes close and she drifts downward again, beneath her pain, into darkness; then she opens her eyes, the lids seeming to snap upward against pressing weight. She grasps the edge of the mattress and pulls while she sits and swings her legs off the bed, and a chill grips her body and shakes it. Her teeth chatter as she walks with hunched shoulders to the bathroom; the toilet seat is cold, her skin is alive, crawling away from its touch, crawling up her back and down her arms, and she lowers her head and mutters: 'Oh Jesus.'

She does not brush her teeth or hair, or look in the mirror. She goes downstairs. There are no railings, and she slides a palm down the wall. She drinks a glass of orange juice, finds a tin with three aspirins behind the rice in the cupboard, swallows them with juice, and phones the Harbor Schooner. Sarah the head waitress answers.

'Is Charlie there?'

'No.'

'Who's tending bar?'

'Sonny.'

'Let me talk to him.'

She ought to tell Sarah, but she does not like to call in sick to women; they always sound like they don't believe her.

'I'm sick,' she says to Sonny. 'I think the flu.'

He tells her to go to bed and take care of herself, and asks if she needs anything.

'No. Maybe I'll come in tomorrow.'

'Get well first.'

'I'll call.'

She takes the glass and pitcher upstairs, breathing quickly as she climbs. The sun angles through her bedroom windows, onto the lower half of the bed. There are shades, but she does not want to darken the room. She puts the pitcher and glass on the bedside table, lies on the damp sheet, pulls up the top sheet and cotton spread, and curls, shivering, on her side. Her two front windows face the lake; she hears voices from there, and motors, and remembers that she has been hearing them since she woke, and before that too, from the sleep she cannot fight. It is taking her now; she wants juice, but every move chills her and she will not reach for it. She stares at the empty glass and wonders why she did not fill it again, drinking would be so much easier, so wonderfully better, if she did not have to sit up and lift the pitcher and pour, so next time she drinks she will refill the glass because then it won't be so hard next time, and if she had a hospital straw, one of bent glass. Vinnie was last week with the tube in his arm and the bandages, but in memory he is farther away than a week, a summer; last night is a week away, going from table to table to table to bar to table to table and driving home, hours of tables and driving. Her memory of making love with Vinnie is clear but her body's aching lethargy rejects it, denies ever making love with anyone, ever wanting to, so that Vinnie last

spring, early when the rivers began to swell with melting snow, is
in focus as he should be: not loving him then she made love because,
it seems to her now, he was something to do, one of a small as-
sortment of choices for a week night; and she remembers him now
without tenderness or recalled passion.

When she wakes again she is on her left side, facing the front
windows, and the room's light has faded. The chills are gone, and
she is hungry. There is ham downstairs, and eggs and cheese and
bread, and leftover spaghetti, but her stomach refuses them all. She
imagines soup, and wants that. But it is down the stairs and she
would have to stand as she opened and heated it, then poured it
into a cup so she could climb again and drink it here; she turns onto
her right side and waits, braced against chills, but they don't come.
Evening sunlight beams through the side window, opposite the foot
of her bed, which is now in the dark spreading across the floor and
dimming the blue walls. As though she can hear it, she senses the
darkness in all the downstairs rooms, and more of it flowing in from
the woods and lake. There are no motors on the water. Voices rise
and waft from lawns touching the beach. She switches on the bedside lamp, pushes herself back and up till she sits against the pillows,
and pours a glass of orange juice. She drinks it in three swallows,
refills the glass, then lies on her back, closes her hot eyes, thinks of
Ray, of danger she cannot feel, and lets the lamp burn so she will
not wake in the dark.

For a while she sleeps, but she is aware that she must not, there
is something she must do, and finally she wakes, her head tossing
on the pillow, legs and arms tense. She reaches for the drawer beside
her, takes the gun, holds it above her with both hands; she pulls
the slide to the rear and eases it forward, watching the bullet enter
the chamber. She lowers the hammer to half-cock and pushes up
the safety. She turns on her side, slips the gun under the pillow,
and goes to sleep holding the checkered wood of its handle.

She wakes from a dream that is lost when she opens her eyes to
light, though she knows it was pleasant and she was not in it, but
watched it. The three windows are black. Steve is looking down at
her, his smell of beer and cigarettes, his red face and arms making
her feel that health, that life even, are chance gifts to the lucky,
kept by the strong, and she was not to have them again.

'Sorry,' he says. 'You want to go back to sleep?'

'No.' Her throat is dry, and she hears a plea in her voice. 'I'm sick.'

'I figured that. Can I do anything?'

'I think I want to smoke.'

He takes cigarette papers from his shirt pocket, a cellophane pouch from his jeans.

'No, a cigarette. In my purse.'

He lights it and hands it to her.

'Could I have some soup?'

'Anything else?'

'Toast?'

'Coming up.'

He goes downstairs, and she smokes, looking at the windows; she cannot see beyond the screens. Neither can her mind: her life is this room, where her body's heat and pain have released her from everyone but Steve, who brings her a bowl of soup on a plate with two pieces of toast. He pushes up the pillows behind her, then pulls a chair near the bed.

'I'm leaving in the morning.'

'What time is it?'

'Almost one.'

She shakes her head.

'That way I beat the traffic.'

'Good idea.'

'I can leave Tuesday, though. Or Wednesday.'

'You're meeting your friends there.'

'They'll keep.'

'No. Go tomorrow, like you planned.'

'You sure?'

'It's just the flu.'

'No fun having it alone.'

'All I do is sleep.'

'Still. You know.'

'I'll be all right.'

'What'll you do about the ex?'

'Maybe he won't come back.'

'Don't bet on it.'

'My father went to see him.'

'Yeah? What did he say?'

'Who, Ray? I don't know.'

'No, your dad.'

'He told him if he harassed me again, he'd take some people out there and break bones.'

'Thing about Ray is he doesn't give a shit.'

'He doesn't?'

'Think about it.'

'He gives a shit about a lot of things.'

'Not broken bones. That little gun you got: if he comes, fire a couple over his head.'

'Why?'

'Because I don't think you could use it on him, and you might just leave it in the drawer. Then there's nothing you can do. So think about scaring him off.'

'I'd use it. You don't know what it's like, a man—what's the *mat*ter with him?'

He shrugs and takes the bowl and plate.

'Think two shots across the bow,' he says and stands; then, leaning over her, he is huge, blocking the ceiling and walls, his chest and beard lowering, his face and breath close to hers; he kisses her forehead and right cheek and smooths the hair at her brow. She watches him cross the room; at the door he turns and says: 'I'll leave this open; mine too. If you need something, give a shout.'

'You've got a nice ass,' she says, and smiles as his eyes brighten and his beard and cheeks move with his grin. She listens to his steps going down, and the running water as he washes her dishes. When he starts upstairs she turns out the lamp. In his room his boots drop to the floor, there is a rustle of clothes, and he is in bed. He shifts twice, then is quiet. She sits against the pillows in the dark; and wakes there, Steve standing beside her, the room sunlit and cool. The lake is quiet.

'You're going?'

'It's time.'

'Have fun.'

'Sure. You want breakfast?'

'No.'

She takes his hand, and says: 'I'll see you in April, I guess. Good hunting and all. Skiing.'

'If you don't find a place, or you want to stay on in spring, that's fine.'

'I know.'

'Well—' His thumb rubs the back of her hand.

'Thanks for everything,' she says.

'You too.'

'The room. Good talks. Whatever.'

'Whatever,' he says, smiling. Then he kisses her lips and is gone.

In early afternoon she phones the Harbor Schooner and tells Charlie, the manager, that she is still sick and can't make it that night but will try tomorrow. She eats a sandwich of ham and cheese, makes a pitcher of orange juice, and brings it upstairs. She reaches the bed weak and short of breath. Through the long hot afternoon she lies uncovered on the bed, asleep, awake, asleep, waking always to the sound of motorboats, the voices of many children, and talk and shouts and laughter of men and women. When the sun has moved to the foot of the bed and the room is darkening, she smells charcoal smoke. She turns on the lamp and lies awake listening to the beginning of silence: the boats are out of the water, most of them on trailers by now; she hears cars leaving, and on the stretch of beach below her windows, families gather, their voices rising with the smells of burning charcoal and cooking meat. Tomorrow she will wake to quiet that will last until May.

She closes her eyes and imagines the frozen lake, evergreens, the silent snow. After school and on weekends boys will clean the ice with snow shovels and play hockey; she will hear only burning logs in the fireplace, will watch them from the living room, darting without sound into and around one another. She will have a Christmas tree, will eat dinner at her parents', but on Christmas Eve she could have them and Margaret here for dinner before midnight Mass. She will live here —she counts by raising thumb and fingers from a closed fist—eight months. Or seven, so she can be out before Steve comes back. Out where? She shuts her eyes tighter, frowning, but no street, no town appears. In the Merrimack Valley she likes Newburyport but not as much since she started working there, and less since Ray moved there. Amesbury and Merrimac are too small, Lawrence is mills and factories, and too many grocery stores and restaurants with Spanish names, and Haverhill: Jesus, Haverhill: some people knew how to live there, her parents did, Haverhill for her father was the police department and their house in the city limits but in the country as well, with the garden her mother and father planted each spring: tomatoes, beans, squash, radishes, beets; and woods beyond the garden, not forest or anything, but enough to walk in for a while before you came to farmland; and her father ice-fished, and fished streams and lakes in spring, the ocean in summer. Everyone joked about living in Haverhill, or almost everyone: the skyline of McDonald's arch and old factories and the one new building on the corner of Main Street and the river, an old folks' home and office building that looked like a gigantic cinder block. But it wasn't that. The Back Bay of Boston was pretty, and the North End was interesting with all those narrow streets and cluttered apartments of Italians, but Jesus, Boston was dirtier than Haverhill and on a grey winter day no city looked good. It was that nothing happened in Haverhill, and she had never lived outside its limits till now, and to go back in spring was going downhill backward. A place would come. She would spend the fall and winter here, and by then she would know where to go.

She looks at the walls, the chest with her purse and cassette player on its top, the closed door of the closet; she will keep this room so she'll have the lake (and it occurs to her that this must have been Steve's, and he gave it up), and she'll hang curtains. She will leave his room, or the back room, alone; will store in it whatever she doesn't want downstairs, that chair with the flowered cover he always sat in, and its hassock, the coffee table with cigarette burns like Timmy's bar; she will paint the peeling cream walls in the kitchen. For the first time since moving in, she begins to feel that more than this one room is hers; not only hers but her: her sense of this seems to spread downward, like sentient love leaving her body to move about the three rooms downstairs, touching, looking, making plans. Her body is of no use to her but to move weakly to the bathroom, to sleep and drink and, when it will, to eat. Lying here, though, is good; it is like the beach or sleeping late, better than those because she will not do anything else, cannot do anything else, and so is free. Even at the beach you have to—what? Go into the water. Collect your things and drive home. Wash salt from suit, shower, wash hair, dry hair. Cook. Eat. But this, with no chills now, no pain unless she moves, which she won't, this doesn't have to end until it ends on its own, and she can lie here and decorate the house, move furniture from one room to another, one floor to another, bring all her clothes from her parents' house, her dresser and mirror, while outside voices lower as the smell of meat fades until all she smells is smoke. Tomorrow she will smell trees and the lake.

She hears a car going away, and would like to stand at the window and look at the darkened houses, but imagines them instead, one by one the lights going out behind windows until the house becomes the shape of one, locked for the winter. She is standing at the chest, getting her cigarettes, when she hears the people next door leaving. *Do it*, she tells herself. She turns out the bedside lamp, crouches at a front window, her arms crossed on its sill, and looks past trees in the front lawn at the dark lake. She looks up at stars. To her right, trees enclose the lake; she cannot see the houses among them. Water laps at the beach and wharf pilings. She can see most of the wharf before it is shielded by the oak; below her, Steve's boat, covered with tarpaulin, rests on sawhorses. Her legs tire, and she weakens and gets into bed, covers with the sheet and spread, and lights a cigarette, the flame bright and large in the dark. She reaches for the lamp switch, touches it, but withdraws her hand. She smokes and sees the bathroom painted mauve.

For a long while she lies awake, filling the ashtray, living the lovely fall and winter: in a sweater she will walk in the woods on brown leaves, under yellow and red, and pines and the blue sky of Indian summer. She will find her ice skates in her parents' basement; she remembers the ponds when she was a child, and wonders how or why she outgrew skating, and blames her fever for making her think this way, but is uncertain whether the fever has made her lucid or foolish. She is considering a snow blower for the driveway, has decided to buy one and learn to use it, when he comes in the crash of breaking glass and a loud voice: he has said something to the door, and now he calls her name. She moves the ashtray from her stomach to the floor, turns on her side to get the gun from under the pillow, then lies on her back.

'Polly?' He is at the foot of the stairs. 'It's me. I'm coming up.'

He has the voice of a returning drunk, boldly apologetic, and she cocks the hammer and points the gun at the door as he climbs, his boots loud, without rhythm, pausing for balance, then quick steps, a pause, a slow step, evenly down the few strides of hall, and his width above his hips fills the door; he is dark against the grey light above him.

'You in here?'

'I've got a gun.'

'No shit? Let me see it.'

She moves her finger from the trigger, and pushes the safety down with her thumb.

'It's pointed at you.'

'Yeah? Where's the light in here?'

'You liked the dark before.'

'I did? That's true. That little apartment we had?'

'I mean June, with that fucking knife.'

'Oh. No knife tonight. I went to the Harbor Schooner—'

'Shit: what *for*.'

'—So I goes Hey: where's Polly? Don't she work here? Sick, they said. To see you, that's all. So I did some shots of tequila and I'm driving up to New Hampshire, and I say what the fuck? So here I am. You going to tell me where the light is?'

His shoulders lurch as he steps forward; she fires at the ceiling above him, and he ducks, his hands covering his head.

'Pol*ly*.' He lowers his hands, raises his head. 'Hey, Polly. Hey: put that away. I just want to talk. That's all. That was an asshole thing I did, that other time. See—'

'Go away.'

Her hand trembles, her ears ring, and she sits up in the gunpowder smell, swings her feet to the floor, and places her left hand under her right, holding the gun with both.

'I just want to ask you what's the difference, that's all. I mean, how was it out here with Steve? You happy, and everything?'

'It was *great*. And it's going to be better.'

'Better. Better without Steve?'

'Yes.'

'Why's that? You got somebody moving in?'

'No.'

'But it was good with Steve here. Great with Steve. So what's the difference, that's what I think about. Maybe the lake. The house? I mean, what if it was with me? Same thing, right? Sleep up here over the lake. Do some fucking. Wake up. Eat. Swim. Work. How come it was so good with Steve?'

'We weren't *mar*ried.'

'Oh. Okay. That's cool. Why couldn't it be us then, out here? What did I ever do anyways?'

'Jesus, what is this?'

'No, come on: what did I do?'

'Nothing.'

'Nothing? I must've done something.'

'You didn't do anything.'

'Then why weren't you happy, like with Steve? I mean, I thought about it a lot. It wasn't that asshole DeLuca.'

'You almost killed him.'

'Bullshit.'

'You could have.'

'You see him?'

'I brought him flowers, is all.'

'See: it wasn't him. And I don't think it was me either. If it was him, you'd be with him, and if it was me, well, you got rid of me, so then you'd be happy.'

'I *am* happy.'

'I don't know, Polly.'

She can see the shape and muted color of his face, but his eyes are shadows, his beard and hair darker; his shoulders and arms move, his hands are at his chest, going down, then he opens his shirt, twists from one side to the other pulling off the sleeves.

'Don't, Ray.'

Flesh glimmers above his dark pants, and she pushes the gun toward it.

'Let's just try it, Polly. Turn on the light, you'll see.' He un-buckles his belt, then stops, raises a foot, holds it with both hands, hops backward and hits the doorjamb, pulls off the boot, and drops it. Leaning there, he takes off the other one, unzips his pants, and they fall to his ankles. He steps out of them, stoops, pushing his shorts down. 'See. No knife. No clothes.' He looks down. 'No hard-on. If you'd turn on a light and put away that hogleg—'

He moves into the light of the door, into the room, and she shakes her head, says No, but it only shapes her lips, does not leave her throat. She closes her eyes and becomes the shots jolting her hands as she pulls and pulls, hears him fall, and still pulls and explodes until the trigger is quiet and she opens her eyes and moves, leaping over him, to the hall and stairs.

In the middle of the night I sit out here in the skiff and I try to think of something else but I can't, because over and over I keep hearing him tell me that time: *Alex, she's the best fuck I've ever had in my life.* I don't want to think about that. But I look back at the house that was Kingsley's and I wish I had put on the lights before I got in the boat, but it wasn't dark yet and I didn't think I'd drift around half the night and have to look back at it with no lights on so it looks like a tomb, with his weights and fishing gear in there. I'll have to get them out. It looks like we're always taking somebody's things out of that house, and maybe it's time to sell it to somebody who's not so unlucky.

He bled to death, so even then she could have done something. I want to hate her for that. I will, too. After he knew he loved her, he didn't talk about her like that anymore, but it was still there between us, what he told me, and he knew I remembered, and sometimes when we were out drinking, me and somebody and him and Polly, and then we'd call it a night and go home, he'd grin at me. What I don't know is how you can be like that with a guy, then shoot him and leave him to bleed to death while you sit outside waiting for your old man and everybody. This morning we put him next to Kingsley and I was hugging Mom from one side and the old man hugging her from the other, and it seemed to me I had two brothers down there for no reason. Kingsley wouldn't agree, and he wouldn't like it that I don't vote anymore, or read the newspapers, or even watch the news. All Ray did was fall in love and not get over it when she got weird the way women do sometimes.

So I sit out here in the skiff and it's like they're both out here with me. I can feel them, and I wish I'd see them come walking across the lake. And I'd say, Why didn't you guys do something else? Why didn't you wait to be drafted, or go to Canada? Why didn't you find another girl? I'd tell them I'm going to sell this—and oh shit it starts now, the crying, the big first one, and I let it come and I shout against it over the water: 'I'm going to *sell* this fucking *house*, you *guys*. And the one in *town*, and I'm moving in with *Mom* and the *old man*; I'm going to get them to sell *theirs* too and get the fuck *out* of here, take them down to *Flor*ida and live in a *con*do. We'll go fishing. We'll buy a boat, and fish.'

GRADUATION

S OMETIMES, OUT IN California, she wanted to tell
her husband. That was after they had been married
for more than two years (by then she was twenty-one) and she had
settled into the familiarity so close to friendship but not exactly that
either: she knew his sounds while he slept, brought some recognition
to the very weight of his body next to her in bed, knew without
looking the expressions on his face when he spoke. As their habits
merged into common ritual, she began to feel she had never had
another friend. Geography had something to do with this too. Waiting for him at the pier after the destroyer had been to sea for five
days, or emerging from a San Diego movie theater, holding his
hand, it seemed to her that the first eighteen years of her life in
Port Arthur, Texas had no meaning at all. So, at times like that,
she wanted to tell him.

She would look at the photograph which she had kept hidden for
four years now, and think, as though she were speaking to him: *I
was seventeen years old, a senior in high school, and I got up that day just
like any other day and ate Puffed Wheat or something with my parents and
went to school and there it was, on the bulletin board*—But she didn't
tell him, for she knew that something was wrong: the photograph
and her years in Port Arthur were true, and now her marriage in
San Diego was true. But it seemed that for both of them to remain
true they had to exist separately, one as history, one as now, and
that if she disclosed the history, then those two truths added together

would somehow produce a lie which in turn would call for more analysis than she cared to give. Or than she cared for her husband to give. So she would simply look at the picture of herself at sixteen, then put it away, in an old compact at the bottom of her jewelry box.

The picture had been cut out of the high school yearbook. Her blonde hair had been short then, an Italian boy; her face was tilted down to one side, she was smiling at the camera, and beneath her face, across her sweater, was written: *Good piece.*

It had been thumbtacked to the bulletin board approximately two years after she had lost her virginity, parked someplace with a boy she loved. When they broke up she was still fifteen, a long way from marriage, and she wanted her virginity back. But this was impossible, for he had told all his friends. So she gave herself to the next boy whose pledge was a class ring or football sweater, and the one after that (before graduation night there were three of them, all with loose tongues) and everyone knew about Bobbie Huxford and she knew they did.

She never found out who put the picture on the bulletin board. When she got to school that day, a group of students were standing in the hall; they parted to let her through. Then she met the eyes of a girl, and saw neither mischief nor curiosity but fascination. A boy glanced at the bulletin board and quickly to the floor, and Bobbie saw the picture. She walked through them, pulled out the thumbtacks, forcing herself to go slowly, taking out each one and pressing it back into the board. She dropped the picture into her purse and went down the hall to her locker.

So at graduation she was not leaving the camaraderie, the perfunctory education, the ball games and dances and drives on a Sunday afternoon; she was leaving a place where she had always felt watched, except when Sherri King had been seduced by an uncle and somehow that word had got out. But the Kings had moved within a month, and Bobbie's classmates went back to watching her again. Still there was nostalgia: sitting on the stage, looking at the audience in the dark, she was remembering songs. Each of her loves had had a song, one she had danced to, pressed sweating and tight-gripped and swaying in dance halls where they served beer to anyone and the juke box never stopped: Nat 'King' Cole singing 'Somewhere Along the Way,' 'Trying' by the Hilltoppers, 'Your Cheatin' Heart' by Joni James, all of them plaintive songs: you drank two or three beers and clenched and dipped and weaved on the dance floor, and you squeezed him, your breasts against his firm narrow chest feeling like your brassiere and wrinkled blouse and his damp shirt weren't even there; you kept one hand on the back of his neck, sweat dripped between your fused cheeks, and you sang in nearly a whisper with Joni or Nat and you gave him a hard squeeze and said in his ear: *I love you, I'll love you forever.*

She had not loved any of them forever. With each one something had gone sour, but she was able to look past that, farther back to the good times. So there was that: sitting on the stage she remembered the songs, the love on waxed dance floors. But nostalgia wasn't the best part. She was happy, as she had been dancing to those songs that articulated her feelings and sent them flowing back into her blood, her heart. This time she didn't want to hold anyone, not even love anyone. She wanted to fly: soar away from everything, go higher than rain. She wanted to leave home, where bright and flowered drapes hung and sunlight moved through the day from one end of the maroon sofa to the other and formed motes in the air but found dustless the coffee table and the Bible that sat on it.

She was their last child, an older brother with eight years in the Army and going for twenty, and an older sister married to a pharmacist in Beaumont, never having gone farther than Galveston in her whole life and bearing kids now like that was the only thing to do.

In the quiet summer afternoons when her mother was taking a nap and her father was at work, she felt both them and the immaculate house stifling her. One night returning from a date she had walked quietly into the kitchen. From there she could hear them snoring. Standing in the dark kitchen she smoked a cigarette, flicking the ashes in her hand (there was only one ash tray in the house and it was used by guests). Then looking at their bedroom door she suddenly wanted to holler: *I drank too much beer tonight and got sick in the john and Bud gave me 7-Up and creme de menthe to settle my stomach and clean my breath so I could still screw and that's what we did:* WE SCREWED. *That's what we always do.*

Now, looking out into the dark, Bobbie wondered if her parents were watching her. Then she knew they were, and they were proud. She was their last child, she was grown now, they had done their duty (college remained but they did not consider it essential) and now in the clean brightly-colored house they could wait with calm satisfaction for their souls to be wafted to heaven. Then she was sad. Because from the anxiety and pain of her birth until their own deaths, they had loved her and would love her without ever knowing who she was.

After the ceremony there was an all-night party at Rhonda Miller's camp. Bobbie's date was a tall shy boy named Calvin Tatman, who was popular with the boys but rarely dated; three days before graduation he had called Bobbie and asked her to be his date for Rhonda's party. The Millers' camp was on a lake front, surrounded by woods; behind the small house there was a large outdoor kitchen, screened on all sides. In the kitchen was a keg of beer, paper cups, and Rhonda's record player; that was how the party began. Several parents were there, drinking bourbon from the grown-ups' bar at one side of the kitchen; they got tight, beamed at the young people jitterbugging, and teased them about their sudden liking for cigarettes and beer. After a while Mr. Miller went outside to the barbecue pit and put on some hamburgers.

At first Bobbie felt kindly toward Calvin and thought since it was a big night, she would let him neck with her. But after Calvin had a few tall cups of beer she changed her mind. He stopped jitterbugging with her, dancing only the slow dances, holding her very close; then, a dance ended, he would join the boys at the keg. He didn't exactly leave her on the dance floor; she could follow him to the keg if she wanted to, and she did that a couple of times, then stopped. Once she watched him talking to the boys and she knew exactly what was going on: he had brought her because he couldn't get another date (she had already known that, absorbed it, spent a long time preparing her face and hair anyway), but now he was saving face by telling people he had brought her because he wanted to get laid.

Then other things happened. She was busy dancing, so she didn't notice for a while that she hadn't really had a conversation with anyone. She realized this when she left Calvin at the beer keg and joined the line outside at the barbecue pit, where Mr. Miller was serving hamburgers. She was last in line. She told Mr. Miller it was a wonderful party, then she went to the table beside the barbecue pit and made her hamburger. When she turned to go back to the kitchen, no one was waiting: two couples were just going in the door, and Bobbie was alone with Mr. Miller. She hesitated, telling herself that it meant nothing, that no one waited for people at barbecue pits. Still, if she went in alone, who would she sit with? She sat on the grass by the barbecue pit and talked to Mr. Miller. He ate a hamburger with her and gave her bourbon and water from the one-man bar he had set up to get him through the cooking. He was a stout, pleasant man, and he told her she was the best-looking girl at the party.

As soon as she entered the kitchen she knew people had been waiting for her. The music and talk were loud, but she also felt the silence of waiting; looking around, she caught a few girls watching her. Then, at her side, Rhonda said: 'Where you been, Bobbie?'

She glanced down at Rhonda, who sat with her boy friend, a class ring dangling from a chain around her neck, one possessive hand on Charlie Wright's knee. She doubted that Rhonda was a virgin but she had heard very little gossip because she had no girl friends. Now she went to the keg, pushed through the boys, and filled a cup.

Some time later, when the second keg had been tapped and both she and Calvin were drunk, he took her outside. She knew by now that everyone at the party was waiting to see if Calvin would make out. She went with him as far as the woods, kissed him standing up, worked her tongue in his mouth until he trembled and gasped; when he touched her breast she spun away and went back to the kitchen, jerking out of his grasp each time he clutched her arm. He was cursing her but she wasn't afraid. If he got rough, they were close enough to the kitchen so she could shout for Mr. Miller. Then Calvin was quiet anyway, realizing that if anyone heard they would know what had happened. When they stepped into the kitchen people were grinning at them. Bobbie went to the beer keg and Calvin danced with the first girl he saw.

When Charlie Wright got drunk he came over and danced with her. They swayed to 'Blue Velvet,' moved toward the door, and stumbled outside. They lay on the ground just inside the woods; because of the beer he took a long time and Bobbie thought of Rhonda waiting, faking a smile, dancing, waiting . . . Charlie told her she did it better than Rhonda. When they returned to the kitchen, Rhonda's face was pale; she did not dance with Charlie for the rest of the night.

At breakfast, near dawn, she sat on the bar and ate bacon and eggs with Mr. Miller, hoping Rhonda would worry about that too. Calvin tried to leave without her, but she had taken his car key, so he had to drive her home. It was just after sunrise, he was drunk, and he almost missed two curves.

'Hell, Calvin,' she said, 'just 'cause you can't make out doesn't mean you got to kill us.'

He swung at her, the back of his open hand striking her cheek-bone, and all the way home she cried. Next day there was not even a bruise.

The lawnmower woke her that afternoon. She listened to it, knowing she had been hearing it for some time, had been fighting it in her sleep. Then she got up, took two aspirins which nearly gagged her, and made coffee and drank it in the kitchen, wanting a cigarette but still unable to tell her parents that she smoked. So she went outside and helped her father rake the grass. The day was hot; bent over the rake she sweated and fought with her stomach and shut her eyes to the pain pulsing in her head and she wished she had at least douched with a Coke, something she had heard about but had never done. Then she wished she had a Coke right now, with ice, and some more aspirin and a cool place in the house to sit very still. She did not want to marry Charlie Wright. Then she had to smile at herself, looking down at the grass piling under her rake. Charlie would not marry her. By this time everyone in school knew she had done it with him last night, and they probably thought she had done it with Calvin too. If she were pregnant, it would be a joke.

That night she told her parents she wanted to finish college as soon as possible so she could earn her own money. They agreed to send her to summer school at L.S.U., and two weeks later they drove her to Baton Rouge. During those two weeks she had seen no one; Charlie had called twice for dates, but she had politely turned him down, with excuses; she had menstruated, felt the missed life flowing as a new life for herself. Then she went away. Sitting in the back of the car, driving out of Port Arthur, she felt incomplete: she had not told anyone she was going to summer school, had not told anyone goodbye.

She went home after the summer term, then again at Thanks-giving, each time feeling more disengaged from her house and the town. When she went home for Christmas vacation, her father met her at the bus station. It was early evening. She saw him as the bus turned in: wiry, a little slumped, wearing the hat that wasn't a Stetson but looked like one. He spoke of the Christmas lights being ready and she tried to sound pleased. She even tried to feel pleased. She thought of him going to all that trouble every Christmas and maybe part of it was for her; maybe it had all started for her delight, long ago when she was a child. But when they reached the house she was again appalled by the lights strung on its front and the lighted manger her father had built years before and every Christmas placed on the lawn: a Nativity absurdly without animals or shepherds or wise men or even parents for the Child Jesus (a doll: Bobbie's) who lay utterly alone, wrapped in blankets on the straw floor of the manger. Holding her father's arm she went into the kitchen and hugged her mother, whose plumpness seemed emblematic of a woman who was kind and good and clean. Bobbie marvelled at the decorated house, then sat down to supper and talk of food and family news. After supper she told them, with even more nervousness than she had anticipated, that she had started smoking and she hoped they didn't mind. They both frowned, then her mother sighed and said:

'Well, I guess you're a big girl now.'

She was. For at L.S.U. she had learned this: you could become a virgin again. She finally understood that it was a man's word. They didn't mean you had done it once; they meant you did it, the lost hymen testimony not of the past but the present, and you carried with you a flavor of accessibility. She thought how much she would have been spared if she had known it at fifteen when she had felt changed forever, having focused on the word *loss* as though an arm or leg had been amputated, so she had given herself again, trying to be happy with her new self, rather than backing up and starting over, which would have been so easy because Willie Sorrells—her first lover—was not what you would call irresistible. Especially in retrospect.

But at L.S.U. she was a virgin; she had dated often in summer and fall, and no one had touched her. Not even Frank Mixon, whom she planned to marry, though he hadn't asked her yet. He was an economics major at Tulane, and a football player. He was also a senior. In June he was going into the Navy as an ensign and this was one of her reasons for wanting to marry him. And she had him fooled.

One night, though, she had scared herself. It was after the Tulane-L.S.U. game, the traditional game which Tulane traditionally lost. It was played in Baton Rouge. After the game Bobbie and Frank double-dated with the quarterback, Roy Lockhart, and his fiancee, Annie Broussard. Some time during the evening of bar-hopping, when they were all high, Roy identified a girl on the dance floor by calling her Jack Shelton's roommate of last year.

'What?' Bobbie said. 'What did you say?'

'Never mind,' Roy said.

'No: listen. Wait a minute.'

Then she started. All those things she had thought about and learned in silence came out, controlled, lucid, as though she had been saying them for years. At one point she realized Frank was watching her, quiet and rather awed, but a little suspiciously too. She kept talking, though.

'You fumbled against Vanderbilt,' she said to Roy. 'Should we call you fumbler for the rest of your life?'

Annie, the drunkest of the four, kept saying: That's *right*, that's *right*. Finally Bobbie said:

'Anyway, that's what *I* think.'

Frank put his arm around her.

'That takes care of gossip for tonight,' he said. 'Anybody want to talk about the game?'

'We tied 'em till the half,' Roy said. 'Then we should have gone home.'

'It wasn't your fault, fumbler,' Annie said, and she was still laughing when the others had stopped and ordered more drinks.

When Frank took Bobbie to the dormitory, they sat in the car, kissing. Then he said:

'You were sort of worked up tonight.'

'It happened to a friend of mine in high school. They ruined her. It's hard to believe, that you can ruin somebody with just talking, but they did it.'

He nodded, and moved to kiss her, but she pulled away.

'But that's not the only reason,' she said.

She shifted on the car seat and looked at his face, a good ruddy face, hair neither long nor short and combed dry, the college cut that would do for business as well; he was a tall strong young man, and because of his size and strength she felt that his gentleness was a protective quality reserved for her alone; but this wasn't true either, for she had never known him to be unkind to anyone and, even tonight, as he drank too much in post-game defeat, he only got quieter and sweeter.

'I don't have one either,' she said.

At first he did not understand. Then his face drew back and he looked out the windshield.

'It's not what you think. It's awful, and I'll never forget it but I've never told anyone, no one knows, they all think—'

Then she was crying into his coat, not at all surprised that her tears were real, and he was holding her.

'I was twelve years old,' she said.

She sat up, dried her cheeks, and looked away from him.

'It was an uncle, one of those uncles you never see. He was leaving someplace and going someplace else and he stopped off to see us for a couple of days. On the second night he came to my room and when I woke up he was doing it—'

'Hush,' he said. 'Hush, baby.'

She did not look at him.

'I was so scared, so awfully *scared*. So I didn't tell. Next morning I stayed in bed till he was gone. And I felt so rotten. Sometimes I still do, but not the way I did then. He's never come back to see us, but once in a while they mention him and I feel sick all over again, and I think about telling them but it's too late now, even if they did something to him it's too late, I can never get it back—'

For a long time that night Frank Mixon held his soiled girl in his arms, and, to Bobbie, those arms seemed quite strong, quite capable. She knew that she would marry him.

Less than a month later she was home for Christmas, untouched, changed. She spent New Year's at Frank's house in New Orleans. In the cold dusk after the Sugar Bowl game they walked back to his house to get the car and go to a party. Holding his arm, she watched a trolley go by, looked through car windows at attractive people leaving the stadium, breathed the smell of exhaust which was somehow pleasing, and the damp winter air, and another smell as of something old, as though from the old lives of the houses they passed. She knew that if she lived in New Orleans only a few months, Port Arthur would slide away into the Gulf. Climbing a gentle slope to his house, she was very tired, out of breath. The house was dark. Frank turned on a light and asked if she wanted a drink.

'God, no,' she said. 'I'd like to lie down for a few minutes.'

'Why don't you? I'll make some coffee.'

She climbed the stairs, turned on the hall light, and went to the guest room. She took off her shoes, lay clothed on the bed, and was asleep. His voice woke her: he stood at the bed, blocking the light from the hall. She propped on an elbow to drink the coffee, and asked him how long she had been asleep.

'About an hour.'

'What did you do?'

'Watched some of the Rose Bowl.'

'That was sweet. I'll hurry and get freshened up so we won't be too late.'

But when she set the empty cup on the bedside table he kissed her; then he was lying on top of her.

'Your folks—'

'They're at a party.'

She was yielding very slowly, holding him off tenderly then murmuring when his hand slipped into her blouse, stayed there, then withdrew to work on the buttons. She delayed, gave in, then stalled so that it took a long while for him to take off the blouse and brassiere. Finally they were naked, under the covers, and her hands on his body were shy. Then she spoke his name. With his first penetration she stiffened and he said It's all right, sweet darling Bobbie, it's all right now—and she eased forward, wanting to enfold him with her legs but she kept them outstretched, knees bent, and gave only tentative motion to her hips. When he was finished she held him there, his lips at her ear; she moved slowly as he whispered; then whimpering, shuddering, and concealing, she came.

'Will you?' he said. 'Will you marry me this June?'

'Oh *yes*,' she said, and squeezed his ribs. 'Yes I will. This is my first time and that other never happened, not ever, it's all over now—Oh I'm so *happy*, Frank, I'm so *happy*—'

THE PITCHER

for Philip

T HEY CHEERED AND clapped when he and Lucky
Ferris came out of the dugout, and when the cheer-
ing and clapping settled to sporadic shouts he had already stopped
hearing it, because he was feeling the pitches in his right arm and
watching them the way he always did in the first few minutes of
his warm-up. Some nights the fast ball was fat or the curve hung
or the ball stayed up around Lucky's head where even the hitters
in this Class C league would hit it hard. It was a mystery that
frightened him. He threw the first hard one and watched it streak
and rise into Lucky's mitt; and the next one; and the next one; then
he wasn't watching the ball anymore, as though it had the power
to betray him. He wasn't watching anything except Lucky's target,
hardly conscious of that either, or of anything else but the rhythm
of his high-kicking wind-up, and the ball not thrown but released
out of all his motion; and now he felt himself approaching that
moment he could not achieve alone: a moment that each time was
granted to him. Then it came: the ball was part of him, as if his
arm stretched sixty feet six inches to Lucky's mitt and slammed the
ball into leather and sponge and Lucky's hand. Or he was part of
the ball.

Now all he had to do for the rest of the night was concentrate
on prolonging that moment. He had trained himself to do that, and
while people talked about his speed and curve and change of pace
and control, he knew that without his concentration they would be

only separate and useless parts; and instead of nineteen and five on the year with an earned run average of two point one five and two hundred and six strikeouts, going for his twentieth win on the last day of the season, his first year in professional ball, three months short of his twentieth birthday, he'd be five and nineteen and on his way home to nothing. He was going for the pennant too, one half game behind the New Iberia Pelicans who had come to town four nights ago with a game and a half lead, and the Bulls beat them Friday and Saturday, lost Sunday, so that now on Monday in this small Louisiana town, Billy's name was on the front page of the local paper alongside the news of the war that had started in Korea a little over a month ago. He was ready. He caught Lucky's throw, nodded to him, and walked with head down toward the dugout and the cheers growing louder behind it, looking down at the bright grass, holding the ball loosely in his hand.

He spoke to no one. He went to the far end of the dugout that they left empty for him when he was pitching. He was too young to ask for that, but he was good enough to get it without asking; they gave it to him early in the year, when they saw he needed it, this young pitcher Billy Wells who talked and joked and yelled at the field and the other dugout for nine innings of the three nights he didn't pitch, but on his pitching night sat quietly, looking neither relaxed nor tense, and only spoke when politeness required it. Always he was polite. Soon they made a space for him on the bench, where he sat now knowing he would be all right. He did not think about it, for he knew as the insomniac does that to give it words summons it up to dance; he knew that the pain he had brought with him to the park was still there; he even knew it would probably always be there; but for a good while now it was gone. It would lie in wait for him and strike him again when he was drained and had a heart full of room for it. But that was a long time from now, in the shower or back in the hotel, longer than the two and a half hours or whatever he would use pitching the game; longer than a clock could measure. Right now it seemed a great deal of his life would pass before the shower. When he trotted out to the mound they stood and cheered and, before he threw his first warm-up pitch, he tipped his cap.

He did not make love to Leslie the night before the game. All season, he had not made love to her on the night before he pitched. He did not believe, as some ballplayers did, that it hurt you the next day. *It's why they call it the box score anyway*, Hap Thomas had said on the bus one night after going hitless; *I left me at least two base hits in that whorehouse last night.* Like most ballplayers in the Evangeline League, Thomas had been finished for a long time: a thirty-six-year-old outfielder who had played three seasons—not consecutively—in Triple A ball, when he was in his twenties. Billy didn't make love the night before a game because he still wasn't used to night baseball; he still had the same ritual that he'd had in San Antonio, playing high school and American Legion ball: he drank a glass of buttermilk then went to bed, where for an hour or more he imagined tomorrow's game, although it seemed the game already existed somewhere in the night beyond his window and was imagining him. When finally he slept, the game was still there with him, and in the morning he woke to it, remembered pitching somewhere between daydream and nightdream; and until time for the game he felt like a shadow cast by the memory and the morning's light, a shadow that extended from his pillow to the locker room, when he took off the clothes which had not felt like his all day and put on the uniform which in his mind he had been wearing since he went to bed the night before. In high school, his classes interfered with those days of being a shadow. He felt that he was not so much going to classes as bumping into them on his way to the field. But in summer when he played American Legion ball, there was nothing to bump into, there was only the morning's wait which wasn't really waiting because waiting was watching time, watching it win usually, while on those mornings he joined time and flowed with it, so that sitting before the breakfast his mother cooked for him he felt he was in motion toward the mound.

And he had played a full season less one game of pro ball and still had not been able to convince his mind and body that the night before a game was far too early to enter the rhythm and concentration that would work for him when he actually had the ball in his hand. Perhaps his mind and body weren't the ones who needed convincing; perhaps he was right when he thought he was not imagining the games, but they were imagining him: benevolent and slow-witted angels who had followed him to take care of him, who couldn't understand they could rest now, lie quietly the night before, because they and Billy had all next day to spend with each other. If he had known Leslie was hurt he could have told her, as simply as a man saying he was beset by the swollen agony of mumps, that he could not make love on those nights, and it wasn't because he preferred thinking about tomorrow's game, but because those angels had followed him all the way to Lafayette, Louisiana. Perhaps he and Leslie could even have laughed about it, for finally it was funny, as funny as the story about Billy's Uncle Johnny whose two hounds had jumped the fence and faithfully tracked or followed him to a bedroom a few blocks from his house, and bayed outside the window: a bedroom Uncle Johnny wasn't supposed to be in, and more trouble than that, because to get there he had left a bedroom he wasn't supposed to leave.

Lafayette was funny too: a lowland of bayous and swamps and Cajuns. The Cajuns were good fans. They were so good that in early season Billy felt like he was barnstorming in some strange country, where everybody loved the Americans and decided to love baseball too since the Americans were playing it for them. They knew the game, but often when they yelled about it, they yelled in French, and when they yelled in English it sounded like a Frenchman's English. This came from the colored section too. The stands did not extend far beyond third and first base, and where the first base stands ended there was a space of about fifty feet and, after that, shoved against each other, were two sections of folding wooden bleachers. The Negroes filled them, hardly noticed beyond the fifty feet of air and trampled earth. They were not too far down the right field line: sometimes when Billy ran out a ground ball he ended his sprint close enough to the bleachers to hear the Negroes calling to him in French, or in the English that sounded like French.

Two Cajuns played for the Bulls. The team's full name was the Lafayette Brahma Bulls, and when the fans said all of it, they said Bremabulls. The owner was a rancher who raised these bulls, and one of his prizes was a huge and dangerous-looking hump-necked bull whose grey coat was nearly white; it was named Huey for their governor who was shot and killed in the state capitol building. Huey was led to home plate for opening day ceremonies, and after that he attended every game in a pen in foul territory against the right field fence. During batting practice the left handers tried to pull the ball into the pen. Nobody hit him, but when the owner heard about it he had the bull brought to the park when batting practice was over. By then the stands were filling. Huey was brought in a truck that entered through a gate behind the colored bleachers, and the Negroes would turn and look behind them at the bull going by. The two men in the truck wore straw cowboy hats. So did the owner, Charlie Breaux. When the Cajuns said his first and last names together they weren't his name anymore. And since it was the Cajun third baseman, E. J. Primeaux, a wiry thirty-year-old who owned a small grocery store which his wife ran during the season, who first introduced Billy to the owner, Billy had believed for the first few days after reporting to the club that he pitched for a man named Mr. Chollibro.

One night someone did hit Huey: during a game, with two outs, a high fly ball that Hap Thomas could have reached for and caught; he was there in plenty of time, glancing down at the pen's fence as he moved with the flight of the ball, was waiting safe from collision beside the pen, looking now from the ball to Huey who stood just on the other side of the fence, watching him; Hap stuck his arm out over the fence and Huey's head; then he looked at Huey again and withdrew his arm and stepped back to watch the ball strike Huey's head with a sound the fans heard behind third base. The ball bounced up and out and Hap barehanded it as Huey trotted once around the pen. Hap ran toward the dugout, holding the ball up, until he reached the first base umpire who was alternately signalling safe and pointing Hap back to right field. Then Hap flipped him the ball and, grinning, raised both arms to the fans behind the first base line, kept them raised to the Negroes as he ran past their bleachers and back to Huey's pen; taking off his cap as he approached the fence where Huey stood again watching, waved his cap once over the fence and horns, then trotted to his position, thumped his glove twice, then lowered it to his knee, and his bare hand to the other, and crouched. The fans were still laughing and cheering and calling to Hap and Huey and Chollibro when two pitches later the batter popped up to Caldwell at short.

In the dugout Primeaux said: 'Hap, I seen many a outfielder miss a fly ball because he's wall-shy, but that's the first time I ever seen one miss because he's *bull*-horn shy.' And Hap said: 'In this league? That's nothing. No doubt about it, one of these nights I'll go out to right field and get bit by a cottonmouth so big he'll chop my leg in two.' 'Or get hit by lightning,' Shep Caldwell said. In June lightning had struck a centerfielder for the Abbeville Athletics; struck the metal peak of his cap and exited into the earth through his spikes. When the Bulls heard the announcement over their public address system, their own sky was cloudy and there were distant flashes; perhaps they had even seen the flash that killed Tommy Lyons thirty miles away. The announcement came between innings when the Bulls were coming to bat; the players and fans stood for a minute of silent prayer. Billy was sitting beside Hap. Hap went to the cooler and came back with a paper cup and sat looking at it but not drinking, then said: 'He broke a leg, Lyons did. I played in the Pacific Coast League with him one year. Forty-one. He was hitting three-thirty; thirty-something home runs; stole about forty bases. Late in the season he broke his leg sliding. He never got his hitting back. Nobody knew why. Tommy didn't know why. He went to spring training with the Yankees, then back to the Pacific Coast League, and he kept going down. I was drafted by then, and next time I saw him was two years ago when he came to Abbeville. We had a beer one night and I told him he was headed for the major leagues when he broke his leg. No doubt about it. He said he knew that. And he still didn't understand it. Lost something: swing; timing. Jesus, he used to hit the ball. Now they fried him in front of a bunch of assholes in Abbeville. How's that for shit.' For the rest of the game most of the players watched their sky; those who didn't were refusing to. They would not know until the next day about the metal peak on Lyons's cap; but two innings after the announcement, Lucky went into the locker room and cut his off. When he came back to the dugout holding the blue cap and looking at the hole where the peak had been, Shep said: 'Hell, Lucky, it never strikes twice.' Lucky said: 'That's because it don't have to,' and sat down, stroking the hole.

Lafayette was only a town on the way to Detroit, to the Tigers; unless he got drafted, which he refused to think about, and thought about daily when he read of the war. Already the Tiger scout had watched Billy pitch three games and talked to him after each one, told him all he needed was time, seasoning; told him to stay in shape in the off-season; told him next year he would go to Flint, Michigan, to Class A ball. He was the only one on the club who had a chance for the major leagues, though Billy Joe Baron would probably go up, but not very far; he was a good first baseman and very fast, led the league in stolen bases, but he had to struggle and beat out drag bunts and ground balls to keep his average in the two-nineties and low three hundreds, and he would not go higher than Class A unless they outlawed the curve ball. The others would stay with the Bulls, or a team like the Bulls. And now Leslie was staying in this little town that she wasn't supposed to see as a town to live in longer than a season, and staying too in the little furnished house they were renting, with its rusted screen doors and its yard that ended in the back at a woods which farther on became a swamp, so that Billy never went off the back porch at night and if he peered through the dark at the grass long enough he was sure he saw cottonmouths.

She came into the kitchen that morning of the final game, late morning after a late breakfast so he would eat only twice before pitching, when he was already—or still, from the night before—concentrating on his twentieth win; and the pennant too. He wanted that: wanted to be the pitcher who had come to a third-place club and after one season had ridden away from a pennant winner. She came into the kitchen and looked at him more seriously than he'd ever seen her, and said: 'Billy, it's a terrible day to tell you this but you said today was the day I should pack.'

He looked at her from his long distance then focussed in closer, forced himself to hear what she was saying, felt like he was even forcing himself to see her in three dimensions instead of two, and said: 'What's the matter, baby?'

'I'm not going.'

'Not going where?'

'San Antonio. Flint. I'm staying here.'

Her perspiring face looked so afraid and sorry for him and determined all at once that he knew he was finished, that he didn't even know what was happening but there would never be enough words he could say. Her eyes were brimming with tears, and he knew they were for herself, for having come to this moment in the kitchen, so far from everything she could have known and predicted; deep in her eyes, as visible as stars, was the hard light of something else, and he knew that she had hated him too, and he imagined her hating him for days while he was on the road: saw her standing in this kitchen and staring out the screen door at the lawn and woods, hating him. Then the picture completed itself: a man, his back to Billy, stood beside her and put his arm around her waist.

'Leslie?' and he had to clear his throat, clear his voice of the fear in it: 'Baby, have you been playing around?'

She looked at him for such a long time that he was both afraid of what she would say, and afraid she wouldn't speak at all.

'I'm in love, Billy.'

Then she turned and went to the back door, hugging her breasts and staring through the screen. He gripped the corners of the table, pushed his chair back, started to rise, but did not; there was nothing to stand for. He rubbed his eyes, then briskly shook his head.

'It wasn't just that you were on the road so much. I was ready for that. I used to tell myself it'd be exciting a lot of the time, especially in the big leagues. And I'd tell myself in ten years it'd be over anyway, some women have to—'

'*Ten?*' Thinking of the running he did, in the outfield on the days he wasn't pitching, and every day at home between seasons, having known long ago that his arm was a gift and it would last until one spring when it couldn't do the work anymore, would become for the first time since it started throwing a baseball just an ordinary arm; and what he could and must do was keep his lungs and legs strong so they wouldn't give out before it did. He surprised himself: he had not known that, while his wife was leaving him, he could proudly and defensively think of pitching in his early thirties. He had a glimpse of the way she saw him, and he was frightened and ashamed.

'All right: fifteen,' she said. 'Some women are married to sailors and soldiers and it's longer. It wasn't the road trips. It was when you were home: you weren't here. You weren't here, with me.'

'I was here all day. Six, seven hours at the park at night. I don't know what that means.'

'It means I'm not what you want.'

'How can you tell me what I want?'

'You want to be better than Walter Johnson.'

From his angle he saw very little of her face. He waited. But this time she didn't speak.

'Leslie, can't a man try to be the best at what he's got to do and still love his wife?' Then he stood: 'Goddamnit who *is* he?'

'George Lemoine,' she said through the screen.

'George *Lemoine*. Who's George *Lemoine?*'

'The dentist I went to.'

'What dentist you went to?'

She turned and looked at his face and down the length of his arms to his fists, then sat at the opposite end of the table.

'When I lost the filling. In June.'

'*June?*'

'We didn't start then.' Her face was slightly lowered, but her eyes were raised to his, and there was another light in them: she was ashamed but not remorseful, and her voice had the unmistakable tone of a woman in love; they were never so serious as this, never so threatening, and he was assaulted by images of Leslie making love with another man. 'He went to the game alone. Sometimes we talked down at the concession stand. We—' Now she looked down, hid her eyes from him, and he felt shut out forever from the mysteries of her heart.

All his life he had been confident. In his teens his confidence and hope were concrete: the baseball season at hand, the season ahead, professional ball, the major leagues. But even as a child he had been confident and hopeful, in an abstract way. He had barely suffered at all, and he had survived that without becoming either callous or naive. He was not without compassion when his life involved him with the homely, the clumsy, the losers. He simply considered himself lucky. Now his body felt like someone else's, weak and trembling. His urge was to lie down.

'And all those times on the road I never went near a whorehouse.'

'It's not the same.'

He was looking at the beige wall over the sink, but he felt that her eyes were lowered still. He was about to ask what she meant, but then he knew.

'So I guess when I go out to the mound tonight he'll be moving in, is that right?'

Now he looked at her, and when she lifted her face, it had changed: she was only vulnerable.

'He has to get a divorce first. He has a wife and two kids.'

'Wait a minute. *Wait* a minute. He's got a wife and two *kids*? How *old* is this son of a bitch?'

'Thirty-four.'

'God*damn* it Leslie! How dumb can you be? He's getting what he wants from you, what makes you think he won't be smart enough to leave it at that? God*damn*.'

'I believe him.'

'You believe him. A dentist anyhow. How can you be married to a ballplayer and fall for a dentist anyhow? And what'll you do for money? You got that one figured out?'

'I don't need much. I'll get a job.'

'Well, you won't have much either, because I'm going over there and kill him.'

'Billy.' She stood, her face as admonitory as his mother's. 'He's got enough troubles. All summer I've been in trouble too. I've been sad and lonesome. That's the only way this could ever happen. You know that. All summer I've been feeling like I was running alongside the players' bus waving at you. Then he came along.'

'And picked you up.'

He glared at her until she blushed and lowered her eyes. Then he went to the bedroom to pack. But she had already done it: the suitcase and overnight bag stood at the foot of the bed. He picked them up and walked fast to the front door. Before he reached it she came out of the kitchen, and he stopped.

'Billy. I don't want you to be hurt; and I know you won't be for long. I hope someday you can forgive me. Maybe write and tell me how you're doing.'

His urge to drop the suitcase and overnight bag and hold her and ask her to change her mind was so great that he could only fight it with anger; and with the clarity of anger he saw a truth which got him out the door.

'You want it all, don't you? Well, forget it. You just settle for what you chose.'

Scornfully he scanned the walls of the living room, then Leslie from feet to head; then he left, out into the sun and the hot still air, and drove into town and registered at a hotel. The old desk clerk recognized him and looked puzzled but quickly hid it and said: 'Y'all going to beat them New Iberia boys tonight?'

'Damn right.'

The natural thing to do now was go to Lemoine's office, walk in while he was looking in somebody's mouth: *It's me you son of a bitch*, and work him over with the left hand, cancel his afternoon for him, send him off to another dentist. What he had to do was unnatural. And as he climbed the stairs to his room he thought there was much about his profession that was unnatural. In the room he turned off the air conditioning and opened the windows, because he didn't want his arm to be in the cool air, then lay on the bed and closed his eyes and began pitching to the batting order. He knew them all perfectly; but he did not trust that sort of perfection, for it was too much like confidence, which was too much like complacency. So he started with Vidrine, the lead-off man. Left-handed. Went with the pitch, hit to all fields; good drag-bunter but only fair speed and Primeaux would be crowding him at third; choke-hitter, usually got a piece of the ball, but not that quick with the bat either; couldn't hit good speed. Fastballs low and tight. Change on him. Good base-runner but he had to get a jump. Just hold him close to the bag. Then Billy stopped thinking about Vidrine on base. Thing was to concentrate now on seeing his stance and the high-cocked bat and the inside of the plate and Lucky's glove. He pushed aside the image of Vidrine crouching in a lead off first, and at the same time he pushed from his mind Leslie in the kitchen telling him; he saw Vidrine at the plate and, beyond him, he saw Leslie going away. She had been sitting in the box seat but now she walked alone down the ramp. Poor little Texas girl. She even sounded like a small town in Texas: Leslie Wells. Then she was gone.

The home run came with one out and nobody on in the top of the third inning after he had retired the first seven batters. Rick Stanley hit it, the eighth man in the order, a good-field no-hit third baseman in his mid-twenties. He had been in the minors for seven years and looked like it: though trimly built, and the best third baseman Billy had ever seen, he had a look about him of age, of resignation, of having been forced—when he was too young to bear it well—to compromise what he wanted with what he could do. At the plate he looked afraid, and early in the season Billy thought Stanley had been beaned and wasn't able to forget it. Later he realized it wasn't fear of beaning, not fear at all, but the strain of living so long with what he knew. It showed in the field too. Not during a play, but when it was over and Stanley threw the ball to the pitcher and returned to his position, his face looking as though it were adjusting itself to the truth he had forgotten when he backhanded the ball over the bag and turned and set and threw his mitt-popping peg to first; his face then was intense, reflexive as his legs and hands and arm; then the play was over and his face settled again into the resignation that was still new enough to be terrible. It spread downward to his shoulders and then to the rest of him and he looked old again. Billy wished he had seen Stanley play third when he was younger and still believed there was a patch of dirt and a bag and a foul line waiting for him in the major leagues.

One of Billy's rules was never to let up on the bottom of the batting order, because when one of them got a hit it hurt more. The pitch to Stanley was a good one. Like many players, Stanley was a poor hitter because he could not consistently be a good hitter; he was only a good hitter for one swing out of every twelve or so; the other swings had changed his life for him. The occasional good one gave the fans, and Stanley too by now, a surprise that always remained a surprise and so never engendered hope. His home run was a matter of numbers and time, for on this one pitch his concentration and timing and swing all flowed together, making him for that instant the hitter of his destroyed dream. It would happen again, in other ball parks, in other seasons; and if Stanley had been able to cause it instead of having it happen to him, he would be in the major leagues.

Billy's first pitch to him was a fast ball, waist high, inside corner. Stanley took it for a strike, with that look on his face. Lucky called for the same pitch. Billy nodded and played with the rosin bag to keep Stanley waiting longer; then Stanley stepped out of the box and scooped up dust and rubbed it on his hands and the bat handle; when he moved to the plate again he looked just as tense and Billy threw the fast ball; Stanley swung late and under it. Lucky called for the curve, the pitch that was sweet tonight, and Billy went right into the wind-up, figuring Stanley was tied up tightly now, best time to throw a pitch into all that: he watched the ball go in fast and groin-high, then fall to the left, and it would have cut the outside corner of the plate just above Stanley's knees; but it was gone. Stanley not only hit it so solidly that Billy knew it was gone before looking, but he got around on it, pulled it, and when Billy found it in the left-centerfield sky it was still climbing above James running from left and LeBlanc from center. At the top of its arc, there was something final about its floodlit surface against the real sky, dark up there above the lighted one they played under.

He turned his back to the plate. He never watched a home run hitter cross it. He looked out at LeBlanc in center; then he looked at Harry Burke at second, old Harry, the manager, forty-one years old and he could still cover the ground, mostly through cunning; make the pivot—how many double plays had he turned in his life?—and when somebody took him out with a slide Billy waited for the cracking sound, not just of bone but the whole body, like a dried tree limb. Hap told him not to worry, old Harry was made of oiled leather. His face looked as if it had already outlived two bodies like the one it commanded now. Never higher than Triple A, and that was long ago; when the Bulls hired him and then the fans loved him he moved his family to Lafayette and made it his home, and between seasons worked for an insurance company, easy money for him, because he went to see men and they drank coffee and talked baseball. He had the gentlest eyes Billy had ever seen on a man. Now Harry trotted over to him.

'We got twenty-one out to get that back for you.'

'The little bastard hit that pitch.'

'Somebody did. Did you get a close look at him?'

Billy shook his head and went to the rubber. He walked the fat pitcher Talieferro on four pitches and Vidrine on six, and Lucky came to the mound. They called him Lucky because he wasn't.

'One run's one thing,' Lucky said. 'Let's don't make it three.'

'The way y'all are swinging tonight, one's as good as nine.' For the first time since he stepped onto the field, Leslie that morning rose up from wherever he had locked her, and struck him.

'Hey,' Lucky said. 'Hey, it's early.'

'Can't y'all hit that fat son of a bitch?'

'We'll hit him. Now you going to pitch or cry?'

He threw Jackson a curve ball and got a double play around the horn, Primeaux to Harry to Baron, who did a split stretching and got Jackson by a half stride.

He went to his end of the bench and watched Talieferro, who for some reason pronounced his name Tolliver: a young big left-handed pitcher with the kind of belly that belonged on a much older man, in bars on weekend afternoons; he had pitched four years at the local college, this was his first season of pro ball, he was sixteen and nine and usually lost only when his control was off. He did not want to be a professional ballplayer. He had a job with an oil company at the end of the season, and was only pitching and eating his way through a Louisiana summer. Billy watched Lucky adjust his peakless cap and dust his hands and step to the plate, and he pushed Leslie back down, for she was about to burst out of him and explode in his face. He looked down at the toe plate on his right shoe, and began working the next inning, the middle of the order, starting with their big hitter, the centerfielder Remy Gauthreaux, who was finished too, thirty years old, but smart and dangerous and he'd knock a mistake out of the park. Low and away to Gauthreaux. Lucky popped out to Stanley in foul territory and came back to the dugout shaking his head.

Billy could sense it in all the hitters in the dugout, and see it when they went to the plate: Talieferro was on, and they were off. It could be anything: the pennant game, when every move counted; the last game of the season, so the will to be a ballplayer was losing to that other part of them which insisted that when they woke tomorrow nothing they felt tonight would be true; they would drive home to the jobs and other lives that waited for them; most would go to places where people had not even heard of the team, the league. All of that would apply to the Pelicans too; it could be that none of it applied to Talieferro: that rarely feeling much of anything except digestion, hunger, and gorging, he had no conflict between what he felt now and would start feeling tomorrow. And it could be that he simply had his best stuff tonight, that he was throwing nearly every pitch the way Stanley had swung that one time.

Billy went to the on-deck circle and kneeled and watched Harry at the plate, then looked out at Simmons, their big first baseman: followed Gauthreaux in the order, a power hitter but struck out about a hundred times a year: keep him off balance, in and out, and throw the fast one right into his power, and right past him too. Harry, choking high on the bat, fouled off everything close to the plate then grounded out to short, and Billy handed his jacket to the batboy and went through cheers to the plate. When he stepped in Talieferro didn't look at him, so Billy stepped out and stared until he did, then dug in and cocked the bat, a good hitter so he had played right field in high school and American Legion when he wasn't pitching. He watched the slow, easy fatman's wind-up and the fast ball coming out of it: swung for the fence and popped it to second, sprinting down the line and crossing the bag before the ball came down. When he turned he saw Talieferro already walking in, almost at the third base line. Harry brought Billy's glove out to the mound and patted his rump.

'I thought you were running all the way to Flint.'

In the next three innings he pitched to nine men. He ended the fifth by striking out Stanley on curve balls; and when Talieferro led off the sixth Billy threw a fast ball at his belly that made him spin away and fall into the dust. Between innings he forced himself to believe in the hope of numbers: the zeros and the one on the scoreboard in right center, the inning number, the outs remaining for the Bulls; watched them starting to hit, but only one an inning, and nobody as far as second base. He sat sweating under his jacket and in his mind pitched to the next three Pelicans, then the next three just to be sure, although he didn't believe he would face six of them next inning, or any inning, and he thought of eighteen then fifteen then twelve outs to get the one run, the only one he needed, because if it came to that, Talieferro would tire first. When Primeaux struck out leading off the sixth, Billy looked at Hap at the other end of the bench, and he wanted to be down there with him. He leaned forward and stared at his shoes. Then the inning was over and he gave in to the truth he had known anyway since that white vision of loss just before the ball fell.

Gauthreaux started the seventh with a single to right, doing what he almost never did: laid off pulling and went with the outside pitch. Billy worked Simmons low and got the double play he needed, then he struck out the catcher Lantrip, and trotted off the field with his string still going, thirteen batters since the one-out walk to Vidrine in the third. He got the next six. Three of them grounded out, and the other three struck out on the curve, Billy watching it break under the shiny blur of the bat as it would in Flint and wherever after that and Detroit too: his leg kicking and body wheeling and arm whipping around in rhythm again with his history which had begun with a baseball and a friend to throw it to, and had excluded all else, or nearly all else, and had included the rest somewhere alongside him, almost out of his vision (once between innings he allowed himself to think about Leslie, just long enough to forgive her); his history was his future too and the two of them together were twenty-five years at most until the time when the pitches that created him would lose their speed, hang at the plate, become hits in other men's lives instead of the heart of his; they would discard him then, the pitches would. But he loved them for that too, and right now they made his breath singular out of the entire world, so singular that there was no other world: the war would not call him because it couldn't know his name; and he would refuse the grief that lurked behind him. He watched the final curve going inside, then breaking down and over, and Lucky's mitt popped and the umpire twisted and roared and pointed his right fist to the sky.

He ran to the dugout, tipping his cap to the yelling Cajuns, and sat between Hap and Lucky until Baron flied out to end the game. After the showers and goodbyes he drove to the hotel and got his still-packed bags and paid the night clerk and started home, out of the lush flatland of marsh and trees, toward Texas. Her space on the front seat was filled as with voice and touch. He turned on the radio. He was not sleepy, and he was driving straight through to San Antonio.

AFTER THE GAME

I WASN'T IN THE clubhouse when Joaquin Quintana went crazy. At least I wasn't there for the start of it, because I pitched that night and went nine innings and won, and the color man interviewed me after the game. He is Duke Simpson, and last year he was our first baseman. He came down from the broadcasting booth, and while the guys were going into the clubhouse, and cops and ushers were standing like soldiers in a V from first to third, facing the crowd leaving the park, I stood in front of the dugout with my jacket on, and Duke and I looked at the camera, and he said: "I'm here with Billy Wells."

This was August and we were still in it, four games back, one and a half out of second. It was the time of year when everybody is tired and a lot are hurt and playing anyway. I wanted a shower and a beer, and to go to my apartment for one more beer and then sleep. I sleep very well after I've pitched a good game, not so well after a bad one, and I sleep very badly the night before I pitch, and the day of the game I force myself to eat. It's one of the things that makes the game exciting, but a lot of times, especially in late season, I long for the time when I'll have a job I can predict, can wake up on the ranch knowing what I'm going to do and that I'm not going to fail. I know most jobs are like that, and the people who have them don't look like they've had a rush of adrenaline since the time somebody ran a stop sign and just missed colliding broadside with them, but there's always a trade-off and, on some days in late season, their lives seem worth it. Duke and I talked about pitching, and our catcher Jesse Wade and what a good game he called behind the plate, so later that night I thought it was strange, that Joaquin was going crazy while Duke and I were talking about Jesse, because during the winter the club had traded Manuel Fernandez, a good relief pitcher, to the Yankees for Jesse. Manuel had been Joaquin's roommate, and they always sat together on the plane and the bus, and ate together. Neither one could speak much English. From shortstop, Joaquin used to call to Manuel out on the mound: *Baja y rapido*.

We ended the interview shaking hands and patting each other on the back, then I went between the cops and ushers but there were some fans waiting for autographs at one end of the dugout, so I went over there and signed three baseballs and a dozen scorecards and said thank you twenty or thirty times, and shook it seemed more hands than there were people, then went into the dugout and down the tunnel to the clubhouse. I knew something was wrong, but I wasn't alert to it, wanting a beer, and I was thinking maybe I'd put my arm in ice for a while, so I saw as if out of the corner of my eye, though I was looking right at it, that nobody was at the food table. There was pizza. Then I heard them and looked that way, down between two rows of lockers. They were bunched down there, the ones on the outside standing on benches or on tiptoes on the floor, stretching and looking, and the ones on the inside talking, not to each other but to whoever was in the middle, and I could hear the manager Bobby Drew, and Terry Morgan the trainer. The guys' voices were low, so I couldn't make out the words, and urgent, so I wondered who had been fighting and why now, with things going well for us, and we hadn't had trouble on the club since Duke retired; he was a good ballplayer, but often a pain in the ass. I went to the back of the crowd but couldn't see, so took off my spikes and stepped behind Bruce Green on a bench. Bruce is the only black on the club, and plays right field. I held his waist for balance as I brought my other foot from the floor. I stay in good running shape all year round, and I am overly careful about accidents, like falling off a bench onto my pitching elbow.

I kept my hands on Bruce's waist and looked over his shoulder and there was Joaquin Quintana, our shortstop, standing in front of his locker, naked except for his sweat socks and jockstrap and his gold Catholic medal, breathing through his mouth like he was in the middle of a sentence he didn't finish. He was as black as Bruce, so people who didn't know him took him for a black man, but Manuel told us he was from the Dominican Republic and did not think of himself as a black, and was pissed off when people did; though it seemed to me he was a black from down there, as Bruce was a black from Newark. His left arm was at his side, and his right forearm was out in front of him like he was reaching for something, or to shake hands, and in that hand he held his spikes. It was the right shoe.

Bruce looked at me over his shoulder.

"They can't move him," he said. Bruce was wearing his uniform pants and no shirt. I came to Boston in 1955, as a minor-league player to be named later in a trade with Detroit, when I was in that organization, and I have played all my seven years of major-league ball with the Red Sox; I grew up in San Antonio, so Bruce is the only black I've ever really known. People were talking to Joaquin. Or the people in front were trying to, and others farther back called to him to have some pizza, a beer, a shower, telling him it was all right, everything was all right, telling him settle down, be cool, take it easy, the girls are waiting at the parking lot. Nobody was wet or wrapped in a towel. Some still wore the uniform and some, like Bruce, wore parts of it, and a few had taken off as much as Joaquin. Most of the lockers were open. So was Joaquin's, and he stood staring at Bobby Drew and Terry Morgan, both of them talking, and Bobby doing most of it, being the manager. He was talking softly and telling Joaquin to give him the shoe and come in his office and lie down on the couch in there. He kept talking about the shoe, as if it was a weapon, though Joaquin held it with his hand under it, and not gripped for swinging, but like he was holding it out to give to someone. But I knew why Bobby wanted him to put it down. I felt the same: if he would just drop that shoe, things would get better. Looking at the scuffed toe and the soft dusty leather and the laces untied and pulled wider across the tongue folded up and over, and the spikes, silver down at their edges, resting on his palm, I wanted to talk that shoe out of his hand too, and I started talking with the others below me, and on the bench across the aisle from me and Bruce, and the benches on the other side of the group around Joaquin.

That is when I saw what he was staring at, when I told him to come on and put down that shoe and let's go get some dinner, it was on me, and all the drinks too, for turning that double-play in the seventh; and Bruce said And the bunt, and Jesse said Perfect fucking bunt, and I saw that Joaquin was not staring at Bobby or Terry, but at nothing at all, as if he saw something we couldn't, but it was as clear to him as a picture hanging in the air right in front of his face.

I lowered myself off the bench and worked my way through the guys, most of them growing quiet while some still tried to break Joaquin out of it. A few were saying their favorite curse, to themselves, shaking their heads or looking at the floor. Everyone I touched was standing tense and solid, but they were easy to part from each other, like pushing aside branches that smelled of sweat. I stepped between Bobby and Terry. They were still dressed, Bobby in his uniform and cap, Terry in his red slacks and white tee shirt.

"Quintana," I said. "Joaquin: it's me, old buddy. It's Billy."

I stared into his eyes but they were not looking back at me; they were looking at something, and they chilled the backs of my knees. I had to stop my hands from going up and feeling the air between us, grabbing for it, pushing it away.

There is something about being naked. Duke Simpson and Tommy Lutring got in a fight last year, in front of Duke's locker, when they had just got out of the shower, and it was not like seeing a fight on the field when the guys are dressed and rolling in the dirt. It seemed worse. Once in a hotel in Chicago a girl and I started fighting in bed and quick enough we were out of bed and putting on our underpants; the madder we got the more clothes we put on, and when she ended the fight by walking out, I was wearing everything but my socks and shoes. I wished Joaquin was dressed.

"Joaquin," I said. "Joaquin, I'm going to take the shoe."

Some of the guys told him to give Billy the shoe. I put my hand on it and he didn't move; then I tried to lift it, and his arm swung a few degrees, but that was all. His bicep was swollen and showing veins.

"Come on, Joaquin. Let it go now. That's a boy."

I put my other hand on it and jerked, and his arm swung and his body swayed and my hands slipped off the shoe. He was staring. I looked at Bobby and Terry, then at the guys on both sides; my eyes met Bruce's, so I said to him: "He doesn't even know I'm here."

"Poor bastard," Bobby said.

Somebody said we ought to carry him to Bobby's couch, and Terry said we couldn't because he was stiff as iron, and lightly, with his fingertips, he jabbed Joaquin's thighs and belly and arms and shoulders, and put his palms on Joaquin's cheeks. Terry said we had to wait for Doc Segura, and Bobby told old Will Hammersley, the clubhouse man, to go tell the press he was sorry but they couldn't come in tonight.

Then we stood waiting. I smelled Joaquin's sweat and listened to his breathing, and looked up and down his good body, and at the medal hanging from his neck, and past his eyes, into his locker: the shaving kit and underwear and socks on the top shelf, with his wallet and gold-banded wristwatch and box of cigars. A couple of his silk shirts hung in the locker, one aqua and one maroon, and a sport coat that was pale yellow, near the color of cream; under it some black pants were folded over the hanger. I wondered what it was like being him all the time. I don't know where the Dominican Republic is. I know it's in the Caribbean, but not where. Over the voices around me, Tommy Lutring said: "Why the *fuck* did we trade *Manuel*?" Then he said: "Sorry, Jesse."

"I wish he was here," Jesse said.

The guys near Jesse patted him on the shoulders and back. Lutring is the second baseman and he loves working with Joaquin. They are something to see, and I like watching them take infield practice. In a game it happens very fast, and you feel the excitement in the moments it takes Joaquin and Tommy to turn a double-play, and before you can absorb it, the pitcher's ready to throw again. In practice you get to anticipate, and watch them poised for the ground-ball, then they're moving, one to the bag, one to the ball, and they always know where the other guy is and where his glove is too, because whoever's taking the throw knows it's coming at his chest, leading him across the bag. It's like the movies I used to watch in San Antonio, with one of those dances that start with a chorus of pretty girls, then they move back for the man and woman: he is in a tuxedo and she wears a long white dress that rises from her legs when she whirls. The lights go down on the chorus, and one light moves with the man and woman dancing together and apart but always together. Light sparkles on her dress, and their shadows dance on the polished floor. I was a kid sitting in the dark, and I wanted to dance like that, and felt if I could just step into the music like into a river, the drums and horns would take me, and I would know how to move.

That is why Tommy said what he did. And Jesse said he wished Manuel was here too, which he probably did but not really, not at the price of him being back with the Yankees where he was the back-up catcher, while here he is the regular and also has our short left field wall to pull for. Because we couldn't do anything and we started to feel like Spanish was the answer, or the problem, and if just somebody could speak it to Joaquin he'd be all right and he'd put down that shoe and use his eyes again, and take off his jockstrap and socks, and head for the showers, so if only Manuel was with us or one of us had learned Spanish in school.

But the truth is the president or dictator of the Dominican Republic couldn't have talked Joaquin into the showers. Doc Segura gave him three shots before his muscles went limp and he dropped the shoe and collapsed like pants you step out of. We caught him before he hit the floor. The two guys with the ambulance got there after the first shot, and stood on either side of him, behind him so they were out of Doc's way; around the end, before the last shot, they held Joaquin's arms, and when he fell Bobby and I grabbed him too. His eyes were closed. We put him on the stretcher and they covered him up and carried him out and we haven't seen him since, though we get reports on how he's doing in the hospital. He sleeps and they feed him. That was three weeks ago.

Doc Segura had to wait thirty minutes between shots, so the smokers had their cigarettes and cigars going, and guys were passing beers and pizza up from the back, where I had stood with Bruce. He was still on the bench, drinking a beer, with smoke rising past him to the ceiling. I didn't feel right, drinking a beer in front of Joaquin, and I don't think Bobby did either. Terry is an alcoholic who doesn't drink anymore and goes to meetings, so he didn't count. Finally when someone held a can toward Bobby he didn't shake his head, but got it to his mouth fast while he watched Doc getting the second needle ready, so I reached for one too. Doc swabbed the vein inside Joaquin's left elbow. This time I looked at Joaquin's eyes instead of the needle: he didn't feel it. All my sweat was long since dried, and I had my jacket off except the right sleeve on my arm.

I know Manuel couldn't have helped Joaquin. The guys keep saying it was because he was lonesome. But I think they say that because Joaquin was black and spoke Spanish. And maybe for the same reason an alcoholic who doesn't drink anymore may blame other people's troubles on booze: he's got scary memories of blackouts and sick hangovers and d.t.'s, and he always knows he's just a barstool away from it. I lost a wife in my first year in professional ball, when I was eighteen years old and as dumb about women as I am now. Her name was Leslie. She left me for a married dentist, a guy with kids, in Lafayette, Louisiana, where I was playing my rookie year in the Evangeline League, an old class C league that isn't there anymore. She is back in San Antonio, married to the manager of a department store; she has four kids, and I hardly ever see her, but when I do there are no hard feelings. Leslie said she felt like she was chasing the team bus all season long, down there in Louisiana. I have had girlfriends since, but not the kind you marry.

By the time Joaquin fell I'd had a few beers and some pizza gone cold, and I was very tired. It was after one in the morning and I did not feel like I had pitched a game, and won it too. I felt like I had been working all day on the beef-cattle ranch my daddy is building up for us with the money I send him every payday. That's where I'm going when my arm gives out. He has built a house on it, and I'll live there with him and my mom. In the showers people were quiet. They talked, but you know what I mean. I dressed then told Hammersley I wanted to go into the park for a minute. He said Sure, Billy, and opened the door.

I went up the tunnel to the dugout and stepped onto the grass. It was already damp. I had never seen the park empty at night, and with no lights, and all those empty seats and shadows under the roof over the grandstand, and under the sky the dark seats out in the bleachers in right and centerfield. Boston lit the sky over the screen in left and beyond the bleachers, but it was a dull light, and above the playing field there was no light at all, so I could see stars. For a long time, until I figured everybody was dressed and gone or leaving and Hammersley was waiting to lock up, I stood on the grass by the batting circle and looked up at the stars, thinking of drums and cymbals and horns, and a man and woman dancing.

CADENCE

to Tommie

H E STOOD IN the summer Virginia twilight, an officer candidate, nineteen years old, wearing Marine utilities and helmet, an M1 rifle in one hand, its butt resting on the earth, a pack high on his back, the straps buckled too tightly around his shoulders; because he was short he was the last man in the rank. He stood in the front rank and watched Gunnery Sergeant Hathaway and Lieutenant Swenson in front of the platoon, talking quietly to each other, the lieutenant tall and confident, the sergeant short, squat, with a beer gut; at night, he had told them, he went home and drank beer with his old lady. He could walk the entire platoon into the ground. Or so he made them believe. He had small, brown, murderous eyes; he scowled when he was quiet or thinking; and, at rest, his narrow lips tended downward at the corners. Now he turned from the lieutenant and faced the platoon. They stood on the crest of a low hill; beyond Hathaway the earth sloped down to a darkened meadow and then rose again, a wooded hill whose black trees touched the grey sky.

'We're going back over the Hill Trail,' he said, and someone groaned and at first Paul fixed on that sound as a source of strength: someone else dreaded the hills as much as he did. Around him he could sense a fearful gathering of resolve, and now the groan he had first clung to became something else: a harbinger of his own failure. He knew that, except for Hugh Munson standing beside him, he was the least durable of all; and since these men, a good half of

them varsity athletes, were afraid, his own fear became nearly un-
bearable. It became physical: it took a penetrating fall into his legs
and weakened his knees so he felt he was not supported by muscle
and bone but by faint nerves alone.

'We'll put the little men up front,' Hathaway said, 'so you long-
legged pacesetters'll know what it's like to bring up the rear.'

They moved in two files, down a sloping trail flanked by black
trees. Hugh was directly behind him. To his left, leading the other
file, was Whalen; he was also short, five-eight or five-seven; but he
was wide as a door. He was a wrestler from Purdue. They moved
down past trees and thick underbrush into the dark of the woods,
and behind him he heard the sounds of blindness: a thumping body
and clattering rifle as someone tripped and fell; there were curses,
and voices warned those coming behind them, told of a branch
reaching across the trail; from the rear Hathaway called: 'Close it
up close it up, don't lose sight of the man in front of you.' Paul
walked step for step beside Whalen and watched tall Lieutenant
Swenson setting the pace, watched his pack and helmet as he started
to climb and, looking up and past the lieutenant, up the wide corridor between the trees, he saw against the sky the crest of the first
hill.

Then he was climbing, his legs and lungs already screaming at
him that they could not, and he saw himself at home in his room
last winter and spring, getting ready for this: push-ups and sit-ups,
leg lifts and squat jumps and deep kneebends, exercises which made
his body feel good but did little for it, and as he climbed and the
muscles of his thighs bulged and tightened and his lungs demanded
more and more of the humid air, he despised that memory of himself, despised himself for being so far removed from the world of
men that he had believed in calisthenics, had not even considered
running, though he had six months to get in condition after signing
the contract with the Marine captain who had come one day like
salvation into the student union, wearing the blue uniform and the
manly beauty that would fulfill Paul's dreams. Now those dreams
were an illusion: he was close to the top of the first hill, his calf and
thigh muscles burning, his lungs gasping, and his face, near sobbing,
was fixed in pain. His one desire that he felt with each breath, each
step up the hard face of the hill, was not endurance: it was deliv-
erance. He wanted to go home, and to have this done for him in

some magical or lucky way that would give him honor in his father's eyes. So as he moved over the top of the hill, Whalen panting beside him, and followed Lieutenant Swenson steeply down, he wished and then prayed that he would break his leg.

He descended: away from the moonlight, down into the shadows and toward the black at the foot of the hill. His strides were short now and quick, his body leaned backward so he wouldn't fall, and once again his instincts and his wishes were at odds: wanting a broken leg, he did not want to fall and break it; wanting to go home, he did not want to quit and pack his seabag and suitcase, and go. For there was that too: they would let him quit. That was the provision which had seemed harmless enough, even congenial, as he lifted his pen in the student union. He could stop and sit or lean against a tree and wait for the platoon to pass and Sergeant Hathaway's bulk to appear like an apparition of fortitude and conscience out of the dark, strong and harsh and hoarse, and he could then say: 'Sir, I want to go home.' It would be over then, he would drift onto the train tomorrow and then to the airport and fly home in a nimbus of shame to face his father's blue and humiliated eyes, which he had last seen beaming at him before the embrace that, four and a half weeks ago, sent him crossing the asphalt to the plane.

It was a Sunday. Sergeants met the planes in Washington and put the men on buses that were green and waxed, and drove them through the last of the warm setting sun to Quantico. The conversations aboard the bus were apprehensive and friendly. They all wore civilian clothes except Paul. At home he had joined the reserve and his captain had told him to wear his uniform and he had: starched cotton khaki, and it was wrinkled from his flight. The sergeants did not look at the uniform or at him either; or, if they did, they had a way of looking that was not looking at him. By the time he reached the barracks he felt that he existed solely in his own interior voice. Then he started up the stairs, carrying seabag and suitcase, guided up by the press of his companions, and as he went down a corridor toward the squad bay he passed an open office and Sergeant Hathaway entered his life: not a voice but a roar, and he turned and stood at attention, seabag and suitcase heavy in each hand, seeing now with vision narrowed and dimmed by fear the raging face, the pointing finger; and he tried for the voice to say Me, sir? but already Hathaway was coming toward him and with both fists struck his chest one short hard blow, the fists then opening to grip his shirt and jerk him forward into the office; he heard the shirt tear; somewhere outside the door he dropped his luggage; perhaps they hit the door-jamb as he was going through, and he stood at attention in the office; other men were there, his eyes were aware of them but he was not, for in the cascade of curses from that red and raging face he could feel and know only his fear: his body was trembling, he knew as though he could see it that his face was drained white, and now he had to form answers because the curses were changing to questions, Hathaway's voice still at a roar, his dark loathing eyes close to Paul's and at the same height; Paul told him his name.

'Where did it happen?'

'Sir?'

'Where did she do it. Where the fuck were you *born*.'

'Lake Charles, Louisiana, sir.'

'Well no shit Lake Charles Louisiana sir, you college idiot, you think I know where that is? Where is it?'

'South of New Orleans sir.'

'South of New Orleans. How *far* south.'

'About two hundred miles sir.'

'Well no shit. Are you a fucking fish? Answer me, candidate shitbird. Are you a fucking fish?'

'No sir.'

'No sir. Why aren't you a fish?'

'I don't know sir.'

'You don't know. Well you better be a Goddamn fish because two hundred miles south of New Orleans is in the Gulf of fucking *Mexico*.'

'West sir.'

'You said south. Are you calling me a liar, fartbreath? I'll break your jaw. You know that? Do you *know* that?'

'Sir?'

'Do you know I can break your Goddamn jaw?'

'Yes sir.'

'Do you want me to?'

'No sir.'

'Why not? You can't use it. You can't Goddamn talk. If I had a piece of gear that wasn't worth a shit and I didn't know how to use it anyway I wouldn't give a good rat's ass if somebody broke it. Stop shaking. Who told you to wear that uniform? I said stop shaking.'

'My captain sir.'

'My *cap*tain. Who the fuck is your captain.'

'My reserve captain sir.'

'Is he a ragpicker?'

'Sir?'

'Is he a *rag*picker. How does he *eat.*'

'He has a hardware store, sir.'

'He's a ragpicker. Say it.'

'He's a ragpicker, sir.'

'I told you to stop shaking. Say my reserve captain is a ragpicker.'

'My reserve captain is a ragpicker, sir.'

Then the two fists came up again and struck his chest and gripped the shirt, shaking him back and forth, and stiff and quivering and with legs like weeds he had no balance, and when Hathaway shoved and released him he fell backward and crashed against a steel wall locker; then Hathaway had him pressed against it, holding the shirt again, banging him against the locker, yelling: 'You can't wear that uniform you shit you don't even know how to wear that uniform you wore it on the Goddamn plane playing Marine Goddamnit— Well you're not a Marine and you'll never be a Marine, you won't make it here one week, you will not be here for chow next Sunday, because you are a shit and I will break your ass in five days, I will break it so hard that for the rest of your miserable fucking life every time you see a man you'll crawl under a table and piss in your skivvies. Give me those emblems. Give them to me! Take them off, take them off, take them off—' Paul's hands rising first to the left collar, the hands trembling so that he could not hold the emblem and collar still, his right hand trying to remove the emblem while Hathaway's fists squeezed the shirt tight across his chest and slowly rocked him back and forth, the hands trembling; he was watching them and they couldn't do it, the fingers would not stop, they would not hold; then a jerk and a shove Hathaway flung him against the locker, screaming at him; and he felt tears in his eyes, seemed to be watching the tears in his eyes, pleading with them to at least stay there and not stain his cheeks; somewhere behind Hathaway the other men were still watching but they were a blur of khaki and flesh: he was enveloped and penetrated by Hathaway's screa and he could see nothing in the world except his fingers wor at the emblems.

Then it was over. The emblems were off, they were in Hath way's hand, and he was out in the corridor, propelled to the doo and thrown to the opposite wall with such speed that he did not even feel the movement: he only knew Hathaway's two hands, one at the back of his collar, one at the seat of his pants. He picked up his suitcase and seabag, and feeling bodiless as a cloud, he moved down the hall and into the lighted squad bay where the others were making bunks and hanging clothes in wall lockers and folding them into foot lockers, and he stood violated and stunned in the light. Then someone was helping him. Someone short and muscular and calm (it was Whalen), a quiet mid-western voice whose hand took the seabag and suitcase, whose head nodded for him to follow the quick athletic strides that led him to his bunk. Later that night he lay in the bunk and prayed dear please God please dear God may I have sugar in my blood. The next day the doctors would look at them and he must fail, he must go home; in his life he had been humiliated, but never never had anyone made his own flesh so uninhabitable. He must go home.

But his body failed him. It was healthy enough for them to keep it and torment it, but not strong enough, and each day he woke tired and rushed to the head where the men crowded two or three deep at the mirrors to shave and others, already shaved, waited outside toilet stalls; then back to the squad bay to make his bunk, the blanket taut and without wrinkle, then running down the stairs and into the cool first light of day and, in formation with the others, he marched to chow where he ate huge meals because on the second day of training Hathaway had said: 'Little man, I want you to eat everything but the table cloth'; so on those mornings, not yet hungry, his stomach in fact near-queasy at the early morning smell of hot grease that reached him a block from the chow hall, he ate cereal and eggs and pancakes and toast and potatoes and milk, and the day began. Calisthenics and running in formation around the drill field, long runs whose distances and pace were at the whim of Lieutenant Swenson, or the obstacle course, or assaulting hills or climbing the Hill Trail, and each day there came a point when his body gave out, became a witch's curse of one hundred and forty-five pounds of pain that he had to bear, and he would look over at Hugh Munson trying to do a push-up, his back arching, his belly drawn to the earth as though gravity had chosen him for an extra, jesting pull; at Hugh hanging from the chinning bar, his face contorted, his legs jerking, a man on a gibbet; at Hugh climbing the Hill Trail, his face pale and open-mouthed and dripping, the eyes showing pain and nothing more, his body swaying like a fighter senseless on his feet; at Hugh's arms taking him halfway up the rope and no more so he hung suspended like an exclamation point at the end of Hathaway's bellowing scorn.

In the squad bay they helped each other. Every Saturday morning there was a battalion inspection and on Friday nights, sometimes until three or four in the morning, Paul and Hugh worked together, rolling and unrolling and rolling again their shelter halves until, folded in a U, they fit perfectly on the haversacks which they had packed so neatly and squarely they resembled canvas boxes. They took apart their rifles and cleaned each part; in the head they scrubbed their cartridge belts with stiff brushes, then put them in the dryer in the laundry room downstairs; and they worked on shoes and boots, spit-shining the shoes and one pair of boots, and saddlesoaping a second pair of boots which they wore to the field; they washed their utility caps and sprayed them with starch and fitted them over tin cans so they would shape as they dried. And, while they worked, they drilled each other on the sort of questions they expected the battalion commander to ask. What *is* enfilade fire, candidate Hugh? Why that, colonel, is when the axis of fire coincides with the axis of the enemy. And can you name the chain of command as well? I can, my colonel, and, sorry to say, it begins with Ike. At night during the week and on Saturday afternoons they studied for exams. Hugh learned quickly to read maps and use the compass, and he helped Paul with these, spreading the map on his foot locker, talking, pointing, as Paul chewed his lip and frowned at the brown contour lines which were supposed to become, in his mind, hills and draws and ridges and cliffs. On Sunday afternoons they walked to the town of Quantico and, dressed in civilian clothes, drank beer incognito in bars filled with sergeants. Once they took the train to Washington and saw the Lincoln Memorial and pretended not to weep; then, proud of their legs and wind, they climbed the Washington Monument. One Saturday night they got happily and absolutely drunk in Quantico and walked home singing love songs.

Hugh slept in the bunk above Paul's. His father was dead, he lived with his mother and a younger sister, and at night in the squad bay he liked talking about his girl in Bronxville; on summer afternoons he and Molly took the train into New York.

'What do you do?' Paul said. He stood next to their bunk; Hugh sat on his, looking down at Paul; he wore a T-shirt, his bare arms were thin, and high on his cheekbones were sparse freckles.

'She takes me to museums a lot.'

'What kind of museums?'

'Art.'

'I've never been to one.'

'That's because you're from the south. I can see her now, standing in front of a painting. Oh Hugh, she'll say, and she'll grab my arm. Jesus.'

'Are you going to marry her?'

'In two years. She's a snapper like you, but hell I don't care. Sometimes I go to mass with her. She says I'll have to sign an agreement; I mean it's not *her* making me, and she's not bitchy about it; there's nothing she can do about it, that's all. You know, agree to raise the kids Catholics. That Nazi crap your Pope cooked up.'

'You don't mind?'

'Naw, it's *Molly* I want. *Her*, man—'

Now in his mind Paul was miles and months away from the squad bay and the smells of men and canvas and leather polish and gun oil, he was back in those nights last fall and winter and spring, showing her the stories he wrote, buying for her Hemingway's books, one at a time, chronologically, in hardcover; the books were for their library, his and Tommie's, after they were married; he did not tell her that. Because for a long time he did not know if she loved him. Her eyes said it, the glow in her cheeks said it, her voice said it. But she never did; not with her controlled embraces and kisses, and not with words. It was the words he wanted. It became an obsession: they drank and danced in night clubs, they saw movies, they spent hours parked in front of her house, and he told her his dreams and believed he was the only young man who had ever had such dreams and had ever told them to such a tender girl; but all this seemed incomplete because she didn't give him the words.

Then one night in early summer she told him she loved him. She was a practical and headstrong girl; the next week she went to see a priest. He was young, supercilious, and sometimes snide. She spent an hour with him, most of it in anger, and that night she told Paul she must not see him again. She must not love him. She would not sign contracts. She spoke bitterly of incense and hocus-pocus and graven images. Standing at Hugh's bunk, remembering that long year of nights with Tommie, yearning again for the sound of his own voice, gently received, and the swelling of his heart as he told Tommie what he had to and wanted to be, he felt divided and perplexed; he looked at Hugh's face and thought of Molly's hand reaching out for that arm, holding it, drawing Hugh close to her as she gazed at a painting. He blinked his eyes, scratched his crew-cut head, returned to the squad bay with an exorcising wrench and a weary sigh.

'—Sometimes she lets me touch her, just the breasts you see, and that's fine, I don't push it. When she lets me I'm Goddamn *grate*ful. Jesus, you got to get a girl again. There's nothing like it. You know that? *Noth*ing. It's another world, man.'

On a hot grey afternoon he faced Hugh on the athletic field, both of them wearing gold football helmets, holding pugil sticks at the ready, as if they were rifles with fixed bayonets. Paul's fists gripped and encircled the smooth round wood; on either end of it was a large stuffed canvas cylinder; he looked into Hugh's eyes, felt the eyes of the circled platoon around him, and waited for Hathaway's signal to begin. When it came he slashed at Hugh's shoulder and neck but Hugh parried with the stick, then he jabbed twice at Hugh's face, backing him up, and swung the lower end of the stick around in a butt stroke that landed hard on Hugh's ribs; then with speed he didn't know he had he was jabbing Hugh's chest, Hathaway shouting now: 'That's it, little man: keep him going, keep him going; Munson get your balance, use your feet, Goddamnit—' driving Hugh back in a circle, smacking him hard on the helmeted ear; Hugh's face was flushed, his eyes betrayed, angry; Paul jabbing at those eyes, slashing at the head and neck, butt stroking hip and ribs, charging, keeping Hugh off balance so he could not hit back, could only hold his stick diagonally across his body, Paul feinting and working over and under and around the stick, his hands tingling with the blows he landed until Hathaway stopped him: 'All right, little man, that's enough; Carmichael and Vought, put on the headgear.'

Paul took off the helmet and handed it and the pugil stick to Carmichael. He picked up his cap from the grass; it lay next to Hugh's, and as he rose with it Hugh was beside him, stooping for his cap, murmuring: 'Jesus, you really like this shit, don't you.'

Paul watched Carmichael and Vought fighting, and pretended he hadn't heard. He felt Hugh standing beside him. Then he glanced at Hathaway, across the circle. Hathaway was watching him.

In the dark he was climbing the sixth and final hill, even the moon was gone, either hidden by trees or clouds or out of his vision because he was in such pain that he could see only that: his pain; the air was grey and heavy and humid, and he could not get enough of it; even as he inhaled his lungs demanded more and he exhaled with a rush and again drew in air, his mouth open, his throat and tongue dry, haunting his mind with images he could not escape: cold oranges, iced tea, lemonade, his canteen of water—He was falling back. He wasn't abreast of Whalen anymore, he was next to the man behind Whalen and then back to the third man, and he moaned and strove and achieved a semblance of a jog, a tottering climb away from the third man and past the second and up with Whalen again, then from behind people were yelling at him, or trying to, their voices diminished, choked off by their own demanding lungs they were cursing him for lagging and then running to catch up, causing a gap which they had to close with their burning legs. Behind him Hugh was silent and Paul wondered if that silence was because of empathy or because Hugh was too tired to curse him aloud; he decided it was empathy and wished it were not.

And now Lieutenant Swenson reached the top, a tall helmeted silhouette halted and waiting against the oppressive and mindless sky, and Paul's heart leaped in victory and resilience, he crested the hill, went happily past Swenson's panting and sweating face, plunged downward, leaning back, hard thighs and calves bouncing on the earth, then Swenson jogged past him, into the lead again and, walking now, brought them slowly down the hill and out of the trees, onto the wide quiet gravel road and again stepped aside and watched them go past, telling them quietly to close it up, close it up, you people, and Paul's stride was long and light and drunk with fatigue; he tried to punch Whalen's arm but couldn't reach him and didn't have the strength to veer from his course and do it—Then Swenson's voice high and clear: "tawn: ten*huhn*,' and he straightened his back and with shoulders so tired and aching that he barely felt the cutting packstraps, he marched to Swenson's tenor cadence, loving now the triumphant rhythm of boots in loose gravel, cooling in his drying sweat, able now to think of water as a promise the night would keep. Then Swenson called out: 'Are you ready, Gunny?' and, from the rear, Hathaway's answering growl: 'Aye, Lieutenant—' and Paul's heart chilled, he had heard the mischievous threat in Swenson's voice and now it came: 'Dou-ble time—' a pause: crunching boots: groans, and then '—*huhn*.'

Swenson ran past him on long legs, swerved to the front of the two files, and slowed to a pace that already Paul knew he couldn't keep. For perhaps a quarter of a mile he ran step for step with Whalen, and then he was finished. His strides shortened and slowed. Whalen was ahead of him and he tried once to catch up, but as he lifted his legs they refused him, they came down slower, shorter, and falling back now he moved to his left so the men behind him could go on. For a moment he ran beside Hugh. Hugh jerked his pale face to the left, looked at him, tried to say something; then he was gone. Paul was running alone between the two files, they were moving past him, some spoke encouragement as they went—hang in there, man—then he was among the tall ones at the rear and still he was dropping back, then a strong hand extended from a gasping shadowed face and took his rifle and went on.

He did not look behind him but he knew: he could feel at his back the empty road, and he was dropping back into it when the last two men, flanking him, each took an arm and held him up. 'You can do it,' they said. 'Keep going,' they said. He ran with them. Vaguely above the sounds of his breathing he could hear the pain of others: the desperate breathing and always the sound of boots, not rhythmic now, for each man ran in step with his own struggle, but anyway steady, and that is what finally did him in: the endlessness of that sound. Hands were still holding his arms; he was held up and pulled forward, his head lolled, he felt his legs giving way, his arms, his shoulders, he was sinking, they were pulling him forward but he was sinking, his eyes closed, he saw red-laced black and then it was over, he was falling forward to the gravel, and then he struck it but not with his face: with his knees and arms and hands. Then his face settled forward onto the gravel. He was not unconscious, and he lay in a shameful moment of knowledge that he would remember for the rest of his life: he had quit before his body failed; the legs which now lay in the gravel still had strength which he could feel; and already, within this short respite, his lungs were ready again. They hurt, they labored, but they were ready.

'He passed out, sir.'

They were standing above him. The platoon was running up the road.

'Who is it?' Hathaway said.

'It's Clement, sir.'

'Leave his rifle here and you men catch up with the platoon.'

'Aye aye, sir.'

There were two of them. They went up the road, running hard to catch up, and he wanted to tell them he was sorry he had lied, but he knew he never would. Then he heard or felt Hathaway squat beside him, the small strong hands took his shoulders and turned him over on his back and unbuckled his chin strap. He blinked up at Hathaway's eyes: they were concerned, interested yet distant, as though he were disassembling a weapon whose parts were new to him; and they were knowing too, as if he were not appraising the condition of Paul's body alone but the lack of will that had allowed it to fall behind, to give up a rifle, to crap out.

'What happened, Clement?'

'I don't know, sir. I blacked out.'

Hathaway's hands reached under Paul's hip, lifted him enough to twist the canteen around, open the flaps, pull it from the cover. The crunching of the platoon receded and was gone up the road in the dark. Hathaway handed him the canteen.

'Take two swallows.'

Paul lifted his head and drank.

'Now stand up.'

He stood, replaced the canteen on his hip, and buckled his chin strap. His shirt was soaked; under it the T-shirt clung to his back and chest.

'Here's your weapon.'

He took the M1 and slung it on his shoulder.

'Let's go,' Hathaway said, and started jogging up the road, Paul moving beside him, the fear starting again, touching his heart like a feather and draining his legs of their strength. But it didn't last. Within the first hundred yards it was gone, replaced by the quick-lunged leg-aching knowledge that there was no use being afraid because he knew, as he had known the instant his knees and hands and arms hit the gravel, that he was strong enough to make it; that Hathaway would not let him do anything but make it; and so his fear was impotent, it offered no chance of escape, and he ran now with Hathaway, mesmerized by his own despair. He tried to re-member the road, how many bends there were, so he could look forward to that last curve which would disclose the lighted streets of what now felt like home. He could not remember how many curves there were. Then they rounded one and Hathaway said, 'Hold it,' and walked toward the edge of the road. Paul wiped sweat from his eyes, blinked them, and peered beyond Hathaway's back and shoulders at the black trees. He followed Hathaway and then he saw, at the side of the road, a man on his hands and knees. As he got closer he breathed the smell.

'Who is it?' Hathaway said.

'Munson.' His voice rose weakly from the smell. Paul moved closer and stood beside Hathaway, looking down at Hugh.

'Are you finished?' Hathaway said.

'I think so.'

'Then stand up.' His voice was low, near coaxing in its demand.

Hugh pushed himself up, stood, then retched again and leaned over the ditch and dry-heaved. When he was done he remained bent over the ditch, waiting. Then he picked up his rifle and stood straight, but he did not turn to face them. He took off his helmet and held it in front of him, down at his waist, took something from it, then one hand rose to his face. He was wiping it with a piece of toilet paper. He dropped the paper into the ditch, then turned and looked at Hathaway. Then he saw Paul, who was looking at Hugh's drained face and feeling it as if it were his own: the cool sweat, the raw sour throat.

'Man—' Hugh said, looking at Paul, his voice and eyes petulant; then he closed his eyes and shook his head.

'We'll run it in now,' Hathaway said.

Hugh opened his eyes.

'I threw up,' he said.

'And you're done.' Hathaway pointed up the road. 'And the barracks is that way.'

'I'll walk.'

'When you get back to New York you can do that, Munson. You can diddle your girl and puke on a six-pack and walk back to the frat house all you want. But here you run. Put on your helmet.'

Hugh slung his rifle on his shoulder and put his helmet on his head.

'Buckle it.'

He buckled it under his chin, then looked at Hathaway.

'I can't run. I threw up.' He gave Paul a weary glance, and looked up the road. 'It's not that I won't. I just can't, that's all.'

He stood looking at them. Then he reached back for his canteen, it rose pale in the moonlight, and he drank.

'All right, Munson: two swallows, then start walking, Clement, let's go.'

He looked at Hugh lowering the canteen, his head back gargling, then his eyes were on the road directly in front of him as he ran up a long stretch then rounded a curve and looked ahead and saw more of the road, the trees, and the black sky at the horizon; he was too tired to lift his head and see the moon and stars and this made him feel trapped on a road that would never end. Before the next curve he reached the point of fatigue he had surrendered to when he fell, and he moved through it into a new plane of struggle where he was certain that now his body would truly fail him, would fold and topple in spite of the volition Hathaway gave him. And then something else happened, something he had never experienced. Suddenly his legs told him they could go as far as he wanted them to. They did not care for his heat-aching head, for his thirst; they did not care for his pain. They told him this so strongly that he was frightened, as though his legs would force him to hang on as they spent the night jogging over Virginia hills; then he regained possession of them. They were his, they were running beside a man who had walked out of the Chosin Reservoir, and they were going to make it. When Paul turned the last bend and saw the street lights and brick buildings and the platoon, which had reached the blacktop road by the athletic field and was marching now, he felt both triumphant and disappointed: he wanted to show Hathaway he could keep going.

They left the gravel and now his feet pounded on the gift of smooth blacktop. They approached the platoon, then ran alongside it, and as they came abreast of Lieutenant Swenson, Hathaway said: 'Lieutenant, you better send a jeep back for Munson. Me and Clement's going to hit the grinder; we had a long rest up the road.' The lieutenant nodded. Paul and Hathaway passed the platoon and turned onto the blacktop parade field and started to circle it. It was a half-mile run. For a while Paul could hear Swenson's fading cadence, then it stopped and he knew Swenson was dismissing the platoon. In the silence of the night he ran alongside Hathaway, listened to Hathaway's breath and pounding feet, glanced at him, and looked up at the full moon over the woods. They left the parade field and jogged up the road between brick barracks until they reached Bravo Company and Hathaway stopped. Paul faced him and stood at attention. His legs felt like they were still running. He was breathing hard; he looked through burning sweat at Hathaway, also breathing fast and deep, his face dripping and red. Hathaway's eyes were not glaring, not even studying Paul: they seemed fixed instead on his own weariness.

'You get in the barracks you get some salt tablets and you take 'em. I don't care if you've been drinking Goddamn Gulf water all your life. Dismissed.'

The rest of the platoon were in the showers. As he climbed the stairs he heard the spraying water, the tired, exultant, and ironic voices. In the corridor at the top of the stairs he stopped and looked at the full-length mirror, looked at his short lean body standing straight, the helmet on his head, the pack with a protruding bayonet handle, the rifle slung on his shoulder. His shirt and patches on his thighs were dark green with sweat. Then he moved on to the water fountain and took four salt tablets from the dispenser and swallowed them one at a time, tilting his head back to swallow, remembering the salt tablets on the construction job when he was sixteen and his father got him the job and drove him to work on the first day and introduced him to the foreman and said: 'Work him, Jesse; make a man of him.' Jesse was a quiet wiry Cajun; he nodded, told Paul to stow his lunch in the toolshed and get a pick and a spade. All morning he worked bare-headed under the hot June sun; he worked with the Negroes, digging a trench for the foundation, and at noon he was weak and nauseated and could not eat. He went behind the shed and lay in the shade. The Negroes watched him and asked him wasn't he going to eat. He told them he didn't feel like it. At one o'clock he was back in the trench, and thirty minutes later he looked up and saw his father in seersucker and straw hat standing with Jesse at the trench's edge. 'Come on up, son,' his father said. 'I'm all right,' and he lifted the pick and dropped more than drove it into the clay at his feet. 'You just need a hat, that's all,' his father said. 'Come on up, I'll buy you one and bring you back to work.' He laid the pick beside the trench, turned to the Negro working behind him, and said, 'I'll be right back.' 'Sure,' the Negro said. 'You get that hat.' He climbed out of the trench and walked quietly beside his father to the car. 'Jesse called me,' his father said in the car. 'He said the nigras told him you didn't eat lunch. It's just the sun, that's all. We'll get you a hat. Did you take salt tablets?' Paul said yes, he had. His father bought him a pith helmet and, at the soda fountain, a Seven-Up and a sandwich. 'Jesse said you didn't tell anybody you felt bad.' 'No,' Paul said. 'I didn't.' His father stirred his coffee, looked away. Paul could feel his father's shy pride and he loved it, but he was ashamed too, for when he had looked up and seen his father on the job, he had had a moment of hope when he thought his father had come to tenderly take him home.

By the time he got out of his gear and hung his wet uniform by the window and wiped his rifle clean and lightly oiled it, the rest of the platoon were out of the showers, most were in their bunks, and the lights would go out in five minutes. Paul went to the shower and stayed long under the hot spray, feeling the sweat and dirt leave him, and sleep rising through his aching legs, to his arms and shoulders, to all save his quick heart. He was drying himself when Whalen came in, wearing shorts, and stood at the urinal and looked over his shoulder at Paul.

'You and Hathaway run all the way in?'

'Yeah.'

'Then the grinder?'

Paul nodded.

'Good,' Whalen said, and turned back to the urinal. Paul looked at his strong, muscled wrestler's back and shoulders. When Whalen passed him going out, Paul swung lightly and punched his arm.

'See you in the morning,' he said.

The squad bay was dark when Paul entered with a towel around his waist. Already most of them were asleep, their breath shallow and slow. There was enough light from the corridor so he could see the rifle rack in the middle of the room, and the double bunks on either side, and the wall lockers against the walls. He went to his bunk. Hugh was sitting on the edge of it, his elbows on his knees, his forehead resting on his palms. His helmet and rifle and pack and cartridge belt were on the floor in front of his feet. He looked up, and Paul moved closer to him in the dark.

'How's it going,' he said softly.

'I threw *up*, man. You see what I mean? That's stupid, Goddamnit. For *what*. What's the point of doing something that makes you puke. I was going to keep running till the Goddamn stuff came up all over me. Is that smart, man?' Hugh stood; someone farther down stirred on his bunk; Hugh took Paul's arm and squeezed it; he smelled of sweat, his breath was sour, and he leaned close, lowering his voice. 'Then you crapped out and I thought good. *Good*, Goddamnit. And man I peeled off and went to the side of the road and waited for it to come up. Then I was going to find you and walk in and drink Goddamn water and piss in the road and piss on all of them.' He released Paul's arm. 'But that Goddamn Doberman pinscher made you run in. Jesus Christ what am I *do*ing here. What am I *do*ing here,' and he turned and struck his mattress, stood looking at his fist on the bed, then raised it and struck again. Paul's hand went up to touch Hugh's shoulder, but stopped in the space between them and fell back to his side. He did not speak either. He looked at Hugh's profiled staring face, then turned away and bent over his foot locker at the head of the bunk and took out a T-shirt and a pair of shorts, neatly folded. He put them on and sat on his locker while Hugh dropped his clothes to the floor and walked out of the squad bay, to the showers.

He got into the lower bunk and lay on his back, waiting for his muscles to relax and sleep to come. But he was still awake when Hugh came back and stepped over the gear on the floor and climbed into his bunk. He wanted to ask Hugh if he'd like him to clean his rifle, but he could not. He lay with aching legs and shoulders and back and arms, and gazed up at Hugh's bunk and listened to his shifting weight. Soon Hugh settled and breathed softly, in sleep.

Paul lay awake, among silhouettes of bunks and wall lockers and rifle racks. They and the walls and the pale windows all seemed to breathe, and to excude the smells of men. Farther down the squad bay someone snored. Hugh murmured in his sleep, then was quiet again.

When the lights went on he exploded frightened out of sleep, swung his legs to the floor, and his foot landed on the stock of Hugh's rifle. He stepped over it and trotted to the head, shaved at a lavatory with Whalen, waited outside a toilet stall but the line was too long and with tightening bowels he returned to the squad bay. Hugh was lying on his bunk. Going past it to the wall locker he said: 'Hey Hugh. Hugh, reveille.' He opened his locker and then looked back; Hugh was awake, blinking, looking at the ceiling.

'Hugh—' Hugh did not look at him. 'Your *gear*, Hugh; what about your *gear*.'

He didn't move. Paul put on utilities and spit-shined boots and ran past him. At the door he stopped and looked back. The others were coming, tucking in shirts, putting on caps. Hugh was sitting on the edge of his bunk, watching them move toward the door. Outside the morning was still cool and Hathaway waited, his boots shining in the sunlight. The platoon formed in front of him and his head snapped toward the space beside Paul.

'Clement, did Munson Goddamn puke and die on the road last night?'

'He's coming, sir.'

He's coming. Well no shit he's coming. What do you people think this is—Goddamn civilian life where everybody crosses the streets on his own time? A platoon is not out of the barracks until every member of that platoon is out of the barracks, and you people are not out of the barracks yet. You are still *in* there with—o-ho—' He was looking beyond them, at the barracks to their rear. 'Well now here he is. You people are here now. Munson, you asshole, come up here.' Paul heard Munson to his left, coming around the platoon; He walked slowly. He entered Paul's vision and Paul watched him going up to Hathaway and standing at attention.

'Well no shit Munson.' His voice was low. 'Well no shit now. Mr. Munson has joined us for chow. He slept a little late this morning. I understand, Munson. It tires a man out, riding home in a jeep. It gets a man tried, when he knows he's the only one who can't hack it. It sometimes gets him so tired he *doesn't even fucking shave!* Who do you think you are that you don't shave! I'll tell you who you are: you are *noth*ing you are *noth*ing you are *noth*ing. The best part of you dripped down your old man's *leg!*' Paul watched Hugh's flushed open-mouthed face; Hathaway's voice was lower now: 'Munson, do you know about the Goddamn elephants. Answer me Munson, or I'll have you puking every piece of chow the Marine Corps feeds your ugly face. Elephants, Munson. Those big grey fuckers that live in the boondocks. They are like Marines, Munson. They stick with the herd. And if one of that herd fucks up in such a way as to piss off the rest of the herd, you know what they do to him? They exile that son of a bitch. They kick his ass out. You know what he does then? Son of a bitch gets lonesome. So everywhere the herd goes he is sure to follow. But they won't let him back in, Munson. So pretty soon he gets so lonesome he goes crazy and he starts running around the boondocks pulling up trees and stepping on troops and you have to go in and shoot him. Munson, you have fucked up my herd and I don't want your scrawny ass in it, so you are going to march thirty paces to the rear of this platoon. Now move out.'

'I'm going home.'

He left Hathaway and walked past the platoon.

'Munson!'

He stopped and turned around.

'I'm going home. I'm going to chow and then I'm going to see the chaplain and I'm going home.'

He turned and walked down the road, toward the chow hall.

'Mun*son*!'

He did not look back. His hands were in his pockets, his head down; then he lifted it. He seemed to be sniffing the morning air. Hathaway's mouth was open, as though to yell again; then he turned to the platoon. He called them to attention and marched them down the road. Paul could see Hugh ahead of them, until he turned a corner around a building and was gone. Then Hathaway, in the rhythm of cadence, called again and again: 'You won't *talk* to Munson talk talk *talk* to Mun-son you won't *look* at Mun-son look look *look* at Mun-son—'

And, in the chow hall, no one did. Paul sat with the platoon,

listened to them talking in low voices about Hugh and, because
he couldn't see him, Hugh seemed to be everywhere, filling the
chow hall.

Later that morning, at close order drill, the platoon was not balanced. Hugh had left a hole in the file, and Paul moved up to fill
it, leaving the file one man short in the rear. Marching in fresh
starched utilities, his cartridge belt brushed clean, his oiled rifle on
his shoulder, and his boot heels jarring on the blacktop, he dissolved
into unity with the rest of the platoon. Under the sun they sweated
and drilled. The other three platoons of Bravo Company were drilling too, sergeants' voices lilted in the humid air, and Paul strode
and pivoted and ignored the tickling sweat on his nose. Hathaway's
cadence enveloped him within the clomping boots. His body flowed
with the sounds. 'March from the waist down, people. Dig in your
heels. That's it, people. Lean back. Swing your arms. That's it,
people—' With squared shoulders and sucked-in gut, his right elbow
and bicep pressed tight against his ribs, his sweaty right palm gripping the rifle butt, Paul leaned back and marched, his eyes on the
clipped hair and cap in front of him; certainty descended on him;
warmly, like the morning sun.

IF THEY KNEW YVONNE

to Andre and Jeb

I GREW UP IN Louisiana, and for twelve years I went to a boys' school taught by Christian Brothers, a Catholic religious order. In the eighth grade our teacher was Brother Thomas. I still have a picture he gave to each boy in the class at the end of that year; it's a picture of Thomas Aquinas, two angels, and a woman. In the left foreground Aquinas is seated, leaning back against one angel whose hands grip his shoulders; he looks very much like a tired boxer between rounds, and his upturned face looks imploringly at the angel. The second angel is kneeling at his feet and, with both hands, is tightening a sash around Aquinas's waist. In the left background of the picture, the woman is escaping up a flight of stone stairs; her face is turned backward for a final look before she bolts from the room. According to Brother Thomas, some of Aquinas's family were against his becoming a priest, so they sent a woman to his room. He drove her out, then angels descended, encircled his waist with a cord, and squeezed all concupiscence from his body so he would never be tempted again. On the back of the picture, under the title *Angelic Warfare*, is a prayer for purity.

Brother Thomas was the first teacher who named for us the sins included in the Sixth and Ninth Commandments which, in the Catholic recording of the Decalogue, forbid adultery and coveting your neighbor's wife. In an introductory way, he simply listed the various sins. Then he focused on what apparently was the most significant: he called it self-abuse and, quickly sweeping our faces, he saw that we understood. It was a mortal sin, he said, because first of all it wasted the precious seed which God had given us for marriage. Also, sexual pleasure was reserved for married people alone, to have children by performing the marriage act. Self-abuse was not even a natural act; it was unnatural, and if a boy did it he was no better than a monkey. It was a desecration of our bodies, which were temples of the Holy Ghost, a mortal sin that resulted in the loss of sanctifying grace and therefore could send us to hell. He walked a few paces from his desk, his legs hidden by the long black robe, then he went back and stood behind the desk again and pulled down on his white collar: the front of it hung straight down from his throat like two white and faceless playing cards.

'Avoid being alone,' he said. 'When you go home from school, don't just sit around the house—go out and play ball, or cut the grass, or wash your dad's car. Do *anything*, but use up your energy. And pray to the Blessed Mother: take your rosary to bed at night and say it while you're going to sleep. If you fall asleep before you finish, the Blessed Mother won't mind—that's what she *wants* you to do.'

Then he urged us to receive the Holy Eucharist often. He told us of the benefits gained through the Eucharist: sanctifying grace, which helped us fight temptation; release from the temporal punishment of purgatory; and therefore, until we committed another mortal or venial sin, a guarantee of immediate entrance into heaven. He hoped and prayed, he said, that he would die with the Holy Eucharist on his tongue.

He had been talking with the excited voice yet wandering eyes of a man repeating by rote what he truly believes. But now his eyes focused on something out the window, as though a new truth had actually appeared to him on the dusty school ground of that hot spring day. One hand rose to scratch his jaw.

'In a way,' he said softly, 'you'd actually be doing someone a favor if you killed him when he had just received the Eucharist.'

I made it until midsummer, about two weeks short of my fourteenth birthday. I actually believed I would make it forever. Then one hot summer night when my parents were out playing bridge, Janet was on a date, and I was alone in the house, looking at *Holiday*

magazine—girls in advertisements drinking rum or lighting cigarettes, girls in bulky sweaters at ski resorts, girls at beaches. girls
on horseback—I went to the bathroom, telling myself I was only
going to piss, lingering there, thinking it was pain I felt but then I
knew it wasn't, that for the first wakeful time in my life it was about
to happen, then it did, and I stood weak and trembling and, shutting
my eyes, saw the faces of the Virgin Mary and Christ and Brother
Thomas, then above them, descending to join them, the awful diaphanous bulk of God.

That was a Tuesday. I set the alarm clock and woke next morning
at six-thirty, feeling that everyone on earth and in heaven had watched
my sin, and had been watching me as I slept. I dressed quickly and
crept past Janet's bedroom; she slept on her side, one sun-dark arm
on top of the sheet; then past the closed door of my parents' room
and out of the house. Riding my bicycle down the driveway I
thought of being struck by a car, so I rode on the sidewalk to church
and I got there in time for confession before Mass. When I got home
Janet was sitting on the front steps, drinking orange juice. I rode
across the lawn and stopped in front of her and looked at her smooth
brown legs.

'Where'd you go?'

'To Mass.'

'Special day today?'

'I woke up,' I said. 'So I went.'

A fly buzzed at my ear and I remembered Brother Thomas quot-
ing some saint who had said if you couldn't stand an insect buzzing
at your ear while you were trying to sleep, how could you stand
the eternal punishment of hell?

'You set the alarm,' she said. 'I heard it.'

Then Mother called us in to breakfast. She asked where I had
been, then said: 'Well, that's nice. Maybe you'll be a priest.'

'Ha,' Daddy said.

'Don't worry, Daddy,' Janet said. 'We don't hate Episcopalians
anymore.'

I got through two more days, until Friday, then Saturday afternoon I had to go to confession again. Through the veil over the
latticed window Father Broussard told me to pray often to the Virgin
Mary, to avoid those people and places and things that were occasions of sin, to go to confession and receive Communion at least

once a week. The tone of his whispering voice was kind, and the confessional itself was constructed to offer some comfort, for it enclosed me with my secret, and its interior was dark as my soul was, and Christ crucified stared back at me, inches from my face. Father Broussard told me to say ten Our Fathers and ten Hail Marys for my penance. I said them kneeling in a pew at the rear, then I went outside and walked around the church to the cemetery. In hot sun I moved among old graves and took out my rosary and began to pray.

Sunday we went to eleven o'clock Mass. Janet and I received Communion, but Mother had eaten toast and coffee, breaking her fast, so she didn't receive. Most Sundays she broke her fast because we went to late Mass, and in those days you had to fast from midnight until you received Communion; around ten in the morning she would feel faint and have to eat something. After Mass, Janet started the car and lit a cigarette and waited for our line in the parking lot to move. I envied her nerve. She was only sixteen, but when she started smoking my parents couldn't stop her.

'I just can't keep the fast,' Mother said. 'I must need vitamins.'

She was sitting in the front seat, opening and closing her black fan.

'Maybe you do,' Janet said.

'Maybe so. If you have to smoke, I wish you'd do it at home.'

Janet smiled and drove in first gear out of the parking lot. Her window was down and on the way home I watched her dark hair blowing in the breeze.

That was how my fourteenth summer passed: baseball in the mornings, and friends and movies and some days of peace, of hope—then back to the confessional where the smell of sweat hung in the air like spewed-out sin. Once I saw the student body president walking down the main street; he recognized my face and told me hello, and I blushed not with timidity but shame, for he walked with a confident stride, he was strong and good while I was weak. A high school girl down the street gave me a ride one day, less than an hour after I had done it, and I sat against the door at my side and could not look at her; I answered her in a low voice and said nothing on my own and I knew she thought I was shy, but that was better than the truth, for I believed if she knew what sat next to her she would recoil in disgust. When fall came I was glad, for

I hoped the school days would break the pattern of my sins. But I was also afraid the Brothers could see the summer in my eyes; then it wasn't just summer, but fall and winter too, for the pattern wasn't broken and I could not stop.

In the confessional the hardest priest was an old Dutchman who scolded and talked about manliness and will power and once told me to stick my finger in the flame of a candle, then imagine the eternal fire of hell. I didn't do it. Father Broussard was firm, sometimes impatient, but easy compared to the Dutchman. The easiest was a young Italian, Father Grassi, who said very little: I doubt if he ever spoke to me for over thirty seconds, and he gave such light penances—three or four Hail Marys—that I began to think he couldn't understand English well enough to know what I told him.

Then it was fall again, I was fifteen, and Janet was a freshman at the college in town. She was dating Bob Mitchell, a Yankee from Michigan. He was an airman from the SAC Base, so she had to argue with Mother for the first week or so. He was a high school graduate, intelligent, and he planned to go to the University of Michigan when he got out. That's what she told Mother, who believed a man in uniform was less trustworthy than a local civilian. One weekend in October Mother and Daddy went to Baton Rouge to see L.S.U. play Ole Miss. It was a night game and they were going to spend Saturday night with friends in Baton Rouge. They left after lunch Saturday and as soon as they drove off, Janet called Bob and broke their date, then went to bed. She had the flu, she said, but she hadn't told them because Mother would have felt it was her duty to stay home.

'Would you bring me a beer?' she said. 'I'll just lie in bed and drink beer and you won't have to bother with me at all.'

I sat in the living room and listened to Bill Stern broadcast Notre Dame and S.M.U. I kept checking on Janet to see if she wanted another beer; she'd smile at me over her book—*The Idiot*—then shake her beer can and say yes. When the game was over I told her I was going to confession and she gave me some money for cigarettes. I had enough to be ashamed of without people thinking I smoked too. When I got home I told her I had forgotten.

'Would you see if Daddy left any?'

I went into their room. On the wall above the double bed was a small black crucifix with a silver Christ (Daddy called it a graven image, but he smiled when he said it); stuck behind the crucifix was a blade from a palm frond, dried brown and crisp since Palm Sunday. I opened the top drawer of Daddy's bureau and took out the carton of Luckies. Then something else red-and-white caught my eye: the corner of a small box under his rolled-up socks. For a moment I didn't take it out. I stood looking at that corner of cardboard, knowing immediately what it was and also knowing that I wasn't learning anything new, that I had known for some indefinite and secret time, maybe a few months or a year or even two years. I stood there in the history of my knowledge, then I put down the cigarette carton and took the box of condoms from the drawer. I had slid the cover off the box and was looking at the vertically arranged rolled condoms when I heard the bedsprings, but it was too late, her bare feet were already crossing the floor, and all I could do was raise my eyes to her as she said: 'Can't you find—' then stopped.

At first she blushed, but only for a second or two. She came into the room, gently took the box from me, put the cover on, and looked at it for a moment. Then she put it in the drawer, covered it with socks, got a pack of cigarettes, and started back to her room.

'Why don't you bring me a beer,' she said over her shoulder. 'And we'll have a little talk.'

When I brought the beer she was propped up in bed, and *The Idiot* was closed on the bedside table.

'Are you really surprised?' she said.

I shook my head.

'Does it bother you?'

'Yes.'

'You're probably scrupulous. You confess enough for Eichmann, you know.'

I blushed and looked away.

'Do you know that some people—theologians—believe a mortal sin is as rare as a capital crime? That most things we do aren't really that evil?'

'They must not be Catholics.'

'Some of them are. Listen: Mother's only mistake is she thinks it's a sin, so she doesn't receive Communion. And I guess that's why she doesn't get a diaphragm—that would be too committed.'

This sort of talk scared me, and I was relieved when she stopped.

She told me not to worry about Mother and especially not to blame Daddy, not to think of him as a Protestant who had led Mother away from the Church. She said the Church was wrong. Several times she used the word love, and that night in bed I thought: love? love? For all I could think of was semen and I remembered long ago a condom lying in the dust of a country road; a line of black ants was crawling into it. I got out of bed, turned on a lamp, and read the *Angelic Warfare* prayer, which ends like this: *O God, Who has vouchsafed to defend with the blessed cord of St. Thomas those who are engaged in the terrible conflict of chastity! grant to us Thy suppliants, by his help, happily to overcome in this warfare the terrible enemy of our body and souls, that, being crowned with the lily of perpetual purity, we may deserve to receive from Thee, amongst the chaste bands of the angels, the palm of bliss. . . .*

Janet didn't do so well in the war. That January she and Bob Mitchell drove to Port Arthur, Texas, and got married by a justice of the peace. Then they went to Father Broussard for a Catholic marriage, but when he found out Janet was pregnant he refused. He said he didn't think this marriage would last, and he would not make it permanent in the eyes of God. My parents and I knew nothing of this until a couple of weeks later, when Bob was discharged from the Air Force. One night they told us, and two days later Janet was gone, up to Michigan; she wrote that although Bob wasn't a Catholic, he had agreed to try again, and this time a priest had married them. Seven months after the Texas wedding she had twin sons and Mother went up there on the bus and stayed two weeks and sent us postcards from Ann Arbor.

You get over your sister's troubles, even images of her getting pregnant in a parked car, just as after a while you stop worrying about whether or not your mother is living in sin. I had my own troubles and one summer afternoon when I was sixteen, alone in the house, having done it again after receiving Communion that very morning, I lay across my bed, crying and striking my head with my fist. It was a weekday, so the priests weren't hearing confessions until next morning before Mass. I could have gone to the rectory and confessed to a priest in his office, but I could not do that, I had to have the veiled window between our faces. Finally I got up and went to the phone in the hall. I dialed the rectory and when Father Broussard answered I told him I couldn't get to church but I had to confess and I wanted to do it right now, on the phone. I barely heard the suspicious turn in his voice when he told me to come to the rectory.

'I can't,' I said.

'What about tomorrow? Could you come tomorrow before Mass, or during the day?'

'I can't, Father. I can't wait that long.'

'Who is this?'

For a moment we were both quiet. Then I said: 'That's all right.' It was an expression we boys used, and it usually meant none of your business. I had said it in a near-whisper, not sure if I could speak another word without crying.

'All right,' he said, 'let me hear your confession.'

I kneeled on the floor, my eyes closed, the telephone cord stretched tautly to its full length:

'Bless me Father, for I have sinned; my last confession was yesterday—' now I was crying silent tears, those I hadn't spent on the bed; I could still talk but my voice was in shards '—my sins are: I committed self-abuse one time—' the word *time* trailing off, whispered into the phone and the empty hall which grew emptier still, for Father Broussard said nothing and I kneeled with eyes shut tight and the receiver hurting my hot ear until finally he said:

'All right, but I can't give you absolution over the phone. Will you come to the rectory at about three?'

'Yes, Father.'

'And ask for Father Broussard.'

'Yes, Father, thank you, Father—' still holding the receiver after he hung up, my eyes shut on black and red shame; then I stood weakly and returned to the bed—I would not go to the rectory— and lay there feeling I was the only person alive on this humid summer day. I could not stop crying, and I began striking my head again. I spoke aloud to God, begging him to forgive me, then kill me and spare me the further price of being a boy. Then something occurred to me: an image tossed up for my consideration, looked at, repudiated—all in an instant while my fist was poised. I saw myself sitting on the bed, trousers dropped to the floor, my shar-pedged hunting knife in my right hand, then with one quick de-termined slash cutting off that autonomous penis and casting it on the floor to shrivel and die. But before my fist struck again I threw that image away. No voices told me why. I had no warning vision of pain, of bleeding to death, of being an impotent freak. I simply knew; it is there between your legs and you do not cut it off.

II

YVONNE MILLET FINALLY put it to good use. We were both nineteen, both virgins; we started dating the summer after our freshman year at the college in town. She was slender, with black hair cut short in what they called an Italian Boy. She was a Catholic, and had been taught by nuns for twelve years, but she wasn't bothered as much as I was. In the parked car we soaked our clothes with sweat, and sometimes I went home with spotted trousers which I rolled into a bundle and dropped in the basket for dry cleaning. I confessed this and petting too, and tried on our dates to keep dry, so that many nights I crawled aching and nauseated into my bed at home. I lay very still in my pain, feeling quasi-victorious: I believed Yvonne and I were committing mortal sins by merely touching each other, but at least for another night we had resisted the graver sin of orgasm. On other nights she took me with her hand or we rubbed against each other in a clothed pantomine of lovemaking until we came. This happened often enough so that for the first time in nearly seven years I stopped masturbating. And Saturday after Saturday I went proudly to confession and told of my sins with Yvonne. I confessed to Father Grassi, who still didn't talk much, but one Saturday afternoon he said: 'How old are you, my friend?'

'Nineteen, Father.'

'Yes. And the young girl?'

I told him she was nineteen. Now I was worried: I had avoided confessing to Father Broussard or the Dutchman because I was afraid one of them would ask about the frequency of our sins, then tell me either to be pure or break up with her and, if I did neither of these, I could not be absolved again. I had thought Father Grassi would not ask questions.

'Do you love her?'

'Yes, Father.'

'At your age I think it is very hard to know if you really love someone. So I recommend that you and your girl think about getting married in two or three years' time and then, my friend, until you are ready for a short engagement and then marriage, I think each of you should go out with other people. Mostly with each other, of course, but with other people too. That may not help you to stay pure, but at least it will help you know if you love each other.'

'Yes, Father.'

'Because this other thing that's going on now, that's not love, you see. So you should test it in other ways.'

I told him I understood and I would talk to my girl about it. I never did, though. Once in a while Yvonne confessed but I have no idea what she told the priest, for she did not see things the way I saw them. One night, when I tried to stop us short, she pulled my hand back to its proper place and held it there until she was ready for it to leave. Then she reached to the dashboard for a cigarette, tapped it, and paused as though remembering to offer me one.

'Don't you want me to do it for you?' she said.

'No, I'm all right.'

She smoked for a while, her head on my shoulder.

'Do you really think it's a worse sin when it happens to you?' she said.

'Yes.'

'Why?'

I told her what the Brothers had taught me.

'You believe that?' she said. 'That God gave you this seed just to have babies with, and if you waste it He'll send you to hell?'

'I guess so.'

'You have wet dreams, don't you?'

'That's different. There's no will involved.'

'What about me? It just happened to me, and I didn't use up any eggs or anything, so where's my sin?'

'I don't know. Maybe sins are different for girls.'

'Then it wouldn't be a sin for me to masturbate either. Right? I don't, but isn't that true?'

'I never thought of that.'

'Well, don't. You think too much already.'

'Maybe you don't think enough.'

'You're right: I don't.'

'I'll tell you why it's a sin,' I said. 'Because it's reserved for married people.'

'Climax?'

'Yes.'

'But you're supposed to be married to touch each other too,' she said. 'So why draw the line at climax? I mean, why get all worked up and then stop and think that's good?'

'You're right. We shouldn't do any of it.'

'Oh, I'm not sure it's as bad as all that.'

'You're not? You don't think it's a sin, what we do?'

'Maybe a little, but it's not as bad as a lot of other things.'

'It's a mortal sin.'

'I don't think so. I believe it's a sin to talk about a girl, but I don't think what you do with her is so bad.'

'All right: if that's what you think, why don't we just go all the way?'

She sat up to throw her cigarette out the window, then she nestled her face on my chest.

'Because I'm scared,' she said.

'Of getting pregnant?'

'I don't think so. I'm just scared of not being a virgin, that's all.'

Then she finished our argument, won it, soaked her small handkerchief in my casuistry. Next morning at breakfast I was tired.

'You're going to ruin your health,' Mother said. 'It was after one when you got home.'

I flexed my bicep and said I was fine. But now Daddy was watching me from his end of the table.

'I don't care about your health,' he said. 'I just hope you know more than Janet did.'

'*Honey*,' Mother said.

'She got it reversed. She started babies before she was married, then quit.'

That was true. Her twin boys were four now, and there were no other children. Bob had finished his undergraduate work and was going to start work on a Ph.D. in political science. Early in the summer Mother had gone up there and stayed two weeks. When she got back and talked about her visit she looked nervous, as though she were telling a lie, and a couple of times I walked into the kitchen where Mother and Daddy were talking and they stopped until I had got what I wanted and left.

'I won't get pregnant,' I said.

'Neither will Yvonne,' Daddy said. 'As long as you keep your pants on.'

Then finally one night in early fall we drove away from her house, where we had parked for some time, and I knew she would not stop me, because by leaving her house she was risking questions from her parents, and by accepting that she was accepting the other risk too. I drove out to a country road, over a vibrating wooden bridge, the bayou beneath us dark as earth on that moonless night, on through black trees until I found a dirt road into the woods, keeping my hand on her small breast as I turned and cut off the ignition and headlights. In a moment she was naked on the car seat, then I was out of my clothes, even the socks, and seeing her trusting face and shockingly white body I almost dressed and took her home but then she said: Love me, Harry, love me—

The Brothers hadn't prepared me for this. If my first time had been with a whore, their training probably would have worked, for that was the sort of lust they focused on. But they were no match for Yvonne, and next morning I woke happier than I had ever been. At school that day we drank coffee and held hands and whispered. That night on the way to her house I stopped at a service station and bought a package of condoms from a machine in the men's room. That was the only time I felt guilty. But I was at least perceptive enough to know why: condoms, like masturbation and whores, were something the Brothers knew about. I left that piss-smelling room, walked into the clear autumn night, and drove to Yvonne's, where they had never been.

For the rest of the fall and a few weeks of winter, we were hot and happy lovers. I marveled at my own joy, my lack of remorse. Once, after a few weeks, I asked her if she ever felt bad. It was late at night and we were sitting at a bar, eating oysters on the halfshell. For a moment she didn't know what I meant, then she smiled.

'I feel wonderful,' she said.

She dipped her last oyster in the sauce, and leaned over the tray to eat it.

'Do we have enough money for more?' she said.

'Sure.'

They were ninety cents a dozen. We watched the Negro open them, and I felt fine, eating oysters and drinking beer at one in the morning, having made love an hour ago to this pretty girl beside me. I looked at her hair and wondered if she ought to let it grow.

'Sometimes I worry though,' she said.

'Getting pregnant?'

'Nope, I never said you had to use those things. I worry about you.'

'Why me?'

'Because you used to think about sins so much, and now you don't.'

'That's because I love you.'

She licked the red sauce from her fingers, then took my hand, squeezed it, and drank some beer.

'I'm afraid someday you'll start feeling bad again, then you'll hate me.'

She was right to look for defeat in that direction, to expect me to move along clichéd routes. But, as it turned out, it wasn't guilt that finally soured us. After a couple of months I simply began noticing things.

I saw that she didn't really like football. She only enjoyed the games because they gave her a chance to dress up, and there was a band, and a crowd of students, and it was fun to keep a flask hidden while you poured bourbon into a paper cup. She cheered with the rest of us, but she wasn't cheering for the same thing. She cheered because we were there, and a young man had run very fast with a football. Once we stood up to watch an end chasing a long pass: when he dived for it, caught it, and skidded on the ground, she turned happily to me and brushed her candied apple against my sleeve. Watch out, I said. She spit on her handkerchief and rubbed the sticky wool. She loved sweets, always asked me to buy her Mounds or Hersheys at the movies, and once in a while she'd get a pimple which she tried to conceal with powder. I felt loose flesh at her waist when we danced, and walking beside her on the campus one afternoon I looked down and saw her belly pushing against her tight skirt; I lightly backhanded it and told her to suck her gut in. She stood at attention, saluted, then gave me the finger. I'm about to start my period, she said. Except for the soft flesh at her waist she was rather thin, and when she lay on her back her naked breasts spread and flattened, as though they were melting.

Around the end of November her parents spent a weekend with relatives in Houston, leaving Yvonne to take care of her sister and brother, who were fourteen and eleven. They left Saturday morning, and that night Yvonne cooked for me. She was dressed up, black cocktail dress, even heels, and she was disappointed when she saw I hadn't worn a coat. But she didn't say anything. She had already fed her brother and sister, and they were in the den at the back of the house, watching television. Yvonne had a good fire in the living room fireplace, and on the coffee table she had bourbon, a pitcher of water, a bucket of ice, and a sugar bowl.

'Like they do in Faulkner,' she said, and we sat on the couch and drank a couple of toddies before dinner. Then she left me for a while and I looked into the fire, hungry and horny, and wondered what time the brother and sister would go to bed and if Yvonne would do it while they were sleeping. She came back to the living room, smiled, blushed, and said: 'If you're brave enough, I am. Want to try it?'

We ate by candlelight: oyster cocktails, then a roast with rice and thick dark gravy, garlic-tinged. We had lemon ice-box pie and went back to the fireplace with second cups of coffee.

'I love to cook,' she said from the record player. She put on about five albums, and I saw that we were supposed to sit at the fire and talk for the rest of the evening. The first album was Jackie Gleason, *Music, Martinis, and Memories*, and she sat beside me, took my hand and sipped her coffee. She rested her head on the back of the couch, but I didn't like to handle a coffee cup leaning back that way, so I withdrew my hand from hers and hunched forward over the coffee table.

'I think I started cooking when I was seven,' she said to my back. 'No, let's see, I was eight—' I looked down at her crossed legs, the black dress just covering her knees, then looked at the fire. 'When we lived in Baton Rouge. I had a children's cookbook and I made something called Chili Concoction. Everybody was nice about it, and Daddy ate two helpings for supper and told me to save the rest for breakfast and he'd eat it with eggs. He did, too. Then I made something called a strawberry minute pie, and I think it was pretty good. I'll make it for you some time.'

'Okay.'

I was still hunched over drinking coffee, so I wasn't looking at her. I finished the coffee and she asked if I wanted more, and that irritated me, so I didn't know whether to say yes or no. I said I guess so. Then watching her leave with my cup, I disliked myself and her too. For if I wasn't worthy of the evening, then wasn't she stupid and annoyingly vulnerable to give it to me? The next album was Sinatra; I finished my coffee, then leaned back so our shoulders touched, our hands together in her lap, and we listened. Once she took a drag from my cigarette and I said keep it, and lit another. The third album was Brubeck. She put some more ice in the bucket, I made toddies, and she asked if I understood *The Bear*. I shrugged and said probably not. She had finished it the day before, and she started talking about it.

'Hey,' I said. 'When are they going to sleep?'

She was surprised, and again I disliked myself and her too. Then she was hurt, and she looked at her lap and said she didn't know, but she couldn't make love anyway, not here in the house, even if they were sleeping.

'We can leave for a while,' I said. 'We won't go far.'

She kept looking at her lap, at our clasped hands.

'They'll be all right,' I said.

Then she looked into my eyes and I looked away and she said: 'Okay, I'll tell them.'

When she came back with a coat over her arm I was waiting at the door, my jacket zipped, the car key in my hand.

We broke up in January, about a week after New Year's. I don't recall whether we fought, or kissed goodbye, or sat in a car staring mutely out the windows. But I do remember when the end started; or, rather, when Yvonne decided to recognize it.

On New Year's Eve a friend of ours gave a party. His parents were out of town, so everyone got drunk. It was an opportunity you felt obliged not to pass up. Two or three girls got sick and had to have their faces washed and be walked outside in the cold air. When Yvonne got drunk it was a pleasant drunk, and I took her upstairs. I think no one noticed: it was past midnight, and people were hard to account for. We lay on the bed in the master bedroom, Yvonne with her skirt pulled up, her pants off, while I performed in shirt, sweater, and socks. She was quiet as we stood in the dark room, taking our pants off, and she didn't answer my whispered Happy New Year as we began to make love, for the first time, on a bed. Then, moving beneath me, she said in a voice so incongruous with her body that I almost softened but quickly got it back, shutting my ears to what I had heard: This is all we ever do, Harry—this is all we ever do.

The other thing I remember about that night is a time around three in the morning. A girl was cooking hamburgers, I was standing in the kitchen doorway talking to some boys, and Yvonne was sitting alone at the kitchen table. There were other people talking in the kitchen, but she wasn't listening; she moved only to tap ashes and draw on her cigarette, then exhaled into the space that held her gaze. She looked older than twenty, quite lonely and sad, and I pitied her. But there was something else: I knew she would never make love to me again. Maybe that is why, as a last form of possession, I told. It could not have been more than an hour later, I was drunker, and in the bathroom I one-upped three friends who were bragging about feeling tits of drunken girls. I told them I had taken Yvonne upstairs and screwed her. To add history to it, I even told them what she had said.

III

Waiting in line for my first confession in five months I felt some guilt but I wasn't at all afraid. I only had to confess sexual intercourse, and there was nothing shameful about that, nothing unnatural. It was a man's sin. Father Broussard warned me never to see this girl again (that's what he called her: this girl), for a man is weak and he needs much grace to turn away from a girl who will give him her body. He said I must understand it was a serious sin because sexual intercourse was given by God to married couples for the procreation of children and we had stolen it and used it wrongfully, for physical pleasure, which was its secondary purpose. I knew that in some way I had sinned, but Father Broussard's definition of that sin fell short and did not sound at all like what I had done with Yvonne. So when I left the confessional I still felt unforgiven.

The campus was not a very large one, but it was large enough so you could avoid seeing someone. I stopped going to the student center for coffee, and we had no classes together; we only saw each other once in a while, usually from a distance, walking between buildings. We exchanged waves and the sort of smile you cut into your face at times like that. The town was small too, so occasionally I saw her driving around, looking for a parking place or something. Then after a while I wanted to see her, and I started going to the student center again, but she didn't drink coffee there anymore. In a week or so I realized that I didn't really want to see her: I wanted her to be happy, and if I saw her there was nothing I could say to help that.

Soon I was back to the old private vice, though now it didn't seem a vice but an indulgence, not as serious as smoking or even drinking, closer to eating an ice cream sundae before bed every night. That was how I felt about it, like I had eaten two scoops of ice cream with thick hot fudge on it, and after a couple of bites it wasn't good anymore but I finished it anyway, thinking of calories. It was a boring little performance and it didn't seem worth thinking about, one way or the other. But I told it in the confessional, so I could still receive the Eucharist. Then one day in spring I told the number of my sins as though I were telling the date of my birth, my height, and weight, and Father Broussard said quickly and sternly: 'Are you sorry for these sins?'

'Yes, Father,' I said, but then I knew it was a lie. He was asking me if I had a firm resolve to avoid this sin in the future when I said: 'No, Father.'

'No what? You can't avoid it?'

'I mean no, Father, I'm really sorry. I don't even think it's a sin.'

'Oh, I see. You don't have the discipline to stop, so you've decided it's not a sin. Just like that, you've countermanded God's law. Do you want absolution?'

'Yes, Father. I want to receive Communion.'

'You can't. You're living in mortal sin, and I cannot absolve you while you keep this attitude. I want you to think very seriously—'

But I wasn't listening. I was looking at the crucifix and waiting for his voice to stop so I could leave politely and try to figure out what to do next. Then he stopped talking, and I said: 'Yes, Father.'

'*What?*' he said. '*What?*'

I went quickly through the curtains, out of the confessional, out of the church.

On Sundays I went to Mass but did not receive the Eucharist. I thought I could but I was afraid that as soon as the Host touched my tongue I would suddenly realize I had been wrong, and then I'd be receiving Christ with mortal sin on my soul. Mother didn't receive either. I prayed for her and hoped she'd soon have peace, even if it meant early menopause. By now I agreed with Janet, and I wished she'd write Mother a letter and convince her that she wasn't evil. I thought Mother was probably praying for Janet, who had gone five years without bearing a child.

It was June, school was out, and I did not see Yvonne at all. I was working with a surveying crew, running a hundred-foot chain through my fingers, cutting trails with a machete, eating big lunches from paper bags, and waiting for something to happen. There were two alternatives, and I wasn't phony enough for the first or brave enough for the second: I could start confessing again, the way I used to, or I could ignore the confessional and simply receive Communion. But nothing happened and each Sunday I stayed with Mother in the pew while the others went up to the altar rail.

Then Janet came home. She wrote that Bob had left her, had moved in with his girlfriend—a graduate student—and she and the boys were coming home on the bus. That was the news waiting for me when I got home from work, Mother handing me the letter as I came through the front door, both of them watching me as I read it. Then Daddy cursed, Mother started crying again, and I took a beer out to the front porch. After a while Daddy came out too and we sat without talking and drank beer until Mother called us to supper. Daddy said, 'That son of a bitch,' and we went inside.

By the time Janet and the boys rode the bus home from Ann Arbor, Mother was worried about something else: the Church, because now Janet was twenty-three years old and getting a divorce and if she ever married again she was out of the Church. Unless Bob died, and Daddy said he didn't care what the Church thought about divorce, but it seemed a good enough reason for him to go up to Ann Arbor, Michigan, and shoot Bob Mitchell between the eyes. So while Janet and Paul and Lee were riding south on the Greyhound, Mother was going to daily Mass and praying for some answer to Janet's future.

But Janet had already taken care of that too. When she got off the bus I knew she'd be getting married again some day: she had gained about ten pounds, probably from all that cheap food while Bob went to school, but she had always been on the lean side anyway and now she looked better than I remembered. Her hair was long, about halfway down her back. The boys were five years old now, and I was glad she hadn't had any more, because they seemed to be good little boys and not enough to scare off a man. We took them home—it was a Friday night—and Daddy gave Janet a tall drink of bourbon and everybody talked as though nothing had happened. Then we ate shrimp *étouffée* and after supper, when the boys were in bed and the rest of us were in the living room, Janet said by God it was the best meal she had had in five years, and next time she was going to marry a man who liked Louisiana cooking. When she saw the quick look in Mother's eyes, she said: 'We didn't get married in the Church, Mama. I just told you we did so you wouldn't worry.'

'You *didn't*?'

'Bob was so mad at Father Broussard he wouldn't try again. He's not a Catholic, you know.'

'There's more wrong with him than that,' Daddy said.

'So I can still get married in the Church,' Janet said. 'To somebody else.'

'But Janet—'

'Wait,' Daddy said. 'Wait. You've been praying for days so Janet could stop living with that son of a bitch and still save her soul. Now you got it—right?'

'But—'

'Right?'

'Well,' Mother said, 'I guess so.'

They went to bed about an hour past their usual time, but Janet and I stayed up drinking gin and tonic in the kitchen, with the door closed so we wouldn't keep anybody awake. At first she just talked about how glad she was to be home, even if the first sign of it was the Negroes going to the back of the bus. She loved this hot old sticky night, she said, and the June bugs thumping against the screen and she had forgotten how cigarettes get soft down here in the humid air. Finally she talked about Bob; she didn't think he had ever loved her, he had started playing around their first year up there, and it had gone on for five years more or less; near the end she had even done it too, had a boyfriend, but it didn't help her survive at all, it only made things worse, and now at least she felt clean and tough and she thought that was the first step toward hope.

The stupid thing was she still loved the philandering son of a bitch. That was the only time she cried, when she said that, but she didn't even cry long enough for me to get up and go to her side of the table and hold her: when I was half out of my chair she was already waving me back in it, shaking her head and wiping her eyes, and the tears that had filled them for a moment were gone. Then she cheered up and asked if I'd drive her around tomorrow, down the main street and everything, and I said sure and asked her if she was still a Catholic.

'Don't tell Mother this,' she said. 'She's confused enough already. I went to Communion every Sunday, except when I was having that stupid affair, and I only felt sinful then because he loved me and I was using him. But before that and after that, I received.'

'You can't,' I said. 'Not while you're married out of the Church.'

'Maybe I'm wrong, but I don't think the Church is so smart about sex. Bob wouldn't get the marriage blessed, so a priest would have told me to leave him. I loved him, though, and for a long time I thought he loved me, needed me—so I stayed with him and tried to keep peace and bring up my sons. And the Eucharist is the sacrament of love and I needed it very badly those five years and nobody can keep me away.'

I got up and took our glasses and made drinks. When I turned from the sink she was watching me.

'Do you still go to confession so much?' she said.

I sat down, avoiding her eyes, then I thought, what the hell, if you can't tell Janet you can't tell anybody. So looking at the screen door and the bugs thumping from the dark outside, I told her how it was in high school and about Yvonne, though I didn't tell her name, and my aborted confession to Father Broussard. She was kind to me, busying herself with cigarettes and her drink while I talked. Then she said: 'You're right, Harry. You're absolutely right.'

'You really think so?'

'I know this much: too many of those celibates teach sex the way it is for them. They make it introverted, so you come out of their schools believing sex is something between you and yourself, or between you and God. Instead of between you and other people.

Like my affair. It wasn't wrong because I was married. Hell, Bob didn't care, in fact he was glad because it gave him more freedom. It was wrong because I hurt the guy.' A Yankee word on her tongue, *guy*, and she said it with that accent from up there among snow and lakes. 'If Bob had stayed home and taken a *Playboy* to the bathroom once in a while I might still have a husband. So if that's a sin, I don't understand sin.'

'Well,' I said. Then looking at her, I grinned and it kept spreading and turned into a laugh. 'You're something, all right,' I said. 'Old Janet, you're something.'

But I still wasn't the renegade Janet was, I wanted absolution from a priest, and next morning while Mother and Daddy were happily teasing us about our hangovers, I decided to get it done. That afternoon I called Father Grassi, then told Janet where I was going, and that I would drive her around town when I got back. Father Grassi answered the door at the rectory; he was wearing a white shirt with his black trousers, a small man with a ruddy face and dark whiskers. I asked if I could speak to him in his office.

'I think so,' he said. 'Do you come from the Pope?'

'No, Father. I just want to confess.'

'So it's you who will be the saint today, not me. Yes, come in.'

He led me to his office, put his stole around his neck, and sat in the swivel chair behind his desk; I knelt beside him on the carpet, and he shielded his face with his hand, as though we were in the confessional and he could not see me. I whispered, 'Bless me Father, for I have sinned,' my hands clasped at my waist, my head bowed. 'My last confession was six weeks ago, but I was refused absolution. By Father Broussard.'

'Is that so? You don't look like a very bad young man to me. Are you some kind of criminal?'

'I confessed masturbation, Father.'

'Yes? Then what?'

'I told him I didn't think it was a sin.'

'I see. Well, poor Father Broussard: I'd be confused too, if you confessed something as a sin and then said you didn't think it was a sin. You should take better care of your priests, my friend.'

I opened my eyes: his hand was still in place on his cheek, and he was looking straight ahead, over his desk at the bookshelf against the wall.

'I guess so,' I said. 'And now I'm bothering you.'

'Oh no: you're no trouble. The only disappointment is you weren't sent by the Pope. But since that's the way it is, then we may just as well talk about sins. We had in the seminary a book of moral theology and in that book, my friend, it was written that masturbation was worse than rape, because at least rape was the carrying out of a natural instinct. What about that?'

'Do you believe that, Father?'

'Do you?'

'No, Father.'

'Neither do I. I burned the book when I left the seminary, but not only for that reason. The book also said, among other things, let the buyer beware. So you tell me about sin and we'll educate each other.'

'I went to the Brothers' school.'

'Ah, yes. Nice fellows, those Brothers.'

'Yes, Father. But I think they concentrated too much on the body. One's own body, I mean. And back then I believed it all, and one day I even wanted to mutilate myself. Then last fall I had a girl.'

'What does that mean, you had a girl? You mean you were lovers?'

'Yes, Father. But I shouldn't have had a girl, because I believed my semen was the most important part of sex, so the first time I made love with her I was waiting for it, like my soul was listening for it—you see? Because I wouldn't know how I felt about her until I knew how I felt about ejaculating with her.'

'And how did you feel? Did you want to mutilate yourself with a can opener, or maybe something worse?'

'I was happy, Father.'

'Yes.'

'So after that we were lovers. Or she was, but I wasn't. I was just happy because I could ejaculate without hating myself, so I was still masturbating, you see, but with her—does that make sense?'

'Oh yes, my friend. I've known that since I left the seminary. Always there is too much talk of self-abuse. You see, even the term is a bad one. Have you finished your confession?'

'I want to confess about the girl again, because when I confessed it before it wasn't right. I made love to her without loving her and the last time I made love to her I told some boys about it.'

'Yes. Anything else?'

'No, Father.'

'Good. There is a line in St. John that I like very much. It is Christ praying to the Father and He says: 'I do not pray that You take them out of the world, but that You keep them from evil.' Do you understand that?'

'I think so, Father.'

'Then for your penance, say alleluia three times.'

Next afternoon Janet and I took her boys crabbing. We had an ice chest of beer and we set it under the small pavilion at the center of the wharf, then I put out six crab lines, tying them to the guard rail. I remembered the summer before she got married Janet and I had gone crabbing, then cooked them for the family: we had a large pot of water on the stove and when the water was boiling I held the gunny sack of live crabs over it and they came falling out, splashing into the water; they worked their claws, moved sluggishly, then died. And Janet had said: *I keep waiting for them to scream*.

It was a hot day, up in the nineties. Someone was water-skiing on the lake, which was saltwater and connected by canal to the Gulf, but we had the wharf to ourselves, and we drank beer in the shade while Paul and Lee did the crabbing. They lost the first couple, so I left the pavilion and squatted at the next line. The boys flanked me, lying on their bellies and looking down where the line went into the dark water; they had their shirts off, and their hot tan shoulders and arms brushed my legs. I gently pulled the line up until we saw a crab just below the surface, swimming and nibbling at the chunk of ham.

Okay, Lee. Put the net down in the water, then bring it up under him so you don't knock him away.'

He lowered the pole and scooped the net slowly under the crab. 'I got him!'

'That's it. You just have to go slow, that's all.'

He stood and lifted the net and laid it on the wharf.

'Look how big,' Paul said.

'He's a good one,' I said. 'Put him in the sack.'

But they crouched over the net, watching the crab push his claws through.

'Poor little crab,' Lee said. 'You're going to die.'

'Does it hurt 'em, Harry?' Paul said.

'I don't know.'

'It'd hurt me,' he said.

'I guess it does, for a second or two.'

'How long's a second?' Lee said.

I pinched his arm.

'About like that.'

'That's not too long,' he said.

'No. Put him in the sack now, and catch some more.'

I went back to my beer on the bench. Paul was still crouching over the crab, poking a finger at its back. Then Lee held open the gunny sack and Paul turned the net over and shook it and the crab fell in.

'Goodbye, big crab,' he said.

'Goodbye, poor crab,' Lee said.

They went to another line. For a couple of hours, talking to Janet, I watched them and listened to their bare feet on the wharf and their voices as they told each crab goodbye. Sometimes one of them would stop and look across the water and pull at his pecker, and I remembered that day hot as this one when I was sixteen and I wanted to cut mine off. I reached deep under the ice and got a cold beer for Janet and I thought of Yvonne sitting at that kitchen table at three in the morning, tired, her lipstick worn off, her eyes fixed on a space between the people in the room. Then I looked at the boys lying on their bellies and reaching down for another crab, and I hoped they would grow well, those strong little bodies, those kind hearts.

ROSE

In memory of Barbara Loden

S OMETIMES, WHEN I see people like Rose, I imagine
them as babies, as young children. I suppose many
of us do. We search the aging skin of the face, the unhappy eyes
and mouth. Of course I can never imagine their fat little faces at
the breast, or their cheeks flushed and eyes brightened from play.
I do not think of them after the age of five or six, when they are
sent to kindergartens, to school. There, beyond the shadows of their
families and neighborhood friends, they enter the world a second
time, their eyes blinking in the light of it. They will be loved or
liked or disliked, even hated; some will be ignored, others singled
out for daily abuse that, with a few adult exceptions, only children
have the energy and heart to inflict. Some will be corrupted, many
without knowing it, save for that cooling quiver of conscience when
they cheat, when they lie to save themselves, when out of fear they
side with bullies or teachers, and so forsake loyalty to a friend. Soon
they are small men and women, with our sins and virtues, and by
the age of thirteen some have our vices too.

There are also those unforgivable children who never suffer at
all: from the first grade on, they are good at schoolwork, at play
and sports, and always they are befriended, and are the leaders of
the class. Their teachers love them, and because they are humble
and warm, their classmates love them too, or at least respect them,
and are not envious because they assume these children will excel
at whatever they touch, and have long accepted this truth. They

come from all manner of families, from poor and illiterate to wealthy and what passes for literate in America, and no one knows why they are not only athletic and attractive but intelligent too. This is an injustice, and some of us pause for a few moments in our middle-aged lives to remember the pain of childhood, and then we intensely dislike these people we applauded and courted, and we hope some crack of mediocrity we could not see with our young eyes has widened and split open their lives, the homecoming queen's radiance sallowed by tranquilized bitterness, the quarterback fat at forty wheezing up a flight of stairs, and all of them living in the same small town or city neighborhood, laboring at vacuous work that turns their memories to those halcyon days when the classrooms and halls, the playgrounds and gymnasiums and dance floors were theirs: the last places that so obediently, even lovingly, welcomed the weight of their flesh, and its displacement of air. Then, with a smile, we rid ourselves of that evil wish, let it pass from our bodies to dissipate like smoke in the air around us, and, freed from the distraction of blaming some classmate's excellence for our childhood pain, we focus on the boy or girl we were, the small body we occupied, watch it growing through the summers and school years, and we see that, save for some strengths gained here, some weaknesses there, we are the same people we first knew as ourselves; or the ones memory allows us to see, to think we know.

People like Rose make me imagine them in those few years their memories will never disclose, except through hearsay: *I was born in Austin. We lived in a garage apartment. When I was two we moved to Tuscaloosa. . . .* Sometimes, when she is drinking at the bar, and I am standing some distance from her and can watch without her noticing, I see her as a baby, on the second or third floor of a tenement, in one of the Massachusetts towns along the Merrimack River. She would not notice, even if she turned and looked at my face; she would know me, she would speak to me, but she would not know I had been watching. Her face, sober or drunk or on the way to it, looks constantly watched, even spoken to, by her own soul. Or by something it has spawned, something that lives always with her, hovering near her face. I see her in a tenement because I cannot imagine her coming from any but a poor family, though I sense this notion comes from my boyhood, from something I learned about America, and that belief has hardened inside me, a stone I

cannot dissolve. Snobbishness is too simple a word for it. I have
never had much money. Nor do I want it. No: it's an old belief,
once a philosophy, which I've now outgrown: no one born to a
white family with adequate money could end as Rose has.

I know it's not true. I am fifty-one years old, yet I cannot feel I
am growing older because I keep repeating the awakening experi-
ences of a child: I watch and I listen, I write in my journal, and
each year I discover, with the awe of my boyhood, a part of the
human spirit I had perhaps imagined, but had never seen or heard.
When I was a boy, many of these discoveries thrilled me. Once in
school the teacher told us of the men who volunteered to help find
the cause of yellow fever. This was in the Panama Canal Zone.
Some of these men lived in the room where victims of yellow fever
had died; they lay on the beds, on sheets with dried black vomit,
breathed and slept there. Others sat in a room with mosquitoes and
gave their skin to those bites we simply curse and slap, and they
waited through the itching and more bites, and then waited to die,
in their agony leaving sheets like the ones that spared their comrades
living in the room of the dead. This story, with its heroism, its
infinite possibilities for human action, delighted me with the pure
music of hope. I am afraid now to research it, for I may find that
the men were convicts awaiting execution, or some other persons
whose lives were so limited by stronger outside forces that the risk
of death to save others could not have, for them, the clarity of a
choice made with courage, and in sacrifice, but could be only a
weary nod of assent to yet another fated occurrence in their lives.
But their story cheered me then, and I shall cling to that. Don't
you remember? When first you saw or heard or read about men
and women who, in the face of some defiant circumstance, fought
against themselves and won, and so achieved love, honor, courage?

I was in the Marine Corps for three years, a lieutenant during a
time in our country when there was no war but all the healthy
young men had to serve in the armed forces anyway. Many of us
who went to college sought commissions so our service would be
easier, we would have more money, and we could marry our girlfriends; in those days, a young man had to provide a roof and all
that goes under it before he could make love with his girl. Of course
there was lovemaking in cars, but the ring and the roof waited
somewhere beyond the windshield.

Those of us who chose the Marines went to Quantico, Virginia, for two six-week training sessions in separate summers during college; we were commissioned at graduation from college, and went back to Quantico for eight months of Officers' Basic School; only then would they set us free among the troops, and into the wise care of our platoon sergeants. During the summer training, which was called Platoon Leaders' Class, sergeants led us, harrassed us, and taught us. They also tried to make some of us quit. I'm certain that when they first lined us up and looked at us, their professional eyes saw the ones who would not complete the course: saw in a young boy's stiffened shoulders and staring and blinking eyes the flaw—too much fear, lack of confidence, who knows—that would, in a few weeks, possess him. Just as, on the first day of school, the bully sees his victim and eyes him like a cat whose prey has wandered too far from safety; it is not the boy's puny body that draws the bully, but the way the boy's spirit occupies his small chest, his thin arms.

Soon the sergeants left alone the stronger among us, and focused their energy on breaking the ones they believed would break, and ought to break now, rather than later, in that future war they probably did not want but never forgot. In another platoon, that first summer, a boy from Dartmouth completed the course, though in six weeks his crew-cut black hair turned gray. The boy in our platoon was from the University of Chicago, and he should not have come to Quantico. He was physically weak. The sergeants liked the smaller ones among us, those with short lean bodies. They called them feather merchants, told them You little guys are always tough, and issued them the Browning Automatic Rifle for marches and field exercises, because it weighed twenty pounds and had a cumbersome bulk to it as well: there was no way you could comfortably carry it. But the boy from Chicago was short and thin and weak, and they despised him.

Our platoon sergeant was a staff sergeant, his assistant a buck sergeant, and from the first day they worked on making the boy quit. We all knew he would fail the course; we waited only to see whether he would quit and go home before they sent him. He did not quit. He endured five weeks before the company commander summoned him to his office. He was not there long; he came into the squad bay where he lived and changed to civilian clothes, packed the suitcase and seabag, and was gone. In those five weeks he had dropped out of conditioning marches, forcing himself up hills in the Virginia heat, carrying seventy pounds of gear—probably half his weight—until he collapsed on the trail to the sound of shouted derision from our sergeants, whom I doubt he heard.

When he came to Quantico he could not chin himself, nor do ten push-ups. By the time he left he could chin himself five quivering times, his back and shoulders jerking, and he could do twenty push-ups before his shoulders and chest rose while his small flat belly stayed on the ground. I do not remember his name, but I remember those numbers: five and twenty. The sergeants humiliated him daily, gave him long and colorful ass-chewings, but their true weapon was his own body, and they put it to use. They ran him till he fell, then ran him again, a sergeant running alongside the boy, around and around the hot blacktop parade ground. They sent him up and down the rope on the obstacle course. He never climbed it, but they sent him as far up as he could go, perhaps halfway, perhaps less, and when he froze, then worked his way down, they sent him up again. That's the phrase: *as far up as he could go.*

He should not have come to Virginia. What was he thinking? Why didn't he get himself in shape during the school year, while he waited in Chicago for what he must have known would be the physical trial of his life? I understand now why the sergeants despised him, this weak college boy who wanted to be one of their officers. Most nights they went out drinking, and once or twice a week came into our squad bay, drunk at three in the morning, to turn on the lights and shout us out of our bunks, and we stood at attention and listened to their cheerful abuse. Three hours later, when we fell out for morning chow, they waited for us: lean and tanned and immaculate in their tailored and starched dungarees and spit-shined boots. And the boy could only go so far up the rope, up the series of hills we climbed, up toward the chinning bar, up the walls and angled poles of the obstacle course, up from the grass by the strength of his arms as the rest of us reached fifty, seventy, finally a hundred push-ups.

But in truth he could do all of it, and that is the reason for this anecdote while I contemplate Rose. One night in our fifth week the boy walked in his sleep. Every night we had fire watch: one of us walked for four hours through the barracks, the three squad bays that each housed a platoon, to alert the rest in case of fire. We heard the story next day, whispered, muttered, or spoken out of the boy's hearing, in the chow hall, during the ten-minute break on a march. The fire watch was a boy from the University of Alabama, a football player whose southern accent enriched his story, heightened his surprise, his awe. He came into our squad bay at three-thirty in the morning, looked up and down the rows of bunks, and was about to leave when he heard someone speak. The voice frightened him. He had never heard, except in movies, a voice so pitched by desperation, and so eerie in its insistence. He moved toward it. Behind our bunks, against both walls, were our wall lockers. The voice came from that space between the bunks and lockers, where there was room to stand and dress, and to prepare your locker for inspection. The Alabama boy stepped between the bunks and lockers and moved toward the figure he saw now: someone squatted before a locker, white shorts and white tee shirt in the darkness. Then he heard what the voice was saying. *I can't find it. I can't find it.* He closed the distance between them, squatted, touched the boy's shoulder, and whispered: *Hey, what you looking for?* Then he saw it was the boy from Chicago. He spoke his name, but the boy bent lower and looked under his wall locker. That was when the Alabama boy saw that he was not truly looking: his eyes were shut, the lids in the repose of sleep, while the boy's head shook from side to side, in a short slow arc of exasperation *I can't find it*, he said. He was kneeling before the wall locker, bending forward to look under it for—what? any of the several small things the sergeant demanded we care for and have with our gear: extra shoelaces, a web strap from a haversack, a metal button for dungarees, any of these things that became for us as precious as talismans. Still on his knees, the boy straightened his back, gripped the bottom of the wall locker, and lifted it from the floor, six inches or more above it, and held it there as he tried to lower his head to look under it. The locker was steel, perhaps six feet tall, and filled with his clothes, boots, and shoes, and on its top rested his packed haversack and helmet. No one in the platoon could have lifted it while kneeling, using only his arms. Most of us could have bear-hugged it up from the floor, even held it there. *Gawd damn*, the fire watch said, rising from his squat; *Gawd damn, lemmee help you with it*, and he held its sides; it was tottering, but still raised. Gently he lowered it against the boy's

204 · ANDRE DUBUS

resistance, then crouched again and, whispering to him, *like to a baby*, he told us, he said: *All rot, now. It'll be all rot now. We'll fin' that damn thing in the mawnin'*; as he tried to ease the boy's fingers from the bottom edge of the locker. Finally he pried them, one or two at a time. He pulled the boy to his feet, and with an arm around his waist, led him to his bunk. It was a lower bunk. He eased the boy downward to sit on it, then lifted his legs, covered him with the sheet, and sat down beside him. He rested a hand on the boy's chest, and spoke soothingly to him as he struggled, trying to rise. Finally the boy lay still, his hands holding the top of the sheet near his chest.

We never told him. He went home believing his body had failed; he was the only failure in our platoon, and the only one in the company who failed because he lacked physical strength and endurance. I've often wondered about him: did he ever learn what he could truly do? Has he ever absolved himself of his failure? His was another of the inspiring stories of my youth. Not *his* story so much as the story of his body. I had heard or read much about the human spirit, indomitable against suffering and death. But this was a story of a pair of thin arms, and narrow shoulders, and weak legs: freed from whatever consciousness did to them, they had lifted an unwieldy weight they could not have moved while the boy's mind was awake. It is a mystery I still do not understand.

Now, more often than not, my discoveries are bad ones, and if they inspire me at all, it is only to try to understand the unhappiness and often evil in the way we live. A friend of mine, a doctor, told me never again to believe that only the poor and uneducated and usually drunk beat their children; or parents who are insane, who hear voices commanding them to their cruelty. He has seen children, sons and daughters of doctors, bruised, their small bones broken, and he knows that the children are repeating their parents' lies: they fell down the stairs, they slipped and struck a table. He can do nothing for them but heal their injuries. The poor are frightened by authority, he said, and they will open their doors to a social worker. A doctor will not. And I have heard stories from young people, college students who come to the bar during the school year. They are rich, or their parents are, and they have about them those characteristics I associate with the rich: they look healthy, as though the power of money had a genetic influence on their very flesh;

beneath their laughter and constant talk there lies always a certain poise, not sophistication, but confidence in life and their places in it. Perhaps it comes from the knowledge that they will never be stranded in a bus station with two dollars. But probably its source is more intangible: the ambience they grew up in: that strange paradox of being from birth removed, insulted, from most of the world, and its agony of survival that is, for most of us, a day-to-day life; while, at the same time, these young rich children are exposed, through travel and—some of them—culture, to more of the world than most of us will ever see.

Years ago, when the students first found Timmy's and made it their regular drinking place, I did not like them, because their lives were so distant from those of the working men who patronize the bar. Then some of them started talking to me, in pairs, or a lone boy or girl, drinking near my spot at the bar's corner. I began enjoying their warmth, their general cheer, and often I bought them drinks, and always they bought mine in return. They called me by my first name, and each new class knows me, as they know Timmy's, before they see either of us. When they were alone, or with a close friend, they talked to me about themselves, revealed beneath that underlying poise deep confusion, and abiding pain their faces belied. So I learned of the cruelties of some of the rich: of children beaten, girls fondled by fathers who were never drunk and certainly did not smoke, healthy men who were either crazy or evil beneath their suits and briefcases, and their punctuality and calm confidence that crossed the line into arrogance. I learned of neglect: children reared by live-in nurses, by housekeepers who cooked; children in summer camps and boarding schools; and I saw the selfishness that wealth allows, a selfishness beyond greed, a desire to have children yet give them nothing, or very little, of oneself. I know one boy, an only child, whose mother left home when he was ten. She no longer wanted to be a mother; she entered the world of business in a city across the country from him, and he saw her for a weekend once a year. His father worked hard at making more money, and the boy left notes on the door of his father's den, asking for a time to see him. An appointment. The father answered with notes on the boy's door, and they met. Then the boy came to college here. He is very serious, very polite, and I have never seen him with a girl, or another boy, and I have never seen him smile.

So I have no reason to imagine Rose on that old stained carpet with places of it worn thin, nearly to the floor; Rose crawling among the legs of older sisters and brothers, looking up at the great and burdened height of her parents, their capacity, their will to love long beaten or drained from them by what they had to do to keep a dwelling with food in it, and heat in it, and warm and cool clothes for their children. I have only guessed at this part of her history. There is one reason, though: Rose's face is bereft of education, of thought. It is the face of a survivor walking away from a terrible car accident: without memory or conjecture, only shock, and the surprise of knowing that she is indeed alive. I think of her body as shapeless: beneath the large and sagging curve of her breasts, she has such sparse curvature of hips and waist that she appears to be an elongated lump beneath her loose dresses in summer, her old wool overcoat in winter. At the bar she does not remove her coat; but she unbuttons it and pushes it back from her breasts, and takes the blue scarf from her head, shakes her graying brown hair, and lets the scarf hang from her neck.

She appeared in our town last summer. We saw her on the streets, or slowly walking across the bridge over the Merrimack River. Then she found Timmy's and, with money from whatever source, became a regular, along with the rest of us. Sometimes, if someone drank beside her, she spoke. If no one drank next to her, she drank alone. Always screwdrivers. Then we started talking about her and, with that ear for news that impresses me still about small communities, either towns or city neighborhoods, some of us told stories about her. Rumors: she had been in prison, or her husband, or someone else in the family had. She had children but lost them. Someone had heard of a murder: perhaps she killed her husband, or one of the children did, or he or Rose or both killed a child. There was talk of a fire. And so we talked for months, into the fall, then early winter, when our leaves are gone, the reds and golds and yellows, and the trees are bare and gray, the evergreens dark green, and beyond their conical green we have lovely early sunsets. When the sky is gray, the earth is washed with it, and the evergreens look black. Then the ponds freeze and snow comes silently one night, and we wake to a white earth. It was during an early snowstorm when one of us said that Rose worked in a leather factory in town, had been there since she had appeared last summer. He knew someone who worked there and saw her. He knew nothing else.

On a night in January, while a light and pleasant snow dusted the tops of cars, and the shoulders and hats and scarves of people coming into Timmy's, Rose told me her story. I do not know whether, afterward, she was glad or relieved; neither of us has mentioned it since. Nor have our eyes, as we greet each other, sometimes chat. And one night I was without money, or enough of it, and she said *I owe you*, and bought the drinks. But that night in January she was in the state when people finally must talk. She was drunk too, or close enough to it, but I know her need to talk was there before vodka released her. I won't try to record our conversation. It was interrupted by one or both of us going to the bathroom, or ordering drinks (I insisted on paying for them all, and after the third round she simply thanked me, and patted my hand); interrupted by people leaning between us for drinks to bring back to booths, by people who came to speak to me, happy people oblivious of Rose, men or women or students who stepped to my side and began talking with that alcoholic lack of manners or awareness of intruding that, in a neighborhood bar, is not impolite but a part of the fabric of conversation. Interrupted too by the radio behind the bar, the speakers at both ends of the room, the loud rock music from an FM station in Boston.

It was a Friday, so the bar closed at two instead of one, we started talking at eleven. Gradually, before that, Rose had pushed her way down the bar toward my corner. I had watched her move to the right to make room for a couple, again to allow a man to squeeze in beside her, and again for some college girls; then the two men to my left went home, and when someone else wedged his arms and shoulders between the standing drinkers at the bar, she stepped to her right again and we faced each other across the corner. We talked about the bartender (we liked him), the crowd (we liked them: loud, but generally peaceful) and she said she always felt safe at Timmy's because everybody knew everybody else, and they didn't allow trouble in here.

"I can't stand fighting bars," she said. "Those young punks that have to hit somebody."

We talked about the weather, the seasons. She liked fall. The factory was too hot in summer. So was her apartment. She had bought a large fan, and it was so loud you could hear it from outside, and it blew dust from the floor, ashes from ashtrays. She liked winter, the snow, and the way the cold made her feel more alive;

but she was afraid of it too: she was getting old, and did not want to be one of those people who slipped on ice and broke a hip.

"The old bones," she said. "They don't mend like young ones."

"You're no older than I am."

"Oh yes I am. And you'd better watch your step too. On that ice," and she nodded at the large front window behind me.

"That's snow," I said. "A light, dry snow."

She smiled at me, her face affectionate, and coquettish with some shared secret, as though we were talking in symbols. Then she finished her drink and I tried to get Steve's attention. He is a large man, and was mixing drinks at the other end of the bar. He did not look our way, so finally I called his name, my voice loud enough to be heard, but softened with courtesy to a tenor. Off and on, through the years, I have tended bar, and I am sensitive about the matter of ordering from a bartender who is making several drinks and, from the people directly in front of him, hearing requests for more. He heard me and glanced at us and I raised two fingers; he nodded. When I looked at Rose again she was gazing down into her glass, as though studying the yellow-filmed ice.

"I worry about fires in winter," she said, still looking down. "Sometimes every night."

"When you're going to sleep? You worry about a fire?"

She looked at me.

"Nearly every night."

"What kind of heat does your building have?"

"Oil furnace."

"Is something wrong with it?"

"No."

"Then—" Steve is very fast; he put my beer and her screwdriver before us, and I paid him; he spun, strode to the cash register, jabbed it, slapped in my ten, and was back with the change. I pushed a dollar toward him, and he thanked me and was gone, repeating an order from the other end of the bar, and a rock group sang above the crowd, a ceiling of sound over the shouts, the laughter, and the crescendo of juxtaposed conversations.

"Then why are you worried?" I said. "Were you in a fire? As a child?"

"I was. Not in winter. And I sure wasn't no child. But you hear them. The sirens. All the time in winter."

"Wood stoves," I said. "Faulty chimneys."

"They remind me. The sirens. Sometimes it isn't even the sirens. I try not to think about them. But sometimes it's like they think about me. They do. You know what I mean?"

"The sirens?"

"*No.*" She grabbed my wrist and squeezed it, hard as a man might; I had not known the strength of her hands. "The flames," she said.

"The flames?"

"I'm not doing anything. Or I'm at work, packing boxes. With leather. Or I'm going to sleep. Or right now, just then, we were talking about winter. I try not to think about them. But here they come, and I can see them. I feel them. Little flames. Big ones. Then—"

She released my wrist, swallowed from her glass, and her face changed: a quick recognition of something forgotten. She patted my hand.

"Thanks for the drink."

"I have money tonight."

"Good. Some night you won't, and I will. You'll drink on me."

"Fine."

"Unless you slip on that ice," nodding her head toward the window, the gentle snow, her eyes brightening again with that shared mystery, their luster near anger, not at me but at what we shared.

"Then what?" I said.

"What?"

"When you see them. When you feel the fire."

"My kids."

"No."

"Three kids."

"No, Rose."

"Two were upstairs. We lived on the third floor."

"Please: no stories like that tonight."

She patted my hand, as though in thanks for a drink, and said: "Did you lose a child?"

"Yes."

"In a fire?"

"A car."

"You poor man. Don't cry."

And with her tough thumbs she wiped the beginning of my tears from beneath my eyes, then standing on tiptoe she kissed my cheek, her lips dry, her cheek as it brushed mine feeling no softer than my own, save for her absence of whiskers.

"Mine got out," she said. "I got them out."

I breathed deeply and swallowed beer and wiped my eyes, but she had dried them.

"And it's the only thing I ever did. In my whole fucking life. The only thing I ever did that was worth a shit."

"Come on. Nobody's like that."

"No?"

"I hope nobody is."

I looked at the clock on the opposite wall; it was near the speaker that tilted downward, like those mirrors in stores, so cashiers can watch people between shelves. From the speaker came a loud electric guitar, repeating a series of chords, then two or more frenetic saxophones blowing their hoarse tones at the heads of the drinkers, like an indoor storm without rain. On that clock the time was two minutes till midnight, so I knew it was eleven thirty-eight; at Timmy's they keep the clock twenty minutes fast. This allows them time to give last call and still get the patrons out by closing. Rose was talking. Sometimes I watched her; sometimes I looked away, when I could do that and still hear. For when I listened while watching faces I knew, hearing some of their voices, I did not see everything she told me: I saw, but my vision was dulled, given distance, by watching bearded Steve work, or the blond student Ande laughing over the mouth of her beer bottle, or old gray-haired Lou, retired from his job as a factory foreman, drinking his shots and drafts, and smoking Camels; or the young owner Timmy, in his mid-thirties, wearing a leather jacket and leaning on the far corner of the bar, drinking club soda and watching the hockey game that was silent under the sounds of rock.

But most of the time, because of the noise, I had to look at her eyes or mouth to hear; and when I did that, I saw everything, without the distractions of sounds and faces and bodies, nor even the softening of distance, of time: I saw the two little girls, and the little boy, their pallid terrified faces; I saw their father's big arm and hand arcing down in a slap; in a blow with his fist closed; I saw the five-year-old boy, the oldest, flung through the air, across the room, to strike the wall and drop screaming to the couch against it. Toward the end, nearly his only sounds were screams; he virtually stopped talking, and lived as a frightened yet recalcitrant prisoner. And in Rose's eyes I saw the embers of death, as if the dying of her spirit had come not with a final yielding sigh, but in a blaze of recognition.

It was long ago, in a Massachusetts town on the Merrimack River. Her husband was a big man, with strongly muscled arms, and the solid rounded belly of a man who drinks much beer at night and works hard, with his body, five days a week. He was handsome, too. His face was always reddish-brown from his outdoor work, his hair was thick and black, and curls of it topped his forehead, and when he wore his cap on the back of his head, the visor rested on his curls. He had a thick but narrow mustache, and on Friday and Saturday nights, when they went out to drink and dance, he dressed in brightly colored pants and shirts that his legs and torso and arms filled. His name was Jim Cormier, his grandfather Jacques had come from Quebec as a young man, and his father was Jacques Cormier too, and by Jim's generation the last name was pronounced *Cormeer*, and he was James. Jim was a construction worker, but his physical strength and endurance were unequally complemented by his mind, his spirit, whatever that element is that draws the attention of other men. He was best at the simplest work, and would never be a foreman, or tradesman. Other men, when he worked with them, baffled him. He did not have the touch: could not be entrusted to delegate work, to plan, to oversee, and to handle men. Bricks and mortar and trowels and chalk lines baffled him too, as did planes and levels; yet when he drank at home every night—they seldom went out after the children were born—he talked about learning to operate heavy equipment.

Rose did not tell me all this at first. She told me the end, the final night, and only in the last forty minutes or so, when I questioned her, did she go further back, to the beginning. Where I start her story, so I can try to understand how two young people married, with the hope of love—even, in those days before pandemic divorce, the certainty of love—and within six years, when they were still young, still in their twenties, their home had become a horror for their children, for Rose, and yes: for Jim. A place where a boy of five, and girls of four and three, woke, lived, and slept in isolation from the light of a child's life: the curiosity, the questions about birds, appliances, squirrels and trees and snow and rain, and the first heart-quickening of love for another child, not a sister or brother, but the boy or girl in a sandbox or on a tricycle at the house down the street. They lived always in darkness, deprived even of childhood fears of ghosts in the shadowed corners of the rooms where they slept, deprived of dreams of vicious and carnivorous monsters. Their young memories and their present consciousness were the tall broad man and his reddening face that shouted and hissed, and his large hands. Rose must have had no place at all, or very little, in their dreams and in their wary and apprehensive minds when they were awake. Unless as a wish: I imagine them in their beds, in the moments before sleep, hoping for Rose to take them in her arms, carry them one by one to the car while the giant slept drunkenly in the bed she shared with him, Rose putting their toys and clothes in the car's trunk, and driving with them far away to a place—what place could they imagine? What place not circumscribed by their apartment's walls, whose very colors and hanging pictures and calendar were for them the dark gray of fear and pain? Certainly, too, in those moments before sleep, they must have wished their father gone. Simply gone. The boy may have thought of, wished for, Jim's death. The younger girls, four and three, only that he vanish, leaving no trace of himself in their home, in their hearts, not even guilt. Simply vanish.

Rose was a silent partner. If there is damnation, and a place for the damned, it must be a quiet place, where spirits turn away from each other and stand in solitude and gaze haplessly at eternity. For it must be crowded with the passive: those people whose presence in life was a paradox; for, while occupying space and moving through it and making sounds in it they were obviously present, while in truth they were not: they witnessed evil and lifted neither an arm nor voice to stop it, they witnessed joy and neither sang nor clapped their hands. But so often we understand them too easily, tolerate them too much: they have universality, so we forgive the man who watches injustice, a drowning, a murder, because he reminds us of ourselves, and we share with him the loyal bond of cowardice, whether once or a hundred times we have turned away from another's suffering to save ourselves: our jobs, our public selves, our bones and flesh. And these people are so easy to pity. We know fear as early as we know love, and fear is always with us. I have friends my own age who still cannot say what they believe, except in the most intimate company. Condemning the actively evil man is a simple matter, though we tend not only to forgive but cheer him if he robs banks or Brink's, and outwits authority: those unfortunate policemen, minions whose uniforms and badges and revolvers are, for many of us, a distorted symbol of what we fear: not a fascist state but a Power, a God, who knows all our truths, believes none of our lies, and with that absolute knowledge will both judge and exact punishment. For we see to it that no one absolutely knows us, so at times the passing blue figure of a policeman walking his beat can stir in us our fear of discovery. We like to see them made into dupes by the outlaw.

But if the outlaw rapes, tortures, gratuitously kills, or if he makes children suffer, we hate him with a purity we seldom feel: our hatred has no roots in prejudice, or self-righteousness, but in horror. He has done something we would never do, something we could not do even if we wished it; our bodies would not obey, would not tear the dress, or lift and swing the axe, pull the trigger, throw the screaming child across the room. So I hate Jim Cormier, and cannot understand him; cannot with my imagination cross the distance between myself and him, enter his soul and know how it felt to live even five minutes of his life. And I forgive Rose, but as I write I resist that compassion, or perhaps merely empathy, and force myself to think instead of the three children, and Rose living there, knowing what she knew. She was young.

She is Irish: a Callahan till marriage, and she and Jim were Catholic. Devout Catholics, she told me. By that, she did not mean they strived to live in imitation of Christ. She meant they did not practice artifical birth control, but rhythm, and after their third year of marriage they had three children. They left the Church then. That is, they stopped attending Sunday Mass and receiving Communion. Do you see? I am not a Catholic, but even I know that they were never truly members of that faith, and so could not have left it. There is too much history, too much philosophy involved, for the matter of faith to rest finally and solely on the use of contraceptives. That was long ago, and now my Catholic friends tell me the priests no longer concern themselves with birth control. But we must live in our own time; Thomas More died for an issue that would have no meaning today. Rose and Jim, though, were not Thomas Mores.

They could not see a single act as a renunciation or affirmation of a belief, a way of life. No. They had neither a religion nor a philosophy; like most people I know, their philosophies were simply their accumulated reactions to their daily circumstance, their lives as they lived them from one hour to the next. They were not driven, guided, by either passionate belief or strong resolve. And for that I pity them both, as I pity the others who move through life like scraps of paper in the wind.

With contraception they had what they believed were two years of freedom. There had been a time when all three of their children wore diapers, and only the boy could walk, and with him holding her coat or pants, moving so slowly beside her, Rose went daily to the laundromat, pushing two strollers, gripping a paper grocery bag of soiled diapers, with a clean bag folded in her purse. Clorox rested underneath one stroller, a box of soap underneath the other. While she waited for the diapers to wash, the boy walked among the machines, touched them, watched them, and watched the other women who waited. The oldest girl crawled about on the floor. The baby slept in Rose's lap, or nursed in those days when mothers did not expose their breasts, and Rose covered the infant's head, and her breast, with her unbuttoned shirt. The children became hungry, or tired, or restless, and they fussed, and cried, as Rose called to the boy to leave the woman alone, to stop playing with the ashtray, the soap, and she put the diapers in the dryer. And each day she felt that the other women, even those with babies, with crawling and barely walking children, with two or three children, and one pregnant with a third, had about them some grace, some calm, that kept their voices soft, their gestures tender; she watched them with shame, and a deep dislike of herself, but no envy, as if she had tried out for a dance company and on the first day had entered a room of slender professionals in leotards, dancing like cats, while she clumsily moved her heavy body clad in gray sweatclothes. Most of the time she changed the diaper of at least one of the children, and dropped it in the bag, the beginning of tomorrow's load. If the baby slept in her stroller, and the older girl and the boy played on the floor, Rose folded the diapers on the table in the laundromat, talking and smoking with the other women. But that was rare: the chance that all three small children could at the same time be peaceful and without need, and so give her peace. Imagine: three of them with bladders and bowels, thirst, hunger, fatigue, and none of them synchronized. Most days she put the hot unfolded diapers in the clean bag and hurried home.

Finally she cried at dinner one night for a washing machine and a dryer, and Jim stared at her, not with anger, or impatience, and not refusal either: but with the resigned look of a man who knew he could neither refuse it nor pay for it. It was the washing machine; he would buy it with monthly payments, and when he had done that, he would get the dryer. He sank posts in the earth and nailed boards across their tops and stretched clotheslines between them. He said in rain or freezing cold she would have to hang the wet diapers over the backs of chairs. It was all he could do. Until he could get her a dryer. And when he came home on those days of rain or cold, he looked surprised, as if rain and cold in New England were as foreign to him as the diapers that seemed to occupy the house. He removed them from the rod for the shower curtain, and when he had cleaned his work from his body, he hung them again. He took them from the arms and back of his chair and laid them on top of others, on a chair, or the edges of the kitchen table. Then he sat in the chair whose purpose he had restored; he drank beer and gazed at the drying diapers, as if they were not cotton at all, but the whitest of white shades of the dead, come to haunt him, to assault him, an inch at a time, a foot, until they won, surrounded him where he stood in some corner of the bedroom, the bathroom, in the last place in his home that was his. His *quercençia*: his cool or blood-smelling sand, the only spot in the bull-ring where he wanted to stand and defend, to lower his head and wait.

He struck the boy first, before contraception and the freedom and new life it promised, as money does. Rose was in the kitchen, chopping onions, now and then turning her face to wipe, with the back of her wrist, the tears from her eyes. The younger girl was asleep; the older one crawled between and around Rose's legs. The boy was three. She had nearly finished the onions and could put them in the skillet and stop crying, when she heard the slap, and knew what it was in that instant before the boy cried: a different cry: in it she heard not only startled fear, but a new sound: a wail of betrayal, of pain from the heart. Wiping her hands on her apron, she went quickly to the living room, into that long and loudening cry, as if the boy, with each moment of deeper recognition, raised his voice until it howled. He stood in front of his seated father. Before she reached him, he looked at her, as though without hearing footsteps or seeing her from the corner of his blurred wet vision, he knew she was there. She was his mother. Yet when he turned his face to her, it was not with appeal: above his small reddened cheeks he looked into her eyes; and in his, as tears ran from them, was that look whose sound she had heard in the kitchen. Betrayal. Accusing her of it, and without anger, only with dismay. In her heart she felt something fall between herself and her son, like a glass wall, or a space that spanned only a few paces, yet was infinite, and she could never cross it again. Now his voice had attained the howl, and though his cheeks were wet, his eyes were dry now; or anyway tearless, for they looked wet and bright as pools that could reflect her face. The baby was awake, crying in her crib. Rose looked from her son's eyes to her husband's. They were dark, and simpler than the boy's: in them she saw only the ebb of his fury: anger, and a resolve to preserve and defend it.

"I told him not to," he said.

"Not to what?"

"Climb on my legs. Look." He pointed to a dark wet spot on the carpet. "He spilled the beer."

She stared at the spot. She could not take her eyes from it. The baby was crying, and the muscles of her legs tried to move toward that sound. Then she realized her son was silent. She felt him watching her, and she would not look at him.

"It's nothing to cry about," Jim said.

"You *slapped* him."

"Not *him*. You."

"Me? That's onions."

She wiped her hands on her apron, brushed her eyes with the back of her wrist.

"Jesus," she said. She looked at her son. She had to look away from those eyes. Then she saw the older girl: she had come to the doorway, and was standing on the threshold, her thumb in her mouth; above her small closed fist and nose, her frightened eyes stared, and she looked as though she were trying not to cry. But, if she was, there could be only one reason for a child so young: she was afraid for her voice to leave her, to enter the room, where now Rose could feel her children's fear as tangibly as a cold draft blown through a cracked windowpane. Her legs, her hips, strained toward the baby's cry for food, a dry diaper, for whatever acts of love they need when they wake, and even more when they wake before they are ready, when screams smash the shell of their sleep. "Jesus," she said, and hurried out of the room where the pain in her son's heart had pierced her own, and her little girl's fearful silence pierced it again; or slashed it, for she felt as she bent over the crib that she was no longer whole, that her height and breadth and depth were in pieces that somehow held together, did not separate and drop to the floor, through it, into the earth itself.

"I should have hit him with the skillet," she said to me, so many years later, after she had told me the end and I had drawn from her the beginning, in the last half-hour of talk.

She could not hit him that night. With the heavy iron skillet, with its hot oil waiting for the onions. For by then something had flowed away from Rose, something of her spirit simply wafting willy-nilly out of her body, out of the apartment, and it never came back, not even with the diaphragm. Perhaps it began to leave her at the laundromat, or in bed at night, at the long day's end not too tired for lust, for rutting, but too tired for an evening of desire that began with dinner and crested and fell and crested again through the hours as they lay close and naked in bed, from early in the night until finally they slept. On the car seat of courtship she had dreamed of this, and in the first year of marriage she lived the dream: joined him in the shower and made love with him, still damp, before they went to the dinner kept warm on the stove, then back to the bed's tossed sheets to lie in the dark, smoking, talking, touching, and they made love again; and, later, again, until they could only lie side by side waiting for their breathing to slow, before they slept. Now at the tired ends of days they took release from each other, and she anxiously slept, waiting for a baby to cry.

Or perhaps it left her between the shelves of a supermarket. His payday was Thursday, and by then the refrigerator and cupboard were nearly empty. She shopped on Friday. Unless a neighbor could watched the children, Rose shopped at night, when Jim was home; they ate early and she hurried to the store to shop before it closed. Later, months after he slapped the boy, she believed his rage had started then, alone in the house with them, changing the baby and putting her in the crib while the other girl and the boy spat and flung food from their highchairs where she had left them, in her race with time to fill a cart with food Jim could afford: she looked at the price of everything she took from a shelf. She did not believe, later, that he struck them on those nights. But there must have been rage, the frightening voice of it; for he was tired, and confused, and overwhelmed by three small people with wills of their own, and no control over the needs of their bodies and their spirits. Certainly he must have yelled; maybe he squeezed an arm, or slapped a rump. When she returned with the groceries, the apartment was quiet: the children slept, and he sat in the kitchen, with the light out, drinking beer. A light from the living room behind him and around a corner showed her his silhouette: large and silent, a cigarette glowing at his mouth, a beer bottle rising to it. Then he would turn on the light and put down his beer and walk past her, to the old car, to carry in the rest of the groceries.

When finally two of the children could walk, Rose went to the supermarket during the day, the boy and girl walking beside her, behind her, away from her voice whose desperate pitch embarrassed her, as though its sound were a sign to the other women with children that she was incompetent, unworthy to be numbered among them. The boy and girl took from shelves cookies, crackers, cereal boxes, cans of vegetables and fruit, sometimes to play with them, but at other times to bring to her, where holding the cart they pulled themselves up on the balls of their feet and dropped in the box, or the can. Still she scolded them, jerked the can or box from the cart, brought it back to its proper place; and when she did this, her heart sank as though pulled by a sigh deeper into her body. For she saw. She saw that when the children played with these things whose colors or shapes drew them so they wanted to sit on the floor and hold or turn in their hands the box or can, they were simply being children whom she could patiently teach, if patience were still an element in her spirit. And that when they brought things to her, to put into the cart, repeating the motions of their mother, they were joining, without fully knowing it, the struggle of the family, and without knowing the struggle that was their parents' lives. Their hearts, though, must have expected praise; or at least an affectionate voice, a gentle hand, to show that their mother did not need what they had brought her. If only there were time: one extra hour of grocery shopping to spend in this gentle instruction. Or if she had strength to steal the hour anyway, despite the wet and tired and staring baby in the cart. But she could not: she scolded, she jerked from the cart or their hands the things they had brought, and the boy became quiet, the girl sucked her thumb and held Rose's pants as the four of them moved with the cart between the long shelves. The baby fussed, with that unceasing low cry that was not truly crying, only wordless sounds of fatigue. Rose recognized it, understood it, for by now she had learned the awful lesson of fatigue, which as a young girl she had never felt. She knew that it was worse than the flu, whose enforced rest at least left you the capacity to care for someone else, to mutter words of love; but that, healthy, you could be so tired that all you wanted was to lie down, alone, shut off from everyone. And you would snap at your husband, or your children, if they entered the room, probed the solace of your complete surrender to silence and the mattress that seductively held your body. So she understood the baby's helpless sounds for *I want to lie in my crib and put my thumb in my mouth and hold Raggedy Ann's dirty old apron and sleep.* The apron was long removed from the doll, and the baby would not sleep without its presence in her hand. Rose understood this, but could not soothe the baby. She could not have soothed her anyway; only sleep could. But Rose could not try, with hugs, with petting, with her softened voice. She was young.

Perhaps her knowledge of her own failures dulled her ears and eyes to Jim after he first struck the boy, and on that night lost for the rest of his life any paternal control he might have exerted in the past over his hands, finally his fists. Because more and more now he spanked them; with a chill Rose tried to deny, a resonant quiver up through her body, she remembered that her parents had spanked her too. That all, or probably all, parents spanked their children. And usually it was the father, the man of the house, the authority and judge, and enforcer of rules and discipline the children would need when they reached their teens. But now, too, he held them by the shoulders, and shook their small bodies, the children sometimes wailing, sometimes frighteningly silent, until it seemed their heads would fly across the room then roll to rest on the floor, while he shook a body whose neck had snapped in two like a dried branch. He slapped their faces, and sometimes he punched the boy, who was four, then five, with his fist. They were not bad children; not disobedient; certainly they were not loud. When Jim yelled and shook them, or slapped or punched, they had done no more than they had in the supermarket, where her voice, her snatching from their hands, betrayed her to the other women. So maybe that kept her silent.

But there was more: she could no longer feel love, or what she had believed love to be. On the few nights when she and Jim could afford both a sitter and a nightclub, they did not dance. They sat drinking, their talk desultory: about household chores, about Jim's work, pushing wheelbarrows, swinging a sledgehammer, thrusting a spade into the earth or a pile of gravel or sand. They listened to the music, watched the band, even drummed their fingers on the table dampened by the bottoms of the glasses they emptied like thirsty people drinking water; but they thirsted for a time they had lost. Or not even that: for respite from their time now, and their knowledge that, from one day to the next, year after year, their lives would not change. Each day would be like the one they had lived before last night's sleep; and tomorrow was a certain and already draining repetition of today. They did not decide to sit rather than dance. They simply did not dance. They sat and drank and watched the band and the dancing couples, as if their reason for dancing had been stolen from them while their eyes had been jointly focused on something else.

She could no longer feel love. She ate too much and smoked too much and drank too much coffee, so all day she felt either lethargic from eating or stimulated by coffee and cigarettes, and she could not recall her body as it had once been, only a few years ago, when she was dating Jim, and had played softball and volleyball, had danced, and had run into the ocean to swim beyond the breakers. The ocean was a half-hour away from her home, yet she had not seen it in six years. Rather than love, she felt that she and Jim only worked together, exhausted, toward a nebulous end, as if they were digging a large hole, wide as a house, deeper than a well. Side by side they dug, and threw the dirt up and out of the hole, pausing now and then to look at each other, to wait while their breathing slowed, and to feel in those kindred moments something of why they labored, of why they had begun it so long ago—not in years, not long at all—with their dancing and lovemaking and finally marriage: to pause and look at each other's flushed and sweating faces with as much love as they could feel before they commenced again to dig deeper, away from the light above them.

On a summer night in that last year, Jim threw the boy across the living room. Rose was washing the dishes after dinner. Jim was watching television, and the boy, five now, was playing on the floor between Jim and the set. He was on the floor with his sisters and wooden blocks and toy cars and trucks. He seldom spoke directly to his father anymore; seldom spoke at all to anyone but his sisters. The girls were too young, or hopeful, or were still in love. They spoke to Jim, sat on his lap, hugged his legs, and when he hugged them, lifted them in the air, talked with affection and laughter, their faces showed a happiness without memory. And when he yelled at them, or shook or spanked them, or slapped their faces, their memory failed them again, and they were startled, frightened, and Rose could sense their spirits weeping beneath the sounds of their crying. But they kept turning to him, with open arms, and believing faces.

"Little flowers," she said to me. "They were like little flowers in the sun. They never could remember the frost."

Not the boy, though. But that night his game with his sisters absorbed him, and for a short while—nearly an hour—he was a child in a home. He forgot. Several times his father told him and the girls to be quiet or play in another room. Then for a while, a long while for playing children, they were quiet: perhaps five minutes, perhaps ten. Each time their voices rose, Jim's command for quiet was abrupt, and each time it was louder. At the kitchen sink Rose's muscles tensed, told her it was coming, and she must go to the living room now, take the children and their blocks and cars and trucks to the boy's bedroom. But she breathed deeply and rubbed a dish with a sponge. When she finished, she would go down to the basement of the apartment building, descend past the two floors of families and single people whose only sounds were music from radios, voices from television, and sometimes children loudly playing and once in a while a quarrel between a husband and wife. She would go into the damp basement and take the clothes from the washing machine, put them in the dryer that Jim was now paying for with monthly installments. Then she heard his voice again, and was certain it was coming, but could not follow the urging of her muscles. She sponged another dish. Then her hands came out of the dishwater with a glass: it had been a jelly jar, and humanly smiling animals were on it, and flowers, and her children liked to drink from it, looked for it first when they were thirsty, and only if it was dirty in the sink would they settle for an ordinary glass for their water, their juice, or Kool-Aid or milk. She washed it slowly, and was for those moments removed; she was oblivious of the living room, the children's voices rising again to the peak that would bring either Jim's voice or his body from his chair. Her hands moved gently on the glass. She could have been washing one of her babies. Her heart had long ago ceased its signals to her; it lay dormant in despair beyond sorrow; standing at the sink, in a silence of her own making, lightly rubbing the glass with the sponge, and her fingers and palms, she did not know she was crying until the tears reached her lips, salted her tongue.

With their wooden blocks, the children were building a village, and a bridge leading out of it to the country: the open spaces of the living-room carpet, and the chairs and couch that were distant mountains. More adept with his hands, and more absorbed too in the work, the boy often stood to adjust a block on a roof, or the bridge. Each time he stood between his father and the television screen, he heard the quick command, and moved out of the way. They had no slanted blocks, so the bridge had to end with two sheer walls; the boy wanted to build ramps at either end, for the cars and trucks to use, and he had only rectangles and squares to work with. He stood to look down at the bridge. His father spoke. He heard the voice, but a few seconds passed before it penetrated his concentration and spread through him. It was too late. What he heard next was not words, or a roar, but a sustained guttural cry, a sound that could be either anguish or rage. Then his father's hands were on him: on him and squeezing his left thigh and left bicep so tightly that he opened his mouth to cry out in pain. But he did not. For then he was above his father's head, above the floor and his sisters, high above the room itself and near the ceiling he glimpsed; and he felt his father's grip and weight shifting and saw the wall across the room, the wall above the couch, so that when finally he made a sound it was of terror, and it came from him in a high scream he heard as he hurtled across the room, seeing always the wall, and hearing his own scream, as though his flight were prolonged by the horror of what he saw and heard. Then he struck it. He heard that, and the bone in his right forearm snap, and he fell to the couch. Now he cried with pain, staring at the swollen flesh where the bone tried to protrude, staring with astonishment and grief at this part of his body. Nothing in his body had ever broken before. He touched the flesh, the bone beneath it. He was crying as, in his memory, he had never cried before, and he not only did not try to stop, as he always had, with pride, with anger; but he wanted to cry this deeply, his body shuddering with it, doubling at his waist with it, until he attained oblivion, invisibility, death. Somehow he knew his childhood had ended. In his pain, he felt relief too: now on this couch his life would end.

He saw through tears but more strongly felt his sisters standing before him, touching him, crying. Then he heard his mother. She was screaming. And in rage. At his father. He had never heard her do that, but still her scream did not come to him as a saving trumpet. He did not want to live to see revenge. Not even victory. Then he heard his father slap her. Through his crying he listened then for her silence. But her voice grew, its volume filled the world. Still he felt nothing of hope, of vengeance; he had left that world, and lived now for what he hoped and believed would be only a very short time. He was beginning to feel the pain in his head and back and shoulders, his elbows and neck. He knew he would only have to linger a while in this pain, until his heart left him, as though disgorged by tears, and went wherever hearts went. A sister's hand held his, and he squeezed it.

When he was above his father's head, the boy had not seen Rose. But she was there, behind Jim, behind the lifted boy, and she had cried out too, and moved: as Jim regained his balance from throwing the boy, she turned him, her hand jerking his shoulder, and when she could see his face she pounded it with her fists. She was yelling, and the yell was words, but she did not know what they were. She hit him until he pushed her back, hard, so she nearly fell. She looked at his face, the cheeks reddened by her blows, saw a trickle of blood from his lower lip, and charged it: swinging at the blood, the lip. He slapped her so hard that she was sitting on the floor, with no memory of falling, and holding and shaking her stunned and buzzing head. She stood, yelling words again that she could not hear, as if their utterance had been so long coming, from whatever depth in her, that her mind could not even record them as they rushed through her lips. She went past Jim, pushing his belly, and he fell backward into his chair. She paused to look at that. Her breath was deep and fast, and he sat glaring, his breathing hard too, and she neither knew nor cared whether he had desisted or was preparing himself for more. At the bottom of her vision, she saw his beer bottle on the floor beside the chair. She snatched it up, by its neck, beer hissing onto her arm and breast, and in one motion she turned away from Jim and flung the bottle smashing through the television screen. He was up and yelling behind her, but she was crouched over the boy.

She felt again what she had felt in the kitchen, in the silence she had made for herself while she bathed the glass. Behind and above her was the sound of Jim's fury; yet she stroked the boy's face: his forehead, the tears beneath his eyes; she touched the girls too, their hair, their wet faces; and she heard her own voice: soft and soothing, so soft and soothing that she even believed the peace it promised. Then she saw, beneath the boy's hand, the swollen flesh; gently she lifted his hand, then was on her feet. She stood into Jim's presence again: his voice behind her, the feel of his large body inches from her back. Then he gripped her hair, at the back of her head, and she shook her head but still he held on.

"His *arm's* broken."

She ran from him, felt hair pulling from her scalp, heard it, and ran to her bedroom for her purse but not a blanket, not from the bed where she slept with Jim; for that she went to the boy's, and pulled his thin summer blanket from his bed, and ran back to the living room. Where she stopped. Jim stood at the couch, not looking at the boy, or the girls, but at the doorway where now she stood holding the blanket. He was waiting for her.

"You crazy fucking bitch."

"*What?*"

"The fucking TV. Who's going to buy one? You? You fucking cunt. You've never had a fucking job in your life."

It was madness. She was looking at madness, and it calmed her. She had nothing to say to it. She went to the couch, opening the blanket to wrap around the boy.

"It's the only fucking peace I've *got.*"

She heard him, but it was like overhearing someone else, in another apartment, another life. She crouched and was working the blanket under the boy's body when a fist knocked loudly on the door. She did not pause, or look up. More knocking, then a voice in the hall: "Hey! Everybody all right in there?"

"Get the fuck away from my door."

"You tell me everybody's all right."

"Get the fuck *away*."

"I want to hear the woman. And the kid."

"You want me to throw you down the fucking stairs?"

"I'm calling the cops."

"Fuck you."

She had the boy in her arms now. He was crying still, and as she carried him past Jim, she kissed his cheeks, his eyes. Then Jim was beside her. He opened the door, swung it back for them. She did not realize until weeks later that he was frightened. His voice was low: "Tell them he fell."

She did not answer. She went out and down the stairs, past apartments; in one of them someone was phoning the police. At the bottom of the stairs she stopped short of the door, to shift the boy's weight in her arms, to free a hand for the knob. Then an old woman stepped out of her apartment, into the hall, and said: "I'll get it."

An old woman with white hair and a face that knew everything, not only tonight, but the years before this too, yet the face was neither stern nor kind; it looked at Rose with some tolerant recognition of evil, of madness, of despair, like a warrior who has seen and done too much to condemn, or even try to judge; can only nod in assent at what he sees. The woman opened the door and held it, and Rose went out, across the small lawn to the car parked on the road. There were only two other cars at the curb; then she remembered that it was Saturday, and had been hot, and before noon she had heard most of the tenants separately leaving for beaches or picnic grounds. They would be driving home now, or stopping to eat. The sun had just set, but most windows of the tenements on the street were dark. She stopped at the passenger door, started to shift the weeping boy's weight, then the old woman was beside her, trying the door, asking for the key. Rose's purse hung from her wrist. The woman's hands went into it, moved in there, came out with the ring of keys, held them up toward the streetlight, and found the one for the car. She opened the door, and Rose leaned in and laid the boy on the front seat. She turned to thank the woman but she was already at the front door of the building, a square back and short body topped by hair like cotton.

Rose gently closed the car door, holding it, making certain it was not touching the boy before she pushed it into place. She ran to the driver's side, and got in, and put the key in the ignition slot. But she could not turn it. She sat in the boy's crying, poised in the moment of action the car had become. But she could not start it.

"Jimmy," she said. "Jimmy, listen. Just hang on. I'll be right back. I can't leave the girls. Do you hear me?"

His face, profiled on the seat, nodded.

"I've got to get them."

She pushed open the door, left the car, closed the door, the keys in her hands, not out of habit this time; no, she clung to them as she might to a tiny weapon, her last chance to be saved. She was running to the building when she saw the flames at her windows, a flare of them where an instant before there had been only lamp-light. Her legs now, her body, were weightless as the wind. She heard the girls screaming. Then the front door opened and Jim ran out of it, collided with her, and she fell on her back as he stumbled and sidestepped and tried to regain balance and speed and go around her. Her left hand grabbed his left ankle. Then she turned with his pulling, his weight, and, on her stomach now, she held his ankle with her right hand too, and pulled it back and up. He fell. She dived onto his back, saw and smelled the gasoline can in his hand, and in her mind she saw him going down to the basement for it, and back up the stairs. She twisted it away from his fingers on the handle, and kneeled with his back between her legs, and as he lifted his head and shoulders and tried to stand, she raised the can high with both hands and brought it down, leaning with it, into it, as it struck his skull. For a moment he was still, his face in the grass. Then he began to struggle again, and said into the earth: "Over now. All over."

She hit him three more times, the sounds hollow, metallic. Then he was still, save for the rise and fall of his back. Beneath his other hand she saw his set of car keys. She scooped them from the grass and stood and threw them across the lawn, whirling now into the screams of the girls, and windows of fire. She ran up the stairs. The white-haired woman was on the second-floor landing. Rose passed her, felt her following, and the others: she did not know how many, nor who they were. She only heard them behind her. No one passed her. She was at the door, trying to turn the knob, while her left arm and hand pressed hot wood.

"I called the fire department," a man said, behind her in the hall.

"So did we," a woman said.

Rose was calling to the girls to open the door.

"They can't," another man said. "That's where the fire is." Then he said: "Fuck this," and pulled her away from the door where she was turning the knob back and forth and calling through the wood to the screams from the rear of the apartment, their bedroom. She was about to spring back to the door, but stopped: the man faced it, then stepped away. She knew his name, or had known it; she could not say it. He lived on the second floor; it was his wife who had said *So did we*. He stepped twice toward the door, then kicked, his leg horizontal, the bottom of his shoe striking the door, and it swung open, through the flames that filled the threshold and climbed the doorjambs. The man leaped backward, his forearms covering his face, while Rose yelled to the girls: *We're coming, we're coming*. The man lowered his head and sprinted forward. Or it would have been a sprint. Certainly he believed that, believed he would run through fire to the girls and get them out. But in his third stride his legs stopped, so suddenly and autonomously that he nearly fell forward into the fire. Then he backed up.

"They'll have a net," he said. He was panting. "We'll get them to jump. We'll get them to a window, and get them to jump."

A man behind Rose was holding her. She had not known it till now. Nor had she known she was straining forward. The man tightly held her biceps. He was talking to her and now she heard that too, and was also aware that people were moving away, slowly but away, down the hall toward the stairs. He was saying, "You can't. All you'll do is get yourself killed."

Then she was out of his hands, as though his fingers were those of a child, and, with her breath held and her arms shielding her face, and her head down, she was in motion, through the flames and into the burning living room. She did not feel the fire, but even as she ran through the living room, dodging flames, running through them, she knew that very soon she would. It meant no more to her than knowing that she was getting wet in a sudden rain. The girls were standing on the older one's bed, at the far side of the room, holding each other, screaming, and watching their door and the hall beyond it where the fire would come. She filled the door, their vision, then was at the bed and they were crying: *Mommy! Mommy!* She did not speak. She did not touch them either. She pulled the blanket from under them, and they fell onto the bed. Running again, she grabbed the blanket from the younger girl's bed, and went into the hall where there was smoke but not fire yet, and across it to the bathroom where she turned on the shower and held the blankets under the spray. They soaked heavily in her hands. She held her breath leaving the bathroom and exhaled in the girls' room. They were standing again, holding each other. Now she spoke to them. Again, as when she had crouched with them in front of Jimmy, her voice somehow came softly from her. It was unhurried, calm, soothing: she could have been helping them put on snowsuits. They stopped screaming, even crying; they only sniffled and gasped as she wound a blanket around each of them, covering their feet and heads too, then lifted them, pressing one to each breast. Then she stopped talking, stopped telling them that very soon, before they even knew it, they would be safe outside. She turned and ran through smoke in the hall, and into the living room. She did not try to dodge flames: if they were in front of her, she spun and ran backward through them, hugging the girls against each other, so nothing of their bodies would protude past her back, her sides; then spun and ran forward again, fearful of an image that entered her mind, though in an instant she expelled it: that she would fall with them, into fire. She ran backward through the door, and her back hit the wall. She bounced off it; there was fire in the hall now, moving at her ankles, and she ran, leaping, and when she reached the stairs she smelled the scorched blankets that steamed around the girls in her arms. She smelled her burned hair, sensed that it was burning still, crackling flames on her head. It could wait. She could wait. She was running down the stairs, and the fire was behind her, above her, and she felt she could run with her girls all night. Then she was on the lawn, and her arms took the girls, and a man wrestled her to the ground and rolled with her, rolled over and over on the grass. When she stood, someone was telling her an ambulance would—But she picked up her girls, unwrapped now, and looked at their faces: pale with terror, with shock, yes; but no burns. She carried them to the car.

"*No*," she heard. It was a man's voice, but one she did not know. Not for a few moments, as she laid the girls side by side on the back seat. Then she knew it was Jim. She was startled, as though she had not seen him for ten years. She ran around the car, got behind the wheel, reached over Jimmy, who was silent now and she thought unconscious until she saw his eyes staring at the dashboard, his teeth gritting against his pain. Leaning over his face, she pushed down the latch on his side. Then she locked her door. It was a two-door car, and they were safe now and they were going to the hospital. She started the engine.

Jim was at her window, a raging face, but a desperate one too, as though standing outside he was locked in a room without air. Then he was motion, on her left, to her front, and he stood at the middle of the car, slapped his hands onto the hood, and pushed. He bulged: his arms and chest and reddened face. With all his strength he pushed, and she felt the car rock backward. She turned on the headlights. The car rocked forward as he eased his pushing and drew breath. Then he pushed again, leaning, so all she could see of him was his face, his shoulders, his arms. The car rocked back and stopped. She pushed the accelerator pedal to the floor, waited two or three seconds in which she either did not breathe or held what breath she had, and watched his face above the sound of the raging engine. Then, in one quick motion, she lifted her foot from the clutch pedal. He was gone as she felt the bumper and grille leap through his resistance. She stopped and looked in the rear-view mirror; she saw the backs of the girls' heads, their long hair; they were kneeling on the seat, looking quietly out the back window. He lay on his back. Rose turned her wheels to the right, as though to back into a parking space, shifted to reverse, and this time without racing the engine, she slowly drove. She did not look through the rear window; she looked straight ahead, at the street, the tenements, the darkening sky. Only the rear tires rolled over him, then struck the curb. She straightened the front wheels and drove forward again. The car bumped over him. She stopped, shifted gears, and backed up: the bump, then the tires hitting the curb. She was still driving back and forth over his body, while beyond her closed windows people shouted or stared, when the sirens broke the summer sky: the higher wail of the police called by the neighbor, and the lower and louder one of the fire engine.

She was in the hospital, and by the time she got out, her three brothers and two sisters had found money for bail. Her parents were dead. Waiting for the trial, she lived with a married sister;

there were children in the house, and Rose shied away from them. Her court-appointed lawyer called it justifiable homicide, and the jury agreed. Long before the trial, before she even left the hospital, she had lost the children. The last time she saw them was that night in the car, when finally she took them away: the boy lying on the front seat, his left cheek resting on it as he stared. He did not move while she drove back and forth over his father. She still does not know whether he knew then, or learned it from his sisters. And the two girls kneeling, their chests leaning on the back of the seat, watching their father appear, then vanish as a bump beneath them. They all went to the same foster home. She did not know where it was.

"Thanks for the drinks," she said, and patted my hand. "Next time you're broke, let me know."

"I will."

She adjusted the blue scaf over her hair, knotted it under her face, buttoned her coat, and put on her gloves. She stepped away from the bar, and walked around and between people. I ordered a beer, and watched her go out the door. I paid and tipped Steve, then left the bottle and glass with my coat and hat on the bar, and moved through the crowd. I stepped outside and watched her, a half-block away now. She was walking carefully in the lightly falling snow, her head down, watching the sidewalk, and I remembered her eyes when she talked about slipping on ice. But what had she been sharing with me? Age? Death? I don't think so. I believe it was the unexpected: chance, and its indiscriminate testing of our bodies, our wills, our spirits. She was walking toward the bridge over the Merrimack. It is a long bridge, and crossing it in that open air she would be cold. I was shivering. She was at the bridge now, her silhouette diminishing as she walked on it. I watched until she disappeared.

I had asked her if she had tried to find her children, had tried an appeal to get them back. She did not deserve them, she said. And after the testimony of her neighbors, she knew she had little hope anyway. She should have hit him with the skillet, she said; the first time he slapped the boy. I said nothing. As I have written, we have talked often since then, but we do not mention her history, and she does not ask for mine, though I know she guesses some of it. All of this is blurred; nothing stands out with purity. By talking to social workers, her neighbors condemned her to lose her children; talking in the courtroom, they helped save her from conviction.

I imagine again those men long ago, sitting among mosquitoes in a room, or sleeping on the fouled sheets. Certainly each of them hoped that it was not the mosquito biting his arm, or the bed he slept on, that would end his life. So he hoped for the men in the other room to die. Unless he hoped that it was neither sheets nor mosquitoes, but then he would be hoping for the experiment to fail, for yellow fever to flourish. And he had volunteered to stop it. Perhaps though, among those men, there was one, or even more, who hoped that he alone would die, and his death would be a discovery for all.

The boy from Chicago and Rose were volunteers too. I hope that by now the man from Chicago has succeeded at something—love, work—that has allowed him to outgrow the shame of failure. I have often imagined him returning home a week early that summer, to a mother, to a father; and having to watch his father's face as the boy told him he had failed because he was weak. A trifling incident in a whole lifetime, you may say. Not true. It could have changed him forever, his life with other men, with women, with daughters, and especially sons. We like to believe that in this last quarter of the century, we know and are untouched by everything; yet it takes only a very small jolt, at the right time, to knock us off balance for the rest of our lives. Maybe—and I hope so—the boy learned what his body and will could do: some occurrence he did not have time to consider, something that made him act before he knew he was in action.

Like Rose. Who volunteered to marry; even, to a degree, to practice rhythm, for her Catholic beliefs were not strong and deep, else she could not have so easily turned away from them after the third child, or even early in that pregnancy. So the life she chose slowly turned on her, pressed against her from all sides, invisible, motionless, but with the force of wind she could not breast. She stood at the sink, holding the children's glass. But *then*—and now finally I know why I write this, and what does stand out with purity—she reentered motherhood, and the unity we all must gain against human suffering. This is why I did not answer, at the bar, when she told me she did not deserve the children. For I believe she did, and does. She redeemed herself, with action, and with less than thirty minutes of it. But she could not see that, and still cannot. She sees herself in the laundromat, the supermarket, listlessly drunk in a nightclub where only her fingers on the table moved to the music. I see her young and strong and swift, wrapping the soaked blankets around her little girls, and hugging them to her, and running and spinning and running through the living room, on that summer night when she was touched and blessed by flames.

THE FAT GIRL

H ER NAME WAS Louise. Once when she was sixteen
a boy kissed her at a barbecue; he was drunk and
he jammed his tongue into her mouth and ran his hands up and
down her hips. Her father kissed her often. He was thin and kind
and she could see in his eyes when he looked at her the lights of
love and pity.

It started when Louise was nine. You must start watching what
you eat, her mother would say. I can see you have my metabolism.
Louise also had her mother's pale blonde hair. Her mother was slim
and pretty, carried herself erectly, and ate very little. The two of
them would eat bare lunches, while her older brother ate sandwiches
and potato chips, and then her mother would sit smoking while
Louise eyed the bread box, the pantry, the refrigerator. Wasn't that
good, her mother would say. In five years you'll be in high school
and if you're fat the boys won't like you; they won't ask you out.
Boys were as far away as five years, and she would go to her room
and wait for nearly an hour until she knew her mother was no longer
thinking of her, then she would creep into the kitchen and, listening to her mother talking on the phone, or her footsteps upstairs, she would open the bread box, the pantry, the jar of peanut
butter. She would put the sandwich under her shirt and go outside
or to the bathroom to eat it.

Her father was a lawyer and made a lot of money and came home
looking pale and happy. Martinis put color back in his face, and at

234 · ANDRE DUBUS

dinner he talked to his wife and two children. Oh give her a potato, he would say to Louise's mother. She's a growing girl. Her mother's voice then became tense: If she has a potato she shouldn't have dessert. She should have both, her father would say, and he would reach over and touch Louise's cheek or hand or arm.

In high school she had two girl friends and at night and on weekends they rode in a car or went to movies. In movies she was fascinated by fat actresses. She wondered why they were fat. She knew why she was fat: she was fat because she was Louise. Because God had made her that way. Because she wasn't like her friends Joan and Marjorie, who drank milk shakes after school and were all bones and tight skin. But what about those actresses, with their talents, with their broad and profound faces? Did they eat as heedlessly as Bishop Humphries and his wife who sometimes came to dinner and, as Louise's mother said, gorged between amenities? Or did they try to lose weight, did they go about hungry and angry and thinking of food? She thought of them eating lean meats and salads with friends, and then going home and building strange large sandwiches with French bread. But mostly she believed they did not go through these failures; they were fat because they chose to be. And she was certain of something else too: she could see it in their faces: they did not eat secretly. Which she did: her creeping to the kitchen when she was nine became, in high school, a ritual of deceit and pleasure. She was a furtive eater of sweets. Even her two friends did not know her secret.

Joan was thin, gangling, and flat-chested; she was attractive enough and all she needed was someone to take a second look at her face, but the school was large and there were pretty girls in every classroom and walking all the corridors, so no one ever needed to take a second look at Joan. Marjorie was thin too, an intense, heavy-smoking girl with brittle laughter. She was very intelligent, and with boys she was shy because she knew she made them uncomfortable, and because she was smarter than they were and so could not understand or could not believe the levels they lived on. She was to have a nervous breakdown before earning her Ph.D. in philosophy at the University of California, where she met and married a physicist and discovered within herself an untrammelled passion: she made love with her husband on the couch, the carpet, in the bathtub, and on the washing machine. By that time much had happened to her and she never thought of Louise. Joan would finally stop growing and begin moving with grace and confidence. In college she would have two lovers and then several more during the six years she spent in Boston before marrying a middle-aged editor who had two sons in their early teens, who drank too much, who was tenderly, boyishly grateful for her love, and whose wife had been killed while rock-climbing in New Hampshire with her lover. She would not think of Louise either, except in an earlier time, when lovers were still new to her and she was ecstatically surprised each time one of them loved her and, sometimes at night, lying in a man's arms, she would tell how in high school no one dated her, she had been thin and plain (she would still believe that: that she had been plain; it had never been true) and so had been forced into the week-end and night-time company of a neurotic smart girl and a shy fat girl. She would say this with self-pity exaggerated by Scotch and her need to be more deeply loved by the man who held her.

She never eats, Joan and Marjorie said of Louise. They ate lunch with her at school, watched her refusing potatoes, ravioli, fried fish. Sometimes she got through the cafeteria line with only a salad. That is how they would remember her: a girl whose hapless body was destined to be fat. No one saw the sandwiches she made and took to her room when she came home from school. No one saw the store of Milky Ways, Butterfingers, Almond Joys, and Hersheys far back on her closet shelf, behind the stuffed animals of her child-hood. She was not a hypocrite. When she was out of the house she truly believed she was dieting; she forgot about the candy, as a man speaking into his office dictaphone may forget the lewd photographs hidden in an old shoe in his closet. At other times, away from home, she thought of the waiting candy with near lust. One night driving home from a movie, Marjorie said: 'You're lucky you don't smoke; it's incredible what I go through to hide it from my parents.' Louise turned to her a smile which was elusive and mysterious; she yearned to be home in bed, eating chocolate in the dark. She did not need to smoke; she already had a vice that was insular and destructive.

She brought it with her to college. She thought she would leave it behind. A move from one place to another, a new room without the haunted closet shelf, would do for her what she could not do for herself. She packed her large dresses and went. For two weeks she was busy with registration, with shyness, with classes; then she began to feel at home. Her room was no longer like a motel. Its walls had stopped watching her, she felt they were her friends, and she gave them her secret. Away from her mother, she did not have to be as elaborate; she kept the candy in her drawer now.

The school was in Massachusetts, a girls' school. When she chose it, when she and her father and mother talked about it in the evenings, everyone so carefully avoided the word boys that sometimes the conversations seemed to be about nothing but boys. There are no boys there, the neuter words said; you will not have to contend with that. In her father's eyes were pity and encouragement; in her mother's was disappointment, and her voice was crisp. They spoke of courses, of small classes where Louise would get more attention. She imagined herself in those small classes; she saw herself as a teacher would see her, as the other girls would; she would get no attention.

The girls at the school were from wealthy families, but most of them wore the uniform of another class: blue jeans and work shirts, and many wore overalls. Louise bought some overalls, washed them until the dark blue faded, and wore them to classes. In the cafeteria she ate as she had in high school, not to lose weight nor even to sustain her lie, but because eating lightly in public had become as habitual as good manners. Everyone had to take gym, and in the locker room with the other girls, and wearing shorts on the volleyball and badminton courts, she hated her body. She liked her body most when she was unaware of it: in bed at night, as sleep gently took her out of her day, out of herself. And she liked parts of her body. She liked her brown eyes and sometimes looked at them in the mirror: they were not shallow eyes, she thought; they were indeed windows of a tender soul, a good heart. She liked her lips and nose, and her chin, finely shaped between her wide and sagging cheeks. Most of all she liked her long pale blonde hair, she liked washing and drying it and lying naked on her bed, smelling of shampoo, and feeling the soft hair at her neck and shoulders and back.

Her friend at college was Carrie, who was thin and wore thick glasses and often at night she cried in Louise's room. She did not know why she was crying. She was crying, she said, because she was unhappy. She could say no more. Louise said she was unhappy too, and Carrie moved in with her. One night Carrie talked for hours, sadly and bitterly, about her parents and what they did to each other. When she finished she hugged Louise and they went to bed. Then in the dark Carrie spoke across the room: 'Louise? I just wanted to tell you. One night last week I woke up and smelled chocolate. You were eating chocolate, in your bed. I wish you'd eat it in front of me, Louise, whenever you feel like it.'

Stiffened in her bed, Louise could think of nothing to say. In the silence she was afraid Carrie would think she was asleep and would tell her again in the morning or tomorrow night. Finally she said Okay. Then after a moment she told Carrie if she ever wanted any she could feel free to help herself; the candy was in the top drawer. Then she said thank you.

They were roommates for four years and in the summers they exchanged letters. Each fall they greeted with embraces, laughter, tears, and moved into their old room, which had been stripped and cleansed of them for the summer. Neither girl enjoyed summer. Carrie did not like being at home because her parents did not love each other. Louise lived in a small city in Louisiana. She did not like summer because she had lost touch with Joan and Marjorie; they saw each other, but it was not the same. She liked being with her father but with no one else. The flicker of disappointment in her mother's eyes at the airport was a vanguard of the army of relatives and acquaintances who awaited her: they would see her on the streets, in stores, at the country club, in her home, and in theirs; in the first moments of greeting, their eyes would tell her she was still fat Louise, who had been fat as long as they could remember, who had gone to college and returned as fat as ever. Then their eyes dismissed her, and she longed for school and Carrie, and she wrote letters to her friend. But that saddened her too. It wasn't simply that Carrie was her only friend, and when they finished college they might never see each other again. It was that her existence in the world was so divided; it had begun when she was a child creeping to the kitchen; now that division was much sharper, and her friendship with Carrie seemed disproportionate and perilous. The world she was destined to live in had nothing to do with the intimate nights in their room at school.

In the summer before their senior year, Carrie fell in love. She wrote to Louise about him, but she did not write much, and this hurt Louise more than if Carrie had shown the joy her writing tried to conceal. That fall they returned to their room; they were still close and warm, Carrie still needed Louise's ears and heart at night as she spoke of her parents and her recurring malaise whose source the two friends never discovered. But on most week-ends Carrie left, and caught a bus to Boston where her boyfriend studied music. During the week she often spoke hesitantly of sex; she was not sure if she liked it. But Louise, eating candy and listening, did not know whether Carrie was telling the truth or whether, as in her letters of the past summer, Carrie was keeping from her those delights she may never experience.

Then one Sunday night when Carrie had just returned from Boston and was unpacking her overnight bag, she looked at Louise and said: 'I was thinking about you. On the bus coming home tonight.' Looking at Carrie's concerned, determined face, Louise prepared herself for humiliation. 'I was thinking about when we graduate. What you're going to do. What's to become of you. I want you to be loved the way I love you. Louise, if I help you, *really* help you, will you go on a diet?'

Louise entered a period of her life she would remember always, the way some people remember having endured poverty. Her diet did not begin the next day. Carrie told her to eat on Monday as though it were the last day of her life. So for the first time since grammar school Louise went into a school cafeteria and ate everything she wanted. At breakfast and lunch and dinner she glanced around the table to see if the other girls noticed the food on her tray. They did not. She felt there was a lesson in this, but it lay beyond her grasp. That night in their room she ate the four remaining candy bars. During the day Carrie rented a small refrigerator, bought an electric skillet, an electric broiler, and bathroom scales.

On Tuesday morning Louise stood on the scales, and Carrie wrote in her notebook: *October 14: 184 lbs*. Then she made Louise a cup of black coffee and scrambled one egg and sat with her while she ate. When Carrie went to the dining room for breakfast, Louise walked about the campus for thirty minutes. That was part of the plan. The campus was pretty, on its lawns grew at least one of every tree native to New England, and in the warm morning sun Louise felt a new hope. At noon they met in their room, and Carrie broiled her a piece of hamburger and served it with lettuce. Then while Carrie ate in the dining room Louise walked again. She was weak with hunger and she felt queasy. During her afternoon classes she was nervous and tense, and she chewed her pencil and tapped her heels on the floor and tightened her calves. When she returned to her room late that afternoon, she was so glad to see Carrie that she embraced her; she had felt she could not bear another minute of hunger, but now with Carrie she knew she could make it at least through tonight. Then she would sleep and face tomorrow when it came. Carrie broiled her a steak and served it with lettuce. Louise studied while Carrie ate dinner, then they went for a walk.

That was her ritual and her diet for the rest of the year, Carrie alternating fish and chicken breasts with the steaks for dinner, and every day was nearly as bad as the first. In the evenings she was irritable. In all her life she had never been afflicted by ill temper and she looked upon it now as a demon which, along with hunger, was taking possession of her soul. Often she spoke sharply to Carrie. One night during their after-dinner walk Carrie talked sadly of night, of how darkness made her more aware of herself, and at night she did not know why she was in college, why she studied, why she was walking the earth with other people. They were standing on a wooden foot bridge, looking down at a dark pond. Carrie kept talking, perhaps soon she would cry. Suddenly Louise said: 'I'm sick of lettuce. I never want to see a piece of lettuce for the rest of my life. I hate it. We shouldn't even buy it, it's immoral.'

Carrie was quiet. Louise glanced at her, and the pain and irritation in Carrie's face soothed her. Then she was ashamed. Before she could say she was sorry, Carrie turned to her and said gently: 'I know. I know how terrible it is.'

Carrie did all the shopping, telling Louise she knew how hard it was to go into a supermarket when you were hungry. And Louise was always hungry. She drank diet soft drinks and started smoking Carrie's cigarettes, learned to enjoy inhaling, thought of cancer and emphysema but they were as far away as those boys her mother had talked about when she was nine. By Thanksgiving she was smoking over a pack a day and her weight in Carrie's notebook was one hundred and sixty-two pounds. Carrie was afraid if Louise went home at Thanksgiving she would lapse from the diet, so Louise spent the vacation with Carrie, in Philadelphia. Carrie wrote her family about the diet, and told Louise that she had. On the plane to Philadelphia, Louise said: 'I feel like a bedwetter. When I was a little girl I had a friend who used to come spend the night and Mother would put a rubber sheet on the bed and we all pretended there wasn't a rubber sheet and that she hadn't wet the bed. Even me, and I slept with her.' At Thanksgiving dinner she lowered her eyes as Carrie's father put two slices of white meat on her plate and passed it to her over the bowls of steaming food.

When she went home at Christmas she weighed a hundred and fifty-five pounds; at the airport her mother marvelled. Her father laughed and hugged her and said: 'But now there's less of you to love.' He was troubled by her smoking but only mentioned it once; he told her she was beautiful and, as always, his eyes bathed her with love. During the long vacation her mother cooked for her as Carrie had, and Louise returned to school weighing a hundred and forty-six pounds.

Flying north on the plane she warmly recalled the surprised and congratulatory eyes of her relatives and acquaintances. She had not seen Joan or Marjorie. She thought of returning home in May, weighing the hundred and fifteen pounds which Carrie had in October set as their goal. Looking toward the stoic days ahead, she felt strong. She thought of those hungry days of fall and early winter (and now: she was hungry now: with almost a frown, almost a brusque shake of the head, she refused peanuts from the stewardess): those first weeks of the diet when she was the pawn of an irascibility which still, conditioned to her ritual as she was, could at any moment take command of her. She thought of the nights of trying to sleep while her stomach growled. She thought of her addiction to cigarettes. She thought of the people at school: not one teacher, not one girl, had spoken to her about her loss of weight, not even about her absence from meals. And without warning her spirit collapsed. She did not feel strong, she did not feel she was committed to and within reach of achieving a valuable goal. She felt that somehow she had lost more than pounds of fat; that some time during her dieting she had lost herself too. She tried to remember what it had felt like to be Louise before she had started living on meat and fish, as an unhappy adult may look sadly in the memory of childhood for lost virtues and hopes. She looked down at the earth far below, and it seemed to her that her soul, like her body aboard the plane, was in some rootless flight. She neither knew its destination nor where it had departed from; it was on some passage she could not even define.

During the next few weeks she lost weight more slowly and once for eight days Carrie's daily recording stayed at a hundred and thirty-six. Louise woke in the morning thinking of one hundred and thirty-six and then she stood on the scales and they echoed her. She became obsessed with that number, and there wasn't a day when she didn't say it aloud, and through the days and nights the number stayed in her mind, and if a teacher had spoken those digits in a classroom she would have opened her mouth to speak. What if that's me, she said to Carrie. I mean what if a hundred and thirty-six is my real weight and I just can't lose anymore. Walking hand-in-hand with her despair was a longing for this to be true, and that longing angered her and wearied her, and every day she was gloomy. On the ninth day she weighed a hundred and thirty-five and a half pounds. She was not relieved; she thought bitterly of the months ahead, the shedding of the last twenty and a half pounds.

On Easter Sunday, which she spent at Carrie's, she weighed one hundred and twenty pounds, and she ate one slice of glazed pineapple with her ham and lettuce. She did not enjoy it; she felt she was being friendly with a recalcitrant enemy who had once tried to destroy her. Carrie's parents were laudative. She liked them and she wished they would touch sometimes, and look at each other when they spoke. She guessed they would divorce when Carrie left home, and she vowed that her own marriage would be one of affection and tenderness. She could think about that now: marriage. At school she had read in a Boston paper that this summer the cicadas would come out of their seventeen year hibernation on Cape Cod, for a month they would mate and then die, leaving their young to burrow into the ground where they would stay for seventeen years. That's me, she had said to Carrie. Only my hibernation lasted twenty-one years.

Often her mother asked in letters and on the phone about the diet, but Louise answered vaguely. When she flew home in late May she weighed a hundred and thirteen pounds, and at the airport her mother cried and hugged her and said again and again: You're so *beautiful*. Her father blushed and bought her a martini. For days her relatives and acquaintances congratulated her, and the applause in their eyes lasted the entire summer, and she loved their eyes, and swam in the country club pool, the first time she had done this since she was a child.

She lived at home and ate the way her mother did and every morning she weighed herself on the scales in her bathroom. Her mother liked to take her shopping and buy her dresses and they put her old ones in the Goodwill box at the shopping center; Louise thought of them existing on the body of a poor woman whose cheap meals kept her fat. Louise's mother had a photographer come to the house, and Louise posed on the couch and standing beneath a live oak and sitting in a wicker lawn chair next to an azalea bush. The new clothes and the photographer made her feel she was going to another country or becoming a citizen of a new one. In the fall she took a job of no consequence, to give herself something to do.

Also in the fall a young lawyer joined her father's firm, he came one night to dinner, and they started seeing each other. He was the first man outside her family to kiss her since the barbecue when she was sixteen. Louise celebrated Thanksgiving not with rice dressing and candied sweet potatoes and mince meat and pumpkin pies, but by giving Richard her virginity which she realized, at the very last moment of its existence, she had embarked on giving him over thirteen months ago, on that Tuesday in October when Carrie had made her a cup of black coffee and scrambled one egg. She wrote this to Carrie, who replied happily by return mail. She also, through glance and smile and innuendo, tried to tell her mother too. But finally she controlled that impulse, because Richard felt guilty about making love with the daughter of his partner and friend. In the spring they married. The wedding was a large one, in the Episcopal church, and Carrie flew from Boston to be maid of honor. Her parents had recently separated and she was living with the musician and was still victim of her unpredictable malaise. It overcame her on the night before the wedding, so Louise was up with her until past three and woke next morning from a sleep so heavy that she did not want to leave it.

Richard was a lean, tall, energetic man with the metabolism of a pencil sharpener. Louise fed him everything he wanted. He liked Italian food and she got recipes from her mother and watched him eating spaghetti with the sauce she had only tasted, and ravioli and lasagna, while she ate antipasto with her chianti. He made a lot of money and borrowed more and they bought a house whose lawn sloped down to the shore of a lake; they had a wharf and a boathouse, and Richard bought a boat and they took friends waterskiing. Richard bought her a car and they spent his vacations in Mexico, Canada, the Bahamas, and in the fifth year of their marriage they went to Europe and, according to their plan, she conceived a child in Paris. On the plane back, as she looked out the window and beyond the sparkling sea and saw her country, she felt that it was waiting for her, as her home by the lake was, and her parents, and her good friends who rode in the boat and waterskied; she thought of the accumulated warmth and pelf of her marriage, and how by slimming her body she had bought into the pleasures of the nation. She felt cunning, and she smiled to herself, and took Richard's hand.

But these moments of triumph were sparse. On most days she went about her routine of leisure with a sense of certainty about herself that came merely from not thinking. But there were times, with her friends, or with Richard, or alone in the house, when she was suddenly assaulted by the feeling that she had taken the wrong train and arrived at a place where no one knew her, and where she ought not to be. Often, in bed with Richard, she talked of being fat: 'I was the one who started the friendship with Carrie, I chose her, I started the conversations. When I understood that she was my friend I understood something else: I had chosen her for the same reason I'd chosen Joan and Marjorie. They were all thin. I was always thinking about what people saw when they looked at me and I didn't want them to see two fat girls. When I was alone I didn't mind being fat but then I'd have to leave the house again and then I didn't want to look like me. But at home I didn't mind except when I was getting dressed to go out of the house and when Mother looked at me. But I stopped looking at her when she looked at me. And in college I felt good with Carrie; there weren't any boys and I didn't have any other friends and so when I wasn't with Carrie I thought about her and I tried to ignore the other people around me, I tried to make them not exist. A lot of the time I could do that. It was strange, and I felt like a spy.'

If Richard was bored by her repetition he pretended not to be. But she knew the story meant very little to him. She could have been telling him of a childhood illness, or wearing braces, or a broken heart at sixteen. He could not see her as she was when she was fat. She felt as though she were trying to tell a foreign lover about her life in the United States, and if only she could command the language he would know and love all of her and she would feel complete. Some of the acquaintances of her childhood were her friends now, and even they did not seem to remember her when she was fat.

Now her body was growing again, and when she put on a maternity dress for the first time she shivered with fear. Richard did not smoke and he asked her, in a voice just short of demand, to stop during her pregnancy. She did. She ate carrots and celery instead of smoking, and at cocktail parties she tried to eat nothing, but after her first drink she ate nuts and cheese and crackers and dips. Always at these parties Richard had talked with his friends and she had rarely spoken to him until they drove home. But now when he noticed her at the hors d'oeuvres table he crossed the room and, smiling, led her back to his group. His smile and his hand on her arm told her he was doing his clumsy, husbandly best to help her through a time of female mystery.

She was gaining weight but she told herself it was only the baby, and would leave with its birth. But at other times she knew quite clearly that she was losing the discipline she had fought so hard to gain during her last year with Carrie. She was hungry now as she had been in college, and she ate between meals and after dinner and tried to eat only carrots and celery, but she grew to hate them, and her desire for sweets was as vicious as it had been long ago. At home she ate bread and jam and when she shopped for groceries she bought a candy bar and ate it driving home and put the wrapper in her purse and then in the garbage can under the sink. Her cheeks had filled out, there was loose flesh under her chin, her arms and legs were plump, and her mother was concerned. So was Richard. One night when she brought pie and milk to the living room where they were watching television, he said: 'You already had a piece. At dinner.'

She did not look at him.

'You're gaining weight. It's not all water, either. It's fat. It'll be summertime. You'll want to get into your bathing suit.'

The pie was cherry. She looked at it as her fork cut through it; she speared the piece and rubbed it in the red juice on the plate before lifting it to her mouth.

'You never used to eat pie,' he said. 'I just think you ought to watch it a bit. It's going to be tough on you this summer.'

In her seventh month, with a delight reminiscent of climbing the stairs to Richard's apartment before they were married, she returned to her world of secret gratification. She began hiding candy in her underwear drawer. She ate it during the day and at night while Richard slept, and at breakfast she was distracted, waiting for him to leave.

She gave birth to a son, brought him home, and nursed both him and her appetites. During this time of celibacy she enjoyed her body through her son's mouth; while he suckled she stroked his small head and back. She was hiding candy but she did not conceal her other indulgences: she was smoking again but still she ate between meals, and at dinner she ate what Richard did, and coldly he watched her, he grew petulant, and when the date marking the end of their celibacy came they let it pass. Often in the afternoons her mother visited and scolded her and Louise sat looking at the baby and said nothing until finally, to end it, she promised to diet. When her mother and father came for dinners, her father kissed her and held the baby and her mother said nothing about Louise's body, and her voice was tense. Returning from work in the evenings Richard looked at a soiled plate and glass on the table beside her chair as if detecting traces of infidelity, and at every dinner they fought.

'Look at you,' he said. 'Lasagna, for God's sake. When are you going to start? It's not simply that you haven't lost any weight. You're gaining. I can see it. I can feel it when you get in bed. Pretty soon you'll weigh more than I do and I'll be sleeping on a trampoline.'

'You never touch me anymore.'

'I don't want to touch you. Why should I? Have you *looked* at yourself?'

'You're cruel,' she said. 'I never knew how cruel you were.'

She ate, watching him. He did not look at her. Glaring at his plate, he worked with fork and knife like a hurried man at a lunch counter.

'I bet you didn't either,' she said.

That night when he was asleep she took a Milky Way to the bathroom. For a while she stood eating in the dark, then she turned on the light. Chewing, she looked at herself in the mirror; she looked at her eyes and hair. Then she stood on the scales and looking at the numbers between her feet, one hundred and sixty-two, she remembered when she had weighed a hundred and thirty-six pounds for eight days. Her memory of those eight days was fond and amusing, as though she were recalling an Easter egg hunt when she was six. She stepped off the scales and pushed them under the lavatory and did not stand on them again.

It was summer and she bought loose dresses and when Richard took friends out on the boat she did not wear a bathing suit or shorts; her friends gave her mischievous glances, and Richard did not look at her. She stopped riding on the boat. She told them she wanted to stay with the baby, and she sat inside holding him until she heard the boat leave the wharf. Then she took him to the front lawn and walked with him in the shade of the trees and talked to him about the blue jays and mockingbirds and cardinals she saw on their branches. Sometimes she stopped and watched the boat out on the lake and the friend skiing behind it.

Every day Richard quarrelled, and because his rage went no further than her weight and shape, she felt excluded from it, and she remained calm within layers of flesh and spirit, and watched his frustration, his impotence. He truly believed they were arguing about her weight. She knew better: she knew that beneath the argument lay the question of who Richard was. She thought of him smiling at the wheel of his boat, and long ago courting his slender girl, the daughter of his partner and friend. She thought of Carrie telling her of smelling chocolate in the dark and, after that, watching her eat it night after night. She smiled at Richard, teasing his anger.

He is angry now. He stands in the center of the living room, raging at her, and he wakes the baby. Beneath Richard's voice she hears the soft crying, feels it in her heart, and quietly she rises from her chair and goes upstairs to the child's room and takes him from the crib. She brings him to the living room and sits holding him in her lap, pressing him gently against the folds of fat at her waist. Now Richard is pleading with her. Louise thinks tenderly of Carrie broiling meat and fish in their room, and walking with her in the evenings. She wonders if Carrie still has the malaise. Perhaps she will come for a visit. In Louise's arms now the boy sleeps.

'I'll help you,' Richard says. 'I'll eat the same things you eat.'

But his face does not approach the compassion and determination and love she had seen in Carrie's during what she now recognizes as the worst year of her life. She can remember nothing about that year except hunger, and the meals in her room. She is hungry now. When she puts the boy to bed she will get a candy bar from her room. She will eat it here, in front of Richard. This room will be hers soon. She considers the possibilities: all these rooms and the lawn where she can do whatever she wishes. She knows he will leave soon. It has been in his eyes all summer. She stands, using one hand to pull herself out of the chair. She carries the boy to his crib, feels him against her large breasts, feels that his sleeping body touches her soul. With a surge of vindication and relief she holds him. Then she kisses his forehead and places him in the crib. She goes to the bedroom and in the dark takes a bar of candy from her drawer. Slowly she descends the stairs. She knows Richard is waiting but she feels his departure so happily that, when she enters the living room, unwrapping the candy, she is surprised to see him standing there.

THE CAPTAIN

For Gunnery Sergeant Jim Beer

H IS SON WORE a moustache. Over and between tan faces and the backs of heads with hair cut high and short, and green-uniformed shoulders and chests and backs, Harry saw him standing with two other second lieutenants at the bar. His black moustache was thick. Only one woman was at happy hour, a blond captain: she had a watchful, attractive face that was pretty when she laughed. Harry stepped forward one pace, then another, and stood with his back to the door, breathing the fragrance of liquor and cigarette smoke, as pleasing to him as the smell of cooking is to some, and feeling through his body the loud talk and laughter and shouts, as though he watched a parade whose music coursed through him. In his own uniform with captain's bars and ribbons, he wanted to stand here and have one Scotch. He did not feel that he stood to the side of the gathered men, but at their head, looking down the axis of their gaiety. A tall man, he did look down at most of them, and he wanted to watch his son from this distance. But there were no waitresses, so he went to the bar and spoke over Phil's shoulder: 'There's one nice thing about a moustache.'

The eyes in the turning face were dark and happy. Then Harry was hugging him, and Phil's arms were around his waist, tighter and tighter, and Phil leaned back and lifted him from the floor, the metal buttons of their blouses clicking together, then scraping as Phil lowered him, and introduced him to the two lieutenants as *my father, Captain LeDuc, retired.* Harry shook hands, not hearing their names, focusing instead on their faces and tightly tailored blouses and the silver shooting badges on their breasts: both wore the crossed rifles and crossed pistols of experts, and above those, like Phil, they wore only the one red and gold ribbon that showed they were in the service during a war they had not seen. He saw them scanning his four rows of ribbons, pretended he had not, and turned to Phil, letting his friends look comfortably at the colored rectangles of two wars and a wound and one act that had earned him a Silver Star. Beside Phil's crossed rifles was the Maltese cross of a sharpshooter. The bartender emptied the astray, and Phil ordered another round and a Scotch and water, and Harry said: 'What happened with the .45?'

'I choked up. What bothers me is knowing I'm better and having to wear this till next year. *Then* I'll—' He smiled and his eyes lowered and rose. 'Jesus.'

'Good,' Harry said. 'If we couldn't forget, we'd never enjoy anything after the age of ten. Or five.'

Phil turned to his friends standing at his left and said he had just told his father he didn't like having to wear the sharpshooter badge until he qualified again next year, and the three of them laughed and joked about rice paddies and Monday and jungle and Charlie, and Harry saw the bartender coming with their drinks and paid him, thinking of how often memory lies, of how so often the lies are good ones. When he was twenty-four years old, he had learned on Guadalcanal that the body could endure nearly anything, and after that he had acted as though he believed it could endure everything: could work without sleep or rest or enough food and water, heedless of cold and heat and illness; could survive penetration and dismemberment, so that death in combat was a matter of bad luck, a man with five bullets in him surviving another pierced by only one. He was so awed by the body's strength and vulnerability that he did nothing at all about prolonging its life. This refusal was rooted neither in confidence nor an acceptance of fate. His belief in mystery and chance was too strong to allow faith in exercising and in controlling what he ate and drank and when he smoked. Phil had forgotten who he was and where he was going; was that how the mind survived? The body pushed beyond pain, and the mind sidestepped. How else could he stand here, comfortable, proud of his son, when his own mind held images this room of cheerful peace could not contain? He raised a knee and drew his pack of cigarettes from his sock, and Phil gave him a light with a Zippo bearing a Marine emblem, and said: 'What's the one nice thing about a moustache?'

'If I have to tell you, you're fucking up on more than the .45.'

'They don't give out badges for that.'

'One girl?'

'No.'

'Good. It's too rough on them.'

'They'll *all* miss me, Pop.'

'I'd rather be in the middle of it. I didn't have a girl, when I was in the Pacific. But, Jesus, I was never warm in the Reservoir, not for one minute, there was always *some*thing cold—'

'Frozen Chosin,' one of the lieutenants said, and drank and eyed Harry's ribbons over the glass.

'—Right: *I* was frozen. *Every*body: we'd come on dead Chi*nese* frozen. And tell you the truth, I didn't think we'd get out, more fucking Chinese than snow, but I'd rather have been freezing my ass off and trying to keep it from getting between a Chinaman's bullet and thin air than back home like your mother. How do you keep waking up every day and doing what there is to do when you know your man is getting shot at? Ha.' He looked from Phil to the two lieutenants watching him, respectfully embarrassed, then back at Phil, whose dark saddened eyes had never looked at him this way before, almost as a father gazing at a son, and in a rush of age he saw himself as father of a man grown enough to give him pity. 'I guess I'm fucking well about to find out.'

'Fucking-A,' Phil said, and clapped his shoulder and turned to his drink.

At three in the morning, a half-hour before the alarm, his heart woke him, its anticipatory beat freezing him as normally caffeine did from that depth of sleep whose paradox he could not forgive: needing each night that respite so badly that finally nothing could prevent his having it, then each morning having to rise from it with coffee and tobacco so that he could resume with hope those volitive hours that would end with his grateful return to the oblivion of dreams. He coughed and swallowed, and coughed again and swallowed that too. Phil was in a sleeping bag on an air mattress in the middle of the small room. Last night after dinner at the officers' club, where they had talked of hunting and today's terrain, they had spread out on Phil's desk a map he got from the sportsmen's club when he drew their hunting area from a campaign hat three nights earlier, and Harry looked, nodded, and listened while Phil, using a pencil as a pointer, told him about the squares of contoured earth on the map that Harry could not only read more quickly, and more accurately, but also felt he knew anyway because, having spent most of his peacetime career at Camp Pendleton, he felt all its reaches were his ground. But he remained amused, and nearly agreed when Phil showed him two long ridges flanking a valley, and said this was the place to get a deer and spend the whole Saturday without seeing one of the other eight hunters who had drawn the same boundaries.

'It'll take us too long to walk in,' Harry said.

'I got the CO's jeep. I told him you were coming to hunt.'

At three-fifteen by the luminous dial of his Marine-issued wristwatch that he felt he had not stolen but retired with him, he quietly left the bed and stood looking down at Phil. He lay on his back, a pillow under his head, all but his throat and face hidden and shapeless in the bulk of the sleeping bag. His face was paled by sleep and the dark, eyeless save for brows and curves, and his delicate breathing whispered into the faint hum, the constant tone of night's quiet. Harry had not watched him sleeping since he was a boy, and now he was pierced as with a remembrance of fatherhood, but of something else too, as old as the earth's dust: in the darkened bedrooms of Phil and the two daughters he had felt this tender dread; and also looking at the face of a woman asleep, even some he did not love when he woke in the night: his children and the women devoid of anger and passion and humor and pain, so that he yearned during their fragile rest to protect them from and for whatever shaped their faces in daylight.

'Lieutenant,' he said, his deep voice, almost harsh, snapping both him and Phil into the day's hunt: 'The good thing about a moustache is you can smell her all night while you sleep, and when you wake up you can lick it again.'

The eyes opened and stared from a face still in repose; the mouth was slower to leave sleep, then it smiled and Phil said: 'You exenlisted men talk dirty.'

They dressed and went quickly down the corridor, rifles slung on their shoulders, Phil carrying in one hand a pack with their breakfast and lunch; they wore pistol belts with canteens and hunting knives, and jeans, and sweat shirts over their shirts, and windbreakers; Harry wore a wide-brimmed straw hat. Still, the act of arming himself to go into the hills made him feel he was in uniform, and as Phil drove the open jeep through fog, Harry shivered and pushed his hat tighter on his head and watched both flanks, an instinct so old and now useless that it amused him. He had learned to use his senses as an animal does, and probably as his ancestors in Canada and New Hampshire had, though not his father, whose avocation was beer and cards and friends in his kitchen or theirs, the men's talk with the first beers and hands of penny ante poker in French and English, then later only in the French that had crossed the ocean centuries before the invention of things, so in the flow of words that Harry never learned he now and then heard engine and car and airplane and electric fan. So in 1936, never having touched a rifle or pistol, he went into the Marine Corps with a taste for beer and a knowledge of poker acquired in his eighteenth year and last at home, when his father said he was old enough to join the table, and he trained with young men who had killed game since boyhood, and would learn cards in the barracks and drinking in bars. Four years later he returned home; in the summer evening he walked from the bus station over climbing and dropping streets of the village to the little house where his father sat on the front steps with a bottle of beer; he had not bathed yet for the dinner that Harry could smell cooking; he had taken off his shirt, and his undershirt was wet and soiled; sweat streaked the dirt on his throat and arms, and he hugged Harry and called to the family, took a long swallow of beer, handed the bottle to Harry, and said: 'I got you a job at the foundry.' Two days later, Harry took a bus to the recruiting office and reenlisted.

The jeep descended into colder air; fog hid the low earth, so that Harry could not judge the distance from the road to the dark bulk of hills on both sides. He stopped looking, and at once felt exposed and alert; he smiled and shook his head and leaned toward the dashboard to light a cigarette. He could see no stars; the wet moon was pallid, distant. He watched the road, grey fog paled and swathed yellow by the headlights, and said: 'There was a battalion cut off, when the Chinese came in.'

'*What?*'

He turned to Phil and spoke away from the rushing air, loudly over the vibrating moan of the jeep: the Chosin Reservoir, the whole Goddamned division was surrounded and a battalion cut off, and they had to go through Chinese to get there and break the battalion out and bring it to the main body. So they could retreat through all those Chinese to the sea. The battalion was pinned down about five miles away, so they started on foot, with a company on each flank playing leapfrog over the hills: two battalions, one of them Royal Marines, and their colonel was in command. A feisty little bastard. 'I've never *liked Li*meys, but the Royal Ma*rines* are *good*.' He guessed he liked Limey troops, it was just the country that pissed him off. The reason Marines had such good liberty in Australia in World War II was the Aussies were off in Africa fighting for England. Even the chaplain probably got laid. 'They loved Ma*rines* and still *do*, and if you ever get a chance to go to Austra*li*a, *take* it.' Their boys were fighting the Goddamn Germans, so it was the Marines keeping Australia safe, and they'd go there for R and R and get all the thanks too. The Limeys were good at that, getting other people to go off and fight in somebody else's yard. 'Do you read *hi*story?'

'Not since *college.*'

'You've *got* to.' He shivered and caught his hat before it blew off, and the jeep climbed into lighter fog. 'If you're going to be a ca*reer* man, you've got to start *study*ing this stuff *now*. Not just *tac*tics and *strat*egy; but how these wars get *start*ed, and *why*, and who *starts* them.'

'I *will*. What about that bat*tal*ion?'

The flank companies kept making contact in the hills, and the troops in the road would assault and clear that hill, then start moving again; but they were moving too slowly, it was one fire fight after another, so the colonel called back for trucks and brought the people down from the hills, and they all mounted up in the trucks and hauled ass down the road till they got hit; then they'd pile out and attack, and when they'd knocked out whatever it was or it had run off to some other hill, they'd hi-diddle-diddle up the road again—

'Holy *shit.*'

'I never felt so *much* like a moving *tar*get.' He rode shotgun in a six-by; the driver was a corporal and he pissed all over himself; he was good, though; he just kept cussing and shifting gears; probably he was praying too; maybe it was all praying: Jesus Christ God*damn*—pissssss—shit *Je*sus—From the front of the six-by he watched the hills, but what good was it to watch where it's going to come from, when you're moving so fast that you know you can't see anything till you draw fire? He felt like he was searching the air for a bullet. He told the corporal he wished he were up there and the Chinese were down here. Probably that was a prayer too —Harry grabbed his hat as the brim slapped the crown; he put it in his lap, and the air was cool on his bald spot. '*De*-fense is *best*, you know. Or don't they *tell* you *that*.' 'Course they don't, Marines always attack; but with helicopters you can go behind them and cut off their line of supply and defend that. 'Read Lid*del Hart*. And learn *Span*ish. That's where it's *go*ing to *be*.'

'*Where*?'

' *Mex*ico to Tie*rra* del *Fue*go. We got the batta*li*on out.'

He twisted and reached behind his left hip for his canteen.

'So the *colo*nel was *right*.'

'*Sure* he was.' He gargled, then swallowed, and drank again and offered the canteen to Phil, who shook his head. 'We *lost* people we might *not* have, if we'd *done* it the *right* way. But we had to *do* it the *fast* way.'

The jeep climbed, and above him the fog was thinning; to his right he could see a ridge outlined clearly against the sky.

'Have you *seen* your *mother* yet?'

'*Last night*. She and the *girls*. We had *din*ner. *Cath*erine's screwed up.'

'Not *dope*?'

'*No*. She doesn't *think* I should *go*. At the same *time* she—' He shrugged, glanced at Harry, then watched the road.

'Loves her *brother*,' Harry said.

'Yes.'

'Just the *wom*en? No *boy* friends?'

'I *don't* think they *like* Marines.'

'*Fuck* 'em.'

'I'll leave *that* to *Cath*erine and *Joyce*.'

'*Easy* now. My *daugh*ters are *vir*gins.'

'*Right*.'

' I wish your *ski*pper had left the *top* on the *jeep*.'

'—*soon* .'

'*What?*'

'To*day* will be *hot*.'

Harry nodded and put on his hat, pressing it down, and watched the suspended motion of fog above the road.

The deer camp duty officer's table was near the fire. He wore hunting clothes and was rankless, as all the hunters were, but was in charge of the camp, logging hunters in and out, and recording their kills, because he had drawn the duty from a hat. A hissing gas lantern was on the table near his log book, and above him shadows cast by the fire danced in trees. Harry and Phil gave him their names and hunting area; he was in his mid-thirties, looked to Harry like a gunnery sergeant or major; they spoke to him about fog and the cold drive, and he wished them luck as they moved away, to the fire where two men squatted with skillets of eggs and others stood drinking coffee from canteen cups. The fire was in a hole; a large coffeepot rested on two stones at the edge of the flames. Harry poured for both of them, shook the pot, and a lance corporal emerged from the darkness; he wore faded green utilities and was eating a doughnut. He took the pot from Harry and shook it, then placed it beside the hole and returned to the darkness. The two men cooking eggs rose and brought the crackling skillets to the edge of the fire's light, where three men sat drinking coffee. The lance corporal came back with a kettle and put it on the stones, then sat cross-legged and smoked. His boots shone in the fire's light. From above, Harry watched him: he liked his build, lean and supple, and the cocky press of his lips, and his wearing his cap visor so low over his eyes that he had to jut out his chin to see in front of him. Phil crouched and held a skillet of bacon over the fire, and Harry stepped closer to the lance corporal; he wanted to ask him why he was in special services, in charge of a hobby shop or gym or swimming pool, drawing duty as a fire-builder and coffee-maker. Looking down at his starched cap and polished boots and large, strong-looking hands, he wished he could train him, teach him and care for him, and his wish became a yearning: looking at Phil wrapping a hand-kerchief around the skillet handle, he wished he could train him too. He circled the lance corporal and sat heavily on the earth beside Phil.

'I *used* to be graceful.'

'Civilians are entitled to a beer gut. We forgot a spatula.'

'Civilian my ass. Here.'

He drew his hunting knife and handed it to Phil; behind him, and beyond the line of trees, a car left the road and stopped. Bacon curled over the knife blade; Phil lifted strips free of the skillet, lowered the pale sides into the grease, and said: 'The eggs will break.'

'I'll cook them.'

'Fried?'

'Lieutenant, I've spent more time in chow lines than you've spent in the Marine Corps.'

Three hunters came out of the trees and stood at the table to his left. The lance corporal flipped his cigarette into the flames and crossed his arms on his knees and watched the kettle.

'They use spatulas,' Phil said.

'True enough. But I will turn the eggs. How they come out is in the hands of the Lord.'

'Bless us o Lord in this thy omelet.'

'Over easy. Do you go to Mass?'

'Sometimes. Do you?'

'On Sundays.'

Across the fire the three men rubbed their hands in the heat. A car left the road, then another, and doors opened and slammed, and voices and rustling, cracking footsteps came through the trees. The lance corporal rose without using his hands and took the coffeepot into the darkness.

'Where does he go?' Harry said.

'He's like an Indian.'

'He's like an Oriental.'

Then he heard the water boiling and, as he looked, steam came from the spout. From the pack he took bread, eggs, and paper plates. Phil spread bacon on a plate, then Harry dug a small hole with the knife and poured in some of the bacon grease and covered it. Kneeling, he fried four slices of bread, then broke six eggs, onehanded, into the skillet and was watching the bubbling whites and browning edges when he heard cars on the road; he glanced up at the dimmed stars and lemon moon; the fog was thinner, and smoke rose darkly through its eddying grey. In the skillet the eggs joined, and he was poised to separate them with his knife, then said: 'Look what we have.'

'Your basic sunnyside pie.'

'It's beautiful.'

He slanted the skillet till grease moved to one side, and with the blade he slapped it over the eggs. He held the skillet higher and watched the yellows, and the milky white circling them; he slid his knife under the right edge, gently moved it toward the center, and stopped under the first yolk. Phil held a paper plate, and Harry tilted the skillet over it, working the knife upward as connected eggs slid over the blade and rim, onto the plate.

'I hate to break it,' Phil said. 'Should we freeze it?'

'In our minds.'

Phil took their cups to the coffeepot; Harry watched him pouring, and waited for him to sit at the plate resting on loose dirt. They did not separate the eggs. On the road, cars approached like a convoy that had lost its intervals, and Harry and Phil ate quietly, slowly, watching the disc become oval, then oblong, then a yellow smear for the last of their bread. Men circled them and the fire. Phil reached for the skillet, and Harry said: 'I'll do it.'

He tossed dirt into it and rubbed the hot metal, then wiped it with a paper towel; he stabbed the knife into the earth and worked it back and forth and deeper, and wiped it clean on his trousers. He held his cigarettes toward Phil, but he was shaking one from his own pack. They sat facing the fire, smoking with their coffee. The lance corporal put on a fresh log, and Harry watched flames licking around its bottom and up its sides; above and around him the voices were incoherent, peaceful as the creaking of windblown trees.

Under a near-fogless sky, a half-hour before dawn, he reached the northern and highest peak of the narrow ridge, and walked with light steps, back and forth and in small circles, until his breathing slowed and his legs stopped quivering. Then he sat facing the bare spine of dirt and rock that dipped and rose and finally descended southward, through diaphanous fog, to the jeep. He heard nothing in the sky or on the earth save his own breathing. He rested his rifle on his thighs and watched both sides of the ridge: flat ground to the east until a mass of iron-grey hills; the valley, broken by a dark stand of trees, was to the west; beyond that was the ridge where Phil hunted.

The air and earth were the grey of twilight; then, as he looked down the western slope, at shapes of rocks and low thickets, the valley and Phil's ridge became colors, muted under vanishing mist: pale green patches of grass and brown earth and a beige stream bed. The trees were pines, growing inside an eastward bend of the stream. Brown and green brush spread up the russet slope of Phil's ridge, and beyond it was the light blue of the sea. Harry stood, was on his feet before he remembered to be quiet and still, and watched the blue spreading farther as fog rose from it like steam. He turned to the scarlet slice of sun crowning a hill. From the strip of rose and golden sky, the horizon rolled toward him: peaks and ridges, gorges and low country, and scattered green of trees among the arid yellow and brown. He faced the ocean, saw whitecaps now, and took off his hat and waved it. On the peak of Phil's ridge he could see only rocks. The sea and sky were pale still; he stood watching as fog dissolved into their deepening blue, the sky brightened, and he could see the horizon. He sat facing it.

At eight o'clock he started walking down the ridge: one soft step, then waiting, looking down both slopes; another step; after three he saw Phil: a flash of light, a movement on the skyline. Then Phil became a tiny figure, and Harry stayed abreast of him. Soon the breeze shifted, came from the sea, and he could smell it. Near midmorning he flushed a doe: froze at the sudden crack of brush, as her bounding rump and darting body angled down the side of the ridge; in the valley she ran south, and was gone.

He sat and smoked and watched a ship gliding past Phil, its stacks at his shoulders. Then he stood and took off his jacket and sweat shirt and hung them from his belt. He caught up with Phil, and stalked again. When the sun was high and sparkling the sea, the ridge dropped more sharply, and he unloaded his rifle and slung it from his shoulder, and went down to the jeep. Phil sat on the hood. Behind him was open country and a distant range of tall hills. Harry sat on the hood and drank from his canteen.

'Saved ammo,' Phil said.

'I almost stepped on a doe.'

'How close?'

'Three steps and a good spit.'

'I've never been that close.'

'Neither have I.'

'Pretty quiet, Pop.'

'She startled me. If she'd been a buck, I would have missed.'

They ate sandwiches, then lay on their backs in the shade of the jeep. Harry rested his hat on his forehead so the brim covered his eyes.

'Are you staying for dinner?' Phil said.

'No. I don't like driving tired.'

'We can go back now, if you want.'

'Let's hunt. What will you do tomorrow?'

'Make sure my toothbrush is packed.'

'No girl?'

'There isn't one. I mean no *one*. So why choose now, right? I'll go out with the guys and get drunk.'

'Only way to go. What time Monday?'

'I don't even want to say.'

'They love getting guys up in the dark.'

His boots were warm. He looked out from under the hat: sunlight was on his ankles now; he looked over his feet at the low end of Phil's ridge.

'Orientals can hide on a parade field. Chinese would crawl all night from their lines to ours. A few feet and wait. All night lying out there, no sound, nothing moving, and just before dawn they'd be on top of us. And *Japanese*: they were like leaves.'

'Except that tank.'

'What tank?'

'Your Silver Star.'

'That was a pillbox.'

'It was?'

'Sure. Did you think I'd go after a tank?'

'Not much difference. Why didn't I know that?'

'Too many war stories, too many Marines; probably a neighbor told *his* kid about a tank.'

'I told *them*. Was it on Tarawa?'

'Yes.'

'At least I got that right.'

'It's not important. It's just something that happened. We were pinned down on the beach. The boxes had interlocking fire. I remember my mouth in the sand, then an explosion to my right front. It was a satchel charge, and a kid named Winslow Brimmer was the one who got it there.'

'Winslow Brimmer?'

'He was a mean little fart from Baltimore. Nobody harassed him about his name. He took whatever was left of his squad to that box, and all but two of them bought it. Then I was running with a flamethrower on my back. If you can call that running.'

'Where did you get the flamethrower?'

'The guy with it was next to me, and he was dead. So I put it on and moved out.'

'Jesus.'

'It was easier than Brimmer's because he had knocked out the one on their left. I had more fresh air than he did.'

'Not much.'

'I can remember doing it, but it's like somebody told me I did it, and that's why I remember. The way it can be after a bad drunk. I don't remember what I felt just before, or what I thought. I remember getting the flamethrower off him and onto me, and that should have taken a while, but it doesn't seem like it. I remember running, but I don't remember hearing anything, not with all those weapons firing, and I don't remember getting there. I was there, and then I burned them. They must have made sounds, but I only remember the smell.'

'Was that when you were wounded?'

'No. That was the next day.'

'I wish I had been there.'

'No you don't. The Navy dropped us in deep water—'

'I know.'

'Dead troops bobbing in it and lying on the reef and the beach. Fuck Tarawa.'

He opened his eyes to the sun, and squinted away from it at the sky. A hawk glided toward the earth, veered away, and climbed west over the ridge.

'You reflected the sun this morning,' he said. 'That's how I saw you.'

'My watch.'

He looked at the chrome band on Phil's wrist.

'Goddamn it, leave that civilian shit at home and get one from supply.'

'It's in my room.'

'Sorry.'

'Okay, Captain.'

He closed his eyes, listening to Phil's breathing. The sun on his face woke him, and he stiffened and pressed his palms against the ground, then knew where he was. Phil was gone. He stood, wiping sweat from his eyes; Phil leaned against the back of the jeep, eating a plum.

'Have some fruit.'

Harry took a peach from the pack and stood beside him.

'Do you want to swap ridges?' Phil said.

'Not unless you do.'

'No, I'm fine.'

'Mine's like home now.'

'We'll probably get back here around six. Thirty minutes to the camp to sign out. Then about forty.'

'Plenty of time. I make it in under three hours. 'Course, there's always the Jesus factor.'

'Like getting a deer.'

'If we do, I'll help you clean it.'

'And take it home with you.'

'Right.'

'All set?'

'Need my hogleg.'

He took the rifle from the back seat and slung it from his shoulder.

'How do you like the .308?' Phil said.

'It's good.'

'Have you zeroed it in?'

'Not this year.'

They walked into the valley and up the hard, cracked earth of the stream bed to the pine trees, and stood in their shade.

'I like the smell of pine,' Harry said. 'Up there I can smell the ocean. Did you see it this morning, when the sun came up?'

'Beautiful.'

'Now we get the sunset. Ready?'

'I'm off.'

'Take care, then.'

'You too.'

They turned from each other and Harry walked out of the trees, into the sunlight, then he lengthened his stride toward the ridge.

ANNA

HER NAME WAS Anna Griffin. She was twenty. Her blond hair had been turning darker over the past few years, and she believed it would be brown when she was twenty-five. Sometimes she thought of dying it blond, but living with Wayne was still new enough to her so that she was hesitant about spending money on anything that could not be shared. She also wanted to see what her hair would finally look like. She was pretty, though parts of her face seemed not to know it: the light of her eyes, the lines of her lips, seemed bent on denial, so that even the rise of her high cheekbones seemed ungraceful, simply covered bone. Her two front teeth had a gap between them, and they protruded, the right more than the left.

She worked at the cash register of a Sunnycorner store, located in what people called a square: two blocks of small stores, with a Chevrolet dealer and two branch banks, one of them next to the Sunnycorner. The tellers from that one—women not much older than Anna—came in for takeout coffees, cigarettes, and diet drinks. She liked watching them come in: soft sweaters, wool dresses, polyester blouses that in stores she liked rubbing between thumb and forefinger. She liked looking at their hair too: beauty parlor hair that seemed groomed to match the colors and cut and texture of their clothing, so it was more like hair on a model or a movie actress, no longer an independent growth to be washed and brushed and combed and cut, but part of the ensemble, as the boots were. They all wore pretty watches, and bracelets and necklaces, and more than one ring. She liked the way the girls moved: they looked purposeful but not harried: one enters the store and stops at the magazine rack against the wall opposite Anna and the counter, and picks up a magazine and thumbs the pages, appearing even then to be in motion still, a woman leaving the job for a few minutes, but not in a hurry; then she replaces the magazine and crosses the floor and waits in line while Anna rings up and bags the cans and bottles and boxes cradled in arms, dangling from hands. They talk to each other, Anna and the teller she knows only by face, as she fills and caps Styrofoam cups of coffee. The weather. Hi. How are you. Bye now. The teller leaves. Often behind the counter, with other customers, Anna liked what she was doing; liked knowing where the pimientos were; liked her deftness with the register and bagging; was proud of her cheerfulness, felt in charge of customers and what they bought. But when the tellers were at the counter, she was shy, and if one of them made her laugh, she covered her mouth.

She took new magazines from the rack: one at a time, keeping it under the counter near her tall three-legged stool, until she finished it; then she put it back and took another. So by the time the girls from the bank glanced through the magazine, she knew what they were seeing. For they always chose the ones she did: *People*, *Vogue*, *Glamour*. She looked at *Playgirl*, and in *Penthouse* she looked at the women and read the letters, this when she worked at night, not because there were fewer customers then but because it was night, not day. At first she had looked at them during the day, and felt strange raising her eyes from the pictures to blink at the parking lot, whose presence of cars and people and space she always felt because the storefront was glass, her counter stopping just short of it. The tellers never picked up those magazines, but Anna was certain they had them at home. She imagined that too: where they lived after work; before work. She gave them large, pretty apartments with thick walls so they only heard themselves; stereos and color television, and soft carpets and soft furniture and large brass beds; sometimes she imagined them living with men who made a lot of money, and she saw a swimming pool, a Jacuzzi.

Near the end of her workday, in its seventh and eighth hours, her fatigue was the sort that comes from confining the body while giving neither it nor the mind anything to do. She was restless, impatient, and distracted, and while talking politely to customers and warmly to the regular ones, she wanted to be home. The apartment was in an old building she could nearly see from behind the counter; she could see the grey house with red shutters next to it. As soon as she left the store, she felt as if she had not been tired at all; only her feet still were. Sometimes she felt something else too, as she stepped outside and crossed that line between fatigue and energy: a touch of dread and defeat. She walked past the bank, the last place in the long building of bank Sunnycorner drugstore department store and pizza house, cleared the corner of the building, passed the dumpster on whose lee side teenagers on summer nights smoked dope and drank beer, down the sloping parking lot and across the street to the old near-yardless green wooden apartment house; up three flights of voices and television voices and the smell that reminded her of the weariness she had just left. It was not a bad smell. It bothered her because it was a daily smell, even when old Mrs. Battistini on the first floor cooked with garlic: a smell of all the days of this wood: up to the third floor, the top of the building, and into the apartment whose smells she noticed only because they were not the scent of contained age she had breathed as she climbed. Then she went to the kitchen table or the bed or shower or couch, either talking to Wayne or waiting for him to come home from Wendy's, where he cooked hamburgers.

At those times she liked her home. She rarely liked it when she woke in it: a northwest apartment, so she opened her eyes to a twilit room and, as she moved about, she saw the place clearly, with its few pieces of furniture, cluttered only with leavings: tossed clothes, beer bottles, potato chip bags, as if her night's sleep had tricked her so she would see only what last night she had not. And sometimes later, during the day or night, while she was simply crossing a room, she would suddenly see herself juxtaposed with the old maroon couch which had been left, along with everything else, by whoever lived there before she and Wayne: the yellow wooden table and two chairs in the kitchen, the blue easy chair in the living room, and in the bedroom the chest of drawers, the straight wooden chair, and the mattress on the floor, and she felt older than she knew she ought to.

The wrong car: a 1964 Mercury Comet that Wayne had bought for one hundred and sixty dollars two years ago, before she knew him, when the car was already eleven years old, and now it vibrated at sixty miles an hour, and had holes in the floorboard; and the wrong weapon: a Buck hunting knife under Wayne's leather jacket, unsheathed and held against his body by his left arm. She had not thought of the car and knife until he put the knife under his jacket and left her in the car, smoking so fast that between drags she kept the cigarette near her face and chewed the thumb of the hand holding it; looking through the wiper-swept windshield and the snow blowing between her and the closed bakery next to the lighted drugstore, at tall Wayne walking slowly with his face turned and lowered away from the snow. She softly kept her foot on the accelerator so the engine would not stall. The headlights were off. She could not see into the drugstore. When she drove slowly past it, there were two customers, one at the cash register and counter at the rear, one looking at display shelves at a side wall. She had parked and turned off the lights. One customer left, a man bareheaded in the snow. He did not look at their car. Then the other one left, a man in a watch cap. He did not look either, and when he had driven out of the parking lot to the highway it joined, Wayne said Okay, and went in.

She looked in the rearview mirror, but snow had covered the window; she looked to both sides. To her right, at the far end of the shopping center, the doughnut shop was open, and in front of it three cars were topped with snow. All the other stores were closed. She would be able to see headlights through the snow on the rear window, and if a cruiser came she was to go into the store, and if Wayne had not already started, she would buy cigarettes, then go out again, and if the cruiser was gone she would wait in the car; if the cruiser had stopped, she would go back into the store for matches and they would both leave. Now in the dark and heater-warmth she believed all of their plan was no longer risky, but doomed, as if by leaving the car and walking across the short space through soft angling snow, Wayne had become puny, his knife a toy. So it was the wrong girl too, and the wrong man. She could not imagine him coming out with money, and she could not imagine tomorrow or later tonight or even the next minute. Stripped of history and dreams, she knew only her breathing and smoking and heartbeat and the falling snow. She stared at the long window of the drugstore, and · she was startled when he came out: he was running, he was alone, he was inside, closing the door. He said *Jesus Christ* three times as she crossed the parking lot. She turned on the headlights and slowed as she neared the highway. She did not have to stop. She moved into the right lane, and cars in the middle and left passed her.

'A *lot*,' he said.

She reached to him, and he pressed bills against her palm, folded her fingers around them.

'Can you see out back?' she said.

'No. Nobody's coming. Just go slow: no skidding, no wrecks. Jesus.'

She heard the knife blade sliding into the sheath, watched yellowed snow in the headlights and glanced at passing cars on her left; she held the wheel with two hands. He said when he went in he was about to walk around like he was looking for something because he was so scared, but then he decided to do it right away or else he might have just walked around the store till the druggist asked what he wanted and he'd end up buying toothpaste or something, so he went down along the side wall to the back of the store—he lit a cigarette and she said *Me too*; she watched the road and taillights of a distant car in her lane as he placed it between her fingers—and he went around the counter and took out the knife and held it at the druggist's stomach: a little man with grey hair watching the knife and punching open the register.

She left the highway and drove on a two-lane road through woods and small towns.

'Tequila,' he said.

In their town all but one package store closed at ten-thirty; she drove to the one that stayed open until eleven, a corner store on a street of tenement houses where Puerto Ricans lived; on warm nights they were on the stoops and sidewalks and corners. She did not like going there, even on winter nights when no one was out. She stopped in front of it, looked at the windows, and said: 'I think it's closed.'

'It's quarter to.'

He went out and tried the door, then peered in, then knocked and called and tried the door again. He came back and struck the dashboard.

'I can't fucking be*lieve* it. I got so much money in my pockets I got no room for my hands, and we got one *beer* at home. Can you believe it?'

'He must've closed early—'

'No shit.'

'—because of the *snow*.'

She turned a corner around a used car lot and got onto the main street going downhill through town to the river.

'I could use some tequila,' she said.

'Stop at Timmy's.'

The traffic lights were blinking yellow so people would not have to stop on the hill in the snow; she shifted down and coasted with her foot touching the brake pedal, drove over the bridge, and parked two blocks from it at Timmy's. When she got out of the car, her legs were weak and eager for motion, and she realized they had been taut all the way home; and, standing at the corner of the bar, watching Johnny McCarthy pour two shots beside the drafts, she knew she was going to get drunk. She licked salt from her hand and drank the shot, then a long swallow of beer that met the tequila's burn as it rose, and held the shot glass toward grinning McCarthy and asked how law school was going; he poured tequila and said *Long but good*, and she drank that and finished her beer, and he poured two more shots and brought them drafts. She looped her arm around Wayne's and nuzzled the soft leather and hard bicep, then tongue-kissed him, and looked down the bar at the regulars, most of them men talking in pairs, standing at the bar that had no stools; two girls stood shoulder to shoulder and talked to men on their flanks. The room was long and narrow, separated from the dining room by a wall with a half-door behind the bar. Anna waved at people who looked at her, and they raised a glass or waved and some called her name, and old Lou, who was drinking beer alone at the other end of the bar, motioned to McCarthy and sent her and Wayne a round. Wayne's hand came out of his jacket and she looked at the bill in it: a twenty.

'Set up Lou,' he said to McCarthy. '*Lou*. Can I buy you a shot?'

Lou nodded and smiled, and she watched McCarthy pour the Fleischmann's and bring it and a draft to Lou, and she wondered if she could tend bar, could remember all the drinks. It was a wonderful place to be, this bar, with her back to the door so she got some of the chill, not all stuffy air and smoke, and able to look down the length of the bar, and at the young men crowded into four tables at the end of the room, watching a television set on a shelf on the wall: a hockey game. It was the only place outside of her home where she always felt the comfort of affection. Shivering with a gulp of tequila, she watched Wayne arm-wrestling with Curt: knuckles white and hand and face red, veins showing at his temple and throat. She had never seen either win, but Wayne had told her that till a year ago he had always won.

'*Pull*,' she said.

His strength and effort seemed to move into the air around her, making her restless; she slapped his back, lit a cigarette, wanted to dance. She called McCarthy and pointed to the draft glasses, then Curt's highball glass, and when he came with the drinks, told him Wayne would pay after he beat Curt. She was humming to herself, and she liked the sound of her voice. She wondered if she could tend bar. People didn't fight here. People were good to her. They wouldn't—A color television. They shouldn't buy it too soon; but when? Who would care? Nobody watched what they bought. She wanted to count the money, but did not want to leave until closing. Wayne and Curt were panting and grunting; their arms were nearly straight up again; they had been going slowly back and forth. She slipped a hand into Wayne's jacket pocket, squeezed the folded wad. She had just finished a cigarette but now she was holding another and wondering if she wanted it, then she lit it and did. There was only a men's room in the bar. 'Draw?' Curt said; 'Draw,' Wayne said, and she hugged his waist and rubbed his right bicep and said: 'I ordered us and Curt a round. I didn't pay. I'm going piss.'

He smiled down at her. The light in his eyes made her want to stay holding him. She walked toward the end of the bar, past the backs of leaning drinkers; some noticed her and spoke; she patted backs, said *Hi How you doing Hey what's happening*; big curly-haired Mitch stopped her: Yes, she was still at Sunnycorner; where had he been? Working in New Hampshire. He told her what he did, and she heard, but seconds later she could not remember; she was smiling at him. He called to Wayne and waved. She said I'll see you in a minute, and moved on. At the bar's end was Lou. He reached for her, raised the other arm at McCarthy. He held her shoulder and pulled her to him.

'Let me buy you a drink.'

'I have to go to the ladies'.'

'Well, go to the ladies' and come back.'

'Okay.'

She did not go. Her shot and their drafts were there and she was talking to Lou. She did not know what he did either. She used to know. He looked sixty. He came every night. His grey hair was short and he laughed often and she liked his wrinkles.

'I wish I could tend bar here.'

'You'd be good at it.'

'I don't think I could remember all the drinks.'

'It's a shot and beer place.'

His arm was around her, her fingers pressing his ribs. She drank. The tequila was smooth now. She finished the beer, said she'd be back, next round was hers; she kissed his cheek: his skin was cool and tough, and his whiskers scraped her chin. She moved past the tables crowded with the hockey watchers; Henry coming out of the men's room moved around her, walking carefully. She went through the door under the television set, into a short hall, glanced down it into the doorless, silent kitchen, and stepped left into the rear of the dining room: empty and darkened. Some nights she and Wayne brought their drinks in here after the kitchen closed and sat in a booth in the dark. The ladies' room was empty. 'Ah.' Wayne was right: when you really had to piss, it was better than sex. She listened to the voices from the bar, wanted to hurry back to them. She jerked the paper, tore it.

Lou was gone. She stood where he had been, but his beer glass was gone, the ashtray emptied. He was like that. He came and went quietly. You'd look around and see him for the first time and he already had a beer; sometime later you'd look around and he was gone. Behind Wayne the front door opened and a blue cap and jacket and badge came in: it was Ryan from the beat. She made herself think in sentences and tried to focus on them, as if she were reading: *He's coming in to get warm. He's just cold.* She waved at him. He did not see her. She could not remember the sentences. She could not be afraid either. She knew that she ought to be afraid so she would not make any mistakes but she was not, and when she tried to feel afraid or even serious she felt drunker. Ryan was standing next to Curt, one down from Wayne, and had his gloves off and was blowing on his hands. He and McCarthy talked, then he left; at the door he waved at the bar, and Anna waved. She went toward Wayne, then stopped at the two girls: one was Laurie or Linda, she couldn't remember which; one was Jessie. They were still flanked by Bobby and Mark. They all turned their backs to the bar, pressed her hands, touched her shoulders, bought her a drink. She said tequila, and drank it and talked about Sunnycorner. She went to Wayne, told McCarthy to set up Bobby and Mark and Jessie—leaning forward: 'Johnny, what is it? Laurie or Linda?' 'Laurie.' She slipped a hand into Wayne's pocket. Then her hand was captive there, fingers on money, his forearm pressing hers against his side.

'I'll get it. Did you see Ryan?'

'Yes.'

She tried to think in sentences again. She looked up at Wayne; he was grinning down at her. She could see the grin, or his eyes, but not both at once. She gazed at his lips.

'You're cocked,' he said. He was not angry. He said it softly, and took her wrist and withdrew it from his pocket.

'I'll do it in the john.'

She wanted to be as serious and careful as he was, but looking at him and trying to see all of his face at once weakened her legs; she tried again to think in sentences but they jumped away from her like a cat her mind chased; when she turned away from him, looked at faces farther away and held the bar, her mind stopped struggling and she smiled and put her hand in his back pocket and said: 'Okay.'

He started to walk to the men's room, stopping to talk to someone, being stopped by another; watching him, she was smiling. When she became aware of it, she kept the smile; she liked standing at the corner of the bar smiling with love at her man's back and profile as he gestured and talked; then he was in the men's room. Midway down the bar McCarthy finished washing glasses and dried his hands, stepped back and folded his arms, and looked up and down the bar, and when he saw nothing in front of her he said: 'Anna? Another round?'

'Just a draft, okay?'

She looked in her wallet; she knew it was empty but she looked to be sure it was still empty; she opened the coin pouch and looked at lint and three pennies. She counted the pennies. Johnny put the beer in front of her.

'Wayne's got—'

'On me,' he said. 'Want a shot too?'

'Why not.'

She decided to sip this one or at least drink it slowly, but while she was thinking, the glass was at her lips and her head tilted back and she swallowed it all and licked her lips, then turned to the door behind her and, without coat, stepped outside: the sudden cold emptied her lungs, then she deeply drew in the air tasting of night and snow. 'Wow.' She lifted her face to the light snow and breathed again. Had she smoked a Camel? Yes. From Lou. Jesus. Snow melted on her cheeks. She began to shiver. She crossed the sidewalk, touched the frosted parking meter. One of her brothers did that to her when she was little. Which one? Frank. Told her to lick the bottom of the ice tray. In the cold she stood happy and clear-headed until she wanted to drink, and she went smiling into the warmth and voices and smoke.

'Where'd you go?' Wayne said.

'Outside to get straight,' rubbing her hands together, drinking beer, its head gone, shaking a cigarette from her pack, her flesh recalling its alertness outside as, breathing smoke and swallowing beer and leaning on Wayne, it was lulled again. She wondered if athletes felt all the time the way she had felt outside.

'We should get some bicycles,' she said.

He lowered his mouth to her ear, pushing her hair aside with his rubbing face.

'We can,' his breath in her ear; she turned her groin against his leg. 'It's about two thousand.'

'No, *Wayne*.'

'Ssshhh. I looked at it, man.'

He moved away, and put a bill in her hand: a twenty.

'Jesus,' she said.

'Keep cool.'

'I've never—' She stopped, called McCarthy, and paid for the round for Laurie and Jessie and Bobby and Mark, and tipped him a dollar. Two thousand dollars: she had never seen that much money in her life, had never had as much as a hundred in her hands at one time: not of her own.

'*Last* call.' McCarthy started at the other end of the bar, taking empty glasses, bringing back drinks. '*Last* call.' She watched McCarthy pouring her last shot and draft of the night; she faced Wayne and raised the glass of tequila: 'Hi, babe.'

'Hi.' He licked salt from his hand.

'I been forgetting the salt,' she said, and drank, looking at his eyes. She sipped this last one, finished it, and was drinking the beer when McCarthy called: 'That's *it*. I'm taking the glasses in *five min*utes. You don't have to go home—'

'—but you can't stay here,' someone said.

'Right. Drink up.'

She finished the beer and beckoned with her finger to McCarthy. When he came she held his hands and said: 'Just a quick one?'

'I can't.'

'Just half a draft or a quick shot? I'll drink it while I put my coat on.'

'The cops have been checking. I got to have the glasses off the bar.'

'What about a roader?' Wayne said.

'Then they'll all want one.'

'Okay. He's right, Anna. Let go of the man.'

She released his hands and he took their glasses. She put on her coat. Wayne was waving at people, calling to them. She waved: '*See* you people. Good *night*, Jessie. Laurie. Good *night*. See you, Henry. Mark. Bobby. Bye-bye, Mitch—'

Then she was in the falling white cold, her arm around Wayne; he drove them home, a block and a turn around the Chevrolet lot, then two blocks, while in her mind still were the light and faces and voices of the bar. She held his waist going up the dark stairs. He was breathing hard, not talking. Then he unlocked the door, she was inside, lights coming on, coat off, following Wayne to the kitchen where he opened their one beer and took a swallow and handed it to her and pulled money from both pockets. They sat down and divided the bills into stacks of twenties and tens and fives and ones. When the beer was half gone he left and came back from the bedroom with four Quaaludes and she said: 'Mmmm' and took two from his palm and swallowed them with beer. She picked up the stack of twenties. Her legs felt weak again. She was hungry. She would make a sandwich. She put down the stack and sat looking at the money. He was counting: '—thirty-five forty forty-five fifty—' She took the ones. She wanted to start at the lowest and work up; she did not want to know how many twenties there were until the end. She counted aloud and he told her not to.

'You don't either,' she said. 'All I hear is ninety-five hundred ninety-five hundred—'

'Okay. In our heads.'

She started over. She wanted to eat and wished for a beer and lost count again. Wayne had a pencil in his hand, was writing on paper in front of him. She counted faster. She finished and picked up the twenties. She counted slowly, making a new stack on the table with the bills that she drew, one at a time, from her hand. She did not keep track of the sum of money; she knew she was too drunk. She simply counted each bill as she smacked it onto the pile. Wayne was writing again, so she counted the last twelve aloud, ending with: '—and forty-*six*,' slamming it onto the fanning twenties. He wrote and drew a line and wrote again and drew another line, and his pencil moved up the columns, touching each number and writing a new number at the bottom until there were four of them, and he read to her: 'Two thousand and eighteen.'

The Quaalude bees were in her head now, and she stood and went to the living room for a cigarette in her purse, her legs wanting to go to the sink at her right but she forced them straight through the door whose left jamb they bumped; as she reached into her purse she heard herself humming. She had thought she was talking to Wayne, but that was in her head, she had told him *Two thousand and eighteen we can have some music and movies now* and she smiled aloud because it had come out as humming a tune she had never heard. In the kitchen Wayne was doing something strange. He had lined up their three glasses on the counter by the sink and he was pouring milk into them; It filled two and a half, and he drank that half. Then he tore open the top of the half-gallon carton and rinsed it and swabbed it out with a paper towel. Then he put the money in it, and folded the top back, and put it in the freezer compartment, and the two glasses of milk in the refrigerator. Then she was in the bedroom talking about frozen money; she saw the cigarette between her fingers as she started to undress, in the dark now; she was not aware of his turning out lights: she was in the lighted kitchen, then in the dark bedroom, looking for an ashtray instead of pulling her sleeve over the cigarette, and she told him about that and about a stereo and Emmylou Harris and fucking, as she found the ashtray on the floor by the bed, which was a mattress on the floor by the ashtray; that she thought about him at Sunnycorner, got horny for him; her tongue was thick, slower than her buzzing head, and the silent words backed up in the spaces between the spoken ones, so she told him something in her mind, then heard it again as her tongue caught up; her tongue in his mouth now, under the covers on the cold sheet, a swelling of joy in her breast as she opened her legs for him and the night's images came back to her: the money on the table and the faces of McCarthy and Curt and Mitch and Lou, and Wayne's hand disappearing with the money inside the carton, and Bobby and Mark and Laurie and Jessie, the empty sidewalk where she stood alone in the cold air, Lou saying: *You'd be good at it.*

The ringing seemed to come from inside her skull, insistent and clear through the voices of her drunken sleep: a ribbon of sound she had to climb, though she tried to sink away from it. Then her eyes were open and she turned off the alarm she did not remember setting; it was six o'clock and she was asleep again, then wakened by her alarmed heartbeat: all in what seemed a few seconds, but it was ten minutes to seven, when she had to be at work. She rose with a fast heart and a headache that made her stoop gingerly for her clothes on the floor and shut her eyes as she put them on. She went into the kitchen: the one empty beer bottle, the ashtray, the milk-soiled glass, and her memory of him putting away the money was immediate, as if he had just done it and she had not slept at all. She took the milk carton from the freezer. The folded money, like the bottle and ashtray and glass, seemed part of the night's drinking, something you cleaned or threw away in the morning. But she had no money and she needed aspirins and coffee and doughnuts and cigarettes; she took a cold five-dollar bill and put the carton in the freezer, looked in the bedroom for her purse and then in the kitchen again and found it in the living room, opened her wallet and saw money there. She pushed the freezer money in with it and slung the purse from her shoulder and stepped into the dim hall, shutting the door on Wayne's snoring. Outside she blinked at sun and cold and remembered Wayne giving her twenty at the bar; she crossed the street and parking lot and, with the taste of beer in her throat and toothpaste in her mouth, was in the Sunnycorner before seven.

She spent the next eight hours living the divided life of a hangover. Drinking last night had stopped time, kept her in the present until last call forced on her the end of a night, the truth of tomorrow; but once in their kitchen counting money, she was in the present again and she stayed there through twice waking, and dressing, and entering the store and relieving Eddie, the all-night clerk, at the register. So for the first three or four hours while she worked and waited and talked, her body heavily and slowly occupied space in those brightly lit moments in the store; but in her mind were images of Wayne leaving the car and going into the drugstore and running out, and driving home through falling snow, the closed package store and the drinks and people at Timmy's and taking the Quaaludes from Wayne's palm, and counting money and making love for so drunk long; and she felt all of that and none of what she was numbly doing. It was a hangover that demanded food and coffee and cigarettes. She started the day with three aspirins and a Coke. Then she smoked and ate doughnuts and drank coffee. Sometimes from the corner of her eye she saw something move on the counter, small and grey and fast, like the shadow of a darting mouse. Her heart was fast too, and the customers were fast and loud, while her hands were slow, and her tongue was, for it had to wait while words freed themselves from behind her eyes, where the pain was, where the aspirins had not found it. After four cups of coffee, her heart was faster and hands more shaky, and she drank another Coke. She was careful, and made no mistakes on the register; with eyes trying to close she looked into the eyes of customers and Kermit, the manager, slim and balding, in his forties; a kind man but one who, today, made her feel both scornful and ashamed, for she was certain he had not had a hangover in twenty years. Around noon her blood slowed and her hands stopped trembling, and she was tired and lightheaded and afraid; it seemed there was always someone watching her, not only the customers and Kermit, but someone above her, outside the window, in the narrow space behind her. Now there were gaps in her memory of last night: she looked at the clock so often that its hands seemed halted, and in her mind she was home after work, in bed with Wayne, shuddering away the terrors that brushed her like a curtain wind-blown against her back.

When she got home he had just finished showering and shaving, and she took him to bed with lust that was as much part of her hangover as hunger and the need to smoke were; silent and hasty, she moved toward that orgasm that would bring her back to some calm mooring in the long day. Crying out, she burst into languor; slept breathing the scent of his washed flesh. But she woke alone in the twilit room and rose quickly from the bed, calling him. He came smiling from the living room, and asked if she were ready to go to the mall.

The indoor walk of the mall was bright and warm; coats unbuttoned, his arm over her shoulder, hers around his waist, they moved slowly among people and smells of frying meat, stopping at windows to look at shirts and coats and boots; they took egg rolls to a small pool with a fountain in its middle and sat on its low brick wall; they ate pizza alone on a bench that faced a displayed car; they had their photographs taken behind a curtain in a shop and paid the girl and left their address.

'You think she'll mail them to us?' Anna said.

'Sure.'

They ate hamburgers standing at the counter, watching the old man work at the grill, then sat on a bench among potted plants to smoke. On the way to the department store they bought fudge, and the taste of it lingered, sweet and rich in her mouth, and she wanted to go back for another piece, but they were in the store: large, with glaring white light, and as the young clerk wearing glasses and a thin moustache came to them, moving past television sets and record players, she held Wayne's arm. While the clerk and Wayne talked, she was aware of her gapped and jutting teeth, her pea jacket, and old boots and jeans. She followed Wayne following the clerk; they stopped at a shelf of record players. She shifted her eyes from one to the other as they spoke; they often looked at her, and she said: Yes. Sure. The soles of her feet ached and her calves were tired. She wanted to smoke but was afraid the clerk would forbid her. She swallowed the taste of fudge. Then she was sad. She watched Wayne and remembered him running out of the drugstore and, in the car, saying *Jesus Christ*, and she was ashamed that she was sad, and felt sorry for him because he was not.

Now they were moving. He was hugging her and grinning and his thigh swaggered against her hip, and they were among shelved television sets. Some of them were turned on, but to different channels, and surrounded by those faces and bodies and colliding words, she descended again into her hangover. She needed a drink, a cigarette, a small place, not all this low-ceilinged breadth and depth, where shoppers in the awful light jumped in and out of her vision.

Timmy's: the corner of the bar near the door, and a slow-sipped tequila salty dog and then one more to close the spaces in her brain and the corners of her vision, stop the tingling of her gums, and the crawling tingle inside her body as though ants climbed on her veins. In her coat pocket, her hand massaged the box of cigarettes; she opened it with a thumb, stroked filters with a finger.

'That's a good advertisement for the Sony,' Wayne said. 'Turning on the RCA next to it.'

She wanted to cry. She watched the pictures on the Sony: a man and a woman in a car, talking; she knew California from television and movies, and they were driving in California: the winding road, the low brown hills, the sea. The man was talking about dope and people's names. The clerk was talking about a guarantee. Wayne told him what he liked to watch, and as she heard hockey and baseball and football and movies she focused so hard on imagining this set in their apartment and them watching it from the couch that she felt like she had closed her eyes, though she had not. She followed them to the cash register and looked around the room for the cap and shoulders of a policeman to appear in the light that paled skin and cast no shadow. She watched Wayne counting the money; she listened to the clerk's pleased voice. Then Wayne had her arm, was leading her away.

'Aren't we taking them?'

He stopped, looked down at her, puzzled; then he laughed and kissed the top of her head.

'We pick them up out back.'

He was leading her again.

'Where are we going now?'

'Records. Remember? Unless you want to spend a fucking fortune on a stereo and just look at it.'

Standing beside him, she gazed and blinked at album covers as he flipped them forward, pulled out some, talked about them. She tried to despise his transistor radio at home, tried to feel her old longing for a stereo and records, but as she looked at each album he held in front of her, she was glutted with spending, and felt more like a thief than she had last night waiting outside the drugstore, and driving home from it. Again she imagined the apartment, saw where she would put the television, the record player; she would move the chest of drawers to the living room and put them on its top, facing the couch where—She saw herself cooking. She was cooking macaroni and cheese for them to eat while they watched a movie; but she saw only the apartment now, then herself sweeping it. Wayne swept it too, but often he either forgot or didn't see what she saw or didn't care about it. Sweeping was not hard but it was still something to do, and sometimes for days it seemed too much to do, and fluffs of dust gathered in corners and under furniture. So now she asked Wayne and he looked surprised and she was afraid he would be angry, but then he smiled and said Okay. He brought the records to the clerk and she watched the numbers come up on the register and the money going into the clerk's hand. Then Wayne led her past the corners and curves of washers and dryers, deeper into the light of the store, where she chose a round blue Hoover vacuum cleaner.

She carried it, boxed, into the apartment; behind her on the stairs Wayne carried the stereo in two boxes that hid his face. They went quickly downstairs again. Anna was waiting. She did not know what she was waiting for, but standing on the sidewalk as Wayne's head and shoulders went into the car, she was anxious and mute. She listened to his breathing and the sound of cardboard sliding over the car seat. She wanted to speak into the air between them, the air that had risen from the floorboard coming home from the mall as their talk had slowed, repeated itself, then stopped. Whenever that happened, they were either about to fight or enter a time of shy loneliness. Now grunting, he straightened with the boxed television in his arms; she grasped the free end and walked backward up the icy walk, telling him Not so *fast*, and he slowed and told her when she reached the steps and, feeling each one with her calves, she backed up them and through the door, and he asked if she wanted him to go up first and she said No, he had most of its weight, she was better off. She was breathing too fast to smell the stairway; sometimes she smelled cardboard and the television inside it, like oiled plastic; she belched and tasted hamburger, and when they reached the third floor she was sweating. In the apartment she took off her coat and went downstairs with him, and they each carried up a boxed speaker. They brought the chest into the living room and set it down against the wall opposite the couch; she dusted its top, and they put the stereo and television on it. For a while she sat on the couch, watching him connect wires. Then she went to the kitchen and took the vacuum cleaner from its box. She put it against the wall and leaned its pipes in the corner next to it and sat down to read the instructions. She looked at the illustrations, and thought she was reading, but she was not. She was listening to Wayne in the living room: not to him, but to speakers sliding on the floor, the tapping touch of a screwdriver, and when she finished the pamphlet she did not know what she had read. She put it in a drawer. Then, so that raising her voice would keep shyness from it, she called from the kitchen: 'Can we go to Timmy's?'

'Don't you want to play with these?'

'No,' she said. When he did not answer, she wished she had lied, and she felt again as she had in the department store when sorrow had enveloped her like a sudden cool breath from the television screens. She went into the living room and kneeled beside him, sitting on the floor, a speaker and wires between his legs; she nuzzled his cheek and said: 'I'm sorry.'

'I don't want to play with them either. Let's go.'

She got their coats and, as they were leaving, she stopped in the doorway and looked back at the stereo and television.

'Should we have bought it all in one place?' she said.

'It doesn't matter.'

She hurried ahead of him down the stairs and out onto the sidewalk, then her feet slipped forward and up and he caught her against his chest. She hooked her arm in his and they crossed the street and the parking lot; she looked to her left into the Sunnycorner, two men and a woman lined at the counter and Sally punching the register. She looked fondly at the warm light in there, the colors of magazine covers on the rack, the red soft-drink refrigerator, the long shelves of bread.

'What a hangover I had. And I didn't make any mistakes.'

She walked fast, each step like flight from the apartment. They went through the lot of Chevrolet pickups, walking single file between the trucks, and now if she looked back she would not be able to see their lawn; then past the broad-windowed showroom of new cars and she thought of their—his—old Comet. Standing on the curb, waiting for a space in traffic, she tightly gripped his arm. They trotted across the street to Timmy's door and entered the smell of beer and smoke. Faces turned from the bar, some hands lifted in a wave. It was not ten o'clock yet, the dining room was just closing, and the people at the bar stood singly, not two or three deep like last night, and the tables in the rear were empty. McCarthy was working. Anna took her place at the corner, and he said: 'You make it to work at seven?'

'How did you know?'

'Oh my *God*, I've got to be at work at seven; another tequila, Johnny.'

She raised a hand to her laughter, and covered it.

'I made it. I made it and tomorrow I don't work till three, and I'm going to have *two* tequila salty dogs and that's *all*; then I'm going to bed.'

Wayne ordered a shot of Fleischmann's and a draft, and when McCarthy went to the middle of the bar for the beer, she asked Wayne how much was left, though she already knew, or nearly did, and when he said *About two-twenty* she was ahead of his answer, nodding but paying no attention to the words, the numbers, seeing those strange visitors in their home, staring from the top of the chest, sitting on the kitchen floor; then McCarthy brought their drinks and went away, and she found on the bar the heart enclosing their initials that she and Wayne had carved, drinking one crowded night when McCarthy either did not see them or pretended not to.

'I don't want to feel bad,' she said.

'Neither me.'

'Let's don't. Can we get bicycles?'

'All of one and most of the other.'

'Do you want one?'

'Sure. I need to get back in shape.'

'Where can we go?'

'The Schwinn place.'

'I mean riding.'

'All over. When it thaws. There's nice roads everywhere. I know some trails in the woods, and one of them goes to a pond. A big pond.'

'We can go swimming.'

'Sure.'

'We should have bought a canoe.'

'Instead of what?'

She was watching McCarthy make a Tom Collins and a gimlet.

'I don't know,' she said.

'I guess we bought winter sports.'

'Maybe we should have got a freezer and a lot of food. You know what's in the refrigerator?'

'You said you didn't want to feel bad.'

'I don't.'

'So don't.'

'What about you?'

'I don't want to either. Let's have another round and hang it up.'

In the morning she woke at six, not to an alarm but out of habit: her flesh alert, poised to dress and go to work, and she got up and went naked and shivering to the bathroom, then to the kitchen, where, gazing at the vacuum cleaner, she drank one of the glasses of milk. In the living room she stood on the cold floor in front of the television and stereo, hugging herself. She was suddenly tired, her first and false energy of the day gone, and she crept into bed, telling herself she could sleep now, she did not have to work till three, she could sleep: coaxing, as though her flesh were a small child wakened in the night. She stopped shivering, felt sleep coming upward from her legs; she breathed slowly with it, and escaped into it, away from memory of last night's striving flesh: she and Wayne, winter-pallid yet sweating in their long, quiet, coupled work at coming until they gave up and their fast dry breaths slowed and the Emmylou Harris album ended, the stereo clicked twice into the silence, a record dropped and Willie Nelson sang 'Stardust.'

'I should have got some ludes and percs too,' he said.

Her hand found his on the sheet and covered it.

'I was too scared. It was bad enough waiting for the *money*. I kept waiting for somebody to come in and blow me away. Even him. If he'd had a gun, he could have. But I should have got some drugs.'

'It wouldn't have mattered.'

'We could have sold it.'

'It wouldn't matter.'

'Why?'

'There's too much to get. There's no way we could ever get it all.'

'A *lot* of it, though. *Some* of it.'

She rubbed the back of his hand, his knuckles, his nails. She did not know when he fell asleep. She slept two albums later, while Waylon Jennings sang. And slept now, deeply, in the morning, and woke when she heard him turning, rising, walking barefooted and heavily out of the room.

She got up and made coffee and did not see him until he came into the kitchen wearing his one white shirt and one pair of blue slacks and the black shoes; he had bought them all in one store in twenty minutes of quiet anger, with money she gave him the day Wendy's hired him; he returned the money on his first payday. The toes of the shoes were scuffed now. She kept the shirt clean, some nights washing it in the sink when he came home and hanging it on a chair back near the radiator so he could wear it next day; he would not buy another one because, he said, he hated spending money on something he didn't want.

When he left, carrying the boxes out to the dumpster, she turned last night's records over. She read the vacuum cleaner pamphlet, joined the dull silver pipes and white hose to the squat and round blue tank, and stepped on its switch. The cord was long and she did not have to change it to an outlet in another room; she wanted to remember to tell Wayne it was funny that the cord was longer than their place. She finished quickly and turned it off and could hear the records again.

She lay on the couch until the last record ended, then got the laundry bag from the bedroom and soap from the kitchen, and left. On the sidewalk she turned around and looked up at the front of the building, old and green in the snow and against the blue glare of the sky. She scraped the car's glass and drove to the laundry: two facing rows of machines, moist warm air, gurgling rumble and whining spin of washers, resonant clicks and loud hiss of dryers, and put in clothes and soap and coins. At a long table women smoked and read magazines, and two of them talked as they shook crackling electricity from clothes they folded. Anna took a small wooden chair from the table and sat watching the round window of the machine, watched her clothes and Wayne's tossing past it, like children waving from a ferris wheel.

THEY NOW LIVE IN TEXAS

for Peggy

W HEN THEY LEFT the party near midnight she felt
sober enough to drive, but in the heated car on the
way home she knew she was not. Her husband was driving with
both hands, and leaning forward, and she could see space between
his shoulders and upper back and the car seat. She looked through
the windshield at the moving reach of their headlights; on both sides
of the road were snowbanks, then woods. She said: "Stephen told
me about his religious experience."

"He had one of those?"

"Before AA."

"Whatever it was, it worked."

When they approached their house, free of neighbors for three
acres, she told her husband she was not drunk but she was not
sober, and asked him to drive the sitter home. He smiled and said
he wasn't sober either but the car didn't seem to know it, and as
he turned he shifted down then accelerated and climbed the long
and sanded driveway.

The girl rose from the couch, turned off the television, and putting
on her parka said the children had gone to bed on time, and had
given her no trouble. The woman thanked and paid her and walked
her to the door, then lay her coat beside her purse on the dining
room table and went down the hall, into the room where her four-
year-old daughter slept among stuffed bears. For moments she stood
looking at her daughter's face in the light from the hall, then she

284 · ANDRE DUBUS

crept out and went into the next room where the six-year-old girl slept with three animals she had loved since she was two: an elephant, a bear, and a rabbit. The woman pulled the blankets to the girl's shoulders and left.

She made a cup of tea with honey and lemon and drank it at the dining room table. She reached across her coat for the cigarettes in her purse as her husband turned into the driveway. In the kitchen he set the alarm, two high beeps behind her, then at the dining room door he stopped and said: "How are you?"

She looked over her left shoulder at him.

"Not sober yet. I'll wait till I am before I go to bed."

"Good plan." He came to her, taking off his coat, and leaned over and kissed her goodnight. Walking down the hall he said: "I should do what you're doing. But I'm wasted."

She watched him go into the girls' rooms, then the bedroom at the hall's end, and close the door. She finished her tea, then left the table and descended two steps into the living room. Last night her husband had brought home two movies because he liked her to have a choice. They had watched the Australian one, *Man of Flowers*, and she could not recall ever seeing a movie so beautiful. All of its music was from *Lucia di Lammermoor* and the movie itself achieved the splendid sadness of opera, for the man of the title was unique, bizarre: she could watch it in the way she listened to music, with a sorrow that uplifted her, for it did not demand empathy. The one they had not watched was a horror movie.

She pressed buttons and inserted the cassette, went to the kitchen and turned on flames under the kettle, then in the bathroom brushed her teeth; but as she poured boiling water into her cup she could taste again onions and tahini. She turned out the kitchen light, and those in the living room, and started the movie and settled on the couch with cigarettes and tea.

The woman in the movie was divorced and lived in Southern California with her children: a girl of about fourteen, and a boy and girl who appeared twelve and nine. They had an almost new car and a small good house and no one mentioned money; the mother did some sort of work, in an office with people, but only a few brief scenes showed it, and either because of the long and frightening action in the home or the Scotch the woman had drunk while she listened to Stephen in the kitchen, the work remained unclear.

The television was at one corner of the room and, to its right, the wall was a long window. The blinds were up, and now and then she glanced from the movie to the snow in front of the house: the white slope, and the scattered shapes of young trees, and, farther right, the sharp bank of the driveway. She knew she ought to lower the blinds, use them against the escaping heat and its cost, but she and her husband had built on this hill so they could look at the sky, and the woods and meadow across the road in front of their house, and she did not lower the blinds. But she stood and, watching the movie, lowered those on the left of the television, and covered the wide sliding glass door to the sundeck.

Something no one could see attacked the mother in her home. Its attacks were in the beginning those of a poltergeist: sounds that woke her, and the source of these sounds could only be another presence, or the malfunctioning of her mind; a jewelry box and evening bag exchanged places on her dressing table; doors closed or opened while the air was still; and sometimes there was nothing tangible, but a force the mother felt, usually in her bedroom, always at night.

Stephen had been sober for one month and four days when he heard a voice in his car as he drove alone one night, and in those moments he felt a strong but good presence in the front seat. Perhaps inside his body too. His face and voice as he told her the story made her believe now that it entered him. Probably he said it had. It loved him. He had never felt so loved, and he released himself to it, and then he wept. The flow of tears felt on his cheeks like the final drops of his agony. The presence drew them from him, as first it had drawn from him not only his struggle against drunkeness, but his very struggle to survive: every effort he had made, every strength he had mustered, since his birth, or even conception. He joyfully surrendered himself to the gift he was receiving: he had never been strong and he would never again need the resolve to be.

Watching a close-up of the mother fearfully closing her eyes for another night, the woman began to cry. She flicked and wiped away tears and focused on the dark bedroom and the face finally asleep, then her tears stopped and her throat dried and her heart felt dry too, a heavy vessel of solid sighs, drawn downward by gravity. She touched her cheeks and knew her make-up was unmarred. If her husband should enter the room now, sit beside her and turn on a lamp, he could not know that she had cried. There was much that he did not need to know, and she envied him now, and many other times, or perhaps only longed for his certainty. He loved her and the girls and most of the time—no: enough of the time—his work. He not only expected nothing else but was content not to. She loved him and her daughters and—enough—her work, and she loved herself too. So her husband loved himself, if that meant being generally happy, and able to live without any of the drugs of her friends: liquor, or therapists or shrinks, or trying to prolong their lives with exercise and atrophied sensuality.

But certainly Stephen had always loved himself. How else explain his years of fighting and failing but always fighting, until the night a voice, a something, visited his car. He knew what the voice said. She understood that, in the kitchen where they leaned against the counter and she vaguely saw and heard friends moving, talking, pouring chablis. But she did not ask him for the words, and he did not offer them. For two years he had not drunk or missed it, and he went to daily mass. He told her of mass and communion in one soft, quick sentence; and though his face did not change color its flesh seemed held by a blush.

The attacks in the movie were vicious now: the thing spoke the mother's name, cursed her, lifted her and flung her against walls and to the ceiling. Her children ran screaming to her room, to her. No one could help; only one person tried. The psychiatrist did not believe her; or he believed she was alone in her room. The medical doctor and the two scientists at the college did not believe her either. Only one man did, a friend not a lover. He sat with her on the final night, and when the thing attacked he cursed it and leaped at it and it threw him across the room. He was unconscious while, for the first time, it raped her. The children held each other just inside her doorway and cried and could not close or even avert their eyes. In the morning the mother and children got into the car and drove away from the house, and the camera moved back from their faces, the mother's last, then from a high distance showed the car traversing a landscape of brown and yellow hills. The scene faded, then words appeared on a blue background: *The events you have just seen occurred in the lives of a real family. They now live in Texas.*

She read the credits then stood and turned off the television and pressed the button to rewind the cassette. Listening to its sound she looked out at the snow. Then she removed the cassette and put it in its case. She sat on the couch and smoked, staring beyond the road at the meadow and trees and stars. She was looking out the window and reaching beside her for another cigarette, when suddenly she knew she was waiting. Quickly she stood and took the ash tray and her tea cup to the kitchen.

VOICES FROM THE MOON

to my sisters, Kathryn and Beth

IT'S DIVORCE THAT did it, his father had said last night. Those were the first words Richie Stowe remembered when he woke in the summer morning, ten minutes before the six-forty-five that his clock-radio was set for; but the words did not come to him as in memory, as something spoken even in the past of one night, but like other words that so often, in his twelve years, had seemed to wait above his sleeping face so that when he first opened his eyes he would see them like a banner predicting his day: *Today is the math test; Howie is going to get you after school. . . . It's divorce that did it*, and he turned off the switch so the radio wouldn't start, and lay in the breeze of the oscillating fan, a lean suntanned boy in underpants, neither tall nor short, and felt the opening of wounds he had believed were healed, felt again the deep and helpless sorrow, and the anger too because he was twelve and too young for it and had done nothing at all to cause it.

Then he got up, dressed in jeans and tee shirt and running shoes, went to his bathroom where a poster of Jim Rice hung behind the toilet, gazed at it while he urinated, studying the strong thighs and arms (in the poster Rice had swung his bat, and was looking up and toward left field), and Richie saw again that moment when Rice had broken his bat without hitting the ball: had checked his swing, and the bat had continued its forward motion, flown out toward first base, leaving Rice holding the handle. This was on television, and Richie had not believed what he had seen until he saw it again, the replay in slow motion.

His bicycle was in his room. He pushed it down the hall, at whose end, opposite his room, was the closed door leading to his father's bathroom and bedroom. He went out the front door and off the slab of concrete in front of it, mounted, and rode down the blacktop street under a long arch of the green branches of trees. As he pedaled and shifted gears he prayed for his anger to leave him, and for his brother Larry, and Brenda, and his father, but as he prayed he saw them: Larry and Brenda when they were married, sitting at the kitchen table with him and his father, Brenda's dark skin darker still from summer, her black hair separating at her shoulders, so that some of it rested on the bare flesh above her breasts. The men were watching her: slender and graceful Larry, who acted and danced, his taut face of angles and edges at the jaw and cheekbones, and a point at the nose; and Richie's father, with Larry's body twenty-two years older, wiry and quick, the face not rounded but softened over the bones.

Then he was at the church, and he locked his bicycle to a utility pole in front of it and went in, early for the seven o'clock Mass, genuflected then kneeled in an empty pew, and gazed at the crucifix, at the suffering head of Christ, but could not stop seeing what he had not seen last night but imagined as he lay in bed while his father and Larry sat and stood and paced on his ceiling, the floor of the living room. He shut his eyes, saw Larry's blanched face looking at his father, and saying *Marry her? Marry her?* and saw his father and Brenda naked in her bed in the apartment she had lived in since the divorce, saw them as he had seen lovemaking in movies, his father on top and Brenda's dark face, her moans, her cries, seeming more in pain than pleasure. As two altar boys and young Father Oberti entered from the left of the altar, Richie stood, praying Please Jesus Christ Our Lord help me, then said to Him: It will be very hard to be a Catholic in our house.

Knowing it would be hard not only in the today and tomorrow of twelve years old, but even harder as he grew older and had to face the temptations that everyone in the family had succumbed to. Even his mother, living a bicycle ride away in her apartment in Amesbury. Though he had never seen her with a man since his father, or heard her mention the name of one. Everyone in the family living in apartments now: his mother, Larry, Brenda, his sister Carol, older than Larry by a year, in her apartment in Boston, never married so not divorced, but at twenty-six had three times broken up with or lost men who lived with her. So only he and his father lived in the large house that to him was three stories, though his father said it was a split-level, the bedrooms and bathrooms on the first floor, then up a short flight of five steps to the kitchen and dining room and the west sundeck, up five more to the undivided one long room they used as two: at one end his father's den with a desk, and at the other the living room with the television; outside that long room, past the glass door, was the east sundeck where they kept the hammock and lawn chairs and grill. Now Brenda would move in, and he must keep receiving the Eucharist daily, must move alone and with the strength of the saints through his high school years, past girls, toward the seminary. Hard enough to stay a Catholic, he prayed; even harder to be a good enough one to be a priest.

He was in bed and near sleep last night when he heard the front door open and knew it was Larry, because he had a key still, then he listened to footsteps: Larry's going up to the kitchen, his father's overhead, coming from the right, from the den. Richie flung back the top sheet, but did not move his feet to the floor. He was sleepy, already it was past ten o'clock, and five times this summer he had turned off the radio when it woke him, gone back to sleep and missed the weekday Mass and waked at nine or later, a failure for the day that had only begun. He pulled the sheet over his chest, settled into the pillow, and listened to their voices in the kitchen, the popping open of beer cans, and their going upstairs to the living room over his bed. He again pushed the sheet away and this time got up; sleepy or no, he would at least go see him, touch him, at least that. He opened his door and was going up the short flight to the kitchen when he heard Larry: "I don't *believe* this."

Richie stood, his hand on the flat banister. His father's voice was low, and neither angry nor sad, but tired: "It's divorce that did it."

"Whose?"

"Yours. Mine. Fucking divorce. You think I chose her?"

"What am I supposed to think?"

"It just happened. It always just happens."

"Beautiful. What happened to will?"

"Don't talk to me about will. Did you will your marriage to end? Did your mother and me? Will is for those bullshit guys to write books about. Out here it's—"

"—Survival of the quickest, right. Woops, sorry son, out of the way, boy, I'm grabbing your ex-wife."

"Out here it's balls and hanging on. I need her, Larry."

Richie imagined them, facing each other in the room, in the blown air from the window fan, as he had seen them all his life, facing each other in quarrels, their arms bent at their sides, fists clenched, save when they gestured and their arms came up with open hands; they never struck the blow that, always, they seemed prepared for; not even his father, when Larry was a boy. Even as Richie stood in dread on the stairs, his fingers and palm pressing down on the banister as if to achieve even more silence from his rigid body, he knew there would be no hitting tonight. His father was not like any other father he knew: at forty-seven, he was still quick of temper, and fought in bars. Yet he had never struck anyone in the family, not even a spanking; *for your kids*, he said, *the tongue is plenty*. Richie backed down the stairs, turned and crept into his room, and softly closed the door.

He stood beneath them and listened for a while, then lay in bed and heard the rest of what came to him through his ceiling when their voices rose, less in anger, it seemed, than in excitement, and his heart beat with it too, and in that beat he recognized another feeling that usually he associated with temptation, with sin, with turning away from Christ: something in him that was aroused, that took pleasure in what he knew, and knew with sadness, to be yet another end of their family.

He prayed against it, incantations of *Lord, have mercy*, as he prayed now in Mass to overcome his anger, his sorrowful loss, and to both endure and help his family. Father Oberti was approaching the Consecration and Richie waited for the miracle, then watched it, nearly breathless, and prayed My Lord and my God to the white Host elevated in Father Oberti's hands, and softly struck his breast. Beneath the Host, Father Oberti's face was upturned and transformed. It was a look Richie noticed only on young priests, and only when they consecrated the bread and wine. In movies he had seen faces like it, men or women gazing at a lover, their lips and eyes seeming near both tears and a murmur of love, but they only resembled what he saw in Father Oberti's face, and were not at all the same. Now Father Oberti lifted the chalice and Richie imagined being inside of him, feeling what he felt as the wine he held became the Blood of Christ. My Lord and my God, Richie prayed, striking his breast, immersing himself in the longing he felt there in his heart: a longing to consume Christ, to be consumed through Him into the priesthood, to stand some morning purified and adoring in white vestments, and to watch his hands holding bread, then God. His eyes followed the descent of the chalice.

From there the Mass moved quickly forward, and he was able to concentrate on it, to keep memory and imagination from returning to last night and tomorrow, or at least from distracting him. Images of his father and Larry and Brenda collided with his prayers, but they did not penetrate him as they had before the Consecration. Even when he was a boy of seven and eight, nothing distracted him from the Consecration and the time afterward, until the Mass ended, and he had believed he was better than the other children. Now, at twelve, he knew he had received a gift, with his First Communion or even before, and that he had done nothing to earn it, and he must be ever grateful and humble about it, or risk losing it.

He rose to approach the altar. With clasped hands resting on his stomach, his head bowed, he walked up the aisle behind three white-haired old women. When it was his turn, he stepped to Father Oberti at the head of the aisle, turned his left palm up, with his right under it, as Father Oberti took a Host from the chalice, raised it, said *Body of Christ*, and Richie said *Amen*. Father Oberti placed the Host on his palm. He looked at it as he turned to go down the aisle. Then with his right thumb and forefinger he put it in his mouth, let it rest on his tongue, then softly chewed as he walked to the pew. He felt that he embraced the universe, and was in the arms of God.

When the Mass ended he kneeled until everyone had left the church. Then he went up to the altar, genuflected, looked up at Christ on the cross, and went around the altar and into the sacristy. The alter boys were leaving, and Father Oberti was in his white shirt and black pants.

"Richie."

"Can I talk to you, Father?"

They watched the altar boys go out the door, onto the lawn.

"What is it?"

"My father and Brenda. My brother's ex-wife? They're getting married."

"Oh my. Oh my, Richie, you poor boy."

Father Oberti sat in a chair and motioned to another, but Richie stood, his eyes moving about the room, sometimes settling on Father Oberti's, but then he nearly cried, so he looked again at walls and windows and floor, telling it as he both heard and imagined last night.

"And, see, Father, the whole family is living outside the Church. In sin. And now Dad and Brenda will be in the house."

"Don't think of it as sin."

He looked at Father Oberti.

"It's even against the law," Richie said. "Massachusetts law. They're going to get married in another state, but Dad's talking to somebody in the—legislature?"

"That's right."

"To try to change the law."

"It's probably a very old law, Richie." Father Oberti did not look shocked, or even surprised, but calm and gentle. "The Church had them too. It was to prevent murder, or the temptation to it."

"Murder?"

"Sure. So that hundreds of years ago your father wouldn't be tempted to kill Larry. To get his wife, and all her land and so forth. It's just an old law, Richie. Don't think of your father and Brenda as sin."

"I'm afraid I'll lose my faith." Heat rose to his face, tears to his eyes, and he looked at the dark blue carpet and Father Oberti's shining black shoes.

"No. This should strengthen it. You must live like the Lord, with His kindness. Don't think of them as sinful. Don't just think of sex. People don't marry for that. Think of love. They are two people who love each other, and as painful as it is for others, and even if it *is* wrong, it's still love, and that is always near the grace of God. Has he been a bad father?"

Richie shook his head.

"Look at me. Don't mind crying. I'm not scolding you."

He wiped away his tears and raised his face and looked into Father Oberti's brown eyes.

"It is very hard to live like Christ. For most of us, it's impossible. The best we can do is try. And two of the hardest virtues for a Christian are forgiveness and compassion. Not judging people. But they are essential parts of love." His hands rose from his lap, and he clasped them in front of his chest, the fingers squeezing. "We can't love without those two. And the message of Christ is love. For everyone. Certainly you will love your father. And his wife. Try to imagine what they feel like, how they comfort each other, how much they love each other, to risk so much to be together. It's not evil. It may be weak, or less strong than the Church wants people to be; than *you* want people to be. And of course you're right. It would be far better if they had fought their love before it grew. But there are much worse things than loving. Much worse, Richie. Be kind, and pray for them, and I will too. I'll pray for you too. And I hope you'll pray for me. People don't think of priests as sinners. Or if they do, they think of sex or drinking. That's very simple-minded. There are sins that are far more complicated, that a priest can commit: pride, neglect, others. He can be guilty of these while ministering sacraments, saying the Mass." His hands parted, reached out, and took Richie's shoulders. "You'll love your father and his wife, and you'll grow up to be a good priest. If it's what you want, and if it's God's will. Don't leave God out of this. Your father and the young lady are in His hands, not yours. You will have some embarrassment. Even some pain. What is that, for a strong boy like you? A devout boy, a daily communicant."

His right hand left Richie's shoulder, and he moved it in a cross between them, then placed his palm on Richie's forehead.

"Thank you, Father."

"We can keep talking."

"No. Thank you, Father."

Father Oberti stood and held out his hand, and Richie shook it.

"I'll see you tomorrow," Father Oberti said.

"Yes."

"Or sooner, if you want."

"No. Tomorrow."

"Good. Go play baseball, and live your life."

Richie lifted his hand in a wave, then turned and left the sacristy, entered the church near the altar, genuflected, looked up at Christ, and went down the aisle. At the door he turned back to the altar, looked at Christ on the cross, then pushed open the heavy brown wooden door, and stepped into warm sunlight and cool air.

On the street near his house, in the shadows under the arch of maples, he saw Melissa Donnelly and her golden retriever. She was two blocks ahead, walking away from him in the middle of the empty street. He pedaled harder three times before he was aware of it, then he slowed but did not touch the brake, and the bicycle kept its quiet speed on the blacktop. Melissa was wearing faded cut-off jeans and sandals, and a blue denim shirt with its sleeves rolled up to her elbows. The dog was named Conroy, and was not on a leash; he zigzagged, nose to ground, in the grass beside the street. When Richie was close, he braked and Melissa looked over her shoulder, then smiled and said: Richie. He said hi and stopped, and walked the bicycle beside her. She was thirteen, three months older than Richie, and he liked her green eyes. Her hair was curls of very light brown, and hung above her shoulders. She wore lipstick.

"Where you going?" she said.

"Home. You walking Conroy?"

"To the field. So I can smoke."

"How did he get his name?"

"He's named for an old friend of my dad's. From the war."

"Which one?"

"Korea."

"Did he die?"

"No. My dad just never saw him again."

Her shirttails were knotted above her waist, showing a suntanned oblong of her stomach. Her legs were smooth and brown. He was looking past the handlebar at her sandaled feet, when the blacktop ended at a weed-grown, deeply rutted trail beside a stand of trees. Beyond the trees was the athletic field.

"Come on," she said, and he followed her through the trees, while Conroy darted ahead and onto the field. On open ground at the edge of the trees they stopped, and Richie stood his bicycle with its stand. Melissa leaned against an oak, looked over each shoulder, then drew a pack of Marlboros from between her breasts and offered it to him. He shook his head.

"Afraid of cancer?"

"I just don't want to smoke."

She shrugged, and he watched her eyes and the cigarette in the middle of her lips as she took a lighter from her pocket. She inhaled and blew smoke and said: "Ah. First since last night."

He imagined her, while he lay in bed before Larry came, or maybe as he stood on the steps or later as he listened in his room, saw her out here under the stars, the glow of her cigarette in the shadows of these trees as Conroy ran in the field.

"Did you walk him last night?"

"Yeah. You'd think they'd catch on. They used to have to tell me to, and now I'm always walking the dog."

"What time were you out here?"

"About ten, I guess. Why?"

"I was wondering what I was doing then."

"You should have been out here. It was beautiful, really. Cool and quiet, and all the stars."

She half-turned toward him. If he moved a hand outward, it would touch her. He folded his arms, then leaned with his side against the tree. He was so close to her now that he could only see her face and throat and shoulders, unless he moved his eyes.

"Where have you been?" she said.

He said to her eyes: "I went to Mass." Then he said to her mouth: "I go every day."

"You do? Why?"

"I want to be a priest."

"Wow."

"It's not just that. I'd go even if I didn't want to be one. Do you receive on Sundays?"

"On Sundays, sure."

"So you believe in it. So do I. That's why I go. Because it's too big not to."

"Too big?"

"You believe it's God? The bread and wine?"

"Yes."

"That's what I mean. It's God, so how can I stay home? When He's there every day."

"I never thought of it like that." The cigarette rose into his vision, and she turned in profile to draw from it. "You feel like you have to go?"

"No. I like it. I love it. It's better than anything. The feeling. Do you think I'm dumb?"

"No. I wish I felt that way."

"Why?"

She shrugged. "The things I do, everybody does them."

He unfolded his arms, and touched her cheek.

"You're so pretty," he said.

"So are you."

His face warmed. "Pretty?"

"Well. You know. Good-looking."

She looked out at the field, finished the cigarette, then called Conroy. He was at the other side of it, near the woods where Richie cross-country skied. Conroy stood still and looked at Melissa's voice. Then he ran toward it.

"Are you going to play softball this morning?" she said.

"Probably. Are you?"

"I don't know."

Conroy stopped on the infield of the softball diamond, sniffed the earth, then moved, with his nose down, to short right field. He straightened, circled three times in the same spot, as though he were drilling himself into it, then squatted, with his four paws close to each other, his tail curled upward, and shat. He cocked his head and watched them, and Melissa said: "Remember that, if you play right field. Are you in a hurry to get home?"

"Not me."

"I'll have another cigarette."

She withdrew her cigarettes from her blouse, and he watched her suntanned hand going down between her breasts, watched as she returned the pack, and imagined her small white breasts, and the brown from the sun ending just above and below them.

"Aren't you playing softball?" he said.

"Late. I have to do housework first."

"Last night—"

When he stopped, she had been frowning about housework, but her face softened and she looked at his eyes, and said: "What?"

"Nothing."

"What's wrong?"

"Maybe I'll tell you sometime."

"Tell me."

"Sometime."

"Promise?"

"Yes. I just wish I had been here."

"Was that it?"

"No."

"You'll tell me?"

"Yes."

He unfolded his arms, lowered them to his sides, where they made him feel as though he were stiffly posing for a picture. Slowly he let them rise, let each hand rest on her shoulders, then move down and lightly hold her biceps. She watched him. Then he swallowed and patted her lean hard arms, and turned away from her, letting his hands slide down to her elbows and away, and he folded his arms on his breast and looked out at the field. Conroy was lying down, chewing a short piece of a branch.

"You've never smoked?" she said.

"No."

"Here. Try."

He looked at her, and she held her cigarette to his lips; he drew on it and inhaled bitter heat and waited to cough as he quickly blew out the smoke, but he did not. Then a dizzying nausea moved through him, and was gone. He shook his head.

"Did you get a kick?"

"Too much of one."

"You have to get used to it. Want another?"

"Woo. Not today."

She smiled at him and ground out the cigarette with her foot, and he watched her toes arch in the sandal. She called Conroy. He came with his head high, holding the stick in his jaws, and Richie walked his bicycle behind Melissa, into the trees, and onto the road. As they walked, the bicycle was between them, and she rested a hand on the seat. In front of his house he stopped.

"So maybe I'll see you later," he said.

"Yes. Maybe tonight too. Father Stowe."

His cheeks were warm again, but he was smiling.

"I feel like a bad girl."

"Why?"

"I gave you your first drag on a cigarette." Then she leaned over the bicycle and with closed lips quickly kissed his mouth, that was open, his lips stilled by surprise, by fear, by excitement. She walked down the road, calling for Conroy, and a block away the dog turned and sprinted toward her, ears back, the stick in his jaws. Richie stood breathing her scents of smoke and lipstick and something else sweet—a cologne or cosmetic—or perhaps he only smelled memory, for it did not fade from the air. He watched her stoop to pet Conroy and nuzzle his ear, then straighten and walk with him, on the side of the road, in the shade of the arching trees.

When she turned into her lawn, he pushed his bicycle up the walk and onto the concrete slab at the front door. He crouched to lock the rear wheel and was very hungry and hoped his father was making pancakes.

II

HE WAS. GREG STOWE had waked when he heard the front door shut behind Richie, and now Richie was nearly an hour late and Greg stood on the narrow east sundeck, which they rarely used because it was shaded by maples and pines and was sunlit only in the middle of the day. But he drank coffee there in the morning, all during the warm months, and often in the colder ones too, in late fall and winter, on windless sunny mornings when the temperature was over twenty. And at night when he knew or believed he was not the same man he was in the morning, he drank beer out there long past midnight, because it was darker, the trees that blocked the sun forming a good black wall between him and the streetlights nearly a hundred yards behind the house. He had bought both lots, so that no one could ever build behind him, and his lawn would always end at streets, not another man's property, and he had left the trees on the back lot, so he had a small woods. Children played there, and teenagers hid and left behind them beer cans and bottles and cigarette butts. But the teenagers always gathered at the same spot, and their trash was contained. He thought it was funny that teenagers, except when they were in a car, did not seem comfortable unless they were stationary in a familiar spot, like an old person, or a dog, in a house.

The front sundeck was good for drinking with friends before dinner, but there was a streetlight, and the lights of other houses, and he could not feel alone there. He liked drinking alone in a place so dark he had to remember the color of his clothes, or wait until his eyes adjusted to discern at least their hue. On those nights, and last night was one of them, time stopped, while his sense of place expanded, so there were moments when the sudden awareness of the dial of his wristwatch, and of where he actually stood, beer in hand, came to him with the startling sense of being wakened by an alarm clock. In the morning, drinking coffee and standing where he had stood the night before, he simply planned his day.

Not this morning, though, for today was a continuation of last night with Larry, interrupted only by his grieving beer-drinking on the deck and a short sleep, and it would resume with Richie as soon as he came home, and end with Carol. So his day was not only already prepared for him, like a road he had to follow (or, more accurately, he thought, an obstacle course), but in truth it could not be planned, for he had no idea—or too many of them—of how, and even when, it would be finished. Nor did he know what he meant by *finished*. What he hoped for was Carol and Larry and Richie and Brenda sitting in his kitchen while he cooked.

But he knew he had as much hope for that as for the traveling he did on the deck at night; he called them his Michelob voyages. He did not have the money for all of them, but he had the money for any one of them, even each of them in turn, if he spaced them by ten or so months and lived out a normal life. He would like to buy a boat with galley and sleeping quarters, learn to repair and maintain it, to navigate, and then go on the Intracostal Waterway, the fifteen hundred and fifty miles from Boston to Florida Bay, then the eleven hundred and sixteen to Brownsville, Texas. His image was of Brenda on the boat, and maybe Richie, and himself on the bridge, simply steering and looking at America. But he did not want to do it as a vacation, something you had to come home from, and at a certain time. Take a year off, Brenda said.

But he could not. He was the sole owner of two ice cream stores; fifteen years ago he had bought them with a partner, and seven years ago he had bought out the partner, who retired and went to Florida and, according to postcards, did nothing but fish. These stores, one of them in an inland town and open all year, with a soda fountain and sandwiches too, and one at Seabrook Beach in New Hampshire, open from Memorial Day weekend till Labor Day, sold homemade ice cream, or as close to it as people could get without doing the work to make it in their own kitchens. Greg had learned that Russians and Americans ate more ice cream than the people of any other countries in the world, and some nights on the deck he amused himself by thinking about opening a store on the Black Sea, at Odessa or Sevastopol.

But he could not leave for a year, or even half of one, not for the Intracoastal Waterway or for any other place—Kenya, Morocco, Greece, Italy, Spain, France, places where he wanted to walk and look, to eat and drink what the natives did—because as well as owning his stores he ran them too. It was something his partner had not had the heart, the drive, to do; and that was Greg's reason for borrowing to buy him out, figuring finally that debt and being alone responsible for everything was better than trying week after week to joke with, tease, and implore a man in an effort to get him to work; when all the time, although Greg liked him, and enjoyed drinking and playing poker with him, and going into Boston to watch games with him, he wanted every workday to kick his ass. So he bought him out, freed him to fish in Florida, a life that sounded to Greg right for the lazy old fart who liked money but not the getting of it, while he himself liked getting it but had little to spend it on, and was not free to spend it on what he would like to.

At night on the east deck, when time relinquished its function in his life, and space lost its distances and limits, he completed his travel on the Intracostal Waterway by sending his boat from Brownsville to the mouth of the Amazon, in the hands of a trustworthy sailor for hire, then flying with Brenda to Rio de Janeiro where they would live the hotel life of sleep and swimming and drinking and eating (and daytime fucking: yes, that) until he was ready for the rigorous part that excluded Richie from the daydream. He would go with Brenda to the mouth of the Amazon, by car or train, however they traveled there. He would rendezvous with his boat and sailor at one of the towns he had looked at as a dot on the globe on his desk. Then he and Brenda would walk west along the river. They would take only canteens, and he would carry a light pack with food for the day. They would wear heavy boots against snakes, and he would wear his .45 at his waist, and carry a machete. They would see anacondas and strange aqua birds and crocodiles. At the day's end the boat would be waiting, and they would board it, and fish, and sip drinks and cook and eat, then lie together gently rocking in the forward cabin with the double bed. Sometimes he imagined the river's bank stripped of trees, and an asphalt road alongside it, with rest areas and Howard Johnson's. But no: it must be jungle, thick living jungle, where each step was a new one, on new earth, so that you could not remember how you felt retracing your steps through the days of your life at home. He went there at night on this deck, and always with the focused excitement, the near-quietude, of love. Only in the mornings with his coffee, or driving from the inland to the beach store, or at other moments during his days, did he ever feel the sadness that he forced to be brief: the knowledge that he would never do it.

If you weren't there, on the job, they either stole from you, at the least by giving away your ice cream to their friends and taking some home as well, or they screwed up in other ways, and the operation went lax, and you had two stores selling ice cream but something was wrong. So he was at both stores every day, and he sometimes worked the counters there too, and washed dishes, and swept floors, all of this to keep things going, Goddamnit, and because he could not be idle while others worked, and every night he was there to close out the register; he took the money with him for night deposit, the .45 in his belt till he was in the car, then on the seat beside him. He carried the pistol in his hand when, at the bank, he walked from the car to the night depository. He had a permit. When he told the police chief, who approved the permit, how much money he carried to the bank each night, the chief asked if he had ever thought of buying a safe. Greg shrugged. He said he liked doing it this way, but that each store did have a safe he used only on nights when he couldn't get there, but anybody could get money from a safe if they wanted to so badly that they'd take the whole damn thing. He alternated the stores, taking the money from the inland one on one night, the beach store on the next, so his manager at one store would not always be last to be relieved of the money, and so last to go home. But most nights, when he reached the second store, his people were still cleaning up anyway, and he helped them with that. Some nights he thought he did not use a safe because he hoped some bastard, or bastards, would try to take his money. His pattern was easy enough to learn, if anyone were interested.

Larry was the only man he knew whom he could trust to do everything, and Larry had never wanted to give himself fully to the stores. During college he had needed his days free, and after college he needed his nights for dance or play rehearsals. This was not a disappointment for Greg; when he felt anything at all about Larry's lack of involvement with the stores, it was relief, for he wanted Larry to be his own man and not spend his life following his father.

He believed the business of fatherhood was to love your children, take care of them, let them grow, and hope they did; and to keep your nose out of their lives. He did not know, and could not remember if he had ever known, whether Larry hoped to be a professional actor or dancer, perhaps even an established one with all the money and its concomitant bullshit, or if he was content to work with the amateur theater and dance companies in the Merrimack Valley. As far as he knew, Larry had never said, and he had never asked, and Larry's face had always been hard for him to read.

But before Brenda, when with no woman or a faceless one for his daydream he rode the Waterway and walked the Amazon on his dark sundeck at night, he had hoped that a time would come when Larry would want or need a break from performing, and would want to work the stores for a few months, and earn much more money, perhaps for an adventure of his own, a shot at New York or Hollywood or wherever else the unlucky bastards born with talent had to go to sell themselves. But not after last night. Probably, after last night, he would not ever show up at the store again, unless it was to collect his final paycheck. As difficult as it was for Greg to believe, as much as his heart and his body refused to accept it, both of them—the heart surrounded by cool fluttering, and the body weary as though it had wrestled through the night while he slept—threatening to quit on him if Larry simply vanished, that was what Larry had said he would do.

Greg had phoned him to come and have a night-cap, at ten at the earliest, saying he had work to do till then. He had no work, unless waiting for Richie to go to bed was work, and finally he supposed it was. Greg had phoned his two managers and told them to put the money in the safes. He did not know what he expected from Larry. An unpredictable conversation or event was so rare in his life that, as well as shyness, guilt, and shame, he felt a thrill that both excited him and deepened his guilt. He brought Larry up to the living room and tried to begin chronologically. He saw his mistake at once, for early in Greg's account Larry saw what was coming and, leaning forward in his chair, said: "Are you going to tell me you've been seeing Brenda?"

"Yes."

"I don't *believe* this."

Greg looked at the floor.

"It's divorce that did it," he said.

"Whose?"

"Yours. Mine." He looked at Larry. "Fucking divorce. You think I chose her?"

"What am I supposed to think?" Larry said, and was out of the chair: he never seemed to stand up from one, there was no visible effort, no pushing against the chair arms, or even a forward thrust of his torso; he rose as a snake uncoils, against no resistance at all, and Greg fixed on that detail, finding in it his son of twenty-five years, holding that vision while the room and Larry and Greg himself faded in a blur of confusion and unpredictability.

"It just happened," Greg said. "It always just happens."

"Beautiful. What happened to will?"

Greg stood and stepped toward him.

"Don't talk to me about will." And they were lost, both of them, in anger, in pride, facing each other, sometimes even circling like fighters, then one would spin away, stride to a window, and stare out at the dark trees of the back lawn; and it was at one of those times when Larry was at the window, smoking, silent, that Greg watched his back and shoulders for a moment, then took their long-emptied and tepid beer cans down to the kitchen, returned with beer and opened and placed one, over Larry's shoulder, onto the windowsill, then opened his own and, standing halfway across the room from Larry, spoke softly to the back of his head.

"You have to know how it started, you have to know the accident. The women, you know: when there's a divorce, they get dropped. You know what I mean. They lose the friends they had through the marriage. The husband's friends. Goddamn if I know why. Doesn't matter if the husband was the asshole. Still it happens. And they're out of his family too. So I'd have her over for dinner. After you guys split up. Her and Richie and me. Shit, I—" Now he did not know, and in a glimpse of his future knew that he never would know, why he had invited her, not even once a week and not only to dinner, but ice-skating and cross-country skiing, always with Richie, and finally canoeing and swimming in lakes, and by June when the ocean was warm enough Richie still went with them, but he and Brenda were lovers. "I just didn't want her to be alone. To feel like the family blamed her."

"The family?" Larry said to the window screen. "You and Richie?"

"Well, Carol's not here. And Mom's—"

"—Come on, Pop."

"Will you let me explain?"

"Go on. Explain." He spoke to the window still, to the dark outside, and Greg was about to tell him to turn around, but did not.

"That's how it started. Or why it started. I'll leave all that analyzing to you. All it does is make your tires spin deeper in the hole."

"That might be good, depending on the hole."

"Jesus. What happened is, sometime in the spring there, I started loving her."

"Great." Now he turned, swallowed from his beer, looked at Greg. "I knew you and Richie were doing things with her. He told me."

"What did you think about it?"

"I tried not to think anything about it. So I thought it was good for Richie. He likes her a lot. I even thought it was good for her."

"But not for me."

"Like I said, I tried not to think anything about it. It looks like one of us should have. Mostly you. What do you mean, you started loving her? Are we talking about fucking?"

"Come on, Larry."

"Well, are we?"

"What do you think?"

"I'm staying on the surface; my little brother and my father have been taking care of my ex-wife."

"You want to hear me say it. Is that it?"

"Isn't that why you called me here?"

Greg pinched his beer can, pressing it together in its middle, and said: "I called you here to say I'm going to marry her."

Like wings, Larry's arms went out from his body, his beer in one hand.

"*Marry* her? *Marry* her?"

"Larry, look; wait, Larry, just stand there. I'll get us a beer. You want something different? I got everything—"

"—You sure the fuck do."

"Come on, Larry. Scotch, rum, tequila, vodka, gin, bourbon, brandy, some liqueurs—"

"—I'll take mescal."

"You'll take tequila."

"And everything else, it seems."

Greg left him standing with his empty can, and carrying his own bent one descended the short staircase, got the tequila from one cabinet, a plate from another, took a lime from the refrigerator and quartered it on the cutting board, put the lime and salt shaker and shot glass and bottle on the plate, then opened himself a beer. Upstairs he walked past Larry and laid the plate on top of the television set near where Larry stood. Greg sat in an armchair across the room.

"Let me talk to you about love," he said.

"Paternal?"

"*Love*, Goddamnit. I don't believe I feel it the way you do."

"Looks like you do. You even chose the same woman."

"I didn't *choose*. Now let me talk. Please. You get to be forty-seven, you love differently. I remember twenty-five. Jesus, you can hardly work, or do anything else; you wake up in the morning and your heart's already full of it. You want to be with her all the time. She can be a liar, a thief, a slut—you don't see it. All you see is her, or what you think is her, and you can walk off a roof with a shingle and hammer in your hands, just thinking about her. But at forty-seven, see, it's different. There's not all that breathlessness. Maybe by then a man's got too many holes in him: I don't know. It's different, but it's deeper. Maybe because it's late, and so much time has been pissed away, and what's left is—is precious. And love—Brenda, for me—is like a completion of who you are. It's got to do with what I've never had, and what I'll never do. Do you understand any of that?"

"All of it," Larry said, and stepped to the television set, and, with his back to Greg, poured a shot of tequila, sprinkled salt onto his thumb, licked it off, drank with one swallow, then put a wedge of lime in his mouth and turned, chewing, to Greg. "But it sounds like you could have had that with anybody."

"No. Those feelings came from her. I didn't feel them before."

"All right. All right, then. But why *marry*, for Christ's sake?"

"I need it. She needs it. It's against the law, in Massachusetts. We'll have to do it some other place. But I'm going to see Brady. See if he can work on changing the law."

"You're bringing this shit to the fucking legislature?"

"Yes."

"God *damn*. Why don't you just fuck her?"

"Larry. Hold on, Larry."

"I *am* holding on, Goddamnit."

Larry's face was reddened, his breath quick; he half-turned toward the television set, picked up the bottle and shot glass, then replaced them without pouring. He looked at Greg, and breathed deeply now, his fists opening and closing at his sides, in front of his pelvis, at his sides. Then, at the peak of a deep breath, he said quietly: "You have to marry her," and exhaled, and in the sound of his expelled breath Greg heard defeat and resignation, and they struck his heart a blow that nearly broke him, nearly forced him to lower his face into his hands and weep.

"Yes," he said. So many times in his life, perhaps all of his life, or so his memory told him, he had stood his ground against opponents: most of them in the flesh, men or women whose intent was to walk right through him, as if he were not there, as if the man he was did not even occupy the space that stood in their way; there had been the other opponents too, without bodies, the most threatening of all: self-pity, surrender to whatever urged him to sloth or indifference or anomie or despair. Always he had mustered strength. But now he felt the ground he held was as vague as a principle that he had sworn to uphold, and he could not remember feeling anything at all about it, yet was defending it anyway because he had said he would. The word *marry* was as empty of emotion for him as, right now, was the image of Brenda's face. And it struck him that perhaps she too, like so much else, like Goddamn near everything else, would become a duty. Because when you fought so much and so hard, against pain like this as well as the knee-deep bullshit of the world, so you could be free to lie in the shade of contentment and love, the great risk was that you would be left without joy or passion, and in the long evenings of respite and solitude would turn to the woman you loved with only the distracted touch, the distant murmurs of tired responsibility. Again he said: "Yes."

"She'll want children, you know," Larry said.

Greg shrugged.

"You'll give them to her?"

"There's always a trade-off."

"What the fuck does that mean?"

"You can't marry a young woman, then turn around and refuse to have kids."

Larry turned to the television, poured tequila, and, ignoring both

salt and lime, drank it, and Greg watched the abrupt upward toss
of his head. Larry put the glass on the plate, his downward motion
with it hard, just hard enough so it did not crack the plate; but the
striking of the thick-bottomed glass on china created in the room a
sudden and taut silence, as though Larry had cocked a gun they
both knew he would not actually use.

"You do that, Pop," he said, facing the corner behind the television. "I'm going."

Then he was walking past Greg and out of the room, and Greg
moved in front of him, and when Larry sidestepped, Greg did too;
Larry stopped.

"Where?" Greg said.

Larry started to go around him but Greg stepped in front of him,
looked at his eyes that were sorrowful and already gone from the
room, as if they looked at a road in headlights, or a bed somewhere
in a stripped and womanless room, or simply at pain itself and the
enduring of it, and Greg thought: *Why they must have looked that way
with Brenda, around the end, they must—*

"Where are you going?"

"Away. And I don't want your blessing. I've already got your
curse."

Then, very fast, and with no touch at all, not even a brush of
arm, of sleeve, he was around Greg and across the short distance
to the stairs, where Greg watched his entire body, then torso and
arms and head, then the head, the hair alone, vanish downward.
He stood listening to Larry's feet going down the second flight. He
listened to the first door, to the entryway and, as it closed, to the
front door open and close, not loudly as with the glass and plate,
but a click that seemed in the still summer night more final than a
slamming of wood into wood.

III

RICHIE PRAYED *Please Jesus Christ Our Lord help us* as he went up
the stairs into the kitchen; then he saw his father standing on the
east sundeck. His back was to Richie, and a coffee mug rested on
the wall, near his hip. Then he turned, smiled, raised the mug to

his lips, blew on the coffee, and drank. Beyond him were the maples that grew near the house, at the edge of the woods.

"Pancake batter's ready," he said. "Bacon's in the skillet. You want eggs too?"

"Sure."

His father stepped into the kitchen, and slid the screen shut behind him; at the stove he turned on the electric burner under the old black iron skillet where strips of bacon lay. From the refrigerator behind him he took a carton of eggs and a half-gallon jar of orange juice, poured a glass of it, and gave it to Richie, who stood a few paces from his father, drinking, waiting, as his father placed a larger iron skillet beside the first one, where grease was spreading from the bacon. His father poured a cup of coffee, lit a cigarette, and Richie knew now it was coming: what he wanted neither to hear, nor his father to be forced to tell. So when his father began, looking from the bacon to Richie, stepping to the counter opposite the stove to stir the batter, back to the stove to look at the bacon and turn on the burner under the second skillet, all the while glancing at Richie, meeting his eyes, and talking about love and living alone, or at least without a wife, and how Richie living here made him happy, very happy, but a man needed a wife too, it was nature's way, and a man wasn't complete without one, and that he, Richie, should also have a woman in the house, that was natural too, and come to think of it natural must come from the word nature, and the needs that Mother Nature put in people; or God, of course, God, Richie stopped him. He said: "I heard you and Larry last night."

For a moment his father stood absolutely still, the spatula in one hand, the cigarette in the other halted in its ascent to his lips. Then he moved again: drew on the cigarette, flicked its ash into the garbage disposal in the sink beside the stove, turned the bacon, leaned the spatula on the rim of the skillet, then faced Richie.

"What do you think?" he said.

"I want you to be happy."

Blushing, his father said: "Well—" He looked at the floor. "Well, son, that's—" He raised his eyes to Richie's. "Thank you," he said. He looked over his shoulder at the bacon, then back at Richie. "You like Brenda?"

"Yes."

"You don't mind her moving in with us? After we're married?"

"No. I like her."

"There must be something."

"Larry."

"Yes."

"Am I going to visit him, like I do Mom?"

His father had not thought about that, Richie saw it in his face, the way it changed as abruptly as when he had stood so still with the spatula and half-raised cigarette, but more completely, deeply: the color rushed out of it, and the lips opened, and he stood staring at Richie's eyes, his mouth, his eyes. Then in two strides his father came to him, was hugging him, so his right cheek and eye were pressed against his father's hard round stomach, his arms held against his ribs by the biceps squeezing his own, the forearms pulling his back toward his father.

"You poor kid," his father said. "Jesus Christ, you poor, poor kid."

Still his father held him, and vaguely he wondered if the cigarette were burning toward the fingers that caressed his back, and he understood that his father had not yet thought about him seeing Larry because there had been so much else, and he would have got around to that too, he always got around, finally, to everything; but there had not been time yet (then he understood too it was not time but relief, peace; there had not been those yet); then against his cheek his father's stomach moved: a soft yet jerking motion, and he knew that above him his father was crying. He had never seen his father cry. Nor did he now. In a while, in his father's embrace, the motion ceased and his father said, in almost his voice, but Richie could hear in it the octave of spent tears: "He's got to come through. Larry. You pray for that, hear? He will. He'll come through, he'll come see us."

Richie nodded against the shirt, the taut flesh; then with a final hug his father squeezed breath out of him and turned back to the stove. Richie waited for him to wipe his tears, but his hands were lifting out bacon and holding a plate covered with paper towel. When he took the batter from the counter, his cheeks and eyes were dry, so maybe as he held Richie he had somehow wiped them; but Richie, already forming the embrace and tears into a memory he knew he would have always, had no memory of his father's hands leaving his back where they petted and pulled. He slid open the screen, stepped onto the sundeck, leaned against its low wall, and watched a gray squirrel climb a maple. The tree was so close that Richie could see the squirrel's eyes and claws as it spiraled up the trunk, in and out of his vision. Near the top it ran outward on a long thick limb, then sat among green leaves, while Richie imagined the tears in his father's eyes, and going down his cheeks, then stopping; then disappearing as though drawn back up his face, into his eyes, lest they be seen.

Saint Peter cried after the cock crowed three times (and still was not under the cross; only Saint John and the women were there, and many times Richie wondered if he would have had the courage to go to the cross), and Christ cried, looking down at Jerusalem, and there must have been other times in the Gospels but he could not remember them now. Four summers ago when he was eight he had come home from the athletic field, bleeding and crying, unable to stop the tears and not caring to anyway, for the boys who had hurt him were teenagers, and the salt taste of blood dripped from his nose to his mouth. It was a Sunday, the family was home, and his father picked him up, listened to his story, blurted, and broken by breaths and sobs, then handed him to Carol and his mother, one holding his torso, the other his legs, and Brenda in front of him, touching a wet cloth to his nose, his lips, and his father and Larry ran out of the house. He twisted out of the arms holding him, away from the three faces he loved and their sweet voices that made him surrender utterly to his pain and humiliation and cry harder; he struck the floor in motion, out of the house, onto his bicycle. His father and Larry were faster than he imagined, but he reached the field in time to see them: each held a bully by the shirt and slapped his face, back and forth, with the palm, the back of the hand, the palm, and the cracks of flesh were so loud that he was frightened yet exultant, standing beside his bicycle, on the periphery of watching children. Then his father and Larry stopped slapping, pushed the boys backward, and they fell and crawled away in the dirt, crying, then stood, holding their bowed heads, and walked away. His father and Larry came toward him, out of the small boys and girls standing still and silent. With a bandanna his father wiped blood from Richie's nose and lips, and with a hand under Richie's chin turned his face upward, studied his nose, touched its bone. Then his father and Larry stood on either side of him, their hands on his shoulders, and he walked his bicycle between them, back to the house.

Watching the squirrel (he could see only the bush of its tail, and a spot of gray between green leaves) he could connect none of this with the mystery of his father's tears: not the actual shedding of them, but the fact that they had to be gone before his father faced him, and gone so absolutely that there was no trace of them, no reddened eyes, or limp mouth, as he had seen on the faces of Carol and his mother. All his instinct told him was that seeing your father cry was somehow like seeing your mother naked, and he had done that once years ago when he had to piss so badly that his legs and back were shivering, and without knocking he had flung open the bathroom door as she stepped out of the shower; as though drawn by it, his eyes had moved to her black-haired vagina, then up to her breasts, and then to her face as she exclaimed his name and grabbed a towel from a rack. He felt the same now as he had felt then: not guilt, as when he had committed an actual sin (using God's name in vain, or impure talk with his friends, yet frightening for him because he knew that soon it would be not words but the flesh that tempted him, and already his penis had urges that made him struggle); so not guilt, but a fearful sense that he had crossed an unexplained and invisible boundary, and whatever lay beyond that boundary was forbidden to him, not by God, but by the breath and blood of being alive.

When his father called him in, he ate heartily, and with relief, and saw that his father did too. And that relief was in his voice, and his father's, when they did speak: of the Red Sox, of Richie's plans for the day—softball in the morning, riding in the afternoon—and what they'd like for dinner. Their voices sounded like happiness. His father asked him if he were jumping or riding on the flat; he said jump, and his father said that'll be ten then, and peeled a bill from a folded stack he drew from his pocket, and Richie, bringing a fork of balanced egg and speared pancake to his mouth, took it with his left hand, and nodded his thanks, then mumbled it through his food. While his father smoked, he cleared the table; his father said I'll wash today, but he said he would, and his father said No, you go on and play ball. By then he had cleaned both iron skillets, the way his father had taught him, without soap, only water and a sponge, and they were drying on the heating burners. He sponged the egg yolk and syrup from the two plates, put them and the flatware in the dishwasher, told his father it wasn't full yet and he'd turn it on tonight when the dinner dishes were in it. He poured the last of the coffee into his father's cup, brought him the cream, and said he was going. He was at the door to his room when his father called: "Brush your teeth, son."

The taste of toothpaste was fading, and he could taste the bacon and syrup again as he rode onto the athletic field and realized that among the faces he scanned, he was looking only for Melissa. She was not there. For the rest of the morning, playing softball with nineteen girls and boys, he watched the trees, where he had stood with her after Mass, watched for her, in the next moment, to emerge in her cut-offs and blue denim shirt. And he watched the road that began at the field and went back to his house and then hers. He watched secretly, while waiting to bat, talking to friends behind the backstop; or standing in left field (because it was Jim Rice's position), he watched between pitches and after plays. When he looked from the outfield to the road, most of it hidden by trees along its sides, or looked at the stand of trees behind the first base line, the grass and earth he stood on seemed never touched before, in this way, by anyone; and that earth seemed part of him, or him part of it, and its cover of soft grass.

He remembered her scents and the taste of her mouth; he no longer tasted the syrup and bacon, save once in the third inning when he belched. He tried to taste her, and inhale her, and he smelled grass and his leather glove, the sweat dripping down his naked chest and sides, the summer air that was somehow redolent of freedom: a warm stillness, a green and blue smell of leaves and grass and pines and the sky itself, though he knew that was not truly part of it, but he did believe he could faintly smell something alive: squirrels that moved in the brush and climbed trunks, and the crows and blackbirds and sparrows that surrounded the softball game in trees, and left it on wings, flying across the outfield to the woods where he cross-country skied, or beyond it to the fields where now the corn was tall.

By the eighth inning, and nearing lunchtime, Melissa had not come. He imagined her pausing with vacuum cleaner, or sponge mop, or dust cloth, to wipe her brow with the back of her sun-browned forearm. He tried to imagine her mind: whether in it she saw him, or softball, or lunch and something cold to drink, and it struck him, and the sole-shaped spots of earth and grass beneath him, that he did not know what she liked to eat and drink. He thought of chili-dogs, hamburgers, grilled cheese with tomato, Coca-Cola, chocolate milk, then realized he was thinking of his own lunches, so he thought of Brenda, of tunafish salad, egg salad, and iced tea; but he could not put those into Melissa's mind. Then, picking up a bat and moving to the on-deck circle (there was no circle, and no one kneeled, waiting to hit; but to him there was a white circle around him), he saw what her mind saw. The image made him smile, yet what he felt was more loving and sorrowful than amused: she wanted a Marlboro. Her mother was in the house, working with her, and more than anything in her life now, Melissa wanted to smoke a cigarette.

IV

IT WAS FITTING, Larry thought, that he should be seeing Brenda in daylight, whose hours had so often haunted him with remorse. As he drove slowly on Main Street, the hands of the old clock outside the clothing store joined at noon, and the whistle at the box factory blew. It blew at seven in the morning, at noon, at twelve-thirty and one, and at five in the afternoon; and sometimes he wondered, with sorrow and anger whose colliding left him finally weary and embittered—a static emotion he believed he should never feel, at twenty-five—whether the timing of the whistle had once ordered every worker in town to factories, and to two shifts for lunch, and then to their homes. That was long ago, when people called the town the Queen Slipper City because the workers made women's shoes; but that market was lost now, to Italian shoes, and the few remaining factories did not need a whistle you could hear wherever you stood inside the town. If you wanted to see factory workers, you had to be parked on one of the old brick streets, outside the old brick factory, when the men and women entered in the morning, left in the afternoon. He imagined those streets in the old days: thousands of men and women carrying lunchboxes, speaking to each other in English, Italian and Greek, Armenian and French,

Polish and Lithuanian, walking toward the factories, disappearing into them at seven o'clock, as if the whistle roared at their backs.

Yet he was the son of an entrepreneur, and worked for him too. His father had worked at a shoe factory as a young boy, long enough to vow that someday he would never again work for another man. Now he made a lot of money selling a frozen tantalizer of people's craving for sweets. It was good ice cream, made by another man who owned and worked his own business in the Merrimack Valley, and Larry's father, by charming him and paying him well, was his only distributor. Ice cream. It seemed to Larry the only delightful food of childhood that adults so loved: they never spoke of, or indulged in, candy and cookies and popsicles, even malts and milkshakes, as they did ice cream. The faces of both men and women became delighted, even mischievous, as they said: Let's go get some *ice* cream. So his father sold it. He was good to his workers, he did not keep them working so few hours a week that he could pay them under the minimum wage, and the young people who worked his counters started at minimum wage, no matter how few their hours were, and his father raised their salaries as soon as he approved of their work. Since he was at the stores every day, working with them, they were soon either gone or making more money. Now his father was planning a way for all workers, above their salaries, to share in the profits, and was working on a four-day week for his daily and nightly managers, because he believed they should be with their young families, and he said there ought to be a way of allowing that and still selling fucking ice cream. This was as deeply as Larry had talked with his father about the philosophy of work in society; but Larry thought of him, a man who seldom read a book, as a good-spirited, money-making, gun-carrying anarchist. And a man now who had violated the lines and distances between them: lines they had drawn and distances created through the years, so they could sit in the same room, in the comfort of acknowledged respect and love.

He crossed the bridge on Main Street, turned right and followed the Merrimack River, glimpsed a sparkle of sun on its moving surface, this river that law and people were allowing to live again as a river ought to, so that now instead of receiving waste along its upriver banks, it was hosting salmon at its mouth. He turned left, passing an old cemetery where once he had walked, reading gravestones, but there were too many dead children and babies there, and he left, his head lowered by images of what were now nuisance illnesses or complications of birth taking the suffering breath from children, and breaking forever the hearts of mothers and fathers. His car climbed under trees and past large old houses and he reached the one where Brenda lived, in an apartment at the rear, on the first floor, and in the lawn behind her kitchen was a birdbath in the middle of a fountain that looked as old as the eighteenth-century tombstones in the cemetery. But he drove on.

Just for a while, up the hill, and around the reservoir where the purple loosestrife was growing now, purple-flowered stalks standing in the marshy ground near the bank; Canada geese were on the water, and across it were tall woods. A long steep hill was there, but you could only see it in winter when the leaves had fallen, and now it was marked by the rising green curve of trees. He turned onto Route 495, three lanes going east to the sea, cutting through wooded hills. Just for a while, so he could breathe against the quickness of breath and coolness beneath his heart that were stage fright before a performance, when he needed it; but, going to see Brenda, it felt too much like the fear and shame he believed he deserved.

He did not know how it started: somewhere in his mind, his spirit, as though on what he called now—and then too, sometimes, then too—those Faustian nights of their marriage, he swayed in feigned drunkenness to a melody he had dreamed. Rose from the couch in pantomime of a tired and drunken husband, waved and sighed goodnight to Brenda and the man they had brought home with them from one of a succession of bars in neighboring towns. In these bars there was music, usually one man or woman with a guitar, and the bar stools had arms and were leather-cushioned, the bar had a padding of leather at its front, and a long mirror behind it, and men and women alone came to drink and hope, but few of them to both hope and believe they would get what he and Brenda trapped them into receiving. Ah, teamwork: he and Brenda, and Mephistopheles. Start talking to a man alone, Brenda sitting between him and Larry, the man at first cordial, guardedly friendly, drawn to Brenda (Larry could see that, over the rim of his glass, in the mirror), but for the first drink or two the man's eyes still moved up and down the mirror, and to the door, for it was Friday night and time was running out and he was wasting it with a married couple. *Run slowly, slowly, horses of the night*. That was Marlowe's Faustus speaking to time, as Mephistopheles approached on it. Yes. The line itself was from Ovid's *Amores*. Yes.

The highway rose to his right while curving to his left and he was going up and around too fast, and he stopped breathing as he shifted down, into the curving descent, and headed north. He breathed again, and slowed for the exit to the New Hampshire beaches. Easy enough, those nights. Lovely enough, was Brenda, so at the bar she had to say very little by way of promise; her eyes spoke to the man, and when Larry went so often to the men's room, she touched the man's hand, murmured to him, and always afterward she told Larry what she said, and always it was nothing, really, or almost nothing: something gentle, something flirtatious, that any woman might say to a man; because, Larry knew, she could no more say *Come home and fuck me* than she could sing an aria. She could dance one, though. Larry also knew, and she admitted it, that she feared risking the man's startled *No way, lady*, and that, equally, or perhaps above all, she delighted in mystery, so long as she was the source of it. The men followed them home for a nightcap.

Only one refused her: a young businessman from Tennessee, on one of those trips to another state, to visit another company, to observe, to comment, to learn, to advise, and the way they spoke of it, you expected to see them wearing field uniforms of some sort, military or civilian, green and new and creased, and to have binoculars hanging from their necks, pistols from their belts. In their living room, the man from Tennessee had passionately kissed her —or returned her kiss—but said *Back home a man can get shot doing this*, and fled to his motel. But the others stayed. Larry had a drink, sitting beside Brenda on the couch; then pleading sudden drunkenness or fatigue or both, he would leave them, shutting the hall door behind him, going the few paces into the bathroom where he would shut that door too, loudly, and stand at the toilet, even at times sway there, because his performance did not stop the moment he left the living room. Whether he used it or not, he flushed the toilet so they would hear that further sound of his drunken decline of consciousness. At the lavatory he stood before the fluorescent-lighted mirror and ran the tap full force, then shut it off and brushed his hair and tossed the brush clattering to the counter that held what he called Brenda's spices: save for his shaving cream and aftershave lotion and deodorant and razor and hairbrush, the surface was nearly covered with bottles and jars, their glass or plastic or perhaps their contents aqua and gold and amber and lilac and white, creams and fluids whose labels he had never read, nor contents sniffed in their containers, because he did not want to alter their effect when he breathed them from her flesh. In the first year of their marriage he had worked hard at cooking something more than broiled chops or fish and steamed vegetables, and had learned too much, so that now he enjoyed meals both a little more and a little less, because after a few bites he could name their seasonings.

Leaving the bathroom, he looked always at the closed door to the living room; beyond it, their voices were lower than the music, so he could hear only Brenda's soft tones, and the man's deeper ones, but no words amid Weather Report or Joni Mitchell or Bonnie Raitt. He walked heavily down the hall, to the bedroom, and shut that door too with force, enough for them to hear if indeed they still listened. Then the music was faint, and he had to concentrate to hear a melody as, at the opposite side of the apartment, he undressed anyway with the sounds of a drunk: sitting in a chair he took off his boots and threw them toward the closet. He left his clothes on the chair, brought cigarettes and lighter to the bedside table, and lay on his back in the dark, naked, warming under blanket and quilt in winter, or a light blanket in fall and spring, and summer was best when he lay under nothing at all, and waited.

He imagined the living room, drew it into the bedroom with him, so he did not see dark walls and light curtains and pale ceiling, the silhouettes of chairs and chest and dressing table with its mirror, but black-haired Brenda on the couch, and the man across the coffee table from her. Some nights they would dance, and that was how she let them know, though most nights she did not have to: her face alone was enough, and they crossed the room to sit beside her on the couch Larry had left. Always she knew how much passion a man could bear before he would risk discovery by the husband. Except with the exploring businessman from Tennessee, haunted by shootings in the hills, or perhaps something else: the Old Testament, or Jesus. *He won't wake till noon*, she would say, her tongue moving on an ear, a throat.

Sometimes his hand slid under the covers, where his erection pushed them into a peak, or on warm nights his hand rose to it, standing in the dark air, and he touched it, held it, but nothing more. Though some nights he did more, and still waited unslaked for Brenda, listening to the faint music, seeing their dance slowing to an embrace, a kiss, their feet still now, only their bodies swaying to the rhythm. Or he listened for the man's feet crossing the floor, the weight of two bodies on the couch. He never heard any sound but music, then a long silence when the cassette ended. He wanted Brenda to put a tape recorder in her purse, leave the purse in the kitchen when they brought someone home, and he would turn on the recorder before he left them and went to the bedroom, and she would bring the purse to the floor by the couch. But she was afraid of the clicking sound when it stopped. He wanted to go out the bedroom window, and around the apartment to the living room; Brenda wanted that too, but they were both afraid a neighbor would see him looking in the window, and call the police. And he was afraid to creep down the hall, and listen at the living room door; each time he wanted to, but was overwhelmed by imagining the man suddenly leaving Brenda to piss, opening the door to find him crouched and erect in the hall.

So he heard and saw her in his mind where, in the third and final year of their marriage, he so often and so passionately saw her with a lover that one night, set free by liquor and Brenda's flesh in his arms, he frightened himself by telling her. She increased both his fear and elation when, without questions or reflection, she said she would do it, and her legs encircled his waist. They were in a dance company then, were performing a dance together, and within the week they were going after rehearsals to bars where no one knew them. On the third night they brought home a young bachelor, a manager of a branch bank, and Larry stayed with them nearly too long, so when he left for the bedroom he pretended drunkenness that was real, and when he lay on the bed the room moved, so he stood and sat and stood, until he heard her light feet in the hall, and he lay on the bed and watched her enter the room and cross it in the dark, and it was worth the fear.

His fear was not of anything concrete; certainly it was not rooted in jealousy, for he shared and possessed those dark recesses of Brenda's spirit, so her apparent infidelity was in truth a deeper fidelity. Also, the fear burned to white ash in what he felt as he waited on those nights. The minutes passed slowly, their seconds piercing him with a thrill like that of a trapezist who, swinging back and forth, lives in those moments of his hands on the bar, his body gaining speed and arc, while also living the two and a half somersaults he will perform, and the moment his hands will meet and grip the empty trapeze swinging toward him, and, if an inch or instant off, his fall to earth. Then she was in the hall, then at the bedroom door, and it swung in and she was framed in it, a cigarette glowing at her side, then she crossed the room. Lying on the bed, he opened his arms. She lay on top of him, her tongue darting and fluttering in his mouth as he unzipped and unbuttoned her clothing, then pushed her up until she was sitting; he lifted his legs around her and off the bed, and stood. He took the cigarette from her and, before putting it out, held it to her lips, then his own, tasting lipstick. He lifted her to her feet and took off her clothes and let them fall to the floor as she began telling him, in the voice she either saved for or only had on these nights, in her throat, but soft, a breathy contralto, and he kneeled and pulled her pants down her smooth hard legs: *kissed me for a long time, and touching my breasts, and I started rubbing his thigh and he put his hand inside my pants—*

Sometimes he believed that first he remarked that part of her, saw in her brown eyes and open lips bridled yet promiscuous lust, and then his visions of her and a lover began. Then he also wondered if he were truly the one who changed the velocity and trajectory of their marriage, sending or leading them to that terrible\ midnight. *Run slowly, slowly, horses of the night.* And he recalled a teacher in college, talking about the mystery of life in general, of plants in the specific, saying that perhaps it was not man's idea to drink and smoke, that rather we were lured by the desire of the tobacco leaf and grape: *smoke me*, they whispered; *drink me.*

Yet it was she who said finally: *There's something dark in us, something evil, and it has to be removed*, and he told her *We can just stop then; we won't even talk about it again, not ever, it'll be something we did one year.* He kept insisting in the face of her gaze that lasted, it seemed, for days and nights: those unblinking eyes, sorrowful yet firm, looking at him as though they saw not his face but his demons; saw them with pity for both him and herself; and seeing his demons reflected in her eyes, he shrank from them, and from her, and from himself. Then he blamed himself for all of it, and pleaded for forgiveness, and the chance to live with her in peace as man and wife, and her eyes and her closed lips told him he understood too little about how far they had gone. Then she told him: *You take too much credit. Or blame. I liked it. I like it. I could do it right now, with you standing there watching.* Her eyes left his and he watched them move about the living room and settle on the couch before they looked at him again. *This isn't our home anymore*, she said. *It isn't anybody's. Or it's too many people's.* Then he grieved and so could not think, not for weeks, then months, as he lived alone and worked for his father and at night rehearsed dances or plays and then went home and wondered, with fear and pain and nothing else, what she was doing that moment, and with whom.

They had lived apart for over a year and were amicably divorced (he did not even have to go to court) and still all he knew, or thought, was that somehow it had to do with his youth: that had he been older (*as my father is*, he thought, driving now past a salt marsh, nearing the sea; *as my father is*) he would not have been so awed and enslaved by her passion, and his too; but without hers his own was ordinary, as it had been before her, as it was since he lost her. So her passion. Older, he believed, he would not have explored it; he would have left it in her depths, like a buried, undetonated bomb. That was all he knew now, and perhaps that had been the source of his fear on those nights, as he lay waiting.

Ahead of him was a bridge over a tidal stream, beyond it was the junction with the road that paralleled the sea; then he saw a farm stand on his side of the bridge, and he slowed and signaled and turned onto the dirt and gravel in front of the stand, a simple place: a rectangular roof resting on four posts and only one wall, at the rear, and in its shade were the boxes of fruit and vegetables, and an old woman behind a counter whose surface was just wide enough to hold a scale and cash register. She spoke to him as he chose tomatoes; she told him they were good, and the corn was picked fresh this morning. He praised the tomatoes and they talked about the long dry spell, and how so much of last summer was cool and rainy, and last fall was more like summer than summer was. He took three large tomatoes that Brenda could eat today and tomorrow, then nine more with graduated near-ripeness that she could place in the kitchen window, to ripen in the sun, and he imagined each of them red on a new day. In his heart he sang: *My true love brought to me three red tomatoes, nine tomatoes ripening*, then he re-membered as a boy hunting grouse, which some natives here called partridges, with his father; and seeing him and his father walking armed into woods made him pause, holding the last tomato above the crisp paper bag. Then he started talking to the woman again, asked how her stand was doing, and she said Pretty well, and weighed the tomatoes and punched the register and said You know how it is, and he said he did, and paid her, and left.

So he did not go to the sea, but back to 495, and to Brenda's, sadly now, the stage fright gone at some time he did not remember. She came to the door barefoot and wearing white shorts and a red tee shirt, and he could not speak. He wanted to hold her very tightly, in silence, then move her backward, with the grace of a dance, to the couch, pull her shirt up past her shoulders and hair and above her head and raised arms, and fumble at her shorts. The couch was a new one; that is, it was a year old. They had sold all the furniture in their apartment, and left it like a box that had contained their marriage.

"I brought you some tomatoes," he said, and handed her the bag; she took it at its top, and the weight lowered her hand.

"Come in the kitchen," she said, and her voice was all right, not impenetrable like her eyes, like her lips had been. They had shown neither surprise nor guilt, nor pity, nor dislike—none of the emo-tions he had imagined as he drove to the house, walked around it to her door at the back. She had finished lunch, and he recognized its traces: jellied madrilène had been in a bowl, cottage cheese and lettuce on a plate, and a small wooden bowl held dressing from her salad. A tall glass was half-filled with tea and melting ice. She offered him some, and he said Yes, that would be good, and at the counter, with her back to him, she squeezed a wedge of lime over a glass, dropped in the wedge, went to the freezer for ice, then set the glass in front of him and poured the tea. She turned her back to him, and exclaimed over the tomatoes as she took them out of the bag, and put the nine in the window and the three in the refrigerator. He said to her body bent at the vegetable bin: "Are you dancing?"

"Only alone."

She straightened, shut the door, then sat opposite him and lit a cigarette from her pack on the table.

"Here?" he said.

"Yes. I'll get back with a company soon. When things are settled."

"Right."

"Are you?"

"We have a performance next week."

"What are you doing?"

"One I choreographed. To Ravel's Piano Concerto in G Major."

"That's ambitious. The whole thing?"

"Second movement. *Adagio Assai.* It's nine and a half minutes."

"It's beautiful. I'd like to see it."

"Would you?"

"Yes."

"Will you?"

"Yes."

He reached to his shirt pocket for a cigarette, but stopped and his hand went to her Benson and Hedges, and holding the gold pack, and shaking out a cigarette, he felt for a moment married to her again, in this apartment, all the darkness left behind them in the other place, as if their only trouble had been renting an apartment that was cursed, evil, that had to be fled or exorcised. Then the illusion ended, and he felt his eyes brimming, and he could not remember what he had come to say. Last night he had wanted to come to her in rage, but he was in too much pain then to drive here, to knock and enter, let alone yell at her what was in his mind. She looked up from tapping ash into the ashtray (it was new too; or a year old) and saw the tears in his eyes, then her hand covered his and she sat rubbing the back of his palm. He could say nothing at all. With the back of his other hand he wiped his eyes. Then he knew why he had come: in love, and simply to look at her, to sit like this, for a few minutes resurrected from their time together before they destroyed their capacity or perhaps their right to share it till one of them died. She was silent. But those dark brown eyes were not: they were wet, and then tears distinct as silver beads went down her dark cheeks. Her full lips, too, were those of a woman whose heart was keening, and he was certain he would never again see her face like this, for him, and he committed it to memory.

"Please don't ever tell him," he said.

She shook her head.

"I know no one can ask that," he said. "Of a lover. A wife."

"You can."

He stood and skirted the small table, and was on his knees, with both arms turning her chair, her body, to face him, and his face was in her lap, her hands moving in his hair; her lap was cotton shorts and the tight flesh of her large strong thighs, and pressing his face to it, he said: "Please, Brenda. Please."

"Never," she said, and as he started to rise, he held her against his chest, and her arms went around him, released him as he stood and looked down at her upturned face. He bent to it, not touching her, and kissed her lips. Then he went out of the kitchen and through the living room and out the door, holding still her unlit cigarette, glimpsed through a blur the birdbath and fountain, turned the corner of the house into the direct light of the sun, and walked fast to his car.

V

IN LATE AFTERNOON Brenda lay on the couch in the living room, barefoot and wearing a leotard, drinking iced tea while her sweat dried and her body cooled. Across the room were two windows facing the back lawn, and at their sides pale blue curtains moved back and forth with the breeze, as though someone stood behind each of them and gently, rhythmically, pushed. She was looking at the curtains and the windows and nothing in particular beyond when she saw Greg: he walked into her vision from the right of the window, where the driveway was. He walked slowly on the grass, profile to her, his hands in the pockets of his khakis, his hard stomach pushing agaisnt his blue shirt and protruding over his belt. Her only movement on the couch was to reach for a cigarette on the coffee table and light it, as she looked at his dark muscular arm—the left one—beneath the short sleeve of his shirt, and at the side of his clean-shaven dark face, slightly bowed, as if with thought or fatigue. She did not know why his arms were so well-muscled; nor why, at forty-seven, his biceps had not begun to flatten, his triceps to sag. He did not know either. She had asked him, had jokingly accused him of clandestine push-ups or isometrics or some other exercise that no one did anymore. Or no one she knew. Nearly all her friends, women and men, had rituals of aerobic exercise, and many now had joined clubs where they used a Nautilus machine. She meant to join one tomorrow. But Greg told her he did nothing at all, had not done a push-up since the Army, and would never do one again on purpose, unless it was to raise himself from a barroom floor out of his own vomit. His vanity about not being vain was endearing. Also, she knew that, at times, the refusal of his arms and legs to age normally gave her confidence in the longevity of his body.

Now, at the fountain and birdbath, he turned from her, and stood looking down at the water that trickled over the sides of the bath, into the stone fountain, watching it as if he saw ideas in its motion. About what, though? Larry and Richie and Carol? His walk along the Amazon? Sometimes when he was tired and a little drunk and bitter, and certain he would never see, much less walk in, that jungle on that river, he said: *Surely by now some sons of bitches have laid a highway*; while Brenda imagined the riverbanks so thick with trees and brush and vines that, after hacking with machetes for the first mile, they would give it up, then travel the river by boat. Still, she would go with him. She would go with him because he wanted to, she would go with him there before Venice and Athens and the Greek islands and Spain, the places where she wanted to walk with him on city and village streets and eat long and leisurely dinners and sleep till lunchtime and make love in the afternoons that only hotels, and especially hotels in a foreign country, could give you. She had done that in Mexico City on her December honeymoon with Larry, and in the afternoons there she never felt that she was distorting daylight by performing a nocturnal act in defiance of schedules and telephones, commitments and errands and chores. In Mexico City, she and Larry knew no one, and did not speak the language anyway. It was odd, she thought, perhaps even sinister, that the world had contrived to give lovers only the night; and the world wanted those nights to be earned, too, by what used to be the sweat of the brow, but was now too often foolish work in rooms with temperatures so regulated that they did not seem to exist on the earth, with her seasons. Then, on the purchased bed, surrounded by the dwelling and the acquisitions that filled it, you could have the night. Yet afternoon was the time she felt most erotic, and before dancing today, she had masturbated on this couch. She would go with Greg first to insects and discomfort because she loved the boy she had found in his older man's body, beneath his man's style. She called it Peter Pan, to herself, and she called him that when he was tired, and a little drunk, and bitter; and on nights when, making love, she sensed it in his body: a tender and humble and grateful presence that seemed to swoon in her arms.

She saw the boy when he took her to his bars. He had two favorites, near his stores, where he drank with men he called his friends, but they could not be, not really. In her life, a friend was a woman you spoke to on the telephone four or five times a week, and bought gifts for, something inexpensive that reminded you of her when you saw it in a shop, and you visited each other and drank coffee or tea or, if at night, a little wine; and you tried to make time at least twice a month for dinner together in a restaurant, or lunch and shopping in Boston, though it was usually once and sometimes not even that because you both had men in your lives, and some of the women had children too. And with your friend you talked, you did not banter; and you knew as much and probably more about her than her husband or lover did, and she knew as much about you. Though no woman knew, or ever would know, about that year with Larry when she learned how heedlessly she could draw someone's life into her own, into the lustful pleasure and wicked dreams of her marriage, when she had learned that the state of being married, which had opened that life to her, was the very state that kept her from being a slut. So she had to take herself, and her slut with her, and go away from the marriage, and Larry; and she had to hold down that part of her being she had, she supposed now, always known was there, but in the nether reaches of her soul, where it was supposed to be, far from the light of sun and moon, to live only in the solitude of masturbation. She had to push it down again, into an oubliette, and keep it covered with the weight of a new life, and then with the solidity of a man who, by chance, or the circumstance of their being in-laws, turned out to be Greg.

So that, by trying to save herself, she had become again a woman she could not have, even two years ago, predicted herself to be. Now she had broken promises so implicit that you never spoke them: *I will not make love with your father, take him from you and you from him, and your home, and Richie, and*—So she was still a scandal to her self, the self who believed in honor, in trying one's best to be a decent human being whose life did not spread harm. Sometimes, for no immediate reason save that her mood suddenly changed, she saw her vagina and its hair as a treacherous web, and with luxurious despair she imagined the faces of women, wives and lovers of men whom she had drawn to her from their places at the bar until they sat across the coffee table from her and Larry on the couch, and when Larry left she drew them across the room and into her body, where she spent them and then expelled them forever from her life. Because she and Larry never brought the same one home twice, even if they saw him again in a bar, even if he came to sit with them, for they were afraid that no man could believe his second night with Brenda was anything but collusion between wife and husband, and so perversion. And once she walked them to the door, she took their lovemaking into her bed, and lived it again with Larry, and as his passion crested hers did too, again, and she embraced both him and the lover, and they grew up and around her, like wisteria.

She did not believe any of these men ever felt used; but she knew they ought to, and most of them would not have gone home with her and Larry, would not have accepted the gambit nightcap, had they known the truth beyond her body, her face. So in those moods she punished herself, whether or not the men knew she deserved it; she punished herself by sustaining and deepening the mood with memories of her lies to the men (how many times had she pretended to be seduced? and how many times had she murmured: *I've never done this before?*) and with imagining the faces of the women who loved them, carvings of betrayal that hung like masks before her eyes.

No: she would never tell that shame to one of her friends but she told everything else and she knew they did too, and that was the friendship. It was as deep as her own feelings about herself, and she could not feel in harmony with the world unless she had that friendship with at least one woman. She was, she thought, more fortunate than most: she had three women she loved. While the men Greg called friends were carpenters and electricians and cops and men who made telephone parts at Western Electric, and Greg only knew them because he liked drinking in the same places they did, stand-up bars where nearly everyone drank beer, and there was no blender and a bartender could work months without using a cocktail shaker, and only kept lemons and limes in the fruit bin, and not many of them, or they would soften and turn brown.

Bartenders called them shot-and-a-beer bars. Brenda liked the ones Greg brought her to; she liked standing at the bar, and watching the men; and she liked the ceiling fans, and not having a jukebox or electronic games, and having the television on only for ballgames or hockey or boxing. She liked the men Greg called his friends too; they were in their forties and fifties and sixties, were near-courtly toward her, lit her cigarettes and were not profane unless Greg was, and then only moderately, never the words she had been hearing from her friends, and saying with them, since her teens. She did not feel superior to them because they worked with their hands. Her father had been a house-painting contractor, but he and one man had done all the work, and they also laid hot top on driveways.

What she did feel was baffled: when she walked into a bar with Greg, and he saw his friends, he called their names, he waved, their faces brightened and they beckoned him and Brenda to the bar, made room for them, bought them drinks, and Greg and the men touched each other. Always. Handshakes and pats on the back and squeezes of biceps, squeezes and rockings of shoulders. Then their strange talk began, or seemed in some mysterious way to continue from the patting and squeezing, and she listened to them, intently because she was baffled, but amused too, because she could listen for two hours or more, and still learn almost nothing about their lives. They talked about their lives, but not the way she and her friends did. She could not tell whether they were married badly or well; and, with some of them, whether they were married at all. She could not tell how they felt about their work, nor most of the time what it even was. She learned these from Greg, in the car going home to her apartment. But they talked about their lives: they told stories about themselves, about mutual friends, or a man they worked with, and when she first went to the bars with Greg she told him she knew now why he called talking to his drinking friends shooting the shit. His drinking friends: he called them that. There were others she had never met, and they were his hunting friends or his fishing friends and some of them were both; but it seemed that, when she was able to keep track of the names in his hunting and fishing stories, there was one man he went with for trout fishing, and two or three for deer hunting, but one of those went deep-sea fishing too, and another may have been his trout fishing friend.

When she became a regular with Greg at the bars, she began to see what was beneath the men's stories, and their teasing each other about their mortality defined by their enlarged stomachs, and their hair graying or vanishing or both; and their other talk that was rarely serious, yet somehow was not dull either. They were trying to be entertaining, and hoping to be entertained. It was the reason they gathered to drink. And she began to think about Richie, as she stood at the bar, and during the days too, when she mused about this difference between men and women she had not remarked so clearly in Larry; for, like her, Larry had three close friends, and they talked seriously about acting and dancing, and death and love, and books they had read and movies they had seen. But in Richie and his friends she saw no difference at all, except alcohol and tobacco, from Greg and his friends. The essence of the friendships was sharing a game or sport or beer-drinking, and she could no more imagine Greg talking soberly and deeply with one of his friends than she could imagine Richie sitting in a living room and talking quietly with one of his about what he wanted and loved and feared.

My God, there was something about boys that domestic life and even civilization itself could not touch, and often they were infuriating and foolish, and yet when they lost that element, as boys or men, they became dull. So as a woman you were left having to choose between a grown boy and a flat American male, and either was liable to drive you mad, but at least with the boy your madness was more homicidal than suicidal, as it was with the other. No wonder the men at the bar, and on the hunting and fishing trips, called themselves *the boys*. They said: *I'm going to have a beer with the boys; I'm going fishing with the boys*, and in their eyes there was a different light, of distance, of reverie, and of fondness, as if they were unfolding a flag they had served when they were young.

And Greg still fought. His friends did not; and after the one fight she saw, they had patted him, squeezed him, and laughed and told him he'd better leave that stuff to the kids, or get himself a younger heart. He had won. He told Brenda once that his ex-wife Joan had said to him, many times: *The trouble with you is nobody's ever beaten you*. Brenda said: Is that true? and he told her he thought it probably was, because he could remember getting the shit kicked out of him, but never losing. She was surprised by the fight she saw, in the bar near the beach store, because she was neither frightened nor scornful nor compassionate. She watched with excitement yet from an odd distance, as though watching two strangers have an equally-matched marital quarrel. The reason for the fight was as shallow as the other exchanges in that bar, and later she knew the true reason was simply a need they had not outgrown. The other man, in his late twenties or early thirties, said to the bartender that she—and he looked down the bar at Brenda—was too young and pretty to have all them old turkeys around her. He said it loudly, and he meant to say it loudly, and Greg was gone from her, was up the bar and turning the man to face him, then they were like two male dogs. They did all but sniff asses and scratch the earth: they growled and snapped and pushed, and she watched, and Greg's friends watched, and everyone else watched, save the bartender who talked too, tried from across the bar to at least try to stop what he knew he could not. Then Greg swung and the other did and they punched and grappled and fell holding each other to the floor, and by then she knew, without knowing how she knew, that also like dogs they would not hurt each other. That was when she understood why they were fighting. They rose from the floor punching, then the young man went backward and down, got up quickly, and men grabbed him from behind, Greg's friends held him, and the two yelled at each other till the bartender, still at his post, yelled louder and told them both to shut the fuck up. Then he told the young man to leave and come back another night when he didn't want trouble. The bartender was not young either. That's probably why he told him to leave, Greg said later, and because anyway the guy had started it and he wasn't a regular. The young man took his change from the bar and left without looking at anyone, and Brenda watched his face as he walked, the blood over one eye and at his mouth. Greg was not bleeding, and he was laughing and buying a round for her and his friends, then he said make it a round for the house, and he overtipped the bartender, as he always did. Once she had told him he tipped too much, from sixty to a hundred percent, and he had said he had the money and the bartenders needed it and worked for it, and if he wanted to save money he'd buy a six-pack or two and drink them at home.

She watched his back; he still looked down at the water in the fountain, and it occured to her that she had never watched him when he was oblivious of her. She had watched him when he pretended not to know she was, while he worked in his stores. But always she knew he felt her eyes on him. Perhaps he did now too. Though she did not think so, for he was a tired-looking man of forty-seven (forty-eight soon, in November) whose back and shoulders and lowered head showed weariness as a face does. Had he known she was watching, he would be standing tall now, and he would have crossed the lawn minutes earlier with quickened movements, for he was proud that she loved him. He had sculpted a style for himself, until he became that style, or most of him did, so he could take money from the world and hold onto enough of it to allow him to walk its streets with at least freedom from want and debt and servitude. On some nights, in her bed, when he had drunk enough, that style fell away like so much dust and he spoke softly to her, his eyes hiding from hers, and told her how happy he was that she loved him, how he woke each morning happy and incredulous that this lovely young woman loved him; told her that when he first saw it lighting her eyes, when he and Richie and she were eating dinners after the marriage, all of his thinking told him what he saw in her eyes could not be there, not for him; and his heart nearly broke in its insistence that he did see what he saw, and that he loved her too. And he said he would not blame her if she woke up one morning knowing it was all a mistake, that he was just someone she had needed for a while, and left him. *Never*, she said to him. *Never*.

Nor did she know why. He was good to her, and he made her laugh. He liked to watch her dance. He had watched Larry, as a father will watch a son perform anything from elocution to baseball to spinning a top. But that was not why he liked to watch her. Nor was it the reason he understood what she was trying to do with her body, and the music, on a stage or here in her living room. His senses told him that. And he knew why she danced, and why she had to keep dancing, while other people—her parents in Buffalo, and her two older sisters whose marriages had taken one to Houston, and the other to Albuquerque, and some of her friends too, though not the close ones—did not understand why she worked so hard at something and was content to remain an amateur. But Greg did. He was neither surprised nor amused when she told him she taught dance to make a living, but she could not remember ever wanting to be a professional dancer, though she had to dance every day, whether she was working with a company or not. She had seen recognition in his eyes. He listened, and nodded his head, and stroked his cheek, then said: *Some people have things like that, and they don't have to make money at it. It's something they have to do, or they're not themselves anymore. If you take it away from them, they'll still walk around, and you can touch them and talk to them. They'll even answer. But they're not there anymore.* She said: *Are you talking about yourself?* His eyes shifted abruptly, toward hers, as if returning from a memory. *Me? No. I was thinking what Richie would be like, if they shut down the stables, and Catholic churches, and banned cross-country skiing.* He had been sitting on this couch, and she had been standing in front of him. Then she sat beside him. *What's yours?* she said. *I don't have one*, he said. *My father did. He was a carpenter.* She said: *I thought he worked for the railroad.* He smiled and touched her cheek. *He did*, he said. *He was a carpenter at home. At night, and on the weekends. God, you should have seen that house grow.*

Now he turned from the fountain, and with her heart she urged him to straighten and stride with energy, but he did not, and he seemed to fade past the window and out of her view. She stood and went to the refrigerator and got two bottles of beer, opened them, went back through the living room, and reached the door before he did. He smiled at her through the screen, and came in, and she kissed him over the bottles, felt his hold on the beer in her left hand, and released it to him; kissing him and feeling the cold bottle leave her fingers, she was struck by a sadness that was sudden yet so familiar now that she did not even have to call it death anymore. She looked up at him.

"I've been watching you," she said.

"And?"

She smiled.

"I was trying to figure out why I love you."

"And?"

"I just do. Come hold me, and tell me about your terrible day."

"How do you know it was terrible?"

"I've been watching you. Come on."

She put her arm about his waist and they went to the couch and sat, and she rested her head on his shoulder.

"Richie this morning," he said, above her head.

"How was he?"

"He's tough."

"That's good."

"I wish to fuck he didn't have to be."

She nodded and nestled against him.

"He'll be all right," he said.

"Larry was here."

"Was it bad?"

"He wasn't. It was."

"Jesus. Tonight I see Carol. After dinner."

She looked at the moving curtains and the birdbath and fountain. Then she said: "I'm lucky. Wickedly lucky."

"How's that?"

"I'm going to enjoy telling my family."

"On the phone."

"No. I'll write letters."

"You'll enjoy that?"

"They never have known me. They might as well keep on, or start trying."

"Do you love them?"

"Sure I do. But I love them better by mail. I need a shower."

"I need another beer. At least."

He went to the kitchen; in the bedroom she pulled the leotard down over her breasts and hips, and stepped out of it as he came in. He arranged two of her four pillows, then lay on the bed, his shoulders propped up so he could drink.

"I've seen worse," he said.

"You've probably fucked worse."

"I have," he said, as she walked away from him, the sadness gone as she felt, because he watched her, the grace of her flesh, and its colors from the sun and her bikini. He had showered here last night, so she lowered the nozzle to keep her hair dry, and waited outside the tub till the water was hot. She stepped in and turned her breasts to the spray and closed her eyes, as she always did, not to keep water from them, but because she shut them to nearly all sensuous pleasures: lying in the sun and dancing alone in her living room and masturbating and making love. Only smoking and drinking and eating were better with your eyes open, and sometimes when she first inhaled or sipped or chewed, she closed her eyes then too. She turned her back to the water and soaped herself, and turned again and rinsed, and stayed, contained by the shower curtain and the hot water, until it began to cool. Then she turned the handle and lifted her arms as cold water struck her breasts and stomach, and she circled in it, her arms above her head, till the cold drew from her an exhaled sound, soft yet shrill, like a bird's. She turned off the water and stepped out, rubbed her cool skin with a thick dark blue towel, then wrapped it around her body, from the tops of her breasts to her thighs, and went to the bedroom.

He had brought her a beer, set on the table at her side of the bed, and the other two pillows were waiting. She lay beside him, leaned against the pillows, and drank. He lit one of her cigarettes and gave it to her, then slid his leg toward hers so they touched. She said: "Maybe next summer I'll be pregnant."

"It's better in winter, when it's not so hot."

"Then maybe next summer I'll have a baby."

"Why not."

"Damned if I know," she said. "So why not."

The ashtray rested on his chest, and moved with his breathing. They lay quietly, as she felt the evening cool coming now to the lawn, and through the window behind the bed. She listened to the silence of the room, and their smoking and swallowing and quiet breath, and she felt held by tranquility and shared solitude, as the hands of her parents had held her on the surface of water when she was a child. She wanted to tell him that, but she did not want to speak. Then she knew that he sensed it anyway, and she lay, her bare leg touching his trousered one, her eyes closed, in the cool silence until he said he had to go now, he had to cook dinner for Richie.

VI

BETWEEN RICHIE'S SQUEEZING thighs and knees, the sorrel mare Jenny turned with the track, and he saw the red barn, then she was cantering straight toward the jump, and over her head he saw Mr. Ripley's white house and a flash of green trees and blue sky beyond its dark gray roof. He fixed his eyes at a point on Mr. Ripley's back wall, directly in line with the middle of the upright posts. He held the reins with both hands, his leather riding crop clutched with his right, angling down and backward over his thigh, and with the kinetic exhilaration that years ago he had mistaken for fear, he glimpsed at the bottom of his vision Jenny's ears and the horizontal rail. Then he was off the earth, flying with her between the uprights, his eyes still on that white point on the wall, his body above the saddle as though he sat on the air they jumped through. When her front feet hit he rocked forward and to the left but only for an instant, then he was in position again, his knees and thighs holding, and he leaned forward and patted her neck as she entered the curve of the oval track, and spoke to her: Good girl, Jenny. Good girl. Then she was around the curve and approaching the other jump; beyond it were the meadow and woods, and he found the top of the pine rising above clumped crowns of deciduous trees, and held his eyes on its cone of green. He listened to Jenny's hooves as their striking vibrated through him like drumbeats, listened to her breathing as he felt it against his legs, and listened to his own quick breath too, and the soft motion of air past his ears: a breeze that was not a breeze, for he and Jenny were its sources, speeding through air so still that no dust stirred from the track before them. Then he was in it, in the air, the pine blurring in the distance, and down now, a smooth forward plunge that pulled his body with it, but this time he held, and when Jenny hit, his body did not jerk forward but flowed with hers, in horizontal cantering speed down the track, as he patted her neck, and spoke his praise. He did not take her into the leftward curve. He was still looking at the pine, and with his left knee he guided her straight on the track, then off it, past the curve and toward the woods. Because Mr. Ripley had said it was awfully hot for both him and Jenny, and if he wanted to, he could jump her for fifteen minutes and then take her on the trail to cool down, and pay only eight dollars instead of the ten for an hour's jumping.

He veered right, away from the pine, and angled her across the meadow, then slowed her to a trot and posted, his body moving up and down in the rhythm of her strides. He looked at the sky above the woods, then around him at the weeds and short grazed-over grass of the meadow. For a quarter of an hour he had smelled Jenny and leather, and now that they were moving slowly, he could smell the grass too. The two-thirty sun (though one-thirty, really: daylight savings time) warmed his velvet-covered helmet, and shone directly on his shoulders and back, like the hot breath or stare of God. For he felt always in God's eye, even when he heard sirens, and knew from their sounds whether it was a fire truck or ambulance or police car, and he imagined houses burning, and bleeding people in crumpled and broken cars, and he knew God saw and loved those who suffered, yet still saw and loved him, and heard his silent prayer for the people at the end of the sirens' long and fading sound. Sister Catherine had taught them that, in the fourth grade: whenever they heard a siren, she told them to bow in prayer at their desks, to pray for those who were suffering now. He reached the entrance to the trail cut into the woods, and Jenny went on her own between the trees, turned left, and slowed to a walk, into the deep cool shade. He settled into the saddle, and shifted his weight to his hips.

He knew that God watched him now, had watched him all day, and last night as he listened on the stairs, then in his room; had watched him on this day from the beginning of time, in the eternal moment that was God's. As soon as He made Adam or started the evolution that would end with people who stood and talked—*and loved*, he thought, *loved*—He had known this day, and also had known what Richie did not: what he would do about it, how he would live with it. Richie himself did not know how he would live with it. Everyone had to bear a cross as Christ did, and he lived to prepare himself for his, but he saw now that he had believed he had already borne the one for his childhood. Nobody had ever said you got one as a child and one or even two when you grew up, but there it was: he had felt spared for a few more years. Two years ago his mother moved out and then they were divorced and he carried that one, got himself nailed to it, hung there in pain and the final despair and then released himself, commended his will and spirit to God, and something in him died—he did not know what —but afterward, like Christ on Easter, he rose again, could love his days again, and the people in them, and he forgave his parents, and himself too for having despaired of them, for believing they could never love anyone and so were unworthy of love, of his love too, and unworthy even of the earth, and its life. Had forgiven himself through confession to Father Oberti one winter morning before the weekday Mass, while snow fell outside, so he had to walk to the church, and snow melted on his boots in the confessional, and he whispered to Father Oberti what he had felt about his mother and

father, and how he had also committed the sin of despair, had
believed that God had turned from him, that he could never again
be happy on this earth, and had wished for his own death, and his
parents' grief; had imagined many times his funeral, and his parents,
standing at opposite sides of the grave, crying. Father Oberti had
said it was a very good confession, and a very mature one for a
young boy. Behind the veil between them, Father Oberti looked
straight ahead, his cheek resting on his hand, and did not know
who Richie was, but Richie had said, at the beginning, *Bless me,
Father, for I have sinned; I'm ten years old.*

Now he had a second cross, its weight pressing down on his
shoulder here on the trail beneath the trees, pressing on his heart,
really, so he thought: *That's it: being sad is the cross.* And he knew
that somehow he must not be sad, even though he was, and he
thought of Larry standing at the fence around the indoor ring in
winter, Sunday after Sunday, and the outdoor ring in warm seasons,
all those Sundays Larry driving him to Ripley Farm and waiting.
Yet he did not have to wait. Most of the children who rode with
Richie were driven to the stables and then picked up, but always
Larry waited, and he did that until Richie was old enough to ride
his bicycle to his lesson, and still in winter or rain Larry drove him.
He had been grateful but had never said so, and he had been grateful
to Larry for teaching him to cross-country ski, and he saw Larry
now skiing beside him, stopping to help him up when he fell on
his back in the snow, his ankles turned with the skis he partly lay
on, and he had never told Larry that either: how Larry had given
him the two sports he most loved. He played softball and touch
football, basketball and hockey with his friends in the neighborhood,
and he played well enough to like these games, but he did not like
the games enough to enjoy them unless he was playing with friends.
This was what he loved: big strong Jenny under him, and the woods
around and above him; and cross-country skiing over the athletic
field and into the woods on the trail marked with orange circles
painted on trees. A small college was near his house, and the college
owned the athletic field and woods, and the trails were marked for
the students; so he saw them sometimes, skied around them or
waited while they skied around him, but they did not disturb him
any more than chipmunks running across the trail did here, or the
male cardinal he saw leaving its perch, or the blue jay, or the two

doves. In riding and skiing he had found an answer to one of his deepest needs, without even knowing he had the need, and so without even seeking an answer. He had learned to make his spiritual solitude physical and, through his flesh, to do this in communion with the snow and evergreens, and the naked trees that showed him the bright sky of winter; and with the body of a horse, and the earth its hooves pounded, the air it breasted, and this woods and his glimpses through leaves of the hot blue sky.

So he wondered what he had ever given Larry, and what he could give him now, what he could do without hurting Brenda, or his father. He patted Jenny's neck, looked between her ears at the winding trail, and looked about him at the woods, with its air that was close and still, yet cool, and he saw the world as a tangle of men and women and boys and girls, thick and wildly growing as this woods; some embraced and some struggled, while all of them reached upward for air and rain and sun. He must somehow move through it, untouched by it, but in it too, toward God. He knew he could do that on a horse, and on cross-country skis, and at Mass when the Consecration sharpened his focus so that he was only aware of himself as a breathing heart, and two knees on the padded kneeler, and two arms resting on the wooden back of the pew in front of him; and then when he took the Body and Blood of Christ from the priest, and placed it on his tongue, and softly chewed as he walked back to his pew. At all those times, he was so free of the world and his life in it that he could have been in another country, in another century; or not even on the earth, and not mortal.

So it was people. They were the cross, and the sadness they brought you, and he could not spend the next five years, till he entered the seminary, on a horse or on skis or at Mass. From Christ he had to receive the strength or goodness or charity or whatever it was to give his father and Brenda more than forgiveness and acceptance. He had to love their days in the house with him, and they had to know he did. And he had to be with Larry outside of the house, as he saw his mother now. Saint Paul had written that all the works were nothing without love. He had to love them all, and he could do that only with Christ, and to receive Christ he could not love Melissa. He knew that from her scents this morning, and her voice, and her kiss.

VII

WHEN CAROL WAS a girl, and her father had spoken to her like this, his face and voice so serious, his speech slow and distinct, as though he studied each word before speaking, she had thought he was stern, and she was frightened. But now she was smiling. She knew she ought not to be, and when she was conscious that again her lips were spread, she drew them in, and tried to return his gaze whose parts were greater than mere seriousness: he was contrite, supplicatory, and he looked trapped too, as if he were lying to her. At twenty-six, she loved him from the distance of a grown daughter, and so more easily, warmly, perhaps more deeply. Yet she felt nostalgia too, a tangible sigh of it in her heart, for the love she had for him when she was a girl: when she believed he was the best father anyone could have, and the most handsome, and that he could do anything on earth she would ever need him to; and she believed that, more than Larry, more even than her mother, she possessed him. When she had outgrown those feelings she had outgrown her fear of him too, and if she had had a choice, she would have chosen the way she loved him now.

She had cleaned her apartment for his visit, and put on a dress, but that was pride, not fear. She had even picked up two blouses and a pair of jeans that had fallen to the closet floor some time ago, and placed them on hangers, and she had slid the closet door shut, which she would have done anyway, but she knew she was doing it to hide two of René's shirts hanging among her clothes, the shirts touching a blouse on one side and a dress on the other, a charade of their owners. All of this was so foolish and, besides, even if he did peer into her closet like some prying detective of a father, which he was not, René's shirts were small enough to be a woman's. So maybe there was still fear, a trace of it, but more likely it was the habitual defense through privacy that one maintained against parents. She had been anxious, though, because of his voice on the phone that morning, and his refusal to tell her why he was coming, save to assure her that the family was in good health, there was nothing to worry about, nothing terrible had happened. Still, when she cleaned her dressing table, she opened the drawer and looked at the vial of cocaine and packet of marijuana. She sat, trying to decide which to employ, before she remembered she had begun by trying to decide whether to use any drug at all. She closed the drawer, stood and glanced about her bedroom whose windows looked out at treetops and down at Beacon Street. She worked for a travel agency and could not afford the apartment but it was worth it and she thought no more about that. She went to the living room, saw on the mantel a Gauloise pack René had forgotten, and brought it to the bedroom and put it in the drawer with the cocaine and marijuana. As she had all her life, she saw this recurrence as a sign: it was meant for her to reach for either the marijuana or the cocaine. But she shut the drawer and sat in the living room, in a wing-backed chair, and waited. Now she was drinking her second Stolichnaya; so was her father, and she watched the level in his glass. She did not want to finish first, and she wished he would hurry.

It was not the vodka that gave her mouth control of itself, so that it smiled when it should not. At times she even laughed, and brought her hand to her mouth, and cleared her throat, and he looked relieved, though puzzled. She felt herself blush too, when she laughed, but there he sat in the old leather-cushioned rocker she had bought from Diana, last year's roommate who had left to live with her boyfriend in Brookline; they had believed they would remain close friends, but Carol had not seen her since winter, and that once was by chance. So the rocking chair often reminded her of Diana, and of the death of friendship that lovers so often caused, and he sat in that chair and talked about Larry and Richie and his friend Brady the state representative, and she not only felt mirthful but could not keep from showing it. Finally his face became more quizzical than anything else, and he stopped talking, looked at her for a moment, then with two swallows finished his drink while she held in her mouth and savored the last of hers.

"You taught me to dance on your toes," she said, and took his glass and went to the kitchen. At the sink she ate his onions and tossed out the ice, put in new cubes, poured vodka from the bottle in the freezer, and forked onions from a jar into the glasses, ground pepper over the ice, then in the doorway she stopped and let the smile come and stay.

"You stood on my feet," he said. "How old were you?"

"Eight. No, nine."

She brought him the drink and sat looking at him.

"That was good," he said.

"It was. Remember, we'd do it late into the night? Even after Mom went to bed. And I thought Mom was jealous. I thought I could see it in her face at breakfast."

"You probably did."

"Was she?"

"I didn't ask."

"Did you ever?"

"Ask if she was jealous? No."

"Ask her anything."

He lit a cigarette, and she knew it was to shift his eyes and his face, and to use his hands, but she quietly waited. How confused they became, these men. For so long she had not known it, even when she first had lovers (not lovers, boys: high school boys), but in college or in her early twenties, she could not recall precisely when, or even what man she had learned it from, she knew with the sudden certainty of one who wakes with the answer to last night's enigma. No matter how old they were, there was something in them that stopped aging at nineteen and, if they loved her, she could summon it from them at will.

"I didn't mean it that way," she said.

"Which way?"

"Trying to blame you. It was affectionate. You see, it's so *funny*. That's why I keep laughing like an idiot. You've always been—you know what you've been. I don't know about you and Mom. But I'm sure of one thing. If you ever asked her how she felt about something, whatever she said wouldn't stop you."

His face reddened and he smiled and looked down at his drink, pinched an onion out of it and put it in his mouth.

"So I'm a selfish bastard," he said, and chewed and watched her. But she knew he did not mean it, for she had seen in his lowered face, and his smile, that look men wore when they knew they were bad boys yet were loved by a woman anyway. At once she saw him in bed with Brenda, and she glanced at his crotch, then looked at her cigarette, drew from it, seeing him as he must be in Brenda, an aging and grateful bear.

"I always thought of you as a bear," she said.

"A bear?"

"A wiry bear. Just wandering through the woods like it's all his. Eating berries. Catching fish. But don't fuck with him."

"Sounds like a grizzly."

"That's when I was a little girl."

"And now?"

"Tonight? A puppy."

"Not even a bear cub?"

"Maybe a cub. Ah, Daddy, you crazy wonderful old thing. Let's dance."

"Dance?"

"Come on."

"I wouldn't know how. Not to your music."

"What if I've got something you can dance to?"

"Jesus. After today—Don't you have anything you want to say?"

"Sure. But I've got Sinatra too."

"No."

"I do. Think you can handle it?"

"I was dancing to Sinatra when—"

"—I know, I know," she said, standing, "when I just wore pants to the beach."

She finished her drink and put out her cigarette, and near the fireplace she kneeled on the carpet and opened the leather cassette box Dennis had given her. He was last fall's lover. Her cassettes were arranged alphabetically, and she took Sinatra and put it in the cassette player on the mantel, and turned to her father. He stood, and said: "Want to roll back the carpet?"

"Take off your shoes," and she reached down to a bent leg and pulled off her sandal, then the other one, watching him sitting to untie and remove his shoes. She crossed the room to him, her arms held out, and he took her hand and waist, and together they turned and swayed and side-stepped between her four chairs, then past them to the rectangular space at one end of the room, near her bedroom door. The song was "My Funny Valentine" and he sang it with Sinatra, softly in her ear; and he was her father, yes, but not of a girl anymore, and as a woman she saw him more clearly, as if her own erotic life had given her an equality or superiority that years alone could not have.

So she saw him as a man too, apart from her mother for two years, alone too much (at least without a woman too much), and he had fallen in love with a very loveable young woman. That was all. And her simple feelings about it made her think she ought

to feel more but could not, because the love she had given others
and taken from them had left her unable or unwilling to look at
the complexity of love; had left her knowing only the tight circle
that surrounded the lovers themselves, so she could feel little more
than recognition of pain touching Larry or Richie. He sang in her
ear, and she rested her head on his chest, and thought that no, it
was not some jaded selfishness; it was being a woman and having
the courage to admit that when you loved, you changed your life,
if that was what it took, and you changed other people's lives, and
you could not let even your own children stop you. Because lovers
had always to be selfish, turned to each other, their backs to the
world, if they wanted to keep their love. As much as she had
wanted Diana to stay, for their friendship and to share the rent,
she had known Diana was right when she moved the few miles
to Brookline, dropped her old life and went to a new one, with
the hope that this time this love would be the one that lived and
grew like a tree. When you had loved several times, there was a
great urge to give up and say it did not exist and had never existed,
had always been a trick of nature to keep itself going, and at those
times you wanted only to take lovers to help you make it through
the nights, as Kristofferson sang. But you had to fight that, even
if you did take the lovers, had to keep alive that part of yourself
that still hoped, believed, so if love did come you would be ready
enough, and strong enough, and then no one could stop you, not
even yourself.

Sinatra started "I Get a Kick Out of You" and her father gently
moved her backward, and danced a slow jitterbug, his hand on her
waist guiding her into a turn, and she circled under their clasped
and shifting hands, faced him, her right hand in his left, their free
arms waving with the beat, his fingers snapping.

"So you fell in love," she said. "So what."

"I'm not sure that's what it is."

"What is it then?"

His eyes were closed now, his head moving from side to side with
the music.

"I don't know. Maybe I never will."

He raised his arm, and she turned toward him and past him,
under his arm, and behind her he turned so when she completed
hers they were facing.

"Why not call it falling in love?" she said.

He pulled her to him, into a slow dance, but faster and with circles like a waltz, and said: "Because at a certain age you don't fall. You just sort of gradually sink."

"Lordy."

"That doesn't mean it's bad."

"What do you call it then?"

"Different. You don't leap anymore. It's solid, though."

"So you sink."

"Something like that. And you know what? I don't care what's wrong with her."

"What's wrong with her?"

"It doesn't matter. I don't care. Comes from age."

They moved apart, holding both hands, then raised their arms and turned from each other, back-to-back, their twisting hands touching, then he took her right with his left, and they danced sideways, back and forth in their rectangle, to the faster beat. At the song's end he swirled with her, then dipped, his left arm supporting her back as beside her he bent his forward knee and leaned with it, as though to kneel. He pulled her up, and held her, and they danced slowly, silently, to "Little Girl Blue." She remembered lunch once with René at a French restaurant that he said was good. He was some sort of chemist and was working in Boston now and all she understood about it was that he might go back to France, and he might not. They were eating paté and she was talking about her father and he said he would like someday to meet him. *No you wouldn't*, she said. He paused, his downturned fork in his left hand, his bread in the right. *Why is that?* She said she had gone to Paris three years ago and when she got back she told her father the Parisians were rude and did not like Americans, and he had said: *If it wasn't for us, they'd be talking German now*. René smiled and said: *Perhaps we would not talk about history*. And she said: *Besides, I don't think he likes men who are fucking his daughter*. He chewed, watching her, then drank wine, and said: *And has he met many of these men? Not if I could help it*, she said, and moving on the carpet with her father's body she knew she would not tell him about René, even if he asked if she were seeing anyone, and for the same reason she had hidden the tracks of René's life into hers: for too long her lovers had seemed from the start ephemeral, no one to arouse his paternal interest; so she had said nothing about any of them, as an adolescent dilettante might decide to stop drawing her parents' enthusiasm toward each new avocation.

"Do you go to Mass at all?" he said.

"Not for years."

"Why?"

"Do you?"

"No," he said. "Why don't you?"

"I don't feel anything there anymore. Is that why you don't go?"

"No. I know it's there. I just can't fit it in."

"Time, you mean?"

"No. My life."

Gracefully he turned and she followed him, on the balls of her feet, her left hand on the back of his neck, her right hand in his left, rising and swinging outward from their circle.

"Richie does, though," he said. "Fits it in."

"Still wants to be a priest?"

"Yes."

"That would be funny. In this family."

"I hope he does it. I tell you, some days I think he ought to go for one of those monasteries. Where nobody talks."

"Trappists."

"That's the one. They make good preserves."

"Great preserves. Daddy?"

"What?"

"Be happy."

"Okay."

"And bring Brenda here for dinner."

"Okay."

"A lot."

"That's very nice."

"No it's not. It's not nice at all. I love you, Daddy. That's all it is."

He hugged her then, and they stood in the music in the room, holding each other, and she felt the life in his chest and hoped it would be long, and happy with love, and she wished more than she had wished for anything, in a very long time, that she could give him those, that they would flow from her heart to his as they stood embraced to a song.

VIII

JOAN'S LOVE HAD died of premature old age. She lived in a small apartment in the town of Amesbury on the Merrimack River. The apartment was on the second floor of a wooden building that years ago had housed a family. She had chosen the place because the other tenants were quiet, retired, and old (at forty-seven she was the youngest) and because her apartment had room for no one but herself to sleep. She had bought a double bed not to share but because she was accustomed to one, and she liked to roll toward its middle and spread out when she was nearing sleep. The closet would not hold all her clothes, but she was as tired of giving them attention as she was of love, and she gave clothes for all seasons to Goodwill. She placed small rugs at either side of the bed, and the rest of the floor was bare. It was old dark wood with slight undulations, and she liked it. There were two windows at the side of the room, and two at the front, and she pushed the dressing table and chest of drawers against walls, clear of the windows. Since she was on the second floor she rarely had to close the Venetian blinds, or even lower them, and nearly always she kept them raised. She liked waking to the blue or gray coming through the windows to her right, and at her feet; and going to sleep looking at their dark, and a gleam from the streetlight half a block away. Three recent and large photographs of her children, in color, hung on the wall above her bed. The other three walls were bare, their flat surfaces interrupted only by a door in one, and two windows in each of the other two. The closet was beside her bed. The two front windows were opposite the foot of the bed, above the short, slanted, blue-shingled roof of the front porch, and past that she could look down on the lawn with its two maples and one oak, and the quiet street.

A chair at the window would clutter the room, so on some nights when she could not sleep for an hour or so past her usual time, she brought a straight-backed chair from the kitchen, and sat at the window, and with the blinds raised she smoked and gazed out at the night, and opened her mind to whatever images came, casting away the ones that brought sorrow or anger or remorse, as deftly as, when snapping beans, she tossed out the ones that were wrinkled. In truth, she could have kept a chair at the window, grown used to its jutting into the little space she had, but she planned to live out her life in this quiet place, alone, and she was cautious about patterns, like becoming the old woman sitting at the window. Old age meant nothing to her; she did not care whether she attained it or not. But she did not want to look like she was living out the last days of a long life, when she was only resting from twenty-seven years of marriage. She meant to keep resting too, until someday a neighbor found her (not too long after death, she hoped), lying on her bed, open-mouthed in final peace (given her with suddenness and without pain, she hoped).

The bedroom was adjacent to the living room, whose door opened to the corridor above the stairs. The living room was small enough too, and she did not have in it a couch anyone could sleep on; she had one armchair with a hassock and floor lamp for reading, a small antique roll-top desk for paying bills and writing an occasional note to Carol, whom she saw less than the other children, and twice a year or so a letter to her brother in Monterey. There were three other chairs in a semicircle facing her armchair, and outside their circle, against the walls, were her bookshelves, filled with fiction written from 1850 to 1950, and of these her favorites were Zola, Kate Chopin's *The Awakening*, and Jean Rhys, de Maupassant, and Colette. There was a television set she rarely watched and a radio and phonograph she played every day, and at night when she came home, with the volume low both day and night, for she always felt she could hear her old neighbors, most of them living alone, either sleeping at night or napping in the afternoon or simply being quiet. She played classical music in daylight, mostly symphonies by Schubert and Mozart and Beethoven and Tchaikovsky, whose sounds changed the very look of the apartment, as tangibly as a fresh coat of paint on the walls. So did Bach's cantatas, and Horowitz playing Scarlatti and Schumann, Chopin and Debussy. Larry and Brenda knew this music, yet when they talked with her about it, they might as well have tried explaining a philosophical abstraction. All she knew was that its deep beauty changed the walls and ceilings and floors of her home. Late at night she liked Billie Holiday and Ella Fitzgerald, Brubeck and Ellington and Charlie Parker, John Coltrane and Sarah Vaughan, and these, as she sat at the window, or leaned back in the armchair in the dark, sculpted her sadness into something strong and lovely.

On her living room wall were framed, glass-covered prints by

Monet and Manet and Cézanne, and a Renoir print hung in the kitchen. Where there was room—on windowsills, the tops of bookshelves, and hanging from the kitchen ceiling—she had put potted plants. The kitchen, with its small working space, and small refrigerator and gas stove, was made for one person, and she ate there, at a table she constantly bumped as she cooked and cleaned. She had bought two chairs for the table, and only Richie or Larry sat in the extra one with any regularity, and once every month or six weeks Carol sat in it, and ate what Joan cooked and was garrulous (and honest, Joan believed) about its flavor.

The sadness that stayed with her was less an emotion than a presence, like the Guardian Angel she had believed in as a child. You never felt the Angel, as you felt shyness or confidence or affection; but often, when you had forgotten about it, you felt it standing beside you, so close that its airy body touched your side, and one large wing enfolded your back. These might be times of danger, to your body or to the self that in childhood you worried most about, the heart and soul that were your name. Or they might be times when you were flirting with the forbidden, pretending to yourself that you would only look but not touch, while knowing that the closer you approached, the more certain was your fall. Now, though, her sadness did not manifest itself only on certain occasions that were connected to it, either directly or by association. Its wing did not wait to touch her when Richie phoned, or when she phoned him, or waited in the car for him to come out of the house and go with her to her apartment; or when she saw a mother with a young son on the sidewalks of the town, or a family with a young son at the restaurant where she worked. No: the wing remained on her back, the body at her side, even when she was in good spirits, alone in her rooms or drinking after work with the other waitresses; her peaceful solitude or talk and laughter were not destroyed, but they were distracted, and so diminished.

She would rather endure carrying Richie in her womb, and the bursting pain of bearing him, than what she had suffered the day she told him and, that same day, left him, and what she had to keep enduring, it seemed, for the rest of her life. She should have left before she conceived him, but she could not wish that, because then he was not alive, and she could not imagine that, nor wish for it, nor survive with her sanity one day in a world he had either left or, because of her, had never joined. Yet a time had come when, still married, and living every day with Richie, she had believed if the phone rang once more, if she drove across the Merrimack to the supermarket one more time, if she cooked one more meal, or if Greg did or said or only started to do or say one of the fifty to one hundred things she could not witness without a boredom that was plummeting toward revulsion, she would go mad. But it was none of these that had defeated her. Nor was it Greg. She could make a list of his parts she disliked, even despised; but any wife could make the same sort of list, any wife who loved; or any husband, for that matter. It was that she had outlived love. A century ago she might have died in childbirth or from the flu, while she was young. Nutrition and medicine had preserved her life, yet without the resilience to love so long. Then each phone call or errand or chore, each grating part of Greg, was love's passing bell.

The restaurant where she worked was owned by Hungarians, the chef had come from an expensive Hungarian restaurant in Boston, and Joan was proud of the good food and low prices that drew from the Merrimack Valley customers who dressed casually and worked for salaries that did not allow luxuries. The restaurant was a white wooden building with two dining rooms and an eight-stool bar, and it was in the shade of trees beside Route 110, a two-lane country road. She could have sat forever at her bedroom window with what Greg sent her twice a month, though she had asked for nothing— at least nothing material—but she worked five nights a week to be with people. She had never been a waitress, and now she was a good one, and she liked the work: liked learning the names and some of the lives of the regular customers, and knowing their drinks before they ordered, so as she turned to each one she could name the drink with a question in her voice. They would nod and praise her memory, and she knew their smiles came from a deeper source: she made them happy by making them feel welcome, by giving them what at least felt like affection, and usually was, beneath the simple exchange of money for food. While she served their tables they talked to her, and often people calling for reservations asked for her station, and always people gave her good tips. She did not need the money, but its meaning gratified her.

The kitchen closed at ten and the bar closed between twelve and one, so when she had cleared all her tables she sat with the other waitresses, at a table near the bar, and drank till closing time. She had always had a little to drink before dinner, when Greg came home, but only as a break from cooking and a greeting to her husband, and the drinks themselves were not important. But now, for the first time in her life, she knew the pleasure of finishing an intense period of fast hard work, and sitting down to drinks with the other workers; their talk was never serious, but gay and laughing, the sounds of release, and each cold drink, each cigarette, soothed her, from her tired feet and legs to her brain, till she felt as if she were talking and laughing from a hammock.

At ten-thirty that night, she was at a table with three women when she glanced down the length of the long dining room, her eyes drawn to its door that opened to the front parking lot, and she saw Larry standing at it, watching her, and knew that was why she had looked and that whatever it was, it was bad. How many times had she felt the tingling heat of lactation in her breast when he was a boy and no longer nursed but was crying in pain? She stood, and the women stopped talking and looked at her.

"It's my son," she said. "I'll see what he wants."

"Call him over," one said, and Joan saw another motioning her to silence, and so she knew that what was in her heart had reached her face too. *Richie. It's Richie*, seeing him dead under a bent bicycle. She was walking toward Larry and he came to her and they stood between the wall and the room of tables covered for tomorrow.

"Is anything wrong?"

"Yes. I need to talk."

"Is anything *wrong. With* somebody."

"No. No, everybody's fine."

"Thank God. I thought something had happened."

"Something did. But everybody's well."

"Good. Then let's hear about it."

She saw Richie in his bed, with whatever he dreamed; now she knew the trouble was love and she felt the hammock again, lifting her, and she sank into its idle swing. She could hear about love from there, without a sigh or the tensing of a muscle. She led him to an empty table opposite the end of the bar, near the television turned to a Red Sox game but without sound, and two empty tables away from her friends, and she seated him with his back to the women, to protect his face.

"Dad called me to the house last night."

"Don't you want a drink?"

"Yes. What's that?"

"Vodka and tonic."

"I'll have one."

She stood, and he reached out a hand that fell short of hers, and said: "Wait. Let me—"

"—Relax, and have a drink. I thought you'd come from the morgue."

She got the drinks from young handsome black-bearded Lee at the bar, and he shook his head at her money. Larry was smoking and staring at the silent ballgame. She sat and he lit her cigarette and said: "Dad and Brenda have been seeing each other. Now they're getting married."

She leaned back in her chair, and studied his face.

"Well," she said, and she saw Greg, foolish and wild, and angry and sweet, both too much and not enough of him to live in the world, let alone with one woman; at least by the time he burned out Brenda he would be nearly dead. "What about you?"

"I'm going fucking nuts. Excuse me. I'm going nuts."

"Don't. At least he didn't take her from you."

"Thanks, Mom."

"You left her or you lost her. That's all. Nothing else matters."

"My father marrying her matters."

"Of course it does. It stinks."

"It's even against the law," he said, and he looked down at his drink, as though ducking his petulance.

"What law?"

"Massachusetts."

"That doesn't surprise me. But it doesn't have anything to do with you. Listen: your father has always been a son of a bitch. That's one reason I loved him for so long."

"Why?"

"Because he never wants to be one. It was exciting, watching him struggle."

"How long would you have stayed? If it weren't for Richie. The accident."

"Richie was no accident."

"Really? You were—" He closed his eyes, his lips quietly counting. "Thirty-five."

"Your father thought it would save us."

"Did you?"

"He could always talk me into things."

"I told him last night I wasn't coming home again. Or to work either."

She nodded, watching him. You knew so much about your children; too much. They changed so little from infancy that, if you dared, you could come very near predicting their lives by the time they started school. At least the important parts: Richie had always been solitary and at peace with it; Carol had wanted happiness whose source was being loved, and she had looked for it with each new friend, had changed her child's play and dress and even speech with these friends, and had never looked for it by doing something she loved, or even doing nothing at all, in her own solitude; and Larry, the one with talents, with real gifts, had always waited for someone—a friend, his family, a teacher—to see those gifts and encourage him. He could no more leave his father now than he could have twenty years ago.

"What do you think?" he said.

"I understand. But I don't think you will."

"Why not?"

"It'll only break your heart, and Richie's, and your father's."

"Not yours?"

"I live here now. You can't work at the stores? Really?"

"No."

"But you don't hate him."

"No."

"You're just hurt."

"Just."

"Want another?"

"All right."

Lee refused her money again, and she thanked him with the freedom she had earned: very early, on this job, she had let men know that she did not want a lover. She had done it with subtlety and, if that wasn't clear, with kindness; and she accepted free drinks because she was a worker there, and a good one.

"I love this time of night," she said to Larry. "You should come in more often, about now."

"Maybe I will."

"We have fun. What about you? Do you have fun?"

"When I'm working."

"At the stores? Or performing?"

"Dancing. Acting. Are you coming next week?"

"Yes. Somebody's working for me. Listen: can I tell you something?"

"After last night, anybody can tell me anything."

"You're a good dancer, a good actor. I've seen you, and I know. I don't have the training to judge like a professional. But I feel it. But you only *want* to be a performer. Then you wait for it to happen. You don't go after it. You let too much get taken from you. You wait too much for things to happen. You think too Goddamn much."

"Jesus."

"You know it's true. I'm not trying to hurt you. I want to tell you something."

"What's that got to do with Dad marrying my Goddamn ex-wife?"

"Look at you. You can't even sound angry when you say that. I think some artists would be set free by all this. No more father, no more job, no ex-wife in the same town. They'd use this like a train to take them away. New York; wherever. Just throw themselves at the world: here I am. What makes me feel so—what gives me pain about you is that you won't. So sometimes I think you got just enough of a gift to be a curse, and not enough to be a blessing. You share that with your father."

"What's his gift?"

"The second part: here I am, world. And the world always sees him. But there's no talent to see. Only the energy, the drive."

"You're sure I won't leave?"

"Yes."

"Me too. I guess that's why I came to see my mommy."

Then he pushed back his chair, started to rise, but she reached across the table and held his wrist till he eased into the chair and slid it forward.

"Stay a while," she said. "Let's talk."

"All right."

"I'm going to keep you here till you smile."

"What time do they close?"

"Time enough. I'll tell you something you don't have to believe tonight, or for a long time. You'll keep working for your father and, after a while, it'll be all right. You'll see him at the store, and you won't think of him with Brenda. There might be a twitch, like some old injury that reminds you it was there. But you won't see the pictures. You probably feel that twitch whenever you see your father anyway, because you've always fought, you two, and you've always loved each other." He nodded, and she saw, so joyfully that she had to force her words to be slow and calm, that he was listening, truly listening, and how many times had she ever been able to tell one of her children something she knew, and to help the child? So much of motherhood was casting lines to children beyond reach, that she could count with less than two digits the times their hands had clutched the rope and pulled. "Finally, at the store, it'll be the same. You'll go get Richie the way I do, sitting in the car, tooting the horn, and you'll bring him to my place for dinner. I'll get a third chair for the table. Then one evening your father will come out to the car while Richie's still inside. He'll look sinful as a scolded boy, and he'll ask you in for a beer. You'll want to curse or cry, but you'll go have the beer instead, and Brenda won't be in the house. Because he will be planning this, because he loves you. You'll just pass the time of day over your beer, and you'll have a second, and when you leave with Richie he'll offer you his hand. You'll shake it. One day after work he'll take you out for drinks and dinner. He'll show up at a play or a dance concert, just him and Richie, and afterward they'll take you someplace for a beer. He'll invite you to Sunday dinner, and you'll go, and everyone will have tense stomachs and be very polite, and Brenda won't kiss or touch your father, but she'll kiss you hello and goodbye. Soon you'll be dropping in and someday it won't even hurt anymore. You and your father will be able to laugh and fight again. Everyone will survive. I told you I'd make you smile."

"Was I?"

"You have tears in your eyes. But there was a smile."

"You know why?"

"No."

"Because I knew all that. When I heard it, I knew I had known it since I woke up this morning."

"Good. You know why I like my waitress friends so much? And what I learned from them? They don't have delusions. So when I'm alone at night—and I love it, Larry—I look out my window, and it comes to me: we don't have to live great lives, we just have to understand and survive the ones we've got. You're smiling again."

"Tears too."

"Wipe them fast, before my friends think something terrible is happening."

IX

AT TEN O'CLOCK Richie's father phoned to say he was still at Carol's and would be home around midnight.

"Are you all right?" his father said.

"Sure."

"Are you going to bed now?"

"After a while."

He put the phone back on the receiver on the kitchen wall and looked at it, then at the clock on the stove. He went down the stairs to his room and took his key ring with the keys to his bicycle lock and the front door and back door; he was passing the open bathroom when he stopped and looked at Jim Rice over the toilet with its raised seat. He went in and brushed his teeth, and his rump tightened against the danger of the bristles and the flavor in his mouth, and his careful brushing of his hair, and tucking in and smoothing of his shirt. He started to pray *Lead us not into temptation* but stopped at *Lead* and hurried out of the house, leaving on lights for his coming back.

Houses were lighted, and leaves of trees near the streetlight, but beneath him the grass was dark and he walked carefully, like a stranger on his lawn. Then he was on the road under the trees, and he could see objects now, distinct in the darkness: shrubs and flowers, and mailboxes near doors, and above him the limbs of trees. He watched the trees where that morning they had talked; then the blacktop ended, and clumsily he stepped through weeds and in and out of ruts, and started to sweat in the warm, close air whose density made him feel he moved through smoke he could neither see nor smell nor taste. He did not risk stumbling loudly through the trees, approaching her like someone frightening or, worse, an awkward boy. He looked up at the treetops against the stars and sky, then left the trail, and went around the trees and stood beside them, in their shadows, and looked at the infield through the backstop screen, and scanned the outfield.

First he saw Conroy, the dog, a blond motion, then a halted silhouette in left center field. He looked to both of Conroy's sides, saw only the expanse of dark grass and the woods past the outfield. Then he stepped out of the shadows, stood in the open, and peered down the edge of the trees. He saw the brightening glow of her cigarette, then it moved down and away from the small figure that was Melissa, profiled, sitting on the ground. Above her, cicadas sang in the trees. At once he moved and spoke her name. Her face jerked toward him, and he said: It's Richie; then he was there, standing above her, looking down at her forehead and her eyes. He could not see their green. He sat beside her, crossed his legs like hers.

"I didn't think you'd still be here," he said.

"Is that why you came late?"

"No. I had to wait for my Dad to call."

"Where is he?"

"Visiting my sister in Boston."

"Can you see Conroy?"

He looked at left field.

"Yes."

"Where?"

"Straight that way."

He pointed his right arm and she touched it with her cheek, sighting down it. Slowly he tightened his bicep so her face would feel its muscles.

"I don't want him in those woods. Once he went in there and wouldn't come out for an hour."

"Look where my finger is."

"Okay, I see him."

"I think he's coming this way."

"He is."

She drew on her cigarette, then tossed it arcing in front of them, and he watched it burn in the grass. He could see its thin smoke, but he could still not see the color of her eyes. She wore the cut-off jeans from this morning and the blue denim shirt with its sleeves rolled up, and the shirttails knotted in front; her skin looked darker.

He had not noticed her shifting, but she had, when she looked down his arm, and now her knee still touched his, and her left arm his right, till one of them moved; and her shoulder rubbed his or rested against it. Beneath the sound of cicadas, his breath was too quick, audible; he tried to slow it, held it for moments after inhaling, and breathed through his nose.

"Why did you have to wait for your father to call?"

"He wanted me to. So I'd know when he'd be home."

"Oh. I thought maybe she was sick or something. Your sister."

"No."

"He sounds nice."

"My dad?"

"Yes."

"I hope so."

"That's a funny thing to say."

He nodded. In her eyes now was a shade of green. Except for tobacco smoke and lipstick, her scents had faded since morning: the cologne or cosmetic was gone. Her clothes and skin too, morning-fresh when she had kissed him, held the smells of the day: its long hot sunlit air, and the restful and pleasant odor of female sweat.

"Why did you say it?"

"Because I want him to be."

"Are you going to tell me?"

"Tell you what?"

He was watching her mouth, and he swallowed, and knew he was lost. If only he could be lost without fear. If only his heart could keep growing larger and larger until he had to hold her, else it would burst through his ribs, if only he could look to the stars —and he did: abruptly lifted his face to the sky—and find in them release from what he felt now, or release to feel it. He looked at her eyes, her nose, her lips.

"You know," she said. "What you told me this morning. that you'd tell me sometime."

"Last night—"

"Go on," she said. "Last night."

"My brother came over, to see my dad. He's twenty-five, and I was in bed. But I got up to tell him hello. I was on the stairs going up to the kitchen, but then I heard what they were saying. So I just stayed and listened. After a while I went back to my room.

It's under the living room, and they were right over me, so I heard it all."

He lay on his back. Then she was beside him, her arm touching his, and he slid his hand under her palm. Slowly and gently he squeezed, and her fingers pressed. When he found that he was trembling, he did not care. He watched the stars, and talked. When he paused after telling her of that morning, of his father's tears he never saw, she said: "You poor guy."

He did not correct her. But he did not feel that way at all. He did not even have to control his voice, for there were no tears in it, nor in his breast. What he felt was the night air starting to cool, and the dew on the grass under his hand holding Melissa's, and under his arms and head and shirt, and only its coolness touching his thick jeans, and the heels of his shoes. He felt Melissa's hand in his, and the beating of his heart she both quickened and soothed, and he smelled the length of her beside him, and heard in the trees the song of cicadas like the distant ringing of a thousand tambourines. He saw in the stars the eyes of God too, and was grateful for them, as he was for the night and the girl he loved. He lay on the grass and the soft summer earth, holding Melissa's hand, and talking to the stars.

TOWNIES

T HE CAMPUS SECURITY guard found her. She wore
a parka and she lay on the footbridge over the pond.
Her left cheek lay on the frozen snow. The college was a small one,
he was the only guard on duty, and in winter he made his rounds
in the car. But partly because he was sleepy in the heated car, and
mostly because he wanted to get out of the car and walk in the cold
dry air, wanted a pleasurable solitude within the imposed solitude
of his job, he had gone to the bridge.

He was sixty-one years old, a tall broad man, his shoulders slumped
and he was wide in the hips and he walked with his toes pointed
outward, with a long stride which appeared slow. His body, whether
at rest or in motion, seemed the result of sixty-one years of erosion,
as though all his life he had been acted upon and, with just enough
struggle to keep going, he had conceded; fifty years earlier he would
have sat quietly at the rear of a classroom, scraped dirt with his
shoe on the periphery of a playground. In a way, he was the best
man to find her. He was not excitable, he was not given to anger,
he was not a man of action: when he realized the girl was dead he
did not think immediately of what he ought to do, of what acts and
words his uniform and wages required of him. He did not think of
phoning the police. He knelt on the snow, so close to her that his
knee touched her shoulder, and he stroked her cold cheek, her cold
blonde hair.

He did not know her name. He had seen her about the campus.

He believed she had died of an overdose of drugs or a mixture of drugs and liquor. This deepened his sorrow. Often when he thought of what young people were doing to themselves, he felt confused and sad, as though in the country he loved there were a civil war whose causes baffled him, whose victims seemed wounded and dead without reason. Especially the girls, and especially these girls. He had lived all his life in this town, a small city in northeastern Massachusetts; once there had been a shoe industry. Now that was over, only three factories were open, and the others sat empty along the bank of the Merrimack. Their closed windows and the dark empty rooms beyond them stared at the street, like the faces of the old and poor who on summer Sundays sat on the stoops of the old houses farther upriver and stared at the street, the river, the air before their eyes. He had worked in a factory, as a stitcher. When the factory closed he got a job driving a truck, delivering fresh loaves of bread to families in time for their breakfast. Then people stopped having their bread delivered. It was a change he did not understand. He had loved the smell of bread in the morning and its warmth in his hands. He did not know why the people he had delivered to would choose to buy bread in a supermarket. He did not believe that the pennies and nickels saved on one expense ever showed up in your pocket.

When they stopped eating fresh bread in the morning he was out of work for a while, but his children were grown and his wife did not worry, and then he got his last and strangest job. He was not an authorized constable, he carried no weapons, and he needed only one qualification other than the usual ones of punctuality and subservience: a willingness to work for very little money. He was so accustomed to all three that none of them required an act of will, not even a moment's pause while he made the decision to take and do the job. When he worked a daylight shift he spent some time ordering possible vandals off the campus: they were usually children on bicycles; sometimes they made him chase them away, and he did this in his long stride, watching the distance lengthen between him and the children, the bicycles. Mostly during the day he chatted with the maintenance men and students and some of the teachers; and he walked the campus, which was contained by an iron fence and four streets, and he looked at the trees. There were trees he recognized, and more that he did not. One of the maintenance men had told him that every kind of New England tree grew here. There was one with thick, low, spreading branches and, in the fall, dark red leaves; sometimes students sat on the branches.

The time he saw three girls in the tree he was fooled: they were pretty and they wore sweaters in the warm autumn afternoon. They looked like the girls he had grown up knowing about: the rich girls who came from all parts of the country to the school, and who were rarely seen in town. From time to time some of them walked the three blocks from the campus to the first row of stores where the commercial part of the town began. But most of them only walked the one block, to the corner where they waited for the bus to Boston. He had smelled them once, as a young man. It was a winter day. When he saw them waiting for the bus he crossed the street so he could walk near them. There were perhaps six of them. As he approached, he looked at their faces, their hair. They did not look at him. He walked by them. He could smell them and he could feel their eyes seeing him and not seeing him. Their smells were of perfume, cold fur, leather gloves, leather suitcases. Their voices had no accents he could recognize. They seemed the voices of mansions, resorts, travel. He was too conscious of himself to hear what they were saying. He knew it was idle talk; but its tone seemed peremptory; he would not have been surprised if one of them had suddenly given him a command. Then he was away from them. He smelled only the cold air now; he longed for their smells again: erotic, unattainable, a world that would never be open to him. But he did not think about its availability, any more than he would wish for an African safari. He knew people who hated them because they were rich. But he did not. In the late sixties more of them began appearing in town and they wore blue jeans and smoked on the street. In the early seventies, when the drinking age was lowered, he heard they were going to the bars at night, and some of them got into trouble with the local boys. Also, the college started accepting boys, and they lived in the dormitories with the girls. He wished all this were not so; but by then he wished much that was happening was not so.

When he saw the three girls in the tree with low spreading branches and red leaves, he stopped and looked across the lawn at them, stood for a moment that was redolent of his past, of the way he had always seen the college girls, and still tried to see them: lovely and nubile, existing in an ambience of benign royalty. Their sweaters and hair seemed bright as the autumn sky. He walked toward them, his hands in his back pockets. They watched him. Then he stood under the tree, his eyes level with their legs. They were all biting silenced giggles. He said it was a pretty day. Then the giggles came, shrill and relentless; they could have been monkeys in the tree. There was an impunity about the giggling that was different from the other graceful impunity they carried with them as they carried the check-books that were its source. He was accustomed to that. He looked at their faces, at their vacant eyes and flushed cheeks; then his own cheeks flushed with shame. It was marijuana. He lifted a hand in goodbye.

He was not angry. He walked with lowered eyes away from the giggling tree, walked impuissant and slow across the lawn and around the snack bar, toward the library; then he shifted direction and with raised eyes went toward the ginkgo tree near the chapel. There was no one around. He stood looking at the yellow leaves, then he moved around the tree and stopped to read again the bronze plaque he had first read and marvelled at his second day on the job. It said the tree was a gift of the class of 1941. He stood now as he had stood on that first day, in a reverie which refreshed his bruised heart, then healed it. He imagined the girls of 1941 standing in a circle as one of the maintenance men dug a hole and planted the small tree. The girls were pretty and hopeful and had sweethearts. He thought of them later in that year, in winter; perhaps skiing while the *Arizona* took the bombs. He was certain that some of them lost sweethearts in that war, which at first he had followed in the newspapers as he now followed the Red Sox and Patriots and Celtics and Bruins. Then he was drafted. They made him a truck driver and he saw England while the war was still on, and France when it was over. He was glad that he missed combat and when he returned he did not pretend to his wife and family and friends that he wished he had been shot at. Going over, he had worried about submarines; other than that, he had enjoyed his friends and England and France, and he had saved money. He still remembered it as a pleasurable interlude in his life. Looking at the ginkgo tree and the plaque he happily felt their presence like remembered music: the girls then, standing in a circle around the small tree on that spring day in 1941; those who were in love and would grieve; and he stood in the warmth of the afternoon staring at the yellow leaves strewn on the ground like deciduous sunshine.

So this last one was his strangest job: he was finally among them, not quite their servant like the cleaning women and not their protector either: an unarmed watchman and patrolman whose job consisted mostly of being present, of strolling and chatting in daylight and, when he drew the night shift, of driving or walking, depending on the weather, and of daydreaming and remembering and talking to himself. He enjoyed the job. He would not call it work, but that did not bother him. He had long ago ceased believing in work: the word and its connotation of fulfillment as a man. Life was cluttered with these ideas which he neither believed nor disputed. He merely ignored them. He liked wandering about in this job, as he had liked delivering bread and had liked the Army; only the stitching had been tedious. He liked coming home and drinking coffee in the kitchen with his wife: the daily chatting which seemed eternal. He liked his children and his grandchildren. He accepted the rest of his life as a different man might accept commuting: a tolerable inconvenience. He knew he was not lazy. That was another word he did not believe in.

He kneeled on the snow and with his ungloved hand he touched her cold blonde hair. In sorrow his flesh mingled like death-ash with the pierced serenity of the night air and the trees on the banks of the pond and the stars. He felt her spirit everywhere, fog-like across the pond and the bridge, spreading and rising in silent weeping above him into the black visible night and the invisible space beyond his ken and the cold silver truth of the stars.

On the bridge Mike slipped and cursed, catching himself on the wooden guard rail, but still she did not look back. He was about to speak her name but he did not: he knew if his voice was angry she would not stop and if his voice was pleading she might stop and even turn to wait for him but he could not bear to plead. He walked faster. He had the singular focus that came from being drunk and sad at the same time: he saw nothing but her parka and blonde hair. All evening, as they drank, he had been waiting to lie with her in her bright clean room. Now there would be no room. He caught up with her and grabbed her arm and spun her around; both her feet slipped but he held her up.

'You asshole,' she said, and he struck her with his fist, saw the surprise and pain in her eyes, and she started to speak but he struck her before she could; and when now she only moaned he swung again and again, holding her up with his left hand, her parka bunched and twisted in his grip; when he released her she fell forward. He kicked her side. He knew he should stop but he could not. Kicking, he saw her naked in the bed in her room. She was slender. She moaned and gasped while they made love; sometimes she came so hard she cried. He stopped kicking. He knew she had died while he was kicking her. Something about the silence of the night, and the way her body yielded to his boot.

He looked around him: the frozen pond, the tall trees, the darkened library. He squatted down and looked at her red-splotched cheek. He lifted her head and turned it and lowered it to the snow. Her right cheek was untouched; now she looked asleep. In the mornings he usually woke first, hung over and hard, listening to students passing in the hall. Now on the snow she looked like that: in bed, on her pillow. Under the blanket he took her hand and put it around him and she woke and they smoked a joint; then she kneeled between his legs and he watched her hair going up and down.

He stood and walked off the bridge and around the library. His body was weak and sober and it weaved; he did not feel part of it, and he felt no need to hurry away from the campus and the bridge and Robin. What waited for him was home, and a two-mile walk to get there: the room he hated though he tried to believe he did not. For he lived there, his clothes hung there, most of all he slept there, the old vulnerable breathing of night and dreams; and if he allowed himself to hate it then he would have to hate his life too, and himself.

He walked without stealth across the campus, then up the road to town. He passed Timmy's, where he and Robin had drunk and where now the girls who would send him to prison were probably still drinking. He and Robin had sat in a booth on the restaurant side. She drank tequila sunrises and paid for those and for his Comfort and ginger, and she told him that all day she had been talking to people, and now she had to talk to him, her mind was blown, her father called her about her grades and he called the dean too so she had to go to the counselor's office and she was in there three hours, they talked about everything, they even got back to the year she was fifteen and she told the counselor she didn't remember much of it, that was her year on acid, and she had done a lot of balling, and she said she had never talked like that with anybody before, had never just sat down and *list*ed what she had done for the last four years, and the counselor told her in all that time she had never felt what she was doing or done what she felt. She was talking gently to Mike, but in her eyes she was already gone: back in her room; home in Darien; Bermuda at Easter; the year in Europe she had talked about before, the year her father would give her when she got out of school. He could not remember her loins, and he felt he could not remember himself either, that his life had begun a few minutes earlier in this booth. He watched her hands as she stirred her tequila sunrise and the grenadine rose from the bottom in a menstrual cloud, and she said the counselor had gotten her an appointment in town with a psychiatrist tomorrow, a woman psychiatrist, and she wanted to go, she wanted to talk again, because now she had admitted it, that she wasn't happy, hadn't been happy, had figured nobody ever could be.

Then he looked at her eyes. She liked to watch him when they made love, and sometimes he opened his eyes and saw on her face that eerie look of a woman making love: as if her eyes, while watching him, were turned inward as well, were indeed watching his thrusting from within her womb. Her eyes now were of the counselor's office, the psychiatrist's office tomorrow, they held no light for him; and in his mind, as she told him she had to stop dope and alcohol and balling, he saw the school: the old brick and the iron fence with its points like spears and the serene trees. All his life this town had been dying. His father had died with it, killing himself with one of the last things he owned: they did not have a garage so he drove the car into a woods and used the vacuum cleaner hose. She said she had never come, not with anybody all these years, she had always faked it; he finished his drink in a swallow and immediately wished he had not, for he wanted another but she didn't offer him one and he only had three dollars which he knew now he would need for the rest of the night; then he refused to imagine the rest of the night. He smiled.

'Only with my finger,' she said.

'I hope it falls off.'

She slid out of the booth; his hand started to reach for her but he stopped it; she was saying something that didn't matter now, that he could not feel: her eyes were suddenly damp as standing she put on her parka, saying she had wanted to talk to him, she thought at least they could talk; then she walked out. He drank her tequila sunrise as he was getting out of the booth. Outside, he stood looking up the street; she was a block away, almost at the drugstore. Then she was gone around the bend in the street. He started after her, watching his boots on the shovelled sidewalk.

Now he walked on the bridge over the river and thought of her lying on the small one over the pond. The wind came blowing down freezing over the Merrimack; his moustache stiffened, and he lowered his head. But he did not hurry. Seeing Robin on the bridge over the pond he saw the dormitory beyond it, just a dormitory for them, rooms which they crowded with their things, but the best place he had ever slept in. The things that crowded their rooms were more than he had ever owned, yet he knew for the girls these were only selected and favorite or what they thought necessary things, only a transportable bit of what filled large rooms of huge houses at home. For four or five years now he had made his way into the dormitory; he met them at Timmy's and they took him back to the dormitory to drink and smoke dope and when the party dissolved one of them usually took him to bed.

One night in the fall before Robin he was at a party there and toward three in the morning nearly all the girls were gone and no one had given him a sign and there were only two girls left and the one college fag, a smooth-shaven, razor-cut boy who dressed better than the girls, went to Timmy's, and even to the bar side of it, the long, narrow room without booths or bar stools where only men drank; he wore a variety of costumes: heels and yellow and rust and gold and red, and drank sloe gin fizzes and smoked like a girl. And Mike, who rarely thought one way or another about fags but disliked them on sight, liked this one because he went into town like that and once a man poured a beer over his head, but he kept going and joking, his necklaces tapping on his chest as he swayed back and forth laughing. That night he came over and sat beside Mike just at the right time, when Mike had understood that the two remaining girls not only weren't interested in him, but they despised him, and he was thinking of the walk home to his room when the fag said he had some Colombian and Mike nodded and rose and left with him. In the room the fag touched him and Mike said twenty-five bucks and put it in his pocket, then removed the fag's fingers from his belt buckle and turned away and undressed. He would not let the fag kiss him but the rest was all right, a mouth was a mouth, except when he woke sober in the morning, woke early, earlier than he ever woke when he slept there with a girl. A presence woke him, as though a large bird had flown inches above his chest. He got up quickly and glanced at the sleeping fag, lying on his back, his bare, smooth shoulders and slender arms above the blanket, his face turned toward Mike, the mouth open, and Mike wanted to kill him or himself or both of them, looking away from the mouth which had consumed forever part of his soul, and with his back turned he dressed. Then quietly opening the door he was aware of his height and broad shoulders and he squared them as glaring he stepped into the corridor; but it was empty, and he got out of the dormitory without anyone seeing him and ate breakfast in town and at ten o'clock went to the employment office for his check.

Through the years he had stolen from them: usually cash from the girls he slept with, taking just enough so they would believe or make themselves believe that while they were drunk at Timmy's they had spent it. Twice he had stolen with the collusion of girls One had gone ahead of him in the corridor, then down the stairs, as he rolled and carried a ten speed bicycle. He rode it home and the next day sold it to three young men who rented a house down the street; they sold dope, and things other people stole, mostly things that kids stole, and Mike felt like a kid when he went to them and said he had a ten-speed. A year later, when a second girl helped him steal a stereo, he sold it at the same house. The girl was drunk and she went with him into the room one of her friends had left unlocked, and in the dark she got the speakers and asked if he wanted any records while he hushed her and took the amplifier and turntable. They carried everything out to her Volvo. In the car he was relieved but only for a moment, only until she started the engine, then he thought of the street and the building where he lived, and by the time she turned on the heater he was trying to think of a way to keep her from taking him home.

All the time she was talking. It was the first time she had stolen anything. Or anything worth a lot of money. He made himself smile by thinking of selling her to the men in the house; he thought of her sitting amid the stereos and television sets and bicycles. Then he heard her say something. She had asked if he was going to sell his old set so he could get some bucks out of the night too. He said he'd give the old one to a friend, and when she asked for directions he pointed ahead in despair. He meant to get out at the corner but when she said Here? and slowed for the turn he was awash in the loss of control which he fought so often and overcame so little, though he knew most people couldn't tell by looking at him or even talking to him. She turned and climbed up the street, talking all the time, not about the street, the buildings, but about the stereo: or the stealing of it, and he knew from her voice she was repeating herself so she would not have to talk about what she saw. Or he felt she was. But that was not the worst. The worst was that he was so humiliated he could not trust what he felt, could not know if this dumb rich girl was even aware of the street, and he knew there was no way out of this except to sleep and wake tomorrow in the bed that held his scent. He had been too long in that room (this was his third year), too long in the building: there were six apartments; families lived in the five larger ones; one family had a man: a pumper of gasoline, checker of oil and water, wiper of windshields. Mike thought of his apartment as a room, although there was a kitchen he rarely used, a bathroom, and a second room that for weeks at a time he did not enter. Some mornings when he woke he felt he had lived too long in his body. He smoked a joint in bed and showered and shaved and left the room, the building, the street of these buildings. Once free of the street he felt better: he liked feeling and smelling clean; he walked into town. The girl stopped the Volvo at another of his sighed directions and touched his thigh and said she would help him bring the stuff in. He said no and loaded everything in his arms and left her.

Robin had wanted to go to his room too and he had never let her and now for the first time grieving for her lost flesh, he wished he had taken her there. Saw her there at nights and on the weekends, the room—rooms: he saw even the second room—smelling of paint; saw buckets and brushes on newspaper awaiting her night and week-end hand, his hand too: the two of them painting while music played not from his tinny-sounding transistor but a stereo that was simply there in his apartment with the certainty of something casually purchased with cash neither from the employment office nor his occasional and tense forays into the world of jobs: dishwashing at Timmy's, the quick and harried waitresses bringing the trays of plates which he scraped and racked and hosed and slid into the washer, hot water in the hot kitchen wetting his clothes; he scrubbed the pots by hand and at the night's end he mopped the floor and the bartender sent him a bottle of beer; but he only worked there in summers, when the students were gone. He saw Robin painting the walls beside him, their brushstrokes as uniform as the beating of their hearts. He was approaching the bar next to the bus station. He did not like it because the band was too loud, and the people were losers, but he often went there anyway, because he could sit and drink and watch the losers dancing without having to make one gesture he had to think about, the way he did at Timmy's when he sat with the girls and was conscious of his shoulders and arms and hands, of his eyes and mouth as if he could see them, so that he smiled—and coolly, he knew—when girl after girl year after year touched his flesh and sometimes his heart and told him he was cool.

He went into the bar, feeling the bass drum beat as though it came from the floor and walls, and took the one untaken stool and ordered a shot of Comfort, out of habit checking his pocket although he knew he had three ones and some change. Everyone he saw was drunk, and the bartender was drinking. Vic was at the end of the bar, wearing a bandana on his head, earring on one ear, big fat arms on the bar; Mike nodded at him. He drank the shot and pushed the glass toward the bartender. His fingers trembled. He sipped the Comfort and lit a cigarette, cold sweat on his brow, and he thought he would have to go outside into the cold air or vomit.

He finished the shot then moved through the crowd to Vic and spoke close to his ear and the gold earring. 'I need some downs.' Vic wanted a dollar apiece. 'Come on,' Mike said. 'Two.' Vic's arm left the bar and he put two in Mike's hand; Mike gave him the dollar and left, out onto the cold street, heading uphill, swallowing, but his throat was dry and the second one lodged; he took a handful of snow from a mound at the base of a parking meter and ate it. He walked on the lee side of buildings now. He was dead with her. He lay on the bridge, his arm around her, his face in her hair. At the dormitory the night shift detectives would talk to the girls inside, out of the cold; they would sit in the big glassed-in room downstairs where drunk one night he had pissed on the carpet while Robin laughed before they went up to her room. The girls would speak his name. His name was in that room, back there in the dormitory; it was not walking up the hill in his clothing. He had two joints in his room and he would smoke those while he waited, lying dressed on his bed. When he heard their footsteps in the hall he would put on his jacket and open the door before they knocked and walk with them to the cruiser. He walked faster up the hill.

LESLIE IN CALIFORNIA

WHEN THE ALARM rings the room is black and grey; I smell Kevin's breath and my eye hurts and won't open. He gets out of bed, and still I smell beer in the cold air. He is naked and dressing fast. I get up shivering in my nightgown and put on my robe and go by flashlight to the kitchen, where there is some light from the sky. Birds are singing, or whatever it is they do. I light the gas lantern and set it near the stove, and remember New England mornings with the lights on and a warm kitchen and catching the school bus. I won't have to look at my eye till the sun comes up in the bathroom. Dad was happy about us going to California; he talked about sourdough bread and fresh fruit and vegetables all year. I put water on the stove and get bacon and eggs and milk from the ice chest. A can of beer is floating, tilting, in the ice and water; the rest are bent in the paper bag for garbage. I could count them, know how many it takes. I put on the bacon and smoke a cigarette, and when I hear him coming I stand at the stove so my back is to the door.

'Today's the day,' he says.

They are going out for sharks. They will be gone five days, maybe more, and if he comes back with money we can have electricity again. For the first three months out here he could not get on a boat, then yesterday he found one that was short a man, so last night he celebrated.

'Hey, hon.'

I turn the bacon. He comes to me and hugs me from behind, rubbing my hips through the robe, his breath sour beer with mint.

'Let me see your eye.'

I turn around and look up at him, and he steps back. His blond beard is damp, his eyes are bloodshot, and his mouth opens as he looks.

'Oh, hon.'

He reaches to touch it, but I jerk my face away and turn back to the skillet.

'I'll never do that again,' he says.

The bacon is curling brown. Through the window above the stove I can see the hills now, dark humps against the sky. Dad liked the Pacific, but we are miles inland and animals are out there with the birds; one morning last week a rattlesnake was on the driveway. Yesterday some men went hunting a bobcat in the hills. They say it killed a horse, and they are afraid it will kill somebody's child, but they didn't find it. How can a bobcat kill a horse? My little sister took riding lessons in New England; I watched her compete, and I was afraid, she was so small on that big animal jumping. Dad told me I tried to pet some bobcats when I was three and we lived at Camp Pendleton. He was the deer camp duty officer one Sunday, and Mom and I brought him lunch. Two bobcats were at the edge of the camp; they wanted the deer hides by the scales, and I went to them saying here, kitty, here, kitty. They just watched me, and Dad called me back.

'It wasn't you,' Kevin says. 'You know it wasn't you.'

'Who was it?'

My first words of the day, and my voice sounds like dry crying. I clear my throat and grip the robe closer around it.

'I was drunk,' he says. 'You know. You know how rough it's been.'

He harpoons fish. We came across country in an old Ford he worked on till it ran like it was young again. We took turns driving and sleeping and only had to spend motel money twice. That was in October, after we got married on a fishing boat, on a clear blue Sunday on the Atlantic. We had twenty-five friends and the two families and open-faced sandwiches and deviled eggs, and beer and wine. On the way out to sea we got married, then we fished for cod and drank, and in late afternoon we went to Dad's for a fish fry with a fiddle band. Dad has a new wife, and Mom was up from Florida with her boy friend. Out here Kevin couldn't get on a boat, and I couldn't even waitress. He did some under-the-table work: carpenter, mechanic, body work, a few days here, a few there. Now it's February, a short month.

'Hon,' he says behind me.

'It's three times.'

'Here. Let me do something for that eye.'

I hear him going to the ice chest, the ice moving in there to his big hands. I lay the bacon on the paper towel and open the door to pour out some of the grease; I look at the steps before I go out. The grease sizzles and pops on the wet grass, and there's light at the tops of the hills.

'Here,' he says, and I shut the door. I'm holding the skillet with a pot holder, and I see he's wearing his knife, and I think of all the weapons in a house: knives, cooking forks, ice picks, hammers, skillets, cleavers, wine bottles, and I wonder if I'll be one of those women. I think of this without fear, like I'm reading in the paper about somebody else dead in her kitchen. He touches my eye with ice wrapped in a dish towel.

'I have to do the eggs.'

I break them into the skillet and he stands behind me, holding the ice on my eye. His arm is over mine, and I bump it as I work the spatula.

'Not now,' I say.

I lower my face from the ice; for awhile he stands behind me, and I watch the eggs and listen to the grease and his breathing and the birds, then he goes to the chest and I hear the towel and ice drop in.

'After, okay?' he says. 'Maybe the swelling will go down. Jesus, Les. I wish I wasn't going.'

'The coffee's dripped.'

He pours two cups, takes his to the table, and sits with a cigarette. I know his mouth and throat are dry, and probably he has a headache. I turn the eggs and count to four, then put them on a plate with bacon. I haven't had a hangover since I was sixteen. He likes carbohydrates when he's hung over; I walk past him, putting the plate on the table, seeing his leg and arm and shoulder, but not his face, and get a can of pork and beans from the cupboard. From there I look at the back of his head. He has a bald spot the size of a quarter. Then I go to the stove and heat the beans on a high flame, watching them, drinking coffee and smoking.

'We'll get something,' he says between bites. 'They're out there.'

Once, before I met him, he was in the water with a swordfish. He had harpooned it and they were bringing it alongside, it was thrashing around in the water, and he tripped on some line and fell in with it.

'We'll get the lights back on,' he says. 'Go out on the town, buy you something nice. A sweater, a blouse, okay? But I wish I wasn't going today.'

'I wish you didn't hit me last night.' The juice in the beans is bubbling. 'And the two before that.'

'I'll tell you one thing, hon. I'll never get that drunk again. It's not even me anymore. I get drunk like that, and somebody crazy takes over.'

I go to his plate and scoop all the beans on his egg yellow. The coffee makes me pee, and I leave the flashlight and walk through the living room that smells of beer and ashtrays and is grey now, so I can see a beer can on the arm of a chair. I sit in the bathroom where it is darkest, and the seat is cold. I hear a car coming up the road, shifting down and turning into the driveway, then the horn. I wash my hands without looking in the mirror; in the gas light of the kitchen, and the first light from the sky, he's standing with his bag and harpoon.

'Oh, hon,' he says, and holds me tight. I put my arms around him, but just touching his back. 'Say it's okay.'

I nod, my forehead touching his chest, coming up, touching, coming up.

'That's my girl.'

He kisses me and puts his tongue in, then he's out the door, and I stand on the top step and watch him to the car. He waves and grins and gets in. I hold my hand up at the car as they back into the road, then are gone downhill past the house. The sun is showing red over the hills, and there's purple at their tops, and only a little green. They are always dry, but at night everything is wet.

I go through the living room and think about cleaning it, and open the front door and look out through the screen. The house has a shadow now, on the grass and dew. There are other houses up here, but I can't see any of them. The road goes winding up into the hills where the men hunted yesterday. I think of dressing and filling the canteen and walking, maybe all morning, I could make a sandwich and bring it in my jacket, and an orange. I open the screen and look up the road as far as I can see, before it curves around a hill in the sun. Blue is spreading across the sky. Soon the road will warm, and I think of rattlesnakes sleeping on it, and I shut the screen and look around the lawn where nothing moves.

THE CURSE

M ITCHELL HAYES WAS forty-nine years old, but when the cops left him in the bar with Bob, the manager, he felt much older. He did not know what it was like to be very old, a shrunken and wrinkled man, but he assumed it was like this: fatigue beyond relieving by rest, by sleep. He also was not a small man: his weight moved up and down in the hundred and seventies and he was five feet, ten inches tall. But now his body seemed short and thin. Bob stood at one end of the bar; he was a large black-haired man, and there was nothing in front of him but an ash tray he was using. He looked at Mitchell at the cash register and said: "Forget it. You heard what Smitty said."

Mitchell looked away, at the front door. He had put the chairs upside down on the table. He looked from the door past Bob to the empty space of floor at the rear; sometimes people danced there, to the jukebox. Opposite Bob, on the wall behind the bar, was a telephone; Mitchell looked at it. He had told Smitty there were five guys and when he moved to the phone one of them stepped around the corner of the bar and shoved him: one hand against Mitchell's chest, and it pushed him backward; he nearly fell. That was when they were getting rough with her at the bar. When they took her to the floor Mitchell looked once at her sounds, then looked down at the duckboard he stood on, or at the belly or chest of a young man in front of him.

He knew they were not drunk. They had been drinking before

they came to his place, a loud popping of motorcycles outside, then walking into the empty bar, young and sunburned and carrying helments and wearing thick leather jackets in August. They stood in front of Mitchell and drank drafts. When he took their first order he thought they were on drugs and later, watching them, he was certain. They were not relaxed, in the way of most drinkers near closing time. Their eyes were quick, alert as wary animals, and they spoke loudly, with passion, but their passion was strange and disturbing, because they were only chatting, bantering. Mitchell knew nothing of the effects of drugs, so could not guess what was in their blood. He feared and hated drugs because of his work and because he was the stepfather of teenagers: a boy and a girl. He gave last call and served them and leaned against the counter behind him.

Then the door opened and the girl walked in from the night, a girl he had never seen, and she crossed the floor toward Mitchell. He stepped forward to tell her she had missed last call, but before he spoke she asked for change for the cigarette machine. She was young, he guessed nineteen to twenty-one, and deeply tanned and had dark hair. She was sober and wore jeans and a dark blue tee shirt. He gave her the quarters but she was standing between two of the men and she did not get to the machine.

When it was over and she lay crying on the cleared circle of floor, he left the bar and picked up the jeans and tee shirt beside her and crouched and handed them to her. She did not look at him. She lay the clothes across her breasts and what Mitchell thought of now as her wound. He left her and dialled 911, then Bob's number. He woke up Bob. Then he picked up her sneakers from the floor and placed them beside her and squatted near her face, her crying. He wanted to speak to her and touch her, hold a hand or press her brow, but he could not.

The cruiser was there quickly, the siren coming east from town, then slowing and deepening as the car stopped outside. He was glad Smitty was one of them; he had gone to high school with Smitty. The other was Dave, and Mitchell knew him because it was a small town. When they saw the girl Dave went out to the cruiser to call for an ambulance, and when he came back he said two other cruisers had those scumbags and were taking them in. The girl was still crying and could not talk to Smitty and Dave. She was crying when a man and woman lifted her onto a stretcher and rolled her out the door and she vanished forever in a siren.

Bob came in while Smitty and Dave were sitting at the bar drinking coffee and Smitty was writing his report; Mitchell stood behind the bar. Bob sat next to Dave as Mitchell said: "I could have stopped them, Smitty."

"That's our job," Smitty said. "You want to be in the hospital now?"

Mitchell did not answer. When Smitty and Dave left, he got a glass of Coke from the cobra and had a cigarette with Bob. They did not talk. Then Mitchell washed his glass and Bob's cup and they left, turning off the lights. Outside Mitchell locked the front door, feeling the sudden night air after almost ten hours of air conditioning. When he had come to work the day had been very hot, and now he thought it would not have happened in winter. They had stopped for a beer on their way somewhere from the beach; he had heard them say that. But the beach was not the reason. He did not know the reason, but he knew it would not have happened in winter. The night was cool and now he could smell trees. He turned and looked at the road in front of the bar. Bob stood beside him on the small porch.

"If the regulars had been here," Bob said.

He turned and with his hand resting on the wooden rail he walked down the ramp to the ground. At his car he stopped and looked over its roof at Mitchell.

"You take it easy," he said.

Mitchell nodded. When Bob got in his car and left, he went down the ramp and drove home to his house on a street that he thought was neither good nor bad. The houses were small and there were old large houses used now as apartments for families. Most of the people had work, most of the mothers cared for their children, and most of the children were clean and looked like they lived in homes, not caves like some he saw in town. He worried about the older kids, one group of them anyway. They were idle. When he was a boy in a town farther up the Merrimack River, he and his friends committed every mischievous act he could recall on afternoons and nights when they were idle. His stepchildren were not part of that group. They had friends from the high school. The front porch light was on for him and one in the kitchen at the rear of the house.

He went in the front door and switched off the porch light and walked through the living and dining rooms to the kitchen. He got a can of beer from the refrigerator, turned out the light, and sat at the table. When he could see, he took a cigarette from Susan's pack in front of him.

Down the hall he heard Susan move on the bed then get up and he hoped it wasn't for the bathroom but for him. He had met her eight years ago when he had given up on ever marrying and having kids, then one night she came into the bar with two of her girl friends from work. She made six dollars an hour going to homes of invalids, mostly what she called her little old ladies, and bathing them. She got the house from her marriage, and child support the guy paid for a few months till he left town and went south. She came barefoot down the hall and stood in the kitchen doorway and said: "Are you all right?"

"No."

She sat across from him, and he told her. Very soon she held his hand. She was good. He knew if he had fought all five of them and was lying in pieces in a hospital bed she would tell him he had done the right thing, as she was telling him now. He liked her strong hand on his. It was a professional hand and he wanted from her something he had never wanted before: to lie in bed while she bathed him. When they went to bed he did not think he would be able to sleep, but she kneeled beside him and massaged his shoulders and rubbed his temples and pressed her hands on his forehead. He woke to the voices of Marty and Joyce in the kitchen. They had summer jobs, and always when they woke him he went back to sleep till noon, but now he got up and dressed and went to the kitchen door. Susan was at the stove, her back to him, and Marty and Joyce were talking and smoking. He said good morning, and stepped into the room.

"What are you doing up?" Joyce said.

She was a pretty girl with her mother's wide cheekbones and Marty was a tall good-looking boy, and Mitchell felt as old as he had before he slept. Susan was watching him. Then she poured him a cup of coffee and put it at his place and he sat. Marty said: "You getting up for the day?"

"Something happened last night. At the bar." They tried to conceal their excitement, but he saw it in their eyes. "I should have stopped it. I think I *could* have stopped it. That's the point. There were these five guys. They were on motorcycles but they weren't bikers. Just punks. They came in late, when everybody else had gone home. It was a slow night anyway. Everybody was at the beach."

"They rob you?" Marty said.

"No. A girl came in. Young. Nice looking. You know: just a girl, minding her business."

They nodded, and their eyes were apprehensive.

"She wanted cigarette change, that's all. Those guys were on dope. Coke or something. You know: they were flying in place."

"Did they rape her?" Joyce said.

"Yes, honey."

"The *fuck*ers."

Susan opened her mouth then closed it and Joyce reached quickly for Susan's pack of cigarettes. Mitchell held his lighter for her and said: "When they started getting rough with her at the bar I went for the phone. One of them stopped me. He shoved me, that's all. I should have hit him with a bottle."

Marty reached over the table with his big hand and held Mitchell's shoulder.

"No, Mitch. Five guys that mean. And coked up or whatever. No way. You wouldn't be here this morning."

"I don't know. There was always a guy with me. But just one guy, taking turns."

"Great," Joyce said. Marty's hand was on Mitchell's left shoulder; she put hers on his right hand.

"They took her to the hospital," he said. "The guys are in jail."

"They are?" Joyce said.

"I called the cops. When they left."

"You'll be a good witness," Joyce said.

He looked at her proud face.

"At the trial," she said.

The day was hot but that night most of the regulars came to the bar. Some of the younger ones came on motorcycles. They were a good crowd: they all worked, except the retired ones, and no one ever bothered the women, not even the young ones with their summer tans. Everyone talked about it: some had read the newspaper story, some had heard the story in town, and they wanted to hear it from Mitchell. He told it as often as they asked but he did not finish it because he was working hard and could not stay with any group of customers long enough.

He watched their faces. Not one of them, even the women, looked at him as if he had not cared enough for the girl, or was a coward. Many of them even appeared sympathetic, making him feel for moments that he was a survivor of something horrible, and when that feeling left him he was ashamed. He felt tired and old, making drinks and change, moving and talking up and down the bar. At the stool at the far end Bob drank coffee and whenever Mitchell looked at him he smiled or nodded and once raised his right fist, with the thumb up.

Reggie was drinking too much. He did that two or three times a month and Mitchell had to shut him off and Reggie always took it humbly. He was a big gentle man with a long brown beard. But tonight shutting off Reggie demanded from Mitchell an act of will, and when the eleven o'clock news came on the television and Reggie ordered another shot and a draft, Mitchell pretended not to hear him. He served the customers at the other end of the bar, where Bob was. He could hear Reggie calling: Hey Mitch; shot and a draft, Mitch. Mitchell was close to Bob now. Bob said softly: "He's had enough."

Mitchell nodded and went to Reggie, leaned closer to him so he could speak quietly, and said: "Sorry, Reggie. Time for coffee. I don't want you dead out there."

Reggie blinked at him.

"Okay, Mitch." He pulled some bills from his pocket and put them on the bar. Mitchell glanced at them and saw at least a ten dollar tip. When he rang up Reggie's tab the change was sixteen dollars and fifty cents, and he dropped the coins and shoved the bills into the beer mug beside the cash register. The mug was full of bills, as it was on most nights, and he kept his hand in there, pressing Reggie's into the others, and saw the sunburned young men holding her down on the floor and one kneeling between her legs, spread and held, and he heard their cheering voices and her screaming and groaning and finally weeping and weeping and weeping, until she was the siren crying then fading into the night. From the floor behind him, far across the room, he felt her pain and terror and grief, then her curse upon him. The curse moved into his back and spread down and up his spine, into his stomach and legs and arms and shoulders until he quivered with it. He wished he were alone so he could kneel to receive it.

SORROWFUL MYSTERIES

W HEN GERRY FONTENOT is five, six, and seven years old, he likes to ride in the car with his parents. It is a grey 1938 Chevrolet and it has a ration stamp on the windshield. Since the war started when Gerry was five, his father has gone to work on a bicycle, and rarely drives the car except to Sunday Mass, and to go hunting and fishing. Gerry fishes with him, from the bank of the bayou. They fish with bamboo poles, corks, sinkers, and worms, and catch perch and catfish. His father wears a .22 revolver at his side, for cottonmouths. In the fall Gerry goes hunting with him, crouches beside him in ditches bordering fields, and when the doves fly, his father stands and fires the twelve-gauge pump, and Gerry marks where the birds fall, then runs out into the field where they lie, and gathers them. They are soft and warm as he runs with them, back to his father. This is in southern Louisiana, and twice he and his father see an open truck filled with German prisoners, going to work in the sugar cane fields.

He goes on errands with his mother. He goes to grocery stores, dime stores, drugstores, and shopping for school clothes in the fall, and Easter clothes in the spring, and to the beauty parlor, where he likes to sit and watch the women. Twice a week he goes with her to the colored section, where they leave and pick up the week's washing and ironing. His mother washes at home too: the bed-clothes, socks, underwear, towels, and whatever else does not have to be ironed. She washes these in a wringer, and the way they come out flattened and drop into the basket. She hangs them on the clothesline in the backyard, and Gerry stands at the basket and hands them to her so she will not have to stoop. On rainy days she dries them inside on racks, which in winter she places in front of space heaters. She listens to the weather forecasts on the radio, and most of the time is able to wash on clear days.

The Negro woman washes the clothes that must be ironed, or starched and ironed. In front of the woman's unpainted wooden house, Gerry's mother presses the horn, and the large woman comes out and takes the basket from the back seat. Next day, at the sound of the horn, she brings out the basket. It is filled with ironed, folded skirts and blouses, and across its top lie dresses and shirts on hangers. Gerry opens the window his mother has told him to close as they approached the colored section with its dusty roads. He smells the clean, ironed clothes, pastels and prints, and his father's white and pale blue, and he looks at the rutted dirt road, the unpainted wood and rusted screens of the houses, old cars in front of them and tire swings hanging from trees over the worn and packed dirt yards, dozens of barefoot, dusty children stopping their play to watch him and his mother in the car, and the old slippers and dress the Negro woman wears, and he breathes her smell of sweat, looks at her black and brown hand crossing him to take the dollar from his mother's fingers.

On Fridays in spring and summer, Leonard comes to mow the lawn. He is a Negro, and has eight children, and Gerry sees him only once between fall and spring, when he comes on Christmas Eve, and Gerry's father and mother give him toys and clothes that Gerry and his three older sisters have outgrown, a bottle of bourbon, one of the fruit cakes Gerry's mother makes at Christmas, and five dollars. Leonard receives these at the back door, where on Fridays, in spring and summer, he is paid and fed. The Fontenots eat dinner at noon, and Gerry's mother serves Leonard a plate and a glass of iced tea with leaves from the mint she grows under the faucet behind the house. She calls him from the back steps, and he comes, wiping his brow with a bandanna, and takes his dinner to the shade of a sycamore tree. From his place at the dining room table, Gerry watches him sit on the grass and take off his straw hat; he eats, then rolls a cigarette. When he has smoked, he brings his plate and glass to the back door, knocks, and hands them to whoever answers. His glass is a jelly glass, his plate blue china, and his knife and fork stainless steel. From Friday to Friday the knife and fork lie at one side of a drawer, beside the compartments that hold silver; the glass is nearly out of reach, at the back of the second shelf in the cupboard for glasses; the plate rests under serving bowls in the china cupboard. Gerry's mother has told him and his sisters not to use them, they are Leonard's, and from Friday to Friday, they sit, and from fall to spring, and finally forever when one year Gerry is strong enough to push the lawn mower for his allowance, and Leonard comes only when Gerry's father calls him every Christmas Eve.

Before that, when he is eight, Gerry has stopped going on errands with his mother. On Saturday afternoons he walks or, on rainy days, rides the bus to town with neighborhood boys, to the movie theater where they watch westerns and the weekly chapter of a serial. He stands in line on the sidewalk, holding his quarter that will buy a ticket, a bag of popcorn, and, on the way home, an ice-cream soda. Opposite his line, to the right of the theater as you face it, are the Negro boys. Gerry does not look at them. Or not directly. he glances, he listens, as a few years later he will do with girls when he goes to movies that draw them. The Negroes enter through the door marked *Colored*, where he supposes a Negro woman sells tickets, then climb the stairs to the balcony, and Gerry wonders whether someone sells them popcorn and candy and drinks up there, or imagines them smelling all the bags of popcorn in the dark beneath them. Then he watches the cartoon and previews of next Saturday's movie, and he likes them but is waiting for the chapter of the serial whose characters he and his friends have played in their yards all week; they have worked out several escapes for the trapped hero and, as always, they are wrong. He has eaten his popcorn when the credits for the movie appear, then a tall man rides a beautiful black or white or palomino horse across the screen. The movie is black and white, but a palomino looks as golden and lovely as the ones he has seen in parades. Sitting in the dark, he is aware of his friends on both sides of him only as feelings coincident with his own: the excitement of becoming the Cisco Kid, Durango Kid, Red Ryder, the strongest and best-looking, the most courageous and good, the fastest with horse and fists and gun. Then it is over, the lights are on, he turns to his friends, flesh again, stands to leave, then remembers the Negroes. He blinks up at them standing at the balcony wall, looking down at the white boys pressed together in the aisle, moving slowly out of the theater. Sometimes his eyes meet those of a Negro boy, and Gerry smiles; only one ever smiles back.

In summer he and his friends go to town on weekday afternoons to see war movies, or to buy toy guns or baseballs, and when he meets Negroes on the sidewalk, he averts his eyes; but he watches them in department stores, bending over water fountains marked *Colored*, and when they enter the city buses and walk past him to the rear, he watches them, and during the ride he glances, and listens to their talk and laughter. One hot afternoon when he is twelve, he goes with a friend to deliver the local newspaper in the colored section. He has not been there since riding with his mother, who has not gone for years either; now the city buses stop near his neighborhood, and a Negro woman comes on it and irons the family's clothes in their kitchen. He goes that afternoon because his friend has challenged him. They have argued: they both have paper routes, and when his friend complained about his, Gerry said it was easy work. Sure, his friend said, you don't have to hold your breath. You mean when you collect? No, man, when I just ride through. So Gerry finishes his route, then goes with his friend: a bicycle ride of several miles ending, or beginning, at a neighborhood of poor whites, their houses painted but peeling, their screened front porches facing lawns so narrow that only small children can play catch in them; the older boys and girls play tapeball on the blacktop street. Gerry and his friends play that, making a ball of tape around a sock, and hitting with a baseball bat, but they have lawns big enough to contain them. Gerry's father teaches history at the public high school, and in summer is a recreation director for children in the city park, and some nights in his bed Gerry hears his father and mother worry about money; their voices are weary, and frighten him. But riding down this street, he feels shamefully rich, wants the boys and girls pausing in their game to know he only has a new Schwinn because he saved his money to buy it.

He and his friend jolt over the railroad tracks, and the blacktop ends. Dust is deep in the road. They ride past fields of tall grass and decaying things: broken furniture, space heaters, stoves, cars. Negro children are in the fields. Then they come to the streets of houses, turn onto the first one, a rutted and dusty road, and breathe the smell. It is as tangible as the dust a car raises to Gerry's face as

it bounces past him, its unmuffled exhaust pipe sounding like gun-
fire, and Gerry feels that he enters the smell, as you enter a cloud
of dust; and a hard summer rain, with lightning and thunder, would
settle it, and the air would smell of grass and trees. Its base is sour,
as though in the heat of summer someone has half-filled a garbage
can with milk, then dropped in citrus fruit and cooked rice and
vegetables and meat and fish, mattress ticking and a pillow, covered
it, and left it for a week in the July sun. In this smell children play
in the street and on the lawns that are dirt too, dust, save for strips
of crisp-looking yellowish grass in the narrow spaces between houses,
and scattered patches near the porches. He remembers the roads
and houses and yards from riding with his mother, but not the
smell, for even in summer they had rolled up the windows. Or
maybe her perfume and cigarettes had fortified the car against the
moment the laundry woman would open the back door, or reach
through the window for her dollar; but he wonders now if his mother
wanted the windows closed only to keep out dust. Women and men
sit on the front porches, as Gerry and his friend slowly ride up the
road, and his friend throws triangular-folded papers onto the yards,
where they skip in rising dust.

It is late afternoon, and he can smell cooking too: hot grease and
meat, turnip or mustard greens, and he hears talk and laughter from
the shaded porches. Everything seems to be dying: cars and houses
and tar paper roofs in the weather, grass in the sun, sparse oaks and
pines and weeping willows draw children and women with babies
to their shade; beneath the hanging tent of a willow, an old man
sits with two crawling children wearing diapers, and Gerry remembers Leonard eating in the shade of the sycamore. Gerry's father
still phones Leonard on Christmas Eve, and last year he went home
with the electric train Gerry has outgrown, along with toy soldiers
and cap pistols and Saturday serials and westerns, a growth that
sometimes troubles him: when he was nine and ten and saw that
other neighborhood boys stopped going to the Saturday movies
when they were twelve or thirteen, he could not understand why
something so exciting was suddenly not, and he promised himself
that he would always go on Saturdays, although he knew he would
not, for the only teenaged boy who did was odd and frightening:
he was about eighteen, and in his voice and eyes was the desperation
of a boy lying to a teacher, and he tried to sit between Gerry and

his friends, and once he did before they could close the gap, and all through the movie he tried to rub Gerry's thigh, and Gerry whispered *Stop it*, and pushed at the wrist, the fingers. So he knew a time would come when he would no longer love his heroes and their horses, and it saddened him to know that such love could not survive mere time. It did not, and that is what troubles him, when he wonders if his love of baseball and football and hunting and fishing and bicycles will die too, and wonders what he will love then.

He looks for Leonard as he rides down the road, where some yards are bordered with colored and clear bottles, half-buried with bottoms up to the sun. In others a small rectangle of flowers grows near the porch, and the smell seems to come from the flowers too, and the trees. He wants to enter one of those houses kept darkened with shades drawn against the heat, wants to trace and define that smell, press his nose to beds and sofas and floor and walls, the bosom of a woman, the chest of a man, the hair of a child. Breathing through his mouth, swallowing his nausea, he looks at his friend and sees what he knows is on his face as well: an expression of sustained and pallid horror.

On summer mornings the neighborhood boys play baseball. One of the fathers owns a field behind his house; he has mowed it with a tractor, and built a backstop of two-by-fours and screen, laid out an infield with a pitcher's mound, and put up foul poles at the edge of the tall weeds that surround the outfield. The boys play every rainless morning except Sunday, when all but the two Protestants go to Mass. They pitch slowly so they can hit the ball, and so the catcher, with only a mask, will not get hurt. But they pitch from a windup, and try to throw curves and knuckleballs, and sometimes they play other neighborhood teams who loan their catcher shin guards and chest protector, then the pitchers throw hard.

One morning a Negro boy rides his bicycle past the field, on the dirt road behind the backstop; he holds a fishing pole across the handlebars, and is going toward the woods beyond left field, and the bayou that runs wide and muddy through the trees. A few long innings later, he comes back without fish, and stops to watch the game. Standing, holding his bicycle, he watches two innings. Then, as Gerry's team is trotting in to bat, someone calls to the boy: Do you want to play? In the infield and outfield, and near home plate, voices stop. The boy looks at the pause, the silence, then nods, lowers his kickstand, and slowly walks onto the field.

'You're with us,' someone says. 'What do you play?'

'I like first.'

That summer, with eight dollars of his paper route money, Gerry has bought a first-baseman's glove: a Rawlings Trapper, because he liked the way it looked, and felt on his hand, but he is not a good first baseman: he turns his head away from throws that hit the dirt in front of his reaching glove and bounce toward his body, his face. He hands the glove to the boy.

'Use this. I ought to play second anyway.'

The boy puts his hand in the Trapper, thumps its pocket, turns his wrist back and forth, looking at the leather that is still a new reddish brown. Boys speak their names to him. His is Clay. They give him a place in the batting order, point to the boy he follows.

He is tall, and at the plate he takes a high stride and a long, hard swing. After his first hit, the outfield plays him deeply, at the edge of the weeds that are the boys' fence, and the infielders back up. At first base he is often clumsy, kneeling for ground balls, stretching before an infielder has thrown so that some balls nearly go past or above him; he is fearless, though, and none of the bouncing throws from third and deep short go past his body. He does not talk to any one boy, but from first he calls to the pitcher: *Come bube, come boy*; calls to infielders bent for ground balls: *Plenty time, plenty time, we got him*; and, to hitters when Gerry's team is at bat: *Good eye, good eye*. The game ends when the twelve o'clock whistle blows.

'That it?' Clay says as the fielders run in while he is swinging two bats on deck.

'We have to go eat,' the catcher says, taking off his mask, and with a dirt-smeared forearm wiping sweat from his brow.

'Me too,' he says, and drops the bats, picks up the Trapper, and hands it to Gerry. Gerry looks at it, lying across Clay's palm, looks at Clay's thumb on the leather.

'I'm a crappy first baseman,' he says. 'Keep it.'

'You kidding?'

'No. Go on.'

'What you going to play with?'

'My fielder's glove.'

Some of the boys are watching now; others are mounting bicycles on the road, riding away with gloves hanging from the handlebars, bats held across them.

'You don't want to play first no more?'

'No. Really.'

'Man, that's some *glove*. What's your name again?'

'Gerry,' he says, and extends his right hand. Clay takes it, and Gerry squeezes the big, limp hand; releases it.

'Gerry,' Clay says, looking down at his face as though to memorize it, or discern its features from among the twenty white faces of his morning.

'Good man,' he says, and turning, and calling goodbyes, he goes to his bicycle, places his fishing pole across the handlebars, hangs the Trapper from one, and rides quickly up the dirt road. Where the road turns to blacktop, boys are bicycling in a cluster, and Gerry watches Clay pass them with a wave. Then he is in the distance, among white houses with lawns and trees; is gone, leaving Gerry with the respectful voices of his friends, and peace and pride in his heart. He has attended a Catholic school since the first grade, so knows he must despise those feelings. He jokes about his play at first base, and goes with his Marty Marion glove and Ted Williams Louisville Slugger to his bicycle. But riding home, he nestles with his proud peace. At dinner he says nothing of Clay. The Christian Brothers have taught him that an act of charity can be canceled by the telling of it. Also, he suspects his family would think he is a fool.

A year later, a Negro man in a neighboring town is convicted of raping a young white woman, and is sentenced to die in the electric chair. His story is the front-page headline of the paper Gerry delivers, but at home, because the crime was rape, his mother tells the family she does not want any talk about it. Gerry's father mutters enough, from time to time, for Gerry to know he is angry and sad because if the woman had been a Negro, and the man white, there would have been neither execution nor conviction. But on his friends' lawns, while he plays catch or pepper or sits on the grass, whittling branches down to sticks, he listens to voluptuous voices from the porches, where men and women drink bourbon and talk of niggers and rape and the electric chair. The Negro's name is Sonny Broussard, and every night Gerry prays for his soul.

On the March night Sonny Broussard will die, Gerry lies in bed and says a rosary. It is a Thursday, a day for the Joyful Mysteries, but looking out past the mimosa, at the corner streetlight, he prays with the Sorrowful Mysteries, remembers the newspaper photographs of Sonny Broussard, tries to imagine his terror as midnight draws near—why midnight? and how could he live that day in his cell?—and sees Sonny Broussard on his knees in the Garden of Olives; he wears khakis, his arms rest on a large stone, and his face is lifted to the sky. Tied to a pillar and shirtless, he is silent under the whip; thorns pierce his head, and the fathers of Gerry's friends strike his face, their wives watch as he climbs the long hill, cross on his shoulder, then he is lying on it, the men with hammers are carpenters in khakis, squatting above him, sweat running down their faces to drip on cigarettes between their lips, heads cocked away from smoke; they swing the hammers in unison, and drive nails through wrists and crossed feet. Then Calvary fades and Gerry sees instead a narrow corridor between cells with a door at the end; two guards are leading Sonny Broussard to it, and Gerry watches them from the rear. They open the door to a room filled with people, save for a space in the center of their circle, where the electric chair waits. They have been talking when the guard opens the door, and they do not stop. They are smoking and drinking and knitting; they watch Sonny Broussard between the guards, look from him to each other, and back to him, talking, clapping a hand on a neighbor's shoulder, a thigh. The guards buckle Sonny Broussard into the chair. Gerry shuts his eyes, and tries to feel the chair, the straps, Sonny Broussard's fear; to feel so hated that the people who surround him wait for the very throes and stench of his death. Then he feels it, he is in the electric chair, and he opens his eyes and holds his breath against the scream in his throat.

Gerry attends the state college in town, and lives at home. He majors in history, and is in the Naval ROTC, and is grateful that he will spend three years in the Navy after college. He does not want to do anything with history but learn it, and he believes the Navy will give him time to know what he will do for the rest of his life. He also wants to go to sea. He thinks more about the sea than history; by Christmas he is in love, and thinks more about the girl than either of them. Near the end of the year, the college president calls an assembly and tells the students that, in the fall, colored boys and girls will be coming to the school. The president is a politician, and will later be lieutenant-governor. There will be no trouble at this college, he says. I do not want troops or federal marshals on my campus. If any one of you starts trouble, or even joins in on it if one of them starts it, I will have you in my office, and you'd best bring your luggage with you.

The day after his last examinations, Gerry starts working with a construction crew. In the long heat he carries hundred-pound bags of cement, shovels gravel and sand, pushes wheelbarrows of wet concrete, digs trenches for foundations, holes for septic tanks, has more money than he has ever owned, spends most of it on his girl in restaurants and movies and night clubs and bars, and by late August has gained fifteen pounds, most of it above his waist, though beneath that is enough for his girl to pinch, and call his Budweiser belt. Then he hears of Emmett Till. He is a Negro boy, and in the night two white men have taken him from his great-uncle's house in Mississippi. Gerry and his girl wait. Three days later, while Gerry sits in the living room with his family before supper, the news comes over the radio: a search party has found Emmett Till at the bottom of the Tallahatchie River; a seventy-pound cotton gin fan was tied to his neck with barbed wire; he was beaten and shot in the head, and was decomposing. Gerry's father lowers his magazine, removes his glasses, rubs his eyes, and says: 'Oh my Lord, it's happening again.'

He goes to the kitchen and Gerry hears him mixing another bourbon and water, then the back screen door opens and shuts. His mother and the one sister still at home are talking about Mississippi and rednecks, and the poor boy, and what were they thinking of, what kind of men *are* they? He wants to follow his father, to ask what memory or hearsay he had meant, but he does not believe he is old enough, man enough, to move into his father's silence in the backyard.

He phones his girl, and after supper asks his father for the car, and drives to her house. She is waiting on the front porch, and walks quickly to the car. She is a petite, dark-skinned Cajun girl, with fast and accented speech, deep laughter, and a temper that is fierce when it reaches the end of its long tolerance. Through generations the Fontenots' speech has slowed and softened, so that Gerry sounds more southern than French; she teases him about it, and often, when he is with her, he finds that he is talking with her rhythms and inflections. She likes dancing, rhythm and blues, jazz, gin, beer, Pall Malls, peppery food, and passionate kissing, with no fondling. She receives Communion every morning, wears a gold Sacred Heart medal on a gold chain around her neck, and wants to teach history in college. Her name is Camille Theriot.

They go to a bar, where people are dancing to the jukebox. The couples in booths and boys at the bar are local students, some still in high school, for in this town parents and bartenders ignore the law about drinking, and bartenders only use it at clubs that do not want young people. Gerry has been drinking at this bar since he got his driver's license when he was sixteen. He leads Camille to a booth, and they drink gin and tonics, and repeat what they heard at college, in the classroom where they met: that it was economic, and all the hatred started with slavery, the Civil War leaving the poor white no one about whom he could say: *At least I ain't a slave like him*, leaving him only: *At least I ain't a nigger*. And after the war the Negro had to be contained to provide cheap labor in the fields. Camille says it might explain segregation, so long as you don't wonder about rich whites who don't have to create somebody to look down on, since they can do it from birth anyway.

'So it doesn't apply,' she says.

'They never seem to, do they?'

'What?'

'Theories. Do you think those sonsabitches—do you think they tied that fan on before or after they shot him? Why barbed wire if he was already dead? Why not baling wire, or—'

The waitress is there, and he watches her lower the drinks, put their empty glasses on her tray; he pays her, and looks at Camille. Her face is lowered, her eyes closed.

Around midnight, when the crowd thins, they move to the bar. Three couples dance slowly to Sinatra; another kisses in a booth. Gerry knows they are in high school when the boy lights a cigarette and they share it: the girl draws on it, they kiss, and she exhales into his mouth; then the boy does it. Camille says: 'Maybe we should go north to college, and just stay there.'

'I hear the people are cold as the snow.'

'Me too. And they eat boiled food with some kind of white sauce.'

'You want some oysters?'

'Can we get there before they close?'

'Let's try it,' he says. 'Did you French-smoke in high school?'

'Sure.'

A boy stands beside Gerry and loudly orders a beer. He is drunk, and when he sees Gerry looking at him, he says: 'Woo. They *did* it to him, didn't they? 'Course now, a little nigger boy like that, you can't tell'—as Gerry stands so he can reach into his pocket— 'could be he'd go swimming with seventy pounds hanging on his neck, and a bullet in his head'—and Gerry opens the knife he keeps sharp for fish and game, looks at the blade, then turns toward the voice: 'Emmett *Till* rhymes with *kill*. Hoo. Hot*damn*. Kill *Till*—'

Gerry's hand bunches the boy's collar, turns him, and pushes his back against the bar. He touches the boy's throat with the point of the knife, and his voice comes yelling out of him; he seems to rise from the floor with it, can feel nothing of his flesh beneath it: 'You like *death? Feel* it!'

He presses the knife until skin dimples around its point. The boy is still, his mouth open, his eyes rolled to his left, where the knife is. Camille is screaming, and Gerry hears *Cut his tongue out! Cut his heart out*! Then she is standing in front of the boy, her arms waving, and Gerry hears *Bastard bastard bastard*, as he watches the boy's eyes and open mouth, then hears the bartender speaking softly: 'Take it easy now. You're Gerry, right?' He glances at the voice; the bartender is leaning over the bar. 'Easy, Gerry. You stick him there, he's gone. Why don't you go on home now, okay?'

Camille is quiet. Watching the point, Gerry pushes the knife, hardly a motion at all, for he is holding back too; the dimple, for an instant, deepens and he feels the boy's chest breathless and rigid beneath his left fist.

'Okay,' he says, and releases the boy's shirt, folds the knife, and takes Camille's arm. Boys at the bar and couples on the dance floor stand watching. There is music he cannot hear clearly enough to name. He and Camille walk between the couples to the door.

Two men, Roy Bryant and John William Milan, are arrested, and through hot September classes Gerry and Camille wait for the trial. Negroes sit together in classes, walk together in the corridors and across the campus, and surround juxtaposed tables in the student union, where they talk quietly, and do not play the jukebox. Gerry and Camille drink coffee and furtively watch them; in the classrooms and corridors, and on the grounds, they smile at Negroes, tell them hello, and get smiles and greetings. The Negro boys wear slacks and sport shirts, some of them with coats, some even with ties; the girls wear skirts or dresses; all of them wear polished shoes. There is no trouble. Gerry and Camille read the newspapers and listen to the radio, and at night after studying together they go to the bar and drink beer; the bartender is polite, even friendly, and does not mention the night of the knife. As they drink, then drive to Camille's house, they talk about Emmett Till, his story they have read and heard.

He was from Chicago, where he lived with his mother; his father died in France, in the Second World War. Emmett was visiting his great-uncle in Money, Mississippi. His mother said she told him to be respectful down there, because he didn't know about the South. One day he went to town and bought two cents' worth of bubble gum in Roy Bryant's store. Bryant's wife Carolyn, who is young and pretty, was working at the cash register. She said that when Emmett left the store and was on the sidewalk, he turned back to her and whistled. It was the wolf whistle, and that night Roy Bryant and his half-brother, John William Milan, went to the great-uncle's house with flashlights and a pistol, said *Where's that Chicago boy*, and took him.

The trial is in early fall. The defense lawyer's case is that the decomposed body was not Emmett Till; that the NAACP had put his father's ring on the finger of that body; and that the fathers of the jurors would turn in their graves if these twelve Anglo-Saxon men returned with a guilty verdict, which, after an hour and seven minutes of deliberation, they do not. That night, with Camille sitting so close that their bodies touch, Gerry drives on highways through farming country and cleared land with oil derricks and gas fires, and on bridges spanning dark bayous, on narrow blacktop roads twisting through lush woods, and gravel and dirt roads through rice fields whose canals shimmer in the moonlight. The windows are open to humid air whose rush cools his face.

When they want beer, he stops at a small country store; woods are behind it, and it is flanked by lighted houses separated by woods and fields. Oyster shells cover the parking area in front of the store. Camille will not leave the car. He crosses the wooden porch where bugs swarm at a yellow light, and enters: the store is lit by one ceiling light that casts shadows between shelves. A man and a woman stand at the counter, talking to a stout woman behind it. Gerry gets three six-packs and goes to the counter. They are only talking about people they know, and a barbecue where there was a whole steer on a spit, and he will tell this to Camille.

But in the dark outside the store, crunching on oyster shells, he forgets: he sees her face in the light from the porch, and wants to kiss her. In the car he does, kisses they hold long while their hands move on each others' backs. Then he is driving again. Twice he is lost, once on a blacktop road in woods that are mostly the conical silhouettes and lovely smell of pine, then on a gravel road through a swamp whose feral odor makes him pull the map too quickly from her hands. He stops once for gas, at an all-night station on a highway. Sweat soaks through his shirt, and it sticks to the seat, and he is warm and damp where his leg and Camille's sweat together. By twilight they are silent. She lights their cigarettes and opens their cans of beer; as the sun rises he is driving on asphalt between woods, the dark of their leaves fading to green, and through the insect-splattered windshield he gazes with burning eyes at the entrance to his town.

DELIVERING

J IMMY WOKE BEFORE the alarm, his parents' sounds
coming back to him as he had known they would
when finally three hours ago he knew he was about to sleep: their
last fight in the kitchen, and Chris sleeping through it on the top
bunk, grinding his teeth. It was nearly five now, the room sunlit;
in the dark while they fought Jimmy had waited for the sound of
his father's slap, and when it came he felt like he was slapping her
and he waited for it again, wished for it again, but there was only
the one clap of hand on face. Soon after that, she drove away.

Now he was ashamed of the slap. He reached down to his morning
hardness which always he had brought to the bathroom so she
wouldn't see the stain; he stopped once to turn off the alarm when
he remembered it was about to ring into his quick breath. Then he
stood and gently shook Chris's shoulder. He could smell the ocean.
He shook Chris harder: twelve years old and chubby and still clumsy
about some things. Maybe somebody else was Chris's father. No.
He would stay with what he heard last night; he would not start
making up more. Somewhere his mother was naked with that son
of a bitch, and he squeezed Chris's shoulder and said: 'Wake up.'
Besides, their faces looked alike: his and Chris's and his father's.
Everybody said that. Chris stared at him.

'Come with me.'

'You're crazy.'

'I need you to.'

'You didn't say anything last night.'

'Come on.'

'You buying the doughnuts?'

'After we swim.'

In the cool room they dressed for the warm sun, in cut-off jeans and T-shirts and sneakers, and went quietly down the hall, past the closed door where Jimmy stopped and waited until he could hear his father's breath. Last night after she left, his father cried in the kitchen. Chris stood in the doorway, looking into the kitchen; Jimmy looked over his head at the table, the beer cans, his father's bent and hers straight, the ashtray filled, ashes on the table and, on the counter near the sink, bent cans and a Seagram's Seven bottle.

'Holy shit,' Chris said.

'You'd sleep through World War III.'

He got two glasses from the cupboard, reaching over the cans and bottle, holding his breath against their smell; he looked at the two glasses in the sink, her lipstick on the rim of one, and Chris said: 'What's the matter?'

'Makes me sick to smell booze in the morning.'

Chris poured the orange juice and they drank with their backs to the table. Jimmy picked up her Winston pack. Empty. Shit. He took a Pall Mall. He had learned to smoke by watching her, had started three years ago by stealing hers. He was twelve then. Would he and Chris see her alone now, or would they have to go visit her at that son of a bitch's house, wherever it was? They went out the back door and around to the front porch where the stacked papers waited, folded and tied, sixty-two of them, and a note on top saying Mr. Thompson didn't get his paper yesterday. 'It's his Goddamn dog,' he said, and cut the string and gave Chris a handful of rubber bands. Chris rolled and banded the papers while Jimmy stood on the lawn, smoking; he looked up the road at the small houses, yellow and brown and grey, all of them quiet with sleeping families, and the tall woods beyond them and, across the road, houses whose back lawns ended at the salt marsh that spread out to the northeast where the breeze came from. When he heard the rolling papers stop, he turned to Chris sitting on the porch and looking at him.

'Where's the car?'

'Mom took it.'

'This early?'

He flicked the cigarette toward the road and kneeled on the porch and started rolling.

'Where'd she go so early?'

'Late. Let's go.'

He trotted around the lawn and pushed up the garage door and went around the pickup; he did not look at Chris until he had unlocked the chain and pulled it from around the post, coiled it under his bicycle seat, and locked it there. His hands were ink-stained.

'You can leave your chain. We'll use mine at the beach.'

He took the canvas sack from its nail on the post and hung it from his right side, its strap over his left shoulder, and walked his bicycle past the truck and out into the sun. At the front porch he stuffed the papers into the sack. Then he looked at Chris.

'We're not late,' Chris said.

'She left late. Late last night.' He pushed down his kickstand. 'Hold on. Let's get these papers out.'

'She left?'

'Don't you start crying on me. Goddamnit, don't.'

Chris looked down at his handlebar.

'They had a fight,' Jimmy said.

'Then she'll be back.'

'Not this time. She's fucking somebody.'

Chris looked up, shaking his head. Shaking it, he said: 'No.'

'You want to hear about it or you just going to stand there and tell me I didn't hear what I heard.'

'Okay, tell me.'

'Shit. I was going to tell you at the beach. Wait, okay?'

'Sixty-two papers?'

'You know she's gone. Isn't that enough for a while?' He kicked up his stand. 'Look. We've hardly ever lived with both of them. It'll be like Pop's aboard ship. Only it'll be her.'

'That's not true.'

'What's not.'

'About hardly ever living with both of them.'

'It almost is. Let's go.'

Slowly across the grass, then onto the road, pumping hard, shifting gears, heading into the breeze and sun, listening for cars to their rear, sometimes looking over his shoulder at the road and Chris's

face, the sack bumping his right thigh and sliding forward but he
kept shoving it back, keeping the rhythm of his pedalling and his
throws: the easy ones to the left, a smooth motion across his chest
like second to first, snapping the paper hard and watching it drop
on the lawn; except for the people who didn't always pay on time
or who bitched at him, and he hit their porches or front doors, a
good hard sound in the morning quiet. He liked throwing to his
right better. The first week or so he had cheated, had angled his
bicycle toward the houses and thrown overhand; but then he stopped
that, and rode straight, leaning back and throwing to his right,
sometimes having to stop and leave his bicycle and get a paper from
under a bush or a parked car in the driveway, but soon he was
hitting the grass just before the porch, unless it was a house that
had a door or wall shot coming, and he could do that with velocity
too. Second to short. He finished his road by scaring himself, hitting
Reilly's big front window instead of the wall beside it, and it shook
but didn't break and when he turned his bicycle and headed back
he grinned at Chris, who still looked like someone had just punched
him in the mouth.

He went left up a climbing road past a pine grove, out of its shade
into the warmth on his face: a long road short on customers, twelve
of them scattered, and he rode faster, thinking of Chris behind him,
pink-cheeked, breathing hard. Ahead on the right he saw Thompson's collie waiting on the lawn, and he pulled out a paper and
pushed the sack behind his leg, then rose from the seat pumping
toward the house, sitting as he left the road and bounced on earth
and grass: he threw the paper thumping against the open jaws, his
front tire gazing the yelping dog as it scrambled away, and he lightly
hand-braked for his turn then sped out to the road again. He threw
two more to his left and started up a long steep hill for the last of
the route: the road cut through woods, in shade now, standing, the
bicycle slowing as the hill steepened near the hardest house of all:
the Claytons' at the top of the hill, a pale green house with a deep
front lawn: riding on the shoulder, holding a paper against the
handlebar, standing, his legs hot and tight, then at the top he sat
to throw, the bicycle slowing, leaning, and with his left hand he
moved the front wheel from side to side while he twisted to his
right and cocked his arm and threw; he stood on the pedals and
gained balance and speed before the paper landed sliding on the

walk. The road wound past trees and fifteen customers and twice that many houses. He finished quickly. Then he got off his bicycle, sweating, and folded the sack and put it in his orange nylon saddlebag, and they started back, Chris riding beside him.

From one house near the road he smelled bacon. At another he saw a woman at the kitchen window, her head down, and he looked away. Some of the papers were inside now. At Clayton's house he let the hill take him down into the shade to flat land and, Chris behind him now, he rode past the wide green and brown salt marsh, its grass leaning with the breeze that was cool and sea-tanged on his face, moving the hair at his ears. There were no houses. A fruit and vegetable stand, then the bridge over the tidal stream: a quick blue flow, the tide coming in from the channel and cove beyond a bend to the north, so he could not see them, but he knew how the cove looked this early, with green and orange charter boats tied at the wharves. An hour from now, the people would come. He and Chris and his father went a few afternoons each summer, with sandwiches and soft drinks and beer in the ice chest, and his father drank steadily but only a six-pack the whole afternoon, and they stood abreast at the rail, always near the bow, the boat anchored a mile or two out, and on lucky days filled a plastic bag with mackerel slapping tails till they died, and on unlucky ones he still loved the gentle rocking of the boat and the blue sea and the sun warmly and slowly burning him. Twice in late summer they had bottom-fished and pulled up cusks from three hundred feet, tired arm turning the reel, cusk breaking the surface with eyes pushed outward and guts in its mouth. His mother had gone once. She had not complained, had pretended to like it, but next time she told them it was too much sun, too smelly, too long. Had she been with that son of a bitch when they went fishing again? The boats headed in at five and his father inserted a cleaning board into a slot in the gunwale and handed them slick cool mackerel and he and Chris cleaned them and threw their guts and heads to the sea gulls that hovered and cried and dived until the boat reached the wharf. Sometimes they could make a gull come down and take a head from their fingers.

They rode past beach cottages and up a one-block street to the long dune that hid the sea, chained their bicycles to a telephone pole, and sprinted over loose sand and up the dune; then walking, looking at the empty beach and sea and breakers, stopping to take off sneakers and shirts, Jimmy stuffing his three bills into a sneaker, then running onto wet hard sand, into the surf cold on his feet and ankles, Chris beside him, and they both shouted at once, at the cold but to the sea as well, and ran until the water pushed at their hips and they walked out toward the sea and low sun, his feet hurting in the cold. A wave came and they turned their backs to it and he watched over his shoulder as it rose; when it broke they dived and he was riding it fast, swallowing water, and in that instant of old sea-panic he saw his father crying; he opened his eyes to the sting, his arms stretched before him, hands joined, then he was lying on the sand and the wave was gone and he stood shouting: 'All *right*.' They ran back into the sea and body-surfed until they were too cold, then walked stiffly up to higher sand. He lay on his back beside his clothes, looked at the sky; soon people would come with blankets and ice chests. Chris lay beside him. He shut his eyes.

'I was listening to the ball game when they came home. With the ear plug. They won, three to two. Lee went all the way. Rice drove in two with a double—' Bright field and uniforms under the lights in Oakland, him there too while he lay on his bunk, watching Lee working fast, Remy going to his left and diving to knock it down, on his knees for the throw in time when they came in talking past the door and down the hall to the kitchen—'They talked low for a long time; that's when they were drinking whiskey and mostly I just heard Pop getting ice, then I don't know why but after a while I knew it was trouble, all that ice and quiet talk and when they popped cans I figured they'd finished the whiskey and they were still talking that way so I started listening. She had already told him. That's what they were talking about. Maybe she told him at the Chief's Club. She was talking nice to him—'

'What did she say?'

'She said—shit—' He opened his eyes to the blue sky, closed them again, pressed his legs into the warm sand, listened to the surf. 'She said I've tried to stop seeing him. She said Don't you believe I've tried? You think I want to hurt you? You know what it's like. I can't stop. I've tried and I can't. I wish I'd never met him. But I can't keep lying and sneaking around. And Pop said Bullshit: you mean you can't keep living here when you want to be fucking him. They didn't say anything for a minute and they popped two more cans, then she said You're right. But maybe I don't have to leave. Maybe if you'd just let me go to him when I wanted to. That's when he started yelling at her. They went at it for a long time, and I thought you'd wake up. I turned the game up loud as I could take it but it was already the ninth, then it was over, and I couldn't stop hearing them anyway. She said Jason would never say those things to her, that's all I know about that son of a bitch, his name is Jason and he's a civilian somewhere and she started yelling about all the times Pop was aboard ship he must have had a lot of women and who did he think he was anyway and she'd miss you and me and it broke her heart how much she'd miss you and me but she had to get out from under his shit, and he was yelling about she was probably fucking every day he was at sea for the whole twenty years and she said You'll never know you bastard you can just think about it for another twenty. That's when he slapped her.'

'Good.'

'Then she cried a little, not much, then they drank some more beer and talked quiet again. He was trying to make up to her, saying he was sorry he hit her and she said it was her fault, she shouldn't have said that, and she hadn't fucked anybody till Jason—'

'She said that?'

'What.'

'Fuck.'

'Yes. She was talking nice to him again, like he was a little kid, then she went to their room and packed a suitcase and he went to the front door with her, and I couldn't hear what they said. She went outside and he did too and after she drove off he came back to the kitchen and drank beer.' He raised his head and looked past his feet at a sea gull bobbing on the water beyond the breakers. 'Then he cried for a while. Then he went to bed.'

'He did?'

'Yes.'

'I've never heard him cry.'

'Me neither.'

'Why didn't you wake me up?'

'What for?'

'I don't know. I wish you had.'

'I did. This morning.'

'What's going to happen?'

'I guess she'll visit us or something.'

'What if they send Pop to sea again and we have to go live with her and that guy?'

'Don't be an asshole. He's retiring and he's going to buy that boat and we'll fish like bastards. I'm going to catch a big fucking tuna and sell it to the Japanese and buy you some weights.'

He squeezed Chris's bicep and rose, pulling him up. Chris turned his face, looking up the beach. Jimmy stepped in front of him, still holding his arm.

'Look: I heard Pop cry last night. For a long time. Loud. That's all the fucking crying I want to hear. Now let's take another wave and get some doughnuts.'

They ran into the surf, wading coldly to the wave that rose until there was no horizon, no sea, only the sky beyond it.

Dottie from tenth grade was working the counter, small and summer-brown.

'Wakefield boys are here,' Jimmy said. 'Six honey dip to go.'

He only knew her from math and talking in the halls, but the way she smiled at him, if it were any other morning, he would stay and talk, and any other day he would ask her to meet him in town tonight and go on some of the rides, squeeze her on the roller coaster, eat pizza and egg rolls at the stands, get somebody to buy them a six-pack, take it to the beach. He told her she was foxy, and got a Kool from her. Cars were on the roads now, but so many that they were slow and safe, and he and Chris rode side by side on the shoulder; Chris held the doughnut bag against the handlebar and ate while Jimmy smoked, then he reached over for the bag and ate his three. When they got near the house it looked quiet. They chained their bicycles in the garage and crept into the kitchen and past the closed door, to the bathroom. In the shower he pinched Chris's gut and said: 'No shit, we got to work on that.'

They put on gym shorts and sneakers and took their gloves and ball to the backyard.

'When we get warmed up I'm going to throw at your face, okay?'

'Okay.'

'You're still scared of it there and you're ducking and you'll get hurt that way.'

The new baseball smooth in his hand and bright in the sun,

smacking in Chris's glove, coming back at him, squeezed high in the pocket and webbing; then he heard the back door and held the ball and watched his father walking out of the shade into the light. He squinted at his father's stocky body and sunburned face and arms, his rumpled hair, and motioned to Chris and heard him trotting on the grass. He was nearly as tall as his father, barely had to tilt his head to look into his eyes. He breathed the smell of last night's booze, this morning's sleep.

'I heard you guys last night,' he said. 'I already told him.'

His father's eyes shifted to Chris, then back.

'She'll come by tomorrow, take you boys to lunch.' He scratched his rump, looked over his shoulder at the house, then at Jimmy. 'Maybe later we'll go eat some lobsters. Have a talk.'

'We could cook them here,' Chris said.

'Sure. Steamers too. Okay: I'll be out in a minute.'

They watched him walk back to the house, then Jimmy touched Chris, gently pushed him, and he trotted across the lawn. They threw fly balls and grounders and one-hop throws from the outfield and straight ones to their bare chests, calling to each other, Jimmy listening to the quiet house too, seeing it darker in there, cooler, his father's closet where in a corner behind blue and khaki uniforms the shotgun leaned. He said, 'Here we go,' and threw at Chris's throat, then face, and heard the back door; his breath quickened, and he threw hard: the ball grazed the top of Chris's glove and struck his forehead and he bent over, his bare hand rubbing above his eye, then he was crying deeply and Jimmy turned to his running father, wearing his old glove, hair wet and combed, smelling of after-shave lotion, and said: 'He's all right, Pop. He's all right.'

ADULTERY

. . . love is a direction and not a state of the soul.
Simone Weil, *Waiting on God*

to Gina Berriault

W HEN THEY HAVE finished eating Edith tells Sharon
to clear the table then brush her teeth and put on
her pajamas; she brings Hank his coffee, then decides she can have
a cup too, that it won't keep her awake because there is a long
evening ahead, and she pours a cup for herself and returns to the
table. When Sharon has gone upstairs Edith says: 'I'm going to
see Joe.'

Hank nods, sips his coffee, and looks at his watch. They have
been silent during most of the meal but after her saying she is going
to see Joe the silence is uncomfortable.

'Do you have to work tonight?' she says.

'I have to grade a few papers and read one story. But I'll read to
Sharon first.'

Edith looks with muted longing at his handlebar moustache, his
wide neck, and thick wrists. She is lighting a cigarette when Sharon
comes downstairs in pajamas.

'Daddy quit,' Sharon says, 'Why don't you quit?'

Edith smiles at her, and shrugs.

'I'm going out for awhile,' she says. 'To see a friend.'

Sharon's face straightens with quick disappointment that borders
on an angry sense of betrayal.

'What friend?'

'Terry,' Edith says.

'Why can't she come here?'

'Because Daddy has work to do and we want to talk.'
'I'll read to you,' Hank says.
Sharon's face brightens.
'What will you read?'
'Kipling.'
' "Rikki-Tikki-Tavi "?'
'Yes: "Rikki-Tikki-Tavi." '

She is eight and Edith wonders how long it will be before Sharon senses and understands that other presence or absence that Edith feels so often when the family is together. She leaves the table, puts the dishes and pots in the dishwasher, and turns it on. She is small and slender and she is conscious of her size as she puts on her heavy coat. She goes to the living room and kisses Hank and Sharon, but she does not leave through the front door. She goes to the kitchen and takes from the refrigerator the shrimp wrapped in white paper; she goes out the back door, into the dark. A light snow has started to fall.

It is seven-thirty. She has told Joe not to eat until she gets there, because she wants to cook shrimp scampi for him. She likes cooking for Joe, and she does it as often as she can. Wreathed in the smells of cooking she feels again what she once felt as a wife: that her certain hands are preparing a gift. But there were times, in Joe's kitchen, when this sense of giving was anchored in vengeful images of Hank, and then she stood in the uncertainty and loss of meaningless steam and smells. But that doesn't happen anymore. Since Joe started to die, she has been certain about everything she does with him. She has not felt that way about anyone, even Sharon, for a long time.

The snow is not heavy but she drives slowly, cautiously, through town. It is a small town on the Merrimack River, and tonight there are few cars on the road. Leaving town she enters the two-lane country road that will take her to Joe. She tightens her seat belt, turns on the radio, lights a cigarette, and knows that none of these measures will slow the tempo of her heart. The road curves through pale meadows and dark trees and she is alone on it. Then there are houses again, distanced from each other by hills and fields, and at the third one, its front porch lighted, she turns into the driveway. She turns on the interior light, looks at her face in the rearview mirror, then goes up the shovelled walk, her face lowered from the snow, and for a moment she sees herself as Joe will see her coming inside with cheeks flushed and droplets in her long black hair. Seeing herself that way, she feels loved. She is thirty years old.

When Joe opens the door she feels the awkward futility of the shrimp in her hand. She knows he will not be able to eat tonight. He has lost thirty pounds since the night last summer when they got drunk and the next day he was sick and the day after and the day after, so that finally he could not blame it on gin and he went to a doctor and then to the hospital where a week later they removed one kidney with its envelope of cancer that had already spread upward. During the X-ray treatments in the fall, five days a week for five weeks, with the square drawn in purple marker on his chest so the technician would know where to aim, he was always nauseated. But when the treatments were finished there were nights when he could drink and eat as he used to. Other nights he could not. Tonight is one of those: above his black turtleneck the pallor of his face is sharpened; looking from that flesh his pale blue eyes seem brighter than she knows they are. His forehead is moist; he is forty years old, and his hair has been grey since his mid-thirties. He holds her, but even as he squeezes her to him, she feels him pulling his body back from the embrace, so she knows there is pain too. Yet still he holds her tightly so his pulling away causes only a stiffening of his torso while his chest presses against her. She remembers the purple square and is glad it is gone now. She kisses him.

'I'm sorry about the shrimp,' he says. 'I don't think I can eat them.'

'It's all right; they'll keep.'

'Maybe tomorrow.'

'Maybe so.'

The apartment is small, half of the first floor of a small two-story house, and it is the place of a man who since his boyhood has not lived with a woman except housekeepers in rectories. The front room where they are standing, holding each other lightly now like dancers, is functional and, in a masculine disorderly way, orderly; it is also dirty. Fluffs of dust have accumulated on the floor. Edith decides to bring over her vacuum cleaner tomorrow. She puts her coat on a chair and moves through the room and down the short hall toward the kitchen; as she passes his bedroom she glances at the bed to see if he rested before she came; if he did, he has concealed it: the spread is smooth. She wonders how he spent his day, but she is afraid to ask. The college is still paying him, though someone else is teaching his philosophy courses that he started in the fall and had to quit after three days. She puts the shrimp in the refrigerator; always, since they were first lovers, when she looks in his refrigerator she feels a tenderness whose edges touch both amusement and pathos. The refrigerator is clean, it has four ice trays, and it holds only the makings of breakfast and cocktail hour. Behind her he is talking: this afternoon he took a short walk in the woods; he sat on a log and watched a cock pheasant walking across a clearing, its feathers fluffed against the cold. The land is posted and pheasants live there all winter. After the walk he tried to read Unamuno but finally he listened to Rachmaninoff and watched the sun setting behind the trees.

While he gets ice and pours bourbon she looks around the kitchen for signs. In the dish drainer are a bowl, a glass, and a spoon and she hopes they are from lunch, soup and milk, but she thinks they are from breakfast. He gives her the drink and opens a can of beer for himself. When he feels well he drinks gin; once he told her he'd always loved gin and that's why he'd never been a whiskey priest.

'Have you eaten since breakfast?'

'No,' he says, and his eyes look like those of a liar. Yet he and Edith never lie to each other. It is simply that they avoid the words cancer and death and time, and when they speak of his symptoms they are looking at the real words like a ghost between them. At the beginning she saw it only in his eyes: while he joked and smiled his eyes saw the ghost and she did too, and she felt isolated by her health and hope. But gradually, as she forced herself to look at his eyes, the ghost became hers too. It filled his apartments: she looked through it at the food she cooked and they ate; she looked through it at the drinks she took from his hand; it was between them when they made love in the dark of the bedroom and afterward when she lay beside him and her eyes adjusted to the dark and discerned the outlines and shapes of the chest of drawers against the wall at the foot of the bed and, hanging above it, the long black crucifix, long enough to hang in the classroom of a parochial school, making her believe Joe had taken with him from the priesthood a crucifix whose size would assert itself on his nights. When they went to restaurants and bars she looked through the ghost at other couples;

it delineated these people, froze their gestures in time. One night, looking in his bathroom mirror, she saw that it was in her own eyes. She wondered what Joe's eyes saw when they were closed, in sleep.

'You should eat,' she says.

'Yes.'

'Do you have something light I could fix?'

'My body.' He pats his waist; he used to have a paunch; when he lost the weight he bought clothes and now all his slacks are new.

'Your head will be light if you take walks and don't eat and then drink beer.'

He drinks and smiles at her.

'Nag.'

'Nagaina. She's the mother cobra. In 'Rikki-Tikki-Tavi.' Would you eat some soup?'

'I would. I was wondering first—' (His eyes start to lower but he raises them again, looks at her) '—if you'd play trainer for a while. Then maybe I'd take some soup.'

'Sure. Go lie down.'

She gets the heating ointment from the medicine cabinet in the bathroom; it lies beside the bottle of sleeping pills. On the shelf beneath these are his shaving cream, razor, after-shave lotion, and stick deodorant. The juxtaposition disturbs her, and for a moment she succumbs to the heavy weariness of depression. She looks at her hand holding the tube of ointment. The hand does not seem to be hers; or, if it is, it has no function, it is near atrophy, it can touch no one. She lowers the hand out of her vision, closes the cabinet door, and looks at herself in the mirror. She is pretty. The past three years show in her face, but still she is pretty and she sips her drink and thinks of Joe waiting and her fingers caress the tube.

In the bedroom Joe is lying on his back, with his shirt off. The bedside lamp is on. He rolls on his belly and turns his face on the pillow so he can watch her. She lights him a cigarette then swallows the last of her bourbon and feels it. Looking at his back she unscrews the cap from the tube; his flesh is pale and she wishes it were summer so she could take him to the beach and lie beside him and watch his skin assume a semblance of health. She squeezes ointment onto her fingers and gently rubs it into the flesh where his kidney used to be. She is overtaken by a romantic impulse which means nothing in the face of what they are facing: she wishes there were no cancer but that his other kidney was in danger and he needed hers and if only he had hers he would live. Her hands move higher on his back. He lies there and smokes, and they do not talk. The first time she rubbed his back they were silent because he had not wanted to ask her to but he had anyway; and she had not wanted to do it but she had, and her flesh had winced as she touched him, and he had known it and she had known that he did. After that, on nights when she sensed his pain, or when he told her about it, she rose from the bed and got the ointment and they were silent, absorbing the achieved intimacy of her flesh. Now his eyes are closed and she watches his face on the pillow and feels what she is heating with her anointed hands.

When she is done she warms a can of vegetable soup and toasts a slice of bread. As she stirs the soup she feels him watching from the table behind her. He belches and blames it on the beer and she turns to him and smiles. She brings him the bowl of soup, the toast, and a glass of milk. She puts ice in her glass and pours bourbon, pouring with a quick and angry turning of the wrist that is either defiant or despairing—she doesn't know which. She sits with him. She would like to smoke but she knows it bothers him while he is eating so she waits. But he does not finish the soup. He eats some of the toast and drinks some of the milk and pretends to wait for the soup to cool; under her eyes he eats most of the soup and finishes the toast and is lifting a spoonful to his mouth when his face is suffused with weariness and resignation which change as quickly to anger as he shakes his head and lowers the spoon, his eyes for a moment glaring at her (but she knows it isn't her he sees) before he pushes back from the table and moves fast out of the kitchen and down the hall. She follows and is with him when he reaches the toilet and standing behind him she holds his waist with one arm and his forehead with her hand. They are there for a long time and she doesn't ask but knows he was here after breakfast and perhaps later in the day. She thinks of him alone retching and quivering over the toilet. Still holding his waist she takes a washcloth from the towel rack and reaches to the lavatory and dampens it; she presses it against his forehead. When he is finished she walks with him to the bedroom, her arm around his waist, his around her shoulder, and she pulls back the covers while he undresses. The telephone is on the bedside table. He gets into bed and she covers him then turning her back to him she dials her home. When Hank answers she says: 'I might stay a while.'

'How is he?'

She doesn't answer. She clamps her teeth and shuts her eyes and raising her left hand she pushes her hair back from her face and quickly wipes the tears from beneath her eyes.

'Bad?' Hank says.

'Yes.'

'Stay as long as you want,' he says. His voice is tender and for a moment she responds to that; but she has been married to him for eight years and known him for the past three and the moment passes; she squeezes the phone and wants to hit him with it.

She goes to the kitchen, the bathroom, and the living room, getting her drink and turning out lights. Joe is lying on his belly with his eyes closed. She undresses, hoping he will open his eyes and see her; she is the only woman he has ever made love with and always he has liked watching her undress; but he does not open his eyes. She turns out the lamp and goes around the bed and gets in with her drink. Propped on a pillow she finishes it and lowers the glass to the floor as he holds her hand. He remains quiet and she can feel him talking to her in his mind. She moves closer to him, smelling mouthwash and ointment, and she thinks of the first time they made love and the next day he bought a second pillow and two satin pillowcases and that night showing them to her he laughed and said he felt like Gatsby with his shirts. She said: Don't make me into that Buchanan bitch; I don't leave bodies in the road. Months later when she went to the hospital to see him after the operation she remembered what she had said. Still, and strangely, there is a sad but definite pleasure remembering him buying the pillow and two satin pillowcases.

Suddenly he is asleep. It happens so quickly that she is afraid. She listens to his slow breath and then, outstretched beside him, touching as much of the length of his body as she can, she closes her eyes and prays to the dark above her. She feels that her prayers do not ascend, that they disseminate in the dark beneath the ceiling. She does not use words, for she cannot feel God above the bed. She prays with images: she sees Joe suffering in a hospital bed with tubes in his body and she does not want him to suffer. So finally her prayer is an image of her sitting beside this bed holding his hand while, gazing at her peacefully and without pain, he dies. But this doesn't touch the great well of her need and she wishes she could know the words for all of her need and that her statement would rise through and beyond the ceiling, up beyond the snow and stars, until it reached an ear. Then listening to Joe's breathing she begins to relax, and soon she sleeps. Some time in the night she is waked by his hands. He doesn't speak. His breath is quick and he kisses her and enters with a thrust she receives; she feels him arcing like Icarus, and when he collapses on her and presses his lips to her throat she knows she holds his entire history in her body. It has been a long time since she has felt this with a man. Perhaps she never has.

II

ALL SHE HAD ever wanted to be was a nice girl someone would want to marry. When she married Hank Allison she was twenty-two years old and she had not thought of other possibilities. Husbands died, but one didn't think of that. Marriages died too: she had seen enough corpses and heard enough autopsies in Winnetka (the women speaking, sipping their drinks, some of them afraid, some fascinated as though by lust; no other conversation involved them so; Edith could feel flesh in the room, pores, blood, as they spoke of what had destroyed or set free one of their kind); so she knew about the death of love as she knew about breast cancer. And, just as she touched and explored her breasts, she fondled her marriage, stroked that space of light and air that separated her from Hank.

He was her first lover; they married a year earlier than they had planned because she was pregnant. From the time she missed her first period until she went to the gynecologist she was afraid and Hank was too; every night he came to her apartment and the first thing he asked was whether she had started. Then he drank and talked about his work and the worry left his eyes. After she had gone to the doctor she was afraid for another week or so; Hank's eyes pushed her further into herself. But after a while he was able to joke about it. We should have done it right, he said—gone to the senior prom and made it in the car. He was merry and resilient. In her bed he grinned and said the gods had caught up with him for all the times he'd screwed like a stray dog.

When she was certain Hank did not feel trapped she no longer felt trapped, and she became happy about having a child. She phoned her parents. They seemed neither alarmed nor unhappy. They liked Hank and, though Edith had never told them, she knew they had guessed she and Hank were lovers. She drove up to Winnetka to plan the wedding. While her father was at work or gone to bed she had prenatal conversations with her mother. They spoke of breast-feeding, diet, smoking, natural childbirth, saddleblocks. Edith didn't recognize the significance of these conversations until much later, in her ninth month. They meant that her marriage had begun at the moment when she was first happy about carrying a child. She was no longer Hank's lover; she was his wife. What had been clandestine and sweet and dark was now open; the fruit of that intimacy was shared with her mother. She had begun to nest. Before the wedding she drove back to Iowa City, where Hank was a graduate student, and found and rented a small house. There was a room where Hank could write and there was a room for the baby, as it grew older. There was a back yard with an elm tree. She had money from her parents, and spent a few days buying things to put in the house. People delivered them. It was simple and comforting.

In her ninth month, looking back on that time, she began to worry about Hank. Her life had changed, had entered a trajectory of pregnancy and motherhood; his life had merely shifted to the side, to make more room. But she began to wonder if he had merely shifted. Where was he, who was he, while she talked with her mother, bought a washing machine, and felt the baby growing inside her? At first she worried that he had been left out, or anyway felt left out; that his shifting aside had involved enormous steps. Then at last she worried that he had not shifted at all but, for his own survival, had turned away.

She became frightened. She remembered how they had planned marriage: it would come when he finished school, got a job. They used to talk about it. Hank lived in one room of an old brick building which was owned by a cantankerous and colorful old man who walked with the assistance of a stout, gnarled, and threatening cane; like most colorful people, he knew he was and he used that quality, in his dealings with student-tenants, to balance his cantankerousness, which he was also aware of and could have controlled but instead indulged, the way some people indulge their vicious and beloved dogs. In the old brick house there was one communal kitchen, downstairs; it was always dirty and the refrigerator was usually empty because people tended to eat whatever they found there, even if the owner had attached a note to it asking that it be spared.

Edith did not cook for Hank in that kitchen. When she cooked for him, and she liked to do that often, she did it in her own apartment, in a tiny stifling kitchen that was little more than an alcove never meant to hold the refrigerator and stove, which faced each other and could not be opened at the same time. Her apartment itself was narrow, a room on one side of a house belonging to a tense young lawyer and his tenser young wife and their two loud sons who seemed oblivious to that quality which permeated their parents' lives. Neither the lawyer nor his wife had ever told Edith she could not keep a man overnight. But she knew she could not. She knew this because they did not drink or smoke or laugh very much either, and because of the perturbed lust in the lawyer's eyes when he glanced at her. So she and Hank made love on the couch that unfolded and became a narrow bed, and then he went home. He didn't want to spend the night anyway, except on some nights when he was drunk. Since he was a young writer in a graduate school whose only demand was that he write, and write well, he was often drunk, either because he had written well that day or had not. But he was rarely so drunk that he wanted to stay the night at Edith's. And, when he did, it wasn't because liquor had released in him some need he wouldn't ordinarily yield to; it was because he didn't want to drive home. Always, though, she got him out of the house; and always he was glad next morning that she had.

He had little money, only what an assistantship gave him, and he didn't like her to pay for their evenings out, so when they saw each other at night it was most often at her apartment. Usually before he came she would shower and put on a dress or skirt. He teased her about that but she knew he liked it. So did she. She liked being dressed and smelling of perfume and brushing her long black hair before the mirror, and she liked the look in his eyes and the way his voice heightened and belied his teasing. She put on records and they had drinks and told each other what they had done that day. She was pretending to be in her first year of graduate school, in American history, so she could be near Hank; she attended classes, even read the books and wrote the papers, even did rather well; but she was pretending. They drank for a while, then she stood between the hot stove and the refrigerator and cooked while he stood at the entrance of the alcove, and they talked. They ate at a small table against the wall of the living room; the only other room was the bathroom. After dinner she washed the dishes, put away leftovers in foil, and they unfolded the couch and made love and lay talking until they were ready to make love again. It all felt like marriage. Even at twenty-seven, looking back on those nights after five years of marriage, she still saw in them what marriage could often be: talk and dinner and, the child asleep, living-room lovemaking long before the eleven o'clock news which had become their electronic foreplay, the weather report the final signal to climb the stairs together and undress.

On those nights in the apartment they spoke of marriage. And he explained why, even on the nights of Iowa winter when his moustache froze as he walked from her door around the lawyer's house and down the slippery driveway to his car, he did not want to spend the night with her. It was a matter of ritual, he told her. It had to do with his work. He did not want to wake up with someone (he said *someone*, not *you*) and then drive home to his own room where he would start the morning's work. What he liked to do, he said (already she could see he sometimes confused like to with have to) was spend his first wakeful time of the day alone. In his room, each working morning, he first made his bed and cleared his desk of mail and books, then while he made his coffee and cooked bacon and eggs on the hot plate he read the morning paper; he read through the meal and afterward while he drank coffee and smoked. By the time he had finished the paper and washed the dishes in the bathroom he had been awake for an hour and a half. Then, with the reluctance which began as he reached the final pages of the newspaper, he sat at his desk and started to work.

He spoke so seriously, almost reverently, about making a bed, eating some eggs, and reading a newspaper, that at first Edith was amused; but she stifled it and asked him what was happening during that hour and a half of quiet morning. He said, That's it: quiet: silence. While his body woke he absorbed silence. His work was elusive and difficult and had to be stalked; a phone call or an early visitor could flush it. She said, What about after we're married? He smiled and his arm tightened her against him. He told her of a roommate he had, when he was an undergraduate. The roommate was talkative. He woke up talking and went to bed talking. Most of the talk was good, a lot of it purposely funny, and Hank enjoyed it. Except at breakfast. The roommate liked to share the newspaper with Hank and talk about what they were reading. Hank was writing a novel then; he finished it in his senior year, read it at home that summer in Phoenix, and, with little ceremony or despair, burned it. But he was writing it then, living with the roommate, and after a few weeks of spending an hour and a half cooking, reading, and talking and then another hour in silence at his desk before he could put the first word on paper, he started waking at six o'clock so that his roommate woke at eight to an apartment that smelled of bacon and, walking past Hank's closed door, he entered the kitchen where Hank's plate and fork were in the drainer, the clean skillet on the stove, coffee in the pot, and the newspaper waiting on the table.

So in her ninth month she began worrying about Hank. What had first drawn her to him was his body: in high school he had played football; he was both too light and too serious to play in college; he was short, compact, and hard, and she liked his poised, graceful walk; with yielding hands she liked touching his shoulders and arms. When he told her he ran five miles every day she was pleased. Later, not long before they were lovers, she realized that what she loved about him was his vibrance, intensity; it was not that he was a writer; she had read little and indiscriminately and he would have to teach her those things about his work that she must know. She loved him because he had found his center, and it was that center she began worrying about in her ninth month. For how could a man who didn't want to spend a night with his lover be expected to move into a house with a woman, and then a baby? She watched him.

When he finished the novel, Sharon was two and they were buying a house in Bradford, Massachusetts, where he taught and where Edith believed she could live forever. Boston was forty minutes to the south, and she liked it better than Chicago; the New Hampshire beaches were twenty minutes away; she had been land-locked for twenty-four years and nearly every summer day she took

Sharon to the beach while Hank wrote; on sunny days when she let herself get trapped into errands or other trifles that posed as commitments, she felt she had wronged herself; but there were not many of those days. She loved autumn—she and Hank and Sharon drove into New Hampshire and Vermont to look at gold and red and yellow leaves—and she loved winter too—it wasn't as cold and windy as the midwest—and she loved the evergreens and snow on the hills; and all winter she longed for the sea, and some days she bundled up Sharon and drove to it and looked at it from the warmth of the car. Then they got out and walked on the beach until Sharon was cold.

Hank was happy about his novel; he sent it to an agent who was happy about it too; but no one else was and, fourteen months later, with more ceremony this time (a page at a time, in the fireplace, three hundred and forty-eight of them) and much more despair, he burned it. That night he drank a lot but was still sober; or sad enough so that all the bourbon did was make him sadder; in bed he held her but he was not really holding her; he lay on his side, his arms around her; but it was she who was holding him. She wanted to make love with him, wanted that to help him, but she knew it would not and he could not. Since sending his novel to the agent he had written three stories; they existed in the mail and on the desks of editors of literary magazines and then in the mail again. And he had been thinking of a novel. He was twenty-six years old. He had been writing for eight years. And that night, lying against her, he told her the eight years were gone forever and had come to nothing. His wide hard body was rigid in her arms; she thought if he could not make love he ought to cry, break that tautness in his body, his soul. But she knew he could not. All those years meant to him, he said, was the thousands of pages, surely over three, maybe over four, he had written: all those drafts, each one draining him only to be stacked in a box or filing cabinet as another draft took its place: all those pages to get the two final drafts of the two novels that had gone into ashes, into the air. He lived now in a total of fifty-eight typed pages, the three stories that lived in trains and on the desks of men he didn't know.

'Start tomorrow,' she said. 'On the new novel.'

For a few moments he was quiet. Then he said: 'I can't. It's three in the morning. I've been drinking for eight hours.'

'Just a page. Or else tomorrow will be terrible. And the day after tomorrow will be worse. You can sleep late, sleep off the booze. I'll take Sharon to the beach, and when I come home you tell me you've written and run with Jack and you feel strong again.'

At the beach next day she knew he was writing and she felt good about that; she knew that last night he had known it was what he had to do; she also knew he needed her to tell him to do it. But she felt defeated too. Last night, although she had fought it, her knowledge of defeat had begun as she held him and felt that tautness which would yield to neither passion nor grief, and she had known it was his insular will that would get him going again, and would deny her a child.

When he finished the novel fourteen months ago she had started waiting for that time—she knew it would be a moment, an hour, a day, no more: perhaps only a moment of his happy assent—when she could conceive. For by this time, though he had never said it, she knew he didn't want another child. And she knew it was not because of anything as practical and as easily solved as money. It was because of the very force in him which had first attracted her, so that after two years of marriage she could think wryly: one thing has to be said about men who've found their center: they're sometimes selfish bastards. She knew he didn't want another child because he believed a baby would interfere with his work. And his believing it would probably make it true

She knew he was being shortsighted, foolish, and selfish; she knew that, except for the day of birth itself and perhaps a day after, until her mother arrived to care for Sharon, a baby would not prevent, damage, or even interrupt one sentence of all those pages he had to write and she was happy that he wrote and glad to listen to on those nights when he had to read them too; those pages she also resented at times, when after burning three hundred and forty-eight of them he lay in despair and the beginnings of resilience against her body she had given him more than three hundred and forty-eight times, maybe given him a thousand times, and told her all the eight years meant to him were those pages. And she resented them when she knew they would keep her from having a second child; she wanted a son; and it would do no good, she knew, to assure him that he would not lose sleep, that she would get up with the baby in the night.

Because that really wasn't why he didn't want a baby; he probably thought it was; but it wasn't. So if she told him how simple it would be, he still wouldn't want to do it. Because, whether he knew it or not, he was keeping himself in reserve. He had the life he wanted: his teaching schedule gave him free mornings; he had to prepare for classes but he taught novels he knew well and could skim; he had summers off, he had a friend, Jack Linhart, to talk, drink, and run with; he had a woman and a child he loved, and all he wanted now was to write better than he'd ever written before, and it was that he saved himself for. They had never talked about any of this, but she knew it all. She almost felt the same way about her life; but she wanted a son. So she had waited for him to sell his novel, knowing that would be for him a time of exuberance and power, a time out of the fearful drudgery and isolation of his work, and in that spirit he would give her a child. Now she had to wait again.

In the winter and into the spring when snow melted first around the trunks of trees, and the ice on the Merrimack broke into chunks that floated seaward, and the river climbed and rushed, there was a girl. She came uninvited in Christmas season to a party that Edith spent a day preparing; her escort was uninvited too, a law student, a boring one, who came with a married couple who were invited. Later Edith would think of him: if he had to crash the party he should at least have been man enough to keep the girl he crashed with. Her name was Jeanne, she was from France, she was visiting friends in Boston. That was all she was doing: visiting. Edith did not know what part of France she was from nor what she did when she was there. Probably Jeanne told her that night while they stood for perhaps a quarter of an hour in the middle of the room and voices, sipping their drinks, nodding at each other, talking the way two very attractive women will talk at a party: Edith speaking and even answering while her real focus was on Jeanne's short black hair, her sensuous, indolent lips, her brown and mischievous eyes. Edith had talked with the law student long enough—less than a quarter of an hour—to know he wasn't Jeanne's lover and couldn't be; his confidence was still young, wistful, and vulnerable; and there was an impatience, a demand, about the amatory currents she felt flowing from Jeanne. She remarked all of this and recalled nothing they talked about. They parted like two friendly but competing hunters after meeting in the woods. For the rest of the night—while talking, while dancing—Edith watched the law student and the husbands lining up at the trough of Jeanne's accent, and she watched Jeanne's eyes, which appeared vacant until you looked closely at them and saw that they were selfish: Jeanne was watching herself.

And Edith watched Hank, and listened to him. Early in their marriage she had learned to do that. His intimacy with her was private; at their table and in their bed they talked; his intimacy with men was public, and when he was with them he spoke mostly to them, looked mostly at them, and she knew there were times when he was unaware that she or any other woman was in the room. She had long ago stopped resenting this; she had watched the other wives sitting together and talking to one another; she had watched them sit listening while couples were at a dinner table and the women couldn't group so they ate and listened to the men. Usually men who talked to women were trying to make love with them, and she could sense the other men's resentment at this distraction, as if during a hand of poker a man had left the table to phone his mistress. Of course she was able to talk at parties; she wasn't shy and no man had ever intentionally made her feel he was not interested in what she had to say; but willy-nilly they patronized her. As they listened to her she could sense their courtesy, their impatience for her to finish so they could speak again to their comrades. If she had simply given in to that patronizing, stopped talking because she was a woman, she might have become bitter. But she went further: she watched the men, and saw that it wasn't a matter of their not being interested in women. They weren't interested in each other either. At least not in what they said, their ideas; the ideas and witticisms were instead the equipment of friendly, even loving, competition, as for men with different interests were the bowling ball, the putter, the tennis racket. But it went deeper than that too: she finally saw that. Hank needed and loved men, and when he loved them it was because of what they thought and how they lived. He did not measure women that way; he measured them by their sexuality and good sense. He and his friends talked with one another because it was the only way they could show their love; they might reach out and take a woman's hand and stroke it while they leaned forward, talking to men; and their conversations were fields of mutual praise. It no longer bothered her. She knew that some women writhed under these conversations; they were usually women whose husbands rarely spoke to them with the intensity and attention they gave to men.

But that night, listening to Hank, she was frightened and angry. He and Jeanne were watching each other. He talked to the men but he was really talking to her; at first Edith thought he was showing off; but it was worse, more fearful: he was being received and he knew it and that is what gave his voice its exuberant lilt. His eyes met Jeanne's over a shoulder, over the rim of a lifted glass. When Jeanne left with the law student and the invited couple, Edith and Hank told them goodbye at the door. It was only the second time that night Edith and Jeanne had looked at each other and spoken; they smiled and voiced amenities; a drunken husband lurched into the group; his arm groped for Jeanne's waist and his head plunged downward to kiss her. She quickly cocked her head away, caught the kiss lightly on her cheek, almost dodged it completely. For an instant her eyes were impatient. Then that was gone. Tilted away from the husband's muttering face she was looking at Hank. In her eyes Edith saw his passion. She reached out and put an arm about his waist; without looking at him or Jeanne she said goodnight to the law student and the couple. As the four of them went down the walk, shrugging against the cold, she could not look at Jeanne's back and hair; she watched the law student and wished him the disaster of bad grades. Be a bank teller, you bastard.

She did not see Jeanne again. In the flesh, that is. For now she saw her in dreams: not those of sleep which she could forget but her waking dreams. In the morning Hank went to his office at school to write; at noon he and Jack ran and then ate lunch; he taught all afternoon and then went to the health club for a sauna with Jack and afterward they stopped for a drink; at seven he came home. On Tuesdays and Thursdays he didn't have classes but he spent the afternoon at school in conferences with students; on Saturday mornings he wrote in his office and, because he was free of students that day, he often worked into the middle of the afternoon then called Jack to say he was ready for the run, the sauna, the drinks. For the first time in her marriage Edith thought about how long and how often he was away from home. As she helped Sharon with her boots she saw Jeanne's brown eyes; they were attacking her; they were laughing at her; they sledded down the hill with her and Sharon.

When she became certain that Hank was Jeanne's lover she could not trust her certainty. In the enclosed days of winter she imagined too much. Like a spy, she looked for only one thing, and she could not tell if the wariness in his eyes and voice were truly there; making love with him she felt a distance in his touch, another concern in his heart; passionately she threw herself against that distance and wondered all the time if it existed only in her own quiet and fearful heart. Several times, after drinks at a party, she nearly asked Jack if Hank was always at school when he said he was. At home on Tuesday and Thursday and Saturday afternoons she wanted to call him. One Thursday she did. He didn't answer his office phone; it was a small school and the switchboard operator said if she saw him she'd tell him to call home. Edith was telling Sharon to get her coat, they would go to school to see Daddy, when he phoned. She asked him if he wanted to see a movie that night. He said they had seen everything playing in town and if she wanted to go to Boston he'd rather wait until the weekend. She said that was fine.

In April he and Jack talked about baseball and watched it on television and he started smoking Parliaments. She asked him why. They were milder, he said. He looked directly at her but she sensed he was forcing himself to, testing himself. For months she had imagined his infidelity and fought her imagination with the absence of evidence. Now she had that: she knew it was irrational but it was just rational enough to release the demons they absorbed her: they gave her certainty. She remembered Jeanne holding a Parliament, waiting for one of the husbands to light it. She lasted three days. On a Thursday afternoon she called the school every hour, feeling the vulnerability of this final prideless crumbling, making her voice as casual as possible to the switchboard operator, even saying once it was nothing important, just something she wanted him to pick up on the way home, and when he got home at seven carrying a damp towel and smelling faintly of gin she knew he had got back in time for the sauna with Jack and had spent the afternoon in Jeanne's bed. She waited until after dinner, when Sharon was in bed. He sat at the kitchen table, talking to her while she cleaned the kitchen. It was a ritual of theirs. She asked him for a drink. Usually she didn't drink after dinner, and he was surprised. Then he said he'd join her. He gave her the bourbon then sat at the table again.

'Are you having an affair with that phony French bitch?'
He sipped his drink, looked at her, and said: 'Yes.'

The talk lasted for days. That night it ended at three in the morning after, straddling him, she made love with him and fell into a sleep whose every moment, next morning, she believed she remembered. She had slept four hours. When she woke to the news on the radio she felt she had not slept at all, that her mind had continued the talk with sleeping Hank. She did not want to get up. In bed she smoked while Hank showered and shaved. At breakfast he did not read the paper. He spoke to Sharon and watched Edith. She did not eat. When he was ready to leave, he leaned down and kissed her and said he loved her and they would talk again that night.

All day she knew what madness was, or she believed she was at least tasting it and at times she yearned for the entire feast. While she did her work and made lunch for Sharon and talked to her and put her to bed with a coloring book and tried to read the newspaper and then a magazine, she could not stop the voices in her mind: some of it repeated from last night, some drawn up from what she believed she had heard and spoken in her sleep, some in anticipation of tonight, living tonight before it was there, so that at two in the afternoon she was already at midnight and time was nothing but how much pain she could feel at once. When Sharon had been in bed for an hour without sleeping Edith took her for a walk and tried to listen to her and said yes and no and I don't know, what do you think? and even heard most of what Sharon said and all the time the voices would not stop. All last night while awake and sleeping and all day she had believed it was because Jeanne was pretty and Hank was a man. Like any cliché, it was easy to live with until she tried to; now she began to realize how little she knew about Hank and how much she suspected and feared, and that night after dinner which she mostly drank she tucked in Sharon and came down to the kitchen and began asking questions. He told her he would stop seeing Jeanne and there was nothing more to talk about; he spoke of privacy. But she had to know everything he felt; she persisted, she harried, and finally he told her she'd better be as tough as her questions were, because she was going to get the answers.

Which were: he did not believe in monogamy. Fidelity, she said. You see? he said. You distort it. He was a faithful husband. He had been discreet, kept his affair secret, had not risked her losing face. He loved her and had taken nothing from her. She accused him of having a double standard and he said no; no, she was as free as she was before she met him. She asked him how long he had felt this way, had he always been like this or was it just some French bullshit he had picked up this winter. He had always felt this way. By now she could not weep. Nor rage either. All she could feel and say was: Why didn't I ever know any of this? You never asked, he said.

It was, she thought, like something bitter from Mother Goose: the woman made the child, the child made the roof, the roof made the woman, and the child went away. Always she had done her housework quickly and easily; by ten-thirty on most mornings she had done what had to be done. She was not one of those women whose domesticity became an obsession; it was work that she neither liked nor disliked and, when other women complained, she was puzzled and amused and secretly believed their frustration had little to do with scraping plates or pushing a vacuum cleaner over a rug. Now in April and May an act of will got her out of bed in the morning. The air in the house was against her: it seemed wet and grey and heavy, heavier than fog, and she pushed through it to the bathroom where she sat staring at the floor or shower curtain long after she was done, then she moved to the kitchen and as she prepared breakfast the air pushed down on her arms and against her body. *I am beating eggs*, she said to herself, and she looked down at the fork in her hand, yolk dripping from the tines into the eggs as their swirling ceased and they lay still in the bowl. *I am beating eggs.* Then she jabbed the fork in again. At breakfast Hank read the paper. Edith talked to Sharon and ate because she had to, because it was morning, it was time to eat, and she glanced at Hank's face over the newspaper, listened to the crunching of his teeth on toast, and told herself: *I am talking to Sharon.* She kept her voice sweet, motherly, attentive.

Then breakfast was over and she was again struck by the seductive waves of paralysis that had washed over her in bed, and she stayed at the table. Hank kissed her (she turned her lips to him, they met his, she did not kiss him) and went to the college. She read the paper and drank coffee and smoked while Sharon played with toast. She felt she would fall asleep at the table; Hank would return in the afternoon to find her sleeping there among the plates and cups and glasses while Sharon played alone in a ditch somewhere down the road. So once again she rose through an act of will, watched Sharon brushing her teeth (*I am watching . . .*), sent her to the cartoons on television, and then slowly, longing for sleep, she washed the skillet and saucepan (*always scramble eggs in a saucepan*, her mother had told her; *they stand deeper than in a skillet and they'll cook softer*) and scraped the plates and put them and the glasses and cups and silverware in the dishwasher.

Then she carried the vacuum cleaner upstairs and made the bed Hank had left after she had, and as she leaned over to tuck in the sheet she wanted to give in to the lean, to collapse in slow motion face down on the half-made bed and lie there until—there had been times in her life when she had wanted to sleep until something ended. Unmarried in Iowa, when she missed her period she wanted to sleep until she knew whether she was or not. Now *until* meant nothing. No matter how often or how long she slept she would wake to the same house, the same heavy air that worked against her every move. She made Sharon's bed and started the vacuum cleaner. Always she had done that quickly, not well enough for her mother's eye, but her mother was a Windex housekeeper: a house was not done unless the windows were so clean you couldn't tell whether they were open or closed; but her mother had a cleaning woman. The vacuum cleaner interfered with the cartoons and Sharon came up to tell her and Edith said she wouldn't be long and told Sharon to put on her bathing suit—it was a nice day and they would go to the beach. But the cleaning took her longer than it had before, when she had moved quickly from room to room, without lethargy or boredom but a sense of anticipation, the way she felt when she did other work which required neither skill nor concentration, like chopping onions and grating cheese for a meal she truly wanted to cook.

Now, while Sharon went downstairs again and made lemonade and poured it in the thermos and came upstairs and went down again and came up and said yes there was a little mess and went downstairs and wiped it up, Edith pushed the vacuum cleaner and herself through the rooms and down the hall, and went downstairs and started in the living room while Sharon's voice tugged at her as strongly as hands gripping her clothes, and she clamped her teeth on the sudden shrieks that rose in her throat and told herself: *Don't:*

she's not the problem; and she thought of the women in supermarkets and on the street, dragging and herding and all but cursing their children along (one day she had seen a woman kick her small son's rump as she pulled him into a drugstore), and she thought of the women at parties, at dinners, or on blankets at the beach while they watched their children in the waves, saying: *I'm so damned bored with talking to children all day—no*, she told herself, *she's not the problem*. Finally she finished her work, yet she felt none of the relief she had felt before; the air in the house was like water now as she moved through it up the stairs to the bedroom, where she undressed and put on her bathing suit. Taking Sharon's hand and the windbreakers and thermos and blanket, she left the house and blinked in the late morning sun and wondered near-prayerfully when this would end, this dread disconnection between herself and what she was doing. At night making love with Hank she thought of him with Jeanne, and her heart, which she thought was beyond breaking, broke again, quickly, easily, as if there weren't much to break any more, and fell into mute and dreary anger, the dead end of love's grief.

In the long sunlit evenings and the nights of May the talk was sometimes philosophical, sometimes dark and painful, drawing from him details about him and Jeanne; she believed if she possessed the details she would dispossess Jeanne of Hank's love. But she knew that wasn't her only reason. Obsessed by her pain, she had to plunge more deeply into it, feel all of it again and again. But most of the talk was abstract, and most of it was by Hank. When she spoke of divorce he calmly told her they had a loving, intimate marriage. They were, he said, simply experiencing an honest and healthful breakthrough. She listened to him talk about the unnatural boundaries of lifelong monogamy. He remained always calm. Cold, she thought. She could no longer find his heart.

At times she hated him. Watching him talk she saw his life: with his work he created his own harmony, and then he used the people he loved to relax with. Probably it was not exploitative; probably it was the best he could do. And it was harmony she had lost. Until now her marriage had been a circle, like its gold symbol on her finger. Wherever she went she was still inside it. It had a safe, gentle circumference, and mortality and the other perils lay outside of it. Often now while Hank slept she lay awake and tried to pray. She wanted to fall in love with God. She wanted His fingers to touch her days, to restore meaning to those simple tasks which now drained her spirit. On those nights when she tried to pray she longed to leave the world: her actions would appear secular but they would be her communion with God. Cleaning the house would be an act of forgiveness and patience under His warm eyes. But she knew it was no use: she had belief, but not faith: she could not bring God under her roof and into her life. He waited her death.

Nightly and fearfully now, as though Hank's adulterous heart had opened a breach and let it in to stalk her, she thought of death. One night they went with Jack and Terry Linhart to Boston to hear Judy Collins. The concert hall was filled and darkened and she sat in the sensate, audible silence of listening people and watched Judy under the spotlight in a long lavender gown, her hair falling over one shoulder as she lowered her face over the guitar. Soon Edith could not hear the words of the songs. Sadly she gazed at Judy's face, and listened to the voice, and thought of the voice going out to the ears of all those people, all those strangers, and she thought how ephemeral was a human voice, and how death not only absorbed the words in the air, but absorbed as well the act of making the words, and the time it took to say them. She saw Judy as a small bird singing on a wire, and above her the hawk circled. She remembered reading once of an old man who had been working for twenty-five years sculpting, out of a granite mountain in South Dakota, a 563-foot-high statue of Chief Crazy Horse. She thought of Hank and the novel he was writing now, and as she sat beside him her soul withered away from him and she hoped he would fail, she hoped he would burn this one too: she saw herself helping him, placing alternate pages in the fire. Staring at the face above the lavender gown she strained to receive the words and notes into her body.

She had never lied to Hank and now everything was a lie. Beneath the cooking of a roast, the still affectionate chatting at dinner, the touch of their flesh, was the fact of her afternoons ten miles away in a New Hampshire woods where, on a blanket among shading pines and hemlocks, she lay in sin-quickened heat with Jack Linhart. Her days were delightfully strange, she thought. Hank's betrayal had removed her from the actions that were her life; she had performed them like a weary and disheartened dancer. Now, glancing at Hank reading, she took clothes from the laundry basket at her feet and folded them on the couch, and the folding of a warm towel was a manifestation of her deceit. And, watching him across the room, she felt her separation from him taking shape, filling the space between them like a stone. Within herself she stroked and treasured her lover. She knew she was doing the same to the self she had lost in April.

There was a price to pay. When there had been nothing to lie about in their marriage and she had not lied, she had always felt nestled with Hank; but with everyone else, even her closest friends, she had been aware of that core of her being that no one knew. Now she felt that with Hank. With Jack she recognized yet leaped into their passionate lie: they were rarely together more than twice a week; apart, she longed for him, talked to him in her mind, and vengefully saw him behind her closed eyes as she moved beneath Hank. When she was with Jack their passion burned and distorted their focus. For two hours on the blanket they made love again and again, they made love too much, pushing their bodies to consume the yearning they had borne and to delay the yearning that was waiting. Sometimes under the trees she felt like tired meat. The quiet air which she had broken in the first hour with moans now absorbed only their heavy breath. At those moments she saw with detached clarity that they were both helpless, perhaps even foolish. Jack wanted to escape his marriage; she wanted to live with hers; they drove north to the woods and made love. Then they dressed and drove back to what had brought them there.

This was the first time in her life she had committed herself to sin, and there were times when she felt her secret was venomous. Lying beside Terry at the beach she felt more adulterous than when she lay with Jack, and she believed her sun-lulled conversation was somehow poisoning her friend. When she held Sharon, salty and cold-skinned from the sea, she felt her sin flowing with the warmth of her body into the small wet breast. But more often she was proud. She was able to sin and love at the same time. She was more attentive to Sharon than she had been in April. She did not have to struggle to listen to her, to talk to her. She felt cleansed. And looking at Terry's long red hair as she bent over a child, she felt both close to her yet distant. She did not believe women truly had friends among themselves; school friendships dissolved into marriages; married women thought they had friends until they got divorced and discovered other women were only wives drawn together by their husbands. As much as she and Terry were together, they were not really intimate; they instinctively watched each other. She was certain that Terry would do what she was doing. A few weeks ago she would not have known that. She was proud that she knew it now.

With Hank she loved her lie. She kept it like a fire: some evenings after an afternoon with Jack she elaborately fanned it, looking into Hank's eyes and talking of places she had gone while the sitter stayed with Sharon; at other times she let it burn low, was evasive about how she had spent her day, and when the two couples were together she bantered with Jack, teased him. Once Jack left his pack of Luckies in her car and she brought them home and smoked them. Hank noticed but said nothing. When two cigarettes remained in the pack she put it on the coffee table and left it there. One night she purposely made a mistake: after dinner, while Hank watched a ball game on television, she drank gin while she cleaned the kitchen. She had drunk gin and tonic before dinner and wine with the flounder and now she put tonic in the gin, but not much. From the living room came the announcer's voice, and now and then Hank spoke. She hated his voice; she knew she did not hate him; if she did, she would be able to act, to leave him. She hated his voice tonight because he was talking to ballplayers on the screen and because there was no pain in it while in the kitchen her own voice keened without sound and she worked slowly and finished her drink and mixed another, the gin now doing what she had wanted it to: dissolving all happiness, all peace, all hope for it with Hank and all memory of it with Jack, even the memory of that very afternoon under the trees. Gin-saddened, she felt beyond tears, at the bottom of some abyss where there was no emotion save the quivering knees and fluttering stomach and cold-shrouded heart that told her she was finished. She took the drink into the living room and stood at the door and watched him looking at the screen over his lifted can of beer. He glanced at her, then back at the screen. One hand fingered the pack of Luckies on the table, but he did not take one.

'I wish you hadn't stopped smoking,' she said. 'Sometimes I think you did it so you'd outlive me.'

He looked at her, told her with his eyes that she was drunk, and turned back to the game.

'I've been having an affair with Jack.' He looked at her, his eyes unchanged, perhaps a bit more interested; nothing more. His lips showed nothing, except that she thought they seemed ready to smile. 'We go up to the woods in New Hampshire in the afternoons. Usually twice a week. I like it. I started it. I went after him, at a party. I told him about Jeanne. I kept after him. I knew he was available because he's unhappy with Terry. For a while he was worried about you but I told him you wouldn't mind anyway. He's still your friend, if that worries you. Probably more yours than mine. You don't even look surprised. I suppose you'll tell me you've known it all the time.'

'It wasn't too hard to pick up.'

'So it really wasn't French bullshit. I used to want another child. A son. I wouldn't want to now: have a baby in this.'

'Come here.'

For a few moments, leaning against the doorjamb, she thought of going upstairs and packing her clothes and driving away. The impulse was rooted only in the blur of gin. She knew she would get no farther than the closet where her clothes hung. She walked to the couch and sat beside him. He put his arm around her; for a while she sat rigidly, then she closed her eyes and eased against him and rested her head on his shoulder.

In December after the summer which Hank called the summer of truth, when Edith's affair with Jack Linhart had both started and ended, Hank sold his novel. On a Saturday night they had a celebration party. It was a large party, and some of Hank's students came. His girl friend came with them. Edith had phoned Peter at the radio station Friday and invited him, had assured him it was all right, but he had said he was an old-fashioned guilt-ridden adulterer, and could not handle it. She told him she would see him Sunday afternoon.

The girl friend was nineteen years old and her name was Debbie. She was taller than Edith, she wore suede boots, and she had long blonde hair. She believed she was a secret from everyone but Edith. At the party she drank carefully (only wine), was discreet with Hank, and spent much time talking with Edith, who watched the face that seemed never to have borne pain, and thought: These Goddamn young girls don't care what they do any more. Hank had said she was a good student. Edith assumed that meant the girl agreed with what he said and told it back to him in different words. What else could come out of a face so untouched? Bland and evil at the same time. Debbie was able to believe it when Hank told her Edith was not jealous. Sometimes Debbie stayed with Sharon while Hank and Edith went out. Hank drove her back to the dormitory; on those nights, by some rule of his own, he did not make love with Debbie. A bit drunk, standing in the kitchen with the girl, Edith glanced at her large breasts stretching the burgundy sweater. How ripe she must be, this young piece. Her nipples thrust against the cashmere. They made love in the car. Hank could not afford motels like Peter could. When Edith was in the car she felt she was in their bed. She looked at the breasts.

'I always wanted big ones,' she murmured.

The girl blushed and took a cigarette from her purse.

'Hank hasn't started smoking again,' Edith said. 'It's amazing.'

'I didn't know he ever did.'

'Until last summer. He wants to live a long time. He wants to publish ten books.'

Edith studied the girl's eyes. They were brown, and showed nothing. A student. Couldn't she understand what she was hearing? That she had come without history into not history, that in a year or more or less she would be gone with her little heart broken or, more than likely, her cold little heart intact, her eyes and lips intact, having given nothing and received less: a memory for Hank to smile over in a moment of a spring afternoon. But then Edith looked away from the eyes. None of this mattered to the girl. Not the parentheses of time, not that blank space between them that one had to fill. It was Edith who would lose. Perhaps the next generation of students would be named Betty or Mary Ann. Well into his forties Hank would be attractive to them. Each year he would pluck what he needed. Salaried and tenured adultery. She would watch them come into her home like ghosts of each other. Sharon would like their attention, as she did now. Edith was twenty-seven. She had ten more years, perhaps thirteen; fifteen. Her looks would be gone. The girls would come with their loose breasts under her roof, and brassiered she would watch them, talk with them. It would not matter to Hank where they had come from and where they were going. He would write books.

She could not read it: the one he sold, the one she had urged him that summer night to begin next day, helping him give birth to it while she gave up a son. When he finished it a month ago and sent it to the agent he gave her the carbon and left her alone with it; it was a Saturday and he went to Jack's to watch football. She tried all afternoon. He needed her to like it; she knew that. He only pretended to care about what she thought of other books or movies. But handing her the manuscript he had boyishly lowered his eyes, and then left. He left because he could not be in the house with her while she read it. When she had read the other one, the one he burned, he had paced about the house and lawn and returned often to watch her face, to see what his work was doing to it. This time he knew better. All of that was in his eyes and voice when he said with such vulnerability that for a moment she wanted to hold him with infinite forgiveness: 'I think I'll go to Jack's and watch the game.'

She tried to recall that vulnerability as she read. But she could not. His prose was objective, concrete, precise. The voice of the book was the voice of the man who last spring and summer had spoken of monogamy, absolved and encouraged her adultery, and in the fall announced that he was having an affair with Debbie. Through the early chapters she was angry. She pushed herself on. Mostly she skimmed. Then she grew sad: this was the way she had wanted it when she first loved him: he would bring her his work and he would need her praise and before anyone else read it the work would be consummated between them. Now she could not read it through the glaze of pain that covered the pages. She skimmed, and when he returned in the evening she greeted him with an awed and tender voice, with brightened eyes; she held him tightly and told him it was a wonderful novel and she thought of how far she had come with this man, how frequent and convincing were her performances.

He wanted to talk about it; he was relieved and joyful; he wanted to hear everything she felt. That was easy enough: they talked for two hours while she cooked and they ate; he would believe afterward that she had talked to him about his book; she had not. Recalling what she skimmed she mentioned a scene or passage, let him in-

terrupt her, and then let him talk about it. Now it would be pub-
lished, and he would write another. Looking at Debbie she wondered
if Peter would leave his wife and marry her. She had not thought
of that before; and now, with images in her mind of herself and
Peter and Sharon driving away, she knew too clearly what she had
known from the beginning: that she did not love Peter Jackman.
All adultery is a symptom, she thought. She watched Debbie, who
was talking about Hank's novel; she had read it after Edith. Hank
brought to his adultery the protocol of a professional. Who *was* this
girl? What was she *do*ing? Did she put herself to sleep in the dormitory with visions of herself and Hank driving away? In her eyes
Edith found nothing; she could have been peering through the windows of a darkened cellar.

'I'm going to circulate,' she said.

In the living room she found Jack, and took his hand. Looking
at his eyes she saw their summer and his longing and she touched
his cheek and beard and recalled the sun over his shoulder and her
hot closed eyes. He did not love Terry but he could not hurt her,
nor leave his children, and he was faithful now, he drank too much,
and often he talked long and with embittered anger about things of
no importance.

'I hope there was *some*thing good,' she said. 'In last summer.'

'There was.' He pressed her hand.

'Doesn't Hank's girl look pretty tonight?' she said.

'I hate the little bitch.'

'So do I.'

Once in Iowa, while Edith was washing clothes at a launderette, a
dreary place of graduate students reading, Mann juxtaposed with
Tide, and stout wives with curlers in their hair, a place she gladly
abandoned when she married Hank and moved into the house with
her own washer and dryer, she met a young wife who was from a
city in the south. Her husband was a student and he worked nights
as a motel clerk. Because they found one for sixty dollars a month,
they lived in a farmhouse far from town, far from anyone. From
her window at night, across the flat and treeless land, she could see
the lights of her closest neighbor, a mile and a half away. She had
a small child, a daughter. She had never lived in the country and
the farmers like to tell her frightening stories. While she was getting

mail from the box at the road they stopped their tractors and talked to her, these large sunburned farmers who she said had grown to resemble the hogs they raised. They told her of hogs eating drunks and children who fell into the pens. And they told her a year ago during the long bad winter a man had hanged himself in the barn of the house she lived in; he had lived there alone, and he was buried in town.

So at night, while her husband was at the motel desk, the woman was afraid. When she was ready for bed she forced herself to turn off all the downstairs lights, though she wanted to leave every light burning, sleep as if in bright afternoon; then she climbed the stairs and turned out the hall light too, for she was trying to train the child to sleep in the dark. Then she would go to bed and, if she had read long enough, was sleepy enough, she'd go to sleep soon; but always fear was there and if she woke in the night—her bladder, a sound from the child, a lone and rare car on the road in front of the house—she lay terrified in the dark which spoke to her, touched her. In those first wakeful moments she thought she was afraid of the dark itself, that if she dispelled it with light her fear would subside. But she did not turn on the light. And as she lay there she found that within the darkness were spaces of safety. She was not afraid of her room. She lay there a while longer and thought of other rooms. She was not afraid of her child's room. Or the bathroom. Or the hall, the stairs, the living room. It was the kitchen. The shadowed corner between the refrigerator and the cupboard. She did not actually believe someone was crouched there. But it was that corner that she feared. She lay in bed seeing it more clearly than she could see her own darkened room. Then she rose from the bed and, in the dark, went downstairs to the kitchen and stood facing the dark corner, staring at it. She stared at it until she was not afraid; then she went upstairs and slept.

On other nights she was afraid of other places. Sometimes it was the attic, and she climbed the stairs into the stale air, past the dusty window, and stood in the center of the room among boxes and cardboard barrels and knew that a running mouse would send her shouting down the stairs and vowed that it would not. The basement was worse: it was cool and damp, its ceiling was low, and no matter where she stood there was always a space she couldn't see: behind the furnace in the middle of the floor, behind the columns supporting the ceiling. Worst of all was the barn: on some nights she woke and saw its interior, a dread place even in daylight, with its beams. She did not know which one he had used; she knew he had climbed out on one of them, tied the rope, put the noose around his neck, and jumped. On some nights she had to leave her bed and go out there. It was autumn then and she only had to put on her robe and shoes. Crossing the lawn, approaching the wide dark open door, she was not afraid she would see him: she was afraid that as she entered the barn she would look up at the beam he had used.

Driving home Sunday night Edith thought of the woman—she could not remember her name, only her story—caught as an adult in the fears of childhood: for it was not the hanged man's ghost she feared; she did not believe in ghosts. It was the dark. A certain dark place on a certain night. She had gone to the place and looked at what she feared. But there was something incomplete about the story, something Edith had not thought of until now: the woman had looked at the place where that night her fear took shape. But she had not discovered what she was afraid of.

In daylight while Hank and Sharon were sledding Edith had driven to the bar to meet Peter. They had gone to the motel while the December sun that stayed low and skirting was already down. When he drove her back to the bar she did not want to leave him and drive home in the night. She kissed him and held him tightly. She wanted to go in for a drink but she didn't ask, for she knew he was late now; he had to return to his wife. His marriage was falling slowly, like a feather. He thought his wife had a lover (she had had others), but they kept their affairs secret from each other. Or tried to. Or pretended to. Edith knew they were merely getting by with flimsy deception while they avoided the final confrontation. Edith had never met Norma, or seen her. In the motels Peter talked about her. She released him and got out of the car and crossed the parking lot in the dark.

She buckled her seatbelt and turned on the radio and cautiously joined the traffic on the highway. But it was not a wreck she was afraid of. The music was bad: repetitious rock from a station for teenagers. It was the only station she could get and she left it on. She had a thirty-minute drive and she did not know why, for the first time in her adult life, she was afraid of being alone in the dark. She had been afraid from the beginning: the first night she left Peter at a parking lot outside a bar and drove home; and now when Sharon was asleep and Hank was out she was afraid in the house and one night alone she heard the washing machine stop in the basement but she could not go down there and put the clothes in the dryer. Sometimes on grey afternoons she was frightened and she would go to the room where Sharon was and sit with her. Once when Sharon was at a birthday party she fell asleep in late afternoon and woke alone with dusk at the windows and fled through the house turning on lights and Peter's disc-jockey program and fire for the teakettle. Now she was driving on a lovely country road through woods and white hills shimmering under the moon. But she watched only the slick dark road. She thought of the beach and the long blue afternoons and evenings of summer. She thought of grilling three steaks in the back yard. She and Hank and Sharon would be sunburned, their bodies warm and smelling of the sea. They would eat at the picnic table in the seven o'clock sun.

She hoped Hank would be awake when she got home. He would look up from his book, his eyes amused and arrogant as they always were when she returned from her nights. She hoped he was awake. For if he was already asleep she would in silence ascend the stairs and undress in the dark and lie beside him unable to sleep and she would feel the house enclosing and caressing her with some fear she could not name.

III

BEFORE JOE RITCHIE was dying they lay together in the cool nights of spring and he talked. His virginal, long-stored and (he told her) near-atrophied passion leaped and quivered inside her; during the lulls he talked with the effusion of a man who had lived forty years without being intimate with a woman. Which was, he said, pretty much a case of having never been intimate with anyone at all. It was why he left the priesthood. Edith looked beyond the foot of the bed and above the chest of drawers at the silhouette of the hanging crucifix while he told her of what he called his failures, and the yearnings they caused.

He said he had never doubted. When he consecrated he knew

that he held the body, the blood. He did not feel proud or particularly humble either; just awed. It was happening in his two lifted hands (and he lifted them above his large and naked chest in the dark), his two hands, of his body; yet at the same time it was not of his body. He knew some priests who doubted. Their eyes were troubled, sometimes furtive. They kept busy: some were athletic, and did that; some read a lot, and others were active in the parish: organized and supervised fairs, started discussion groups, youth groups, pre-Cana groups, married groups, counselled, made sick calls, jail calls, anything to keep them from themselves. Some entered the service, became chaplains. One of them was reported lost at sea. He had been flying with a navy pilot, from a carrier. The poor bastard, Joe said. You know what I think? He wanted to be with that pilot, so he could be around certainty. Watch the man and the machine. A chaplain in an airplane. When I got the word I thought: That's it: in the destructive element immerse, you poor bastard.

Joe had loved the Eucharist since he was a boy; it was why he became a priest. Some went to the seminary to be pastors and bishops; they didn't know it, but it was why they went, and in the seminary they were like young officers. Some, he said, went to pad and shelter their neuroses—or give direction to them. They had a joke then, the young students with their fresh and hopeful faces: behind every Irish priest there's an Irish mother wringing her hands. But most became priests because they wanted to live their lives with God; they had, as the phrase went, a vocation. There were only two vocations, the church taught: the religious life or marriage. Tell that to Hank, she said; he'd sneer at one and laugh at the other. Which would he sneer at? Joe said. I don't really know, she said.

It was a difficult vocation because it demanded a marriage of sorts with a God who showed himself only through the volition, action, imagination, and the resultant faith of the priest himself; when he failed to create and complete his union with God he was thrust back upon himself and his loneliness. For a long time the Eucharist worked for Joe. It was the high point of his day, when he consecrated and ate and drank. The trouble was it happened early in the morning. He rose and said Mass and the day was over, but it was only beginning. That was what he realized or admitted in his mid-thirties: that the morning consecration completed him but it didn't last; there was no other act during the day that gave him that completion, made him feel an action of his performed in time and mortality had transcended both and been received by a God who knew his name.

Of course while performing the tasks of a parish priest he gained the sense of accomplishment which even a conscripted soldier could feel at the end of a chore. Sometimes the reward was simply that the job was over: that he had smiled and chatted through two and a half hours of bingo without displaying his weariness that bordered on panic. But with another duty came a reward that was insidious: he knew that he was a good speaker, that his sermons were better than those of the pastor and the two younger priests. One of the younger priests should have been excused altogether from speaking to gathered people. He lacked intelligence, imagination, and style; with sweaty brow he spoke stiffly of old and superfluous truths he had learned as a student. When he was done, he left the pulpit and with great relief and concentration worked through the ritual, toward the moment when he would raise the host. When he did this, and looked up at the Eucharist in his hands, his face was no longer that of the misfit in the pulpit; his jaw was solemn, his eyes firm. Joe pitied him for his lack of talent, for his anxiety each Sunday, for his awareness of each blank face, each shifting body in the church, and his knowledge that what he said was ineffectual and dull.

Yet he also envied the young priest. In the pulpit Joe loved the sound of his own voice: the graceful flow of his words, his imagery, his timing, and the tenor reaches of his passion; his eyes engaged and swept and recorded for his delight the upturned and attentive faces. At the end of his homily he descended from the pulpit, his head lowered, his face set in the seriousness of a man who has just perceived truth. His pose continued as he faced the congregation for the Credo and the prayers of petition; it continued as he ascended the three steps to the altar and began the offertory and prepared to consecrate. In his struggle to rid himself of the pose, he assumed another: he acted like a priest who was about to hold the body of Christ in his hands, while all the time, even as he raised the host and then the chalice, his heart swelled and beat with love for himself. On the other six days, at the sparsely attended week-day masses without sermons, he broke the silence of the early mornings only with prayers, and unaware of the daily communicants, the same people usually, most of them old women who smelled of sleep and cleanliness and time, he was absorbed by the ritual, the ritual became him, and in the privacy of his soul he ate the body and drank the blood; he ascended; and then his day was over.

The remaining hours were dutiful, and he accepted them with a commitment that nearly always lacked emotion. After a few years he began to yearn; for months, perhaps a year or more, he did not know what he yearned for. Perhaps he was afraid to know. At night he drank more; sometimes the gin curbed his longings that still he wouldn't name; but usually, with drinking, he grew sad. He did not get drunk, so in the morning he woke without hangover or lapse of memory, and recalling last night's gloom he wondered at its source, as though he were trying to understand not himself but a close friend. One night he did drink too much, alone, the pastor and the two younger priests long asleep, Joe going down the hall to the kitchen with less and less caution, the cracking sound of the ice tray in his hands nothing compared to the sound that only he could hear: his monologue with himself; and it was so intense that he felt anyone who passed the kitchen door would hear the voice that resounded in his skull. In the morning he did not recall what he talked about while he drank. He woke dehydrated and remorseful, his mind so dissipated that he had to talk himself through each step of his preparation for the day, for if he didn't focus carefully on buttoning his shirt, tying his shoes, brushing his teeth, he might fall again into the shards of last night. His sleep had been heavy and drunken, his dreams anxious. He was thankful that he could not recall them. He wished he could not recall what he did as he got into bed: lying on his side he had hugged a pillow to his breast, and holding it in both arms had left consciousness saying to himself, to the pillow, to God, and perhaps aloud: I must have a woman. Leaving the rectory, crossing the lawn to the church in the cool morning, where he would say mass not for the old ladies but for himself, he vowed that he would not get drunk again.

It was not his holding the pillow that frightened him; nor was it the words he had spoken either aloud or within his soul: it was the fearful and ascendant freedom he had felt as he listened to and saw the words. There was dew on the grass beneath his feet; he stopped and looked down at the flecks of it on his polished black shoes. He stood for a moment, a slight cool breeze touching his flesh, the early warmth of the sun on his hair and face, and he felt a loving and plaintive union with all those alive and dead who had at one time in their lives, through drink or rage or passion, suddenly made the statement whose result they had both feared and hoped for and had therefore long suppressed. He imagined a multitude of voices and pained and determined faces, leaping into separation and solitude and fear and hope. His hand rose to his hair, grey in his thirties. He walked on to the church. As he put on his vestments he looked down at the sleepy altar boy, a child. He wanted to touch him but was was afraid to. He spoke gently to the boy, touched him with words. They filed into the church, and the old women and a young couple who were engaged and one old man rose.

There were ten of them. With his gin-dried mouth he voiced the prayers while his anticipatory heart beat toward that decision he knew he would one day reach, and had been reaching for some time, as though his soul had taken its own direction while his body and voice moved through the work of the parish. When the ten filed up to receive communion and he placed the host on their tongues and smelled their mouths and bodies and clothes, the sterile old ones and the young couple smelling washed as though for a date, the boy of after-shave lotion, the girl of scented soap, he studied each face for a sign. The couple were too young. In the wrinkled faces of the old he could see only an accumulation of time, of experience; he could not tell whether, beneath those faces, there was a vague recollection of a rewarding life or weary and muted self-contempt because of moments denied, choices run from. He could not tell whether any of them had reached and then denied or followed an admission like the one that gin had drawn from him the night before. Their tongues wet his fingers. He watched them with the dread, excitement, and vulnerability of a man who knows his life is about to change.

After that he stayed sober. The gin had done its work. Before dinner he approached the bottle conspiratorially, held it and looked at it as though it contained a benevolent yet demanding genie. He did not even have to drink carefully. He did not have to drink at all. He drank to achieve a warm nimbus for his secret that soon he would bare to the pastor. In the weeks that followed his drunken night he gathered up some of his past, looked at it as he had not when it was his present, and smiling at himself he saw that he had been in trouble, and the deepest trouble had been his not knowing that he was in trouble. He saw that while he was delivering his sermons he had been proud, yes; perhaps that wasn't even sinful; perhaps it was natural, even good; but the pride was no longer significant. The real trap of his sermons was that while he spoke he had acted out, soberly and with no sense of desperation, the same yearning that had made him cling to the pillow while drunk. For he realized now that beneath his sermons, even possibly at the source of them, was an abiding desire to expose his soul with all his strengths and vanities and weaknesses to another human being. And, further, the other human being was a woman.

Studying himself from his new distance he learned that while he had scanned the congregation he had of course noted the men's faces; but as attentive, as impressed, as they might be, he brushed them aside, and his eyes moved on to the faces of women. He spoke to them. It was never one face. He saw in all those eyes of all those ages the female reception he had to have: grandmothers and widows and matrons and young wives and young girls all formed a composite woman who loved him.

She came to the confessional too, where he sat profiled to the face behind the veiled window, one hand supporting his forehead and shielding his eyes. He sat and listened to the woman's voice. He had the reputation of being an understanding confessor; he had been told this by many of those people who when speaking to a priest were compelled to talk shop; not theirs: his. Go to Father Ritchie, the women told him at parish gatherings; that's what they all say, Father. He sat and listened to the woman's voice. Usually the sins were not important; and even when they were he began to sense that the woman and the ritual of confession had nothing to do with the woman and her sin. Often the sins of men were pragmatic and calculated and had to do with money; their adulteries were restive lapses from their responsibilities as husbands and fathers, and they confessed them that way, some adding the assurance that they loved their wives, their children. Some men confessed not working at their jobs as hard as they could, and giving too little time to their children. Theirs was a world of responsible action; their sins were what they considered violations of that responsibility.

But the women lived in a mysterious and amoral region which both amused and attracted Joe. Their sins were instinctual. They raged at husbands or children; they fornicated or committed adultery; the closest they came to pragmatic sin was birth control, and few of them confessed that anymore. It was not celibate lust that made Joe particularly curious about their sexual sins: it was the vision these sins gave him of their natures. Sometimes he wondered if they were capable of sinning at all. Husbands whispered of one-night stands, and in their voices Joe could hear self-reproach that was rooted in how they saw themselves as part of the world. But not so with the women. In passion they made love. There was no other context for the act. It had nothing to do with their husbands or their children; Joe never said it in the confessional but it was clear to him that it had nothing to do with God either. He began to see God and the church and those activities that he thought of as the world—education, business, politics—as male and serious, perhaps comically so; while women were their own temples and walked cryptic, oblivious, and brooding across the earth. Behind the veil their voices whispered without remorse. Their confessions were a distant and dutiful salute to the rules and patterns of men. He sat and listened to the woman's voice.

And his reputation was real: he was indeed understanding and kind, but not for God, not for the sacrament that demanded of him empathy and compassion as God might have; or Christ. For it was not God he loved, it was Christ: God in the flesh that each morning he touched and ate, making his willful and faithful connection with what he could neither touch nor see. But his awareness of his duty to imitate Christ was not the source of his virtues as a confessor. Now, as he prepared to leave the priesthood, he saw that he had given kindness and compassion and understanding because he had wanted to expose that part of himself, real or false, to a faceless nameless woman who would at least know his name because it hung outside the confessional door. And he understood why on that hungover morning he had wanted to touch the altar boy but had been afraid to, though until then his hands had instinctively gone out to children, to touch, to caress; on that morning he had been afraid he would not stop at a touch; that he would embrace the boy, fiercely, like a father.

He did not lose his faith in the Eucharist. After leaving the priesthood he had daily gone to Mass and received what he knew was the body and blood of Christ. He knew it, he told Edith, in the simplest and perhaps most profound way: most profound, he said, because he believed that faith had no more to do with intellect than love did; that touching her he knew he loved her and loving her he touched her; and that his flesh knew God through touch as it had to; that there was no other way it could; that bread and wine becoming body and blood was neither miracle nor mystery, but natural, for it happened within the leap of the heart of man toward the heart of God, a leap caused by the awareness of death. Like us, he had said. Like us what? she said, lying beside him last spring, his seed swimming in her, thinking of her Episcopal childhood, she and her family Christian by skin color and pragmatic in belief. When we make love, he said. We do it in the face of death. (And this was in the spring, before he knew.) Our bodies aren't just meat then; they become statement too; they become spirit. If we can do that with each other then why can't we do it with God, and he with us? I don't know, she said; I've never thought about it. Don't, he said; it's too simple.

After they became lovers he continued going to daily Mass but he stopped receiving communion. She offered to stop seeing him, to let him confess and return to his sacrament. He told him no. It was not that he believed he was sinning with her; it was that he didn't know. And if indeed he were living in sin it was too complex for him to enter a confessional and simply murmur the word *adultery*; too complex for him to burden just any priest with, in any confessional. He recognized this as pride: the sinner assuming the anonymous confessor would be unable to understand and unwilling to grapple with the extent and perhaps even the exonerating circumstances of the sin, but would instead have to retreat and cling to the word *adultery* and the divine law forbidding it. So he did not confess. And there were times at daily Mass when he nearly joined the others and received communion, because he felt that he could, that it would be all right. But he did not trust what he felt: in his love for Edith he was untroubled and happy but he did not trust himself enough to believe he could only be happy within the grace of God. It could be, he told her, that his long and celibate need for earthly love now satisfied, he had chosen to complete himself outside the corridor leading to God; that he was not really a spiritual man but was capable of, if not turning his back on God, at least glancing off to one side and keeping that glance fixed for as long as he and

Edith loved. So he did not receive, even though at times he felt that he could.

If she were not married he was certain he would receive communion daily while remaining her lover because, although he knew it was rarely true, he maintained and was committed to the belief that making love could parallel and even merge with the impetus and completion of the Eucharist. Else why make love at all, he said, except for meat in meat, making ourselves meat, drawing our circle of mortality not around each other but around our own vain and separate hearts. But if she were free to love him, each act between them would become a sacrament, each act a sign of their growing union in the face of God and death, freed of their now-imposed limitations on commitment and risk and hope. Because he believed in love, he said. With all his heart he believed in it, saw it as a microcosm of the Eucharist which in turn was a microcosm of the earth-rooted love he must feel for God in order to live with certainty as a man. And like his love for God, his love for her had little to do with the emotion which at times pulsated and quivered in his breast so fiercely that he had to make love with her in order to bear it; but it had more to do with the acts themselves, and love finally was a series of gestures with escalating and enduring commitments.

So if she were free to love him he could receive communion too, take part without contradiction in that gesture too. And if their adultery were the classic variety involving cuckoldry he would know quite simply it was a sin, because for his own needs he would be inflicting pain on a man who loved his wife. But since her marriage was not in his eyes a marriage at all but an arrangement which allowed Hank to indulge his impulses within the shelter of roof, woman, and child which apparently he also needed, the sin—if it existed—was hard to define. So that finally his reason for not receiving communion was his involvement in a marriage he felt was base, perhaps even sordid; and, in love as he was, he reeked or at least smelled faintly of sin, which again he could neither define nor locate; and indeed it could be Hank's sin he carried about with him and shared. Which is why he asked her to marry him.

'It's obvious you love Hank,' he said.

'Yes,' she said, her head on his bare shoulder; then she touched his face, stroked it.

'If you didn't love him you would divorce him, because you could keep Sharon. But your love for him contradicts its purpose. It empties you without filling you, it dissipates you, you'll grow old in pieces.'

'But if I were divorced you couldn't be married in the church. What about your Eucharist? Would you give that up?'

'I'd receive every day,' he said. 'Who would know? I'd go to Mass and receive the Eucharist like any other man.'

'I don't think you're a Catholic at all.'

'If I'm not, then I don't know what I am.'

IV

SHE WAKES FRIGHTENED beside Joe and looks in the grey light at the clock on the bedside table—six-forty. Joe is sleeping on his back, his mouth open; his face seems to have paled and shrunk or sagged during the night, and his shallow breath is liquid. She quietly gets out of bed. Her heart still beats with fright. This is the first time she has ever spent the night with Joe, or with any of her lovers; always the unspoken agreement with Hank was that for the last part of the night and the breakfast hour of the morning the family would be together under one roof; sometimes she had come home as late as four in the morning and gotten into bed beside Hank, who slept; always when he came home late she was awake and always she pretended she was asleep.

She dresses quickly, watching Joe's face and thinking of Sharon sleeping and hoping she will sleep for another half-hour; although if she wakes and comes down to the kitchen before Edith gets home, Edith can explain that she has been to the store. Yet she knows that discovery by Sharon is not what she really fears, that it will probably be another seven years before Sharon begins to see what she and Hank are doing. At the thought of seven more years of this her fear is instantly replaced by a rush of despair that tightens her jaws in resignation. Then she shakes her head, shakes away the image of those twenty-eight seasons until Sharon is fifteen, and continues to dress; again she is afraid. She needs a cigarette and goes to the kitchen for one; at the kitchen table she writes a note telling Joe she will be back later in the morning. She plans to clean his apartment but does not tell him in the note, which she leaves propped against the bedside clock so he will see it when he wakes and will not have to call her name or get up to see if she is still with him. She writes only that she will be back later and that she loves him. She assumes it is true that she loves him, but for a long time now it has been difficult to sort out her feelings and understand them.

As now, driving home, and knowing it is neither discovery by Sharon nor rebuke by Hank that makes her grip on the wheel so firm and anxious that the muscles of her arms tire from the tension. For she knows Hank will not be disturbed. He likes Joe and will understand why she had to stay the night; although, on the road now, in the pale blue start of the day, her decision to sleep with Joe seems distant and unnecessary, an impulse born in the hyperbole of bourbon and night. She wishes she had gone home after Joe was asleep. But if she is home in time to cook breakfast, Hank will not be angry. So why, then, driving through the streets of a town that she now thinks of as her true home, does she feel like a fugitive? She doesn't know.

And yet the feeling persists through breakfast, even though she is in luck: when she enters the kitchen she hears the shower upstairs; she brings a glass of orange juice upstairs, stopping in her room long enough to hang up her coat and change her sweater and pants; then she goes to Sharon's room. Sharon sleeps on her back, the long brown hair spread on the pillow, strands of it lying on her upturned cheek; her lips are slightly parted and she seems to be frowning at a dream. The room smells of childhood: the neutral and neuter scents of bedclothes and carpet and wood, and Edith recalls the odors of Joe's apartment, and of Joe. She sits on the side of the bed, pausing to see if her weight will stir Sharon from the dream and sleep. After a while she touches Sharon's cheek; Sharon wakes so quickly, near startled, that Edith is saddened. She likes to watch Sharon wake with the insouciance of a baby, and she regrets her having to get up early and hurry to school. Sharon pushes up on her elbows, half-rising from the bed while her brown eyes are blinking at the morning. Edith kisses her and gives her the juice. Sharon blinks, looks about the room, and asks what time it is.

'There's plenty of time,' Edith says. 'Would you like pancakes?'

Sharon gulps the juice and says yes, then pushes back the covers and is waiting for Edith to get up so she can swing her feet to the floor. Edith kisses her again before leaving the room. In the hall she is drawn to the sound of the shower behind her, needs to say something to Hank, but doesn't know what it is; with both loss and relief she keeps going down the hall and the stairs, into the kitchen.

Hank and Sharon come down together; by this time Edith has made coffee, brought the *Boston Globe* in from the front steps and laid it at Hank's place; the bacon is frying in the iron skillet, the pancake batter is mixed, and the electric skillet is heated. Her eyes meet Hank's. He does not kiss her good-morning before sitting down; that's no longer unusual but this morning the absence of a kiss strikes her like a mild but intended slap. They tell each other good-morning. Since that summer three years ago she has felt with him, after returning from a lover, a variety of emotions which seem unrelated: vengeance, affection, weariness, and sometimes the strange and frightening lust of collusive sin. At times she has also felt shy, and that is how she feels this morning as he props the paper on the milk pitcher, then withdraws it as Sharon lifts the pitcher and pours into her glass. Edith's shyness is no different from what it would be if she and Hank were new lovers, only hours new, and this was the first morning she had waked in his house and as she cooked breakfast her eyes and heart reached out to him to see if this morning he was with her as he was last night. He looks over the paper at her, and his eyes ask about Joe. She shrugs then shakes her head, but she is not thinking of Joe, and the tears that cloud her eyes are not for him either. She pours small discs of batter into the skillet, and turns the bacon. Out of her vision Hank mumbles something to the paper. She breathes the smells of the batter, the bacon, the coffee.

When Hank and Sharon have left, Edith starts her work. There is not much to do, but still she does not take time to read the paper. When she has finished in the kitchen she looks at the guest room, the dining room, and the living room. They are all right; she vacuumed yesterday. She could dust the bookshelves in the living room but she decides they can wait. She goes upstairs; Sharon has made her bed, and Edith smooths it and then makes the other bed where the blankets on her side are still tucked in. The bathroom is clean and smells of Hank's after-shave lotion. He has left hair in the bathtub and whiskers in the lavatory; she picks these up with toilet paper. She would like a shower but she wants to flee from this house. She decides to shower anyway; perhaps the hot water and warm soft lather will calm her. But under the spray she is the same, and she washes quickly and very soon is leaving the house, carrying the vacuum cleaner. On the icy sidewalk she slips and falls hard on her rump. For a moment she sits there, hoping no one has seen her; she feels helpless to do everything she must do; early, the day is demanding more of her than she can give, and she does not believe she can deal with it, or with tomorrow, or the days after that either. She slowly stands up. In the car, with the seatbelt buckled around her heavy coat, she turns clumsily to look behind her as she backs out of the driveway.

At Joe's she moves with short strides up the sidewalk, balancing herself against the weight of the vacuum cleaner. She doesn't knock, because he may be sleeping still. But he is not. As she pushes open the front door she sees him sitting at the kitchen table, wearing the black turtleneck. He smiles and starts to rise, but instead turns his chair to face her and watches her as, leaving the vacuum cleaner, she goes down the hall and kisses him, noting as she lowers her face his weary pallor and the ghost in his eyes. In spite of that and the taste of mouthwash that tells her he has vomited again, she no longer feels like a fugitive. She doesn't understand this, because the feeling began when she woke beside him and therefore it seems that being with him again would not lift it from her. This confuses and frustrates her: when her feelings enter a terrain she neither controls nor understands she thinks they may take her even further, even into madness. She hugs Joe and tells him she has come to clean his apartment; he protests, but he is pleased.

He follows her to the living room and sits on the couch. But after a while, as she works, he lies down, resting his head on a cushion against the arm of the couch. Quietly he watches her. She watches the path of the vacuum cleaner, the clean swath approaching the layers and fluffs of dust. She feels the touch of his eyes, and what is behind them. When she is finished she moves to the bedroom and again he follows her; he lies on the bed, which he has made. For a while she works in a warm patch of sunlight from the window. She looks out at the bright snow and the woods beyond: the spread and reaching branches of elms and birches and maples and tamaracks are bare; there are pines and hemlocks green in the sun. She almost stops working. Her impulse is to throw herself against the window,

cover it with her body, and scream in the impotent rage of grief.
But she does not break the rhythm of her work; she continues to
push the vacuum cleaner over the carpet, while behind her he watches
the push and pull of her arms, the bending of her body, the movement of her legs.

When she has vacuumed and dusted the apartment and cleaned
the bathtub and lavatory she drinks coffee at the kitchen table while
he sits across from her drinking nothing, then with apology in his
voice and eyes he says: 'I called the doctor this morning. He said
he'd come see me, but I told him I'd go to the office.'

She puts down her coffee cup.

'I'll drive you.'

He nods. Looking at him, her heart is pierced more deeply and
painfully than she had predicted: she knows with all her futile and
yearning body that they will never make love again, that last night's
rushed and silent love was their last, and that except to pack his
toilet articles and books for the final watch in the hospital, he will
not return to his apartment she has cleaned.

It is night, she is in her bed again, and now Hank turns to her, his
hand moving up her leg, sliding her nightgown upward, and she
opens her legs, the old easy opening to the hand that has touched
her for ten years; but when the nightgown reaches her hips she does
not lift them to allow it to slip farther up her body. She is thinking
of this afternoon when the priest came to the room and she had to
leave. She nodded at the priest, perhaps spoke to him, but did not
see him, would not recognize him if she saw him again, and she
left and walked down the corridor to the sunporch and stood at the
windows that gave back her reflection, for outside the late afternoon
of the day she cleaned Joe's apartment was already dark and the
streetlights and the houses across the parking lot were lighted. She
smoked while on the hospital bed Joe confessed his sins, told the
priest about her, about the two of them, all the slow nights and
hurried afternoons, and she felt isolated as she had when, months
ago, he had begun to die while, healthy, she loved him.

Since breakfast her only contact with Hank and Sharon was calling a sitter to be waiting when Sharon got home, and calling Hank
at the college to tell him she was at the hospital and ask him to feed
Sharon. Those two phone calls kept her anchored in herself, but

the third set her adrift and she felt that way still on the sun-porch: Joe had asked her to, and she had phoned the rectory and told a priest whose name she didn't hear that her friend was dying, that he was an ex-priest, that he wanted to confess and recieve communion and the last sacrament. Then she waited on the sun-porch while Joe in confession told her goodbye. She felt neither anger nor bitterness but a vulnerability that made her cross her arms over her breasts and draw her sweater closer about her shoulders, though the room was warm. She felt the need to move, to pace the floor, but she could not. She gazed at her reflection in the window without seeing it and gazed at the streetlights and the lighted windows beyond the parking lot and the cars of those who visited without seeing them either, as inside Joe finally confessed to the priest, any priest from any rectory. It did not take long, the confession and communion and the last anointing, not long at all before the priest emerged and walked briskly down the corridor in his black overcoat. Then she went in and sat on the edge of the bed and thought again that tomorrow she must bring flowers, must give to this room scent and spirit, and he took her hand.

'Did he understand everything?' she said.

He smiled. 'I realized he didn't have to. It's something I'd forgotten with all my thinking: it's what ritual is for: nobody has to understand. The knowledge is in the ritual. Anyone can listen to the words. So I just used the simple words.'

'You called us adultery?'

'That's what I called us,' he said, and drew her face down to his chest.

Now she feels that touch more than she feels Hank's, and she reaches down and takes his wrist, stopping the hand, neither squeezing nor pushing, just a slight pressure of resistance and his hand is gone.

'I should be with him,' she says. 'There's a chair in the room where I could sleep. They'd let me: the nurses. It would be a help for them. He's drugged and he's sleeping on his back. He could vomit and drown. Tomorrow night I'll stay there. I'll come home first and cook dinner and stay till Sharon goes to bed. Then I'll go back to the hospital. I'll do that till he dies.'

'I don't want you to.'

She looks at him, then looks away. His hand moves to her leg again, moves up, and when she touches it resisting, it moves away and settles on her breast.

'Don't,' she says. 'I don't want to make love with you.'

'You're grieving.'

His voice is gentle and seductive, then he shifts and tries to embrace her but she pushes with her hands against his chest and closing her eyes she shakes her head.

'Don't,' she says. 'Just please don't. It doesn't mean anything any more. It's my fault too. But it's over, Hank. It's because he's dying, yes—' She opens her eyes and looks past her pushing hands at his face and she feels and shares his pain and dismay; and loving him she closes her eyes. 'But you're dying too. I can feel it in your chest just like I could feel it when I rubbed him when he hurt. And so am I: that's what we lost sight of.'

His chest still leans against her hands, and he grips her shoulders. Then he moves away and lies on his back.

'We'll talk tomorrow,' he says. 'I don't trust this kind of talk at night.'

'It's the best time for it,' she says, and she wants to touch him just once, gently and quickly, his arm or wrist or hand; but she does not.

In late afternoon while snow clouds gather, the priest who yesterday heard Joe's confession and gave him the last sacrament comes with the Eucharist, and this time Edith can stay. By now Hank is teaching his last class of the day and Sharon is home with the sitter. Tonight at dinner Sharon will ask as she did this morning: Is your friend dead yet? Edith has told her his name is Mr. Ritchie but Sharon has never seen him and so cannot put a name on a space in her mind; calling him *your friend* she can imagine Joe existing in the world through the eyes of her mother. At breakfast Hank watched them talking; when Edith looked at him, his eyes shifted to the newspaper.

When the priest knocks and enters, Edith is sitting in a chair at the foot of the bed, a large leather chair, the one she will sleep in tonight; she nearly lowers her eyes, averts her face; yet she looks at him. He glances at her and nods. If he thinks of her as the woman in yesterday's confession there is no sign in his face, which is young: he is in his early thirties. Yet his face looks younger, and there is about it a boyish vulnerability which his seriousness doesn't hide. She guesses that he is easily set off balance, is prone to concern about trifles: that caught making a clumsy remark he will be anxious for the rest of the evening. He does not remove his overcoat, which is open. He moves to the bed, his back to her now, and places a purple stole around his neck. His hands are concealed from her; then they move toward Joe's face, the left hand cupped beneath the right hand which with thumb and forefinger holds the white disc.

'The body of Christ,' he says.

'Amen,' Joe says.

She watches Joe as he closes his eyes and extends his tongue and takes the disc into his mouth. His eyes remain closed; he chews slowly; then he swallows. The priest stands for a moment, watching him. Then with his right palm he touches Joe's forehead, and leaves the room. Edith goes to the bed, sits on its edge, takes Joe's hand and looks at his closed eyes and lips. She wants to hold him hard, feel his ribs against hers, has the urge to fleshless insert her ribs within his, mesh them. Gently she lowers her face to his chest, and he strokes her hair. Still he has not opened his eyes. His stroke on her hair is lighter and slower, and then it stops; his hands rest on her head, and he sleeps. She does not move. She watches as his mouth opens and she listens to the near gurgling of his breath.

She does not move. In her mind she speaks to him, telling him what she is waiting to tell him when he wakes again, what she has been waiting all day to tell him but has not because once she says it to Joe she knows it will be true, as true as it was last night. There are still two months of the cold and early sunsets of winter left, the long season of waiting, and the edges of grief which began last summer when he started to die are far from over, yet she must act: looking now at the yellow roses on the bedside table she is telling Hank goodbye, feeling that goodbye in her womb and heart, a grief that will last, she knows, longer than her grieving for Joe. When the snow is melted from his grave it will be falling still in her soul as it is now while she recalls images and voices of her ten years with Hank and quietly now she weeps, not for Joe or Sharon or Hank, but for herself; and she wishes with all her splintered heart that she and Hank could be as they once were and she longs to touch him, to cry on his broad chest, and with each wish and each image her womb and heart toll their goodbye, forcing her on into the pain that waits for her, so that now she is weeping not quietly but with shuddering sobs she cannot control, and Joe wakes and opens his eyes and touches her wet cheeks and mouth. For a while she lets him do this. Then she stops crying. She kisses him, then wipes her face on the sheet and sits up and smiles at him. Holding his hand and keeping all nuances of fear and grief from her voice, because she wants him to know he has done this for her, and she wants him to be happy about it, she says: 'I'm divorcing Hank.'

He smiles and touches her cheek and she strokes his cool hand.

A FATHER'S STORY

M Y NAME IS Luke Ripley, and here is what I call my
life: I own a stable of thirty horses, and I have young
people who teach riding, and we board some horses too. This is in
northeastern Massachusetts. I have a barn with an indoor ring, and
outside I've got two fenced-in rings and a pasture that ends at a
woods with trails. I call it my life because it looks like it is, and
people I know call it that, but it's a life I can get away from when
I hunt and fish, and some nights after dinner when I sit in the dark
in the front room and listen to opera. The room faces the lawn and
the road, a two-lane country road. When cars come around the
curve northwest of the house, they light up the lawn for an instant,
the leaves of the maple out by the road and the hemlock closer to
the window. Then I'm alone again, or I'd appear to be if someone
crept up to the house and looked through a window: a big-gutted
grey-haired guy, drinking tea and smoking cigarettes, staring out at
the dark woods across the road, listening to a grieving soprano.

My real life is the one nobody talks about anymore, except Father
Paul LeBoeuf, another old buck. He has a decade on me: he's sixty-
four, a big man, bald on top with grey at the sides; when he had
hair, it was black. His face is ruddy, and he jokes about being a
whiskey priest, though he's not. He gets outdoors as much as he
can, goes for a long walk every morning, and hunts and fishes with
me. But I can't get him on a horse anymore. Ten years ago I could
badger him into a trail ride; I had to give him a western saddle, and

he'd hold the pommel and bounce through the woods with me, and be sore for days. He's looking at seventy with eyes that are younger than many I've seen in people in their twenties. I do not remember ever feeling the way they seem to; but I was lucky, because even as a child I knew that life would try me, and I must be strong to endure, though in those early days I expected to be tortured and killed for my faith, like the saints I learned about in school.

Father Paul's family came down from Canada, and he grew up speaking more French than English, so he is different from the Irish priests who abound up here. I do not like to make general statements, or even to hold general beliefs, about people's blood, but the Irish do seem happiest when they're dealing with misfortune or guilt, either their own or somebody else's, and if you think you're not a victim of either one, you can count on certain Irish priests to try to change your mind. On Wednesday nights Father Paul comes to dinner. Often he comes on other nights too, and once, in the old days when we couldn't eat meat on Fridays, we bagged our first ducks of the season on a Friday, and as we drove home from the marsh, he said: For the purposes of Holy Mother Church, I believe a duck is more a creature of water than land, and is not rightly meat. Sometimes he teases me about never putting anything in his Sunday collection, which he would not know about if I hadn't told him years ago. I would like to believe I told him so we could have philosophical talk at dinner, but probably the truth is I suspected he knew, and I did not want him to think I so loved money that I would not even give his church a coin on Sunday. Certainly the ushers who pass the baskets know me as a miser.

I don't feel right about giving money for buildings, places. This starts with the Pope, and I cannot respect one of them till he sells his house and everything in it, and that church too, and uses the money to feed the poor. I have rarely, and maybe never, come across saintliness, but I feel certain it cannot exist in such a place. But I admit, also, that I know very little, and maybe the popes live on a different plane and are tried in ways I don't know about. Father Paul says his own church, St. John's, is hardly the Vatican. I like his church: it is made of wood, and has a simple altar and crucifix, and no padding on the kneelers. He does not have to lock its doors at night. Still it is a place. He could say Mass in my barn. I know this is stubborn, but I can find no mention by Christ of maintaining buildings, much less erecting them of stone or brick, and decorating them with pieces of metal and mineral and elements that people still fight over like barbarians. We had a Maltese woman taking riding lessons, she came over on the boat when she was ten, and once she told me how the nuns in Malta used to tell the little girls that if they wore jewelry, rings and bracelets and necklaces, in purgatory snakes would coil around their fingers and wrists and throats. I do not believe in frightening children or telling them lies, but if those nuns saved a few girls from devotion to things, maybe they were right. That Maltese woman laughed about it, but I noticed she wore only a watch, and that with a leather strap.

The money I give to the church goes in people's stomachs, and on their backs, down in New York City. I have no delusions about the worth of what I do, but I feel it's better to feed somebody than not. There's a priest in Times Square giving shelter to runaway kids, and some Franciscans who run a bread line; actually it's a morning line for coffee and a roll, and Father Paul calls it the continental breakfast for winos and bag ladies. He is curious about how much I am sending, and I know why: he guesses I send a lot, he has said probably more than tithing, and he is right; he wants to know how much because he believes I'm generous and good, and he is wrong about that; he has never had much money and does not know how easy it is to write a check when you have everything you will ever need, and the figures are mere numbers, and represent no sacrifice at all. Being a real Catholic is too hard; if I were one, I would do with my house and barn what I want the Pope to do with his. So I do not want to impress Father Paul, and when he asks me how much, I say I can't let my left hand know what my right is doing.

He came on Wednesday nights when Gloria and I were married, and the kids were young; Gloria was a very good cook (I assume she still is, but it is difficult to think of her in the present), and I liked sitting at the table with a friend who was also a priest. I was proud of my handsome and healthy children. This was long ago, and they were all very young and cheerful and often funny, and the three boys took care of their baby sister, and did not bully or tease her. Of course they did sometimes, with that excited cruelty children are prone to, but not enough so that it was part of her days. On the Wednesday after Gloria left with the kids and a U-

Haul trailer, I was sitting on the front steps, it was summer, and I was watching cars go by on the road, when Father Paul drove around the curve and into the driveway. I was ashamed to see him because he is a priest and my family was gone, but I was relieved too. I went to the car to greet him. He got out smiling, with a bottle of wine, and shook my hand, then pulled me to him, gave me a quick hug, and said: 'It's Wednesday, isn't it? Let's open some cans.'

With arms about each other we walked to the house, and it was good to know he was doing his work but coming as a friend too, and I thought what good work he had. I have no calling. It is for me to keep horses.

In that other life, anyway. In my real one I go to bed early and sleep well and wake at four forty-five, for an hour of silence. I never want to get out of bed then, and every morning I know I can sleep for another four hours, and still not fail at any of my duties. But I get up, so have come to believe my life can be seen in miniature in that struggle in the dark of morning. While making the bed and boiling water for coffee, I talk to God: I offer Him my day, every act of my body and spirit, my thoughts and moods, as a prayer of thanksgiving, and for Gloria and my children and my friends and two women I made love with after Gloria left. This morning offertory is a habit from my boyhood in a Catholic school; or then it was a habit, but as I kept it and grew older it became a ritual. Then I say the Lord's Prayer, trying not to recite it, and one morning it occured to me that a prayer, whether recited or said with concentration, is always an act of faith.

I sit in the kitchen at the rear of the house and drink coffee and smoke and watch the sky growing light before sunrise, the trees of the woods near the barn taking shape, becoming single pines and elms and oaks and maples. Sometimes a rabbit comes out of the treeline, or is already sitting there, invisible till the light finds him. The birds are awake in the trees and feeding on the ground, and the little ones, the purple finches and titmice and chickadees, are at the feeder I rigged outside the kitchen window; it is too small for pigeons to get a purchase. I sit and give myself to coffee and tobacco, that get me brisk again, and I watch and listen. In the first year or so after I lost my family, I played the radio in the mornings. But I overcame that, and now I rarely play it at all. Once in the mail I received a questionnaire asking me to write down everything

I watched on television during the week they had chosen. At the end of those seven days I wrote in *The Wizard of Oz* and returned it. That was in winter and was actually a busy week for my television, which normally sits out the cold months without once warming up. Had they sent the questionnaire during baseball season, they would have found me at my set. People at the stables talk about shows and performers I have never heard of, but I cannot get interested; when I am in the mood to watch television, I go to a movie or read a detective novel. There are always good detective novels to be found, and I like remembering them next morning with my coffee.

I also think of baseball and hunting and fishing, and of my children. It is not painful to think about them anymore, because even if we had lived together, they would be gone now, grown into their own lives, except Jennifer. I think of death too, not sadly, or with fear, though something like excitement does run through me, something more quickening than the coffee and tobacco. I suppose it is an intense interest, and an outright distrust: I never feel certain that I'll be here watching birds eating at tomorrow's daylight. Sometimes I try to think of other things, like the rabbit that is warm and breathing but not there till twilight. I feel on the brink of something about the life of the senses, but either am not equipped to go further or am not interested enough to concentrate. I have called all of this thinking, but it is not, because it is unintentional; what I'm really doing is feeling the day, in silence, and that is what Father Paul is doing too on his five-to-ten-mile walks.

When the hour ends I take an apple or carrot and I go to the stable and tack up a horse. We take good care of these horses, and no one rides them but students, instructors, and me, and nobody rides the horses we board unless an owner asks me to. The barn is dark and I turn on lights and take some deep breaths, smelling the hay and horses and their manure, both fresh and dried, a combined odor that you either like or you don't. I walk down the wide space of dirt between stalls, greeting the horses, joking with them about their quirks, and choose one for no reason at all other than the way it looks at me that morning. I get my old English saddle that has smoothed and darkened through the years, and go into the stall, talking to this beautiful creature who'll swerve out of a canter if a piece of paper blows in front of him, and if the barn catches fire and you manage to get him out he will, if he can get away from you, run back into the fire, to his stall. Like the smells that surround them, you either like them or you don't. I love them, so am spared having to try to explain why. I feed one the carrot or apple and tack up and lead him outside, where I mount, and we go down the driveway to the road and cross it and turn northwest and walk then trot then canter to St. John's.

A few cars are on the road, their drivers looking serious about going to work. It is always strange for me to see a woman dressed for work so early in the morning. You know how long it takes them, with the makeup and hair and clothes, and I think of them waking in the dark of winter or early light of other seasons, and dressing as they might for an evening's entertainment. Probably this strikes me because I grew up seeing my father put on those suits he never wore on weekends or his two weeks off, and so am accustomed to the men, but when I see these women I think something went wrong, to send all those dressed-up people out on the road when the dew hasn't dried yet. Maybe it's because I so dislike getting up early, but am also doing what I choose to do, while they have no choice. At heart I am lazy, yet I find such peace and delight in it that I believe it is a natural state, and in what looks like my laziest periods I am closest to my center. The ride to St. John's is fifteen minutes. The horses and I do it in all weather; the road is well plowed in winter, and there are only a few days a year when ice makes me drive the pickup. People always look at someone on horseback, and for a moment their faces change and many drivers and I wave to each other. Then at St. John's, Father Paul and five or six regulars and I celebrate the Mass.

Do not think of me as a spiritual man whose every thought during those twenty-five minutes is at one with the words of the Mass. Each morning I try, each morning I fail, and know that always I will be a creature who, looking at Father Paul and the altar, and uttering prayers, will be distracted by scrambled eggs, horses, the weather, and memories and daydreams that have nothing to do with the sacrament I am about to receive. I can receive, though: the Eucharist, and also, at Mass and at other times, moments and even minutes of contemplation. But I cannot achieve contemplation, as some can; and so, having to face and forgive my own failures, I have learned from them both the necessity and wonder of ritual.

For ritual allows those who cannot will themselves out of the secular to perform the spiritual, as dancing allows the tongue-tied man a ceremony of love. And, while my mind dwells on breakfast, or Major or Duchess tethered under the church eave, there is, as I take the Host from Father Paul and place it on my tongue and return to the pew, a feeling that I am thankful I have not lost in the forty-eight years since my first Communion. At its center is excitement; spreading out from it is the peace of certainty. Or the certainty of peace. One night Father Paul and I talked about faith. It was long ago, and all I remember is him saying: Belief is believing in God; faith is believing that God believes in you. That is the excitement, and the peace; then the Mass is over, and I go into the sacristy and we have a cigarette and chat, the mystery ends, we are two men talking like any two men on a morning in America, about baseball, plane crashes, presidents, governors, murders, the sun, the clouds. Then I go to the horse and ride back to the life people see, the one in which I move and talk, and most days I enjoy it.

It is late summer now, the time between fishing and hunting, but a good time for baseball. It has been two weeks since Jennifer left, to drive home to Gloria's after her summer visit. She is the only one who still visits; the boys are married and have children, and sometimes fly up for a holiday, or I fly down or west to visit one of them. Jennifer is twenty, and I worry about her the way fathers worry about daughters but not sons. I want to know what she's up to, and at the same time I don't. She looks athletic, and she is: she swims and runs and of course rides. All my children do. When she comes for six weeks in summer, the house is loud with girls, friends of hers since childhood, and new ones. I am glad she kept the girl friends. They have been young company for me and, being with them, I have been able to gauge her growth between summers. On their riding days, I'd take them back to the house when their lessons were over and they had walked the horses and put them back in the stalls, and we'd have lemonade or Coke, and cookies if I had some, and talk until their parents came to drive them home. One year their breasts grew, so I wasn't startled when I saw Jennifer in July. Then they were driving cars to the stable, and beginning to look like young women, and I was passing out beer and ashtrays and they were talking about college.

When Jennifer was here in summer, they were at the house most days. I would say generally that as they got older they became quieter, and though I enjoyed both, I sometimes missed the giggles and shouts. The quiet voices, just low enough for me not to hear from wherever I was, rising and falling in proportion to my distance from them, frightened me. Not that I believed they were planning or recounting anything really wicked, but there was a female seriousness about them, and it was secretive, and of course I thought: love, sex. But it was more than that: it was womanhood they were entering, the deep forest of it, and no matter how many women and men too are saying these days that there is little difference between us, the truth is that men find their way into that forest only on clearly marked trails, while women move about in it like birds. So hearing Jennifer and her friends talking so quietly, yet intensely, I wanted very much to have a wife.

But not as much as in the old days, when Gloria had left but her presence was still in the house as strongly as if she had only gone to visit her folks for a week. There were no clothes or cosmetics, but potted plants endured my neglectful care as long as they could, and slowly died; I did not kill them on purpose, to exorcise the house of her, but I could not remember to water them. For weeks, because I did not use it much, the house was as neat as she had kept it, though dust layered the order she had made. The kitchen went first: I got the dishes in and out of the dishwasher and wiped the top of the stove, but did not return cooking spoons and pot holders to their hooks on the wall, and soon the burners and oven were caked with spillings, the refrigerator had more space and was spotted with juices. The living room and my bedroom went next; I did not go into the children's rooms except on bad nights when I went from room to room and looked and touched and smelled, so they did not lose their order until a year later when the kids came for six weeks. It was three months before I ate the last of the food Gloria had cooked and frozen: I remember it was a beef stew, and very good. By then I had four cookbooks, and was boasting a bit, and talking about recipes with the women at the stables, and looking forward to cooking for Father Paul. But I never looked forward to cooking at night only for myself, though I made myself do it; on some nights I gave in to my daily temptation, and took a newspaper or detective novel to a restaurant. By the end of the second year, though, I had stopped turning on the radio as soon as I woke in the morning, and was able to be silent and alone in the evening too, and then I enjoyed my dinners.

It is not hard to live through a day, if you can live through a moment. What creates despair is the imagination, which pretends there is a future, and insists on predicting millions of moments, thousands of days, and so drains you that you cannot live the moment at hand. That is what Father Paul told me in those first two years, on some of the bad nights when I believed I could not bear what I had to: the most painful loss was my children, then the loss of Gloria, whom I still loved despite or maybe because of our long periods of sadness that rendered us helpless, so neither of us could break out of it to give a hand to the other. Twelve years later I believe ritual would have healed us more quickly than the repetitious talks we had, perhaps even kept us healed. Marriages have lost that, and I wish I had known then what I know now, and we had performed certain acts together every day, no matter how we felt, and perhaps then we could have subordinated feeling to action, for surely that is the essence of love. I know this from my distractions during Mass, and during everything else I do, so that my actions and feelings are seldom one. It does happen every day, but in proportion to everything else in a day, it is rare, like joy. The third most painful loss, which became second and sometimes first as months passed, was the knowledge that I could never marry again, and so dared not even keep company with a woman.

On some of the bad nights I was bitter about this with Father Paul, and I so pitied myself that I cried, or nearly did, speaking with damp eyes and breaking voice. I believe that celibacy is for him the same trial it is for me, not of the flesh, but the spirit: the heart longing to love. But the difference is he chose it, and did not wake one day to a life with thirty horses. In my anger I said I had done my service to love and chastity, and I told him of the actual physical and spiritual pain of practicing rhythm: nights of striking the mattress with a fist, two young animals lying side by side in heat, leaving the bed to pace, to smoke, to curse, and too passionate to question, for we were so angered and oppressed by our passion that we could see no further than our loins. So now I understand how people can be enslaved for generations before they throw down their tools or use them as weapons, the form of their slavery—the cotton fields, the shacks and puny cupboards and untended illnesses—absorbing their emotions and thoughts until finally they have little or none at all to direct with clarity and energy at the owners and legislators. And I told him of the trick of passion and its slaking: how during what we had to believe were safe periods, though all four children were conceived at those times, we were able with some coherence to question the tradition and reason and justice of the law against birth control, but not with enough conviction to soberly act against it, as though regular satisfaction in bed tempered our revolutionary as well as our erotic desires. Only when abstinence drove us hotly away from each other did we receive an urge so strong it lasted all the way to the drugstore and back; but always, after release, we threw away the remaining condoms; and after going through this a few times, we knew what would happen, and from then on we submitted to the calendar she so precisely marked on the bedroom wall. I told him that living two lives each month, one as celibates, one as lovers, made us tense and short-tempered, so we snapped at each other like dogs.

To have endured that, to have reached a time when we burned slowly and could gain from bed the comfort of lying down at night with one who loves you and whom you love, could for weeks on end go to bed tired and peacefully sleep after a kiss, a touch of the hands, and then to be thrown out of the marriage like a bundle from a moving freight car, was unjust, was intolerable, and I could not or would not muster the strength to endure it. But I did, a moment at a time, a day, a night, except twice, each time with a different woman and more than a year apart, and this was so long ago that I clearly see their faces in my memory, can hear the pitch of their voices, and the way they pronounced words, one with a Massachusetts accent, one midwestern, but I feel as though I only heard about them from someone else. Each rode at the stables and was with me for part of an evening; one was badly married, one divorced, so none of us was free. They did not understand this Catholic view, but they were understanding about my having it, and I remained friends with both of them until the married one left her husband and went to Boston, and the divorced one moved to Maine. After both those evenings, those good women, I went to Mass early while Father Paul was still in the confessional, and received his absolution. I did not tell him who I was, but of course he knew, though I never saw it in his eyes. Now my longing for a wife comes only once in a while, like a cold: on some late afternoons when I am alone in the barn, then I lock up and walk to the house, daydreaming, then suddenly look at it and see it empty, as though for the first time, and all at once I'm weary and feel I do not have the energy to broil meat, and I think of driving to a restaurant, then shake my head and go on to the house, the refrigerator, the oven; and some mornings when I wake in the dark and listen to the silence and run my hand over the cold sheet beside me; and some days in summer when Jennifer is here.

Gloria left first me, then the Church, and that was the end of religion for the children, though on visits they went to Sunday Mass with me, and still do, out of a respect for my life that they manage to keep free of patronage. Jennifer is an agnostic, though I doubt she would call herself that, any more than she would call herself any other name that implied she had made a decision, a choice, about existence, death, and God. In truth she tends to pantheism, a good sign, I think; but not wanting to be a father who tells his children what they ought to believe, I do not say to her that Catholicism includes pantheism, like onions in a stew. Besides, I have no missionary instincts and do not believe everyone should or even could live with the Catholic faith. It is Jennifer's womanhood that renders me awkward. And womanhood now is frank, not like when Gloria was twenty and there were symbols: high heels and cosmetics and dresses, a cigarette, a cocktail. I am glad that women are free now of false modesty and all its attention paid the flesh; but, still, it is difficult to see so much of your daughter, to hear her talk as only men and bawdy women used to, and most of all to see in her face the deep and unabashed sensuality of women, with no tricks of the eyes and mouth to hide the pleasure she feels at having a strong young body. I am certain, with the way things are now, that she has very happily not been a virgin for years. That does not bother me. What bothers me is my certainty about it, just from watching her walk across a room or light a cigarette or pour milk on cereal.

She told me all of it, waking me that night when I had gone to sleep listening to the wind in the trees and against the house, a wind so strong that I had to shut all but the lee windows, and still the house cooled; told it to me in such detail and so clearly that now, when she has driven the car to Florida, I remember it all as though I had been a passenger in the front seat, or even at the wheel. It started with a movie, then beer and driving to the sea to look at the waves in the night and the wind, Jennifer and Betsy and Liz. They drank a beer on the beach and wanted to go in naked but were afraid they would drown in the high surf. They bought another six-pack at a grocery store in New Hampshire, and drove home. I can see it now, feel it: the three girls and the beer and the ride on country roads where pines curved in the wind and the big deciduous trees swayed and shook as if they might leap from the earth. They would have some windows partly open so they could feel the wind; Jennifer would be playing a cassette, the music stirring them, as it does the young, to memories of another time, other people and places in what is for them the past.

She took Betsy home, then Liz, and sang with her cassette as she left the town west of us and started home, a twenty-minute drive on the road that passes my house. They had each had four beers, but now there were twelve empty bottles in the bag on the floor at the passenger seat, and I keep focusing on their sound against each other when the car shifted speeds or changed directions. For I want to understand that one moment out of all her heart's time on earth, and whether her history had any bearing on it, or whether her heart was then isolated from all it had known, and the sound of those bottles urged it. She was just leaving the town, accelerating past a night club on the right, gaining speed to climb a long, gradual hill, then she went up it, singing, patting the beat on the steering wheel, the wind loud through her few inches of open window, blowing her hair as it did the high branches alongside the road, and she looked up at them and watched the top of the hill for someone drunk or heedless coming over it in part of her lane. She crested to an open black road, and there he was: a bulk, a blur, a thing running across her headlights, and she swerved left and her foot went for the brake and was stomping air above its pedal when she hit him, saw his legs and body in the air, flying out of her light, into the dark. Her brakes were screaming into the wind, bottles clinking in the fallen bag, and with the music and wind inside the car was his sound, already a memory but as real as an echo, that car-shuddering thump as though she had struck a tree. Her foot was back on the accelerator. Then she shifted gears and pushed it. She ejected the cassette and closed the window. She did not start to cry until she knocked on my bedroom door, then called: 'Dad?'

Her voice, her tears, broke through my dream and the wind I heard in my sleep, and I stepped into jeans and hurried to the door, thinking harm, rape, death. All were in her face, and I hugged her and pressed her cheek to my chest and smoothed her blown hair, then led her, weeping, to the kitchen and sat her at the table where still she could not speak, nor look at me; when she raised her face it fell forward again, as of its own weight, into her palms. I offered tea and she shook her head, so I offered beer twice, then she shook her head, so I offered whiskey and she nodded. I had some rye that Father Paul and I had not finished last hunting season, and I poured some over ice and set it in front of her and was putting away the ice but stopped and got another glass and poured one for myself too, and brought the ice and bottle to the table where she was trying to get one of her long menthols out of the pack, but her fingers jerked like severed snakes, and I took the pack and lit one for her and took one for myself. I watched her shudder with her first swallow of rye, and push hair back from her face, it is auburn and gleamed in the overhead light, and I remembered how beautiful she looked riding a sorrel; she was smoking fast, then the sobs in her throat stopped, and she looked at me and said it, the words coming out with smoke: 'I hit somebody. With the *car*.'

Then she was crying and I was on my feet, moving back and forth, looking down at her, asking *Who? Where? Where?* She was pointing at the wall over the stove, jabbing her fingers and cigarette at it, her other hand at her eyes, and twice in horror I actually looked at the wall. She finished the whiskey in a swallow and I stopped pacing and asking and poured another, and either the drink or the exhaustion of tears quieted her, even the dry sobs, and she told me; not as I tell it now, for that was later as again and again we relived it in the kitchen or living room, and, if in daylight, fled it on horseback out on the trails through the woods and, if at night, walked quietly around in the moonlit pasture, walked around and around it, sweating through our clothes. She told it in bursts, like she was a child again, running to me, injured from play. I put on boots and a shirt and left her with the bottle and her streaked face and a cigarette twitching between her fingers, pushed the door open

468 · ANDRE DUBUS

against the wind, and eased it shut. The wind squinted and watered
my eyes as I leaned into it and went to the pickup.

When I passed St. John's I looked at it, and Father Paul's little
white rectory in the rear, and wanted to stop, wished I could as I
could if he were simply a friend who sold hardware or something.
I had forgotten my watch but I always know the time within minutes, even when a sound or dream or my bladder wakes me in the
night. It was nearly two; we had been in the kitchen about twenty
minutes; she had hit him around one-fifteen. Or her. The road was
empty and I drove between blowing trees; caught for an instant in
my lights, they seemed to be in panic. I smoked and let hope play
its tricks on me: it was neither man nor woman but an animal, a
goat or calf or deer on the road; it was a man who had jumped away
in time, the collision of metal and body glancing not direct, and he
had limped home to nurse bruises and cuts. Then I threw the
cigarette and hope both out the window and prayed that he was
alive, while beneath that prayer, a reserve deeper in my heart,
another one stirred: that if he were dead, they would not get Jennifer.

From our direction, east and a bit south, the road to that hill and
the night club beyond it and finally the town is, for its last four or
five miles, straight through farming country. When I reached that
stretch I slowed the truck and opened my window for the fierce air;
on both sides were scattered farmhouses and barns and sometimes
a silo, looking not like shelters but like unsheltered things the wind
would flatten. Corn bent toward the road from a field on my right,
and always something blew in front of me: paper, leaves, dried
weeds, branches. I slowed approaching the hill, and went up it in
second, staring through my open window at the ditch on the left
side of the road, its weeds alive, whipping, a mad dance with the
trees above them. I went over the hill and down and, opposite the
club, turned right onto a side street of houses, and parked there, in
the leaping shadows of trees. I walked back across the road to the
club's parking lot, the wind behind me, lifting me as I strode, and
I could not hear my boots on pavement. I walked up the hill, on
the shoulder, watching the branches above me, hearing their leaves
and the creaking trunks and the wind. Then I was at the top, looking
down the road and at the farms and fields; the night was clear, and
I could see a long way; clouds scudded past the half-moon and stars,
blown out to sea.

I started down, watching the tall grass under the trees to my right, glancing into the dark of the ditch, listening for cars behind me; but as soon as I cleared one tree, its sound was gone, its flapping leaves and rattling branches far behind me, as though the greatest distance I had at my back was a matter of feet, while ahead of me I could see a barn two miles off. Then I saw her skid marks: short, and going left and downhill, into the other lane. I stood at the ditch, its weeds blowing; across it were trees and their moving shadows, like the clouds. I stepped onto its slope, and it took me sliding on my feet, then rump, to the bottom, where I sat still, my body gathered to itself, lest a part of me should touch him. But there was only tall grass, and I stood, my shoulders reaching the sides of the ditch, and I walked uphill, wishing for the flashlight in the pickup, walking slowly, and down in the ditch I could hear my feet in the grass and on the earth, and kicking cans and bottles. At the top of the hill I turned and went down, watching the ground above the ditch on my right, praying my prayer from the truck again, the first one, the one I would admit, that he was not dead, was in fact home, and began to hope again, memory telling me of lost pheasants and grouse I had shot, but they were small and the colors of their home, while a man was either there or not; and from that memory I left where I was and while walking in the ditch under the wind was in the deceit of imagination with Jennifer in the kitchen, telling her she had hit no one, or at least had not badly hurt anyone, when I realized he could be in the hospital now and I would have to think of a way to check there, something to say on the phone. I see now that, once hope returned, I should have been certain what it prepared me for: ahead of me, in high grass and the shadows of trees, I saw his shirt. Or that is all my mind would allow itself: a shirt, and I stood looking at it for the moments it took my mind to admit the arm and head and the dark length covered by pants. He lay face down, the arm I could see near his side, his head turned from me, on its cheek.

'Fella?' I said. I had meant to call, but it came out quiet and high, lost inches from my face in the wind. Then I said, 'Oh God,' and felt Him in the wind and the sky moving past the stars and moon and the fields around me, but only watching me as He might have watched Cain or Job, I did not know which, and I said it again, and wanted to sink to the earth and weep till I slept there in the weeds. I climbed, scrambling up the side of the ditch, pulling at clutched grass, gained the top on hands and knees, and went to him like that, panting, moving through the grass as high and higher than my face, crawling under that sky, making sounds too, like some animal, there being no words to let him know I was here with him now. He was long; that is the word that came to me, not tall. I kneeled beside him, my hands on my legs. His right arm was by his side, his left arm straight out from the shoulder, but turned, so his palm was open to the tree above us. His left cheek was clean-shaven, his eye closed, and there was no blood. I leaned forward to look at his open mouth and saw the blood on it, going down into the grass. I straightened and looked ahead at the wind blowing past me through grass and trees to a distant light, and I stared at the light, imagining someone awake out there, wanting someone to be, a gathering of old friends, or someone alone listening to music or painting a picture, then I figured it was a night light at a farmyard whose house I couldn't see. *Going*, I thought. *Still going*. I leaned over again and looked at dripping blood.

So I had to touch his wrist, a thick one with a watch and expansion band that I pushed up his arm, thinking *he's left-handed*, my three fingers pressing his wrist, and all I felt was my tough fingertips on that smooth underside flesh and small bones, then relief, then certainty. But against my will, or only because of it, I still don't know, I touched his neck, ran my fingers down it as if petting, then pressed, and my hand sprang back as from fire. I lowered it again, held it there until it felt that faint beating that I could not believe. There was too much wind. Nothing could make a sound in it. A pulse could not be felt in it, nor could mere fingers in that wind feel the absolute silence of a dead man's artery. I was making sounds again; I grabbed his left arm and his waist, and pulled him toward me, and that side of him rose, turned, and I lowered him to his back, his face tilted up toward the tree that was groaning, the tree and I the only sounds in the wind. Turning my face from his, looking down the length of him at his sneakers, I placed my ear on his heart, and heard not that but something else, and I clamped a hand over my exposed ear, heard something liquid and alive, like when you pump a well and after a few strokes you hear air and water moving in the pipe, and I knew I must raise his legs and cover him and run to a phone, while still I listened to his chest, thinking *raise with what? cover with what?* and amid the liquid sound I heard the heart, then lost it, and pressed my ear against bone, but his chest was quiet, and I did not know when the liquid had stopped, and do not know now when I heard air, a faint rush of it, and whether under my ear or at his mouth or whether I heard it at all. I straightened and looked at the light, dim and yellow. Then I touched his throat, looking him full in the face. He was blond and young. He could have been sleeping in the shade of a tree, but for the smear of blood from his mouth to his hair, and the night sky, and the weeds blowing against his head, and the leaves shaking in the dark above us.

I stood. Then I kneeled again and prayed for his soul to join in peace and joy all the dead and living; and, doing so, confronted my first sin against him, not stopping for Father Paul, who could have given him the last rites, and immediately then my second one, or I saw then, my first, not calling an ambulance to meet me there, and I stood and turned into the wind, slid down the ditch and crawled out of it, and went up the hill and down it, across the road to the street of houses whose people I had left behind forever, so that I moved with stealth in the shadows to my truck.

When I came around the bend near my house, I saw the kitchen light at the rear. She sat as I had left her, the ashtray filled, and I looked at the bottle, felt her eyes on me, felt what she was seeing too: the dirt from my crawling. She had not drunk much of the rye. I poured some in my glass, with the water from melted ice, and sat down and swallowed some and looked at her and swallowed some more, and said: 'He's dead.'

She rubbed her eyes with the heels of her hands, rubbed the cheeks under them, but she was dry now.

'He was probably dead when he hit the ground. I mean, that's probably what killed—'

'Where was he?'

'Across the ditch, under a tree.'

'Was he—did you see his face?'

'No. Not really. I just felt. For life, pulse. I'm going out to the car.'

'What for? Oh.'

I finished the rye, and pushed back the chair, then she was standing too.

'I'll go with you.'

'There's no need.'

'I'll go.'

I took a flashlight from a drawer and pushed open the door and held it while she went out. We turned our faces from the wind. It was like on the hill, when I was walking, and the wind closed the distance behind me: after three or four steps I felt there was no house back there. She took my hand, as I was reaching for hers. In the garage we let go, and squeezed between the pickup and her little car, to the front of it, where we had more room, and we stepped back from the grill and I shone the light on the fender, the smashed headlight turned into it, the concave chrome staring to the right, at the garage wall.

'We ought to get the bottles,' I said.

She moved between the garage and the car, on the passenger side, and had room to open the door and lift the bag. I reached out, and she gave me the bag and backed up and shut the door and came around the car. We sidled to the doorway, and she put her arm around my waist and I hugged her shoulders.

'I thought you'd call the police,' she said.

We crossed the yard, faces bowed from the wind, her hair blowing away from her neck, and in the kitchen I put the bag of bottles in the garbage basket. She was working at the table: capping the rye and putting it away, filling the ice tray, washing the glasses, emptying the ashtray, sponging the table.

'Try to sleep now,' I said.

She nodded at the sponge circling under her hand, gathering ashes. Then she dropped it in the sink and, looking me full in the face, as I had never seen her look, as perhaps she never had, being for so long a daughter on visits (or so it seemed to me and still does: that until then our eyes had never seriously met), she crossed to me from the sink and kissed my lips, then held me so tightly I lost balance, and would have stumbled forward had she not held me so hard.

I sat in the living room, the house darkened, and watched the maple and the hemlock. When I believed she was asleep I put on *La Boheme*, and kept it at the same volume as the wind so it would not wake her. Then I listened to *Madame Butterfly*, and in the third act had to rise quickly to lower the sound: the wind was gone. I looked at the still maple near the window, and thought of the wind leaving farms and towns and the coast, going out over the sea to die on the waves. I smoked and gazed out the window. The sky was darker, and at daybreak the rain came. I listened to *Tosca*, and at six-fifteen went to the kitchen where Jennifer's purse lay on the table, a leather shoulder purse crammed with the things of an adult woman, things she had begun accumulating only a few years back, and I nearly wept, thinking of what sandy foundations they were: driver's license, credit card, disposable lighter, cigarettes, checkbook, ballpoint pen, cash, cosmetics, comb, brush, Kleenex, these the rite of passage from childhood, and I took one of them—her keys—and went out, remembering a jacket and hat when the rain struck me, but I kept going to the car, and squeezed and lowered myself into it, pulled the seat belt over my shoulder and fastened it and backed out, turning in the drive, going forward into the road, toward St. John's and Father Paul.

Cars were on the road, the workers, and I did not worry about any of them noticing the fender and light. Only a horse distracted them from what they drove to. In front of St. John's is a parking lot; at its far side, past the church and at the edge of the lawn, is an old pine, taller than the steeple now. I shifted to third, left the road, and, aiming the right headlight at the tree, accelerated past the white blur of church, into the black trunk growing bigger till it was all I could see, then I rocked in that resonant thump she had heard, had felt, and when I turned off the ignition it was still in my ears, my blood, and I saw the boy flying in the wind. I lowered my forehead to the wheel. Father Paul opened the door, his face white in the rain.

'I'm all right.'

'What happened?'

'I don't know. I fainted.'

I got out and went around to the front of the car, looked at the smashed light, the crumpled and torn fender.

'Come to the house and lie down.'

'I'm all right.'

'When was your last physical?'

'I'm due for one. Let's get out of this rain.'

'You'd better lie down.'

'No. I want to receive.'

That was the time to say I want to confess, but I have not and will not. Though I could now, for Jennifer is in Florida, and weeks have passed, and perhaps now Father Paul would not feel that he must tell me to go to the police. And, for that very reason, to confess now would be unfair. It is a world of secrets, and now I have one from my best, in truth my only, friend. I have one from Jennifer too, but that is the nature of fatherhood.

Most of that day it rained, so it was only in early evening, when the sky cleared, with a setting sun, that two little boys, leaving their confinement for some play before dinner, found him. Jennifer and I got that on the local news, which we listened to every hour, meeting at the radio, standing with cigarettes, until the one at eight o'clock; when she stopped crying, we went out and walked on the wet grass, around the pasture, the last of sunlight still in the air and trees. His name was Patrick Mitchell, he was nineteen years old, was employed by CETA, lived at home with his parents and brother and sister. The paper next day said he had been at a friend's house and was walking home, and I thought of that light I had seen, then knew it was not for him; he lived on one of the streets behind the club. The paper did not say then, or in the next few days, anything to make Jennifer think he was alive while she was with me in the kitchen. Nor do I know if we—I—could have saved him.

In keeping her secret from her friends, Jennifer had to perform so often, as I did with Father Paul and at the stables, that I believe the acting, which took more of her than our daylight trail rides and our night walks in the pasture, was her healing. Her friends teased me about wrecking her car. When I carried her luggage out to the car on that last morning, we spoke only of the weather for her trip—the day was clear, with a dry cool breeze—and hugged and kissed, and I stood watching as she started the car and turned it around. But then she shifted to neutral and put on the parking brake and unclasped the belt, looking at me all the while, then she was coming to me, as she had that night in the kitchen, and I opened my arms.

I have said I talk with God in the mornings, as I start my day, and sometimes as I sit with coffee, looking at the birds, and the woods. Of course He has never spoken to me, but that is not something I require. Nor does He need to. I know Him, as I know the part of myself that knows Him, that felt Him watching from the wind and the night as I knelt over the dying boy. Lately I have taken to arguing with Him, as I can't with Father Paul, who, when he hears my monthly confession, has not heard and will not hear anything of failure to do all that one can to save an anonymous life, of injustice to a family in their grief, of deepening their pain at the chance and mystery of death by giving them nothing—no one—to hate. With Father Paul I feel lonely about this, but not with God. When I received the Eucharist while Jennifer's car sat twice-damaged, so redeemed, in the rain, I felt neither loneliness nor shame, but as though He were watching me, even from my tongue, intestines, blood, as I have watched my sons at times in their young lives when I was able to judge but without anger, and so keep silent while they, in the agony of their youth, decided how they must act; or found reasons, after their actions, for what they had done. Their reasons were never as good or as bad as their actions, but they needed to find them, to believe they were living by them, instead of the awful solitude of the heart.

I do not feel the peace I once did: not with God, nor the earth, or anyone on it. I have begun to prefer this state, to remember with fondness the other one as a period of peace I neither earned nor deserved. Now in the mornings while I watch purple finches driving larger titmice from the feeder, I say to Him: I would do it again. For when she knocked on my door, then called me, she woke what had flowed dormant in my blood since her birth, so that what rose from the bed was not a stable owner or a Catholic or any other Luke Ripley I had lived with for a long time, but the father of a girl.

And He says: I am a Father too.

Yes, I say, as You are a Son Whom this morning I will receive; unless You kill me on the way to church, then I trust You will receive me. And as a Son You made Your plea.

Yes, He says, but I would not lift the cup.

True, and I don't want You to lift it from me either. And if one of my sons had come to me that night, I would have phoned the police and told them to meet us with an ambulance at the top of the hill.

Why? Do you love them less?

I tell Him no, it is not that I love them less, but that I could bear the pain of watching and knowing my sons' pain, could bear it with pride as they took the whip and nails. But You never had a daughter and, if You had, You could not have borne her passion.

So, He says, you love her more than you love Me.

I love her more than I love truth.

Then you love in weakness, He says.

As You love me, I say, and I go with an apple or carrot out to the barn.

ABOUT THE AUTHOR

Andre Dubus, who has recovered from an accident that cost him a leg in July 1986, lives in Haverhill, Massachusetts, in that Merrimack River country northwest of Boston he has made his own. He writes something every day—day in, night out. Baseball, which he cannot do without, helps sustain him. He's been a peacetime Marine Corps captain, a member of the Iowa Writer's Workshop, a college teacher, and a Guggenheim Fellow. The author of seven previous books of fiction, and the winner of the *Boston Globe's* first annual Laurence L. Winship Award (1975), he became a MacArthur Fellow in July 1988.

V I N T A G E
CONTEMPORARIES

VINTAGE
CONTEMPORARIES

___ **The Stars at Noon** by Denis Johnson	$5.95	394-75427-1
___ **Asa, as I Knew Him** by Susanna Kaysen	$4.95	394-74985-5
___ **Lulu Incognito** by Raymond Kennedy	$7.95	394-75641-X
___ **Steps** by Jerzy Kosinski	$5.95	394-75716-5
___ **A Handbook for Visitors From Outer Space**		
by Kathryn Kramer	$5.95	394-72989-7
___ **The Garden State** by Gary Krist	$7.95	679-72515-6
___ **House of Heroes and Other Stories** by Mary LaChapelle	$7.95	679-72457-5
___ **The Chosen Place, the Timeless People**		
by Paule Marshall	$6.95	394-72633-2
___ **A Recent Martyr** by Valerie Martin	$7.95	679-72158-4
___ **The Consolation of Nature and Other Stories**		
by Valerie Martin	$6.95	679-72159-2
___ **The Beginning of Sorrows** by David Martin	$7.95	679-72459-1
___ **Suttree** by Cormac McCarthy	$6.95	394-74145-5
___ **California Bloodstock** by Terry McDonell	$8.95	679-72168-1
___ **The Bushwhacked Piano** by Thomas McGuane	$5.95	394-72642-1
___ **Nobody's Angel** by Thomas McGuane	$6.95	394-74738-0
___ **Something to Be Desired** by Thomas McGuane	$4.95	394-73156-5
___ **To Skin a Cat** by Thomas McGuane	$5.95	394-75521-9
___ **Bright Lights, Big City** by Jay McInerney	$5.95	394-72641-3
___ **Ransom** by Jay McInerney	$5.95	394-74118-8
___ **Story of My Life** by Jay McInerney	$6.95	679-72257-2
___ **Mama Day** by Gloria Naylor	$8.95	679-72181-9
___ **The All-Girl Football Team** by Lewis Nordan	$5.95	394-75701-7
___ **Welcome to the Arrow-Catcher Fair** by Lewis Nordan	$6.95	679-72164-9
___ **River Dogs** by Robert Olmstead	$6.95	394-74684-8
___ **Soft Water** by Robert Olmstead	$6.95	394-75752-1
___ **Family Resemblances** by Lowry Pei	$6.95	394-75528-6
___ **Norwood** by Charles Portis	$5.95	394-72931-5
___ **Clea & Zeus Divorce** by Emily Prager	$6.95	394-75591-X
___ **A Visit From the Footbinder** by Emily Prager	$6.95	394-75592-8
___ **Mohawk** by Richard Russo	$8.95	679-72577-6
___ **The Risk Pool** by Richard Russo	$8.95	679-72334-X
___ **Rabbit Boss** by Thomas Sanchez	$8.95	679-72621-7
___ **Anywhere But Here** by Mona Simpson	$6.95	394-75559-6
___ **Carnival for the Gods** by Gladys Swan	$6.95	394-74330-X
___ **The Player** by Michael Tolkin	$7.95	679-72254-8
___ **Myra Breckinridge and Myron** by Gore Vidal	$8.95	394-75444-1
___ **The Car Thief** by Theodore Weesner	$6.95	394-74097-1
___ **Breaking and Entering** by Joy Williams	$6.95	394-75773-4
___ **Taking Care** by Joy Williams	$5.95	394-72912-9
___ **The Easter Parade** by Richard Yates	$8.95	679-72230-0
___ **Eleven Kinds of Loneliness** by Richard Yates	$8.95	679-72221-1
___ **Revolutionary Road** by Richard Yates	$8.95	679-72191-6

Now at your bookstore or call toll-free to order: 1-800-733-3000
(credit cards only).